I0819839

Lost in Translation, Presumption, and Interpretation

Adam, Noah, and the Ancient Mesopotamian Mythology of the Creation and the Flood

With Arabic Transliterations, and Arabic and English Translations of Relevant Passages from the Ancient Literature and the Hebrew Genesis

Saad D. Abulhab

Blautopf Publishing

B l a u t o p f Publishing
blautopfpublishing.com
New York

Colophon
English text set in *Cambria*, and *Calibri*
Arabic text set in *Arabetics Latte. PF Nuyork Arabic,* and *Arial*
Hebrew text set in *SBL Hebrew*

Publisher's Cataloging-in-Publication Data

Lost in Translation, Presumption, and Interpretation:
Adam, Noah, and the Ancient Mesopotamian Mythology of the Creation and the Flood.
With Arabic Transliterations, and Arabic and English Translations of Relevant Passages from the Ancient Literature and the Hebrew Genesis / Saad D. Abulhab
p. cm.
1. Adam (Biblical figure) 2. Noah (Biblical figure). 3. Gilgamesh
4. Bible stories, Hebrew -- O.T. Genesis
5. Epic poetry, Assyro-Babylonian -- History and criticism
6. Epic poetry, Assyro-Babylonian -- Translations into English
7. Epic poetry, Assyro-Babylonian -- Translations into Arabic
I. Title.

BS580.A4 A23 2020
221.924–dc22
Library of Congress Control Number: 2020935896
CIP

ISBN: 978-0984984398 (hardcover)
ISBN: 979-8630345981 (paperback)

First Edition

Printed by Lightning Source©, an INGRAM© company

28 26 24 22 20 8 7 6 5 4 3 2 1

DEDICATION

To the many wonderful and loving people in my life, family, relatives, friends, and colleagues, whose generous and vital moral, intellectual, and material support over the years have made it possible for me to live a very happy, meaningful, challenging, and productive life.

TABLE OF CONTENTS

Introduction

The common, biblical beliefs in an initial, single human creation, and a subsequent survival of a punishing, catastrophic flood were among the key forming pillars of the Near East monotheist religions. The other key pillar was, arguably, the belief in the existence of a one, supreme god and creator. However, neither the two stories of human creation and catastrophic flood, nor the belief in one supreme god, were originally introduced by these monotheist religions. Key inscriptions from ancient Mesopotamia have clearly indicated that various versions of these beliefs were commonplace for thousands of years before. Despite the differences in details, and at times ambiguities, the monotheist faiths seem to have derived their defining themes from one source: early Mesopotamian mythology. Unfortunately, several key inscriptional facts supporting this hypothesis were lost in the current transliterations, translations, and interpretations of the ancient texts. The work presented in this book attempts to highlight these historical facts.

According to Genesis in the Old Testament, the first monotheist human was a god-created being named Adam, a long-lived male who supposedly lasted for almost a thousand years. We are told in Genesis that Adam had spawned several, similarly long-lived generations, before the arrival of his great, great grandson, Noah. At some point during Noah's time, god became unhappy with the humans and decided to limit their age to 120 years, but eventually decided to eliminate them all together, by enacting a total and catastrophic flood on earth. Noah and his immediate family members were the only survivors of this flood, according to Genesis, making him, in reality, the actual first human (i.e. Adam II) and father of humanity. Only after the passing of a few of Noah's generations, the lower human age limit was apparently applied.

The suggestion by monotheists that the early generations of the first human had lived a long life, similar to that of a typical Mesopotamian god, should swing the door wide open to reasonable scientific speculation and questioning as to who Adam and Noah really were, and how they were initially perceived by both the early Mesopotamians and monotheists. In Genesis, we were not only told that Adam was formed with a blood similar to that of a god, repeating a similar claim by the Babylonian Creation Epic, but he was also proclaimed "as one of us" by the god. The huge age difference between Adam and his immediate generations on one side, and that of a typical human on the other, is not a secondary factor to ignore. Genesis' justification for this human age discrepancy was neither consistent nor satisfactory.

Despite the many references to the one god in Genesis, *Yihwa Alhim* (God the Almighty), the reader is left confused whether this god was the only god present in the universe. One concludes after reading Genesis that the writer was not actually a believer in one god, the key defining pillar of a monotheistic faith. While Genesis' passages stating that Adam was formed with god's blood and became one of the gods can be argued, its explicit claim about the existence of sons of god (i.e. gods) cannot be disputed. Genesis claimed that because the sons of god took many human daughters as wives, god decided to limit the human age to 120 years.

The Quran, the other major monotheist book, generally acknowledged the two stories of Adam and Noah told by Genesis. However, it did not offer any details regarding ages or immediate generations. Although it is widely believed that the Quran had adopted the two stories from Genesis, examining some key relevant details in the Quran reveals access to additional, different sources. These sources seem to be rooted in some sort of an early collective folklore memory carried on over the centuries by the ancient populations of the greater Arabian Peninsula, including the Fertile Crescent. For example, the shape, dimensions, passengers, and resting location of the Noah arc in the Quran were not only completely different than those of the Old Testament, but also conforming with the ancient Mesopotamian literature. As for the one god concept, the Quran was surely clearer and more confident and decisive, compared to Genesis.

Pinpointing when and where the first monotheist religion was established in the Near East, or who was the first monotheist, cannot be attested by any ancient inscriptional evidence. However, it is safe to assume that sometime during the first millennium BCE, a Mesopotamian, presumably named Abram, was preaching some sort of a monotheistic message. This can be attested by reading passages from the Hebrew Old Testament, and more importantly by the circumstantial evidence presented by the eventual emergence of several prominent monotheist religions in the area attributing their competing, and sometimes conflicting, new beliefs to an Abraham. Abram's name was updated by god to Abraham after he migrated from Mesopotamia, according to Genesis. Namely, the emergence over a thousand-year time period (possibly 600 BCE-600CE) of the so-called Abrahamic religions: Judaism, Mandaean, Christianity, and Islam.

All but a few key monotheist characters and events were believed to be taken place, or connected with, ancient Mesopotamia. To trace the root of the early monotheist god, one must start with the Mesopotamian gods. Specifically, one must look into the supreme Mesopotamian god, *anu*, the god of sky and havens, who was very likely the one god referenced by early monotheists, with some character modifications. Curiously, the root Arabic word *alu* of which the first monotheist god name was derived from, is clearly related to the root word *anu*, linguistically and in meaning. The word *ilu* is the generic Akkadian word used in the meaning of god or deity. In fact, the god *anu*/anum was routinely referred to in major Mesopotamian texts, like the Code of Hammurabi, as *ilu/ilum*. In other words, the Hebrew god of Genesis, *alhim/ilhim*, is linguistically related to *anum/ilum*. The optional ending letter *m* was typically used for emphasis in ancient Arabic from Yemen to Iraq. The letter *h* was likely added in the same manner it was added to update the name *abram/ibram* to *abraham/ibrahim*. Studying the history of monotheism should be conducted within the frames of early Mesopotamian culture. Analyzing relevant ancient Mesopotamian texts is undoubtedly the best way to obtain factual clues about the evolution of monotheism.

To conduct a balanced and neutral study of the above topics, I have offered in this book new, original translations of the relevant texts regarding the first gods, first humans, and the story of the flood in four major ancient Mesopotamian inscriptions, and in Hebrew Genesis of the Old Testament. These original translations utilized both the modern etymological dictionaries of the Akkadian and Sumerian languages, and the historical Arabic language etymological references. Linguistic text analysis is the best, and possibly the only available methodology to speculate with some degree of accuracy about the common traditional beliefs of the pre-monotheist people in the Near East region. The old Arabic etymological references, which were written more than a thousand years ago, brilliantly analyzed Arabic words' roots and offered ancient, extinct meanings. These references should be considered as primary tools for the translation of any and all early Arabic (i.e. the so-called Semitic) texts.

Specifically, I have provided in this book new, original Arabic transliterations, and Arabic and English translations for about 250 line entries from *The Babylonian Creation Epic--Enuma Elish* (~1750-1200 BCE), *The Adapa Epic* (~1700 BCE), *The Sumerian Creation Myth --Eridu Genesis* (~1600 BCE), and Genesis of the Hebrew Old Testament. For convenience, I have also included my original Arabic transliterations, and Arabic and English translations for about 350 line entries from the Standard Babylonian edition of *The Epic of Gilgamesh* (~1300-1000 BCE), which were published in one of my books back in 2016. Based on my readings and analysis of the literary evidence presented in the above sources, I will share below several key, fact-driven observations indicating the undeniable ancient Mesopotamian roots of the one god, Adam, Noah, and the flood narratives.

To the Ancient Mesopotamians, the creation of early gods was the key to the creation of the humans and the universe. The god Anu, a third generation god, was the first god to be born, not formed, as a perfect god. The first couple of gods formed, *Lahmu* and *Lihamu*, whose names literally translate to "*mass of flesh*", were imperfect deities. The second improved, formed couple, *Ashar* and *Qishar*, whose names literally translate to *bone* and *skin*, were not related to the first gods but were formed like them from scratch. They were the parents of Anu. However, while the father *Ashar* was not consistently given a deity title in the Babylonian literature, his son Anu, who became later the god of heavens, was not only given this title but was the only one referred to by using the word *ilum* (i.e. the god) alone, in the meaning of "the god". Despite the rise of several other important gods over a period of thousands of years, Anu continued to be recognized as the supreme god of the land.

According to the *Babylonian Creation Epic*, the forming of the first human came about to solidify the outcome of a major inner war between the high ranking gods, and to alleviate the hard work typically assigned to lower ranking gods. The epic stated that the first human was formed partially from the blood of a punished, sacrificed god to do the tedious hard work of the lower gods. In other words, the first human/partial god, *lullu* or *amilu* whose name literally means "hard worker", was assigned hard work as a punishment. Clearly, the main characteristics of the first man according to the Babylonian creation story, including his blood, age, and function, are identical to those of Adam in the Hebrew Genesis.

Many scholars refer to the ancient Mesopotamian *Adapa Epic* as a possible missing link to the story of Adam. They do have a point. Based on the historical Arabic etymological references, the word *adapa* could also be *adaba*, which is identical to the word *adama*, linguistically and in meaning. However, the main details of the story of Adapa do not fit with those of the story of Adam. It is true that Adapa was forgiven by the god Anu for defying him, just as Adam was forgiven by the Hebrew god *alhim*, but Adapa was neither punished to do the hard work of the land nor granted a long life. He was just sent back to where he came from, like Gilgamesh was. The story of Gilgamesh is the only Mesopotamian story that can be compared to some extent to that of Adapa. Gilgamesh like Adapa, had the opportunity to eat the food of eternal life, after a difficult journey in the wild waters of the oceans, but lost it.

The story of Noah and the flood is a fundamental pillar of monotheism. Noah according to the Abrahamic faiths was the actual father of all nations, practically assuming the role of Adam. Unlike the story of Adam, Noah's story was unquestionably an ancient Mesopotamian folk story. It is fully attested in several pre-monotheist inscriptions, based on modern discoveries. Even though the details of the story in these ancient inscriptions do not match those of the Hebrew Genesis, my reading revealed several details matched those given in the Quran, the other major monotheistic book. This indicates that the key stories of the monotheistic faiths were in fact adapted, with a varied extent and/or interpretations, from a cache of historical folk tales that were preserved over a very long period of time.

First, my reading revealed that the ancient Mesopotamians have used a nickname for the main character in the flood story that was identical in meaning to the eventual nickname, Noah. That nickname was *rawqu*, meaning "the distant" or "the withdrawn", which is identical in meaning, according to the Arabic historical references, to the word *nawḥu*, for Noah. Incidentally, this evidence flatly rejects any notion that the name Noah was an actual first or given name.

Second, my reading confirmed the circular/cylindrical shape (i.e. *fulk*) of the vessel used by Noah as given in the Quran. It also confirmed Genesis description that it was a covered vessel sealed, inside and outside, with closed compartments. However, the dimensions given in Genesis, which were those of a standard long ship, did not only contradict with those alluded in the Quran and confirmed by the old inscription, but also with the shape name offered by Genesis itself, *tibah* or *tibat* (ie. chest). Possibly, the writer of Genesis had freely speculated about the meaning of *tibah* and conceptualized the dimensions of a long coffin, the other standard old Arabic meaning of the word *tibah*, instead of the actual less-used meaning, chest. The Greek translated *tibah* as *κιβωτός, meaning* "box, chest, coffin".

Third, my reading confirmed that the mountain which presumably held the vessel was indeed the one given in the Quran (i.e. *al-Jawdiyy)*. In the standard Babylonian edition of *The Epic of Gilgamesh*, the name was either *niṣir* or *nimuš*. The meaning of these two names according to old Arabic are "the keeper for good" or "the keeper of good secret", respectively. These meanings are the same meanings for *al-Jawdiyy*, which means "doer of good" or "keeper of good". I have speculated few years ago that *Mount al-Jawdiyy* is in fact one of the *Ajyād* mountain chain surrounding Macca. One mountain in this chain was named *al-Amīn* before Islam, meaning "the keeper", and was later re-named *Abu-Qbays*, because it was commonly believed that it was the source of the holly black stone of *Kaʿbah*.

After examining the older Sumerian version of the flood story in *The Eridu Genesis*, I was able to confirm my speculation beyond any doubt. In the line about the mountain holding the vessel, the older Sumerian inscription used *mount BAL* meaning "the keeper mountain," and immediately explained it as *mount DILMON-NA*, meaning "the black rock mountain". It explained further that this mountain was located in the land of the house of *god*[god]*Šamaš*, or the land of the departing (setting) of the sun. Mecca, which was already a holy place for thousands of years before Islam, is located in western Arabia, southwest of Mesopotamia. It is far more geologically-logical destination for any Mesopotamian catastrophic flood, compared to that of the Hebrew Genesis destination, *uru-rut*, or *uru-ruḍ* (i.e. seat (land) of the rivers), the historical kingdom of *Arārāt*.

Curiously, the story of the flood in Gilgamesh revealed open hostility by god *Enlil* toward the humans, and indirectly toward god *Idim*, the Sumerian counterpart of god *Ea* (or *Ḥea*), the "father" of humanity. According to the modern Assyriology dictionaries and the historical Arabic manuscripts, the word *Enlil* (i.e. *En-lil*) means the lord (i.e. father) of *lil*, where *lil* is linguistically associated with foolishness, evil, ghosts, chaos, wind, and turbulences. Meanwhile, the words *Idim* (from root word *adama*) and *Ea* (or *Ḥea*) are associated with life, water, fertility, and creation. This story of animosity and jealousy is almost identical to the Quranic story of animosity between *Iblīs* (Satan: the father of the genies and fools), whose name is linguistically and functionally identical to *Enlīl*, and *Ādam* (the father of humans). It also support my earlier observation that the Quran had access to additional sources, other than Genesis, and brings up the likelihood that the monotheist characters Adam and Satan were simply the Mesopotamian gods *Idim* and *Enlil*, downgraded. Even the fact that the word *Ḥewa* (i.e. Eve) of Genesis is identical linguistically and in meaning, functionality, and action with *Ḥea* should not be overlooked. After all, it was *Ḥea*, the father of the living, who misled Adapa to defy god *Anu*, just like *Ḥewa*, the mother of the living, did with Adam.

The subject of death and life was in the center of the stories of Adam and Noah as they were told in all relevant and related ancient Mesopotamian and Near Eastern literature. People have never managed to understand or accept death as a living fact, in the past or present . This was especially true in ancient times, where the mystery of life and death was only explained through the actions of reward and punishment by a supreme force. Not understanding and/or accepting a fact can surely open the doors wide to presumptions and interpretations. This in turn becomes an ideal environment to produce rich, dramatic, confusing, and conflicting fictional tales.

In the following chapters, I will discuss in more details my new and old readings of the relevant lines in the old inscriptions as presented in this book, and in Genesis. In Part 1, I will provide the common Latin (and Hebrew when applicable) transliterations as provided by the scholars, and then add my own equivalent Arabic transliterations along with my English and Arabic translations. My English translations will attempt to follow the linguistic spirit of the texts rather than attempting to utilize grammatically correct usages. In Part 2, I will also include the referenced words entries from the modern Akkadian and Sumerian dictionaries in addition to those of the historical Arabic etymological references.

1

Adam and the Early Mesopotamian Creation Mythology

The hypothesis of a creation of an initial single human from scratch, is the central thematic and philosophical element of monotheism, whether it was originated in Mesopotamia or elsewhere. It embodies the fundamental tenets of the monotheistic concepts of creation and supreme creator. It explains the nature of the first created human and the destiny of humanity. It determines the roots of punishment and rewards in relation to the one god. Whether the first human was created from scratch by a supreme intelligence, or evolved naturally, characterizes the validity of human awareness, and the essence and order of intelligence itself. Singling out ancient Mesopotamia for this study is crucial, since today the term monotheism became synonym to the so-called Abrahamic monotheism of the three major world religions, Judaism, Christianity, and Islam, which are believed to be originated from that area. Although the Hebrew Old Testament does not seem to be the sole monotheist source consulted for the topic of human creation in Islam and Christianity, it should nonetheless be the key one to examine, because it was the earliest one.

Modern readings in the literary work of ancient Mesopotamia, comprising modern Iraq and most of Syria today, indicate that the story of the first Monotheist human, Adam, shares key details with several stories of the ancient literature. The nature of the first human was neither clear nor consistent in both. However, the struggle between good and evil, and the contrast of death and eternal life, were the main hallmarks of all these stories. When taking into account that these ancient folk tales were circulated for thousands of years, matching the exact, identical name of the first human, Adam, becomes less important, and not the only definitive factor to trace back his story. Particularly since all the names used for the major characters in these time periods, gods, humans, or mixed beings, were methodological, descriptive names or nick names, rather than actual names. According to the inscriptions, most of these characters were referred to by different names in various historical time periods and/or geographical localities.

In this study, several ancient stories will be examined to understand the nature of the first human and the mythological settings surrounding his creation, and to extract any possible linkages to the prevailing, modern story of Adam. Most emphasis will be on similarities and common elements between these stories as evident through various readings of inscriptions and manuscripts. Translations that are primarily based on *actual* historical dictionaries, like the old etymological Arabic references, are crucial to arrive to the correct readings. In all these stories, one should concentrate on their three main narrative elements: the nature of the initial first human, his immortality status, and the events shaping the outcomes. One should also keep in mind the fact that while many pre-historic ancient stories had survived, none had ever being retold intact. Different versions of identical ancient stories were likely introduced over the centuries and millenniums, after being influenced by the unique factors of specific geographical locations and historical periods.

There are three key elements in the monotheist story of Adam. First, he was initially a divine creature created from scratch by god, in terms of blood, look and immortality status. Second, his immortality status was threatened by unintentional and uncontrolled circumstances. Third, these circumstances involved an open conflict between good and evil forces. As for the first element, the Hebrew Genesis was solidly clear that Adam was not only created with the blood of a god but he also had the look and feel of a god. Current translations of line 1:26 in Genesis claim it said "*Let us make man in our image, after our likeness*".* However, while the first relevant Hebrew word in the line, *bi-ṣalamnū*, correctly meant "in our image", the second word, *ka-damwutnū*, could not have meant "*as our likeness*". Surely, the word *dumyatu* can mean "*image*" in old Arabic and Hebrew, and one can hypothesize it could also mean "*likeness*", but using two words with identical meanings after each other would be an unneeded repetition. This word was clearly related to the root Arabic words *damū* and *damā*, meaning blood. Therefore, *ka-damwutnū* can either mean "*as our blood*" or "*as a piece of our blood*". Similarly, the phrase *bi-damwūt ilhim ʿsah ʾatū* in line 5:1 meant "*with a blood of god he made him*" or "*with a piece of god's blood he made him*", not "*in the likeness of God he made him*".† Furthermore, to emphasize his divine status, the Hebrew Genesis quoted God addressing Adam in line 3:22 saying "*Adam had become as one of us*", just before he was offered to eat from the "*Tree of life*" to acquire the long life of a typical god, living for a millennium.‡ Below is an original reading by the author from the Hebrew Genesis, lines 1:26, 3:22, and 5:1, respectively:§

> *And God said: 'let us make human(s) in our image, as a piece of our blood, and let them benefit by the fish of the sea, and by the fowl of the air, and by the cattle, and by all the earth, and by every creeping thing that is creeping upon the earth.' And God created the human(s) in his own characteristic, in the characteristic of god he created him, male and female he created them. ....*
>
> *And God Almighty said: 'Here, Adam had become as one of us, calling for good and evil, and he even may put forth his hand,' and he (Adam) took part of the tree of life, and ate, and lived for long. ......*
>
> *This is the book of the generations of Adam. In the day God created Adam, with a piece of God's blood he made him. Male and female he created them, and blessed them, and called their name Adam, in the day of their creation. ....*

The Quran, on the other hand, did not offer any details or comment regarding Adam's age, blood type, look, or immortality status. According to the Quran, the first human was formed from clay or mud, but he was also created from *ʿalaq*, an old Arabic word meaning blood.** The Quran further said that this human was formed from clay and blood, first, but he was given an image afterwards.†† By saying "he was given an image" but avoiding any further details about that image, or the blood type, the Quran was simply being consistent with a central teaching in Islam: the look and nature of god is unknown to us, and one should not even speculate about it. However, and despite his classification as the first prophet by Muslim scholars, there is no single reference in the Quran explicitly referring to Adam as a prophet; he was only referred to as being a chosen one, along with Noah and a couple more prophets and their immediate sons, and that was interpreted as being a prophet.‡‡ On the contrary, the Quran gave Adam a godly status by saying he was created from mud but was then filled

---

*Genesis (1:26) וַיֹּאמֶר אֱלֹהִים נַעֲשֶׂה אָדָם בְּצַלְמֵנוּ

†Genesis (5:1) בִּדְמוּת אֱלֹהִים עָשָׂה אֹתוֹ

‡Genesis (3:22) לָדַעַת טוֹב וָרָע וְעַתָּה פֶּן-יִשְׁלַח יָדוֹ וְלָקַח גַּם מֵעֵץ הַחַיִּים וְאָכַל וָחַי לְעֹלָם וַיֹּאמֶר יְהוָה אֱלֹהִים הֵן הָאָדָם הָיָה כְּאַחַד מִמֶּנּוּ

§For additional translations and transliterations details, see Part 1.5 and Part 2.4 of this book.

**Quran (96:2) خلق الإنسان من علق

††Quran (7:11) ولقد خلقناكم ثم صورناكم ثم قلنا للملائكة اسجدوا لآدم فسجدوا إلا إبليس لم يكن من الساجدين

‡‡Quran (3:33) إن الله اصطفى آدم ونوحا وآل إبراهيم وآل عمران على العالمين

with the spirit or soul of a god. The Quran even emphasized this status by stating god had asked all divine characters of heaven to prostrate to him, a worship act reserved for gods, not the prophets. By substituting god's blood with god's spirit, the Quran reaffirmed Adam as a creature of godly characteristics, consistent with how the Hebrew Genesis described him, rather than a common human.* According to the Quran, only Jesus was created in an arguably-similar process as Adam, with a divine sprit blow and without two parents.† Aside from the Quran, most early Muslim scholars believed Adam was a giant living for a millennium. In other words, he was not a normal human.

The immortality status of Adam and the event surrounding his desire to attain it, marked the additional two central elements of his monotheist story. The premise of the first element was that his disobedience of god, even if unintended or caused by misinformation, was the reason behind human mortality. In both the Hebrew Genesis and the Quran, Adam risked his eternal life because he defied the god after becoming a victim of deception, but he was forgiven afterwards. However, following his forgiveness in Genesis, Adam was given a very long life, rather than the eternal life he was seeking when he ate from the forbidden tree. God invited him to eat from the "*Tree of Life*", to live a long life, not eternal life. The Hebrew word לְעֹלָם in line 3:22 means "*for a very long*" not "*forever*" as most current translations claim. In the Quran, the topic of Adam's age was left open, allowing Muslim scholars to speculate that he had lived the age claimed by Genesis without offering any details.

The Hebrew Genesis further detailed how the later human generations lost their ability to attain a very long life and why their age was limited to 120 years. It explained that because many *sons of gods* mated with many pretty human daughters and had mixed children, the god became angry seeing his soul being attached to too many partial humans.‡ Genesis's explanation, of course, openly contradicted the concept of one god, which monotheism routinely pride itself for pioneering, since the sons of gods were gods as the following reading by the author of lines 6:1-3 clearly suggests:§

> *And because the society of the humans became huge, on the crust of the earth, and daughters were born to them, the sons of God sheltered the daughters of the humans because they were beautiful, and they took as women (spouses) for them, whomever they wanted. And the Almighty said: 'My soul shall not abide for long in a human, in a mischievous; he is flesh,' and his days were (since) hundred and twenty years.*

The events surrounding Adam's loss of immortality marked the second key element of the story of Adam, where he is depicted as a victim of an evil character plotting to hurt him and/or end humanity. The conflict between good and evil is the main theme here. Both Genesis and the Quran explained how that evil character deceived Adam and his wife to disobey god's order to bring punishment upon him. While Genesis represented this character by a (satanic?) serpent, the Quran identified it as *Iblīs* (i.e Satan) and explained he is a *gin* (i.e. ghost) who was once among god's divine characters but was later expelled from heaven because he defied god, by refusing to prostrate to Adam. According to the Quran, Satan was the father of all *gins* and Adam was the father of all humans**. Muslims believe Satan (i.e. *al-Shayṭān*) was formed from fire, unlike Adam who was

---

*Quran (38:71-72) إذ قال ربك للملائكة إني خالق بشرا من طين. فإذا سويته ونفخت فيه من روحي فقعوا له ساجدين

†Quran (3:59) إن مثل عيسى عند الله كمثل آدم خلقه من تراب ثم قال له كن فيكون

‡Genesis (6:1) וַיְהִי כִּי-הֵחֵל הָאָדָם לָרֹב עַל-פְּנֵי הָאֲדָמָה וּבָנוֹת יֻלְּדוּ לָהֶם (6:2) וַיִּרְאוּ בְנֵי-הָאֱלֹהִים אֶת-בְּנוֹת הָאָדָם כִּי טֹבֹת הֵנָּה וַיִּקְחוּ לָהֶם נָשִׁים מִכֹּל אֲשֶׁר
בָּחָרוּ (6:3) וַיֹּאמֶר יְהוָה לֹא-יָדוֹן רוּחִי בָאָדָם לְעֹלָם בְּשַׁגַּם, הוּא בָשָׂר וְהָיוּ יָמָיו מֵאָה וְעֶשְׂרִים שָׁנָה

§For additional translations and transliterations details, see Part 1.5 and Part 2.4 of this book

**Quran (18:50) وإذ قلنا للملائكة اسجدوا لآدم فسجدوا إلا إبليس كان من الجن ففسق عن أمر ربه أفتتخذونه وذريته أولياء من دوني وهم لكم عدو بئس للظالمين بدلا

formed from clay. It is important to observe here that in the monotheist story of Adam, the conflict was initially between Satan, as the force of evil, and the God, as the force of good, not between Satan and Adam. Adam was a victim, first. Only after the god said "*Adam had become as one of us*" that Adam started to take the role of a messenger/force of good, like the god, as we saw earlier when reading line 3:22 of Genesis.

Undoubtedly, the story of Adam must have been substantially based, at least partially, on several previously circulating folk stories involving its main characters and key events, from the greater Mesopotamia region, which includes most of the Fertile Crescent today. Observing the main elements of the story, and examining the key functionalities and name meanings of its main characters should easily reveal their actual attested identities. A name of a character can change significantly over the millenniums since it is only a nickname, but its characteristics and roles only evolve slightly into different ones to fit the religious and geopolitical desires in various historical time periods. A good example is Satan, which the Quran called *Iblīs* or *al-Shayṭān*. He is without the slightest doubt *godEnlil* of Mesopotamia, himself, who was also known as *godAmurri* and *godEllil*. A strait forward analysis of all his nicknames, and his key roles, revealed he was the lord of *gins* (ghosts) in ancient Mesopotamia, a creator of storms and chaos, an angry stubborn god who threatens and blusters, an instigator of jealousy, hate, and skepticism, and a desperate, crazy, fool devil.* These are the characteristics of Satan after he was expelled from heaven, according to the narrative of the Quran. In fact, the story of the flood in the standard Babylonian edition of the Epic of Gilgamesh clearly revealed his roles as such, as the following reading by the author of lines 157-206 from Tablet 11 show below. Notice the evil role played by *GodEnlil* in his attempt to annihilate humanity by the flood, through an eyewitness account told by *Uta-Napištim* (Noah) to Gilgamesh, describing what he saw and heard immediately after leaving the vessel at the top of *Mt. Nimuš* (also *Mt. Niṣir*).

> *I lifted up an offering (sheep) to the four cardinal directions [to the four seas] and sacrificed (it). I held incense (session) in the top of [around] the mountain peak. I fumed (smoked) seven and (then) seven (more) flasks. In their underneath (in the flasks or in the fire beneath them), I threw, in portions (gradually), reed, cedar wood, and myrtle leaves scent. The gods smelled the savour. The gods smelled the sweet {soothing} savour. The gods gathered, like scorpions (hypocrites) [flies], over [around] the giver of the gratitude (the sacrifice). The lady of god (Aruru), immediately, at her arrival, she belittled their majesties the hypocrites of godAnim; she made them like her laughingstock: 'The gods, herein, let them have (wear) the lapis lazuli stones of my interior [bottom] (i.e. my feces), (so) I should not forget them. These days, herein, I shall mourn forever, (so) I should not forget them. The gods should come to the incense (session), (but) The godEnlil should not come to the incense (session). That is (because) he had not restrained himself (he acted carelessly), he established the Deluge, and he fated (destined) my people to the pileup ruin [to the ruin]'. The god Enlil, immediately, at his arrival, he saw the raft; godEnlil toughened (became angry). He was filled with rage of (at) the gods, the Igigi gods (the underground jins or ghosts): 'Over here (bring over here), the escaped living being [Over here (bring out here), the living being]. No man should survive in the pileup ruin [the ruin]'. The godNinurta let go [held and let go] his mouth (tongue), shouting. He said to god Enlil the warrior (hero): 'Who other than god Ea can accomplish (such) matter (plan)? For godEa had acquired all the skills [the experiences]'. GodEa let go [held and let go] his mouth (tongue), shouting. He said to Enlil the warrior (hero): 'You are the most revered of the gods, a warrior (hero). How, how could you not restrain yourself (how could you act carelessly), (and) instate the Deluge? (on) The one of a sin (on the perpetrator of a sin), impose the equal of [equalize (match)] his sin. (on) The one of evil-doing [of offence] (on the perpetrator of evil-doing [of offence]), impose the equal of*

---

*For more details, see Part 2.5 of this book: References, Nicknames, and Meanings for Idim and Enlil.

[equalize (match)] his evil-doing [his offence]. Loosen up, so it would not be broken; tighten up, so it would not be loose. Rather than you instate the Deluge, a ferocious creature [a lion] could rise (appear) to eliminate the offenders (the disobedient). Rather than you instate the Deluge, a sly creature [a wolf] could rise (appear) to eliminate the offenders (the disobedient). Rather than you instate the Deluge, a famine could settle (pervade) to slaughter (to sweep) the land. Rather than you instate the Deluge, The ^{god}Erra (Errakal) could rise (appear) to slaughter (sweep) the land {the offenders (the disobedient)}. I, myself, did not disclose the internal (hidden) deal [judgement] of their majesties the gods. I made Atra-Hasis (Uta-Napištim) experience (see) a dream, he heard the internal (hidden) deal [judgement] of the gods. And now, the guidance (the decision) is (up) to his guider (his owner) (i.e. Ea)'. (then) The god IDIM (god EA) went up to the heart of the raft. He held my hands, he took me out. He pulled out the female (my wife) (and) made her squat at my side. He turned [touched] our fronts [our foreheads], standing still between us, granting us: 'In the past, Uta-Napištim (was) a human being. From now on, Uta-Napištim and his woman (his wife), let them have a destiny like preceding (bygone) gods. Let it be for them that Uta-Napištim shall dwell far away, in (at) the mouth (source) of the rivers'. (and so) They took (put) me far away at the mouth (source) of the rivers, they made me settle.

Compare Enlil's evil role in the standard Babylonian version quote above, with his good role in the following reading by the author, below, of lines C9-C10 and E1-E11 from a Sumerian version of the flood story, the Eridu Genesis (also known as the Sumerian Creation Myth), which is dated to around a millennium earlier.* It seems that around 700-1000 BCE, ^{God}*Enlil* was on his way to become the future Satan. Notice that in the later version, ^{God}*Idim* was the one boarding the raft and granting *Uta-Napištim* the eternal life, not ^{God}*Enlil* as most translations claim today. The name ^{God}*Idim* in line 11:199 was not a scribe error as most scholars claimed. It was the correct one! In the earlier version, it was ^{God}*Enlil* who granted the eternal life to *Zisudra* (i.e. *Zi Sudra: one with cycled or eternal life*), an earlier Sumerian nickname for *Uta-Napištim*:

.... The god (^{god}Anu), ^{god}Enlil [The confronter ^{god}Enlil], ^{god}Enki (^{god}EA), ^{goddess}Ninhursaga the pure, the gods [god of heaven (^{god}Anu)], blessed, declared as beneficial (designated) that the keeper of a pure earth shall be the confronter ^{god}Enlil. ....

That of the heaven conferred that he (the human) shall benefit from that of the earth, he shall be the one doing its tedious functions (hard work). The confronter ^{god}Enlil of the heaven conferred that he (the human) shall benefit from that of the earth, be doing its tedious functions (hard work). The small animal creatures descended the land, rushing descended. Zisudra the king, in front of the confronter ^{god}Enlil frightened he pleaded, stretched the floor (prostrated) in obedience. The confronter ^{god}Enlil touched Zisudra, ..., addressed (loudly): "The age (life) of an aging (bygone) god, blessed (granted) him." A long-lasting life of an aging (bygone) god, they blessed (awarded), descended (brought down). Back to that (since then), Zisudra the king, keeper (preserver) of the small animal creatures (and) the livestock of mankind's breathing life (the farm animals), they left (in his place) confined (isolated). (at) Mt. Bal (the keeper [triumph] mountain: Mt. al-Amin or Mt. Abu Qbays in Mecca), Mt. dilmun-na (the black rock mountain: Mt. Daylamiyya or Mt. Abu Qbays in Macca), (at) the land of [where] the house of ^{god}Shamash [the departing (setting) of the sun], they blessed (awarded) him the long age (life) (i.e. they settled him there forever).

The conflict of good and evil in the flood story of standard Babylonian edition of the Gilgamesh epic was between two Mesopotamian gods, *Enlil* and *Idim*, who was called *Ea* later on, the creator of the first human (i.e *luʿullu* or *ʿamilu*) according to the Babylonian Creation Epic, as shall be seen later. This human creator god versus human destroyer go conflict is identical to the conflict seen in the

*For additional translations and transliterations details, see Part 1.4 and Part 2.3 of this book

monotheist story of Adam, between the creator god and Satan. For the sake of identifying characters, it should not make a difference whether it was about annihilating humans by eliminating Adam or Noah. Looking at the two characters abstractly, Noah was Adam II. The monotheist story of Adam simply replaced the human creator, *godIdim*, with the supreme god of heavens, *godAnu* or *Alu* (also called *godAnum, godAnim,* or *Alum*), which the Hebrew Genesis called *Alahim*, adding final Arabic letter *mīm* for emphasis, and the Quran called *Allah*. This is expected since monotheism is about *one* supreme god. The god *Idim* became Adam and was simply downgraded to a super human of godly status in the reluctant Hebrew Genesis. A millennium later, the more assertive Quran only identified him as the father of humans without calling him god or prophet, but it hinted to his super divine status, as someone who other divine characters of heaven were required to prostrate to. Today, Adam is identified by most Muslim scholars as a prophet, and is even given the same long godly age claimed in the Hebrew Genesis. Additionally, it is very important to observe here that the names Adam and *Idim* are linguistically correlated.*

The gods *Enlil* and *Idim* were not the only gods keeping their divine roles under monotheism, in addition to the one supreme god of heavens *Anu* or *Alu*. Two important groups of gods working collectively, but separately, to serve the gods, also did. One of them was the *Anunnaki* group comprising of good soldier gods working under the command of *GodAnu*, both on earth and in heaven. The other one was the *Igigi* group working under the command of *GodEnlil*. This group initially comprised of good gods living in heaven and working with the *Anunnaki* to help *GodAnu*, just as Enlil was, but eventually most of them became bad gods following *Enlil*'s steps and living underground. This was evident in their role as the soldiers of *GodEnlil* in the Gilgamesh Epic flood story. In an almost identical fashion, Genesis and the Quran spoke about god's Angels (or *al-mala'ikah*), working in close proximity to the god, as a group. They spoke about the underground characters of *Gog* and *Magog* (in the Quran they were called *Yājūj* and *Mājūj*). In the Quran, one of god's angels, *Jibra'īl*, was even the one revealing the words of the Quran to prophet Muhammad. The Quran also spoke about good and bad underground *gins* (ghosts) as the generations of *Iblīs* (Satan). It is quite clear from their identical roles and characteristics that the Mesopotamian *Anunnaki* gods simply became the "*Angles of God*" and the *Igigi* gods became the *gins*, or the "*Gog* and *Magog*", under the new monotheist order. Again this was necessary to introduce the new *one* god concept. Once again, as with Adam, the names *Gog*, *Magog* and *Igigi* are linguistically correlated.†

At present, we do not have a single ancient Mesopotamian story with all the details of the Hebrew Genesis story of Adam, but we do know about several earlier stories including important bits and pieces from that story. Anyway, most stories should have some degree of originality even when they are similar to previous ones, and Adam's Hebrew story should not be an exception. Many scholars attempted to link the Adam story directly to specific earlier Mesopotamian stories. Korpel thinks it was a Canaanite story originally, citing another story with similar characters and events, which was discovered few years ago on several Ugaritic Cuneiform tablets from the late thirteen century BCE.‡ The main god in that story was *El* and was supposedly living on Mt. Ararat, otherwise known as the mountain where Noah settled according to the Hebrew Genesis and possibly the Gilgamesh Epic. At some point, god *El* expelled an Evil god named *Hurun* because he wanted to replace him, and in revenge *Hurun* transformed the *Tree of Life* to a *Tree of Death* and enveloped the whole world in a poisonous fog. God *El* then dispatched a good god named *Adam*, who was depended on the *Tree of*

*For more details, see Part 2.5 of this book: References, Nicknames, and Meanings for Idim and Enlil

†ibid. Page 144-47.

‡Marjo C. A. Korpel and Johannes C. DeMoor. *Adam, Eve, and the Devil: A New Beginning* (Hebrew Bible Monographs), 29, Apr 2014.

Life to maintain his immortality, so that he would fight *God Hurun* and restore the tree back. However, *God Hurun* transformed himself into a serpent and bit Adam, making him mortal forever. Eventually, *God Hurun* uprooted the Tree of Death after he was forced by the gods, and the goddess of Sun sent Adam a good woman to start the process of human reproduction.

Unfortunately, I was not able to personally examine the transliterations of the Ugaritic tablets that were used by Korpel, but I am confident her overall translation and story outline are accurate. I also think her speculation of a linkage between that story and the story of Adam is very valid. The main elements of the Ugaritic and Genesis stories are identical. The conflict was between god and Satan, with Adam being a victim, and *Hurun*'s goal was to hurt or eliminate Adam. The characters involved were almost identical in names: the *Tree of life*, *hilil* (i.e the serpent), *El* (i.e *Alu*, *Alhim*, or *Allah*), Adam, and *Hurun,* (i.e Satan). The name *Hurun* was clearly another nick name of Satan (i.e *Enlil*), likely pronounced *Ḥurun* and derived from the Arabic root word *ḥrn*, which means "the stubborn or the unruly".* The word *hilīl* or *hilāl* is derived from Arabic root word *hll* and which means "male serpent", among many other meanings.† The most significant fact attested by the Ugaritic story is that the main characters, Adam and Satan, were indeed gods, just as concluded in this study. Also, this story clearly corroborated several unique details from the story of Adam in Genesis and the Quran, and indicated that the Quran must have had additional sources, other than Genesis. Still, this Ugaritic story does not seem to be the direct source of the monotheist story of Adam because the events of the two stories are significantly different. Rather, these stories must have *independently* referenced various earlier Mesopotamian based mythological stories, involving the gods *Anu*, *Idim*, and *Enlil*.

Some scholars thought the Myth of Adapa, a Mesopotamian story on a tablet dated from around 1700 BCE, was the earlier version of the biblical story of Adam. Their main argument was that the name Adam could be a later pronunciation of the name *Adapa* (*Adafa*) or *Adaba* . These scholars have a good point: the Sumerian letter sound *f* was often replaced with the Akkadian letter sound *b*, and they are anyway interchangeable in early Arabic. Also the letter sound *b* is interchangeable with the letter sound *m*, in early Arabic so that *Adaba* could have easily been pronounced *Adama* and then Adam. However, it is very clear that the key elements of this story and even its main character, *Adapa*, do not fit at all with those of the monotheist story of Adam. There was no conflict between good and evil or even between gods. There was no deception or even defiance of god's order. In the end, *Adapa* remained a mortal human. If any, in terms of its main character and outcome, the ending and key hero character of this story resemble that of the story of Gilgamesh, who was the king of Eridu's neighboring city of *Shuruppak* (*Shurubba'ak*) after his meeting with *Uta-Napištim* (Noah). Below are two relevant readings by the author from the tablet of the Myth of Adapa, lines 1:1-18, 12:11, and 2:57-70, and from the flood story in the Epic of Gilgamesh, Tablet 11, lines 207-307.‡

Myth of Adapa, lines 1:1-18, 12:11, and 2:57-70:

> His (Adapa's) shout (command) is like the shout (command) of an enraged (angry) god. He (god Ea) crowned (assigned) him wide knowledge, the heavy obligation of the earth, all of it. To that one (to Adapa), he gave him expertise, (but) he did not give him eternal life. In his days, in those years, the affable son of Eridu, god Ea built him as a model in the mankind. The affable, (whom) no one could [would] obstruct (challenge) his shout (command). The determined, the extra sensing of (the listener

---

*حرن (الصَحَاح في اللغة) فرسٌ حَرونٌ: لا ينقاد، وإذا اشتدَّ به الجريُ وقف. وقد حَرَنَ يَحْرُنُ حُروناً. وحَرُنَ بالضم، أي صار حَروناً. ويقال: حَرَنَ في البيع، إذا لم يزد ولم يُنقِص.

†هلل (لسان العرب) والهِلالُ: الحيَّة ما كان، وقيل: هو الذكر من الحيّات؛

‡For additional translations and transliterations details, see Part 1.2 and Part 2.2 of this book

to) ^{gods}Anunnaki, was he. Ready (prepared), hands-clean, anointed, a seeker of responsibilities. With the cooks, he does the cooking. With the cooks of Eridu, he does the cooking. The food and water of Eridu he makes daily. In his clean hands, he throws down (spreads) the dining sheet. And without him, the dining sheet is not separated (removed). (one time) He steered a ship, doing the fishing, the (bird) hunting of Eridu. At that time, Adapa the son of Eridu, |while {wherein}| ^{god}Ea in bed, in chamber, he attended to Eridu's repletion (feeding), daily. ....

(^{god}Anu said:) "Adapa, the son of ^{god}Ea, has crossed [broke] the edges of the south wind." ....

(^{god}Anu said:) Why ^{god}Ea, (to) the not honored [chosen] mankind, that of heaven and earth (their inner working), he handed it to him (enabled him to it)? (in) A heart of void land [unknown], he set him in; he himself (^{god}Ea), he had done (that) to him. We, what shall we do with him? Food of (eternal) life, let him take, to eat. Food of (eternal) life, they let him take, (but) he did not eat. Water of (eternal) life, they let him take, (but) he did not drink. A dress, they let him take, (and) he dressed (himself). Oil, they let him take, (and) he oiled (himself). ^{god}Anu got confused, he shouted in (from) around him (Adapa): "Come, Adapa, why are you not eating, not drinking? People shall not be living (eternally), no matter how (the days) are turned around". (Adapa answered:) "^{god}Ea, my lord, spoke (loudly): 'don't eat, don't drink'." (^{god}Anu said:) "Take him, return him to his dwelling-place."

Epic of Gilgamesh Tablet 11, lines 207-307:

.... And now, who will assemble the gods for (achieving) that [for you]? The (eternal) life that you aim [want] to be given, (come) Work hard for (it), do not lay down (sleep) for six days and seven nights". He sat in between his legs (crouched). Sleep, like dust [Ambergris perfume], is spreading (blowing) over [around] him. Uta-Napištim said to her, to his woman (wife): 'Look at this young man who intends (wants) (eternal) life! Sleep, like dust [Ambergris perfume], is spreading (blowing) over [around] him'. His woman (wife) said to him, to Uta-Napištim: 'Divert him [Touch him], let the man be startled (awakened). Let him go back (through) the road he went (came), in safety. Let him go back (through) the great gate he exited, to his land'. Uta-Napištim said to her, to his woman (wife): 'Human is deceitful, he can deceive you. Go on, leave him his breads; set (put) them by his head, and the day in which he laid down (he slept) (through), document it in a brick (in a stone)'. She left him his breads; she set (put) them by his head, and the day in which he laid down (he slept) (through), she showed [marked] it in a brick (in a stone). The first [His first] bread was dry. The second was leathery (rubbery), the third was damp (soggy). His fourth, its Anise loaf oozed (sweated). The fifth brought in (produced) [was reached (stricken) by] mould. The sixth was baked and dried (fresh). (while) The seventh was tender, he (Uta-Napištim) diverted [touched] him, the man got startled (awakened). Gilgamesh said to him, to Uta-Napištim the withdrawn and distant (Noah): 'As soon as sleep settled over [around] me, Immediately [Rudely], you diverted me [touched me], disturbed (aroused) me'. Uta-Napištim said to him, to Gilgamesh: 'Come, Gilgamesh, mark [count] your breads, and for each day that you laid down [slept], let it have (give it) your mark [count] (for the bread) for that (day) [for you]. Your first bread was dry. The second was leathery (rubbery), the third was damp (soggy). The fourth one, your Anise loaf oozed (sweated). The fifth one, brought in (formed) [was reached (was struck) by] mold, the sixth was baked and dried (fresh). (while) The seventh was tender, I, myself diverted [touched] you {you got startled (awoke)}'. Gilgamesh said to him, to Uta-Napištim the withdrawn and distant (Noah): 'How, how should I proceed, Ut ZI (the life-given one: Uta-Napištim), where should I go? The Gripper has seized my organs. In my bed's room [my bed-chamber], death dwells. And wherever I will set |my foot [my face]|, there he is: death!'. Uta-Napištim said to him, to Ur-šánabi (the protector of eternity), the shipwright: 'O Ur-šánabi, may the gulf extract you (get rid of you), may the crossing boat reject you. That (gulf), where many adventures (took place) at its shores, tremble in fear (when) at its shore! The man who you came ahead of (you led; you brought here), his full body is covered with matted hair. His hides (animal leather clothes) took away (lessened) the entwined and polished look of his organs (of his body). Take him, Ur-šánabi, to the washtub of highness [washtub of purity] of his lords [Take him,

Ur-šánabi, direct him [bring him] to the washtub of highness [washtub of purity]]. Let him clean [rub off] his fullness (his whole body) in the waters, like a high one [a pure one] (like a god). Let him get rid of his hides (animal leather clothes), let the sea take them over [carry (bring) them away]. (with) Fine oil (perfume), anoint (massage) his body {for him}. Let him have his head band (his turban) made anew (be renewed). Let him have a robe dressed, befitting his dignity. (and) Until he goes (home) to his city, until he arrives to his way (finds his way home), the robe should not be afflicted by untidiness (should not become untidy); it should stay intact, new' Ur-šánabi took him to the washtub of highness [washtub of purity] of his lords. [Ur-šánabi took him, he directed him [he brought him] to the washtub of highness [washtub of purity]]. He cleaned [rubbed off] in the waters his fullness (his whole body), like a high one [a pure one] (like a god). He got rid of his hides (animal leather clothes), the sea took them over [carried (brought) them away] (with) Fine oil (perfume), he anointed (massaged) his body. His head band (his turban) was made anew (was renewed). He was dressed in a robe befitting his dignity, (making sure,) until he goes (home) to his city, until he arrives to his way (finds his way home), the robe should not be afflicted by untidiness (should not become untidy); it should stay intact, new. Gilgamesh and Ur-šánabi boarded the raft. They prepared (equipped) [put (launched)] the round raft, which they had (previously) boarded. His woman (wife) said to him, to Uta-Napištim: 'Gilgamesh rushed [jostled], endured, (and) incurred (struggled). What (little) have you given him (as) he returns (back) to his land?' As he, Gilgamesh, moved (unleashed) his punting-pole, (and as) the raft moved closer to the shore, Uta-Napištim said to him, to Gilgamesh: 'Gilgamesh, you came, you endured, (and) you incurred (struggled). What (little) have I given you (as) you return (back) to your land? I shall reveal, Gilgamesh, a matter of secret, and I shall tell you (about) an inner (hidden) deal of the gods, for (regarding) that (matter) [for you (only)]. It is a weed like a knife sharpener, located |under the Abzu|. Its (fine) thorns [Its file (rasp)] will scrape (make) your hands like a skinless (huskless) berry. If that weed [After that weed], your hands reach to it, |.......... you will gain the eternal life|'. Gilgamesh, immediately, in hearing that (when he heard that). He uncovered [opened] a waterway |......... to the ABZU|. He flipped upside down (threw downward into the Abzu) stones [tied] tightened (fastened) to [in] his feet [lower legs]. They (the stones) made him arrive (pulled him deep) to the Abzu .... He found his plant [the plant]; he swept it away (pulled it out) .... He cut loose the stones fastened in his feet [lower legs]. The sea threw him away (ejected him) to the shore. Gilgamesh said to him, to Ur-šánabi, the shipwright: 'O, Ur-šánabi, this weed is the plant of deliverance (salvation) [the plant for (against) hardship]. For a man, it delivers the living breath [the wink (spark) [trickle (flow)] of life] (the heartbeat) in his heart. I shall carry it [bring it] to Uruk-of-the-cattles-site [Uruk-of-the-alter]. I shall feed the weed to an old man, to test. If [(only) After it] the old man grew into a young man. I, myself, shall eat it to go back to my youth {to that of my youth (the age of my youth)}'. After 20 journeys (leagues), they broke a (bread) piece (they took a meal break). After 30 journeys (leagues), they stopped by a watering place. Gilgamesh saw the source of its fresh (cold) waters. He went to the middle of the waters to refresh. A snake smelled the scent of the weed. Quietly, it raised, it snatched [snapped] (ate) the weed. On its return, it got rid of (sloughed) a skin. Every day, Gilgamesh sat down crying. Over [Around] the surrounding of his nose (his cheeks), his tears rushed {went} down. |Gilgamesh said to him,| to Ur-šánabi, the shipwright: 'For whom of mine, Ur-šánabi, my arms struggled (endured). For whom of mine, the blood of my heart roiled (boiled). I have not secured (I have not achieved) a well done job to {in} (for) my own, (but) to the ferocious creature of the ground (den) (the snake), I have achieved a well done job. Now, after 20 journeys (leagues), the high (sea) tide is proceeding too fast. The (underground) tunnel, to uncover it [as I was uncovering it], I threw (down) ropes into it, step by step. What can I find that is placed to accompany (guide) me, so I, myself, can feel (my way down) to it? And I had [also] left the raft at the shore (now)'.

There were many ancient Mesopotamian gods, called by many different names, but only one supreme god, the god of heavens, who was called only by one name, *Anu* or *Alu* (sometimes *Anum*, *Anim*, or *Alum* after adding the optional *m* for the emphasis). In Akkadian, the sounds for *n* and *l* were often interchangeable. Since the Cuneiform symbol for *Anu* was the same as for the word *Alu* for *god*, many times, his name was not preceded by the usual *diğir* sign for deity, as it was the case for all other gods. Over the millenniums many new Mesopotamian gods were born and many old ones died or faded. Some gods were regional ones, while others, like *Idim* and *Enlil* were more universal, even when they were called by different nick names. Mesopotamian gods behaved like humans, in terms of aging, emotion, revenge, morality, and even sexual desires. They had wives, daughters and sons. They were males and females. This is why the Hebrew Genesis claim that Adam was formed in the image and blood of god, is not a strange or surprising claim. In fact, the ancient Babylonian Creation Epic, also referred to as *Enuma Eliš*, was primarily a creation epic of the Mesopotamian gods. Few lines in the tablets described the creation of the first human, and earth prior to the emergence of the gods, but most of the lines were about the struggles between the gods and the emergence of the grandson of *GodAnu*, *Marduk*, the powerful future god of Babylonia, who had supposedly created the heavens and placed his grandfather *GodAnu* there, as we shall see later. Below is an excerpt reading by the author from the Babylonian Creation Epic, Tablet 1, lines 1-73, detailing the events surrounding the creation of the early Mesopotamian gods, the key characters prior to their creation, the crowning of *GodAnu's son*, *GodEA* (i.e. *GodIdim*):*

> *When high above, had not been raised, heavens [When high above, had not been called heavens], (and) down below, the land terrain had not been mentioned by name. (that time) Abzu (of underground fresh water basin), their (the gods) foremost (chief) and creator, (and) maker Tiamat (of salt water sea), the one who gave birth to all of them (the gods), (were) downloading (penetrating into each other) their waters, as one; (and) The fields (pastures) were not depleted; the marshes [reeds] were not sought after [widespread]. When the gods were not revealed (made visible), anyone (none, were not mentioned by name, were not assigned destinies, they (Abzu and Tiamat) built (made/formed) the gods close to the. They revealed (made visible) godLahmu and godessLahamu, mentioned (them) by name{s} {mentioned them}. Until when (As soon as) they grew up, becoming huge [becoming old], they made Ashshar and godessQishar, they increased over them (over Lahmu and Lahamu); they delayed the days (their dying days), perpetuated the years (centuries?) (their ages). godAnu, their newborn male, became an equal of his fathers; Ashshar made alike his first-born, godAnu, and godAnu begat his alike, godNudimud. godNudimud of [for] his fathers, {he} was their speaker [leader] by name; dexterous of knowledge, percipient (insightful), robust of vigor (strength), bold (daring), a magnitude [a big difference] from (over) the begetter of his father, Ashshar. He has no equal in (among) the gods, his brethren {his fathers}. The brethren gods debated [faced] each other. They ignored (disregarded) Tiamat (and) exalted (intensified) {high} their debate {zealotry}. They made the mind of Tiamat go [go insane]. With rituals (protocols), they fostered the closeness of the gathered brethren (gods assembly). Abzu could not rob [lower] their voice, and Tiamat was silent in front of them. Their doing brought harm [defeat] over her. Their way (method), (that) they were carrying out (executing), was unpleasant (i.e. their practices). Thereupon, Abzu, the creator of the great gods [the community of gods], ordered godMummu, his confidant, saying to him: "Confidant godMummu, the one who pleases my innermost, come, let us [so that we] go after (to) Tiamat." They went, they sat {they were poured out} in front of the sea. Directing (pointing, telling) his matters [concerns] regarding the gods, their first-born sons. Abzu collected (worked) his mouth, saying to her {said to her} {said with loud voice to her}, to pure Tiamat: "Their way (their practice) brought harm [defeat] on me. By day not at ease (relaxed), I am. By night not a bit sleeping (dozing off), I am. Let me (I want to) wipe (them) out. Let me (I want to) stultify their way (their practice). Let avoidance (quiet) be set, let us [so that we] sleep a bit (doze off), we ourselves." Tiamat, immediately, in (upon) hearing him [that], she felt hurt [became furious], saddened over her consort (mate) {inter-connector}. She shouted hurtfully. Her opinions were raised loudly [She raised loudly her opinions]. She brought (put) the rage [evil] to her gut (inside her): "What? We, ourselves, wipe out what we build [built]? Let-it-be harmful, their way (practice),*

*For additional translations and transliterations details, see Part 1.1 and Part 2.1 of this book

let us [so that we] correct [endure] kindly {tastefully}]". godMummu analyzed (explained; elaborated; added), advising Abzu. His Mummu [His worker (officer)], the confidant, was an irrational (unwise) advisor: [The confidant was irrational (unwise), an advisor, his Mummu [his worker (officer)]:] [The confidant was irrational (unwise), his Mummu [his worker (officer)] the advisor:] "Wipe out, my father! This way (gods' way) is a disregard. By day, let-you-be to (in) it at ease (relaxed). By night, let-you-be to (in) it a bit asleep (dozed off)." Abzu followed (agreed with) him. His face became red and yellow (from anger), (that is) because he hid (harbored) rages [evils] toward the gods, his sons {toward his sons}. GodMummy encircled (embraced) his thick neck (Abzu's), to seat his knees (to make him kneel), to kiss him. Everything their meeting hid (harbored), was repeated (leaked) to the gods, their first-born sons. The gods heard (that) (and) became disordered. They kept quiet, (and) were sitting in silence. The one surpassing in knowledge, the ready (prepared) one, the out-standing (rising) one, GodEa, the percipient (insightful) of everything, pursued their plots. He allocated for it, (and) the plan for all, he enforced it [kept it secret]. He outsmarted [diverted] (tricked) him. The dominance (supremacy) [surpass] of his spell was great [refined (immaculate)]. He awaited and temporized [recited on] him. He (Abzu) relaxed in the waters. Sleep enveloped him. He was dozed off pleasantly. He (godEA) made Abzu dozed off, enveloped by sleep. GodMummy, the advisor, was slowly stiffened (by seizure). He (godEA) separated (opened) his straps (Abzu's), slipped away (slided) his pure gold crown (Abzu's). He carried his (fearsome) aura (Abzu's). He (godEA), himself, dressed (surrounded himself with it). (then) He suppressed Abzu, slaughtered him (spelled his blood). He confined [spared] GodMummu, left (him) on top of him (Abzu). (and) He enforced his dwelling over (the body of) Abzu. He threw [rotted] GodMummu (over him), restrained (tied) his rope. Right after he suppressed his rages [his (Abzu's) evils], he reached his goal.

Three important Mesopotamian mythological believes are revealed from the above story. First, the world before the creation of the gods was one flat earth with a constantly intermingling sweet water river (or lake), controlled by a male creature called *Abzu*, and a very huge salt water sea (ocean), controlled by a very, very huge mother creature called *Tiamat*. The earth was already there as evident by line 1.6, and the fact that Abzu was waiting for Tiamat sitting on the ocean coast with his helper god! Based on their incorrect translations of line 1.6, scholars claimed there was no vegetation or pastures at that time, but the line actually said there were plentiful then. Second, the first couple of god-like creatures formed by Abzu and Tiamat was not a perfect one, prompting them to form a second improved couple. While the first couple, *Laḫmu* and *Liḫamu*, was formed from flesh alone, the second one, *godAshshar and godessQishar*, included bones and skin, as the linguistic meanings of their names clearly indicate. The second couple, whose names were preceded by the god symbols unlike the first one, but the highest ranking god was still not one of them. The first truly perfect god was their son, *godAnu*, the first born, not formed, god, who was eventually crowned as the supreme god of heaven. Still, some scholars believe that the strong northern Mesopotamian Assyrians (or *al-ʾĀshūriyūn*) had derived their name after *godAshshar, godAnu's father,* which may indicate they thought he should have been the highest ranking god, instead. Third, the Mesopotamian gods were as brutal as humans, except for *GodAnu*, who was above this brutality. Only his son and grandson were involved in brutal fights. His son, *GodEa*, killed Abzu, as we saw in the story above. His grandson, Marduk, killed Tiamat, and erected the heavens by stretching her skin upward, let the Tigris and Euphrates rivers flow through her eyes, and created the mountains of Ararat from her breasts, as the following reading by the author from the Babylonian Creation Epic, Tablet 4 lines 135-140, and Tablet 5 lines 53-62, describes:*

.... The lord (i.e. *Marduk*) retreated, deliberating (examining) the 'stone lump' (the corpse). He extracted [divided] the mighty organs (parts), building logical replies (solutions). He peeled (slit) her

*For additional translations and transliterations details, see Part 1.1 and Part 2.1 of this book

like a fired (BBQed: masqoof) fish to her two (parts) (i.e. he slit her from her back into two connected halves, as Iraqis prepare a carp fish for their "masqoof" (roofed: roof-like) dish, before sticking it vertically on its side with its belly cavity facing open wood fire flame). He set flat her two (connected) halves (cavity down, skin up), made (from them) as roof, heavens: he stretched (extended) [lifted] the cortex (the skin), fixed the boundaries (the extent). Her waters were not lifted up, they (the waters), he made (them) flow. ....

.... He set in her head, poured (heaped) a 'mountain' over her. He slit [opened] a deep slit (an abyss), waters burst (poured) out. He uncovered [made flow] ultra-sweet waters in (from) her face's two (eyes), let it (made it) cover (flood) [so that it covered (flooded)]. He filled (blocked) her nostrils, left (alone) her mouth dent [opening]. He poured (heaped) in (from) her breasts mountains in between. He lowered (leveled) the buttocks to the swelling (level) of the vulva. He twisted and extended her tail (toward her buttocks), flipped (it) upside down (downward), evenly. He |........| the Abzu underneath her feet [lower legs]. |He set in her crotch [hole] (as) a marker (pointing to) [a reference point of] heavens. He pressed down her two halves, stuck [suppressed] (them) to the earth. ....

The current translations of Tablet 4, lines 137-140, are quite peculiar. For example, sticking with the limited options of the mostly speculated meanings offered by the modern Assyriology dictionaries, two prominent scholars, Lambert, and decades later Foster, gave similar meaningless, illogical translations of these lines. Their erroneous readings are unfortunately common, as in a lot of other modern translations of Akkadian literature, and are the direct result of their refusal to recognize the true identity of the Akkadian language as an *early Arabic language* that must be primarily deciphered using the old etymological Arabic manuscripts. To explain his unconvincing translation of line 4:138, Foster offered a meaningless footnote explanation saying "*that is, he made the sky to hold the waters*". Readers can compare the translations below and judge on their own:

Lambert: *He split her into two like a dried fish: one half of her he set up and stretched out as the heavens. He stretched the skin and appointed a watch, with the instruction not to let her waters escape.*

Foster:* *He split her into two, like a fish for drying. Half of her he set up and made, as cover, heaven (that is, he made the sky to hold the waters). He stretched out the hide and assigned watchmen, and ordered them not to let her waters escape.*

Author: *He peeled (slit) her like a fired (BBQed: masqoof style) fish to her two (parts)*†*. He set flat her two (connected) halves (cavity down, skin up), made (from them) as roof, heavens: he stretched (extended) [lifted] the cortex (the skin), fixed the boundaries (the extent); her waters were not lifted up, they (the waters), he made (let them) flow.*

The first human in the Babylonian Creation Epic was created to alleviate the burden of the hard work previously done by the gods, particularly by the *Anunnaki* and *Igidi* working gods groups. Accordingly, he was formed by *God*Ea (i.e *God*Idim) from a piece of blood taken from a punished god, whose blood was spilled for that purpose. The two story elements above are very similar to those of the story of Adam, who was supposedly created from god's blood and was ordered to do the hard work of the land after his expulsion, as a punishment. It is not clear whether the Mesopotamian first human, *lullu* (i.e *luʿullu* or *ʿamilu*), was formed as one or many humans. Logically speaking, one human/god would not have been able to perform the difficult, tedious work done previously by

---

*Benjamin R. Foster. Before the Muses: An anthology of Akkadian Literature. Second Edition. 1996. Vol I, Page 376.

†i.e. He slit her from her back into two connected halves like a *Masqoof* fish, as the Iraqis do, even today, when preparing their BBQed style carp fish dish, by sticking all fish vertically on their sides using sticks and arranging them in circles, making sure both of their belly cavities and backs are facing the open wood fire flames, sidewise. The word *Masqoof* literally means roofed or roof-like shape.

many gods. The immortality status of the first humans was also not clear, but they were likely immortal since they were created from the blood of an immortal god. To be accurate, the Mesopotamian gods were not actually immortal, living forever, but rather practically immortal, living for a very long periods of time. As stated earlier, many of them do die either naturally or by slaying, according to the ancient mythology. The following reading by the author of Tablet 6, lines 1-30, details the creation of the first human according to the Babylonian Creation Epic. The story starts with ^{God}*Marduk* asking the assembly of gods after he killed Tiamat to tell him who instigated her to go to war with his group of gods:

> ^{god}*Marduk*, upon his hearing gods' speech, he carried on, inside him, building logical replies (solutions). He let go [collected and let go] his mouth, addressing (loudly) ^{god}*Ea*, giving (little by little) what he finalized (decided) in his heart, (as) a directive: "I shall drain (shed) blood, I shall have [form] bones, I shall extract [create] a savage creature, (and) let-it-be to him 'man', its kind. I shall build a savage man. Let-it-be to him the tedious functions (hard work) burden of the gods; they, let-it-be to them rest. I shall make-to-two the inner ways (order) of the gods, I shall make (it) logical. As one (equal), let-it-be the weight (status/importance). To (As) two, let-it-be to them the division". ^{god}*Ea* clarified to him, addressing him (about) a matter. That is because (Regarding) the resting of the gods, he seconded him the mind (thought): "Let one, a brother of theirs, be given up (sacrificed). Let-him-be slaughtered (while healthy) so that people may emerge. Let their majesties the gods assemble. Let that of mischief (wickedness) be given up (sacrificed) so that they would worry [be suppressed]". ^{god}*Marduk* assembled their majesties the gods. Kindly, he spoke with high voice (firmly), giving the details [orders]. He let go [collected and let go] his mouth, (as) the gods surrounded [squeezed] him. The king, telling the matter to the ^{gods}*Anunnaki*: "Let-it-be to him a proof (fact), your up-front (direct) testimony. Bring forth proofs (facts) resonating (responding) with me. Who built up (drummed for) the battle, {and} mixed it up on Tiamat, (and) rushed the war? Let that who built up (drummed for) the battle be given up. His mischief, I shall penalize him for it {let-him-be for it penalized}, (while) you sit comfortably". Their majesties the gods, the ^{gods}*Igigi*, clarified to him, to the *Lugal-dimmer-ankia* (king of gods of heaven and earth), king of the gods, their lord: "^{God}*Qingu* was the one who built up (drummed for) the battle, {and} mixed it up on Tiamat, (and) rushed the war". (then) They suppressed him (^{God}*Qingu*), restrained (tied) him {restrained (tied up)}, facing (him) (in front of) ^{God}*Ea*. They imposed on him the equal of the mischief (wickedness); they shed his blood. From his blood, he (^{god}*Ea*) built mankind. He imposed upon (the mankind) the tedious functions (hard work) of the gods. He liberated the gods. Right after ^{god}*Ea*, the amazing, built mankind, (and) imposed upon (them) the tedious functions (hard work) of the gods that is for them— ......

In conclusion, the first monotheist human, Adam, was originally a god, in the Mesopotamian mythology, just as the Hebrew Genesis reluctantly revealed, and the assertive Quran slightly hinted. Specifically, he was the pre-monotheist, Sumerian god, *Idim*, who was also called ^{God}*Ea* and many other nicknames over the millenniums. The names *Idim* and *Adam* are even linguistically related, according to early Arabic root words analysis. As a Mesopotamian god, *Idim* was the creator of the first human, and the father of his immediate generations, as he was sometimes referred to in the ancient literature. He was the preserver of life on earth, and the protector of humans against the evil designs of their, and his arch enemy, ^{God}*Enlil*, the future monotheist Satan. The names and roles of these two important divine characters, ^{God}*Idim* and ^{God}*Enlil*, were etched too deep in the collective folk memory of the peoples of the greater Mesopotamia and the Near East, to be completely erased by the new monotheist order. The early monotheists had likely eased in their new believes to the peoples of the region by incorporating these two second highest ranking gods under the supreme god of heavens, ^{God}*Anu* (or ^{God}*Alu*), as new altered divine characters. The top god, ^{God}*Anu,* was then given the post-monotheist role of the one and only god, *Alhim* or *Allah*, consistent with the key theme of the Monotheist faiths. Several important narrative details involving the events, characters, and roles in the Hebrew Genesis story of Adam must have predated it for many centuries. The story in the Quran omitted much of the details in Genesis, but included a few unique details on its own. However, all of these ancient stories seem to be independent, original stories borrowing only bits and pieces from each other.

2

Noah and the Mesopotamian Mythology of Flood and Survival

The story of Noah (Hebrew and Arabic: *Nūḥ* or *Nawḥ*) was the second most important story of the Near East monotheist faith after the story of Adam, if not the most important one, since Noah became the actual father of humanity after the flood, and he and two of his descendants, Shem (i.e. *Sām*), and Abram (Hebrew: Abraham and Arabic: *Ibrāhīm*), were the key early monotheist characters. According to the Hebrew Old Testament, Noah, who was the tenth in descent from Adam, was the immediate father of Shem, who in turn was supposedly the father of the so-called Semitic people. And Abraham, who was the ninth in descent from Noah was the father of the Abrahamic religions, as recognized by Judaism, Christianity and Islam.

Unlike with the Hebrew Genesis' Adam story, the theme of the Noah story was not about human immortality, but rather about human mortality and the punishing fate for a wicked humanity. Noah according to Genesis was a mortal man. However, the two stories share several parallel details. Taking into account the claim by Genesis that Noah lived 950 years,* he becomes effectively more immortal than Adam, who supposedly lived 930 years after eating from the tree of life, in order to live forever! Unlike with Adam's age, the Quran explicitly agreed with Genesis, this time around, regarding Noah's godly age.† The declaration by Genesis that the human age was limited to 120 year only a couple of generations *after* Noah, the direct, pure descendant of the divine Adam, further emphasizes his contradicting monotheist classification as a human. Furthermore, the Genesis' Noah story, like Adam's, also involved the elements of human punishment and the conflict between good and evil, but this time it involved a good angry god set on eliminating humanity versus the evil "wicked" humans, rather than a good god versus the evil, human-hating Satan. However, Noah, like Adam, was also an innocent, but chosen, victim caught within uncontrolled events driven by a conflict between good and evil, in this new story.

The above elements' similarities between the two stories in Genesis should not be surprising, since the Noah story was clearly a reset of the Adam story, with few new twists. It was about the cleansing of humanity and the introduction of a new, pure father of humanity, a decisively human character though, even if theoretically. However, these similarities have much deeper roots. Modern inscriptional discoveries have shown beyond any doubt that the monotheist story of Noah was adapted, almost entirely, from a much older story with these story elements. The main character of the older story, *Uta-Napištim*, meaning "*the one given life or eternal life*", was clearly Noah, as he was often referred to as *ru-ū-qu*, a nickname with identical meaning to *nūḥu*, or *nūḥ*, meaning "*the withdrawn, the distant, the pure, the far away, or the resigned*".‡ In the flood story of the Gilgamesh

*Genesis (9:29) וַיִּהְיוּ כָּל-יְמֵי-נֹחַ תְּשַׁע מֵאוֹת שָׁנָה וַחֲמִשִּׁים שָׁנָה וַיָּמֹת

†Quran (29: 14) ولقد أرسلنا نوحا إلى قومه فلبث فيهم ألف سنة إلا خمسين عاما فأخذهم الطوفان وهم ظالمون

‡Saad D. Abulhab. The Epic of Gilgamesh: Selected Readings from its Original Early Arabic Language. New York: Blautopf Publishing, 2016. Page 161-163.

Epic, at least in its Akkadian version, *Uta-Napištim*, a decisively human character who was eventually rewarded an "eternal" life, was the victim of a conflict between a good god, his creator and protector, and an evil one bent on harming humanity, just as it was the case in the Adam story of Genesis. The ancient story though did not claim *Uta-Napištim* became effectively the new father of humanity after the flood.

Even though most current translations of the story of Noah from the Hebrew Genesis *effectively* declared him as *Adam II*, the father of *all nations*, the actual relevant Hebrew texts do not support that. Notably, scholars translated line 10:5 in Genesis as follows: "*Of these were the isles of the nations divided in their lands, every one after his tongue, after their families, in their nations*".[*] However, the Hebrew word used in that line, *goyim* (i.e. Arabic root word جوي for *alien, outsider,* or *foreigner*), did not always mean "*nation*" in the ancient Hebrew manuscripts. Future use of this word in that meaning should not be applied retroactively by scholars. The phase words *hā-jawyim* and *bi-jawyihim* mean "*the aliens*" and "*in their alienation*", respectively. The above line was referring to the flood survivors, Noah's immediate generations, as *aliens, outsiders,* or *foreigners*, being isolated in patches of new, *foreign* lands, rather than their original lands before the flood. To further understand the meaning of the word *goyim* in that line, one should examine its usages in other lines. For example, examine author's translations of lines 12:2-6 and 19:6 in Genesis, below.[†] These lines referred to Abram the father of monotheism, a *migrant* (i.e. *alien or outsider*) according to Genesis who left Ur in southern Mesopotamia to settle in the foreign land of Canaan. He was presumably blessed by god in this new land to become a very successful and worthy man, and the father of the future kings of Canaan. According to lines 12:5, Abram's name was changed by god to *Abraham* because he was chosen to became *metaphorically and symbolically* the father of the *numerous aliens* of Canaan, the majority people of Canaan, in addition to becoming a miracle biological father of a few ones of his own. In line 12:6, god assigned him and his direct descendants to be the leaders of these *numerous aliens* of Canaan. Neither lines meant that he had fathered numerous biological generations replacing the native Canaanite majority! Outsider or foreigner is a relative term since for an outsider, the majority *insiders* in a new land are all *outsiders*!

Genesis (10:5; 10:32)

> *Of these, apart, were the aliens marked (divided) in their lands—each man according to his tongue—according to their families in their alienation. .... These are the families of the sons of Noah according to their generations in their alienation, and from these had the aliens expanded (spread) in the after-the-flood earth.*

Genesis (12:2-6; 19:6)

> *'And I will make you to a great alien, and I will bless you, and make your name great as it (the name) will become a blessing. And I shall give my covenant, between me and you, and I shall give you a fortune, a plenty of plenty.' And Abram fell on his face, and God spoke to him to say: 'I hereby shall give you my covenant, that is you shall be a father of the numerous aliens. And your name shall not be called, after that, Abram, but your name shall become Abraham, for a father of the numerous aliens, we shall give (establish) you. And I shall give you the utmost freshness (the freshest water), a plenty of plenty, and we shall give you (establish you) to aliens, and kings, they shall choose from you.*
> .... *And you shall become for me a kingdom of priests and a holy alien (outsider).' These are the words that you shall speak to the children of Israel.'*

---

[*]Genesis (10:5) מֵאֵלֶּה נִפְרְדוּ אִיֵּי הַגּוֹיִם בְּאַרְצֹתָם אִישׁ לִלְשֹׁנוֹ לְמִשְׁפְּחֹתָם בְּגוֹיֵהֶם

[†]For additional translations and transliterations details, see Part 1.5 and Part 2.4 of this book

As fascinating as the monotheist story of Noah may seem to many, the earlier versions of this story were as captivating and even more magnificent, from a philosophical, linguistic, and historical perspective. The original flood story, as it was told by *Uta-Napištim* to Gilgamesh in the standard Babylonian edition of the Epic of Gilgamesh, which made George Smith (1840-1876), the young British Assyriologist who first translated it, take off his clothes in shock and happiness thousands of years later, was indeed *"far more bloodcurdling than the one in the Old Testament"*.[*] Most scholars, poets, and journalists, like *The New Yorker* Journalist Joan Acocella, believe today that Smith *"had discovered what was then, and still is, the longest poem in the world, 'Gilgamesh'"*.[†] Poet and scholar Michael Schmidt who had recently published a book about Gilgamesh and the various translations of the epic[‡] thinks, as Acocella explained, *"that a poem that exists in a pile of broken pieces, in an extremely dead language, would be something that translators would run away from, in a hurry. The very opposite is the case. Presumably because it is, as Schmid writes, such an 'uncertain, porous' thing, translators are drawn to it."*[§] However, the language and storylines in the standard edition of the Gilgamesh epic clearly indicate it was rather a novel or a literary epic, including only sporadic poems. Readers can appreciate the mastery language of this literary work when examining the eerie but beautiful images invoked in the following reading by the author of the devastating seven days of the flood as told by *Uta-Napištim* in Tablet 11, lines 90-136:

> *Of that day, I looked from far (observed) its condition (weather). That day, to the one observing carefully, had fright (was frightening). I entered to inside of the raft; I casted (sealed) my door. To the caster (sealer) of the raft, Puzur-Kurgal (Enlil's defector), the shipwright, I let to rest (I gave up) the palace of majesty, (and) even its contents. All time long, before dawn, (starting) at the earliest morning dark white, a black cloud rose (showed) over the far horizon. The [god]Askar (Haddad: god of darkness and thunder) thundered (threatened loud) inside it. The [god]Sullat (god of looting) and the [god]Hanish (god of captivity) went in the front. They went with (led) the officers (soldiers) over mountains and land. The god Ninurta (of fire and war) passed by, burning the ships and weirs. The Anunnaki (god Anim's angles on earth) roamed with [unleashed] the torches. With their black, white, and orange/red (tiger colors: Arabs death colors), they spotted the land. (as) The spoiling (ruining) act (force) of the god Askar was taking over [encroaching] the sky. All that was dark white, to a pitch-dark (color) returned. He pressed (crushed) the land, like /an oil compressor/ camel he (repeatedly) circled it. In one day, the wind [storm] .... Immediately [with a grudge], the Deluge was swallowing (submerging) .... of the lands. Like (in) a battle, the sand took over [encroached] the people. A brother could not see his (own) brother. People could not connect with each other in the pileup ruin [the ruin] {the entrapment}. The Deluge frightened (even) the gods. They left [rushed], they went up to the haven of [god]Anim. The gods were like hiding hyenas, waiting [lying down] in the hideouts. (as) The [goddess]Istar was reading aloud {as if} a testimony (witness statement), the lady of god {the sweetheart of gods} screamed (while weeping) [raised up] an honest (candid) outcry: '(indeed) Like his first day, to the mud, let him (the human) be returned to it! That is because I, myself, in front of {in the assembly of} the gods, had shouted: O, the one of horror (war). How could I had shouted in front of {in the assembly of} the gods: O, the one of horror (war), (and) declared a battle for the annihilation of my people. It is I, myself, who give birth to the breed of people (now) Like the breeds of fish, they fill the sea!' The gods, particularly the Anunnaki, were crying with her The gods were taken over (were overwhelmed), while sitting, by crying {With noisy exhaustion, they were crying with her}. Their lips were dry {became dark} as a result of dehydration. For six days and nights {and seven nights}, the hell of the Deluge came by, peeling the (face of) earth (turning it) to a flat water-covered land {the hell of thunder came by, the Deluge /was peeling/ the earth (turning it) to a flat water-covered land} . At the arrival of the seventh day, it was*

[*]Joan Acocella. Beyond the Waters of Death: The making of 'Gilgamesh'. *The New Yorker*. Book review. October 14, 2019. Pg. 74

[†]ibid. Pg. 72

[‡]Michael Schmidt. Gilgamesh: The Life of a Poem. Princeton. 2019.

[§]Joan Acocella. Beyond the Waters of Death: The making of 'Gilgamesh'. *The New Yorker*. Book review. October 14, 2019. Pg. 76

(finally) quiet, the battle of the Deluge {the battle of the Deluge quieted}. It, which had labored [had pushed and pounded] like a female in the first pregnancy (labor). The sea pulled back (down) (subsided), fell still, the worst {the tempest} of the Deluge ended. I observed that day {the sea}, complete quiet (silence) had set in, and all people had returned back (turned) to clay. Like an open (empty) land, the valleys were leveled.

Surely, even the most complete version of the epic of Gilgamesh at hand contains plenty of uncertainty, plenty of porous passages scattered around in "a *pile of broken mud tablet pieces*". The difficulty involved in deciphering the ancient language used in the various versions of the epic, and the damaged, missing text lines and sections on its many tablets, are the main reasons behind this uncertainty. However, while the original challenging language of the epic can be very hard to decipher with absolute certainty, it is definitely not an "*extremely dead language*". In fact, after examining, understanding, and feeling its original linguistic style, one would conclude otherwise. Unfortunately, most of the current, poetic Western translations of the epic have failed to capture its actual spirit and literary flavor, either because they used inaccurate raw translations, or artificially injected these translations with their Western literary or even biblical styles. Also, most of these translations rely on the speculated linguistic tools compiled over the past 100 years by numerous western Assyriologists. These tools can be useful, but they fail many times to provide correct meanings since they do not even recognize the actual language of the texts: early Arabic. The early, ancient Arabic language, just like the old Arabic language, is not an "*extremely dead language*" today. Those who can read it can still appreciate it. Even though I disagree with Foster regarding the identity of the ancient Babylonian language of the text, I fully understand his lack of "*patience with clueless folks who think that they can translate the epic without going to the trouble of mastering Babylonian, though they are welcome to retell it*".*

Despite the striking differences in their story details, the theme topic of the Gilgamesh and Hebrew Genesis flood stories was the same: the complex topic of life, death, punishment, and human wickedness. The few unique story details offered in the Quran, though, agrees clearly with the ancient Mesopotamian versions, Sumerian and Akkadian. The study in the rest of this chapter will include select readings from several versions and will point out translation accuracy and differences. First, to appreciate the language of the original Mesopotamian story and understand its key theme, a full translation by the author is provided below of the section in Tablet 10, lines 297-322,† detailing the actual reason behind the anger of the gods and their desire to punish, not eradicate humanity. The lines starts with *Uta-Napištim* (Noah) addressing Gilgamesh after he arrived to his vicinity, following a dangerous and exhausting trip through the rough seas in pursuit of eternal life. While current translations, notably the one by Andrew George, have captured some of the images and facts of this section, many mainly emphasized poetry and failed to capture the moral, philosophical, and tragic facts of its main theme.

You are aging [attenuating]; what are you finding (gaining)? Slowly, you are hurting [tiring] your own. You are filling your intestines with severe hunger {exhaustion hunger}. You are bringing the faraway closer, your (final) dates [days]. A man is like a snapped off [an eliminated] reed in a canebrake, |that| is his fate [his afterward (his future)]. The entwined and polished (well-built) young man, the entwined and polished (well-built) young woman. Hurriedly (prematurely), death abducts |even their lives|. No one sees death. No one, of this death, sees its face. No one, of this death, hears its scream (voice). The burst [This undefeatable force] of death is the destroyer [eliminator] of man (mankind). As long as we build {he

*Joan Acocella. Beyond the Waters of Death: The making of 'Gilgamesh'. *The New Yorker*. Book review. October 14, 2019. Pg. 76

†Saad D. Abulhab. The Epic of Gilgamesh: Selected Readings from its Original Early Arabic Language. New York: Blautopf Publishing, 2016.

builds} a palace. As long as we acquire [monopolize] (more) property. As long as brothers snatch [confiscate] {As long as brothers snatch [confiscate] inheritance share}. As long as viciousness and immorality [animosity and hatred] spreads [exists] in the land. As long as the river got energized (rose) (and) carried (brought) the flood. (and) The departing provider [The loved one] floated in the river (with) His face staring (at) the face of the sun. At once (instantly), he does not have anything. The abducted and the dead, they are like {they are like the form of} brothers of one semen-drop (like twin). Of death, they (the gods) did not draw (determine) the shape of its figure. They had not granted the eternity of savage [early] man, as a grant, in the land {(but) They had granted the equality of savage [early] man, from the beginning}. Their majesties the Anunnaki (godAnim's angles on earth), their majesties the gods, were in assembly. GoddessMamitum {Mami} (goddess of death), (after) repeatedly inquiring [discussing in detail] the decree with them {their decree}, gave her decree. They (the gods) established (set) death and life. Of death, they had not made known (revealed) its dates [days]" {Of death, they had not made known (revealed) its dates [days]; they made them known (revealed them), differently"}.

The above translation by the author makes it very clear that the ancient flood story, just like the monotheist one, was *not* about the sad and tragic horror of death or about a devastating destruction occurring without reasons, as most current translations of the story make it sounds like. The story was *not* about the beautiful but poetic images of floating mayflies, or drifting dragonflies, down a flooded river, with their faces gazing at the sun. This story was about the faces of the bloated bodies of dead providers and loved ones swept by the sea of a flooded river, with their open eyes staring at the sun! It is about a fragile, but stubborn and arrogant human not realizing that his fate can be, within moments, the same as that of a *"snapped off [eliminated] reed in a canebrake"*. This story was *not* about the uncertainties of random ordinary events taking place *"at some time"*, or about questioning *"how long"* these event should be taking place. This story was about the gods electing to use a swift punishing flood against a wicked humanity *as long as* people continue to be greedy and build palaces on the expense of the poor, *as long as* brothers confiscate the inheritance shares of their brothers, and *as long as "viciousness and immorality [animosity and hatred] spreads [exists] in the land"*. To compare other readings, examine below two of the popular translations missing the theme of that section of Tablet 10, the first by Andrew George and the second by Maureen Kovacs:

At some time we build a household, At some time we start a family, At some time the brothers divide, {At some time the brothers divide shares,} At some time feuds arise in the land. At some time the river rose (and) brought the flood, the mayfly floating on the river. Its countenance was gazing on the face of the sun, Then all of a sudden nothing was there! The abducted and the dead, how alike they are! They cannot draw the picture of death. The dead do not greet man in the land. {Mortal man is imprisoned. After they blessed me,} The Anunnaki, the great gods, were in assembly, Mammitum, who creates destiny, made a decree with them: {made a decree:} Death and life they did establish, The day of death they did not reveal'

For how long do we build a household? For how long do we seal a document! For how long do brothers share the inheritance? For how long is there to be jealousy in the land(!)! For how long has the river risen and brought the overflowing waters, so that dragonflies drift down the river!' The face that could gaze upon the face of the Sun, has never existed ever. How alike are the sleeping(!) and the dead. The image of Death cannot be depicted. (Yes, you are a) human being, a man (?)! After Enlil had pronounced the blessing,'" the Anunnaki, the Great Gods, assembled. Mammetum, she who forms destiny, determined destiny with them. They established Death and Life, but they did not make known 'the days of death'".

After reading over various old versions of the flood stories, one can immediately notice how historically-inaccurate the Genesis story version was regarding details, compared to the ancient Mesopotamian versions, and to less extent to the Quranic version. The most striking differences are about the shape and dimension of Noah vessel, the identities of those who boarded the vessel with him, the name of the mountain holding the vessel, and the geographic location of that mountain. Even more striking was how scholars who translated the Gilgamesh versions, and are aware of the worthy Islamic scholarship details regarding this story, have failed to effectively point out some of these differences.

Hebrew Genesis correctly called Noah's vessel a *tibah* or *tibat*, meaning "box, chest, coffin", since it was a sealed and covered vessel, not a ship. The Greek also correctly translated *tibah* as *κιβωτός*, in the same meaning. In old Arabic *tibat* and *tābūt* mean coffin, too. However, it seems that the writer of Genesis chose the meaning coffin, as a long covered body coffin, and interpret that as to indicate that the vessel was a regular long, narrow ship, not a floating chest. As a result, that original writer, or possibly another future writer, felt the need to elaborate further to convince his readers, by throwing in exact dimensions: L300 x H30 x W50!* Likely, the writer was not aware of the story in the standard edition of the Epic of Gilgamesh. This may indicate that Genesis was only introduced in the second half of the first millennium BCE, when access to Gilgamesh literature was fading. According to the standard edition, Noah's vessel was definitely a roundish, covered floating raft, like a covered deep bowl, with a 10 x 10 units rim and depth, as the readings of Tablet 11, lines 28-31 and 58-59 by the author show below.† The Quran confirmed this roundish shape by calling it a "*fulk*".

> *"The raft that you will build, for her, let her capacity (size) be extended (large), for her, let her breadth [depth] and basin [stretch] be corresponding (equal). Like an Abzu (a hill [a hunch] [a bowl] [an arc]) to it, its roof (should look)". ....*
>
> *....... An acre (the area of) its circle, as much as 10 Nindans [10 Nindans each,] the height of its walls. As much as 10 Nindans equaled (extended) the rim of its top [the diameter of its surrounding] [As much as 10 Nindans [10 Nindans each] equaled (extended) the edges of its top [surrounding]].....*

The identities of those boarding Noah vessels, people and animals, were also different in the Genesis story. It seems that the writer of Genesis wanted to serve some of the political goals around that time. Genesis removed the open human dimension of the original story in favour of a tribal one, by suggesting that only Noah and his immediate sons and wives boarded the vessel, and all other people died. Lines 6:19-20 in Genesis claimed that Noah boarded *"every living thing of all flesh"*, reinforcing the monotheist claim that the flood was not a localized event but a global one necessitating the rescue of *all* creatures on earth.‡ On the other hand, the standard edition of Gilgamesh indicated that there was a well-organized collective effort directed by a fair, undiscriminating leader, *Uta-Napištim*, to build the vessel by a group of skilled supporters who presumably boarded it afterwards, and that the rescued animals were mainly farm animals. A king who was apparently very concerned with preserving his people's accumulative wealth, his skilled subjects, and the farm animals needed for their future survival, and even some wild creatures. The fact that the animals were mainly farm animals is clearly confirmed by lines E9-10 of the Sumerian version of the flood story, the Eridu Genesis, which called him *"the king, keeper (preserver) of the small animal creatures (and) the livestock of mankind's breathing life (the farm animals)"*. Readers can examine below the original translations by the author of Tablet 11, lines 49-57, 69-75, and 79-84, respectively:§

---

*Genesis (6:15) וזה אֲשֶׁר תַּעֲשֶׂה אתה שְׁלֹשׁ מאות אַמָּה ארך הַתֵּבָה חֲמִשִּׁים אַמָּה רָחְבָּהּ וּשְׁלֹשִׁים אַמָּה קוֹמָתָהּ

†Saad D. Abulhab. The Epic of Gilgamesh: Selected Readings from its Original Early Arabic Language. New York: Blautopf Publishing, 2016.

‡Genesis (6:19) וּמִכָּל-הָחַי מִכָּל-בָּשָׂר שְׁנַיִם מִכֹּל, תָּבִיא אֶל-הַתֵּבָה--לְהַחֲיֹת אִתָּךְ: זָכָר וּנְקֵבָה, יִהְיוּ (6:20) מֵהָעוֹף לְמִינֵהוּ, וּמִן-הַבְּהֵמָה לְמִינָהּ, מִכֹּל רֶמֶשׂ הָאֲדָמָה, לְמִינֵהוּ--שְׁנַיִם מִכֹּל יָבֹאוּ אֵלֶיךָ, לְהַחֲיוֹת

§Saad D. Abulhab. The Epic of Gilgamesh: Selected Readings from its Original Early Arabic Language. New York: Blautopf Publishing, 2016.

At the door of Atra-Hasis (the one with sharp sense: Uta-Napištim), a crowd was gathering. The carpenter proceeding with his axe. The reed cutter proceeding with his cudgel (club). .... proceeding with his maple wood club. The young strong men |carrying| .... The elders carrying (in baskets) ropes. The rich [the master] proceeding with the tar (bitumen, asphalt). The working poor brought in |....| the needed (necessary) hard labor. In the fifth day, I did (I put) its external structure: ....

For the subjects (workers), I barbecued fattened camels. I slaughtered young sheep (for them), every day (with) Beer, grain drink, and barley wine, I irrigated (hydrated) my subjects (workers), like the waters of a river (do). They were preparing (for) a festival [a festival gathering] like (the festival of) the New Year's Day. At sun's rise (sunrise), I put my hand on miscellaneous parts (of the raft). Before sun's high (noon), the raft was ready.............

All what I had, I loaded aboard it (onboard). All what I had of silver metal, I loaded aboard it (onboard). All what I had of gold metal, I loaded aboard it (onboard). All what I had of livestock (cattle) beings (farm animals), all of them, I loaded aboard it (onboard). I grabbed (rushed) to the inside of the raft all my kith and kin. Herds of the wild, creatures of the wild, my subjects (workers), I grabbed (rushed) all (in).

The most controversial part of the Noah story, in both ancient and monotheist versions, was the name and location of the mountain that finally held his vessel. Let's examine below the relevant texts from four key versions of the story:

From the Quran (11:44)*

.... and it leveled (settled) on the al-Jawdiyy ......

From the Hebrew Genesis (8:4)†

And the coffin (chest) rested in the seventh month, on the seventeenth day of the month, on the mountains of Ararat (country of rivers—the ancient country of Ararat).

From the Stander Edition of the Epic of Gilgamesh, Tablet 11, Lines 137-156 and 204-206‡

I opened a breathing hole, a beam of light fell (landed) over [around] the surrounding of my nose. I sank (squatted), I sat down crying. Over [around] the surroundings of my nose (my cheeks), the tears came (down). I scanned the edges of the sea space (expanse) {the sea sky (horizon)}. On as many as 12 {14} (edges) [On each of the 12 {14} (edges)], a high land mass rose (appeared). On {Mount} Naymūs [{Mount} Naydhīr] (keeper of the good (secret): Mt. al-Amin or Mt. Abu Qbays in Mecca), the raft levelled (rested; ended) [anchored]. Mount Naymūs [Naydhīr] held (kept) the raft; to the fast water, it did not give up. First day, second day, Mount Naymūs [Naydhīr] held (kept) the raft; to the fast water, it did not give up. Third day, fourth day, Mount Naymūs [Naydhīr] held (kept) the raft; to the fast water, it did not give up. Fifth day, Sixth day, Mount Naymūs [Naydhīr] held (kept) the raft; to the fast water, it did not give up. At the arrival of the seventh day, I lifted a dove, I set it free. The dove went, it returned [(kept) circling around]. A wet land had not appeared to it [became available to him], it was frustrated [it went back and forth]. I lifted a swallow, I set it free. The swallow went, it returned [(kept) circling around]. A wet land had not appeared to it [became available to him], it was frustrated [it went back and forth]. I lifted a raven, I set it free. The raven went, it saw waters sediments. It was eating, cruising (roving), tracking (aiming), it was not frustrated [it did not go back and forth].

From now on, Uta-Napištim and his woman (his wife), let them have a destiny like preceding (bygone) gods. Let it be for them that Uta-Napištim shall dwell far away, in (at) the mouth (source) of the rivers'. (and so) They took (put) me far away at the mouth (source) of the rivers, they made me settle.

---

*Quran (11:44) وقيل يا أرض ابلعي ماءك ويا سماء أقلعي وغيض الماء وقضي الأمر واستوت على الجودي وقيل بعدا للقوم الظالمين

†Genesis (8:4) וַתָּנַח הַתֵּבָה בַּחֹדֶשׁ הַשְּׁבִיעִי בְּשִׁבְעָה-עָשָׂר יוֹם לַחֹדֶשׁ עַל הָרֵי אֲרָרָט

‡Saad D. Abulhab. The Epic of Gilgamesh: Selected Readings from its Original Early Arabic Language. New York: Blautopf Publishing, 2016.

From the Sumerian Eridu Genesis, Lines E9-E11

> *Back to that (since then), Zisudra the king, keeper (preserver) of the small animal creatures (and) the livestock of mankind's breathing life (the farm animals), they left (in his place) confined (isolated). (at) Mt. Bal (the keeper [triumph] mountain), Mt. dilmun-na (the black rock mountain: Mt. Daylamiyya or Mt. Abu Qbays in Macca), (at) the land of [where] the house of godShamash [the departing (setting) of the sun], they blessed (awarded) him the long age (life) (i.e. they settled him there forever).*

The above four references to the story are taken from early sources dated back to around 2000 BCE–650 CE, which makes them the ideal tools to help us understand where exactly the ancient people of the Near East thought the vessel had landed, and what was the fate of Noah.

One should first observe from the above readings that while the Quran and the two ancient Mesopotamian references explicitly named the mountain, Genesis only gave a geographical location, the *mountains of Arrṭ*. Clearly, this refers to a chain of mountains named *Arrṭ* or a chain of mountains in a country named *Arrṭ*. Because of the lack of vowels in ancient Hebrew, the word *Arrṭ* was not exactly pronounced, but it was likely either *Araraṭ, Aruruṭ*, or *Arruṭ*, and it was surely referring to the ancient mountainous country of Ararat, now part of east Turkey, as the location. The word *Arrṭ* in Genesis is derived from *UrRuṭ* meaning *"the country or land of the rivers"*, an Assyrian name. The word *Ur* means city or country, and the word *ruṭ* is borrowed, and altered, from the Greek word *rud* for river. The geographical area given by Genesis, Ararat, where most of the feeding rivers for the Tigris and Euphrates flow, is the same area given by the standard edition of the Epic of Gilgamesh as the future home of *Uta-Napištim* (i.e. Noah), as he explicitly explained when saying *"they took (put) me far away at the mouth (source) of the rivers, they made me settle"*. Obviously, according to his words, it was *not* where his vessel and its passengers landed!

Fortunately, the geographic location where the vessel landed, according to the ancient Mesopotamian beliefs, was clearly revealed by the names of the holding mountain provided explicitly in the two ancient Mesopotamian references above, and by the Quran. The standard edition named it *Mt. Naymūs or Mt. Naydhīr.* meaning *"the keeper of good mountain"*. The Sumerian Eridu Genesis called it *Mt. Bal*, meaning *"the keeper mountain"*, and *Mt. dilmun-na*, meaning *"the black rock mountain"*. The Quran named it *al-Jawdiyy*, also meaning *"the keeper"*. This word is a singular of *Ajyād*, the well-known name of the *Ajyād* mountain chain surrounding Mecca. This clearly leads us to the pre-Islamic *Mt. al-Amīn*, meaning *"the trusted keeper mountain"*, which is one of the peaks of the *Ajyād* mountain chain of Mecca, now called *Mt. Abu Qbays.* Before and after Islam, this mountain is believed by the Arabs to be the source of the black stone of *Kaʿbah.* It was also called *Mt. Daylamiyya*, a name even linguistically similar to the Sumerian name *Mt. dilmun-na*. In Sumerian, the noun word *na* means stone, and in Arabic the adjective word *dilmun*, from root word *dlm*, means black. The adjective preceded the noun as it is often done in Sumerian. Verifying this conclusion about the geographical area of the mountain, line E11 of the Sumerian Eridu Genesis even explained that it is where the sun sets, and God*Shamash* lives! That is west Arabia where Mecca is located. All this is astonishing but not surprising. Mecca was a holy destination for thousands of years before Islam. One of its many nick names, the Akkadian name *Bayt Yaqīn* meaning *the house of persuasion, rightness, or truth*, was explicitly marked in the Babylonian world map, in the far southwest corner relative to the city of Babylon. Even today, Muslims call it *Bayt Allāh*, meaning *the house of God.*[*]

---

[*]For additional information see: Saad D. Abulhab. The Epic of Gilgamesh: Selected Readings from its Original Early Arabic Language. New York: Blautopf Publishing, 2016. Pages 163-166.

3

The Case for Early Arabia and Arabic Language

The key aspect of my readings of the texts of ancient Near East languages stems from my evidence-backed conclusion that these languages should be classified and read as early Arabic. I will explore here this central point by replying to a new theory with an opposite understanding of early Arabia and the Arabic language, put forth by Ahmad al-Jallad, a scholar of ancient Near East languages and scripts. In a recent debate with al-Jallad, a self-described Semitic linguist, he proclaimed that exchanging the term 'Semitic' for 'early Arabic' or 'early *fuṣḥā*' is "simply a matter of nomenclature."* While his interpretation of the term Semitic sounds far more moderate than that of most Western philologists and epigraphists, it is not only fundamentally flawed and misleading, but also counterproductive. Most scholars, unfortunately, continue to misinform their students and the scholarly community by alluding to a so-called Semitic mother language, as a scientific fact. In a recent article, al-Jallad complained that most Arab scholars "rely almost exclusively on classical-Arabic dictionaries" to decipher ancient Arabic inscriptions written in Musnad and other scripts, but he neglects to see how relying exclusively on modern inscriptions-driven, limited-in-scope linguistic tools have produced erroneous and distorted translations, as we shall demonstrate later on.†

To put the above claim by al-Jallad in context, it is important to point out his overall views regarding the history of the Arabic language. He believes "various ancient forms of Arabic were present many centuries before the rise of Classical Arabic, in places such as Syria and Jordan," and that "the language may have originated there and then migrated south—suggesting that the 'corrupt' forms of Arabic spoken around the region may, in fact, have lineages older than classical Arabic." His key assertion that Arabic was born in the south Levant and spread southward is the latest of a barrage of current Western scholarly theories aimed at smearing and dismantling the brilliant scholarly work of numerous Islamic Arab linguists and historians, over more than a thousand years. Luckily, al-Jallad's speculative theory is only shared by a small group of Western scholars, including his colleague and mentor MacDonald, an accomplished Oxford scholar who, himself, has been working for years on exaggerated, questionable linguistic classifications of old Arabic. It is not surprising therefore why MacDonald rushed to accuse potential critics of al-Jallad's new theory of hidden motives, by claiming "his theory will inevitably meet a lot of opposition, mainly for non-academic reasons."‡

Ironically, while al-Jallad believes that using the coined, never-attested term Semitic, as a classification basis, is a matter of flexible terminology, he and most Western scholars demand strict, attested terminology use as a prerequisite for the classifications of early Arabs and Arabic language. Accordingly to them, one can only classify various ancient populations of the Arabian Peninsula and

* In a debate with al-Jallad via academia.edu on Sept 17, 2019.
† A New History of Arabia, Written in Stone. Muhanna, Elias. *The New Yorker*. May 23, 2018
‡ ibid

the Fertile Crescent as Arabs if they were explicitly identified as such in inscriptions. The earliest Arabs, we are told, should be traced to around 853 BCE, the date of the oldest Assyrian inscription found mentioning the word 'arab'. Presumably, these Arabs occupied the desert area extending from Mesopotamia in the East to the Sinai Peninsula in the west (i.e. mainly the southern Levant desert). Many repeatedly cite this inscription to support their absurd classification of the Arabs as merely the nomads of the vast Arabian deserts.

Citing his readings of a cache of Musnad Safaitic inscriptions from the Jordanian desert, al-Jallad, with a small group of scholars, wants to take the above absurdity a bit further. His belief that the Arabs originated in the southern Levant then migrated south to arabize the rest of the Arabian Peninsula would reverse the remarkable scholarly conclusions by numerous historians and linguists, past and present, who believed the Arabs originated in southern Arabia and migrated North. At least, other scholars who cite the Assyrian inscription do not imply the geographical territory of the early Arabs was limited to the Levant-Mesopotamian dessert area. This new theory by al-Jallad contradicts the overwhelming facts of history, geography, anthropology, and linguistics. Unlike al-Jallad's unsubstantiated assumptions, the early prominent historians who lived during a much closer time era have documented the clear trend of prior migration north. They backed their work by plenty of details, some of which can easily be verified by modern discoveries. The facts of geography confirm the past, gradual desertification of the Arabian Peninsula leading to northward migrations. There is nothing significantly unique to the Levant desert, geographically or otherwise, to separate it from the vast Arabian deserts of the peninsula. Nomads roamed this area as one in the past, and they even do today. Even the anthropological discoveries of the earliest human bones in the African Horn area suggest close-by Yemen was likely the original source of early migrations. Most importantly, the inscriptional, linguistic evidence from ancient Mesopotamia and the Levant revealed that the languages of northern Arabia were substantially similar to those of the rest of the peninsula, including ancient Yemen.

To be sure, neither the new Safaitic inscriptions cited by al-Jallad, nor his readings of them are remarkable enough to necessitate a reversal of the established scholarly conclusions. In the past century, scholars have read plenty of Safaitic Musnad inscriptions, without finding their language to be significantly distinct from the languages of other Musnad inscriptions found throughout Arabia, including Yemen. The Safaitic script was a relatively young script, confined to a smaller geographic area, compared to the rest of the Musnad family of scripts. It was used for writing north-western Arabic regional dialects' texts, at a much later Arabic linguistic evolution stage. Inscriptional evidence of the early languages of southern Arabian Peninsula indicated that theses languages have shared most of their words' roots and general meanings with the languages of the northern Arabian Peninsula and the Fertile Crescent. Sharing a substantial number of attested, common words *is* the key factor in determining Arabic linguistic classifications and origins. Pointing out a few unique grammatical features shared with modern Arabic, as al-Jallad does, *is not* the key factor.

Listening to a very interesting and informative lecture by al-Jallad, I could not help but to observe how torn and conflicted he was, on the topic of the Arabic language history.* Discussing the early languages of Yemen, he claimed they are "as distantly related to Arabic as Hebrew and Aramaic are related to Arabic". One should ask what Arabic was he referring to. If he meant the Arabic of the

* The Rise of Arabic: From an Epic Past to an Evidence-Based History. A lecture by Dr. Ahmad Al-Jallad, Sofia Chair of Arabic at Ohio State University. Dār al-'Āthār al-'Islāmiyyah, Kuwait, December 16, 2019.

Safaitic inscriptions then he is clearly wrong. If he meant the modern standard Arabic, then quoting Ibn Khaldūn would be a more accurate way to describe the differences between the old Yemen language, the pre-Islamic Arabic language of central Hijaz, and the modern standard Arabic of his time during the 14th century CE. Ibn Khaldūn wrote *".. the Muḍar tongue and Ḥimīr tongue were in a similar situation before the changes that occurred to many of the words of Ḥimīr tongue among the people of Muḍar. This is evident through available historical quotes, in contradiction with those who assume through ignorance that the two were one language and attempt to measure the Ḥimīr language based on the measurements of the Muḍar language and its grammar rules ..... The language of Ḥimīr is another language that differs from the language of Muḍar in many of its conditions, words' roots, and vowels, as the language of the Arabs in our time differs from the language of Muḍar."*[*] He clearly believed the three languages were all substantially Arabic languages but in different developmental stages, with the Yemen language being the oldest, original one.

The contradictions of al-Jallad's hypothesis that Arabic was originated in the southern Levant, not Yemen, are quite clear. To support his valid point that invoking "nomenclature is often (always?) ideological" and can therefore be bias, he gave an example to demonstrate how most scholars would observe the "developmental trajectory" of old English into modern English, but deny that for modern Arabic. He correctly stated that while *"modern English does not even resemble the West Saxon dialect of English"*, we would not *"look at modern English and say, English just appeared out of nowhere"*. However, shortly after, to justify his theory that the Arabic language was not originated in Yemen, he read a couple brief sentences from ancient Yemen inscriptions and complained that their language *does not even resemble* modern Arabic! It seems that al-Jallad wants to play both sides of the argument; contradicting his own linguistic evolution example, he denied the Arabic language its own "developmental trajectory" and implied it appeared "out of nowhere". He is yet to tell us where did his original Levant Arabic come from.

Advocating objectivity, al-Jallad said *"I want to be neutral, I don't want to make assumptions about what people may have called their languages".* This is a good point. Speakers of the original Italian called it "vulgar" Latin, but this should not prevent us from classifying it Early Italian. Even today, we call most Arabian Peninsula people 'Saudis', but this is irrelevant for their actual classification. It does not matter if the Akkadians never called their language Arabic. If it is substantially Arabic, then it is ancient Arabic; "if it looks like a duck, swims like a duck, and quacks like a duck, then it probably *is* a duck." However, while al-Jallad rightfully pointed out that ancient classifications should not be based on what people have called their languages, he had endorsed previously the notion that the Arabs (and therefore their language) are as old as the oldest inscription explicitly *calling* them with that name.[†] Continuing with his objectivity claim, al-Jallad said *"let's just talk in linguistic terms. We are looking for packages of linguistic features, like 'lam yaʿud'; that is an Arabic feature, it only occurs in Arabic, we don't find it in any other Semitic language"*. Once again, after he rightfully dismissed the notion that *"if the inscription does not have 'al', it is not Arabic"*, and observed that the definitions of the Arabic language in the twentieth century *"are anchored in ideology and nit-picking than they are in linguistic facts"*, he nit-picked, himself, by complaining about the absence of the Arabic *lam*. Incidentally, it is not true that other Semitic Languages did not use the *lam* feature. The standard edition of the Epic of Gilgamesh in the Akkadian language, which I believe al-Jallad would classify as a non-Arabic, Semitic language, have used it in Tablet II, line 77, for example.

---

[*] Ibn Khaldūn. Ta'rīkh Ibn Khaldūn. Part I, Chapter 47.

[†] Early Arabic Linguistic Classification. Chapter 16: *The Earliest Stages of Arabic and its Linguistic Classification.* Ahmad al-Jallad. 2018.

The hypocrisy of modern Western scholarship regarding Arabia and the Arabs is most apparent in its contradicting manipulation of the term Arabic language. While scholars hypothesize about the existence of an imaginary, unattested, mother language with the *invented name* 'Semitic', they demand that the existence of a real, ancient language with the *actual name* 'Arabic' must be attested first by inscriptional evidence, throughout its developmental stages. It gets even worse! While the invented Semitic language was sub-classified into many imaginary languages: Proto-Semitic, West-Semitic, East Semitic, .. etc, Arabic was denied any such meaningful classifications or sub-classifications. According to al-Jallad's Semitic tree, Arabic was a lonely "child" of Central Semitic, which in turn was branched from West Semitic.* Other scholars think Arabic branched from a presumed Arabic-Safaitic language, which in turn was branched from a vaguely-termed, West Semitic entity named "North Arabian", not even "North Arabic".†

Even with the emergence of Arabic as an established, fully-documented and explicitly-defined literary language after the introduction of the Quran, it was miss-classified into ambiguous and confusing sub-classifications. Western scholars classified the Arabic language of literary texts into: Classical Arabic (CA), Standard Classical Arabic (SCA), and Modern Standard Arabic (MSA). Accordingly, CA was the language of the Umayyad and Abbasid literary texts between the 7th and 9th centuries, and SCA was a standardized form of CA originating from the orthography of the Quraysh tribe of Macca, with MSA, the widely used language for formal Arabic communications today, being its direct descendant. Notice, we are not told where did CA come from. Also notice, the language of the Quran, the most important linguistic reference of the Arabic language, and pre-Islamic poetry were left out of the above classifications, possibly to open it up to scholarly interpretations! Clearly, the above coined classifications are not only meaningless and arbitrarily, but also designed to question the historical integrity and continuity of the Arabic language. It is quite misleading to claim CA was originated from the orthography of the Quraysh.

On the other hand, the early scholars and linguists of Arabic simply classified the language of the Quran as a formal, clear language (i.e. Fuṣḥā) representing the collective tongues or orthography of the entire people of the Arabian Peninsula, with Quraysh orthography chosen in the few instances when there was orthographic disagreements. According to these scholars, the Fuṣḥā language of the Quran, then, was rooted in the Ancient Arabic Language, and was fully linked to the rich Fuṣḥā language of its time, like the pre-Islamic Arabic poetry. Their solid linguistic classification makes it clear that at the time of the Quran, the Arabic language comprised of slightly varied formal languages (i.e. Fuṣḥā) spoken only by literate elite minorities, side-by-side a wide variety of locally-spoken dialects, exactly like it is today. It is logically impossible to assume that the sophisticated Fuṣḥā language of the Quran was evolved overnight. Claiming this language was used for a few centuries and must be defined by such a short time period implies that. It is also logically impossible to assume that this complex language was used by any certain local population for their day-to-day conversations. In a way, Fuṣḥā for the Arabic language is like Hochdeutsch for the German language!

Given how inaccurate and groundless the current definition of CA is, it is often ignored and many would use the term 'Classical Arabic' to simply denote Fuṣḥā. I will do exactly that. To reiterate, Fuṣḥā (past and present) represented the collective orthographic experience of the Arabic speaking

* Early Arabic Linguistic Classification. Chapter 16: *The Earliest Stages of Arabic and its Linguistic Classification*. Ahmad al-Jallad. 2018

† The Semitic Languages. Edited by John Huehnergard and Na'ama Pat-El. Chapter 1: Introduction to the Semitic Languages and their History. Routledge Family Language Series. Oxon & New York, 2019.

people, transcending geographic and historical boundaries. It did not represent a specific language in the sense of a daily spoken language by a specific group or region. It is rather a linguistic methodology used by the literate elite to document the Arabic language text in a clear, undisputed, verified, and inclusive manner, consistent with what is accepted as a so-called pure or formal language, at a certain time period and location. Fuṣḥā had no fixed grammar rules (as Ibn Khaldūn noted!) but rather an evolving grammar influenced by styles, scripts, mediums, and the writing systems utilized, geographically and historically. The great work of the Abbasid grammarians was extremely useful, but it was only intended to document and control the evolution of Fuṣḥā. With the above understanding of CA as a formal documentation language, not linked to a historical time period or geographical locality, it would be natural to assume the existence of earlier, substantially similar languages, and to identify them as early CA languages.

Fortunately, modern inscriptional discoveries have clearly revealed that earlier forms of the Classic Arabic language of the Quran and the pre-Islamic poetry have existed for at least a millennium and a half before. The Akkadians recorded their literary work and formal communications using a language with undisputed Arabic words and slightly similar grammar. A lot of the archaic grammar used by the written Akkadian language can even be seen in the pre-Islamic poetry and the Quran. The fact that it was not identical to the modern Arabic grammar is completely irrelevant. This is the essence of linguistic evolution. Ancient languages, spoken or formal, are not supposed to exactly resemble their modern corresponding ones. The key point here is that the Akkadians have invented a grammar methodology to formally record text, effectively creating a formal, reference language (i.e. early Fuṣḥā), which was not used as a day-to-day spoken language by various Mesopotamian localities, then. To support the above, I ask the reader to examine the following early classical Arabic poem from Tablet 10, Line 62 & 63, of the standard edition of the Epic pf Gilgamesh (~1000 BCE):*

ذا سغبا لغب ليعدل كاء ذا   إن عسر خيا وعسر ليفح كاء ذا

The script developed by the early Akkadian Arabs, whether it was originally borrowed or invented, was undoubtedly the most elaborate script used by the Arabs to record their language, until the emergence of the modern, soft vowels enhanced Arabic script in the 8th century. This Cuneiform script integrated detailed vowels information to allow for precise pronunciations, making it a far better script to facilitate any early Arabic linguistic research than al-Jallad's "favourite", ill-equipped Greek script.† In fact, the Greek script would surely distort the pronunciations of Arabic words, just as the Latin script, Western scholar's favourite script to transliterate historical Arabic texts, would. For example, scholars translated the text of the *Umm al_Jimāl* Nabatean inscription (~250 CE) *solely* on their reading of its inexact translation in a nearby Greek inscription. Misreading the Arabic Nabataean text, they translated it as "*This is the Stelle of Fihru, son of Shullai, teacher of Jadhimat, king of Tanūkh*" when in fact it said "*This is the soul and tomb of Fr', son of Shullai, teacher/commander of Jadhimat, the one who made Tanūkh reign (crowned it)*". The name *Fihru* did not exist in the Nabataean inscription. There was no letter *hā*. The word was actually *qbr* for *qabr*, meaning tomb. Together with the previous word *nafsu*, it formed the familiar phrase *nafs-u-qabr* seen on numerous tombs in north eastern Arabia, where the deceased was likely from. The name *Fihru* was *assumed* based on scholars' pronunciation of the word ΦΕΡΟΥ in the Greek inscription, because they neglected tracing the following slightly damaged word, which was the actual name.

---

* Saad D. Abulhab. *The Epic of Gilgamesh: Selected Readings from its Original Early Arabic Language: Including a New Translation of the Flood Story.* New York: Blautopf. 2016.

† The Rise of Arabic: From an Epic Past to an Evidence-Based History. A lecture by Dr. Ahmad Al-Jallad, Sofia Chair of Arabic at Ohio State University. Dār al-'Āthār al-'Islāmiyyah, Kuwait, December 16, 2019.

This word was *Fr'*, for *Fara'*, or *Firu'*, or *Farā*. Similarly, the clear word *mmlk*, (i.e. *mumallik*) for "the one who established kingdom of" was simply read *mlk*, for *malik*, meaning king, because the Greek inscription translated it that way! Scholars ignored the second undisputedly clear letter *m*.

A correct transliteration of the *Umm al_Jimāl* inscription matters. It is one of only three Nabataean inscriptions from the early centuries of the first millennium with clear Classical Arabic passages. The three inscriptions also confirmed important historical and linguistic facts regarding Arabic and Arabs. Unfortunately, the other two inscriptions, *al-Namārah* (327 CE) and *ʿAyn Abdāt* (~88 CE) were also misread and misinterpreted. Some scholars like al-Jallad even questioned whether the language of *al-Namārah* is Classical Arabic, simply because it did not fit the arbitrary definition of CA. As for *ʿAyn Abdāt*, scholars continue to circulate false, mediocre translations of its two lines of vertical classical Arabic poem, and distort their rhyming verses. With an astonishing lack of a minimal linguistic understanding of how the eloquent and sophisticated Classical Arabic poetry work, they managed to translate its rather simple, philosophical two poetry lines, as three plain sentences without a slightest hint of Arabic poetic style.

The *ʿAyn Abdāt* inscription starts with three Aramaic dialect text lines inscribed by a man named *Jrm Ilhi*. In the first two he asked to praise those who would read a prayer to god. In the third, he informs readers that he gave an offering to god *Abdāt*. Then, he inscribes two lines of Classical Arabic poetry explaining how death is inevitable regardless of offering or status since it is here to get us, but he does not want death because it is like a wound that tortures you but does not let you perish. He was likely a reincarnation believer complaining that one would not perish after death, or possibly, he was complaining about the suffering caused by the death of a loved one. Most current translations, however, missed the point of this poem, which was clearly about death, not god. Here is one of these translations: *For he [Obodas -the god] acts [expecting] no reward nor predilection. Though death has often sought us out, he afforded it no occasion; though I have often encountered wounding, he has not let it be my destruction.** For those who want to judge on their own, below are the two poetry lines:

فيفعلُ لا فدا ولا أثرا　　　فكان هنا يبغنا

الموتُ لا أبغهُ من هنا　　　أدد جرحُ لا يردنا

To reinforce his theory that the Arabic language originated in the Levant, al-Jalad reminded us that the early Arabic script was also originated there since it was simply an evolved Nabataean script, a familiar claim put forward by Western scholars in the past century. He claimed "all this rich Arabic written heritage (i.e. Musnad) was dead-end" and "everything "died off" to conclude that "the way to write Arabic happened here in the Nabataean kingdom". The Nabataeans, he explained, were "Arabic speakers", "who did not write their language" and "they did all their business using the Aramaic language and the Aramaic script". This may sound convincing at first, but it contradicts inscriptional evidence, which revealed the Nabataeans used a distinct dialect of the Arabic language, in addition to Aramaic, and a distinct script that was possibly older than the Aramaic script. The Nabataean and Aramaic scripts were likely derived from Musnad or Phoenician, an ancient script closely related to Musnad, which itself was influenced by the cuneiform Ugaritic alphabet. Inscriptions also revealed Musnad coexisted for a long time, with the new, developing writing systems in northern Arabia, and at least one Musnad style, Saba'i of the Yemen, survived intact till Islam. The death of the Musnad script was decreed by the Muslim leaders who decided in favour of the newer Arabic script, to record the Quran. Like many Western scholars, al-Jallad overlooks how the early Arabs classified the

* Hoyland, Robert G. *Arabia and the Arabs: From the Bronze Age to the Coming of Islam*. London: Routledge. 2001

Nabataeans. According to them, they were the *settled* Arab farmers and dwellers of cities. Early scholars talked about the Nabataeans of Iraq (i.e Akkadians) and explained they were much older than the Nabataeans of the Levant. They even mentioned the Nabataeans of Uman and Bahrain!

In all likelihood, the early Arabic script, Jazm, was independently invented by Musnad, possibly Safaitic, scribes who were heavily influenced by the success of the prominent Nabataean script in the Northern Arabian region, and by other Aramaic-linked scripts in the area, including Mesopotamia. There is plenty of evidence to support this when examining the early Arabic inscriptional timelines, minimized shapes, reduced glyphs, expanded alphabetic mapping, and cursive style. The strict manner in which the glyphs of early Arabic styles connect across the horizontal line, is unique, indicating it was designed from scratch, not evolved. The name given by the early Arabs who used this style was *khaṭṭ al-Jazm*, literally meaning 'the horizontal line of cut or deducted shapes'. This name conforms with the claims put by early Arabic scholars that this script was invented, not evolved. The early Arabic script was not fully developed until it was adopted by the emerging Islamic state. Therefore, studying the early history of Arabic script should include the study of inscriptions and manuscripts of the early Islamic period.

Invoking nomenclature is often ideological, as al-Jallad noted, but the use of the term "Semitic" is *not* "simply a matter of nomenclature". Identifying the actual language of an ancient inscription is essential to deciphering it correctly. It is key to arriving at meaningful, more precise transliterations and translations. Classifying an inscription as an early Arabic inscription, rather than Semitic, leads us to use the old etymological Arabic references, which were based on past compilations of actual words' roots and usages, as primary tools. The modern linguistic dictionaries created by compiling speculated words and meanings, based on limited number of inscriptions, can be useful as secondary tools. Relying solely on these modern dictionaries can produce distorted, erroneous, and weird readings, like the one we read above for the *ʿAyn Abdāt* inscription.

Western scholars claim that relying solely on compiled lists of attested words' meanings, derivations, and grammatic usages from inscriptions is the only scholarly method to decipher ancient Near East texts, and produce verified language classifications. However, most data in these compiled lists are speculated (i.e. unattested and unverified). al-Jallad believes his searchable, limited-in-scope compiled list from the south Levant Safaitic inscriptions was key to the validity of his new theory; we are told his new Arabia history is "written on stone", after all! Certainly, the language of these inscriptions was undeniably Arabic as it can easily be verified through the Arabic etymological tools. Using his list can be helpful, but relying on it as an alternative to the historical references can be damaging. Examining one of his many Safaitic inscriptions' translations can illustrate this point, and would be the best way to conclude. Compare his translation below with the likely, coherent translation based on the Arabic references. Strangely, Al-Jallad wants the readers to accept his notion that a wild female wolf was actually named *Mn*! Clearly, he speculated rather than consulting the root word *mnn* in the Arabic historical manuscripts.

ṭrd h-ḏ'b ẓlʿ m-mn ʿkd yglḥ [طرد هذئب ضلع ممن عكد يجلح]
<u>al-Jallad's translation:</u> *He drove away the wolf, which was seeking to mate from Mn after it attacked.*[*]
<u>Arabic-based translation:</u> *The wolf chased around, he wanted to mate with the weak one, he kept on attacking [or: he then attached*

[*] A Dictionary of the Safaitic Inscriptions. Ahmad Al-Jallad and Karolina Jaworska. Studies in Semitic Languages and Linguistics, Vol 98. 2019

Part 1

Translations and Arabic Transliterations of Relevant Passages

Reading Guide

Red or Light-shaded words are presumably Sumerian words

[ ] Alternative transliterations or translations

{ } Words or lines from another tablet copy

( ) Alternative words meanings or clarification nots

... Missing words or lines

| | Assumed words or lines for lost text

Letters Substitutions Guides

al-Jibūrī Letters Substitutions Rules

From: *Qamūs al-Lughah al-Akkadiyyah al-ʿArabiyyah*

Akkadian Arabic throat letters (أ، ح، هـ، ع، غ، ض، ظ، ث، ذ) **=> Hamzah** (') **=> ē, ī, ū, û , ā, â**

e.g. ba'lum = bēlum بعل | ẖaqlum = ēqlum حقل | ĝrub = ērub غرب

Nūn (n) **with sukūn** (stop) **+ Arabic lip letter** (b, p, m) **=> Arabic lip letter repeated** (bb, pp, mm)

e.g. kanpum => kappum | anpum => appum

Letter with sukūn (stop) **+ Arabic teeth letter** (t, d, ṭ, s, š) **=> Lām + Arabic teeth letter** (t, d, ṭ, s, š)

e.g. išdu => ildu | išṭur => ilṭur | iššī => ilšī | ištakan => iltakan | ušubtu => ušultu

Mīm (m) **+ Arabic teeth letter** (t, d, ṭ, s, š) **=> Nūn** (n) **+ Arabic teeth letter** (t, d, ṭ, s, š)

e.g. imdud => indud | imtu => intu | amiš => aniš | imtanum => intanum

Rā' (r) **+ Nūn** (n) **=> Nūn** (n) **+ Nūn** (n) **=> NūnNūn** (nn)

e.g. arnu => annu | ibqurnisu => ibqunnisu

Two assimilated letters => Nūn (n) **with sukūn** (stop) **+ One assimilated letter**

e.g. inazziq => inanziq | inaddi => inandi | immagar => imangar | nammuri => nanmuri

Two words joind by two assimilated letters L1-L2 => One word, repeated assimilated letter L2

e.g. şit-šamaši => şissamiši | sinm-yattum => sinyyatum | umam-kal => umakkal

Strong Sumerian letter sounds => Akkadian letter sounds

ث => ش   ذ => ط   ذ => ئ   ذ => ز   ظ => ص   ض => ص   ق <=> ك

Arabic Letters Substitutions

From: *Lisān al-ʿArab*

ت <=> ظ	س (+ ق،ط،غ،خ،غ) => ص	ز <=> س	أ <=> ع
ت <=> ض	س <=> ش	ز <=> ص	أ <=> هـ
ذ <=> ث	س <=> ت	ك <=> ق	ب <=> م
ذ <=> ض	ف <=> ب	م <=> ن	د <=> ط
	ت <=> ط	ن => ر	د <=> ذ

Latin Arabic Letters Substitutions

Compiled by the Author through his Research

Latin Letter	Possible Arabic Letter(s)	Latin Letter	Possible Arabic Letter(s)
A (àáāâ)	ا أ آ ع هـ	S	س ش ص ظ
B	ب	Š	ش س ذ ض ث ظ
D	د ذ ض ط	Ṣ	ص ض ظ
E (èē)	أ إ ي ح ع غ هـ	T	ت ط ث ذ
G	ج ق غ	Ṭ	ط ت
H (ẖ)	خ ح هـ	U (úū)	ؤ و ع
I (íī)	إ ي ع ح هـ	W	و
K	ك ق خ	Y	ي
L	ل	Z	ز ذ ص ظ
M	م	ʾ Hamzah	أ ع غ ح هـ ض ظ ث ذ
N	ن	a	◌َ
P	ف ب	e	◌َ
Q (ḵ)	ق ك	i	◌ِ
R	ر	u	◌ُ

1

Relevant Readings from the Babylonian Creation Epic

1.1

e-nu-ma e-liš la na-bu-ú šá-ma-mu

حينما عليتْ [عليذْ] لا نبُئو سمَامُ {سمَام}

حينما عالياً، ما رُفِعت السماوات،

[حينما عالياً، ما نودِيت السماوات،]

When high above, had not been raised, heavens,
[When high above, had not been called heavens,]

1.2

šap-liš am-ma-tum šu-ma la zak-rat

سفِلتْ [سفلِذْ] أمتُمْ {أبتُمْ} سمُا لا ذكْرَتْ

أسفلاً، تضاريس الارضُ ما ذُكِرَت إسْماً (بالاسم)،

down below, the land terrain had not been mentioned by name.

1.3

ZU.AB-ma reš-tu-ú za-ru-šú-un

ذارُؤذنْ عبزُما {عبْزُ} {عبْزُما} {عبْزو} ريسّتو

(حينها) عبْزَ (ذا العبَزِ، حوض المياه الجوفية العذبة)، ذارُؤهم (خالق الآلهة) القيّوم (القائم عليهم)،

(that time) Abzu (of underground fresh water basin), their (the gods) foremost (chief) and creator,

1.4

mu-um-mu ti-amat mu-al-li-da-at gim-ri-šú-un

مومْ تيمَات [طيمَات] مُألِدتْ {مُملَدتْ} جمرِذُنْ

(و) الفاعلة تَيمات (ذات الطَمّةْ او التَمّةْ، بحرالمياه المالحة)، والدةْ (مُنجبة) (الآلهة) كلّهم،

(and) maker Tiamat (of salt water sea), the one who gave birth to all of them (the gods),

1.5

$\text{A}^{\text{meš}}$-šú-nu iš-te-niš i-ḫi-qu-ú-ma

آميس ذنْ {مؤوذنْ} إسْتنِتْ {إسْتُنِتْ} [إسْتنِذْ {إسْتُنِذْ}] يُحيقوما {يُحيقْما}

(كانو) يحيقو (يُنزلو او يولجو ببعض) مياهم، واحداً؛

(were) downloading (penetrating into each other) their waters, as one;

1.6

gi-pa-ra la ki-iṣ-ṣu-ru ṣu-ṣa-a la še-'u-ú

جبَرا لا قصِرُ {قصُرُ} {قصرا} [كصِرُ {كصُرُ} {كصُرا}] صُصا {صُصئا} لا سَعو {سَعي} [شعو {شعي}]

(و) الحقول (المراعي) ما كانت قاصرة (ما كانت ضئيلة أومُستنفذة)، الاهوار [غابات القصب] ما كانت مُسعيا (لها) [متفشية ومنتشرة].

(and) the fields (pastures) were not depleted, the marshes [reeds] were not sought after [widespread].

1.7

e-nu-ma DINGIR.DINGIR la šu-pu-u ma-na-ma

حينما دنجر.دنجر {دنجر ميس} لا شُفُوَ [شوفُو] مَنما

حينما الآلهة ما بُرزو (ما ظهرو)، ايآ ما (ايآ كان)،

When the gods were not revealed (made visible), anyone (none),

1.8

šu-ma la zuk-ku-ru ši-ma-tú la ši-i-mu

سُما لا ذُكُرو سِماتو {سِماتا} لا سيمو

ما ذُكرو إسماً (بالاسم)، ما علّمو سماتاً (عُيّنو مصائرا)،

were not mentioned by name, were not assigned destinies,

1.9

ib-ba-nu-ú-ma DINGIR.DINGIR qé-reb-šú-un

إبنُوما {إبنُوَ} {إبنُما} دنجر.دنجر {دنجر ميس} قَربْذُنْ

(عبزُ وتيمات) بَنيا (اصطنعا) الآلهة قُربُهم؛

they (Abzu and Tiamat) built (made/formed) the gods close to them;

1.10

^{d}làḫ-mu ^{d}la-ḫa-mu uš-ta-pu-ú šu-mi iz-zak-ru

دنجرلحْمُو {و} دنجرلحامو أُشتَفُوَ {شْتَفُوَ} سُمي {سُما} إذّكْرو {ذونْ إذّكْرو}

أبرَزو (أظهَرو) هما الهلحمو والهةلحامو، ذكَرو بالاسماء {بالاسم} {ذكَروهم}.

they revealed (made visible) ^{god}Lahmu and ^{godess}Lahamu, mentioned by name{s} {mentioned them}.

1.11

a-di ir-bu-ú i-ši-ḫu

عَدي [عَتي] {عَديما [عَتيما]} إربُو يذيحو [يذيخو] [يشيخو]

حتى حينَ (بينما) نَمو، أخذو يكبرو [أخذو يشيخو]،

Until when (As soon as) they grew up, becoming huge [becoming old],

1.12
an-šár ᵈki-šár ib-ba-nu-u e-li-šu-nu at-ru
أنشار (أشّار) {و} دنجرقشار إبنُوما {إبنَو} {إبنَما} عليذُنو أتْرو

بَنَيا أشّار والهةقشار، أزادو عليهم (على لحمو ولحامو)؛

they made Ashshar and godessQishar, they increased over them (over Lahmu and Lahamu);

1.13
ur-ri-ku UDmeš uṣ-ṣi-bu MU.AN.NAmeš
أرّكو {أرّكي} أودْميس [عودْميس] أُصّبو {وصّبو} مُوْنَمِيس {مُوْمِيس}

أخّرو الايام (أيامهم اي مواعيد فناءهم)، أدامو السنين (المئات أوالقرون؟) (سنينهم اي أعمارهم).

they delayed the days (their dying days), perpetuated the years (centuries?) (their ages).

1.14
ᵈa-num a-pil-šu-nu ša-nin AD.AD-šú
دنجرأنُوم [دنجرعَنومْ] أفلذُنُ ثانِنْ {ثانينْ} {ثانينَ} أدْ. أدْذو [عَدْ. عَدْذو]

الهأنو، وليدهم، ثُنّيَ (ضُوهِيَ) آباءه؛

godAnu, their newborn male, became an equal of his fathers;

1.15
an-šár ᵈa-num bu-uk-ra-šu ú-maš-šil-ma
أنشار دنجرأنُوم [دنجرعَنومْ] بُكْر ذو أُمثِلَمَ

أشّار ماثَلَ (جعل مماثلا) ابنه البِكر، الهأنو،

Ashshar made alike his first-born, godAnu,

1.16
ù ᵈa-num tam-ši-la-šú ú-lid ᵈnu-dím-mud
و دنجرأنُوم [دنجرعَنومْ] تَمْثِلَذو أُلِدْ دنجرنُوْديمُدْ

والهأنو وَلَدَ (أنجب) مثيله، الهنُوْديمُد.

and godAnu begat his alike, godNudimud.

1.17
ᵈnu-dím-mud šá ADmeš-šú šá-liṭ-su-nu šu-ma
دنجرنُوْديمُدْ ذا أَدْميس ذو [عَدْميس ذو] سالطْنُنْ سُما {ذوو}

الهنُوْديمُدْ ذا [الى] آبائه، كان سَليطَهم (متحدثهم) [قائدهم] بالاسم {هو}؛

godNudimud of [for] his fathers, {he} was their speaker [leader] by name;

1.18
pal-ka uz-nu ḫa-sis e-mu-qan pu-un-gul
فَلْقَ أُذْنُ {أُذْنَ} حَسِسْ حُمْقَنْ فُنْجلْ {فُجْلْ}

حاذقُ علم (معرفة)، حاسٌّ (سميعً بصيرً، عليمً)، غليظ عزما،
dexterous of knowledge, percipient (insightful), robust of vigor (strength),

1.19

gu-uš-šur ma-a'-diš a-na a-lid abī(ad)-šú an-šár

جُسْرْ مأدذْ[مأدتْ] {مادذْ[مادتْ]} أنَ آلدْ أدْذو [عَدْذو] أنشار

جسور (مقدام)، مبلغاً [غيرً] عن والد أبيه، أشّار.
bold (daring), a magnitude [a big difference] from (over) the begetter of his father, Ashshar.

1.20

la i-ši ša-ni-na ina DINDIR^{meš} at-ḫe-e-šú

لا إإذي [إإتي] ثانينْ {ثانينَ} إنَ دنجرمِيس أتْخيذو {أدْمِيسذو [عَدْمِيسذو]}

ما أوتيَ (ما له) ثانيا في (فيما بين) الآلهة، تأخيّته (مُتآخيه){أباءه}.
He has no equal in (among) the gods, his brethren {his fathers}.

1.21

in-nen-du-ma at-ḫu-ú DINGI.DINGIR^{ni}

إنّعَنْدُما [إنعمْدُما] أتْخُوَ دنجر.دنجرني {دنجر.دنجرنو}

الألهة المتآخين عاندو [واجهو] بعضهم البعض.
The brethren gods debated [faced] each other.

1.22

e-šu-ú ti-amat-ma na-ṣir-šu-nu iš-tap-pu

إعشو تيَمَتْما {تيَماتما} {تيَمات} [طيَمات] {طيَماتما {طيَماتما} {طيَمات}] ناظرْذنْ {مَطرْذنْ [مَصرْذنْ]} إشْتعفو {إشْتعفلما}

تجاهلو تيمات (و) علّو (صعّدو) {عاليا} مناظرتهم {حدّيتهم (حدّية جدالهم)}.
They ignored (disregarded) Tiamat (and) exalted (intensified) {high} their debate {zealotry}.

1.23

dal-ḫu-nim-ma ša ti-amat ka-ra-sa

دَلْهُنِمَ ذا تيَمات [طيَمات] {تُووت؟} كَرسَا

أذْهبو [جننو] عقل تيمات.
They made the mind of Tiamat go [go insane].

1.24

i-na šu-'a-a-ri šu-u'-du-ru qé-reb an-durun-na

إنَ شُعاري ذُؤدُرو قرِبْ أنْدرُونّ

بالشعائر (عبر مراسيم المناظرة) رَعْو (عززو) قُرب [تقارب] الأنْدُرونّ (المتآخين المجتمعين) (مجمع الآلهة).
With rituals (protocols), they fostered the closeness of the gathered brethren (gods assembly).

1.25

la na-ši-ir Apsû(zu.ab) ri-gim-šú-un

لا نسرْ {نَنْسرِّي} عبزْ {عَبزوَ} رِجمْذُنْ

ما نسرَ (ما استطاع ان يسلب) [ما استطاع ان يخفض] صوتهم، عَبزْ.

Abzu could not rob [lower] their voice,

1.26

ù ti-amat šu-qám-mu-mat i-na IGI-šu-un

وتَيمات [طَيَمات] ذُقمُّتْ [ذُكَمُّتْ] [تُقَمُّتْ [تكَمُّتْ]] إنَ إجيذُنْ

وتيمات كانت صامتة في وجههم (أمامهم).

and Tiamat was silent in front of them,

1.27

im-tar-ṣa-am-ma ep-še-ta-šu-un e-li-ša

إمْتَرضَمّ [إمْتَرصَمّ] عفْسِتاذُنْ [عَفْشِتاذُنْ] عَليذا

فعلتهم جلبت الأذى [القهر] عليها.

Their doing brought harm [defeat] over her.

1.28

la ṭa-bat al-kát-su-nu šu-nu-ti i-ga-me-la

لا طابَتْ أَلْكَتّنْ {أَلْكَذُنْ} ذُنوتي يجمِّلا

ما طابت (ما كانت طيبة) طريقتهم (التي) هم كانو يمارسون (ينفذون) (أي ممارساتهم).

Their way (method), (that) they were carrying out (executing), was unpleasant (i.e. their practices).

1.29

e-nu-šu Apsû(zu.ab) za-ri DINGI.DINGIR ra-bí-ù-tim

حينْذو عَبزْ ذارِء دنجر.دنجر ربِؤتِمْ [ربوّتِم]

حينئذ، عَبزْ، خالق سمو (عظمة) الآلهة [جماعة الآلهة]،

Thereupon, Abzu, the creator of the great gods [the community of gods],

1.30

is-si-ma ^{d}mu-um-mu suk-kal-la-šu i-zak-kar-šu

إسَّمَا دنجرمومْ سقّلذو يذكَرذو

أمرَ إلهمُوم، مُعتَمَده، ذاكرا له (قائلا له):

ordered ^{god}Mummu, his confidant, saying to him:

1.31

^{d}mu-um-mu suk-kal-lu mu-ṭib-ba ka-bat-ti-ia

دنجرمومْ سُقلّو مُطِيبا كَبَتِيّا [كَبَدِيّا]

مُعْتَمَد إلهمُومٌ، مُطَيِّبُ لبّيَ،

"Confidant godMummu, the one who pleases my innermost;

1.32

al-kám-ma ṣe-ri-iš ti-amat i ni-il-li-ik

ألْكَما ظِهْرِيتْ [ظِهْرِيذْ] تَيمات [طَيّمات] {تَووَتِ؟} يا نئلِكْ

تَرَسّلْ (تعالَ)، دعنا [حتّى؛ كَيْما] نَتَرَسّلْ خلف (الى) تيمات

come, let us [so that we] go after (to) Tiamat."

1.33

il-li-ku-ma qu-ud-mi-iš ta-ma-tum ú-ši-bu

إلِّكُما قُدْمِيتْ [قُدْمِيذْ] {قُدْمَتْ [قُدْمَذْ]} تيمَتْمْ [طَيمَتْمْ] {تيَمات [طَيّمات]} {تَووَتِ؟} أُأْثِبو {سَكْبْ}

تَرَسّلا (ذهبا)، جلَسَا {سُكِبا (صُبّا)} قُدّام (أمام) البحر {(أمام) تيمات}

They went, they sat {they were poured out} in front of the sea.

1.34

a-ma-a-ti im-tal-li-ku aš-šum DINDIR.DINGIR bu-uk-ri-šu-un

أماتي [هَماتي] يمْتَلِّكُ [يمْتَلّأكُ] [يمتأَلِّكُ] أذُّمْ [هَذُّمْ] دنجر.دنجر {دنجرميسنو} بُكريذُنْ

مُتَوجها (مُشيرا الى، مُسردا) أموره [همومه] هذا لأن (بسبب، بخصوص) الآلهة، أبناءهم الأوائل،

Directing (pointing, telling) his matters [concerns] regarding the gods, their first-born sons,

1.35

Apsû(zu.ab) pa-a-šu i-pu-šam-ma

عَبْزُ فاءَذو [فاهَذو] إعِبُشَما

عَبزُ جمع (شغّلَ) فَمَه،

Abzu collected (worked) his mouth,

1.36

a-na ti-amat el-le-tam-ma i-zak-kar-ši

أنَ تيَمات [طَيَمات] علِيّتَما يذَكّرْذي {إذّكّرْذو} {مُوَذي}

قائلا لها {قال لها}{صاح لها}، الى الطاهرة تيمات:

saying to her {said to her} {said with loud voice to her}, to pure Tiamat:

1.37

im-tar-ṣa-am-ma al-kát-su-nu e-li-ia

إمْتَرْضَمَّ [إمْتَرصَمَّ] ألْكَتّنْ عَليا

طريقتهم (ممارستهم) جلبت الأذى [القهر] عليّ.

Their way (their practice) brought harm [defeat] on me.

1.38
ur-ri-iš la šu-up-šu-ḫa-ku mu-ši-iš la ṣa-al-la-ku
عُريتْ [عُريذْ] لا سُفْسحاْكو مُسيتْ [مُسيذْ] لا ظلّأكو

مساءاً لا مرتاح أنا أكن؛ ليلاً لا غافيا أنا أكن.

By day not at ease (relaxed), I am; by night not a bit sleeping (dozing off), I am.

1.39
lu-uš-ḫal-liq-ma al-kát-su-nu lu-sa-ap-pi-iḫ
لأتْحلقْما ألْكتّنْ لأسفّهْ

"لأزيلْ(هم) (لأبيد(هم))، لأسفّهْ طريقتهم (ممارستهم)

“Let me (I want to) wipe (them) out, let me (I want to) stultify their way (their practice).

1.40
qu-lu liš-ša-kin-ma i ni-iṣ-lal ni-i-ni
قُلو {قوْلو} [قهْلو {قهْلو}] ليسكّنْما يا نظْلّلْ نحنْ [نينْ]

ليسكُن (ليعّم) التجافي (الهدوء)، دعنا [حتى؛ كيْما] نغفي قليلا نحنْ."

Let avoidance (quiet) be set, let us [so that we] sleep a bit (doze off), we ourselves.”

1.41
ti-amat an-ni-ta i-na še-me-e-ša
تيمات [طيمات] آنيتّا إنَ سمْعيذا {سمْعيذو}

تيمات، حالا، حينَ سمْعِه [سمْعِ ذلك]،

Tiamat, immediately, in (upon) hearing him [that],

1.42
i-zu-uz-ma il-ta-si e-lu ḫar-me-ša
إعزْزْما [إإزْزْما] إلتأسيَ علو حرْمذا {خامرذا}

عزّزت (تألمت) [إشتدت]، تأسّت (حزنت) على حرمِها (قرينها) {مُخالطها (مُولجها)}،

she felt hurt [became furious], saddened over her consort (mate) {inter-connector},

1.43
is-si-ma mar-ṣi-iš ug-gu-gát e-diš-ši-ša
إسّما مرْضتْ [مرْضذْ] [مرصتْ [مرْصذْ]] أجُجتْ [عجُجتْ] حديثيذا [حدسيذا]

صاحت بألم، رفعت [رفعت] بصوت عالي أراءها،

she shouted hurtfully, her opinions were raised loudly [she raised loudly her opinions],

1.44
le-mut-ta it-ta-di a-na kar-ši-ša
لئمْتَ إتأديَ أنَ كرْشيذا

جلبَت (وضعت) اللؤمة (الغيظ) [الشر] الى كرشها (داخلها):
she brought (put) the rage [evil] to her gut (inside her):

1.45
mi-na-a ni-i-nu šá ni-ib-nu-ú nu-uš-ḫal-laq-ma
منا نحنُ [نينُ] ذا نبْنو نُتْحلَّقم

"ماذا؟ نحن أنفسنا نُزيلُ (نُبيدُ) ما نبني [بنينا]؟
"What? We, ourselves, wipe out what we build [built]?

1.46
al-kàt-su-nu lu šum-ru-ṣa-at-ma i ni-iš-du-ud ṭa-biš
ألْكَتّنْ لو {لوو} ذُمْرُضَتْما [ذُمْرُصَتْما] {تُمْرُضَتْما [تُمْرُصَتْما]} يا نسْدُدْ [نشْدُدُ] طابتْ [طابِذْ] { ذوقاتْ [ذوقاذْ]}
(و)لتكن مؤذية، طريقتهم (ممارستهم)؛ دعنا [حتى؛ كيْما] نُسدِدْ (نُصلحْ، نُقوّمْ) [نتحمّل] بطيبة {بذوق}"
Let-it-be harmful, their way (practice); let us [so that we] correct [endure] kindly {tastefully}]"

1.47
i-pul-ma dmu-um-mu ZU.AB i-ma-al-lik
إفِلْما دنجرمُومُ عبْزُ {عبْزا} يملّكْ [يمألّكْ] [يملاِكْ]

تخلّلَ (حلّ؛ وضح، أكثرَ) الهمُومُ، يوجه (موجّها) عبْزُ {عبزا}؛
godMummu analyzed (explained; elaborated; added), advising Abzu;

1.48
suk-kal-lum la ma-gi-ru mi-lik mu-um-mi-šu
سُقّلُمْ لا مَجرُ {مَجرا} ملكْ [مِإلكْ] [ملاِكْ] مُومذو

مُومّهُ [عامله]، المُعتمَدُ، كان موجّهْ غير عاقل (متهور):
[المُعتمَدُ كان غير عاقل (متهور)، (كـ)موجّهاً، مُومّهُ [عامله]]:
[المُعتمَدُ كان غير عاقل (متهور)، مُومّهُ [عامله] الموجّه]:
His Mummu [His worker (officer)], the confidant, was an irrational (unwise) advisor:
[The confidant was irrational (unwise), an advisor, his Mummu [his worker (officer)]]:
[The confidant was irrational (unwise), his Mummu [his worker (officer)] the advisor]:

1.49
ḫul-li-qam-ma a-bi al-ka-ta e-ši-ta
حلْقّما أبي ألكتا عشيتا {ألكتمْ عشيتمْ} {عشيتو}

"أزلْ (أبدْ)، أبي! هذه الطريقة، تجاهل.
"Wipe out, my father! this way is a disregard.

1.50

ur-ri-iš lu-ú šup-šu-ḫa-at mu-šiš lu-ú ṣal-la-at

عُريتْ [عُريذْ] لوَ [لهوَ] سُفْسحتْ مُسيتْ [مُسيذْ] لو {لوو [لهو]} ظلّأتْ {نأخاتْ [نأحاتْ]}

مساءاً، لتكن (انت) له (به) مرتاح؛ ليلاً، لتكن (انت) له (به) غافيا."

By day, let-you-be to (in) it at ease (relaxed); by night, let-you-be to (in) it a bit asleep (dozed off)."

1.51

iḫ-du-šum-ma ZU.AB im-me-ru pa-nu-šu

إحْدوُذُمّا عفزو {عبزْ} إمّعْرو فنوذو

عبزْ تبعه (وافقه)، وجهه تمعّرَ (أصبح احمر بصفار من الغضب)؛

Abzu followed (agreed with) him, his face became red and yellow (from anger);

1.52

aš-šum lem-né-e-ti ik-pu-du a-na DINGIR.DIGIR ma-re-e-šu

أذْمْ [هذُّمْ] لئَمْنيتي إكْفُدوَ [إكْفُتو] أنَ دنجر.دنجر مأريذو {دُمو. دُموذو} {دُمومبسذو}

هذا لانه أضمر (اخفى) اللآمة (الغيظ) [الشرور] للآلهة، أبناءه {على أبناءه}.

(that is) because he hid (harbored) rages [evils] toward the gods, his sons {toward his sons}.

1.53

^{d}mu-um-mu i-te-dir ki-šad-su

دنجرمومْ إإتطرْ [إإتدرْ] قِسدْذو

إلهمومْ أحاط (طوّق) رقبته الغليظة،

^{God}Mummy encircled (embraced) his thick neck,

1.54

uš-ba-am-ma bir-ka-a-šú ú-na-áš-šaq ša-a-šu

يُثْبمّا بِرْكاذو يُنَسّقْ ذا أذو

يُجْلِسْ (ليُجلِسْ) ركبتيه (ليجعله يجثي)، يُقبّلْ (ليقبّلْ) له.

to seat his knees (to make him kneel), to kiss him.

1.55

mim-mu-ú ik-pu-du pu-uḫ-ru-uš-šun

مِمّو إكْفُدوَ [إكْفُتو] فُهْرُذُمْ

كُلما أضمر (أخفى) إجتماعهم،

Everything their meeting hid (harbored),

1.56

a-na DINGIR.DINGIR bu-uk-ri-šu-nu uš-tan-nu-ni

أنَ دنجر.دنجر {دنجرمبس} بُكريذُنْ {بُكريذُنُما} أُثْتَنْني

كُرِّرَ (سُرِّبَ) الى الآلهة، أبناءهم الأوائل.

was repeated (leaked) to the gods, their first-born sons.

1.57

iš-mu-nim-ma DINGIR.DINGIR i-dul-lu

إسْمُعْنِما دنجر.دنجر {دنجر^ميس} إعِدلّو

سمعو الآلهة (ذلك)، إرتبكو،

The gods heard (that) (and) became disordered,

1.58

qu-lu iṣ-ba-tu šá-qu-um-míš uš-bu

قْلوَ {قُولوَ} [قْهلوَ {قْهلوَ}] إضْبَطْو ذُقُمّذْ [ذُكُمّتْ] أُثْبو

لزمو الهدوء، كانو جالسين [جلسو] بصمت.

they kept quiet, were sitting in silence.

1.59

šu-tur uz-na it-pe-šu te-le-ú

سُطْرْ أُذْنَ {أُذْنْ} {أُذْنِ} إتْبِتو [عتفسو] طَلَعو {طَلَعي} [تَلَعو {تَلَعي}]

المتجاوز في العلم (المعرفة)، المُستعد [الفاعل]، الطالع (البارزُ)،

The one surpassing in knowledge, the ready (prepared) one, the out-standing (rising) one,

1.60

^{d}é-a ḫa-sis mi-im-ma-ma i-še-'a-a šib-qí-šu-un

دنجرحيا حَسِسْ ممّما إسَعا سِبْقيذُنْ

إلهحيا، حاسٌّ كل شيء، سعي (وراء) مؤامرتهم.

^{God}Ea, the percipient (insightful) of everything, pursued their plots.

1.61

ib-šim-šum-ma uṣ-rat ka-li ú-kin-šu

إبْثيمذُما {إبْثيذُما} [إبْذيمذُما {إبْذيذُما}] أُصورتْ [وْصُرَتْ] كَل أُإكِنْذو

خصص لها [أوجد لها] (و) خطة كل شيء، طبقها [أخفاها].

He allocated for it, (and) the plan for all, he enforced it [kept it secret].

1.62

ú-nak-kil-šu šu-tu-ra ta-a-šu el-lum

أُنَقِّل [أُنَكِّل] ذو سُطرا تعا ذو علُّمْ

فاقه دهاء وحيلة [حرفه] (خدعه)؛ سيطرة [تجاوز] تعويذته (سحره) عال [عظيم].

He outsmarted [diverted] (tricked) him; the dominance (supremacy) [surpass] of his spell was great [refined (immaculate)].

1.63
im-nu-šum-ma ina mê(a.meš) ú-šap-ši-iḫ
إمْنُذْما إنَ {أنَ} آمِيس {مَيي} أُسَفْسِحْ

إنتظره وماطله [تلى عليه]؛ إسترخى (عبز) في {على} المياه.

He awaited and temporized [recited on] him; he (Abzu) relaxed in the waters.

1.64
šit-tu ir-te-ḫi-šu ṣa-lil ṭu-ub-ba-tiš
شتّ إرْتحيذو ظَلِلْ طُبّاتِتْ [طُبّاتِذْ]

أداره (غشاه) النوم؛ كان غافيا قليلا بمسرّة.

Sleep enveloped him; he was dozed off pleasantly.

1.65
ú-šá-aṣ-lil-ma Apsû(zu.ab) re-ḫi šit--tum
أُتَظْلِلْمَ عبزُ {عبزم} {عبْزُو} {عبزا} رَحي شتُّم

جعل عبز غافيا قليلا، مُداراً (مغشيا) بالنوم؛

He made Abzu dozed off, enveloped by sleep;

1.66
dmu-um-mu tam-la-ku da-la-piš ku-ú-ru
دنجرمُومُّ تَمْلَكْ دلَفِتْ [دلَفِذْ] قُور [كُورُ]

إلهمُومُّ، الموجّه، شَنِج ببطئ.

GodMummy, the advisor, was slowly stiffened (by seizure).

1.67
ip-ṭur rik-si-šu iš-ta-ḫaṭ a-ga-šu
إفْطُوْر رِكْسيذو إسْتَحطْ [إشْتحطْ] عقاذو

فصَلَ (فتح) حزامه، مَلَصَ تاج ذهبه الخالص.

He separated (opened) his straps, slipped away (slided) his pure gold crown.

1.68
me-lam-mi-šu it-ba-la šu-ú ú-ta-di-iq
مَلَمّذو [معَلَمّذو] إتْبَلا [إتْبعَلا] ذوو أُتحَدِقْ

حمَلَ هالته (المخيفة)؛ هو، نفسه، أرتدى (احاط نفسه بها).

He carried his (fearsome) aura; he, himself, dressed (surrounded himself with it).

1.69
ik-mi-šu-ma ZU.AB i-na-ra-áš-šu
إكْميذومَ عبزُ {عبزم} {عبزا} إنَحرادو [إنهرادو]

كبح [قمع] عبزْ، نحره (أراق دمه).

He suppressed Abzu, slaughtered him (spelled his blood).

1.70

^{d}mu-um-mu i-ta-sìr eli(ugu)-šú ip-tar-ka

[دنجر]مُوُمُّ إِأتَسِرْ [إتأسرْ] عُجُذو إفْتَرْكا [إفْتَرْقا] [إتّرْكا]

حبس [أبقى] [إله]مُومٌّ، ترك(ه) فوقه (فوق عبز).

He confined [spared] ^{God}Mummu, left (him) on top of him (Abzu).

1.71

ú-kin-ma UGU ZU.AB šu-bat-su

أُإكِنْمَ عُجُ عَبزُ {علي عبز} ثُبَتْذو

فرض مقامه فوق (جثة) عبزْ؛

He enforced his dwelling over (the body of) Abzu;

1.72

^{d}mu-um-mu it-ta-maḫ ú-kal ṣer-ret-su

[دنجر]مُوُمُّ إتّمَحْ [إتّمَهْ] أُكَلْ {أُكَلَ} صرَتّذو {صَرَّتو}

رمى [عَفّنَ] [إله]مُومٌّ (عليه)، قيّد (شدّ) حبله.

He threw [rotted] ^{God}Mummu (over him), restrained (tied) his rope.

1.73

ul-tu lem-né-e-šu ik-mu-ú i-sa-a-du

أُلْتُ لَمْنيذو إكْمو إأسادو

أولما (حالما) كبح [قمع] غيظه [شروره (شرور عبز)]، بلغ (حيا) غايته؛

Right after he suppressed his rages [his (Abzu's) evils], he reached his goal;

1.74

^{d}é-a uš-ziz-zu er-net-ta-šú UGU ga-ri-šú

[دنجر]حيا أُتْزِئْزو عِرْنَتاذو عُجْ جارِؤذو

[إله]حيا فرَقَ (إنتزع) [ربح] إنتصاره على متحديه (أعداءه).

^{God}Ea extracted [won] his victory over his challengers (enemies).

1.75

qer-biš ku-um-mi-šú šup-šu-ḫi-iš i-nu-úḫ-ma

قَرْبِتْ كُمّذو سُفْسُحِتْ [سُفْسُحِذْ] إإنحْما [إإنخْما]

إضطجع مرتاحا داخل قُبّته.

He laid down comfortably inside his dome.

1.76

im-bi-šum-ma ZU.AB ú-ad-du-ú eš-re-e-ti

إمْبِيذُوما [إنْبَيذُوما] عَبزْ أُأدو عَشْريتي

دعاها عَبزْ (طاسة)، (و)عُملت أجزاء [(و)عَملها أجزاء]،

He called it Abzu (bowl), (and) it was made parts (sections) [he made it parts (sections)],

1.77

áš-ru-uš-šu gi-pa-ra-šú ú-šar-šid-ma

أشْرُتْذو جِبَراذو أُتَرْصِدْما

حيثها (حيث فيها) هُيئ حقله (ميدانه) [ديره] [هَيّئ حقله (ميدانه) [ديره]]،

wherein his field [cloister] was prepared [he prepared his field [cloister]],

1.78

^{d}é-a u ^{d}dam-ki-na ḫi-ra-tuš ina rab-ba-a-te uš-bu

[دنجر]حيا و [دنجر]دَمْكينا [دأَمْكينا] خيرَتْذ إنَ رَبّاتَ {رَبّاتُ} أُثْبو

(وحيث فيه) [إله]حيا و [إلهة]دَمكينا، زوجته، كانو مقيمين بسمو (بعظمة) [أقامو بسمو (بعظمة)].

(and wherein) Ea and Damkina, his wife, were settled [settled] in majesty.

.

.

.

4.135

i-nu-úḫ-ma be-lum šá-lam-taš i-bar-ri

إإنْحما بَعلْمْ سَلَمْتَتْ [سَلَمْتَذْ] يبرّيَ

تنحى (أبتعد) الرب (أي مردوخ)، يتداول (يدرس) "كتلة الحجر" (الجثة).

The lord (i.e. Marduk) retreated, deliberating (examining) the 'stone lump' (the corpse).

4.136

UZU.ku-bu ú-za-a-zu i-ban-na-a nik-la-a-ti

عضو.كُبو أُزأزْ يبّنا نِقْلات [نكلات]

إنتزع [قسّم] الاعضاء (الاجزاء) هائلة الحجم، يبني اجابات (حلول) منطقية.

He extracted [divided] the mighty organs (parts), building logical replies (solutions).

4.137

iḫ-pi-ši-ma ki-ma nu-un maš-te-e a-na ši-ni-šu

إحْفيذما كيما نُنْ مَشْتي أنَ ثنيتُ

قَشَرها (شقّها) مثل سمكة مشوية (مسقوفة) لاثنينها (لنصفيها) (اي شقها من ظهرها لنصفين متصلين عبر البطن).

He peeled (slit) her like a fired (BBQed: masqoof) fish to her two (parts) (i.e. he slit her from her back into two connected halves, as Iraqis prepare a carp fish for their "masqoof" (roofed: roof-like) dish, before sticking it vertically on its side with its belly cavity facing open wood fire flame).

4.138

mi-iš-lu-uš-ša iš-ku-nam-ma šá-ma-mi uṣ-ṣal-lil

مِثْلوتّا إسْكُنَما سَمَام أُظَلِلْ

أسكنَ (وضع) نصفيها (جوفها للاسفل وجلدها للاعلى)، أُظَلِّلْ (جعل منهما كسقف،) السماوات:

He set flat her two (connected) halves (cavity down, skin up), made (from them) as roof, heavens:

4.139

iš-du-ud pár-ka ma-aṣ-ṣa-ra ú-šá-aṣ-bit

إشْدُدْ فَرْكا مَصارا أُتَضْبِط

شدَّ (مَدَّ) [رفعَ] القشرة (الجلد)، ضَبَطَ الحدود (حدّدَ المدى)،

He stretched (extended) [lifted] the cortex (the skin), fixed the boundaries (the extent),

4.140

me-e-ša la šu-ṣa-a {ṣu-ṣa-a} šu-nu-ti {šu-nu-tú} um-ta-'i-ir

مَييذا لا شُصا {صُصا} ذُنوتي {ذُنوتو} [ثُنوتي {ثُنوتو}] أمْتأر

مياهها ما رُفعت، هم (المياه)، أسالَ (هو).

Her waters were not lifted up, they (the waters), he made (them) flow.

.

.

.

5.53

iš-kun SAG.DU-sa ina U|GU-š|u KUR-a iš-pu-uk

إسكُن سجدوتا إنَ |عُجُذو| كورا إسْفُكْ

أسكنَ (وضع) رأسها، صَبّ (كوّم) "جبلا" فيما فوقها.

He set in her head, poured (heaped) a 'mountain' over her.

5.54

nag-bu up-te-et-ta A-ú it-tas-bi

نَقْبْ أُفتتا [أُفتحتا] آو إتّسبي [أتسأبي] [إتّصبي] [أتصأبي]

شقّ [فتح] فتحة عميقة (هوّة)، تدفقت المياه.

He slit [opened] a deep slit (an abyss), waters burst (poured) out.

5.55

ip-te-e-ma i-na IGI+2-šá p|u-ra-at-ta| i-di-ig-lat

إفْتيَما [إفْتحَما] إنَ إجي+2 ذا فُراتا يادّجْلَتْ

بيّنَ [أجرى] من إثنين وجهها (عينيها) مياه شديدة العذوبة، دَعَها (جعلها) [حتّى؛ كيْما] غطّت (فاضت)

He uncovered [made flow] ultra-sweet waters in (from) her face's two (eyes), let it (made it) cover (flood) [so that it covered (flooded)].

5.56

na-ḫi-ri-šá up-te-ḫa-a |PU|.TAG-šú e-te-ez-ba

نَخِيريذا أُفتَحا |فو|.طعجذو [|فو|.تعقذو] إعتَزْبا

ملئ (سدّ) منخاريها، ترك بعج [فتحة] فمها (لحاله).

He filled (blocked) her nostrils, left (alone) her mouth dent [opening].

5.57

iš-pu-uk ina ṣir-ti-šá š|a-de|-e bé-ru-ti

إسْفُكْ إنَ صِرتيذا سادِيي بيّرْتي [بينْتي]

صبَّ (كوّم) في (من) ثدييها جبالا فيما بين.

He poured (heaped) in (from) her breasts mountains in between.

5.58

nam-ba-a' up-ta-li-šá ana ba-ba-lim kup-pu

نَمْباع أُفْتَلِسا [أُفْتَلِذا] أنَ بَبَلِمْ كُفّو [كُبّو] [قبّو]

أخفض (ساوى) العجز الى (مستوى) ورم الشرج.

He lowered (leveled) the buttocks to the swelling (level) of the vulva.

5.59

e-gir zib-bat-sa dur-ma-ḫi-|iš| ú-rak-kis-ma

إعَجِرْ زِبّتذا [ذِبّتذا] دُرْمَهِت [دُرْمَهِذْ] أُركِسْما [أُرَكِزْما]

لويَ ومدّ ذنبها (نحو عجزها)، قلبه رأسا على عقب (نكّسه الى الاسفل) باستواء.

He twisted and extended her tail (toward her buttocks), flipped (it) upside down (downward), evenly.

5.60

|...|-ú ZU.AB šá-pal še-pu-uš-šu

|...|و عبزْ سَفَل ظيفْتو

|...| العبزُ أسفل (تحت) أقدامها [سيقانها].

|...| the Abzu underneath her feet [lower legs].

5.61

|iš-kun ḫa|l-la-šá re-ta-at šá-ma-mi

|إسْكُنْ خَلّ|ذا رَتَتْ سَمَامِ

|أسْكنَ (وضع) منْفرجُها [ثقبها]| (كـ)إشارة (توماً الى) [علامة مرجعية الى] السماوات.

|He set in her crotch [hole] (as) a marker (pointing to) [a reference point of] heavens.

5.62

|meš-la-šá| uṣ-ṣal-li-la er-ṣe-ti uk-tin-na

مثْلاذا أُظَللا إرْضتي أُكْتنا

أطبقَ نصفيها، ألصق [أخضع] أرضا.

He pressed down her two halves, stuck [suppressed] (them) to the earth.

.

.

.

6.1

ᵈAMAR.UTU zik-ri DINGIR.DINGER ina še-mi-šú

دنجرأمَر.أُتو ذِكري دنجر.دنجر إنَ سَمع ذو

إلهمردوخ، عند سمعه حديث الآلهة،

ᵍᵒᵈMarduk, upon his hearing gods' speech,

6.2

ub-bal ŠÀ-ba-šú i-ban-na-a nik-la-a-te

أبَلْ [أُبَّعَلْ] شأيذو [سأيذو] يبّنا نِقلات [نِكلاتِ]

حَمَلَ (باشر)، داخله، يبني اجابات (حلول) منطقية.

he carried on, inside him, building logical replies (solutions).

6.3

ep-šu pi-i-šú a-na ᵈÉ.A i-qab-bi

إعَفْشُ [إعَفْسُ] فِيذو أنَ دنجرحيا يقَبي

أطلق [جمع وأطلق] فمه، مخاطبا بصوت عالي إلهحيا،

He let go [collected and let go] his mouth, addressing (loudly) ᵍᵒᵈEa,

6.4

šá i-na ŠÀ-bi-šú uš-ta-mu-ú i-nam-din mil-ku

ذا إنَ شأيذو [سأيذو] أُسْتمو ينَمْدنْ ملْكُ

يعطي (شيئاً فشيئاً) الذي أتمَّ (قرر) في داخله، (كـ)توجيها:

Giving (little by little) what he finalized (decided) in his heart, (as) a directive:

6.5

da-mi lu-uk-ṣur-ma eṣ-mé-ta lu-šab-ši-ma

دَمي لأُقصُرْما [لأُكْصُرْما] عصْمَيتا [عظْمَيتا] لأُتبْذيما

لأُسْتَنفذْ (لأُريقْ) دماً، لأمتلك [لأُكوّنْ] عظاما،

I shall drain (shed) blood, I shall have [form] bones,

6.6

lu-uš-ziz-ma lul-la-a lu-ú a-me-lu MU-šu

لأُتْزِئزْما لُعْلا [لُعْلُعَا] لوو [لهو] عَميلُ مؤذو

لأُفْرِقَ (لأَنتزع) [لأخلق] كائن متوحش، (و) ليكن له "رَجُل" صنفه؛

I shall extract [create] a savage creature, (and) let-it-be to him "man", its kind;

6.7

lu-ub-ni-ma LÚ.U$_{18}$.LU-a a-melu

لأَبْنِيما لُعْلا [لُعْلُعَا] عَميلْ

لأبنيَ رجل متوحش.

I shall build a savage man.

6.8

lu-ú en-du dul-u DINGER.DINGER-ma šu-nu lu-ú pa-áš-*ẖu*

لوو [لهو] عدُّ [عنْدُ] دولُو دنجر.دنجرمَ ذُنْ لوو [لهو] فَسْحْ

ليكن له عبء دول (رتابة عمل) الآلهة؛ هم، لتكن لهم الراحة.

Let-it-be to him the tedious functions (hard work) burden of the gods; they, let-it-be to them rest.

6.9

lu-šá-an-ni-ma al-ka-kát DINGER.DINGER lu-u-nak-kil

لأُثَنيمَ ألْكَكَتْ دنجر.دنجر لأُنَكِّلْ [لأُنَقِّلْ]

لأُثنّي (لأجعل اثنين) شِعاب (نظام) الآلهة، لأجعلْ(ها) منطقيه:

I shall make-to-two the inner ways (order) of the gods, I shall make (it) logical:

6.10

iš-ten-niš lu kub-bu-tu-ma a-na ši-na lu-ú zi-zu

إسْتَنِتْ [إسْتَنِذْ] لو كُبْتُما أنَ ثينا لوو [لهو] زئزْ

واحدا (متساويا)، ليكن الثقل (الاعتبار والاهمية)؛ لإثنين، لتكن لها [لهم] الفرقة."

As one (equal), let-it-be the weight (status/importance); to (as) two, let-it-be to them the division."

6.11

i-pul-šu-ma ^{d}É.A a-ma-tú i-qab-bi-šú

إإفلْذُما ^{دنجر}حيا أماتُو يقبيذو

^{اله}حيا وضّح له، يخاطبه (بصوت عالي)، (عن) أمرا؛

^{god}Ea clarified to him, addressing him (about) a matter;

6.12

áš-šú tap-šu-uḫ-ti šá DINGER.DINGER-ma ú-šá-an-na-áš-šú ṭé-e-mu

أذّو [هذّو] تَفْسُحْتي دنجر.دنجرما أُثَنَّاذو [أُثَنَّأذو] طعِمْ [طيمْ]

هذا بسبب (بخصوص) راحة الآلهة، ثنّاه (ثنّى له) العقل (الفكر):
That is because (Regarding) the resting of the gods, he seconded him the mind (thought):

6.13

li-in-na-ad-nam-ma iš-tin a-ḫu-šu-un
لينَدْنَما إسْتِنْ أخوذُنْ

"ليُعطى (ليُفدى) واحدا، أخيهم،
"Let one, a brother of theirs, be given up (sacrificed),

6.14

šu-ú li-ab-bit-ma UN^{MEŠ} lip-pat-qu
لوو [لهو] ليعَبِطما [ليأبِتما] عُنْميس ليفتَقْو

ليكن له ان يُنحر (سليما) لينبثقو الناس.
Let-him-be slaughtered (while healthy) so that people may emerge.

6.15

lip-ḫu-ru-nim-ma DINGER.DINGER GAL^{MEŠ}
ليفْهُرْنيما دنجر.دنجر جَلْميس

ليجتمعو جلالات الآلهة،
Let their majesties the gods assemble,

6.16

ša an-ni li-in-na-din-ma šu-nu lik-tu-nu
ذا عَنِّ [أَنِّ] [أَرْنِ] لينَّدِنْما ذُنْ ليكْتُنو

ليُعطى (ليُفدى) صاحب الخباثة (الخطيئة)، ليقلقو (ليخضعو) هم"
Let that of mischief (wickedness) be given up (sacrificed) so that they would worry [be supressed]."

6.17

^{d}AMAR.UTU ú-paḫ-ḫir-ma DINGER.DINGER GAL^{MEŠ}
دنجرأمَر.أُتو أُفَهِرْما دنجر.دنجر جَلْميس

الهمردوخ جمع جلالات الآلهة.
^{god}Marduk assembled their majesties the gods.

6.18

ṭa-biš ú-ma-'a-ár i-nam-din ter-ti
طابِتْ [طابِذْ] أُمَأَرْ ينَدِنْ تيرتي [تِئرْتي]

بطيبة، تكلم بنبرة عالية (بحزم)، يعطي التفاصيل [الأوامر].
Kindly, he spoke with high voice (firmly), giving the details [orders].

6.19

ep-šú pi-i-šú DINGER.DINGER ú-paq-qu-šú

إعَفْشُ [إعفْسُ] فيّذو دنجر.دنجر أُفاقوذو

أطلق [جمع وأطلق] فمه، (بينما) الآلهة أحاطو به.

He let go [collected and let go] his mouth, (as) the gods surrounded [squeezed] him.

6.20

LUGAL a-na ^{d}a-nun-na-ki a-ma-ta i-zak-kar

لُجَلْ أنَ دنجرأنُنَّكي أمَتا يذَكَرْ

الملك، ذاكراً الأمر الى آلهةأنونكي:

The king, telling the matter to the ^{gods}Anunnaki:

6.21

lu-ú ki-nam-ma maḫ-ru-ú nim-bu-ku-un

لوو كينَما مَخْرو نمبُكُنْ

لتكن له أثباتا (حقيقة)، شهادتكم المقدّمة (المباشرة)،

Let-it-be to him a proof (fact), your up-front (direct) testimony,

6.22

ki-na-a-ti at-ta-ma-a i-nim-ma-a it-ti-ia

كيناتي أتّما ينئِما أتيا

آتو إثباتات (حقائق) تتجاوب معي:

Bring forth proofs (facts) resonating (responding) with me:

6.23

man-nu-um-ma šá ib-nu-ú tu-qu-un-tu

مَنما ذا إبْنو تُقُنْتْ

من ذا الذي بنى (هيئ) المعركة،

Who built up (drummed for) the battle,

6.24

ti-amat ú-šá-bal-ki-tú-ma {úš-bal-ki-tu-ma} {ú-bal-ki-tu-ma} ik-ṣu-ru ta-ḫa-zu

{و} تيَمات [طيَمات] أتابَلْكيتُما {أتبَلْكيتُما} {أبَلْكيتُما} إقْصرو [إكْصُرو] تَحزْ

(و) ألبَسها (خَلطها على) تيمات، (و) عجّل الحرب؟

{and} mixed it up on Tiamat, (and) rushed the war?

6.25

li-in-na-ad-nam-ma šá ib-nu-ú tu-qu-un-tu

ليندْنَما ذا إبْنو تُقُنْتْ

لِيُعطى (لِيُفدى) الذي بنى (هيئ) المعركة،

Let that who built up (drummed for) the battle be given up,

6.26

ár-nu-uš-šú lu ú-šá-áš-šá-a {lu-ša-áš-ša-a-áš-ša-a} {lu-ú šu-uš-taš-šá-a} pa-šá-ḫiš tuš-ba

أرنتْذو لو أُساسّا {لأُسّاسّا} {لوو ذُستَسّا} فسحتْ [فَسَحذ] تُشْبا

خباثته (خطيئته)، سوف أعاقبه لها {ليكن لها مُعاقبا}، (بينما) تَجلسو(انتم) براحة."

His mischief, I shall penalise him for it {let-him-be for it penalized}, (while) you sit comfortably."

6.27

i-pu-lu-šu-ma ^{d}í-gì-gì DINGER.DINGER GAL^{MEŠ}

إإفلوذُما ^{دنجر}إججي دنجر.دنجر جَلْ^{ميس}

جلالات الآلهة، ^{الآلهة}إججي، وضّحو له،

Their majesties the gods, the ^{gods}Igigi, clarified to him,

6.28

a-na ^{d}LUGAL-DÌM.ME.ER-AN.KI.A malik DINGER.DINGER be-la-šú-un

أنَ ^{دنجر}لُجَلْ دِمِّرْ أنكيا مَلِكْ دنجر.دنجر بَعلَذُن

الى لُجل دمرعنكيا (ملك آلهة السماء والارض)، ملك الآلهة، ربهم:

To Lugal-dimmer-ankia (king of gods of heaven and earth), king of the gods, their lord:

6.29

^{d}kin-gu-ma šá ib-nu-ú tu-qu-un-tu

^{دنجر}قنْجُما ذا إبْنُو تُقُنْتُ

^{اله}قنجا ذا الذي بنى (هيئ) المعركة،

"^{God}Qingu was the one who built up (drummed for) the battle,

6.30

ti-amat ú-šá-bal-ki-tú-ma {úš-bal-ki-tu-ma} {ú-bal-ki-tu-ma} ik-ṣu-ru ta-ḫa-zu

{و} تَيمات [طيَمات] أُتابَلكيتُما {أُتبَلكيتُما} {أُبَلْكيتُما} إقْصرو [إكْصُرُو] تَحزَ

(و) ألبَسَها (خلطها على) تيمات، (و) عجّل الحرب."

{and} mixed it up on Tiamat, (and) rushed the war."

6.31

ik-mu-šu-ma maḫ-riš ^{d}É.A ú-kal-lu-šú

إكْموذُما مَخْرِتْ ^{دنجر}حيا أُكلُّذو {أُكلُّذْ}

كبحوه [قمعوه]، قيدوه {مقيدا} بواجهة (أمام) ^{اله}حيا.

They suppressed him, restrained (tied) him {restrained (tied up)} facing (in front of) ^{God}Ea.

6.32

an-nam i-me-du-šu-ma da-me-šú ip-tar-'u-u

أنّمْ [عنّمْ] [أرنَمْ] إعّمَدوذُما دَمَذو إفْتَرْؤو

أقاموه (أقاموعليه معادل) الخباثة (الخطيئة)؛ أراقو دمَه.

They imposed on him the equal of the mischief (wickedness); they shed his blood.

6.33

ina da-me-šú ib-na-a a-me-lu-tú

إنَ دَمَذو إبّنا عَميلْتو

بدمه (من دمه)، بنى (إلهحيا) البشر،

From his blood, he (godEa) built mankind,

6.34

i-mid dul-li DINGER.DINGER-ma DINGER.DINGER um-taš-šìr

إعّمِدْ دوليَ دنجر.دنجرما دنجر.دنجر أُمْتَسِرْ

فرض (عليه) دول (رتابة عمل) الآلهة؛ حرر الآلهة.

He imposed upon (him) the tedious functions (hard work) of the gods; he liberated the gods.

6.35

ul-tu a-me-lu-tu ib-nu-u dÉ.A er-šú

أُلْتْ عَميلْتو إبْنُوَ دنجرحيا عَرْسو [عَرْشو]

أولّما (حالا بعدما) بنى إلهحيا، المُدهِش، البشر،

Right after godEa, the amazing, built mankind,

6.36

dul-lu šá DINGER.DINGER i-mi-du-ni šá-a-šú

دولْ ذا دنجر.دنجر إعّمِدْنيَ ذا أذو

(و) فرض (عليهم) دول (رتابة عمل) الآلهة التي لهم --

(and) imposed upon (them) the tedious functions (hard work) of the gods that is for them—

2

Relevant Readings from the Myth of Adapa

1.2

qi-bit-su ki-ma qi-bit ilu lu-u-ma(?)-ti(?).

قيبِتْذو كيما قيبِتْ إلو لؤماتي

صَرْخته (أمره) (صرخة أدفا) مثل صرخة (أمر) أله غاضب.

His (Adapa's) shout (command) is like the shout (command) of an enraged (angry) god.

1.3

uz-na rapaš-tum ú-šak-lil-šu u-ṣu-rat mâti kul-lu-mu

أُذْنَ رَبَسْتُمْ [رَبَضْتُمْ] [رَفَذْتُمْ] أُتَكَلِلْذو أُصَرتْ مأتِ كُلُمْ

(الإلهحيا) كلّله (أودعه) علمٌ واسعٌ (معرفة شاملة)، وصرٌ (عهد أو واجب) الارض الثقيل كُلّه.

He (^{god}Ea) crowned (assigned) him wide knowledge, the heavy obligation of the earth, all of it.

1.4

ana šu-a-tu ni-me-qa iddin-šu napiš-tam da-er-tam {darî-tam} ul iddim-šu

أَنَ ذآتُ نيمَقا إدّنْذو نَفِسْتَمْ دائِرْتَمْ {دَئريتَمْ} أُلْ إدّمْذو [إدّنْذو]

الى ذاك (لأدَفا) أعطى خبرة (مهارة)، ما أعطى الحياة الدائمة (الأبدية).

To that one (to Adapa), he gave him expertise, (but) he did not give him eternal life.

1.5

ina u-me-šu-ma {û-me-šú-ma} ina ša-na-a-ti ši-na-a-ti ab-kal-lum mâr $^{\hat{a}l}$Eridu

إنَ أُوميتوما إنَ سَناتي ذيناتي أبْكَلَمْ [أفْكَلَمْ] [أبْجَلَمْ] مأرْ ألوإريدو

في أيامه، في تلكم السنين، إبن بلدأريدو الخلوق [النبيل]،

In his days, in those years, the affable son of Eridu,

1.6

^{d}E-a ki-ma rid(?)-di ina a-me-lu-ti ib-ni-šú

إلهحيا كيما ريدِ [رئِدْ] إنَ عميلُتي إبنيذو

بناه (خلقه) إلهحيا كرائد (كقدوة) في البشر.

^{god}Ea built him as a model in the mankind.

1.7

ab-kal-lum qi-bit-su ma-am-man ul ú-šam-sak

أبْكَلُمْ [أفْكَلُمْ] [أبْجَلُمْ] قيبتو مَمنْ ألْ أتَمْسَكْ [يتَمْسَكْ]

الخلوق [النبيل]، (الذي) ما أعاق (عارض) [لم يعيق (يعارض)] صَرْخته (أمره) أيا كان (أحداً)،

The affable, (whom) no one could [would] obstruct (challenge) his shout (command).

1.8

li-e-um at-ra ḫa-si-sa {At-ra-ḫa-si-sa} ša ^{d}A-nun-na-ki šú-ma

لعيُمْ عترا حسسا [عَتْرَحسسا] ذا الآلهةعنُناكي ذوما

الحريصْ (شديد الارادة)، مُرهفُ حسّ الآلهةعنُناكي (المسْتَمعْ للآلهة عنُناكي)، كان هو.

The determined, the extra sensing of (the listener to) the ^{gods}Anunnaki, was he.

1.9

ib-bu el-lam qa-ti pa-ši-šu muš-te-'-u par-ši {par-ṣi}

إبُّ علَمْ قاتي بَسِسُ مُسْتَعُو فرْسِ [فَرْصِ] {فَرْضِ}

متهيأ، طاهر اليدين، مدهون، ساعي واجبات.

Ready (prepared), hands-clean, anointed, a seeker of responsibilities.

1.10

it-ti nu-ḫa-tim-me nu-ḫa-tim-mu-ta ip-pu-uš

إتي نُحتَمي نُحتَمتا يعفُسْ [يعفُشْ]

مع الطباخين، يعمل (يؤدي) الطبخ.

With the cooks, he does the cooking.

1.11

it-ti nu-ḫa-tim-me ša mâr ^{âl}Eridu |nu-ḫa-tim-mu-ta ip-pu-uš|$^{KI-MIN}$

إتي نُحاتَمي ذا ألوإريدو |نُحتَمتا يعفُسْ [يعفُشْ]|كمنْ

مع طباخين بلدأريدو، يعمل (يؤدي) الطبخ.

With the cooks of Eridu, he does the cooking.

1.12

a-ka-la u me-e ša ^{âl}Eridu û-mi-šam-ma ip-pu-uš

أكَلا و ميي ذا ألوإريدو أُوميتَمّا يعفُسْ [يعفُشْ]

أكل وشرب بلدأريدو، يعمل يوميا.

The food and water of Eridu he makes daily.

1.13

ina qa-ti-šu el-li-ti pa-aš-šu-ra i-rak-kas

إنَ قاتيذو علّت بذُرا يركَسْ

بيديه الطاهرتين يرمى اسفلا (فرش) السُفرة (سفرة الطعام)

In his clean hands, he throws down (spreads) the dining sheet.

1.14

u ba-lu-uš-šu pa-aš-šu-ra ul ip-paṭ-ṭar

و بَلوتّو بذُرا ألْ إفطّرْ

وبدونه، ما فُصلت (عُزلتْ) السُفرة (سفرة الطعام).

And without him, the dining sheet is not separated (removed).

1.15

elippa u-ma-ḫar bâ'iru-tu {bâ'iru-tam} da-ku-tu {da-ku-tam} ša ^{âl}Eridu ip-pu-uš

علبّا أُمخر بئرتو {بئرتمْ} دأكتو {دأكتمْ} ذا ألوإريدو يعفسْ [يعفشْ]

(ذات مرّة) أبحر قفة (سفينة)، يعمل (يؤدي) النخز (صيد السمك)، القتل (صيد الطيور) لـ بلدأريدو.

(one time) He steered a ship, doing the fishing, the (bird) hunting of Eridu.

1.16

e-nu-mi-šu A-da-pa mâr ^{âl}Eridu

حينُميذو أدابا [أدافا] مأرْ ألوإريدو

حينها (حينذاك)، أدابْ [أدافْ] إبن بلدأريدو،

At that time, Adapa the son of Eridu,

1.17

|...|-ur {|...|-ar} ^{d}E-a ina ma-ia-li {ma-aia-li} ina ša-da-di

|...| إلهحيا إنَ مأياك إنَ سَدَد

|عندما{حيثما}| إلهحيا في السرير، في الحجرة،

|while {wherein}| ^{god}Ea in bed, in chamber,

1.18

û-mi-šam-ma ši-ga-ar ^{âl}Eridu iš-ša-ar

أُوميتما سجَرْ ألوإريدو إسّرْ

حافظ على (تولى) (هو) إشباع (إطعام) بلدأريدو يوميا.

he attended to Eridu's repletion (feeding), daily.

.

.

.

2.11

A-da-pa ma-ar ^{d}E-a ša šu-ú-ti ka-ap-pa-ša iš-te-bi-ir

أدافا [أدابا] مأرْ إلهحيا ذا سؤتي كَفّتا إتّعبْرْ [إستَعبْرْ] [إستَبرْ]

أدابُ [أدافُ]، إبن إلهحيا، عبر (شق ومضى عبر) [حزر (عرف كنه)] طرفي الجنوب (جمع جنب: أي ريح الجنوب)

"Adapa, the son of ^{god}Ea, has crossed [broke] the edges of the south wind."

.

.

.

2.57

am-mi-ni ^{d}E-a a-mi-lu-ta la ba-ni-ta ša ša-me-me

أمّنيَ إلهحيا عَميلتا لا بَنيتا [بَنئتا] ذا سَمِمِ

من ماذا (لماذا) إلهحيا، (لـ)بشرا غير مُشرّف [مفضّل]، ما للسماء

why ^{god}Ea, (to) the not honoured [chosen] mankind, that of heaven

2.58

u ir-ṣi-e-ti ú-ki-il-li-in-ši li-ib-ba

وإرْضيتِ أُكلنْذي لبّا

والارض (دواخلهما)، سلّمها له (أمكنه منها)؟ (في) قلبْ (وسط)

and earth (their inner working), he handed it to him (enabled him to it)? (in) A heart

2.59

ka-ap-ra iš-ku-un-šu šu-ú-ma i-te-pu-us-su

قَفْرا [كَفْرا] [قَبْرا] إسكُنْذو ذووما إتعْفستو [إتعْفشتو]

قفر (أرض خالية) [المجهول]، أسكنه (وضعه)؛ هو بنفسه (إلهحيا)، هو قد فعل به (ذلك).

of void land [unknown], he set him in; he himself (^{god}Ea), he had done (that) to him.

2.60

ni-nu mi-na-a ni-ip-pu-us-su a-ka-al ba-la-ṭi

نِحْنُ [نينُ] مِنا نِعفّسُ [نِعفّشُ] أكَلْ بَلَطِ

نحن، ماذا سوف نفعل به؟ أكْلُ الحياة (الدائمة)،

We, what shall we do with him? Food of (eternal) life,

2.61

li-ga-ni-šu-um-ma li-kul |a|-ka-al ba-la-ṭi

لِيْقانيذُما لِيإكُلْ أكَلْ بَلَطِ

أُخّذوهْ (دَعُوهُ يأخذ)، ليأكل. أكْلُ الحياة (الابدية)،

let him take, to eat. Food of (eternal) life,

2.62

il-gu-ni-šu-um-ma ú-ul i-ku-ul me-e ba-la-ṭi

إلقونيذُما أُل إإكُلْ مَيي بلَط

أَخَّذوهْ (دَعَوْهْ يأخذ)، (لكنه) ما أكَلَ. ماء الحياة (الدائمة)،

they let him take, (but) he did not eat. Water of (eternal) life,

2.63

il-gu-ni-šu-um-ma ú-ul il-ti lu-ba-ra

إلقونيذْما أُل إلْتي [إسْتي] لبْارا [لُبْانا]

أَخَّذوه (دَعَوْهْ يأخذ)، (لكنه) ما نَدي (شَرَبْ). ثوبا،

they let him take, (but) he did not drink. A dress,

2.64

il-gu-ni-šu-um-ma it-ta-al-ba-aš ša-am-na

إلقونيذْما إتلْبَسْ سَمْنا

أَخَّذوهْ (دَعَوْهْ يأخذ)، (ف) لَبَسَ (نفسه). دهنا،

they let him take, (and) he dressed (himself). Oil,

2.65

il-gu-ni-šu-um-ma it-ta-ap-ap-ši-iš

إلقونيذْما إتَبْبَسسْ

أَخَّذوه (دَعَوْهْ يأخذ)، (ف) دهن (نفسه).

they let him take, (and) he oiled (himself).

2.66

id-gu-ul-šu-um-ma ^{d}A-nu iṣ-ṣi-iḫ i-na mu-ḫi-šu

إدْجلْذْما [إدْغلْذْما] إلهأنو [إلهعَنو] إصيّحْ إنَ مُحذّو [مُخذّو]

إلتَبَسَ إلهأنّو، صاح في محيطه (محيط أدابْ):

^{god}Anu got confused, he shouted in (from) around him (Adapa):

2.67

al-k(m) A-da-pa am-mi-ni la ta-ku-ul la ta-al-ti-ma

أَلْكَمْ أدافا [أدابا] إمنِ لا تأكل لا تَلْتيما [تَسْتيما]

"تعال أدابُ [أدافُ]، من ماذا (لماذا) لا تأكل، لا تندي (تشرب)؟

"Come, Adapa, why are you not eating, not drinking?

2.68

la ba-al-ṭa-ta-a ni-ši da-a-la-ti ^{d}E-a be-li

لا بَلْطاتآ نِئس دآلاتي إلهحيا بَعْلي

لن يصبحو أحياءا (للأبد) الناس، (ما) دارت (الايام)." "^إله^حيا، ربي،

People shall not be living (eternally), no matter how (the days) are turned around". "godEa, my lord,

2.69

iq-ba-a la ta-ka-al la ta-ša-at-ti

إقْبا لا تأكل لا تَستي

قال (بصوت عالي): لا تأكل، لا تندي (تشرب)".

spoke (loudly): 'don't eat, don't drink'."

2.70

li-i-ga-šu-ma |te|-ir-ra-šu a-na ga-ga-ri-šu

لييقاذوما تيئْراذو أنَ قَقاريذو

"خُذووه، أعيدوه الى مُستقرّه."

"Take him, return him to his dwelling-place."

Relevant Readings from the Epic of Gilgamesh*

Tablet 10

297 *You are aging [attenuating]; what are you finding (gaining)?*
298 *Slowly, you are hurting [tiring] your own*
299 *You are filling your intestines with severe hunger {exhaustion hunger}*
300 *You are bringing the faraway closer, your (final) dates [days]*
301 *A man is like a snapped off [an eliminated] reed in a canebrake, |that| is his fate [his afterward (his future)]*
302 *The entwined and polished (well-built) young man, the entwined and polished (well-built) young woman*
303 *Hurriedly (prematurely), death abducts |even their lives|*
304 *No one sees death*
305 *No one, of this death, sees its face*
306 *No one, of this death, hears its scream (voice)*
307 *The burst [This undefeatable force] of death is the destroyer [eliminator] of man (mankind)*
308 *As long as we build {he builds} a palace*
309 *As long as we acquire [monopolize] (more) property*
310 *As long as brothers snatch [confiscate] {As long as brothers snatch [confiscate] inheritance share}*
311 *As long as viciousness and immorality [animosity and hatred] spreads [exists] in the land*
312 *As long as the river got energized (rose) (and) carried (brought) the flood*
313 *(and) The departing provider [The loved one] floated in the river*
314 *(with) His face staring (at) the face of the sun*
315 *At once (instantly), he does not have anything*
316 *The abducted and the dead, they are like {they are like the form of} brothers of one semen-drop (like twin)*
317 *Of death, they (the gods) did not draw (determine) the shape of its figure*
318 *They had not granted the eternity of savage [early] man, as a grant, in the land {(but) They had granted the equality of savage [early] man, from the beginning}*
319 *Their majesties the Anunnaki (god Anim's angles on earth), their majesties the gods, were in assembly*

---

*For Latin and Arabic transliterations consult: Saad D. Abulhab. The Epic of Gilgamesh: Selected Readings from its Original Early Arabic Language. New York: Blautopf Publishing, 2016.

320 *Goddess Mamitum {Mami} (goddess of death), (after) repeatedly inquiring [discussing in detail] the decree with them {their decree}, gave her decree*

321 *They (the gods) established (set) death and life*

322 *Of death, they had not made known (revealed) its dates [days]" {Of death, they had not made known (revealed) its dates [days]; they made them known (revealed them), differently"}*

Tablet 11

1 *Gilgamesh said to him, to Uta-Napištim the withdrawn and distant (Noah):*

2 *"(as) I stare at you, Uta-Napištim*

3 *Your capacity (size) is not different (exceptional), you are like me*

4 *And you are not different (exceptional), you are like me*

5 *Burning (eager) is my heart [inner flame] to conduct a battle*

6 *|But| my hand had dropped (paralyzed) over [around] your site*

7 *How, how had you stood in the assembly of gods, (and) seeked {seeked to reach} the eternal life?"*

8 *Uta-Napištim said to him, to Gilgamesh:*

9 *"I shall reveal to you, Gilgamesh, a matter of secret*

10 *And I shall tell you (about) an inner (hidden) deal [judgement] of the gods, for (regarding) that (matter) [for you (only)]*

11 *The city of Shuruppak (riverside [soft land] valley [groove]), a town that you know yourself*

12 *The city that is located in the Euphrates depression (valley)*

13 *It is that (one) (that) {It is the city (that)} the gods were lodged [had ended] near it {near}*

14 *|Till| their hearts carried (decided) on setting the Deluge, their majesties the gods*

15 *The god Anim, their father, finalized (approved)*

16 *Their king (leader) was the fighter (hero) god Enlil,*

17 *Their officer (chamberlain) was the god Ninurta*

18 *Their puppet (servant) was the god Ennugi (the follower; the servant)*

19 *God Ea, the god Ninsiku (one who waters and fertilizes), was finalized (overpowered) with (by) them (the three gods)*

20 *(thus) He repeated (leaked for good deed) their matter [their determination (plan)] to (via) the reed fence:*

21 *"Reed fence, reed fence! Brick wall, brick wall!*

22 *Listen, O reed fence! Beware, O brick wall!*

23 *Man of Shuruppak, son of the people (tribe) of Tutu*

24 *Stay [Do not leave] home, build a wooden raft (Noah's raft: a closed round floater, with arched floor and roof, and equal diameter and depth)*

25 *Abandon [Free yourself from] seeking (to save) wealth, seek (to save) lives*

26 *Spurn land property, revive [keep on] the soul [life]*

27 *Safeguard the livestock (cattle) beings (the farm animals), all of them, inside the raft*

28 *The raft that you will build*

29 *For her, let her capacity (size) be extended (large)*

30 *For her, let her breadth [depth] and basin [stretch] be corresponding (equal)*

31 *Like an Abzu (a hill [a hunch] [a bowl] [an arc]) to it, its roof (should look)"*

32 *I, myself, understood [was guided] (instinctively), I said to god Ea, my lord:*

33 *"I shall accept (I shall obey), O lord, what you say, exactly:*

34 *I, myself, shall do the job*

35 *How should I leave the city, the subjects and the elderly?"*
36 *God Ea let go [held and let go] his mouth (tongue), shouted {shouted (loudly)}*
37 *He said {Saying} to his servant, to me:*
38 *"And you shall say (loudly), verbatim, to them:*
39 *Clearly, the god Enlil [Since the god Enlil] is rejecting me [harboring animosity and hatred toward me]*
40 *I shall not stay (live) in your city*
41 *In god Enlil's den (dwelling-place), I shall not set my feet [my lower legs]*
42 *I shall go back to the Abzu, I shall live with god Ea, my master*
43 *To you (for your sake), I shall ask him to bestow upon you [to shower you] the rush (the abundance)*
44 *Plenty of birds, flocks of fishes*
45 *.................. the joy of ease and wealth*
46 *Before dawn, I shall ask him to bestow upon you [shower you] eggs [dried bread]*
47 *At night, I shall ask him to bestow upon you [shower you] a flow of yogurt [wheat]"*
48 *All time long, before dawn, (starting) at the earliest morning dark white*
49 *At the door of Atra-Hasis (the one with sharp sense: Uta-Napištim), a crowd was gathering*
50 *The carpenter proceeding with his axe*
51 *The reed cutter proceeding with his cudgel (club)*
52 *................. proceeding with his maple wood club*
53 *The young strong men |carrying| ....*
54 *The elders carrying (in baskets) ropes*
55 *The rich [the master] proceeding with the tar (bitumen, asphalt)*
56 *The working poor brought in |....| the needed (necessary) hard labor*
57 *In the fifth day, I did (I put) its external structure:*
58 *An acre (the area of) its circle, as much as 10 Nindans [10 Nindans each,] the height of its walls*
59 *As much as 10 Nindans equaled (extended) the rim of its top [the diameter of its surrounding] [As much as 10 Nindans [10 Nindans each] equaled (extended) the edges of its top [surrounding]]*
60 *I did (I put) its (internal) dividers, to them (the dividers), I drew (designed) them:*
61 *I supported it (the raft) by (adding) 6 parts (decks)*
62 *I divided it (horizontally) to 7 parts (sections)*
63 *I divided its interior belly (vertically) to 9 parts (compartments)*
64 *Water (sealing) plugs on its waists (sides), I squeezed (I pushed and pounded) for it {to let it have}*
65 *I observed (examined) its half sphere (concave) size and did (put) the needed hard labor: 1 Sar (3x3600 mass units) of raw bitumen, I threw in portions (gradually) to the oven*
66 *3 Sar (3x3600) {6 Sar (6x3600} volume units of melted bitumen (asphalt), I |coated| on the inside*
67 *Set aside (aside from) one Sar (3600 mass units) of grain that the bread making consumed [that they consumed as bread]*
68 *2 Sar (2x360 mass units) of grain that the shipwright set aside (stored)*
69 *For the subjects (workers), I barbecued fattened camels*
70 *I slaughtered young sheep (for them), every day*
71 *(with) Beer, grain drink, and barley wine,*
72 *I irrigated (hydrated) my subjects (workers), like the waters of a river (do)*

73 *They were preparing (for) a festival [a festival gathering] like (the festival of) the New Year's Day*
74 *At sun's rise (sunrise), I put my hand on miscellaneous parts (of it)*
75 *Before sun's high (noon), the raft was ready*
76 *|Moving the raft to the waters| was very difficult*
77 *We kept pulling the ship harness ropes, from top and bottom [We kept carrying [moving (bringing)] the ship slip-away (rolling) logs, from back and front]*
78 *Until its harness (rope) belt [Until two thirds of it] went in the waters*
79 *All what I had, I loaded aboard it (onboard)*
80 *All what I had of silver metal, I loaded aboard it (onboard)*
81 *All what I had of gold metal, I loaded aboard it (onboard)*
82 *All what I had of livestock (cattle) beings (farm animals), all of them, I loaded aboard it (onboard)*
83 *I grabbed (rushed) to the inside of the raft all my kith and kin*
84 *Herds of the wild, creatures of the wild, my subjects (workers), I grabbed (rushed) all (in)*
85 *The god Shamash had set the grace period (deadline):*
86 *'Before dawn, dried bread [eggs]; at night, he will shower [bless] with a flow of wheat [yogurt]*
87 *Enter to the inside of the raft, cast (seal) your door {the raft}'*
88 *He stressed (repeated) |again| the grace period:*
89 *'Before dawn, dried bread [eggs]; at night, he will bestow upon [shower] a flow of wheat [yogurt'*
90 *Of that day, I looked from far (observed) its condition (weather)*
91 *That day, to the one observing carefully, had fright (was frightening)*
92 *I entered to inside of the raft; I casted (sealed) my door*
93 *To the caster (sealer) of the raft, Puzur-Kurgal (Enlil's defector), the shipwright*
94 *I let to rest (I gave up) the palace of majesty, (and) even its contents*
95 *All time long, before dawn, (starting) at the earliest morning dark white*
96 *A black cloud rose (showed) over the far horizon*
97 *The god Askar (Haddad: god of darkness and thunder) thundered (threatened loud) inside it*
98 *The god Sullat (god of looting) and the god Hanish (god of captivity) went in the front*
99 *They went with (led) the officers (soldiers) over mountains and land*
100 *The god Ninurta (of fire and war) passed by, burning the ships and weirs*
101 *The Anunnaki (god Anim's angles on earth) roamed with [unleashed] the torches*
102 *With their black, white, and orange/red (tiger colors: Arabs death colors), they spotted the land*
103 *(as) The spoiling (ruining) act (force) of the god Askar was taking over [encroaching] the sky*
104 *All that was dark white, to a pitch-dark (color) returned*
105 *He pressed (crushed) the land, like |an oil compressor| camel he (repeatedly) circled it*
106 *In one day, the wind [storm] ....*
107 *Immediately [with a grudge], the Deluge was swallowing (submerging) .... of the lands*
108 *Like (in) a battle, the sand took over [encroached] the people*
109 *A brother could not see his (own) brother*
110 *People could not connect with each other in the pileup ruin [the ruin] {the entrapment}*
111 *The Deluge frightened (even) the gods*
112 *They left [rushed], they went up to the haven of god Anim*
113 *The gods were like hiding hyenas, waiting [lying down] in the hideouts*
114 *(as) The goddess Istar was reading aloud {as if} a testimony (witness statement)*

115 *The lady of god {the sweetheart of gods} screamed (while weeping) [raised up] an honest (candid) outcry:*
116 *'(indeed) Like his first day, to the mud, let him (the human) be returned to it!*
117 *That is because I, myself, in front of {in the assembly of} the gods, had shouted: O, the one of horror (war)*
118 *How could I had shouted in front of {in the assembly of} the gods: O, the one of horror (war)*
119 *(and) declared a battle for the annihilation of my people*
120 *It is I, myself, who give birth to the breed of people*
121 *(now) Like the breeds of fish, they fill the sea!'*
122 *The gods, particularly the Anunnaki, were crying with her*
123 *The gods were taken over (were overwhelmed), while sitting, by crying*
124 *{With noisy exhaustion, they were crying with her}*
125 *Their lips were dry {became dark} as a result of dehydration*
126 *For six days and nights {and seven nights}*
127 *The hell of the Deluge came by, peeling the (face of) earth (turning it) to a flat water-covered land*
128 *{The hell of thunder came by, the Deluge |was peeling| the earth (turning it) to a flat water-covered land}*
129 *At the arrival of the seventh day*
130 *It was (finally) quiet, the battle of the Deluge*
131 *{The battle of the Deluge quieted}*
132 *It, which had labored [had pushed and pounded] like a female in the first pregnancy (labor)*
133 *The sea pulled back (down) (subsided), fell still, the worst {the tempest} of the Deluge ended*
134 *I observed that day {the sea}, complete quiet (silence) had set in*
135 *And all people had returned back (turned) to clay*
136 *Like an open (empty) land, the valleys were leveled*
137 *I opened a breathing hole, a beam of light fell (landed) over [around] the surrounding of my nose*
138 *I sank (squatted), I sat down crying*
139 *Over [around] the surroundings of my nose (my cheeks), the tears came (down)*
140 *I scanned the edges of the sea space (expanse) {the sea sky (horizon)}*
141 *On as many as 12 {14} (edges) [On each of the 12 {14} (edges)], a high land mass rose (appeared)*
142 *On {Mount} Naymūs [{Mount} Naydhīr] (keeper of the good (secret): Mt. al-Amīn (al-Jawdiyy), one of the peaks of the Ajyād mountains chain in Mecca), the raft levelled (rested; ended) [anchored]*
143 *Mount Naymūs [Naydhīr] held (kept) the raft; to the fast water, it did not give up*
144 *First day, second day, Mount Naymūs [Naydhīr] held (kept) the raft; to the fast water, it did not give up*
145 *Third day, fourth day, Mount Naymūs [Naydhīr] held (kept) the raft; to the fast water, it did not give up*
146 *Fifth day, Sixth day, Mount Naymūs [Naydhīr] held (kept) the raft; to the fast water, it did not give up*
147 *At the arrival of the seventh day*
148 *I lifted a dove, I set it free*
149 *The dove went, it returned [(kept) circling around]*

150 *A wet land had not appeared to it [became available to him], it was frustrated [it went back and forth]*
151 *I lifted a swallow, I set it free*
152 *The swallow went, it returned [(kept) circling around]*
153 *A wet land had not appeared to it [became available to him], it was frustrated [it went back and forth]*
154 *I lifted a raven, I set it free*
155 *The raven went, it saw waters sediments*
156 *It was eating, cruising (roving), tracking (aiming), it was not frustrated [it did not go back and forth]*
157 *I lifted up an offering (sheep) to the four cardinal directions [to the four seas] and sacrificed (it)*
158 *I held incense (session) in the top of [around] the mountain peak*
159 *I fumed (smoked) seven and (then) seven (more) flasks*
160 *In their underneath (in the flasks or in the fire beneath them), I threw, in portions (gradually), reed, cedar wood, and myrtle leaves scent*
161 *The gods smelled the savor*
162 *The gods smelled the sweet {soothing} savor*
163 *The gods gathered, like scorpions (hypocrites) [flies], over [around] the giver of the gratitude (the sacrifice)*
164 *The lady of god (Aruru), immediately, at her arrival*
165 *She belittled their majesties the hypocrites of god Anim; she made them like her laughingstock:*
166 *'The gods, herein, let them have (wear) the lapis lazuli stones of my interior [bottom] (i.e. my feces), (so) I should not forget them*
167 *These days, herein, I shall mourn forever, (so) I should not forget them*
168 *The gods should come to the incense (session)*
169 *(but) The god Enlil should not come to the incense (session)*
170 *That is (because) he had not restrained himself (he acted carelessly), he established the Deluge*
171 *And he fated (destined) my people to the pileup ruin [to the ruin]'*
172 *The god Enlil, immediately, at his arrival*
173 *He saw the raft; Enlil toughened (became angry)*
174 *He was filled with rage of (at) the gods, the Igigi gods (the underground jinns or ghosts):*
175 *'Over here (bring over here), the escaped living being [Over here (bring out here), the living being]*
176 *No man should survive in the pileup ruin [the ruin]'*
177 *The god Ninurta let go [held and let go] his mouth (tongue), shouting*
178 *He said to Enlil the warrior (hero):*
179 *'Who other than the god Ea can accomplish (such) matter (plan)?*
180 *For the god Ea had acquired all the skills [the experiences]'*
181 *The god Ea let go [held and let go] his mouth (tongue), shouting*
182 *He said to Enlil the warrior (hero):*
183 *'You are the most revered of the gods, a warrior (hero)*
184 *How, how could you not restrain yourself (how could you act carelessly), (and) instate the Deluge?*
185 *(on) The one of a sin (on the perpetrator of a sin), impose the equal of [equalize (match)] his sin*
186 *(on) The one of evil-doing [of offence] (on the perpetrator of evil-doing [of offence]), impose the equal of [equalize (match)] his evil-doing [his offence]*

187 *Loosen up, so it would not be broken; tighten up, so it would not be loose*
188 *Rather than you instate the Deluge*
189 *A ferocious creature [A lion] could rise (appear) to eliminate the offenders (the disobedient)*
190 *Rather than you instate the Deluge*
191 *A sly creature [A wolf] could rise (appear) to eliminate the offenders (the disobedient)*
192 *Rather than you instate the Deluge*
193 *A famine could settle (pervade) to slaughter (to sweep) the land*
194 *Rather than you instate the Deluge*
195 *The god Erra (Errakal) could rise (appear) to slaughter (sweep) the land {the offenders (the disobedient)}*
196 *I, myself, did not disclose the internal (hidden) deal [judgement] of their majesties the gods*
197 *I made Atra-Hasis experience (see) a dream, he heard the internal (hidden) deal [judgement] of the gods*
198 *And now, the guidance (the decision) is (up) to his guider (his owner) (i.e. Ea)'*
199 *(then) The god IDIM (the one who waters the soil: god EA) went up to the heart of the raft*
200 *He held my hands, he took me out*
201 *He pulled out the female (my wife) (and) made her squat at my side*
202 *He turned [touched] our fronts [our foreheads], standing still between us, granting us:*
203 *'In the past, Uta-Napištim (was) human being*
204 *From now on, Uta-Napištim and his woman (his wife), let them have a destiny like preceding (bygone) gods*
205 *Let it be for them that Uta-Napištim shall dwell far away, in (at) the mouth (source) of the rivers'*
206 *(and so) They took (put) me far away at the mouth (source) of the rivers, they made me settle*
207 *And now, who will assemble the gods for (achieving) that [for you]?*
208 *The (eternal) life that you aim [want] to be given,*
209 *(come) Work hard for (it), do not lay down (sleep) for six days and seven nights"*
210 *He sat in between his legs (crouched)*
211 *Sleep, like dust [Ambergris perfume], is spreading (blowing) over [around] him*
212 *Uta-Napištim said to her, to his woman (wife):*
213 *'Look at this young man who intends (wants) (eternal) life!*
214 *Sleep, like dust [Ambergris perfume], is spreading (blowing) over [around] him'*
215 *His woman (wife) said to him, to Uta-Napištim:*
216 *'Divert him [Touch him], let the man be startled (awakened)*
217 *Let him go back (through) the road he went (came), in safety*
218 *Let him go back (through) the great gate he exited, to his land'*
219 *Uta-Napištim said to her, to his woman (wife):*
220 *'Human is deceitful, he can deceive you*
221 *Go on, leave him his breads; set (put) them by his head*
222 *And the day in which he laid down (he slept) (through), document it in a brick (in a stone)'*
223 *She left him his breads; she set (put) them by his head*
224 *And the day in which he laid down (he slept) (through), she showed [marked] it in a brick (in a stone)*
225 *The first [His first] bread was dry*
226 *The second was leathery (rubbery), the third was damp (soggy)*
227 *His fourth, its Anise loaf oozed (sweated)*
228 *The fifth brought in (produced) [was reached (stricken) by] mold*

229 *The sixth was baked and dried (fresh)*

230 *(while) The seventh was tender, he (Uta-Napištim) diverted [touched] him, the man got startled (awakened)*

231 *Gilgamesh said to him, to Uta-Napištim the withdrawn and distant (Noah):*

232 *'As soon as sleep settled over [around] me,*

233 *Immediately [Rudely], you diverted me [touched me], disturbed (aroused) me'*

234 *Uta-Napištim said to him, to Gilgamesh:*

235 *'Come, Gilgamesh, mark [count] your breads*

236 *And for each day that you laid down [slept], let it have (give it) your mark [count] (for the bread) for that (day) [for you]*

237 *Your first bread was dry*

238 *The second was leathery (rubbery), the third was damp (soggy)*

239 *The fourth one, your Anise loaf oozed (sweated)*

240 *The fifth one, brought in (formed) [was reached (was struck) by] mold, the sixth was baked and dried (fresh)*

241 *(while) the seventh was tender, I, myself diverted [touched] you {you got startled (awoke)}'*

242 *Gilgamesh said to him, to Uta-Napištim the withdrawn and distant (Noah):*

243 *'How, how should I proceed, Ut ZI (the life-given one: Uta-Napištim), where should I go?*

244 *The Gripper has seized my organs*

245 *In my bed's room [my bed-chamber], death dwells*

246 *And wherever I will set |my foot [my face]|, there he is: death!'*

247 *Uta-Napištim said to him, to Ur-šánabi (the protector of eternity), the shipwright:*

248 *'O Ur-šánabi, may the gulf extract you (get rid of you), may the crossing boat reject you*

249 *That (gulf), where many adventures (took place) at its shores, tremble in fear (when) at its shore!*

250 *The man who you came ahead of (you led; you brought here)*

251 *His full body is covered with matted hair*

252 *His hides (animal leather clothes) took away (lessened) the entwined and polished look of his organs (of his body)*

253 *Take him, Ur-šánabi, to the washtub of highness [washtub of purity] of his lords [Take him, Ur-šánabi, direct him [bring him] to the washtub of highness [washtub of purity]]*

254 *Let him clean [rub off] his fullness (his whole body) in the waters, like a high one [a pure one] (like a god)*

255 *Let him get rid of his hides (animal leather clothes), let the sea take them over [carry (bring) them away]*

256 *(with) Fine oil (perfume), anoint (massage) his body {for him}*

257 *Let him have his head band (his turban) made anew (be renewed)*

258 *Let him have a robe dressed, befitting his dignity*

259 *(and) Until he goes (home) to his city,*

260 *Until he arrives to his way (finds his way home),*

261 *The robe should not be afflicted by untidiness (should not become untidy); it should stay intact, new'*

262 *Ur-šánabi took him to the washtub of highness [washtub of purity] of his lords*

263 *[Ur-šánabi took him, he directed him [he brought him] to the washtub of highness [washtub of purity]]*

264 *He cleaned [rubbed off] in the waters his fullness (his whole body), like a high one [a pure one] (like a god)*

265 *He got rid of his hides (animal leather clothes), the sea took them over [carried (brought) them away]*
266 *(with) Fine oil (perfume), he anointed (massaged) his body*
267 *His head band (his turban) was made anew (was renewed)*
268 *He was dressed in a robe befitting his dignity*
269 *(making sure,) Until he goes (home) to his city,*
270 *Until he arrives to his way (finds his way home),*
271 *The robe should not be afflicted by untidiness (should not become untidy); it should stay intact, new*
272 *Gilgamesh and Ur-šánabi boarded the raft*
273 *They prepared (equipped) [put (launched)] the round raft, which they had (previously) boarded*
274 *His woman (wife) said to him, to Uta-Napištim:*
275 *'Gilgamesh rushed [jostled], endured, (and) incurred (struggled)*
276 *What (little) have you given him (as) he returns (back) to his land?'*
277 *As he, Gilgamesh, moved (unleashed) his punting-pole*
278 *(and as) The raft moved closer to the shore*
279 *Uta-Napištim said to him, to Gilgamesh:*
280 *'Gilgamesh, you came, you endured, (and) you incurred (struggled)*
281 *What (little) have I given you (as) you return (back) to your land?*
282 *I shall reveal, Gilgamesh, a matter of secret*
283 *And I shall tell you (about) an inner (hidden) deal of the gods, for (regarding) that (matter) [for you (only)]*
284 *It is a weed like a knife sharpener, located |under the Abzu|*
285 *Its (fine) thorns [Its file (rasp)] will scrape (make) your hands like a skinless (huskless) berry*
286 *If that weed [After that weed], your hands reach to it*
287 *|.......... you will gain the eternal life|'*
288 *Gilgamesh, immediately, in hearing that (when he heard that)*
289 *He uncovered [opened] a waterway |......... to the ABZU|*
290 *He flipped upside down (threw downward into the Abzu) stones [tied] tightened (fastened) to [in] his feet [lower legs]*
291 *They (the stones) made him arrive (pulled him deep) to the Abzu ....*
292 *He found his plant [the plant]; he swept it away (pulled it out) .....*
293 *He cut loose the stones fastened in his feet [lower legs]*
294 *The sea threw him away (ejected him) to the shore*
295 *Gilgamesh said to him, to Ur-šánabi, the shipwright:*
296 *'O, Ur-šánabi, this weed is the plant of deliverance (salvation) [the plant for (against) hardship]*
297 *For a man, it delivers the living breath [the wink (spark) [trickle (flow)] of life] (the heartbeat) in his heart*
298 *I shall carry it [bring it] to Uruk-of-the-cattles-site [Uruk-of-the-alter]*
299 *I shall feed the weed to an old man, to test*
300 *If [(only) After it] the old man grew into a young man*
301 *I, myself, shall eat it to go back to my youth {to that of my youth (the age of my youth)}'*
302 *After 20 journeys (leagues), they broke a (bread) piece (they took a meal break)*
303 *After 30 journeys (leagues), they stopped by a watering place*
304 *Gilgamesh saw the source of its fresh (cold) waters*
305 *He went to the middle of the waters to refresh*

306 *A snake smelled the scent of the weed*
307 *Quietly, it raised, it snatched [snapped] (ate) the weed*
308 *On its return, it got rid of (sloughed) a skin*
309 *Every day, Gilgamesh sat down crying*
310 *Over [Around] the surrounding of his nose (his cheeks), his tears rushed {went} down*
311 *|Gilgamesh said to him,| to Ur-šánabi, the shipwright:*
312 *'For whom of mine, Ur-šánabi, my arms struggled (endured)*
313 *For whom of mine, the blood of my heart roiled (boiled)*
314 *I have not secured (I have not achieved) a well done job to {in} (for) my own*
315 *(but) To the ferocious creature of the ground (den) (the snake), I have achieved a well done job*
316 *Now, after 20 journeys (leagues), the high (sea) tide is proceeding too fast*
317 *The (underground) tunnel, to uncover it [as I was uncovering it], I threw (down) ropes into it, step by step*
318 *What can I find that is placed to accompany (guide) me, so I, myself, can feel (my way down) to it?*
319 *And I had [also] left the raft at the shore (now)'*
320 *After 20 journeys (leagues), they broke a (bread) piece (they took a meal break) {.................... meal [meal break]}*
321 *After 30 journeys (leagues), they stopped by a watering place*
322 *(finally) They arrived to the center of Uruk-of-the-cattles-site [alter]*
323 *Gilgamesh said to him, to Ur-šánabi, the shipwright:*
324 *'Go up, O Ur-šánabi, in (to) the top of [around] the wall of Uruk, go in all directions*
325 *Explore the protecting apparatus, the brickwork of its waterways (gutters) [Explore the protecting apparatus, examine the brickwork]*
326 *After all (indeed) [(see) If (in fact)] its brickwork is not kiln-fired*
327 *And its foundation, the seven messengers have not laid out*
328 *Three Sar and a half is (equals) Uruk area'"*

Tablet 10

297 أنت تهْرمُ [تهْزلُ]؛ ماذا تلقي (تُحْرز) (انت)؟
298 ببطئ (أنت) تؤذي [تُتْعب] ذاتك
299 (أنت) تملئ مصارينك جوع شديد {جوع إعياء وتعب}
300 (أنت) تُقَرّب البعيد، (تقرب) مواعيدك [أيامُك] (الاخيرة)
301 الرجل ذا مَثلُ قَصبَةِ أجمة (قصبة هور) مكسورة [مَقصية]، |ذلك| حُكمه (مَصيره) [ما بعده (مستقبله)]
302 الشاب المفتول المصقول (المجدول)، الشابة المفتولة والمصقولة (المجدولة)
303 بعجلة (قبل الاوان)، |حتى حياتهمْ| يَسلبُ الموت
304 لا أحدا يرى الموت
305 لا أحدا، لهذا الموت، يرى وجههُ
306 لا أحدا، لهذا الموت، يسمع صرخته (صوته)
307 أجيجُ الموت [بطش الموت الذي لا يقهر] هو قاهر [قاصي] الرجل
308 طالما (كلما) نحن نبتني {هو يبتني} صرحا

309 طالما (كلما) نحن نقتني [نحتكر] مُلكا (اضافيا)

310 طالما (كلما) ينتزع [يستحوذ] الاخوان {طالما (كلما) يتنازع [يستحوذ] الاخوان ميراثا}

311 طالما (كلما) تظهر (تنتشر) [تتواجد] الزَعارةُ (الشراسة وسوء الخلق) [العداوة والبغضاء] في الصُقع (الارض)

312 طالما (كلما) نشط (انطلق) (إرتفع) النهر، (و)حمِل (جلب) العلو (الفيض)

313 (و)طاف المُعيل الراحل [الحبيب] في النهر

314 وجهه يحدّق بوجه الشمس

315 أول بأول (حالا، بلحظة)، لا يظهر [لا يوجد] له (لا يملك) اي شيء

316 المخطوف و الميت، كأنهم أخا مذِمة (نُطْفة) {كأنهم بهيئة أخا مذِمة (تؤم)}

317 للموت، هم (الآلهة) لم يرسمو شكل قوامه

318 أبدية الرجل المتوحش [البدائي]، ما وهبتها (الآلهة) هبتاً في الصُقعِ (الارض) {(لكن) مساواة الرجل المتوحش [البدائي]، وهبتها (الآلهة) أولا (من البداية)}

319 جلالات أنونّ كي (ملائكة الإله أنو في الارض)، جلالات الآلهة، كانو مجتمعين

320 الآلهة مَميتم {مَمي} (آلهة الموت)، مُستخبرتا [متناولتنا (بالتفصيل)] القرار معهم {قرارهم}، أعطت قرارها

321 هم أقامو (وضعو) الموت والحياة

322 للموت، (هم) ما عرّفو (كشفو) مواعيده [أيامه]" {للموت، (هم) ما عرّفو (كشفو) مواعيده [أيامه]؛ (هم) عرّفوها (كَشفوها) بطريقة ثانية (اخرى)"}

Tablet 11

1 جشْجمَش قال اليه، الى أُتانفسْتم البعيد المُتنحي (نوح):

2 "(عندما) أتمعن النظر فيك، (يا) أُتانفسْتم

3 قُدرتُك (حجمك) ليس مختلف (استثنائي)، مثلي أنت

4 و أنت لست مختلفاً (استثنائياً)، مثليَ أنت

5 مجْمرُ (مفحمٌ) قلبي [لهبي] على [الى] إنجاز معركة

6 |ولكن| يدي سقطت (شُلّت) فوق [حول] مقامك

7 كيف، كيف أنت وقفت في مجلسُ الآلهة، (و) سَعيتَ {سعيت الوصول الى} الحياة الابدية ؟"

8 أُتانفسْتم قال اليه، الى جشْجمَش:

9 "لأُكاشفُك، يا جشْجمَش، أمرَ سر

10 و لأُخبركَ (عن) غامضَ شأن (فعل) [حكم] الآلهة، لذاك (الامر) [لكَ]

11 مدينة شُربّأك [شُربّعَك] (قاطع [بعج، وادي] ضفاف النهر [الارض اللينة])، المدينة التي تعرفها انت

12 |المدينة التي في| مُنْخَفض (غور) نهرالفرات ساكنة (واقعة)

13 |هي تلك (التي)| {هي المدينة (التي)} كانت الآلهة ماكثةً [انتهو قُربُها [قريباً (منها)}

14 حتى حمل (أراد) قلبهم قيام الطوفان، جلالاتُ الآلهَة

15 |الإله أنيم، ابيهم، أتّمَ (وافق)

16 ملكهم كان الإله المحارب (البطل) إنليل

17 مستخدمهم (حاجبهم) كان الإله ننورة

18 أمعتهم (خادمهم) كان الإله عنج (التابع؛ الخادم)

19 الإله حيا، الإله الناسكُ (الذي يُسقي ويُخصب)، كان مغلوبا معهم

20 (لذا) كرّرَ (سرّب لفعل الخير) أمرهم [همّتهم (خطتهم)] الى (عبر) جدار القصب:

21 "ياسياج القصب، ياسياج القصب! يا جدار الحجر، يا جدار الحجر!

22 إسمع ياسياج القصب! إنتبه يا جدار الحجر

23 يا رجل شُربكا [شُربّعكا] بن قوم تُوتْ

24 إلتزم (لاتبرح) الصرح (البيت)، إبني عوّامة (جارية)

25 (عوّامة (فُلْك [فُلْكَة]) نوح: سفينة خشبية مدورة اسطوانية مغلقة تشبه الكُفّة، الطَبْقَة، القَصعة، العُلبة، او الصحيفة، لها ارضية وسقف مقوسين، وقطر وعمق متساويين)

26 أُترُك [تحرّر من] السَعيَ لحفظ المال والاملاك [الغنى]، إسعى (لحفظ) الأنفُس (الارواح)

27 إنبُذْمَ العقار، إحْيِ [إحفظ] النفس [الحياة]

28 أسلِم (إحفَظ) نُعُمُ الأنفاس (أنفاس (كائنات) الأنْعام (المواشي والدواجن)) كلها في داخل العوّامة

29 العوّامة هذه التي ستبنيَ أنتَ

30 لتكن لها ممتدة (كبيرة) قدرتها (حجم استيعابها)

31 ليكن لها متماثل (متساوٍ)، وسعها [عمقها] وحوضها [امتدادها]

32 مثل عبزَ ([أكمة (تلّة) [طاسة] [حدْبة] [قوس]) لها، غطائها"

33 انا نفسي عَرفتَمَ [إهتديتُمَ] (تلقائيا)، قلت الى الإله حيا، ربّيَ:

34 "سأقبل (سأطيع) يا رب ما تَقولَ، حرفيا

35 سأؤدي انا نفسي الانجاز

36 كيف سأفلُّ (سأترك) المدينة، الرعية والشيبة ؟"

37 الإله حَيا أطلق [جمع وأطلق] فمه (لسانه)، ضاجاً {صارخا (مُلقنا)}

38 قال {قائلا} الى خادمه، اليّ:

39 "وأنت ستقول (بصوت عالي) حرفيا لهم:

40 من الواضح [مُذ ان أصبح] الإله إنليل ينبذني [يضمر العداوة والبغضاء لي]

41 سوف لن أقيم (انا) في مدينتكم

42 في جُحر (مُستَقر) الإله إنليل سوف لن أسكن (أثبت) قدميّ [ساقي]

43 سوف أعود (انا) الى العَبز، سوف أُقيم مع الإله حَيا، ربّي

44 اليكمُ (من اجلكم)، سأتوسله ان يَنعمكم [يُمطركم] التزاحم [التناهش] (الكثرة (الخير))

45 خصبَ (كثرةً) من الطيور، أسرابً من الاسماك

46 .... فرحة اليُسر والغنى

47 في السَحْر (قبيل الصبح)، إسأتوسله ان يَنعمكم [يُمطركم]] الخبز اليابس [البيض

48 في الليل، سأتوسله ان يَنعمكم [يُمطركم] سيل من القمح [الخَثرة (اللبن)]"

49 كُلَّمَ (طوال) السَحر (قبيل الصبح)، عند (منذ) أوّل بياض الصُبح الداكن

50 على باب أتْرَ حَسِسْ (حاد الحس (المعرفة بالمحيط): كنية لعطا نفستم)، يتجمع تجمعاً

51 النجار ماضيا بفأسه

52 قاطع القصب ماضيا بهراوته

53 .... ماضيا بهراوته المصنعوة من خشب الاسفندان

54 الشباب الاشداء |يحملون| ....

55 المسنين (الشيبة) يحملون (بالزبل) الحبال

56 الثري [السيد] ماضيا بالقير

57 المعدم [الكادح الفقير] جلب |....| العمل المُضني المتطلب

58 في اليوم الخامس إتأديت (وضعت) بنيانها (هيكلها الخارجي):

59 فدان (مساحة) دائرتها، حوالي 10 نندان إرتفاع [10 نندان إرتفاع كل من] حياطينُها

60 حوالي 10 نندان ساوى (امتدّ) طوق عاليها (فوهتها) [قطر محيطها] [حوالي 10 نندان ساوت (امتدّت) {10 نندان ساوت (امتدّت)} اطراف عاليها [محيطها]]

61 أديت (وضعت) فواصلها (الداخلية)، لها (لهذه الفواصل) انا رسمتها (صممتها):

62 دعمتُها الى (عبر اضافة) ستةً [6 أجزاء] [6 اطراف] (سقوف)

63 قسمتها (عرضيا) الى سبعةً [7 اجزاء] [7 اطراف] (اقسام)

64 قسمت قربتها (بطنها) الى تسعةً [9 اجزاء] [9 اطراف]

65 سدّادت مياه عند خواصرها (جوانبها الخارجية)، كبَسْتُ (ضَغطْتُ ودقّيْتُ) لها {كبسْتُ، لتكن لها}

66 رأيت (تفحصت) حجم كورها (تقعرها) و أديت (وضعت) العمل المُضني المطلوب:

67 3 سأر (3600×3 وحدة وزن) قير (خام) رميت على شكل دفعات (تدريجيا) الى الفرن

68 3 سأر (3600×3 وحدة حجم) {6 سأر (3600×3 وحدة حجم)} زفت (قير مائع) |أطليت| على داخلها

69 3 سأر (3600×3 وحدة وزن) (من) الحبوب ما كان يحمل (بالزبائل) حمالي النقل بالشوكة (النقالة)

70 ضع جانبا (فيما عدا) سأر (3600 وحدة وزن) من الحبوب التي استهلكها عمل الخبز الحواري [أكلوها خبزا حواري]

71 2 سأر (3600×2 وحدة وزن) من الحبوب ما أفرزَ (خزّن) الملّاح

72 الى الرعية (العمال) شويت النوق المسمّنة (المعلوفة)

73 ذبحتُ [أسجيت (مدّدتُ)] (لهم) العَدويّة (صغار الغنم)، كل يوم

74 جعة (بيرة)، شرابُ حبوب، ونبيذ شعير!

75 سقيت (رويت) رعيتي (عمالي)، مثلما (تفعل) مياهُ نهرٍ

76 هم كانو يهيؤ (الى) إحتفال [تجمُّعْ إحتفالي] مثل (احتفال) يوم العام الجديد

77 عند شروق الشمس، وضعت يدي على اجزاء متفرقة (لها)

78 قبل إرتفاع الشمس (منتصف النهار)، كانت العوّامة مهيئة

79 |نَقل العوّامة الى المياه| كان صعبا جدا

80 بقينا نسحب حبال لجام السفينة، من الاعلى و الاسفل

81 [بقينا نحمل [ننقل (نجلب)] دحاريج (نقل) السفينة المنزلقة، من الخلف والمقدمة]

82 حتى ترسلَ (ذهب) سَنفُها (حزام (حبل) اللجام) [ثلثاها] |في المياه|

83 كُلما أؤتيتُ (مَلكتُ) حَمّلتُها (العوّامة)

84 كُلما أؤتيتُ (مَلكتُ) من معدن الفضة حَمّلتُها

85 كُلما أؤتيتُ (مَلكتُ) من معدن الذهب حَمّلتُها

86 كُلما أؤتيتُ (مَلكتُ) من نُعمُ الأنفاس (أنفاس (كائنات) الأنْعام (المواشي والدواجن)) حَمّلتُها {اخفيتها}، كلها

87 إنتزعت (أرسلت) الى داخل العوامة كل مُقربيّ وسلالتي (ابنائي)

88 قطعان البرية، كائنات (دواب) البرية، أبناء رعيتي (عمالي)، إنتزعت (أرسلتُ) كلهم (فيها)

89 إله الشمس حَدّدَ المهلة الزمنية:

90 'في السَحَر (قبيلَ الصبح) خبزٌ يابس [بَيضٌ]؛ في الليل سيزُخُّ [سيَنْعَم] بسيلٍ من الطحين [الخُثرة (اللبن)]

91 أُدْخُل الى قلب العوّامة، صُبْ (أقفل باحكام) بابَك {العوّامة}'

92 أكدَّ (كرر) هو |للمرة الثانية| المهلة الزمنية:

93 'في السَحَر (قبيلَ الصبح) خبز يابس [بَيضٌ]؛ في الليل سينْعَمُ [سيزُخّ] سيل من القمح [الخُثرة (اللبن)]'

94 لذاك اليوم، نظرت عن بعيد حاله (مناخه)

95 (ذلك اليوم، الى من يتمعن بدقة، أوتي (له) رعب (كان مرعب)

96 دخلتُ الى قلب العوّامة، صَبيّت (أغلقت باحكام) بابي

97 الى مُغلقُ العوّامة، فُزُرْ كُرجَلْ (سيد الجن، إنليل) (المنشق عن إنليل)، الملّاحُ

98 آويت (أعطيت) قصر الجلالة، (و)حتى محتوياته

99 كُلَّمَ (طوال) السَحر (قبيل الصبح)، عند (منذ) أوّل بياض الصُبح الداكن

100 عَلَتْ (ظهرت فوق) أول تخوم السماء (الأفق) غيمة سوداء

101 الإله عسْكُر [عسْقُر] (إله الظلام والرعد) في قلبها رَعد (توعَدَ صارخا)

102 الإله سَلّاتْ (إله السلب والنهب) و الأله حانشْ (إله السبي) ترسّلا (ذهبا) في المقدمة

103 ترسّلو (قادو) المستخدمين (الجنود) جبالا وارض

104 الإله هراكَل (فوق الجبّار) كان يُذري (يكتسح) الدحاريج (دحاريج نقل ورسو السفن)

105 استرسل (جاء) الإله ننُورةَ (اله النار والحرب)، يحرق المواخر (السفن والسدود)

106 أنُنّ كي (ملائكة الإله أنو في الارض) طافو بالمشاعل [أطلقو المشاعل]

107 بسوادهم وبياضهم وحمرتهم (الوان النمر: الوان الموت عند العرب)، رقّطو الارض

108 (بينما) سحْرُ (فسادُ) الإله عسْكُر [عسْقُر] كان يبوء (يحوز على) [يبغي (يطغي على)] السماء

109 كلّما كان أبيضا داكنا، الى سواد معتم عادَ

110 عَصُرَ (سحق) أصقاع الارض مثل جملُ |معصرة الزيت| دار حولها (مرارا)

111 في يوم واحد، .... الريحُ [العاصفة] ....

112 حالا [بعدوانية]، كان الطوفان يبتلع .... أصقاع الارض

113 كما (في) معركةٍ، باءَ (حاز) [بغي (طغي)] الترابُ (الرمل) فوق الناسَ

114 لم يستطع الاخ ان يرى أخيه

115 لم يستطع الناس ان يتواصلو ببعضهم في دمار التكدس [الدمار] {الحَبسةِ}

116 أخاف الطوفان (حتى) الآلهة

117 أقلعو [أسرعو]، ارتفعو الى سماء الإله أنيم

118 الآلهة كانت مختبئة كالضباع، متربّصة [مستلقية] في المخابئ

119 (بينما) الإلهة إستار كانت تقرأ بصوت عالي بيان (شهادة) {كأنما بيان (شهادة)}

120 رقيقة وجميلة الإله {حبيبة الآلهة} صرخت باكيتا [رفعت] صرخةً صادقة (صريحة):

121 '(حقا) كأولُ يومه، الى الطين، ليكن له (قد) عادَ!

122 ذلك لانني انا نفسي، في مقدمة (أمام) {في مجمع} الآلهة، كنت قد زئرتُ (صرخت): يا هولة [حولة] (الى الحرب)

123 كيف لي أن زئرتُ (صرخت) في مقدمة (أمام) {في مجمع} الآلهة: يا هولة [حولة] (الى الحرب)

124 (و)دَعوتُ الى معركة لإبادة بشريا

125 إني انا نفسي من يولد ذُرية البشر

126 (الان) هم مثل ذريات الاسماك يملؤون البحر!'

127 الآلهة، بالذات أنَنكي، كانو يبكون معها

128 الآلهة كانو مغلوبين (غاصّين)، وهم جالسين، بالبكاء {بإعياء صاخب كانو يبكون معها}

129 ذَبُلت (يبست) {دَكُنت} شفاههم نتيجة الاجتفاف

130 لستة ايام وليالي {وسبعة ليالي}

131 تَرسّل (جاء) سعير (أجيج) الطوفان، لمحوةٍ (ارض مغطاة بالماء) يَقشطُ (وجه) الارض {تَرسّل (جاء) سعير (أجيج) الرعد، لمحوةٍ (ارض مغطاة بالماء) كانت عاصفة الطوفان |تَقشطُ| (وجه) الارض}

132 عند مجيء سابعُ يوم

133 (اخيرا) هادئة كانت هي، معركة الطوفان {هدأت عاصفة |الطوفان|}

134 هذه التي مَخضت [ضغطت وضربت] مثل انثى في اول حمل (مخاض)

135 تنحى (انحسر) البحر، بهت (خمد)، شدّة (محنة) {إعصار} الطوفان انتهت {انتهى}

136 تأملت يومها {البحر}، هدوء (صمت) مطبق

137 وكل البشر عادو الى الطين

138 مثل عراء (فضاء الارض) اصبحت الوديان مستوية

139 فتحت متنفسا (ثقب)، حزمة ضوء وقعت فوق محيط أنفي (خدي)

140 غصت (قرفصت)، جلست ابكي

141 فوق محيط أنفي (خدي) ترسّل (سال) الدمع

142 تأملت اطراف فضاء {سماء} البحر

143 على حوالي 12 {حوالي 14} (طرف) [على كل من 12 {14} (طرفا)]، إعْتلى (ظَهَر) مرتفع ارضي

144 على {جبل} نَيْموس {نَيْظير} (حافظُ (سرّ) الخير: الجبل الامين (الجودي)، احد قمم سلسلة جبال أجياد في مكة) إتمَدت (إستوت: إعتدلت؛ إستقرت؛ إنتهت) [(إرتكَزت (رست؛ استقرت)] العوّامة

145 جبلُ نَيْموس {نَيْظير} إلتزمَ (حَفظَ) العوّامة، الى الماء السريع لم يعطي (يستسلم)

146 يوما واحدا، يوما ثانيا، جبلُ نَيْموس {نَيْظير} إلتزمَ (حَفظَ) العوّامة، الى الماء السريع لم يعطي (يستسلم)

147 ثالثا يوم، رابعا يوم، جبلُ نَيْموس {نَيْظير} إلتزمَ (حَفظَ) العوّامة، الى الماء السريع لم يعطي (يستسلم)

148 خامسُ يوم، سادسا يوم، جبلُ نَيْموس {نَيْطير} إلتزَمَ (حَفظَ) العوّامة، الى الماء السريع لم يعطي (يستسلم)

149 عند مجيء سابعِ يوم

150 تَرَسّل (ذهب) طير الحمام، (ثم) عادَ [(بقي) يحومَ (يدور)]

151 أرض نزيزة ما ظهرت له [تواجدت له] {اشرفت (ظهرت) له}، قُهر (أُحبط) [بقي ذاهبا وآيبا]

152 رفعت طير سنونو، حررته

153 تَرَسّل (ذهب) طير السنونو، (ثم) عادَ [(بقي) يحومَ (يدور)]

154 أرض نزيزة ما ظهرت له [تواجدت له] {اشرفت (ظهرت) له}، قُهر (أُحبط) [بقي ذاهبا وآيبا]

155 رفعت غُراب، حررته

156 تَرَسّل (ذهب) الغراب، رآى رُسُب المياه

157 كان يأكلُ، يسيحُ، يتواتر (يحدّ البصر)، ما قُهر (أُحبط) [ما بقي ذاهبا وآيبا]

158 رفعت ذبيحة الى جهات الارض الاربعة [الى البحار الاربعة] واتقيت (ضحيت)

159 اقمت بخور في اعالي [حوالي] زيقورة (قمة) الجبل

160 دخّنْتُ (بخّرْتُ) سبعة و (ثم) سبعة قوارير (اخرى)

161 في اسفلهم (في قعر القوارير او في النار تحت القوارير)، رميت بدفعات (تدريجيا)، قصب، خشب عرن، و عطر ورق الآس

162 الآلهة شمّت عطر طيب (حلوٌ)

163 الآلهة، كالعقارب (المنافقين)، تجمعت فوق [حول] سيد (معطي) الشكُر (العرفان)

164 رقيقة وجميلة الإله (أرورْ) ، أول بأول (فورا)، عند وصولها

165 استخَفّت بجلالات منافقين الإله أنيم، جعلتهم مثل اضحوكتها:

166 ’الآلهةُ هنا [هذه]، ليكن لهم (ليلبسو) أحجار لازورْد باطنيا [إستيا] (جعاميصيَ)، يجب ان لا (كي لا) أنساها

167 الأيام هنا [هذه]، لأندب (لأرثي) {سأندب (سأرثي)} على مدى الدهر، يجب ان لا (كي لا) أنساها

168 لتترسل (لتأتي) الآلهة الى البخور

169 الإله إنليل يجب ان لا يترسل (يأتي) الى البخور

170 هذا أنه (ذلك لأنه) ما تَماسكَ (تّصرّف بتهوّر)، أقام الطوفان

171 و منّى (جعل قَدَرً) ناسيَ الى دمار التكدس [الدمار]‘

172 الإله إنليل، أول بأول (فورا)، عند وصوله

173 رأى العوّامة، تعزز (تصلب) الإله إنليل

174 إمتلئ غضبا من الآلهة، آلهة يجيجِ (ياجوج وماجوج: جن باطن الارض):

175 ’هاهنا (إجلبو) الكائن الحي الخارج (الهارب) [هاهنا أخرجو [إجلبو] الكائن الحي]

176 يجب ان لا يحيى رجل في دمار التكدس [الدمار]‘

177 الإله ننورة أطلق [ضَمّ وأطلق] فمه، ضاجاً {صارخا}

178 قال الى المحارب (البطل) الإله إنليل:

179 ’من ذا الذي غير الإله حيا (يستطع ان) يحقق (مثل) هذا الامر [المخطط]؟

180 فالإله حيا قد اكتسب كل المهارات [الخبرات]‘

181 الإله حيا أطلق [ضمّ وأطلق] فمه (لسانه)، ضاجاً {صارخا}

182 قال الى المحارب (البطل) الإله إنليل:

183 'أنت أبجَل (عظيم) الآلهة، محاربً (بطل)

184 كيف، كيف لا تتماسك (كيف تتصرف بتهّور)، (و) تقيم الطوفان؟

185 (على) صاحبُ (فاعلُ) الخطيئة، إعتمد (افرض معادل) [ساوي] خطيئته

186 (على) صاحبُ (فاعلُ) فعل الشر [الاعتداء] إعتمد (افرض معادل) [ساوي] فعل شرّه [اعتداءه]

187 أرخي، يجب ان لا (كي لا) يصبح مقطوعا؛ شدْ، يجب ان لا (كي لا) يصبح راخيا

188 بدلاً من ان تقيم الطوفان

189 لينتصب (ليظهر) كائنً مفترسً [اسدً] ليُبيدْ الناس المُسيئين

190 بدلاً من ان تقيم الطوفان

191 لينتصب (ليظهر) ذئب [داهيةً] ليُبيدْ الناس المُسيئين

192 بدلاً من ان تقيم الطوفان

193 ليُقيمُ (ليعمّ) الجفاف، ليذبح (ليكتسح) الارض (الصّقع)

194 بدلاً من ان تقيم الطوفان

195 لينهض (ليظهر) الإله هرا (هراكَل) ليذبح (ليكتسح) الارض {الناس المُسيئين}

196 انا، نفسي، لم أكشف غامضُ شأن (فعل) [حكم] جلالاتُ الآلهَة

197 انا جعلت أترَ حَسيسْ يختبر (يرى) حلماً، هو سمعَ غامضُ شأن (فعل) [حكم] الآلهَة

198 اما الآن (ف)لآمره (الإله إديم) الامرُ '

199 (بعد ذلك) صعد الإله إديم (ساقي الارض: الإله حيا) الى قلب العوّامة

200 مَسكَ يداي، إنتزعني لي

201 انتزع الإمرأة (زوجتي) (و) أجلَسها القرفصاء، بجنبي

202 لَفتَ (أدار) [لَمسَ] واجهتينا [جبينينا]، يقف ساكنْ بيننا، يهبُنا:

203 'في السابق، أُتانَفستم (كان) بشر

204 اما الآن، أُتانَفستم و إمرأته (زوجته)، ليكن لهم مصير مثل (مصير) آلهة ماضين (راحلين)

205 ليكن لهم أن يقيمُ أتانَفستم بعيدا، في (عند) فم (منبع) الانهار'

206 (وهكذا) ألقوني (أخذوني) بعيدا، في فم (منبع) الانهار، أأوَوْني

207 اما الآن، الى ذلك (من اجل ذلك) [إليك (من اجلك)]، من (ذا الذي) سيجمع الآلهة؟

208 الحياةَ التي تصبو [تبغي] أن تُعطى (لك) أنت،

209 (هيا) أكبْ لها، إياك أن [لا] تستلقي (تنَم) لستة ايام وسبعة ليالي"

210 كأنما جلس في ما بين فردتيه (رجليه) (قرفصَ)

211 النوم، مثل غبار [طيب العنبر] ينتشر فوقه [حوله]

212 أُتانَفستم قال اليها، الى إمرأته (زوجته):

213 'أنظري الى (هذا) الرجل الشاب الذي ينوي (يطلب) الحياة (الابدية)!

214 النوم، مثل غبار [طيب العنبر] ينتشر فوقه [حوله]'

215 إمرأته (زوجته) قالت اليه، الى أُتانَفسْتم:
216 'إلفتْه (أدرِهْ) [إلمسْهُ] ليَفزْ (ليستيقظ) الرجل
217 ليرجع (عبر) الطريق (الذي) ترسّلَ (جاء)، بالسلامة
218 ليرجع (عبر) الباب العظيم (الذي) خرج (منه)، الى أرضه'
219 أُتانَفسْتم قال اليها، الى إمرأته (زوجته):
220 'البشر منافق، (قد) يخدعك
221 هيا (أكبي)، اتركي له خُبْزاته، ضعيها عند رأسه
222 واليوم الذي إستلقى به (نامَه)، وثّقيه في حجر'
223 هي، تركت له خُبْزاتَه، وضعتها عند رأسه
224 واليوم الذي إستلقى به (نامَه)، عرّفتْه [علّمته] في حجر
225 الخُبزة [خُبزَتُه] الاولى كانت ذابلة (يابسة)
226 الثانية كانت جلدية (ملساء)، الثالثة كانت رَطبة (مبْتَلّة)
227 الرابعة رَشّحَت (عَرقَت) رغيفة يانسونها
228 الخامسة جلبت (أنْتَجتْ) [وصلها (أصابها)] العفن
229 السادسة كانت مطبوخة ومجففة (جاهزة للأكل)
230 (بينما) السابعة في طراوتها، لَفَتهُ (أداره) [لمسَه] (أُتانَفستْم)، فزَّ (استيقظ) الرَجل
231 جِشْجمَش قال اليه، الى أُتانَفستم البعيد المُتنحي (نوح):
232 'حالما سكن النومُ فوقي [حولي]،
233 حالا [بفضاضة]، انت لفَتّني (أدرْتني) [لَمَسْتني]، أزعَجتني (أنهَضتني)'
234 أُتانَفستم قال اليه، الى جِشْجمَش:
235 'ترسّلْ (تعالَ) (يا) جِشْجمَش، علّمْ [عدد] خُبزاتكَ
236 واليوم الذي إسْتَلْقَيتَ به (نَمْتَه)، ليكن له (إعطيه) تعليمُك [عدُّكَ] (للخبز) لذاك (اليوم) [لكَ]
237 خُبزتُكَ الاولى كانت ذابلة (يابسة)
238 الثانية كانت جلدية (ملساء)، الثالثة كانت رَطبة (مبْتَلّة)
239 الرابعة، رَشّحَت (عَرقَت) رغيفة يانسونك
240 الخامسة جلبت (أنْتَجتْ) [وصلها (أصابها)] العفن، السادسة كانت مطبوخة ومجففة (جاهزة للأكل)
241 (بينما) السابعة في طراوتها، لَفَتُّكَ (أدرتك) [لمَسْتَك] أنا نفسي {فزّيت (استيقظت) أنت}'
242 جِشْجمَش قال اليه، الى أُتانَفستم البعيد المُتنحي (نوح):
243 'كيف، كيف لي ان أواصل، أتْ ذي (مؤتى الحياة) (أُتانَفستم)، اي مكانٍ لاذهَبْ؟
244 حجز أعضائيا القابضُ (الموت)
245 في غرفة سريري [أريكَتي] يقيمُ الموت
246 وحيث سأضع [سأثبّت] |قدمي [وَجهي]|، هو ذا الموت!'
247 أُتانَفسْتم قال اليه، الى عُرْسنَب (حامي الابدية) الملاح:
248 '(يا) عُرْسنَب، ليُخرجكَ (ليتخلص منك) الخورُ، ليَنبذكَ المعْبرُ (سفينة العبور)

249 هذا (الخور) الذي (جرت) في سواحله العديد من المغامرات (رواح ومجيء) [الشدائد]، إرتَعدْ (خوفا) (من) ساحله

250 الرجل الذي ترسّلت (مَضيت) أمامه (قُدْتَ)

251 إكتَسي (تغطى بشعر متعقّد) ملؤ (كاملُ) قوامه (جسده)

252 جلوده الحيوانية إستأصلت (قللت) مجدولية (بُرْم وصَقْل) أعضاءه (جسده)

253 إلتَقيه (خُذْهُ)، (يا) عُرْسَنَب، الى ناموس (وعاء العلْم: حوض العلو [النقاء]) أربابه (آلهته) [إلتَقيه (خُذْهُ)، (يا) عُرْسَنَب، إرْشده الى الناموس (وعاء العلْم: حوض العلو [النقاء])]

254 لينَظّف [ليفَرك] في الماء، مثل عالٍ [نقيٍ] (إله)، ملؤهُ (كامله)

255 ليتخلص من جلوده الحيوانية، ليتَولّاها [ليحملها (ليجلبها)] البحر (بعيدا)

256 (و) طيبَ (عطرٍ) إدلك {إدلك له} جسمه

257 ليكن له مُجددا {مُجددْ} نطاق رأسه (عمامته)

258 عباءةً ليكن له، مرتديا، قدْرَ (بما يناسب) وقاره

259 (و)حتّى يترَسّل (يذهب) الى مدينته،

260 حتّى يصلُ الى (يجدُ) طريقه،

261 العباءة، يجب ان لا يَصلْها (يُصيبها) شعَثَ (تجعد وسخ وتشقق)؛ يجب ان تبقى غير منقوصة (مَصونةً) جديدةً'

262 لقاهُ (أخَذهُ)، عُرْسَنَب، الى ناموس (وعاء العلْم: حوض العلو [النقاء]) أربابه (آلهته) [لقاهُ (أخَذهُ)، عُرْسَنَب، أرْشدَهُ [جلَبَهُ] الى الناموس (وعاء العلْم: حوض العلو [النقاء])]

263 نَظّفَ [فَركَ] في الماء، مثل عالٍ [نقيٍ] (إله)، ملؤهُ (كامله)

264 تَخلّصَ من جلوده الحيوانية، تَولّاها [حملها (جلبها)] البحر (بعيدا)

265 دَلكَ جسمَهُ طيبَ (عطرٍ)

266 جَدّدَ (أستَحْدَثَ) نطاق رأسه (عمامته)

267 عباءةً، كان مرتديا، ضَبَطْ (بما يناسب) وقاره

268 (ف)حتّى يترَسّل (يذهب) الى مدينته،

269 حتّى يصلُ الى (يجدُ) طريقه،

270 العباءة، يجب ان لا يَصلْها (يُصيبها) شعَثَ (تجعد وسخ وتشقق)؛ يجب ان تبقى غير منقوصة (مَصونةً) جديدةً

271 جِشْجِمَش و عُرْسَنَب علَوْ (ركبو) العوّامة

272 هيؤْ (أعدّو) [وضعو في الماء] العوّامة المدورة التي هم (كانو قد) إعتَلَوْ (ركبو) (من قبل)

273 إمرأته (زوجته) قالت اليه، الى أُتانفسْتم:

274 'جِشْجِمَشْ دَوّى (دَبّ) [تزاحم]، ناح (عانى)، جَرّ الخُطى (تَجشم)

275 أيّما (نزرٌ قليلٌ) آتيتَهُ (أعطيه) (وهو) يرجع الى أرضه ؟'

276 وبينما هو، جِشْجِمَش، (قد) حرّكَ (أطْلَقَ) المرْدي (خشبة التّسْير)

277 (و)العوامة اقتربت الى الساحل

278 أُتانَفسْتم قال اليه، الى جِشْجِمَش:

279 '(يا) جِشّجِمَشْ، (أنت) تَرَسّلتَ (جئتَ)، نُحتَ (عانيتَ)، جَرّيت الخُطى (تَجَشّمْتَ)

280 أيّما (نزرٌ قليلٌ) آتيتُكَ (أعطيتك) (وانت) ترجع الى أرضك؟

لأكْشفُ، يا جِشْجمَش، أمرُ سرِ
و لأخْبرَكَ (عن) غامضْ شأن (فعل) الآلهة، لذاك (الامر) [لكَ]
عُشبٌ هو مثل مَحد (السكاكين)، | في اعماق الأبزَ| ساكنٌ
شوكه (الناعم) [مبْرَده] سيكْشطُ (سيجْعَلْ) يداك كثمرة عليق (ملطاء)
اذا ما العُشب هذا، له تَصِلُ يداكَ
|....... ستحصل على الحياة الابدية|'
جِشْجمَشْ، حالا، حين (عند) سَمع ذلك
كشَفَ [فتح] منفذا مائيا |........... الى العَبْزْ|
قلَبَ رأسا على عقب [نكّسَ الى الاسفل] (رمى الى العَبْزْ) صخور مربوطة الى [في] قدميه [سيقانه]
(الصخور) أوْصلته (سَحبته عميقا) الى العَبْزْ ....
هو وجدَ عُشْبَه [العشب]، إقتلعه ......
قَطع الصخور المربوطة في قدميه [سيقانه]
القاهُ (قذفه) البحر الى الساحل
جِشْجمَش قال اليه، الى عُرْسنَب الملّاح:
'يا عُرْسنَب، هذا العُشبُ عُشْبُ الخلاص (النجاة) [عُشبُ الشدّة (الضيق)]
للرجل، (هذا العشب) يُوصلُ (يَمنحُ) الى قلبه نفَسُ العيشُ (الحياة) [ومض [دلَف] الحياة (نبض القلب)]
سأحمله [سأجلبه] الى عُروك مقام المناسم والانعام [عُروك مذبح القرابين]
سأأكلْ العُشبَ عجوزاً، لأجرِبْ
(فقط) بعدما [اذا ما] العجوزُ صَغُرَ (صار) شاباً
أنا، نفسي، سأأكله لأعود الى شبابيا {الى ما لشبابي (الى عهد شبابي)}'
على (بُعْدَ) 20 رحلة (فرسخ) كَسرو كسرة (خبز) (أخذو استراحة للأكل)
على (بُعْدَ) 30 رحلة (فرسخ) نزلو نوبةً (موْرِد: منهل)
جِشْجمَش رأى بئرٌ (منبعٌ) مياهه العذبة (الباردة)
هب الى وسط المياه لينتعش
ثعبانٌ شمَّ نفس (رائحةَ) العشب
إرتفع بهدوء، خَبطَ [نهَش] العُشب
في (عند) عودته، تخلص من (سلخ) جلدً
في كل يوم، جِشْجمَش جلس يبكي
فوق [حول] محيط أنفه دبّ (انهمر) {ترسّل (سال)} دمعُهُ
|جِشْجمَش قال اليه،| الى عُرْسنَب الملّاح:
'الى مَنْ (ذا الذي) ليَ، عُرْسنَب، عانت (كافحت) يداي
الى مَن (ذا الذي) ليَ، تَحاملَ غيظا (غَلي) دمُ قلبيا
أنا ما ضَمنت (أنجزت) عملا متقنا الى {في} ذاتي
(ولكن) الى كائنِ الجُحْر المفترس (الثعبان)، أنا أنجزت عملا متقنا

315 (اما) الآن، على (بَعْدَ) 20 رحلة (فرسخ)، فموج (البحر) العالي يمضي بسرعة
316 المنفذ (الارضي)، لكَيْ أكْشفُه، رميت به حبال خطوة بخطوة
317 أيّ شيئاً سآتيَ (سأجد)، مَوْضوعاً ليرافقني (ليوجهني)، كي أحسُّ انا نفسي (طريقي) له
318 و (قد) تركت انا [ايضا] العوّامة في (عند) الساحل'
319 على (بَعْدَ) 20 رحلة (فرسخ) كَسَرو كسرة (خبز) (أخذو استراحة للأكل) {................. وجبة غذاء [إستراحة غذاء]}
320 على (بَعْدَ) 30 رحلة (فرسخ) نزلو نوبةً (مَوْرِد: منهل)
321 (أخيرا) وصلو الى مركز عُروك مقام المناسم والانعام [مذبح القرابين]
322 جِشْجِمَش {جش تَكْ} قال اليه، الى عُرْسَنَب الملّاح:
323 'إصعدْ، يا عُرْسَنَب، في اعالي [حوالي] سور عُروك، ترسَّلْ (إذهبْ) في كل الاتجاهات
324 إستطلعْ نظام الحماية، طابوق المصبّات <المصافي> (المرازيب) [إستطلعْ نظام الحماية، تفحّصْ الطابوق]
325 بَعدَ إذْ (حقا ان) [إنظر اذا ما] طابوقه ليس آجرة (طابوق مطبوخ في فرن)
326 و اسُسُه ما وضعَ المرسلون السبعة
327 1 سأر (جزء كبير) مدينة، 1 سأر حقول [بساتين]، 1 سأر حفرة طين، شطر (نصفِ سأر) معبد إسْتار
328 3 سأر وشطر (نصفِ سأر) (تساوي) مساحة عُروك'"

Relevant Readings from the Sumerian Eridu Genesis

.A.11

an ^{d}en-lil$_{2}$ ^{d}en-ki ^{d}nin-hur-saĝ-ĝa$_{2}$-ke$_{4}$

عَنْ دنجرإنليل دنجرعَنْكي دنجرنِنْ خورسَجا- كحِ

المعترض الهإنليل، الهعنكي (الهحيا)، (و) الهةنن خرْسجا الطاهرة (الهةإرْوَرْ)،

The confronter ^{god}Enlil, ^{god}Enki, (and) ^{goddess}Ninhursaga, the pure,

A.12

saĝ gig$_{2}$-ga mu-un-dim$_{2}$-eš-a-ba

سَغْ جِجا مُنْ-طيمْ-أذ-ابا [اما]

(ل)ذوي الرؤوس (العقول) المظلمة (البشر)، أنعموهم جبلو لهم.

(to) the dark-headed (dark-minded) (people), they blessed them (and) fashioned for them.

A.13

niĝ$_{2}$-gilim ki-ta ki-ta mu-lu-lu

نِجلِمْ قعيتا قعيتا ملُؤ لو [مؤلولو]

كائنات صغار حيوانات الارض، ملؤو (بها) الارض.

They filled the land (with) small animal creatures.

A.14

maš$_{2}$-anše niĝ$_{2}$-ur$_{2}$-4 edin-na me-te-a-aš bi$_{2}$-ib$_{2}$-ĝal$_{2}$

ميشْ-عنْش [ميسْ-عنْس] نِج-عرّ-4 عدنا ميتَعا-أذ ببْجَل

ماشية العمل [قطعان الماشية]، كائنات القوائم الاربعة، أكفو (بـ)منافعها المقام.

The working cattle [The cattle herds], the four-legged creatures, they sufficed the site (with) their benefits.

.
.
.

C.7

kug ^{d}inana-ke$_{4}$ uĝ$_{3}$-bi-še$_{3}$ a-nir mu-|un-ĝa$_{2}$-ĝa$_{2}$|

كوق [خوق] الهةإنانا-كح عجْ-بحتَ آ-نعرْ منْ-جاجا

الواسعة [واسعة الفرج]، الهةإنانا (الهةعشتار) باركت، أجاءت الناس (دعت على الناس)، مبحوحتا، صرخة حرب.
The wide one [the one with wide vulva], ^{goddess}Inana (^{goddess}Ishtar), blessed, brought on (called for) the people, hoarse-voiced, a war scream.

C.8

^{d}en-ki šag$_4$ ni$_2$-te-na-ke$_4$ ad i-ni-|in-gi$_4$-gi$_4$|

دنجرعنْكي شأقْ نئي-تعنا-كح أدْ ينِنْ-جيء جيء [ينِنْ-قيئ قيئ]

قلبُ الهعنكي (الهحيا) بَعُد، أرتخى (برَدَ)، طاهرا، يسترجع الحنين (القديم).
^{god}Enki's heart went far (back), became cool, pure, recalling back the (early) yearning.

C.9

an ^{d}en-lil$_2$ ^{d}en-ki ^{d}nin-hur-saĝ-ĝa$_2$-|ke$_4$|

أنْ دنجرإنليل [عنْ دنجرإنليل] دنجرعنْكي الهةنِنْ خورسَجا - كِح

الإله (الهأنو)، الهإنليل [المعترض الهإنليل]، الهعنكي (الهحيا)، الهةننخرْسجا الطاهرة،
The god (^{god}Anu), ^{god}Enlil [The confronter ^{god}Enlil], ^{god}Enki (^{god}EA), ^{goddess}Ninhursaga the pure,

C.10

diĝir an ki-ke$_4$ mu an ^{d}en-lil$_2$ mu-|un-pad$_3$|

دنجر دنجر [دنجر عنْ] قِع-كِح مُعْ عنْ دنجرإنليل مُنْفأدْ

الآلهة [إله السماء (الهأنو)] باركو، أفادو (حددو) ان يكن حافظ (ضامن) الارض الطاهرة (مطهّر الارض) المعترض الهإنليل.
the gods [the god of heaven (^{god}Anu)], blessed, declared as beneficial (designated) that the keeper of a pure earth shall be the confronter ^{god}Enlil.

.
.
.

E.1

zi an-na zi ki-a i$_3$-pad$_3$-de$_3$-en-ze$_2$-en za-zu-da he$_2$-em-da-la$_2$

ذي عنا ذي قعِيا يفأدنْذنْ زَزُدا هيَمْ-دألا

ذي (الذي في) السماء أسدى (خصص) أن يستفد هو (البشر) من ذي (الذي في) الارض، ان يتداولها (يقوم بعملها الرتيب) هو
That of the heaven conferred that he (the human) shall benefit from that of the earth, he shall be the one doing its tedious functions (hard work).

E.2

an ^{d}en-lil$_2$ zi an-na zi ki-a i$_3$-pad$_3$-de$_3$-ze$_2$-en za-da-ne-ne im-da-la$_2$

عَنْ دنجرإنليل ذي عنا ذي قعيا يفأديذنْ زَدانني يمْدألا

المعترض الهإنليل ذي (الذي في) السماء، أسدى (خصص) أن يستفد (البشر) من ذي (الذي في) الارض، ان يتداولها (يقوم بعملها الرتيب)."

The confronter ^{god}Enlil of the heaven conferred that he (the human) shall benefit from that of the earth, be doing its tedious functions (hard work).

E.3

niĝ$_{2}$-gilim-ma ki-ta ed$_{3}$-de$_{3}$ im-ma-ra-ed$_{3}$-de$_{3}$

نجْ-جلما قعيتا عدّي يمْأرا-عدّي

كائنات صغار الحيوانات أغارت (نزلت الى) الارض، تَسرعُ (مسرعة) أغارت (نزلت).

The small animal creatures descended the land, rushing descended.

E.4

zi-ud-su$_{3}$-ra$_{2}$ lugal-am$_{3}$

ذي سْدرا لُجَلَمْ

ذي سُدرا الملك،

Zisudra the king,

E.5

igi an ^{d}en-lil$_{2}$-la$_{2}$-še$_{3}$ giri$_{17}$ ki su-ub ba-|gub|

إجي عَنْ دنجرإنليك-لعَتَ جئري قعِ صَبْ با-جوبْ

أمام المعترض إنليلْ، خاشيا تضرَعَ، أنحدر أرضا بطاعة.

in front of the confronter ^{god}Enlil frightened he pleaded, stretched the floor (prostrated) in obedience.

E.6

an ^{d}en-lil$_{2}$ zi-ud-su$_{3}$-ra$_{2}$ mi$_{2}$-e-|eš$_{2}$$^{?}$|..... dug$_{4}$-|ga|

عَنْ دنجرإنليك ذي سْدرا معَشْ ..... ضُجّا

المعترض إلهإنليل، دَعَك (لَمَسَ) ذي سُدرا، ....، خاطب (بصوت عالي):

The confronter ^{god}Enlil touched Zisudra, ..., addressed (loudly):

E.7

til$_{3}$ diĝir-gin$_{7}$ mu-un-na-šum$_{2}$-mu

طيكْ دنجر-جعنْ منّا-ذْمو

"عمرُ (حياة) إله طاعن بالسن (ماضٍ)، أنعموه."

"The age (life) of an aging (bygone) god, blessed (granted) him."

E.8

zi da-ri$_{2}$ diĝir-gin$_{7}$ mu-un-<na>-ab-ed$_{3}$-de$_{3}$

ذي دأرِ [دهْرِ] دنجر-جعن منّا-أبْعَدّي

حياة دهر (كحياة دهر) إله طاعن بالسن (ماضٍ) أنْعَمو أنْزَلو.

A long-lasting life of an aging (bygone) god, they blessed (awarded), descended (brought down).

E.9

ud-ba zi-ud-su$_3$-ra$_2$ lugal-am$_3$

عُدْبَ ذي سُدرا لُجَلَمْ

عودةً لذا (منذ ذلك الوقت)، ذي سُدرا الملك،

Back to that (since then), Zisudra the king,

E.10

mu niĝ$_2$-gilim-ma numun nam-lu$_2$-ulu$_3$ uru$_3$ ak

مُعْ نِجلِما نُعُمُنْ نَمْ لُعْلُ عِرو عَكْ

ضامٌّ (حافظ) كائنات الحيوانات الصغيرة (و) نُعَمُ حياة نفس الانسان (ألانعام: المواشي والدواجن)، تركو (في مكانه) مُحَدَدْ (معزول).

keeper (preserver) of the small animal creatures (and) the livestock of mankind's breathing life (the farm animals), they left (in his place) confined (isolated).

E.11

kur-bal kur dilmun-na ki ^{d}utu e$_3$-še$_3$ mu-un-til$_3$-eš

قُورْ- بَلْ [كُور- بَلْ] قُورْ [كُورْ] دِلْمُونا [دِلْمُنْ- نأ] قِعِ [دنجر]أضو حيّتَ مُنْ-طيلْ-أذْ

(في) جبل الحفْظ [الظَفْر] (جبل الأمين أو جبل ابو قبيس في مكة)، جبُل الحجر الاسود (جبل دَيْلَمي أو جبل ابو قبيس في مكة)، أرضُ (حيث) مستقر (بيت) [إله]الشمس [أرضُ (حيث) خروج (غروب) الشمس]، أنعموه طول العُمر (الحياة) (أي: أسكنوه للابد).

(at) Mt. Bal (the keeper [triumph] mountain: Mt. al-Amin or Mt. Abu Qbays in Mecca), Mt. dilmun-na (the black rock mountain: Mt. Daylamiyya or Mt. Abu Qbays in Macca), (at) the land of [where] the house of ^{god}Shamash [the departing (setting) of the sun], they blessed (awarded) him the long age (life) (i.e. they settled him there forever).

Relevant Readings from the Hebrew Old Testament

Genesis 1.26

וַיֹּאמֶר אֱלֹהִים נַעֲשֶׂה אָדָם בְּצַלְמֵנוּ כִּדְמוּתֵנוּ וְיִרְדּוּ בִדְגַת הַיָּם וּבְעוֹף הַשָּׁמַיִם וּבַבְּהֵמָה וּבְכָל הָאָרֶץ וּבְכָל הָרֶמֶשׂ הָרֹמֵשׂ עַל הָאָרֶץ

ويأمر ألهيم نعسه أدم بصلمنو كدموتنو ويردو بدجت هيم وبعوف هشميم [هسميم] وببهمه وبكل هأرص وبكل هرمس هرمس عل هأرص

وقال الإله: "لنعمل أدم (بشر) بصورتنا، كعلقتنا (كقطعة من دمنا)، ولينتفعو بصيد البحر، وبطائر السماء، وبالبهائم، وبكل الارض، وبكل دابة دابّةً على الارض."

And God said: 'let us make human(s) in our image, as a piece of our blood, and let them benefit by the fish of the sea, and by the fowl of the air, and by the cattle, and by all the earth, and by every creeping thing that is creeping upon the earth.'

Genesis 1.27

וַיִּבְרָא אֱלֹהִים אֶת-הָאָדָם בְּצַלְמוֹ בְּצֶלֶם אֱלֹהִים בָּרָא אֹתוֹ זָכָר וּנְקֵבָה בָּרָא אֹתָם

ويبرأ ألهيم أت-هأدم بعلمو بعلم ألهيم برأ أتو ذكر ونقبه برأ أتم

وخلق الإله الأدم (البشر) هذا بسمته، بسمة الإله خلق هذا، ذكر وأنثى خلق هذم (البشر).

And God created the human(s) in his own characteristic, in the characteristic of god he created him, male and female he created them.

Genesis 2.7

וַיִּיצֶר יְהוָה אֱלֹהִים אֶת-הָאָדָם עָפָר מִן הָאֲדָמָה וַיִּפַּח בְּאַפָּיו נִשְׁמַת חַיִּים וַיְהִי הָאָדָם לְנֶפֶשׁ חַיָּה

وييصر يهوه ألهيم أت-هأدم عفر من هأدمه ويفح بأفيو نشمت [نسمت] حييم ويهي هأدم لنفش [لنفس] حيه

وصير (جعل) الإله تعالى آدمَ هذا تراب من قشرة الارض، ونفح (نفخ) بأنفه نسمة حياة، وأصبح آدم نفسا حيّة.

Then God Almighty rendered Adam a dust from the earth's crust, and blew into his nose a breath of life, and Adam became a living soul.

.
.
.

Genesis 2.21

וַיַּפֵּל יְהוָה אֱלֹהִים תַּרְדֵּמָה עַל הָאָדָם וַיִּישָׁן וַיִּקַּח אַחַת מִצַּלְעֹתָיו וַיִּסְגֹּר בָּשָׂר תַּחְתֶּנָּה

ويفل يهوه ألهيم تردمه عل هأدم وييشن [وييسن] ويقح أحت مصلعتيو [مضلعتيو] ويسجر بسر تحتنه

وأسقط الإله تعالى سبات على آدم، فأسِنَ (فغُشي عليه)، وأستخلص (انتزع) واحدا من أضلاعه، وملئ لحم تحته (بجهاته الستة: بمكانه).

And God Almighty befallen a coma upon Adam, and he fainted, and he took one of his ribs, and filled flesh in its (six) sides (its place).

Genesis 2.22

וַיִּבֶן יְהוָה אֱלֹהִים אֶת-הַצֵּלָע אֲשֶׁר לָקַח מִן הָאָדָם לְאִשָּׁה וַיְבִאֶהָ אֶל הָאָדָם

ويبن يهوه ألهيم أت-هصلع [هضلع] أشر لقح من هأدم لأشه [لأسه] ويبأه أل هأدم

وبنى الإله تعالى الضلع هذا، الذي أُخذ من آدم، لإنسه (لإمرأة)، وبوأها لآدم هذا.

And God Almighty built the rib, which was taken from Adam, into a woman, and he assigned her to Adam.

Genesis 2.23

וַיֹּאמֶר הָאָדָם זֹאת הַפַּעַם עֶצֶם מֵעֲצָמַי וּבָשָׂר מִבְּשָׂרִי לְזֹאת יִקָּרֵא אִשָּׁה כִּי מֵאִישׁ לֻקְחָה זֹּאת

ويأمر هأدم زأت [ذأت] هفعم عصم [عظم] معصمي [معظمي] وبسر مبسري يقرأ أشه [أسه] كي مأيش [مأيس] لقحت زأت [ذأت]

وقال آدم: "هذه المليئة بعظم من عظامي ولحم من لحمي ستدعى إنسة (إمرأة)، لأن من إنسٍ (إمرءٍ) أُخذَت هذه."

And Adam said: 'This one who is filled with a bone of bones and flesh of my flesh shall be called woman because she was taken out of man, this one.'

Genesis 2.24

עַל-כֵּן יַעֲזָב אִישׁ אֶת-אָבִיו וְאֶת-אִמּוֹ וְדָבַק בְּאִשְׁתּוֹ וְהָיוּ לְבָשָׂר אֶחָד

عل-كن يعزب أيش [أيس] أت-أبيو وأت-أمو ودبق بأشتو [بأستو] وهيو لبسر أحد

على ما كان (عليه) يترك إنسا (إمرأً) أبوه هذا وأمه هذا ويكون لاسقا بإنسته [بأمرأته]، فقد كانو للحم (لجسد) واحد.

Therefore, a man would leave his father and his mother, and be stuck to his woman, as they were to (of) one flesh.

Genesis 2.25

וַיִּהְיוּ שְׁנֵיהֶם עֲרוּמִּים הָאָדָם וְאִשְׁתּוֹ וְלֹא יִתְבֹּשָׁשׁוּ

ويهيو شنيهم [ثنيهم] عروميم هأدم وأشتو [وأستو] ولا يتكششو

و (عليه) يكونا اثناهم عاريان، آدم وإنسته (إمرأته)، ولا يخجلو (من بعض).

And (therefore) they would both be naked, Adam and his woman, and would not be shy (of each other).

.
.
.

Genesis 3.20

וַיִּקְרָא הָאָדָם שֵׁם אִשְׁתּוֹ חַוָּה כִּי הִוא הָיְתָה אֵם כָּל חָי

ويقرأ هأدم شم [سم] أشتو [أستو] حوه كي هوأ هيته أم كل حي

ودعى آدم اسم إنسته (إمرأته) حواء، لأنها كانت أم كل حي.

And Adam called his woman name Hawa (Eve) because she was the mother of all living.

Genesis 3.21

וַיַּעַשׂ יְהוָה אֱלֹהִים לְאָדָם וּלְאִשְׁתּוֹ כָּתְנוֹת עוֹר וַיַּלְבִּשֵׁם

ويعس يهوه ألهيم لأدم ولأشتو [ولأستو] كتنوت عور ويلبشم [ويلبسم]

وعمل الإله تعالى لآدم ولإنسته (لإمرأته) ملابس جلد وألبسهم.

And God Almighty made for Adam and for his woman garments of skins and clothed them.

Genesis 3.22

וַיֹּאמֶר יְהוָה אֱלֹהִים הֵן הָאָדָם הָיָה כְּאַחַד מִמֶּנּוּ לָדַעַת טוֹב וָרָע וְעַתָּה פֶּן-יִשְׁלַח יָדוֹ וְלָקַח גַּם מֵעֵץ הַחַיִּים וְאָכַל וָחַי לְעֹלָם

ويأمر يهوه ألهيم هن هأدم هيه كأحد ممنو لدعت طوب ورع وعته فن-يشلح يدو ولقح جم معص هحييم وأكل وحي لعلم

وقال الإله تعالى: "هنا قد أصبح آدم كواحد منا، في دعوة الخير والشر، وحتى فليشلح (فليمد) يده." وأخد (آدم) مقدار [نتوء (غصن)] من شجرة الحياة وأكل وحيا طويلا.

And God Almighty said: 'Here, Adam had become as one of us, in calling for good and evil, and he even may put forth his hand,' and he (Adam) took part of the tree of life, and ate, and lived for long.

.
.
.

Genesis 5.1

זֶה סֵפֶר תּוֹלְדֹת אָדָם בְּיוֹם בְּרֹא אֱלֹהִים אָדָם בִּדְמוּת אֱלֹהִים עָשָׂה אֹתוֹ

ذه سفر تولدت أدم بيوم برأ ألهيم أدم بدموت ألهيم عسه أتو

هذا كتاب مواليد آدم. في يوم خلق الإله آدم، بعلقة (بقطعة من دم) الإله عمل هذا.

This is the book of the generations of Adam. In the day God created Adam, with a piece of God's blood he made him.

Genesis 5.2

זָכָר וּנְקֵבָה בְּרָאָם וַיְבָרֶךְ אֹתָם וַיִּקְרָא אֶת-שְׁמָם אָדָם בְּיוֹם הִבָּרְאָם

ذكر ونقبه برأم ويبرك أتم ويقرأ أت-شمم [سمم] أدم بيوم هبرأم.

ذكرً وأنثى، خلقهم، وبارك هذم، ودعى أسمهم هذا آدم يوم خلْقهم.

Male and female he created them, and blessed them, and called their name Adam, in the day of their creation.

Genesis 5.3

וַיְחִי אָדָם שְׁלֹשִׁים וּמְאַת שָׁנָה וַיּוֹלֶד בִּדְמוּתוֹ כְּצַלְמוֹ וַיִּקְרָא אֶת-שְׁמוֹ שֵׁת

ويحي أدم شلشيم [ثلثيم] ومئت شنه [سنه] ويولد بدموتو كصلمو ويقرأ أت-شمو [سمو] شث

وحيا آدم ثلاثين و مئة سنة، وأنجب ولدا بعلقته (بقطعة من دمه)، كصورته، ودعى اسمه هذا (المولود) شث.

And Adam lived a hundred and thirty years, and begot a son with a piece of his blood, as his image, and called his name, Seth.

Genesis 5.4

וַיִּהְיוּ יְמֵי אָדָם אַחֲרֵי הוֹלִידוֹ אֶת-שֵׁת שְׁמֹנֶה מֵאֹת שָׁנָה וַיּוֹלֶד בָּנִים וּבָנוֹת

ويهيو يمي أدم أحري هوليدو أت-شث شمنه [ثمنه] مئت شنه [سنه] ويولد بنيم وبنوت

وكانت أيام آدم بعدما ولدَ شث هذا ثمنمائة سنة، وولد أبناء وبنين.

And the days of Adam after he begot this Seth were eight hundred years;, and he begot sons and daughters.

Genesis 5.5

וַיִּהְיוּ כָּל יְמֵי אָדָם אֲשֶׁר חַי תְּשַׁע מֵאוֹת שָׁנָה וּשְׁלֹשִׁים שָׁנָה וַיָּמֹת

ويهيو كل يمي أدم أشر حي تشع [تسع] مئوه شنه [سنه] وشلشيم [وثلثيم] شنه [سنه] ويمت

وكانت كل أيام آدم، حيث حيا، تسعمائة سنة وثلاثين سنة، ومات.

And total days that Adam lived were nine hundred and thirty years; and he died.

.
.
.

Genesis 6.1

וַיְהִי כִּי הֵחֵל הָאָדָם לָרֹב עַל פְּנֵי הָאֲדָמָה וּבָנוֹת יֻלְּדוּ לָהֶם

ويهي كي هحل هأدم لرب عل فني هأدمه وبنوت يلدو لهم

و لأن المجتمع من البشر اصبح ضخم على وجه قشرة الارض، وبنات ولدت لهم،

And because the society of the humans became huge on the crust of the earth, and daughters were born to them,

Genesis 6.2

אוּ בְנֵי הָאֱלֹהִים אֶת-בְּנוֹת הָאָדָם כִּי טֹבֹת הֵנָּה וַיִּקְחוּ לָהֶם נָשִׁים מִכֹּל אֲשֶׁר בָּחָרוּ

أو بني هألهيم أت-بنوت هأدم كي طبت هنه ويقحو لهم نشيم [نسيم] مكل أشر بحرو

آوا أبناء الأله بنات البشر هذا، لانهن طيبات (حسناوات)، وأخذو لهم نساء (زوجات) من كل من أرادو.

the sons of God sheltered the daughters of the humans because they were beautiful, and they took as women for them whomever they wanted.

Genesis 6.3

וַיֹּאמֶר יְהוָה לֹא יָדוֹן רוּחִי בָאָדָם לְעֹלָם בְּשַׁגַּם הוּא בָשָׂר וְהָיוּ יָמָיו מֵאָה וְעֶשְׂרִים שָׁנָה

ويأمر يهوه لا يدون روحي بأدم لعلم بشجم هوأ بسر وهيو يميو مئت وعسريم [وعشريم] شنت [سنت]

وقال تعالى: "لا تدن روحي طويلا في بشر، في خبيث؛ هو لحم"، و كانت ايامه (بعد ذلك) مئة وعشرين عاما.

And Almighty said: ‘My soul shall not abide for long in a human, in a mischievous; he is flesh,’ and his days were (since) hundred and twenty years.

.

.

Genesis 6.14

עֲשֵׂה לְךָ תֵּבַת עֲצֵי גֹפֶר קִנִּים תַּעֲשֶׂה אֶת-הַתֵּבָה וְכָפַרְתָּ אֹתָהּ מִבַּיִת וּמִחוּץ בַּכֹּפֶר

عسه لك تبت عصي غفر [جبر] قنيم تعسه أت-هتبه وكفرت أته مبيت ومحوص [ومحوط] بكفر

"إعمل لك تابوت (صندوق مغطى) اشجار صمغ [عصي قصب]، حجُراتً (لاقسام) ستعمل التابوت، واطلي هذا، جوفا (داخلا) و محيطا (خارجا)، بقير.

Make yourself a coffin (chest) of glue trees [reed sticks], (to) compartments you shall make this coffin (chest), and you shall coat it, inside and outside, with pitch.

Genesis 6.15

וְזֶה אֲשֶׁר תַּעֲשֶׂה אֹתָהּ שְׁלֹשׁ מֵאוֹת אַמָּה אֹרֶךְ הַתֵּבָה חֲמִשִּׁים אַמָּה רָחְבָּהּ וּשְׁלֹשִׁים אַמָּה קוֹמָתָהּ

وذه أشر تعسه أته شلش [ثلث] مئوت أمه أرك [أرخ] هتبه حمشيم [خمسيم] أمه رحبه وشلشيم [وثلثيم] أمه قومته

وهذا الذي ستعمل أنت: ثلثمائة ذراع طول التابوت، خمسين ذراع وسعه (عرضه)، و ثلاثين ذراع قوامه (ارتفاعه).

And this is what you will do: three hundred cubits the length of the coffin (chest), fifty cubits the its breadth, and thirty cubits its height .

Genesis 6.16

צֹהַר תַּעֲשֶׂה לַתֵּבָה וְאֶל אַמָּה תְּכַלֶּנָּה מִל-מַעְלָה וּפֶתַח הַתֵּבָה בְּצִדָּהּ תָּשִׂים תַּחְתִּיִּם שְׁנִיִּם וּשְׁלִשִׁים תַּעֲשֶׂה

صهر تعسه لتبه وإل أمه تكلنه [تخلنه] مل-معله وفتح هتبه بصده تسيم تحتيم شنيم [ثنيم] وشلشيم [وثلثيم] تعسم

ضوء ستعمل للتابوت ولذراع تدخله من الاعلى، وفتحة التابوت بجانبه ستعلّم، (طابق) سفلي، ثاني، وثالث ستعمل."

A light you shall make for the coffin (chest), and to a cubit, you shall make it enter from the top; and the opening of the coffin (chest), on its side you, shall mark; with lower, a lower, second, and third ones (stories) you shall make.

.

.

.

Genesis 8.4

וַתָּנַח הַתֵּבָה בַּחֹדֶשׁ הַשְּׁבִיעִי בְּשִׁבְעָה-עָשָׂר יוֹם לַחֹדֶשׁ עַל הָרֵי אֲרָרָט

وتنح هتبه بحدش [بحدث] هشبيعي [هسبيعي] بشبعه-عسر [بسبعه-عشر] يوم لحدش [لحدث] عل هري أررط

واعتمد (رسى) التابوت بالشهر السابع، باليوم 17 من الشهر، على جبال أررط (أرْ- رَطْ، أرارطو، أرارتو، أراراد، أرارات: بلاد الانهار—بلاد أرارات التأريخية).

And the coffin (chest) rested in the seventh month, on the seventeenth day of the month, on the mountains of Ararat (the country of rivers—the ancient country of Ararat).

.
.
.

Genesis 9.29

וַיִּהְיוּ כָּל יְמֵי נֹחַ תְּשַׁע מֵאוֹת שָׁנָה וַחֲמִשִּׁים שָׁנָה וַיָּמֹת

ويهيو كل يمي نح تشع [تسع] مئوت شنه [سنه] وحمشيم [وخمسيم] شنه [سنه] ويمت

وكانت كل أيام نوح تسعمائة سنة وخمسين سنة، ومات.

And all the days of Noah were nine hundred and fifty years, and he died.

.

Genesis 10.5

מֵאֵלֶּה נִפְרְדוּ אִיֵּי הַגּוֹיִם בְּאַרְצֹתָם אִישׁ לִלְשֹׁנוֹ לְמִשְׁפְּחֹתָם בְּגוֹיֵהֶם

مأله بفردو أيي هجويم بأرصتم [بأرضتم] أيش [أيس] للشنو [للسنو] لمشفحتم بجويهم

من هؤلاء، على انفصال، علّمَ الغرباء في أراضيهم—(كل) رجل حسب لسانه—حسب عوائلهم في غربتهم.

Of these, apart, were the aliens marked (divided) in their lands—each man according to his tongue—according to their families in their alienation.

.
.
.

Genesis 10.32

אֵלֶּה מִשְׁפְּחֹת בְּנֵי נֹחַ לְתוֹלְדֹתָם בְּגוֹיֵהֶם וּמֵאֵלֶּה נִפְרְדוּ הַגּוֹיִם בָּאָרֶץ אַחַר הַמַּבּוּל

أله مشفحت بني نح لتولدتم بجويهم ومأله بقردو هجويم بأرص [بأرض] أحر [أخر] همبول

هذه عوائل أبناء نوح، حسب ولاداتهم في غربتهم، ومن هذه توسع (انتشر) الغرباء في ارض مابعد الطوفان.

These are the families of the sons of Noah according to their generations in their alienation, and from these had the aliens expanded (spread) in after-the-flood earth.

.
.
.

Genesis 12.2

וְאֶעֶשְׂךָ לְגוֹי גָּדוֹל וַאֲבָרֶכְךָ וַאֲגַדְּלָה שְׁמֶךָ וֶהְיֵה בְּרָכָה

وأعسك لجوي جدول وأبرخك [وأبركك] وأجدله شمك [سمك] وهيه برخه [بركه]

"وأعملك لغريب مُعظّم (شديد العظمة)، وأباركك، وأعظّمُ اسمك فيكون بركة.

'And I will make you to a great alien, and I will bless you, and make your name great as it (the name) will become a blessing.

.
.
.

Genesis 17.2

וְאֶתְּנָה בְרִיתִי בֵּינִי וּבֵינֶךָ וְאַרְבֶּה אוֹתְךָ בִּמְאֹד מְאֹד

وأتنه بريتي بيني وبينك وأربه أوتك بمأد مأد

وسآتي عهدي، بيني وبينك، وسآتيك النصيب، بالوافر الوافر."

And I shall give my covenant, between me and you, and I shall give you a fortune, a plenty of plenty.'

Genesis 17.3

וַיִּפֹּל אַבְרָם עַל-פָּנָיו וַיְדַבֵּר אִתּוֹ אֱלֹהִים לֵאמֹר

ويفل أبرم عل فنيو ويدبر أتو ألهيم لأمر

ووقع أبراهيم على وجهه، وتكلم اليه الإله ليقل:

And Abram fell on his face, and God spoke to him to say:

Genesis 17.4

אֲנִי הִנֵּה בְרִיתִי אִתָּךְ וְהָיִיתָ לְאַב הֲמוֹן גּוֹיִם

أني هنه بريتي أتك وهييت لأب همون جويم

"أنا هنا آتيك عهدي، وذلك ان ستكن لأب الكثير من غرباء.

'I hereby shall give you my covenant, that is you shall be a father of the numerous aliens.

Genesis 17.5

וְלֹא יִקָּרֵא עוֹד אֶת שִׁמְךָ,אַבְרָם וְהָיָה שִׁמְךָ אַבְרָהָם כִּי אַב הֲמוֹן גּוֹיִם נְתַתִּיךָ

ولا يقرأ عود أت شمك أبرم وهيه شمك [سمك] أبرهم كي أب همون جويم نتتيك

ولن يدعى بعد هذا اسمك ابرام، وسيكون اسمك ابراهيم، اذ أبا الكثير من غرباء، سنْعْطيك (سنجْعلْك).

And your name shall not be called, after that, Abram, but your name shall become Abraham, for a father of the numerous aliens, we shall give (establish) you.

Genesis 17.6

וְהִפְרֵתִי אֹתְךָ בִּמְאֹד מְאֹד וּנְתַתִּיךָ לְגוֹיִם וּמְלָכִים מִמְּךָ יֵצֵאוּ

وهفرتي آتك بمأد مأد ونتتيك لجويم وملكيم ممك يصأو

وسآتيك العذوبة الشديدة (بالماء العذب)، بالوافر الوافر، وسنْعْطيك (سنجْعلْك) لغرباء، و ملوكا سيختارو منك.

And I shall give you the utmost freshness (the freshest water), a plenty of plenty, and we shall give you (establish you) to aliens, and kings, they shall choose from you.

.
.

.

Exodus 19.6

וְאַתֶּם תִּהְיוּ-לִי מַמְלֶכֶת כֹּהֲנִים וְגוֹי קָדוֹשׁ אֵלֶּה הַדְּבָרִים אֲשֶׁר תְּדַבֵּר אֶל בְּנֵי יִשְׂרָאֵל

وأتم تهيو لي مملكت كهنيم وجوي قدوش [قدوس] أله هدبريم أشر تدبر أل بني يسرأل

وأنتم ستصبحو لي مملكة كَهَنة وغريب مقدس." هذه الكلمات التي ستتكلم الى بني إسرائيل.

And you shall become for me a kingdom of priests and a holy alien (outsider).' These are the words that you shall speak to the children of Israel.'

Part 2

Words' Roots and other References

1

Part 1-1 References

1.1

حين (مقاييس اللغة) الحاء والياء والنون أصلٌ واحد، ثم يحمل عليه، والأصل الزمان. فالحِينُ الزّمان قليله وكثيره.

علو (مقاييس اللغة) *العين واللام والحرف المعتل ياءً كان أو واواً أو ألفاً، أصلٌ واحد يدلُّ على السموّ والارتفاع، لا يشذُّ عنه شيء. ومن ذلك العَلاء والعَلْوَ. ويقولون: تعالى النهار، أي ارتفع .

علا (لسان العرب) عُلو كلّ شيء وعِلوه وعَلوه وعُلاوته وعالِيه وعالِيَته: أرفعُه، يتعدّى إليه الفعلُ بحَرْف وبغير حَرف كقولك قعَدْتُ عُلوه وفي عُلوه. وتعالى: ترفَّع؛ والعا والسافلُ: بمنزلة الأعْلى والأسفل؛

نبأ (مقاييس اللغة) النون والباء والهمزة قياسه الإتيانُ من مكانٍ إلى مكان. ومن هذا القياس النَبأ: الخبر، لأنَّه يأتي من مكان إلى مكان. والمُنبئ: المُخبِر. وأنبأته ونبّأته. والنَّبأة الصَوت. وهذا هو القياس، لأنَّ الصوتَ يجيءُ من مكانٍ إلى مكان. ومن هَمَز النبيَّ فلأنه أنبأ عن الله تعالى.

نبَا (القاموس المحيط) نَبَا بَصَرُهُ نُبُوّاً ونُبِيّاً ونَبْوَةً، والنَّباوَةُ: ما ارْتَفَعَ من الأرض كالنَّبْوَة والنَّبِيِّ،

نبا (الصّحاح في اللغة) نَبا الشيء عنّي يَنْبو، أي تجافى وتباعد. والنَبوَةُ والنَباوَةُ: ما ارتفع من الأرض. فإنْ جعلت النَبيَّ مأخوذاً منه، أي أنه شُرِّفَ على سائر الخلق فأصلُه غير الهمز، وتصغيره نُبَيٌّ، والجمع أنْبياءُ .

نبأ (لسان العرب) النَّبأُ: الخبر، والجمع أنْبَاءٌ، وإنَّ لفلان نَبأً أي خبراً. وقيل: النَّبيُّ مشتق من النَّبَاوة، وهي الشيءُ المُرْتَفِعُ .

نبا (لسان العرب) والنَّبْوةُ: الارْتِفاع. ابن سيده: النَّبْوُ العُلُوُّ والارْتِفاعُ، وقد نبا. والنَّبْوةُ والنَّباوةُ والنبيُّ: ما ارتَفع من الأرض. وفي الحديث: فأُتي بثلاثة قِرَصةٍ فوُضِعت على نَبيٍّ أي على شيء مرتفع من الأرض، من النَّباوة والنَّبْوة الشرَفِ المُرْتَفِع من الأَرض؛ وقال الزجاج: القراءة المجتمع عليها في النبيين والأنبياء طرح الهمز، وقد همز جماعة من أهل المدينة جميع ما في القرآن من هذا، واشتقاقه من نَبأ وأَنبأَ أي أخبر، قال: والأَجود ترك الهمز لأن الاستعمال يُوجب أنّ ما كان مهمُوزاً من فعيل فجمعه فُعَلاء مثل ظريف وظُرفاء، فإذا كان من ذوات الياء فجمعه أَفْعِلاء نحو غنيّ وأَغْنياء ونَبيٍّ وأَنْبياء، بغير همز، فإذا همَزْت قلت نَبيء ونُبَآء كما تقول في الصحيح، قال: وقد جاءَ أَفعلاء في الصَّحيح، وهو قليل، قالوا خَميسٌ وأَخْمِساء ونَصِيبٌ وأَنْصِباء، فيجوز أن يكون نَبيّ من أَنبأْت مما ترك همزه لكثرة الاستعمال، ويجوز أن يكون من نبا يَنْبُو إذا ارتفع، فيكون فَعِيلاً من الرِّفْعة.

سمم (لسان العرب) وسَمامةُ الرجل͏ وكلّ شيء وسَماوتُه: شخصُه، وقيل: سَماوتُه أعلاه.

سمو (مقاييس اللغة) السين والميم والواو أصلٌ يدل على العُلُوّ. يقال سَمَوْت، إذا علوت. وسَما بصرُه: عَلا. وسَما لي شخصٌ: ارتفع حتى استثبتُه. وسَمَاوةُ الهلال وكلّ شيء: شخصُهُ، والجمع سَماوٌ. والعرب تُسمّي السَحاب سماءً، والمطرَ سماءً، فإذا أُريدَ به المطرُ جُمع على سُمِيّ. والسَّماءة: الشَّخص. والسماء: سقف البيت. وكلُّ عالٍ مطلٍّ سماء، حتى يقال لظهر الفرس سَماء. ويتّسِعون حتّى يسمُّوا النّبات سماء.ويقال إن أصل "اسمٍ" سِمْو، وهو من العلوّ، لأنّه تنويهٌ ودَلالةٌ على المعنى .

سما (لسان العرب) السُّمُوُّ: الارْتِفاعُ والعُلُوُّ، تقول منه: سَمَوتُ وسَمَيْتُ مثل عَلَوْت وعَلَيْت وسَلَوْت وسَلَيْت؛ عن ثعلب. وسَما الشيءُ يَسْمُو سُمُوّاً، فهو سام: ارْتَفَع. وسماءُ كلِّ شيء: أَعلاهُ، مذكَّر. والسَّماءُ: سقفُ كلّ شيء وكلِّ بيتٍ. والسمواتُ السبعُ سماءٌ، والسمواتُ السبْع: أَطباقُ الأَرَضِينَ، وتُجْمَع سَماءً وسَمواتٍ. وقال الزجاج: السماءُ في اللغة يقال لكلِّ ما ارتفع وعَلا قدْ سَما يَسْمُو.

1.2

سفل (مقاييس اللغة) السين والفاء واللام أصلٌ واحد، وهو ما كان خلافَ العلوّ. فالسُّفل سُ͏فل الدارِ وغيرها. والسُّفول: ضدّ العُلُوّ.

أمت (مقاييس اللغة) الهمزة والميم والتاء أصلٌ واحد لا يقاس عليه، وهو الأَمْتُ، قال الله تعالى: لا تَرَى فِيهَا عِوَجاً ولاَ أَمْتاً [طه 107]. قال الخليل: العِوَج والأَمْتُ بمعنىً واحد. وقال آخرون – وهو ذلك المعنى – إنَ الأَمْتَ أن يغلُظ مكانٌ ويَرِق مكان. أمت (الصّحَاح في اللغة) الأَمْتُ: المكان المرتفع. وأمْتُ النِباك وهي التلال الصغار. وقوله تعالى: " لا تَرى فيها عِوَجاً ولا أَمْتاً"، أي لا انخفاضَ فيها ولا ارتفاع.
أمت (لسان العرب) أَمتَ الشيءَ يَأْمِتُه أَمْتاً، وأَمَتَه: قَدَّرَهُ وحَزَرَه. والأَمْتُ المكانُ المرتفع. وشيءٌ مأْمُوتٌ: معروف. والأَمْتُ الانْخفاضُ، والارْتفاعُ، والاختلافُ في الشيء. والأَمْتُ الرَّوابي الصِّغار.
أبت (لسان العرب) أَبِتَ اليومُ يَأْبِتُ ويَأْبُتُ أَبْتاً وأُبوتاً، وأَبِتَ، بالكسر، فهو أَبِتٌ وآبِتٌ وأَبْتٌ: كله بمعنى اشتدَّ حَرُّه وغَمُّه، وسَكَنَتْ ريحه؛ قال رؤْبة: من سافعاتٍ وهَجِيرٍ أَبْتِ وهو يومٌ أَبْتٌ، وليلةٌ أَبْتَةٌ، وكذلك حَمْتٌ، وحَمْتَةٌ، ومَحْتٌ، ومَحْتَةٌ: كل هذا في شدّة الحرّ؛ وأَنشد بيت رؤْبة أيضاً. وأَبْتَةُ الغَضَب: شدَّتُه وسَوْرَتُه.
أبس (مقاييس اللغة) الهمزة والباء والسين تدلّ على القهر، يقال منه أبَسَ الرجُلُ الرجُلَ، إذا قَهَره. قال: والأبس: كلّ مكانٍ خشنٍ. ويقال أَبَسْت بمعنى حَبَسْت وتأبس الشيءُ تغيّر .

ذكر (لسان العرب) الذِّكْرُ: الحِفْظُ للشيء تَذْكُرُه. والذِّكْرُ أيضاً: الشيء يجري على اللسان. والذِّكْرُ جَرْيُ الشيء على لسانك، وقد تقدم أَن الذِّكْرَ لغة في الذكر، ذَكَرَهُ يَذْكُرُه ذِكْراً وذُكْراً؛ الأَخيرة عن سيبويه. وقوله تعالى: واذكروا ما فيه؛ قال أَبو إِسحق: معناه ادْرُسُوا ما فيه. وتَذَكَّرَهُ واذَّكَرَهُ وادَّكَرَهُ واذْدَكَرَهُ، قلبوا تاء افْتَعَلَ في هذا مع الذال بغير إِدغام؛

1.3

أبز (مقاييس اللغة) قال الفرّاء: الأَبَزَى والقَفَزَى اسمان من أبز الفرسُ وقفَزَ. والأَبْزُ الوثْب.
الأَفْزُ (القاموس المحيط) الأَفْزُ: الوَثْبُ، كأنه مَقْلُوبٌ من الوَفْزِ.
ضفز (لسان العرب) أبو زيد: الضَّفْزُ والأَفْزُ العَدْوُ. يقال: ضَفَزَ يَضْفِزُ وأَفَزَ يأْفِزُ، وقال غيره: أَبَزَ وضَفَزَ بمعنى واحد .

رأس (لسان العرب) رَأْسُ كلِّ شيء: أَعلاه، والجمع في القلة أَرْؤُسٌ وآراسٌ على القلب، ورُؤُوس في الكثير، ولم يقلبوا هذه، ورؤْسٌ: الأَخيرة على الحذف؛ والرَّئِيس سَيِّدُ القوم، والجمع رُؤَساء، وهو الرَّأْسُ أَيضاً، ويقال رَيِّسٌ مثل قَيِّم بمعنى رَئِيس؛
رأس (العباب الزاخر) ورئيس القوم: سَيِّدُهم ووالي أمورهم، ويقال -أيضاً-: رَيِّسٌ -مثال قَيِّم- على الإدغام،

ذرأ (مقاييس اللغة) الذال والراء والهمزة أصلان: أحدهما لونٌ إلى البياض، والآخر كالشَّي يُبذَرُ ويُزْرَع .
ذرأ (الصّحَاح في اللغة) ذرأ الله الخلق يذرؤُهُم ذرءاً. خَلَقَهُمْ .
ذَرَأَ (القاموس المحيط) ذَرَأَ، كجَعَلَ: خَلَقَ،

1.4

موم (لسان العرب) وقد مَوَّمَها: عَمِلَها .
طمم (لسان العرب) طَمَّ الماءُ يَطِمُّ طَمّاً وطُموماً: عَلا وغَمَر. وكلُّ ما كَثُر وعلا حتى غَلب فقد طَمَّ يطِمُّ. وطَمَّ الشيءَ يَطُمُّه طَمّاً: غَمَره. وقيل: الطِّمُّ البَحْرُ والرِّمُّ الثرى. والطَّمُّ، بالفتح: هو البحر فكُسِرت الطاء ليزدوج مع الرِّمّ. وروى ابن الكلبي عن أَبيه قال: إِنما سُمِّي البحرُ الطِّمَّ لأَنه طَمَّ على ما فيه، والرِّمُّ ما على ظهر الأَرض من فُتاتها، أرادوا الكثرة من كل شيء.
التَّيْمُ (القاموس المحيط) وأرضٌ تَيْماءُ: قَفْرَةٌ مُضِلَّةٌ مُهْلِكَةٌ، أو واسعَةٌ. والتَّيْماءُ: الفَلاةُ،

ولد (لسان العرب) وولَدته الأُم تَلِدُه مَوْلِداً. والمُوَلَّد: المُحْدَثُ من كل شيء ومنه المُوَلَّدُونَ من الشعراء إِنما سموا بذلك لحدوثهم .

جمر (مقاييس اللغة) الجيم والميم والراء أصلٌ واحدٌ يدلُّ على التجمُّع. وهذا جميرُ القوم أي مجتمعُهم. وقد أجْمَرَ القوم على الأمر اجتمَعُوا.

1.5

موه (مقاييس اللغة) الميم والواو والهاء أصلٌ صحيح واحد، ومنه يتفرَّع كَلِمُه، وهي المَوه أصل بناء الماء، وتصغيرهُ مُوَيْه، قالوا: وهذا دليلٌ على أنّ الهمزة في الماء بدل من هاء. يقال: مَوَّهْتُ الشَّيء، كأنّك سقيته الماء. وموّهت الشّيء: طَلَيْتُه بفضَّة أو ذهب، كأنّهم يجعلون ذلك بمنزلة ما يُسقّاه. وقالوا: ما أحسَنَ مُوهَةَ وجهه، أي ترقرُق ماءِ الشَّباب فيه. ويقال في النسبة إلى ماه ماهيٌّ ومائيٌّ، وإلى ماءٍ مائيٌّ* وماويّ.
موه (الصّحَاح في اللغة) الماءُ: الذي يُشْرَبُ، والهمزة فيه مُبْدَلَةٌ من الهاء في موضع اللام، وأصله مَوَهٌ بالتحريك، لأنّه يجمع على أَمْواهٍ في القِلَّة ومياهٍ في الكثرة، وتصغيره مُوَيْهٌ، فإذا أنّثته قلت ماءةٌ.
الماءُ (القاموس المحيط) الماءُ والمهُ والماءةُ، وهَمْزَةُ الماءِ مُنْقَلِبَةٌ عن هاءٍ: م، وسُمِعَ: اسْقِنِي ماً، بالقَصْرِ
أاءَ (القاموس المحيط) وأوتُ الأَ◌ديم: دَبَغْتُهُ به، والأصل: أوْتٌ، فهو مَؤُوءٌ، والأَصْلُ: مَأْ◌ووءٌ.
مأي (لسان العرب) مَأَيْتُ في الشيء أَمْأَى مَأْياً: بالغتُ. ومَأَوْتُ الجِلْدَ والدَّلوَ والسِّقاءَ مَأْواً ومَأَيْتُ السقاءَ مَأْياً إِذا وَسَّعْته ومددته حتى يتسع.

حيق (مقاييس اللغة) الحاء والياء والقاف كلمةٌ واحدة، وهو نُزولُ الشيء بالشيء، يقال حاق به السُّوءُ يَحِيق.
حيق (لسان العرب) وحاقَ بهم: في كلام العرب عادَ عليهم ما استهزؤوا به، وجاء في التفسير: أحاط بهم نزل بهم، قال: ومنه قوله عز وجل: ولا يَحِيق المَكْرُ السَّيِّءُ إلا بأَهله، أَي لا يَرجِع عاقبةُ مكروهه إلا عليهم. وحاق فيه السيفُ حَيْقاً: كحاكَ.

أسس (لسان العرب) الأُسُّ والأَسَس والأَساس: كل مُبْتَدإِ شيءٍ. وكان ذلك على أُسِّ الدهر وأَسِّ الدهر وإِسِّ الدهر، ثلاث لغات، أَي على قِدَم الدهر ووجهه، ويقال: على است الدهر.
أَسْتُ (القاموس المحيط) أَسْتُ الدَّهْرِ: قِدَمُه .

1.6

الجَبْرُ (القاموس المحيط) وتجَبَّرَ: تكَبَّر، و~ الشَّجرُ: اخضَرَّ وأوْرَقَ، و~ الكلأُ: أُكِلَ ثم صَلَحَ قليلاً،
جبر (لسان العرب) وتَجَبَّرَ النبتُ والشجر: اخضَرَّ وأَوْرَق وظهرت فيه المَشْرةُ وهو يابس، وتَجَبَّرَ النبت أَي نبت بعد الأَكل. وتَجَبَّرَ النبت والشجر إِذا نبت في يابسه الرَّطْبُ. وتَجَبَّرَ الكلأُ أُكِلَ ثم صلح قليلاً بعد الأَكل .

قصر (مقاييس اللغة) القاف والصاد والراء أصلانِ صحيحان، أحدهما يدلُّ على ألا يبلُغ الشَّيءُ مداه ونهايتَه، والآخر على الحَبْس.
القَصْرُ (القاموس المحيط) القَصْرُ والقِصَرُ، كعِنَبٍ: خِلافُ الطُّولِ،
قصر (لسان العرب) والاقْتِصارُ على الشيء: الاكتفاء به. وتَقاصَرتْ نَفْسُه: تضاءلت. وتَقاصَر الظلُّ: دنا وقَلَصَ.
كصر (لسان العرب) أَبو زيد: الكَصِيرُ لغة في القَصِير لبعض العرب.

صيص (لسان العرب) ابن الأَعرابي: أَصاصَت النَّخلة إِصاصةً وصَيَّصَت تَصْييصاً إِذا صارت شِيصاً، قال: وهذا من الصِّيصِ لا من الصِّيصَاء، يقال: من الصِّيصَاء صَأْصَت صِيصَاءً. والصِّيصُ والصِّيصَاءُ: لُغةٌ في الشِّيص والشِّيصَاء.
الصِّيصُ (القاموس المحيط) الصِّيصُ، بالكسر: الشِّيصُ، وكلُّ شيء امتَنَع به وتُحُصِّنَ به، فهو صِيصةٌ، ومنه قيل للحصون: الصَّياصِي؛
شيص (لسان العرب) ويقال: أَشاصَ به إِذا رفَعَ أَمرَه إِلى السلطان؛
شصا (الصِّحَاح في اللغة) شصا بصرُه يشصو شُصُوّاً: شَخَصَ. وأَشْصاه صاحبه: رفعه. وفي المثل: إذا ارْجَحَنَّ شاصِياً فارفعْ يداً، أي إذا سقط ورفع رجليه فاكْفُفْ عنه. وشصا السحاب، أي ارتفع في الهواء .
شصا (لسان العرب) يقال للميت إِذا انتفخ فارتفعت يداه ورجلاه: قد شَصَى يَشْصِي (* قوله «قد شصى يشصي إلخ» ضبط في المحكم والتهذيب والصحاح من باب رمى، وفي القاموس شصي كرضي، قال شارحه: وقد ضبط الفعل مثل رمى يرمي على ما هو في النسخ وصحح عليه فقول المصنف كرضي محل تأمل). شُصِيّاً، فهو شاصٍ؛ حكاه عن الكسائي؛ قال ابن سيده: والمعروف يَشْصُو. المحكم: شَصا برجله شُصِيّاً رفعها. الليث: شَصَتِ السَّحابةُ تَشْصُو إِذا ارتفعت في نُشُوئِها، وشصا السحاب.
شَصِيَ (القاموس المحيط)
شَصِيَ المَيِّتُ، كرَضِيَ ودَعا، شُصِيّاً، كصُلِيٍّ: ارْتَفَعَتْ يَداهُ ورِجْلاهُ .

شعا (لسان العرب) أَشْعَى القومُ الغارةَ إِشْعاءً: أَشْعَلُوها. وغارةٌ شَعْواءُ: فاشِيةٌ متفرِّقة؛ وشعيَت الغارةُ تشْعَى شعاً إِذا انتشَرت، فهي شَعْواءُ، كما يقال عَشِيَتِ المرأَة تَعْشَى عَشاً فهي عَشْواء. والشاعِي: البعيدُ. والشَّعْوُ انتِفاشُ الشَّعَر. والشُّعَى: خُصَلُ الشَّعَرِ المُشْعانِّ. والشَّعْوانة الجُمَّةُ من الشَّعَر المُشْعانّ. وشجرة شَعْواءُ: مُنْتَشِرة الأَغصان. وأَشْعَى به: اهْتَمَّ؛ قال أَبو خراش: أَبْلِغْ عَلِيّاً، أَذَلَّ اللهُ سَعْيَهُمُ أَن البَكْرَ الذي أَشْعَوْا به هَمَلُ قال ابن جني: هو من قولهم غارةٌ شَعْواءُ، ورُوِي: أَسْعَوْا به، بالسين غير معجمة، وقد تقدم. الأَصمعي: جاءت الخيلُ شَواعِيَ وشَوائِعَ أَي متفرقةً؛

سعا (لسان العرب) والسَّعْيُ: القَصْدُ، وبذلك فُسِّرَ قوله تعالى: فاسْعَوْا إِلى ذِكْرِ الله؛ وليسَ من السَّعْي الذي هو العَدْوُ، وقرأَ ابن مسعود: فامْضُوا إِلى ذكْرِ الله، وقال: لو كانَتْ من السَّعْيِ لسَعَيْتُ حتى يَسْقُط رِدائي. قال الزجاج: السَّعْيُ والذَّهابُ بمعنى واحدٍ لأَنك تقولُ للرجل هو يَسْعَى في الأَرض، وليس هذا باشْتداد. وقال الزجاج: أَصلُ السَّعْيِ في كلام العرب التصرُّف فيكل عَمَلٍ؛ وأَسْعَى غيرَه: جَعَله يَسْعَى؛ وقد روي بيتُ أَبي خِراش: أَبْلِغْ عَلِيّاً، أَطالَ اللهُ ذُلَّهُمُ أَنَّ البَكْرَ الذي أَسْعَوْا به هَمَلٌ أَسْعَوْا وأَشْعَوْا.

1.7

شوف (مقاييس اللغة) الشين والواو والفاء أصلٌ واحد، وهو يدلُّ على ظهور وبُروز. من ذلك قول العرب: تَشَوَّفَت الأوعالُ، إذا علَتْ مَعاقل الجبال.

1.8

سمت (لسان العرب) السَّمْتُ: حُسْنُ النَّحْوِ في مَذْهَبِ الدِّينِ، والفعلُ سَمَتَ يَسْمُ◌ِتُ سَمْتاً، وإنه لحَسَنُ السَّمْت أي حَسَنُ القَصْدِ والمَذْهَب في دينه ودنْياه. والسَّمْتُ الطريقُ؛ وسَمْتُ الطريقِ: قَصْدُه. وفي حديث عمر، رضي الله عنه: فينظرون إلى سَمْتِه وهَدْيه أي حُسْنِ هيئته ومَنْظَرِه في الدين، وليس من الحُسْنِ والجمال؛ وقيل: هو من السَّمْتِ الطريق .

سوم (لسان العرب) والسُّومَةُ والسِّيمةُ والسِّيماء والسِّيمياءُ: العلامة. وسَوَّمَ الفرسَ: جعل عليه السِّيمة. وسامني الرجلُ بسِلْعته سَوْماً: وذلك حين يذكر لك هو ثمنها، والاسم من جميع ذلك السُّومَةُ والسِّيمَةُ. وسُمْتُكَ بَعِيرَك سِيمةً حسنة، وإنه لغالي السِّيمةِ.

1.9

بني (لسان العرب) والبَنْيُ نَقيضُ الهَدْم، بَنى البَنَّاءُ البِناءَ بَنْياً وبِنَاءً وبِنًى، مقصور، وبُنياناً وبِنْيَةً وبِنايةً وابتَناه وبَنَّاه؛ وبَنَى الرجلَ: اصْطَنَعَه؛

قرب (الصّحاح في اللغة) وأقْرَبْتُ السيفَ: جعلتُ له قِراباً. وأقْرَبْتُ القدحَ، من قولهم قَدَحٌ قَرْبانُ، إذا قارب أن يمتلئَ، وجُمْجُمَة قَرْبى، وقَدَحان قَرْبانانِ؛ والجمع قِرابٌ. والقِرْبَة ما يُستقى فيه الماء؛ والجمع في أدنى العدد قِرْبات وقِرَبات، وللكثير قِرَبٌ. والقَرابة القُربى في الرحم، وهو في الأصل مصدرٌ. تقول: بيني وبينه قَرابة، وقُرْبٌ، وقُرْبى ومَقْرَبَةٌ، وقُرْبَةٌ، وقُرُبَةٌ بضم الراء.
قرب (لسان العرب) القُرْبُ نقيضُ البُعْدِ. وفي الحديث: إن لَقِيتَني بقُراب الأَرضِ خطيئةً أي بما يقارِبُ مِلأَها، وهو مصدرُ قارَبَ يُقارِبُ. وأقْرَبْتُ القَدَحَ، مِنْ قولهم: قَدَح قَرْبانُ إذا قارَبَ أن يمتلئَ؛ وقَدَحانِ قَرْبانانِ والجمع قِرابٌ، مثل عَجْلانَ وعِجالٍ؛ تقول: هذا قَدَحٌ قَرْبانُ ماءً، وهو الذي قد قارَبَ الامتِلاءَ. ويقال: لو أنَّ لي قُرابَ هذا ذَهَباً أي ما يُقارِبُ مِلأَه. وأَقْرَبَتِ الحاملُ، وهي مُقْرِبٌ: دنا وِلادُها، وجمعها مَقاريبُ، كأنهم توهموا واحدَها على هذا، مِقْراباً؛ والقُرْبُ الخاصِرة، والجمع أقرابٌ؛ وقال الشَّمَرْدَلُ: يصف فرساً: لاحِقُ القُرْبِ، والأَياطِلِ نَهْدٌ، * مُشْرِفُ الخَلْقِ في مَطاه تَمامُ التهذيب: فرسٌ لاحِقُ الأَقْرابِ، يَجْمَعُونه؛ وإنما له قُرْبانِ لسَعته، كما يقال شاة ضَخْمَةُ الخَواصِر، وإنما لها خاصِرتانِ؛ وقَرَبَتِ الشمسُ للمغيب: كَكَرَبَتْ؛ وزعم يعقوب أن القاف بدل مِن الكاف.
الكَرْبُ (القاموس المحيط) وكارَبَهُ: قارَبَهُ. والكَرَبَةُ، مُحَرَّكَةً: الزِّرُّ يكونُ فيه رأسُ عَمُودِ البَيْتِ. أو كَرْبُها، أي: نَحْوُها وقُرابُها.
كرب (لسان العرب) وكَرَبَ الأَمْرُ يَكْرُبُ كُرُوباً: دَنا. وكلُّ دانٍ قريبٍ، فهو كارِبٌ. والكَرْبُ: القُرْبُ.

1.10

لحم (مقاييس اللغة) اللام والحاء والميم أصلٌ صحيح يدلُّ على تداخُلٍ، كاللَّحمِ الذي هو متداخِلٌ بعضُه في بعض. من ذلك اللَّحْم. ويقال لَحَمْتُ اللَّحمَ عن العظم: قشرتُه.
اللَّحْمُ (القاموس المحيط) اللَّحْمُ، ويُحَرَّكُ م ج: ألْحُمٌ ولُحومٌ ولِحامٌ ولُحْمانٌ. واللَّحْمَةُ: القِطْعَةُ منه، وبالضم: القَرابةُ، وما سُدِيَ به بين سَدَى الثَّوْبِ، وما يُطْعَمُهُ البازي مما يَصِيدُهُ، ويُفْتَحُ فيهما. والمَلْحَمَةُ: الوَقْعَةُ العظيمةُ القَتْلِ. ولَحْمُ كُلِّ شيءٍ: لُبُّهُ.

1.11

أدي (مقاييس اللغة) الهمزة والدّال والياء أصلٌ واحد، وهو إيصال الشيء إلى الشيء أو وصوله إليه من تلقاء نفسه.
عدو (مقاييس اللغة) العين والدال والحرف المعتل أصلٌ واحدٌ صحيحٌ يرجع إليه الفروعَ كلّها، وهو يدلُّ على تجاوُزٍ في الشيء وتقدُّمٍ لما ينبغي أن يقتصر عليه.
عدا (لسان العرب) والتَّعَدِّي مُجاوَزَةُ الشيء إِلى غَيْرِه، يقال: عَدَّيْتُه فتَعَدَّى أي تجاوزَ.

عتا (لسان العرب) عَتَّى: بمعنى حتَّى، هُذَلِيَّةٌ وثَقَفِيَّة، وقرأ بعضهم: عَتَّى حينٍ؛ أي حتى حينٍ. كلُّ العربِ يَقُولون حتى إلاّ هُذَيلاً وثَقِيفاً فإنهم يقولون عَتَّى.
عدو (مقاييس اللغة) العين والدال والحرف المعتل أصلٌ واحدٌ صحيحٌ يرجع إليه الفروعَ كلّها، وهو يدلُّ على تجاوُزٍ في الشيء وتقدُّمٍ لما ينبغي أن يقتصر عليه.
عدا (لسان العرب) وعَدَا الأَمرَ يَعْدُوه وتَعَدَّاه، كلاهما: تَجاوَزَة. ويقال: ما يَعْدُو فلانٌ أَمْرَك أي ما يُجاوِزه. والتَّعَدِّي: مُجاوَزَةُ الشيء إِلى غَيْرِه، يقال: عَدَّيْتُه فتَعَدَّى أي تَجاوزَ.

ربي/أ (مقاييس اللغة) الراء والباء والحرف المعتل وكذلك المهموز منه يدلُّ على أصلٍ واحد، وهو الزّيادة والنَّماء والعُلُوّ. تقول مِن ذلك: ربا الشّيءُ يربُو، إذا زاد .
ربا (الصّحاح في اللغة) رَبا الشيءُ يَرْبو رَبْواً، أي زاد .

ذيح (لسان العرب) ابن الأثير في حديث عَلِيٍّ: كان الأَشعثُ ذا ذَيْحٍ؛ الذَّيحُ: الكِبْرُ .

1.12

قشر (مقاييس اللغة) والقِشْرة الجلدة المقشورة .
قش (مقاييس اللغة) القاف والشين كلماتٌ على غير قياس. فالقَشُّ: القشْر.

نشر (لسان العرب) ونَشَر اللهُ الميت يَنْشُره نَشْراً ونُشوراً وأَنْشره فنَشَر الميتُ لا غير: أَحياه؛ قال الأَعشى: حتى يقولَ الناسُ مما رأَوْا: يا عَجَباً للميّت النّاشِرِ وفي التنزيل العزيز: وانْظُرْ إِلى العظام كيف ننشرها؛ قرأَها ابن عباس: كيف نُنْشِرُها، وقرأَها الحسن: نَنْشُرها؛ وقال الفراء: من قرأَ كيف نُنشِرها، بضم النون، فإِنْشارُها إِحياؤُها، واحتج ابن عباس بقوله تعالى: ثم إِذا شاء أَنْشَرَه، قال: ومن قرأَها نَنْشُرها وهي قراءة الحسن فكأَنه يذهب بها إِلى النَّشْر والطيِّ، والوجه أَن يقال: أَنشَرَ اللهُ الموتى فنَشَرُوا هُمْ إِذا حَيُوا وأَنشَرهم اللهُ أَي أَحْياهم؛ وأَنشد الأَصمعي لأَبي ذؤيب: لو كان مِدْحَةُ حَيٍّ أَنشرَتْ أَحداً، أَحْيا أَبُوّتَكَ الشُّمَّ الأَماديحُ قال: وبعض بني الحرث كان به جَرَب فنَشَر أَي عاد وحَيِي. ومنه الحديث: لا رَضاعَ إِلا ما أَنشر اللحم وأَنبت العظم (* قوله« الا م أنشر اللحم وأنبت العظم» هكذا في الأصل وشرح القاموس. والذي في النهاية والمصباح: الا ما أنشر العظم وأنبت اللحم) أَي شدّه وقوّاه من الإِنْشار الإِحْياء. والنَّشْر الحياة. ونَشَرت الأَرض تنشُر نُشُوراً: أَصابها الربيعُ فأَنبتت. وما أَحْسَنَ نَشْرَها أَي بَدْءَ نباتها. والنَّشْر أَيضاً: مصدر نشَرت الخشبة بالمِنْشار نَشْراً. والنَّشْر خلاف الطيّ. نشَر الثوبَ ونحوه يَنْشُره نَشْراً ونَشَّره: بَسطه. وكلُّ شيء أَخذته غضّاً، فقد نَشَرته وانْتَشَرته، ومَرْجِعه إِلى النَّشْر ضدّ الطيّ، ويروى بالباء الموحدة والسين المهملة. وتنَشَّر الشيءُ وانتَشَر: انبَسط. وانْتَشَر النهارُ وغيره: طال وامْتَدّ.
أشر (لسان العرب) الأَشَرُ: المَرَح. وأَشِرَ النخل أَشَراً كثُر شُرْبُه للماء فكثرت فراخه. وأَشَرَ الخَشَبة بالمِئْشار، مهموز: نَشَرها، والمئشار: ما أُشِرَ به.

وتر (لسان العرب) والتَّواتُرُ التتابُعُ، وقيل: هو تتابع الأَشياء وبينها فَجَواتٌ وفَتَراتٌ.
أتر (لسان العرب) الأُتْرُور: لغة في التُّؤْرُور مقلوب عنه .
تأر (لسان العرب) أَتأَر إِليه النَّظَرَ: أَحَدَّه. وأَتأَره بصره: أَتبَعه إِياه، بهمز الأَلفين غير ممدودة؛ قال بعض الأَغفال: وأَتأَرَتْني نَظْرة الشَّفيرِ. وأَتأَرتُه بصري: أَتبَعْته إِياه. ومنه يقال: أَتأَرتُ إِليه النظر أَي أَدمته تارةً بعد تارةٍ.

1.13

ركا (لسان العرب) وأَرْكَيْت في الأَمْر: تأَخَّرْت. ابن الأَعرابي: ركاه إِذا أَخَّره. قال: ومعنى قوله اركُوا هذَيْن أَي أَخِّرُوا

أود (لسان العرب) وآد الشيءُ أَوْداً: رجع؛ ويقال: آد النهارُ يؤُود أَوْداً إِذا رجع في العشيّ؛
عود (لسان العرب) وعاد إِليه يَعُودُ عَوْدَةً وعَوْداً: رجع. والعِيدُ: كلُّ يوم فيه جَمْعٌ، واشتقاقه من عاد يَعُود كأَنهم عادوا إِليه؛ وأَما قول أَبي النجم: حتى إِذا الليلُ تَجَلَّى أَصْحَمُه، وانْجابَ عن وجْهٍ أَغَرَّ أَدْهَمُه، وتَبِعَ الأَحْمَرَ عَوْدٌ يَرْجُمُه فإِنه أَراد بالأَحمر الصبح، وأَراد بالعود الشمس.

مأي (لسان العرب) مَأَيتُ في الشيء أَمْأَى مَأْياً: بالغتُ. الكسائي: كان القوم تسعة وتسعين فأَمْأَيْتُهم، بالأَلف، مثل أَفعلتُهم، وكذلك في الأَلف آلَفْتُهم، وكذلك إِذا صاروا هم كذلك قلت: قد أَمْأَوْا وآلفُوا إِذا صاروا مائةً أَو أَلفاً. الجوهري: وأَمْأَيْتُها لك جعلتها مائةً. وأَمْأَتِ الدراهمُ والإِبلُ والغنمُ وسائر الأَنواع: صارت مائةً، وأَمْأَيْتُها مِائةً. وشارطَتُه مُماآةً أَي على مائةٍ؛ عن ابن الأَعرابي، كقولك شارطته مُؤالفةً.
مأى (الصّحاح في اللغة) ومائةٌ من العدد، وأصله مِئًى مثال مِعًى، والهاء عوض من الياء. وإذا جمعت بالواو والنون قلت: مِئُونَ بكسر الميم، وبعضهم يقول: مُؤُون بالضم. قال ابن السكيت: قال الأخفش: ولو قلت مِئاتٌ، لكان جائزاً. وأَمْأَى القوم: صاروا مائةً. وأَمْأَيْتُهُمْ أنا. أبو زيد: أَمْأَتْ غنمُ فلان، إذا صارت مائةً. وأَمْأَيْتُها لك: جعلتها مائةً.

ePSD: me'atu
meat [100] wr. me-at "100" Akk. me'atu

قرن (لسان العرب) والقَرْنُ في قوم نوح: على مقدار أَعمارهم؛ وقيل: القَرْنُ أَربعون سنة بدليل قول الجَعْدِي: ثلاثة أَهْلِينَ أَفْنَيْتُهم، وكانَ الإِلهُ هو المُسْتاسا وقال هذا وهو ابن مائة وعشرين سنة، وقيل: القَرْن مائة سنة، وجمعه قُرُون. وفي الحديث: أَنه مسح رأْس غلام وقال عِشْ قَرْناً، فعاش مائة سنة.

الوَصْبُ (القاموس المحيط) ووصَبَ يَصِبُ وُصوباً: دامَ، وثَبَتَ، كأَوْصَبَ، و~ على الأَمْرِ: واظَبَ، وأَحْسَنَ القِيامَ عليه.
وصب (مقاييس اللغة) الواو والصاد والباء: كلمةٌ تدلُّ على دَوامِ شيء. ووَصَبَ الشَّيءُ وصوباً: دام.

1.14

الإِبِلُ (القاموس المحيط) وأُبُلَّتُه، بِضَمَّتَيْنِ مُشَدَّدَةً: أَصْحابُه وقَبيلَتُه. وناقَةٌ أَبِلَةٌ: مبارَكةٌ في الوَلَدِ.
أبل (لسان العرب) وأَبَّل الرجلَ: كأَبَّنه؛ عن ابن جني؛ اللحياني: أَبَّنْت الميت تأْبيناً وأَبَّلْته تأْبيلاً إِذا أَثنيت عليه بعد وفاته.

أفل (مقاييس اللغة) قال الخليل: وإذا استقرّ اللّقاح في قَرار الرّحِم فقد أفَل. والأصل الثاني الأفيل، وهو الفصيل، والجمع الإفَال. قال الأصمعي: الأفيل ابنُ المخاض وابن اللبون، الأنثى أفيلة، فإذا ارتفع عن ذلك فليس بأفيل.
افل (لسان العرب) وسَبُعَةٌ آفِل وآفلة: حامل. قال الليث: إذا استقر اللّقاح في قرار الرّحِم قيل قد أفَلَ، ثم يقال للحامل آفِل.
فلا (لسان العرب) فلا الصَّبيَّ والمُهْرَ والجَحْش فَلْواً وفِلاءً (* قوله« وفلاء» كذا ضبط في الأصل، وقال في شرح القاموس: وفلاء كسحاب، وضبط في المحكم بالكسر.) وأفْلاه وافْتلاه: عَزَله عن الرَّضاع وفصَله. والفَلُوُّ والفُلُوُّ والفِلْوُ: الجَحش والمُهر إذا فطم؛

ثني (لسان العرب) والثِّنْيُ: واحد أَثْناء الشيء أي تضاعيفه؛ والاثْنان: ضعف الواحد. وقال الفراء في قوله عز وجل: اللهُ نَزَّلَ أحسَن الحديث كتاباً مُتشابِهاً مَثانِيَ؛ أي مكرراً أي كُرِّرَ فيه الثوابُ والعقابُ؛
ثني (مقاييس اللغة) الثاء والنون والياء أصلٌ واحد، وهو تكرير الشَّيء مرّتين، أو جعلُه شيئين متواليَين أو متباينين، وذلك قولك ثَنَيْت الشَّيءَ ثَنْياً.
يروى: "ثُنْيانُنا إن أتاهُمْ كانَ بَدْأهُم". والثِّنَى: الأمْرُ يعادُ مرّتين.
سنن (لسان العرب) وقد سَنَنْتُه أَسُنُّه سَنّاً إذا صوَرته. وبَنى القوم بيوتهم على سَنَنٍ واحد أي على مثال واحد.

الإِدُّ (القاموس المحيط) والأَدُّ والإِدُّ والآدُ: الغَلَبَةُ، والقُوَّةُ.
أدا (لسان العرب) وآداهُ على كذا يُؤْدِيهِ إيداءً: قَوّاه عليه وأعانَه. ومَنْ يُؤْدِيني على فلان أي من يُعِينني عليه؛ يقال: آدِني عليه، بالمد، أي قَوِّني.
العَدُّ (القاموس المحيط) و~ الغُلامُ: شَبَّ، وغَلُظَ.

1.15

مثل (مقاييس اللغة) الميم والثاء واللام أصلٌ صحيح يدلُّ على مناظرَة الشَّيءِ للشيء.
مثل (لسان العرب) مِثل: كلمةُ تَسْوِيَةٍ. يقال: هذا مِثْله ومَثَله كما يقال شِبْهه وشَبَهُه بمعنىً؛ والتِّمْثال: اسم للشيء المصنوع مشبَّهاً بخلق من خلق الله.

بكر (مقاييس اللغة) الباء والكاف والراء أصلٌ واحدٌ يرجع إليه فرعان هما منه. فالأوّل أوّلُ الشيء وبَدْؤُه. والبِكْرُ من كلِّ أمرٍ أولُه.
بكر (الصّحَاح في اللغة) وبِكْرُها ولدُها. والذكر والأنثى فيه سواء.

1.16

دوم (لسان العرب) والدَّيُّومُ: الدائمُ منه كما قالوا قَيُّوم.
دامَ (القاموس المحيط) والمُدامُ: المَطَرُ الدائمُ. دامَ يَدُومُ ويَدامُ دَوْماً ودَواماً ودَيْمومةً، ودِمْتَ، بالكسر. تَدُومُ نادِرَةٌ. والدَّيُّومُ والدَّوْمُ: الدائمُ.
ودام: سَكَنَ، ومنه: الماءُ الدائمُ، والدِيمَةُ، بالكسر: مَطَرٌ يَدومُ في سُكونٍ بلا رَعْدٍ وبَرْقٍ . وأرض مَدِيمَةٌ ومُدَيَّمَةٌ: أصابتها الدِّيَمُ، وأصلها الواو؛
نوي (لسان العرب) ونَوَّيْته تَنْوِيةً أي وَكَلْته إلى نِيَّتِه. ونوِيُّك: صاحبُك الذي نيته نيّتك؛ ونَواهُ للهُ: حفظه؛

1.17

سلط (لسان العرب) السَّلاطةُ: القَهْرُ، وقد سَلَّطه اللهُ فتَسَلَّطَ عليهم، والاسم سُلْطة، بالضم. والسُّلْطانُ الحُجَّةُ والبُرْهان. وقال أبو بكر: في السلطان قولان: أحدهما أن يكون سمي سلطاناً لتَسلِيطِه، والآخر أن يكون سمي سلطاناً لأنه حجة من حُجَج الله. وسُلْطانُ كل شيء: شِدَّتُه وحِدَّتُه وسَطْوَتُه، قيل من اللسانِ السَّلِيطِ الحديدِ.
سلط (مقاييس اللغة) السينُ واللام والطاء أصلٌ واحدٌ، وهو القوّة والقهر. من ذلك السَّلاطة، من التسلط وهو القَهْر، ولذلك سمّي السُّلْطان سلطاناً. والسلطان الحُجّة. والسَّليط من الرجال: الفصيح اللسان الذَّرِب.

ذا (الصّحَاح في اللغة) قال سيبويه: إن ذَا وحدها بمنزلة الذي. وأما ذو الذي بمعنى صاحِبٍ فلا يكون إلاَّ مضافاً.
ذا (لسان العرب) قال أبو العباس أحمد بن يحيى ومحمد بن زيد: ذا يكون بمعنى هذا، ومنه قول الله عز وجل: مَنْ ذا الذي يَشْفَع عِنده إلا بإذنه؛ أي مَنْ هذا الذي يَشْفَع عِنده؛ قالا: ويكون ذا بمعنى الذي ، قالا: ويقال هذا دو صَلاحٍ ورأيتُ هذا ذا صَلاحٍ ومررت بهذا ذي صَلاحٍ، ومعناه كله صاحِب صَلاح.

ša
lu [PERSON] wr. lu2; mu-lu; mu-lu2; lu10; lu6 "who(m), which; man; (s)he who, that which; of; ruler; person"
Akk. amēlu; ša

1.18

فلق (لسان العرب) وأَفْلَقَ في الأمر إذا كان حاذقاً به. وجاء بعُلَقَ فُلَقَ أي بعجب عجيب.
فلق (الصّحَاح في اللغة) والفِلْقُ بالكسر: الداهيةُ والأمرُ العجبُ. تقول منه: أفْلَقَ الرجلُ وافْتَلَقَ. وشاعرٌ مُفْلِقٌ: قد جاء بالفِلْقِ. والفَليقَةُ: الداهيةُ.

أذن (مقاييس اللغة) الهمزة والذال والنون أصلان متقاربان في المعنى، متباعدان في اللفظ، أحدهما أُذُنُ كلّ ذي أُذُن، والآخر العِلم؛ ويقال للرجل السامع من كلّ أحدٍ أُذُنٌ. قال الله تعالى: وَمِنْهُمُ الَّذِينَ يُؤْذُونَ النَّبِيَّ وَيَقُولُونَ هُوَ أُذُنٌ.
أذن (لسان العرب) أَذِنَ بالشيء إِذْناً وأَذَناً وأَذانةً: عَلِم .

حسس (لسان العرب) الحِسُّ والحَسِيسُ: الصوتُ الخفيُّ؛ والحِسُّ، بكسر الحاء: من أَحْسَسْتُ بالشيء. حسَّ بالشيء يَحُسُّ حَسّاً وحِسّاً وحَسِيساً وأَحسَّ به وأَحسَّه: شعر به؛ وتقول: ما أَحْسَسْتُ بالخبر وما أَحْسْت وما حَسِيتُ ما حِسْتُ أي لم أعرف منه شيئاً (*عبارة المصباح: وأحس الرجل الشيء إحساساً علم به، وربما زيدت الباء فقيل: أحسّ به على معنى شعر به. وقال أبو معاذ: التَحَسُّسُ شبه التسمع والتبصر؛ قال: والتجَسُّسُ، بالجيم، البحث عن العورة، قاله في تفسير قوله تعالى: ولا تجَسَّسوا ولا تحَسَّسُوا. ابن الأعرابي: تجَسَّسْتُ الخبر وتحَسَّسْتُه بمعنى واحد. وتَحَسَّسْتُ من الشيء أي تَخَبَّرت خبره. وحَسَّ منه خبراً وأَحسَّ، كلاهما: رأَى. وعلى هذا فسر قوله تعالى: فلما أَحسَّ عيسى منهم الكُفْرَ. وحكى اللحياني: ما أَحسَّ منهم أَحداً أي ما رأَى. ويقال: هل أَحسَست صاحبك أي هل رأيته؟ وهل أَحْسَسْت الخبر أي هل عرفته وعلمته.

جسس (لسان العرب) الجَسُّ: اللَّمْسُ باليد. وجَسَّ الشخص بعينه: أَحدَّ النظر إليه ليَسْتَبِينه ويَسْتَثْبِته؛ قال ابن سيده: والجَواسُّ عند الأَوائل الحَواسُّ.

فجل (مقاييس اللغة) وكلُّ شيء عَرَّضته فجَلْتَه.
فجل (لسان العرب) وفَجِلَ الشيء وفَجَلَ يَفْجُل فَجْلا وفَجَلاً: استرخى وغَلُظ. وإِياه عنى بقوله وهو مجهز السفينة يهجو رجلاً: أَشْبَهُ شيء بجُشاء الفُجْل ثِقْلاً على ثِقْل، وأَيّ ثِقَل والفنجلة والفَنْجَلى: مِشية فيها استرخاء يسحب رجله على الأَرض؛ وقال صخر بن عمير:فإِنْ تَرَيْني في المَشيب والعِلَه، فصِرتُ أَمشي القَعْوَلى والفَنْجلَه، وتارةً أَنْبُتُ نَبْتاً نَقْثَله النَّقْثَلة: مِشية الشيخ يُثِير التراب إِذا مشى.

بجل (لسان العرب) التَّبجيل: التعظيم. بَجَّل الرجلَ: عَظَّمه. ورجل بَجَال وبَجِيل: يُبَجِّله الناسُ، وقيل: هو الشيخ الكبير العظيم السيد مع جَمال ونُبل، وقد بَجُل بَجالة وبُجُولاً،

1.19

جسر (مقاييس اللغة) الجيم والسين والراء يدلُّ على قوّة وجُرأة. فالجَسْرة: الناقة القوية، ويقال هي الجريئة على السَّير. وصُلْبٌ جَسْرٌ أي قويّ.
جسر (الصّحاح في اللغة) والجَسْرُ بالفتح: العظيم من الإبل وغيرها؛ والأنثى جَسْرَةٌ. وجَسَرَ على كذا يَجْسُرُ جَسارَةً وتجاسَرَ عليه، أي أقدم. والجَسورُ: المقدام .
جسر (لسان العرب) جَسَرَ يَجْسُرُ جُسُوراً وجَسارة: مضى ونفذ. وجَسَرَ على كذا يَجْسُر جَسارةً وتَجاسَر عليه؛ أَقدم. والجَسُورُ: المِقْدامُ. ورجل جَسْر وجَسُورٌ: ماضٍ شجاعٌ، والأُنثى جَسْرَةٌ وجَسُورٌ وجَسُورةٌ. ورجل جَسْرٌ: جسيمٌ جَسُورٌ شجاع.

مادَ (القاموس المحيط) و~ الرجلُ: تَبَخْتَرَ، وزارَ، و~ قومَهُ: مارَهُم،
مأد (لسان العرب) ويقال للغصن إِذا كان ناعماً يهتز: هو يَمْأَدُ مَأْداً حسناً. ومأَد النباتُ والشجر يمأَدُ مأْداً: اهتز وتروّى وجرى فيه الماء،
ميد (لسان العرب) ماد الشيء يَميد: زاغ وزكا؛ ومِدْته وأَمَدْته: أَعْطيْته. وماد إِذا تَجِر، وماد: أَفْضَل. ومَيْدٌ: بمعنى غير أَيضاً، وقيل: هي بمعنى على كما تقدم في بَيْد. ومادَ الشيءُ يَميدُ مَيْداً: تحرك ومال. وماد يَميدُ إِذا تثنَّى وتبختر. ومادت الأَغْصان: تمايلت. ويقال: لم أَدر ما مِيداءُ ذلك أَي لم أَدر ما مَبْلَغه وقياسه، وكذلك ميتاؤه، أَي لم أَدر ما قَدْرُ جانبيه وبُعْده؛ ومَيْد: لغة في بَيْد بمعنى غير، وقيل: معناهما على أَنْ؛ وفي الحديث: أَنا أَفْصَحُ العَرَب مَيْدَ أَنِّي مِنْ قُرَيْشٍ ونشأْتُ في بني سعد بن بكر؛ وفسره بعضهم: من أَجْلِ أَني. وفي الحديث: نحن الآخِرون السابقون مَيْدَ أَنَّا أُوتينا الكتابَ من بَعْدهم .
ميد (مقاييس اللغة) وأمّا قوله صلى الله عليه وآله وسلم: "مَيدَ أنّا أوتينا الكتابَ مِن بعدهم"، أي غير أنا، أو على أنا، فهو لغة في بَيْد أنَا .

1.20

أخا (لسان العرب) وما كنتَ أخاً ولقد تأَخَّيت وآخَيت وأَخَوْت تأْخُو أُخُوَّة وتآخيا، على تفاعَلا، وتأَخَّيت أَخاً أَي اتَّخذْت أَخاً. وتأَخَّى الرجل: اتَّخذه أَخاً أَو دعاه أَخاً. والآخِيَّة، بالمدّ والتشديد، واحدة الأَواخي: عُودٌ يُعَرَّض في الحائط ويُدْفن طرَفاه فيه ويصير وسطه كالعُروة تُشدّ إِليه الدابَّة؛ وقال ابن السكيت: هو أَن يُدْفن طرَفا قِطْعة من الحبْل في الأَرض وفيه عُصَيَّة أَو حُجَير ويظهر منه مثل عُرْوة تُشدّ إِليه الدابة، وقيل: هو حَبْل يُدْفن في الأَرض ويَبْرُز طَرفه فيشدُّ به. قال أَبو منصور: سمعت بعضَ العرب يقول للحبْل الذي يُدْفن في الأَرض مَثْنِيّاً ويَبْرُز طرَفاه الآخران شبه حلقة وتشدّ به الدابة آخِيَّةٌ. وقال أَعرابي لآخر: أَخِّ لي آخِيَّةً أَربط إِليها مُهْري؛ وإِنما تُؤَخَّى الآخِيَّةُ في سُهولة الأَرضين لأَنها أَرْفق بالخيل من الأَوْتاد الناشِزة عن الأَرض، وهي أَثبت في الأَرض السَّهْلة من الوَتِد. ويقال للأَخِيَّة: الإِدْرَوْنُ، والجمع الأَدارين.

ندر (لسان العرب) والأَندَرُون فِتْيان من مواضع شتى يجتمعون للشُّرب؛ قال عمرو بن كلثوم: ولا تُبقي خُمور الأَندَرينا واحدهم أَندَرِيٌّ، لمَّا نسَب الخمرَ إلى أهل القرية اجتمعتْ ثلاث ياءات فخفَّفها للضرورة، كما قال الراجز: وما عِلْمي بِسِحْرِ البابِلِينا وقيل: الأَندَرُ قرية بالشام فيها كروم فجمَعها الأَندَرِين، تقول إذا نسَبتَ إليها: هؤلاء الأَندَرِيُّون. قال: وكأَنه على هذ المعنى أَراد خمور الأَندَرِيِّين فخفَّف ياء النسبة، كما قولوا الأَشْعَرِين بمعنى الأَشعريين. وفي حديث عليٍّ، كرم لله وجهه: أَنه أَقبل وعليه أَندَرْوَرْدِيَّةٌ؛ قيل: هي فوق التُّبَّان ودون السراويل تُغطي الركبة، منسوبة إلى صانع أَو مكانٍ. أَبو عمرو: الأَندَرِيّ الحَبْل الغليظ؛ وقال لبيد: مَمَرٌّ كَكَرِّ الأَندَرِيِّ شتيم.

1.21

أمد (مقاييس اللغة) الهمزة والميم والدال، الأمد: الغاية. كلمةٌ واحدة لا يقاس عليها .
مد (مقاييس اللغة) الميم والدال أصلٌ واحدٌ يدلُّ على جَرِّ شيءٍ في طول، واتِّصال شيء بشيء في استطالة .
مدد (لسان العرب) ومَدَّه في الغيِّ والضلال يَمُدُّه مَدًّا ومَدَّ له: أَمْلَى له وتركه. وفي التنزيل العزيز: ويمُدُّهم في طغيانهم يَعْمَهُون؛ أَي يُمْلي ويَلِجُّهم؛ قال: وكذلك مدَّ الله له في العذاب مَدًّا. قال: وأَمَدَّه في الغي لغة قليلة.
عمد (مقاييس اللغة) العين والميم والدال أصلٌ كبير، فروعه كثيرة ترجع إلى معنىً، وهو الاستقامة في الشيء، منتصباً أو ممتداً، وكذلك في الرَّأي وإرادةِ الشيء. من ذلك عَمَدْتُ فلاناً وأنا أَعْمِدُه عَمْداً، إذا قصدتُ إليه. قال الخليل: والعَمْد: أنْ تعمِد الشَّيءَ بعمادٍ يُمسِكه ويَعتمِد عليه. قال ابن دُرَيد: عَمَدْت الشَّيءَ: أسندتُه. وعَميد القوم: سيِّدهم ومُعْتَمَدُهم الذي يعتمِدونه إذا حَزَبهم [أمرٌ] فزعوا إليه. قال الخليل: العَمْد: أن تكابِد أمراً بِجِدٍّ ويقين. تقول: فعلت ذلك عَمْداً وَعَمْدَ عين، وَتعمَّدت له وفعلته مُعتمِداً، أي متعمّداً.ومن الباب: السَّنام العَمِدُ [عَمِدَ] يَعْمَد عَمَداً.
ويقولون: الزمْ عُمْدَتَك، أي قَصْدَك.
عند (لسان العرب) والمُعانَدَةُ والعِنادُ: أَن يَعْرِفَ الرجلُ الشيء فيأْباه ويميل عنه؛ ويقال: هو يمشي وَسَطاً لا عَنَداً. وعَنَدَ الدمُ يَعْنُد إِذا سال في جانب. وعانِدَةُ الطريق: ما عُدِلَ عنه فعَنَدَ؛ والعَنَدُ الاعتراض؛ والعَنَدُ، بالتحريك: الجانب. وعانَدَ فلانٌ فلاناً إِذا جانبه. والعُنُودُ: كأَنه الخِلافُ والتَّباعُدُ والترك؛ ويقال: استَعْنَدَني فلان من بين القوم أَي قَصَدَني.

1.22

عشا (لسان العرب) تقول: أَوْطَأْتني عَشْوَةً أَي أَمراً مُلتَبِساً، وذلك إِذا أَخْبَرْته بما أَوْقَعْته به في حَيْرَةٍ أَو بَلِيَّة. والعُشْوة، بالضم والفتح والكسر: الأَمْرُ المُلْتَبس.
عشو (مقاييس اللغة) العين والشين والحرف المعتل أصلٌ صحيحٌ يدلُّ على ظلامٍ وقِلَّةِ وُضوحٍ في الشيء، ثم يفرَع منه ما يقاربُه. من ذلك العِشاء، وهو أوَّل ظلامِ الليل. وعَشْواءُ الليل: ظُلمتُه. والتَّعاشي: التَّجاهُل في الأمر.
عسا (لسان العرب) وعَسا الليلُ: اشتدت ظُلْمته؛ وعَسا النباتُ عُسُوّاً: غَلُظَ واشْتَدَّ؛
عسو/ي (مقاييس اللغة) العين والسين والحرف المعتل أصلٌ صحيحٌ يدلُّ على قوّةٍ واشتدادٍ في الشَّيء. يقال: عَسَا الشَّيءُ يعسو، إذا اشتدّ.
عتا (لسان العرب) عَتَا يَعْتُو عُتُوّاً وعِتِيّاً: اسْتَكْبَرَ وجاوَزَ الحَدَّ،
أَذِيَ (القاموس المحيط) أَذِيَ به، كبَقِيَ، بالكسر أَذًى وتأذَّى،

نظر (لسان العرب) والمَنْظَرةُ موضع الرَّبيئةِ. غيره: والمَنظَرةُ موضع في رأْس جبل فيه رقيب ينظر العدوّ يَحْرُسه. الجوهري: والمَنظَرةُ المَرْقَبة. وناظُورُ الزرع والنخل وغيرهما: حَافِظُه؛ وفي الحديث: إِن الله لا يَنْظُر إِلى صُوَرِكم وأَموالكم ولكن إِلى قلوبكم وأَعمالكم؛ فجعل نَظَرهُ إِلى ما هو للسِّرِّ واللُّبِّ، وهو القلب والعمل؛ قال عُرْوَةُ بن الوَرْد: إِذا بَعُدُوا لا يأْمَنُونَ اقْتِرابَهُ، تَشَوُّفَ أَهلِ الغائبِ المُتَنَظَّرِ وقوله أَنشده ابن الأَعرابي: ولا أَجْعَلُ المعروفَ حِلَّ أَلِيَّةٍ، ولا عِدَةً في النَّاظِرِ المُتَغَيَّبِ فسره فقال: الناظر هنا على النَّسَب أَو على وضع فاعل موضع مفعول؛ هذا معنى قوله، ومَثَّله بِسِرٍّ كاتم أَي مكتوم. والنَّظْرةُ الهيئةُ. وتناظَرت الدَّاران: تقابلتا. ونَظَرَ إِليك الجبلُ: قابلك. والتَّنَظُّرُ توقّع الشيء. ابن سيده: والتَّنَظُّرُ تَوَقُّعُ ما تَنْتَظِرُهُ. والنَّظِرَةُ، بكسر الظاء: التأْخير في الأَمر. والتَّناظُرُ: التَّراوُضُ في الأَمر. ونَظِيرُك: الذي يُراوِضُك وتُناظِرُهُ، وناظَرَه من المُناظَرَة. والنَّظِيرُ: المِثْلُ، وقيل: المثل في كل شيء. وفلان نَظِيرُك أَي مِثْلُك لأَنه إِذا نَظَر إِليهما النَّاظِرُ رآهما سواءً. الجوهري: ونَظِيرُ الشيء مِثْلُه. وحكى أَبو عبيدة: النِّظْر والنَّظِير بمعنًى مثل النِّدِّ والنَّدِيدِ؛ والنَّظْرةُ سُوءُ الهيئة. وفيه نَظْرَةٌ أَي قبح؛
رجم (لسان العرب) والرَّجْمُ الهِجْرانُ، والرَّجْمُ الطَّرْدُ، والرَّجْمُ الظن، والرجم السَّب والشتم. والمَراجِمُ: الكَلِمُ القَبيحة. وتَراجَموا بينهم بمَراجِمَ: تراموْا. ولسان مِرْجَمٌ إِذا كان قَوَّالاً.
ظر (مقاييس اللغة) الظاء والراء أصلٌ صحيحٌ واحدٌ يدلُّ على حَجَرٍ محدَّد الطَّرَف. وأظرَّ الرَّجُل: مَشَى على الظِّرَار. ويقال المَظَرَّةُ: الحجر يُقدح به .
نصر (لسان العرب) النَّصر: إِعانة المظلوم؛ والانتصار: الانتقام. والمُسْتَنْصِر السَّائل. ووقف أَعرابيّ على قوم فقال: انْصُرُوني نَصَركم الله أَي أَعطُوني أَعطاكم الله.
مصر (لسان العرب)والمِصْرُ الحاجز والحَدُّ بين الشيئين؛ ويقال: اشترى الدار بِمُصُورها أَي بحدودها. والمِصْرُ الحدّ في كل شيء، وقيل: المصر الحَدُّ في الأَرض خاصة. والمِصْران الكوفةُ والبصرةُ؛
صرر (لسان العرب) وكلُّ شيء جمعته، فقد، صَرَرْته؛ ومنه قيل للأَسير: مَصْرُور لأَن يَدَيْه جُمِعتا إِلى عُنقه؛

بصر (لسان العرب) وأَبْصَرْتُ الشيءَ: رأيته. وبَصرُ القلب: نَظَرهُ وخاطره. وقال ابن بزرج: أَبْصِرْ إِلَيَّ أي انظر إِلَيَّ، وقيل: أَبصِرْ إِلَيَّ أي التفتْ إِلَيَّ. والبَصْرَتان الكوفة والبصرة.
بصر (الصّحاح في اللغة) والبُصْرُ بالضم: الجانبُ والحرفُ من كلّ شيء.
مسر (لسان العرب) مَسَرَ الشيءَ يَمْسُرُه مَسْراً: استخرجه من ضيق، والمَسْرُ فعل الماسِر. ومَسَرْتُ به ومَحَلْتُ به أي سَعَيْتُ به. والماسِرُ: الساعي .
نسر (الصّحاح في اللغة) والناسورُ بالسين والصاد جميعاً: عِلَّةٌ تحدث في مآقي العين، يَسْقي فلا ينقطع.

شعف (لسان العرب) شَعَفَةُ كلِّ شيء: أعلاه. وشعَفةُ الجبل، بالتحريك: رأسه، والجمع شَعَفٌ وشِعافٌ وشُعوفٌ وهي رؤوس الجبال. وشَعَفْتُ البعيرَ بالقَطِرانِ إذا شَعَلته به. وشعَفه الهَوى إذا بلغ منه، وفلان مَشْعُوفٌ بفلانة، وقراءة الحسن شَعَفَها، بالعين المهملة، هو من قولهم شُعِفْتُ بها كأنه ذَهَبَ بها كل مَذهب، وقيل: بطَنها حُباً. وشعَفه حُبُّها يَشْعَفُه إذا ذهب بفؤاده مثل شعفه المرض إذا أذابه. وشعَفه الحُبُّ: أحرق قلبه، وقيل: أمرضه. وبه شُعافٌ أي جُنون. ومعنى شُعِفَ بفلان إذا ارتفع حُبُّه إلى أعلى المواضع من قلبه، قال: وهذا مذهب الفرّاء، وقال غيره: الشَّعَفُ الذُّعر، فالمعنى هو مَذعُورٌ خائف قَلِقٌ. الشَّعَفُ: شِدَّةُ الفزَع حتى يذهب بالقلب؛
شعف (مقاييس اللغة) الشين والعين والفاء يدلُّ على أعالي الشيء ورأسه. فالشَّعَفة: رأس الجبل، والجمع شَعَفات وشَعَفٌ. وضُرب فلانٌ على شَعفات رأسه، أي أعالي رأسه.
شعب (لسان العرب) الشَّعْبُ: الجمعُ، والتَّفريقُ، والإِصلاحُ، والإِفسادُ: ضِدٌّ. وتَشَعَّبَتْ أغصانُ الشجرة، وانْشَعَبَتْ: انْتَشَرت وتفرَّقَتْ. والتَّشَعُّبُ التفرُّق. وانْشَعَبَ الطريقُ: تَفَرَّقَ؛ وانشعَبَ به القولُ: أَخَذ به من مَعْنًى إِلى مَعْنًى مُفارِقٍ للأَولِ؛ وشُعَبُ الجبالِ: رُؤُوسُها؛ وقيل: ما تفرَّقَ من رؤوسها. وفي حديث ابن مسعود: الشَّبابُ شُعْبة من الجُنون، إِنما جَعَله شُعْبَةً منه، لأَنَّ الجُنون يُزِيلُ العَقْلَ، وكذلك الشَّبابُ قد يُسرِعُ إِلى قِلَّةِ العَقْلِ، لِما فيه من كثرة المَيْلِ إِلى الشَّهوات، والإِقْدامِ على المَضارِّ. قال أبو أُسامة: هذه الطَّبقات على ترتيب خَلْق الإِنسان، فالشَّعبُ أَعظَمُها، مُشْتَقٌّ من شَعْب الرَّأْس .
سعب (لسان العرب) وانْسَعبَ الماءُ وانْثَعبَ إِذا سالَ. وتَسَعَّبَ الشيءُ: تَمَطَّط. والسَّعْبُ كلُّ ما تَسعَّبَ من شرابٍ أَو غيره.
سعف (لسان العرب) السَّعَفُ: أَغصانُ النخلة، وأَكثر ما يقال إِذا يبست، وإِذا كانت رَطْبة، فهي الشَّطْبةُ؛
سعف (مقاييس اللغة) السين والعين والفاء أصلان متباينان، يدلُّ أحدُهما على يُبْس شيء وتشعُّثه. والتَّشعيثُ: التفريق والتميز، كانْشعاب الأنهار والأغصان؛
شأف (لسان العرب) شَئِفَ صدرُه عليَّ شَأَفاً: غَمِرَ. والشأْفَةُ العداوةُ؛ والشآفةُ العداوةُ؛ وفي الأفعال: شَئِفْتُ الرجل شآفةً، بالمد، أبغضته، وقلب شَئِفٌ؛ وأَنشد: يا أَيُّها الجاهلُ، أَلاَ تَنْصَرِفْ، ولم تُداوِ قَرْحَةَ القلب الشَّئِفْ أبو زيد: شَئِفْت له شأَفاً إِذا أبغضته.
شأب (لسان العرب) الشَّآبِيبُ مِن المَطَر: الدُّفعاتُ. وشُؤْبُوبُ العَدْو مثله. ابن سيده: الشُّؤْبُوبُ: الدُّفْعة من المطر وغيره .
شبا (القاموس المحيط) شَبا: عَلا، و~ وجْهُه: أضاءَ بعدَ تَغَيُّرٍ، و~ الفَرَسُ: قامتْ على رِجْلَيْها، و~ النارَ: أوْقَدها. و~ الشَّجَرُ: طالَ والتَفَّ نَعْمَةً،
سبأ (الصّحاح في اللغة) أبو زيد: سَبأْتُهُ بالنار أحرقتُهُ.
شبا (لسان العرب) والشَّبْوَ: الأذى. وجاريةٌ شَبْوَةٌ: جريئة كثيرة الحركة فاحشةٌ.
شفف (لسان العرب) شَفَّه الحُزْنُ والحُبُّ يَشُفُّه شَفّاً وشُفوفاً: لذَعَ قَلْبَه، وقيل أَنحله، وقيل أَذْهَبَ عقله؛ واسْتَشَفَّه هو: رأَى ما وراءه. وقد شَفَفْتَ عليه تَشِفُّ أَي زِدْتَ عليه؛ والشفشفة: الارتعادُ والاختلاط. والشَّفْشفةُ: سُوء الظنّ مع الغَيْرة .
سفف (الصّحاح في اللغة) السَفيف: حِزامُ الرَحْل. وسَفيفةٌ من خوص: نسيجةٌ من خوص. وقد سَفَفْتُ الخوصَ أَسُفُّهُ بالضم سَفّاً وأَسْفَفْتُهُ أيضاً، أي نسجتُه. وسَفْسَاف التراب: ما تهى منه. وسَفْسَافُ الدقيق عند النخل: هو ما يرتفع من غباره.
لعا (لسان العرب) ولعاً كلمة يُدعَى بها للعاثر معناها الارتفاع؛

1.23

كرش (الصّحاح في اللغة) الكَرِشُ لكلِّ مُجْتَرٍّ بمنزلة المعدة للإنسان تؤنِّثها العرب.
كرش (مقاييس اللغة) الكاف والراء والشين أصلٌ صحيح يدلُّ على تَجمُّعٍ وجَمْع.
كرس (مقاييس اللغة) الكاف والراء والسين أصلٌ صحيح يدلُّ على تلبُّد شيءٍ فوق شيءٍ وتجمُّعه.
كرس (العباب الزاخر) والانْكِراس: الانْكِباب، وقد انْكَرَسَ في الشَّيْءِ: إذا دَخَلَ فيه مُنْكَبّاً،
كرس (لسان العرب) تكَرَّسَ الشيءُ وتكارَسَ: تراكَمَ وتلازَبَ. وتكرَّس أُسُّ البناء: صَلُبَ واشتدَّ. ابن الأَعرابي: كَرِس الرجل إِذا ازدحمَ عِلمه على قلبه؛ قال ابن عباس: كُرْسِيُّه عِلْمه،
قرش (مقاييس اللغة) القاف والراء والشين أصلٌ صحيح يدلُّ على الجمع والتجمُّع. فالقَرْش: الجمع، يقال تَقَرَّشوا، إذا تجمَّعوا.
كرث (مقاييس اللغة) الكاف والراء والثاء، ليس فيه إلاّ كَرَثَهُ الأمرُ، إذا بلغ منه المَشقَّة.
كرث (لسان العرب) كَرَثَه الأَمْرُ يَكْرِثُه ويَكْرُثُه كَرْثاً، وأَكْرَثَه: ساءه واشتدَّ عليه، وبَلَغ منه المَشَقَّة،
قرس (لسان العرب) وقَرَسَ البَرْدُ يَقْرِس قَرْساً: اشتدَ، وفيه لغة أُخرى قَرِس قَرَساً؛

دله (لسان العرب) الدَّلَهُ والدَّلَهُ: ذهابُ الفُؤاد من هَمٍّ أَو نحوه كما يَدْلَهُ عقل الإِنسان من عشق أَو غيره، وقد دَلَهَهُ الهَمُّ أَو العِشقُ فتدَلَّه. والمرأَةُ تَدَلَّهُ على ولدها إِذا فَقَدَتْه. ودُلِّهَ الرجلُ: حُيِّرَ، ودَلَّه عقلَه تَدْليهاً. والمُدَلَّهُ الذي لا يحفظ ما فعل ولا ما فُعِلَ به.

والتَّدَلُّه ذهابُ العقل من الهوى؛ أنشد ابن بري: ما السّنُّ إلا غَفْلَةُ المُدَلَّهِ ويقال: دَلَّهَهُ الحُبُّ أي حَيَّره وأدْهَشه، ودَلِهَ هو يَدْلَهُ. ابن سيده: وَدَلَهَ يَدْلَهُ دُلُوهاً سَلا.

دله (مقاييس اللغة) الدال واللام والهاء أَصيلٌ يدلُّ على ذَهاب الشّيء. يقال ذهب دَمُ فُلانٍ دَلْهاً، أي بُطْلاً. وَدَلَّهَ عقله الحُبُّ وغيرُه، أي أذهب .

الدَّلْهُ (القاموس المحيط) ودَلِهَ، كفَرِحَ: تَحَيَّرَ، أو جُنَّ عِشْقاً أو غَمًّا.

1.24

شور (لسان العرب) والشَّارَة والشُّوْرَة: الحُسْن والهيئة واللِّباس، وقيل: الشُّوْرَة الهيئة. والشَّوْرَة: الجَمال الرائع. والشَّوْرَة: الخَجْلَة. والشَّيِّر: الجَمِيل. وأشار إِليه وشَوَّر: أَومأَ، يكون ذلك بالكفّ والعين والحاجب؛ وأَشارَ إِليه باليَدِ: أَومأَ، وأَشارَ عليه بالرَّأْي. وأَشار يُشِير إِذا ما وَجَّه الرَّأْي. ويقال: فلان جيِّد المَشُورة والمَشْوَرَة، لغتان. قال الفراء: المَشُورة أَصلها مَشْوَرَة ثم نقلت إِلى مَشُورة لخفَّتها. اللَّيث: المَشْوَرَة مفْعَلَة اشتُقَّ من الإِشارة، ويقال: مَشُورة. أَبو سعيد: يقال فلان وَزِيرُ فلان وشَيِّرُه أَي مُشاوِرُه، وجمعه شُوَرَاءُ. وقصيدة شَيِّرَة أي حسناء.وشيءٌ مَشُورٌ أي مُزَيَّنٌ؛ الفراء: إِنه لحسن الصُّورة والشُّوْرَة، وإِنه لحسَن الشَّوْر والشَّوار، واحده شَوْرَة وشَوارة، أَي زينته. وشُرتُه: زَيَّنْتُه، فهو مَشُور.

سعر (مقاييس اللغة) السين والعين والراء أصل واحدٌ يدل على اشتعال [الشيء] واتّقاده وارتفاعه. قال ابن السِّكيت: ويقال سَعَرهم شَرّاً، ولا يقال أسْعَرَهُم.ومن هذا الباب: السُّعْر، وهو الجنون، وسمّي بذلك لأنّه يَسْتعِر في الإنسان. ويقولون ناقة مسعورة. وذلك لِحدّتها كأنّها مجنونة. فأمّا سِعْر الطعام فهو من هذا أيضاً؛ لأنّه يرتفع ويعلو. فأمَّا مساعِر البعير فإنَّها مشاعِرُهُ.

شعر (الصّحاح في اللغة) والشَعائِرُ: أعمالُ الحجِّ.

شعر (لسان العرب) شَعَرَ به وشَعُرَ يَشْعُر شِعْراً وشَعْراً وشِعْرَةً ومَشْعُورَةً وشُعُوراً وشُعُورَةً وشِعْرَى ومَشْعُوراءَ ومَشْعُوراً؛ الأَخيرة عن اللحياني، كله: عَلِمَ. والشِّعْرُ منظوم القول. وشِعارُ الحج: مناسكه وعلاماته وآثاره وأَعماله، جمع شَعِيرَة، وكل ما جعل عَلَماً لطاعة الله عز وجل كالوقوف والطواف والسعي والرمي والذبح وغير ذلك؛

دعر (مقاييس اللغة) الدال والعين والراء أصلٌ واحد يدلُّ على كراهةٍ وأذىً، وأصله الدُّخَان؛

دعر (لسان العرب) ورجل دُعَرَةٌ: فيه ذلك، وحكاه كراع ذُعْرَة، بالذال المعجمة وسكون العين، وذُعَرَةٌ؛

درأ (العباب الزاخر) واندَرَأ: أي اطلع مفاجأة. وتدارَأْتُم أي اختلفتم وتدافعتم، وكذلك ادّارأتم؛ أصله تدارأتم، فأُدغمت التاء في الدال واجتُلِبَتِ الأف ليصح الابتداء بها.

ذأر (لسان العرب) ذَئِرَ الرجلُ: فَزِعَ.

ذعر (لسان العرب) الذُّعْرُ، بالضم: الخَوْفُ والفَزَعُ، وهو الاسم. ذَعَرَهُ يَذْعَرُهُ ذَعْراً فانْذَعَرَ، وهو مُنْذَعِرٌ، وأَذْعَرَه، كلاهما: أَفزعنه وصيره إِلى الذُّعْرِ؛

عدر (لسان العرب) والعُدْرةُ الجُرأَة والإِقدام.

ودر (لسان العرب) وَدَّر الرجل تَوْديراً: أَوقعه في مَهْلكة. ابن الأَعرابي: تهَوَّل في الأَمر وتورَّط وتوَدَّر بمعنى مال .

مالَ (القاموس المحيط) مالَ إليه مَيْلاً ومَمالاً ومَمِيلاً وتَمْيالاً ومَيَلاناً ومَيْلولَةً: عَدَلَ، فهو مائِلٌ ج: مالَةٌ ومُيَّلٌ، كرُكَّعٍ. ومالَهُ وأمالَهُ إليه ومَيَّلَهُ فاستَمَالَ. وأمالَ: رَعَى الخَلَّةَ. و~ بنا الطريقُ: قَصَدَ. و~ بقَلْبِه: أمالَهُ. "والمائِلاتُ" في الحديثِ: اللاتِي يَمِلْنَ خُيَلاءَ، و"المُمِيلاتُ": اللاتِي يُمِلْنَ قُلوبَنا إليهِنَّ، أو يُمِلْنَ المَقانِعَ لتَظْهَرَ وُجوهُهُنَّ وشُعُورُهُنَّ.

1.25

نشر (لسان العرب) ونَشَر الخشبة ينشُرها نشراً: نَحتها، وفي الصحاح: قطعها بالمِنْشار.

نسر (لسان العرب) نَسَرَ الشيءَ: كشَطَه.

نسر (مقاييس اللغة) النون والسين والراء أصلٌ صحيح يدلُّ على اختلاس* واستلاب. منه النَّسْر: تناوُلُ شيءٍ من طعام. ونَسَرَهُ، كأنَّه شيءٌ يسيرٌ استلبَه. ومنه النَّسْر، كأنَّه ينسُرُ الشَّيء. والمِنْسَر خيل ما بين المائة إلى المائتين وهو القياس، كأنّه إنما جاء لينسرَ شيئاً، أي يختطفه ويَستلبَه. ويقال: بَلِ المِنْسَر لا يمرُّ بشيءٍ إلا قلعه.

رجم (لسان العرب) والرَّجْمُ الهِجْرانُ، والرَّجْمُ الطَّرْدُ، والرَّجْمُ الظن، والرجم السَّب والشتم. والمَراجمُ: الكلِمُ القَبيحة. وتَراجَموا بينهم بمَراجِمَ: تَرامَوْا. ولسان مِرْجَمٌ إِذا كان قَوَّالاً.

1.26

كمم (لسان العرب) قال العجاج: بَل لو شَهِدتَ الناسَ إِذ تُكُمُّوا بِغُمَّةٍ، لو لم تُفَرَّج غُمُّوا وتُكُمُّوا أَي أُغْمِيَ عليهم وغُطُّوا. قال ابن الأَثير: كَمَكَمْت الشيء إذا أَخفيته. وكَمَمْت الشيء: غَطَّيته. والمِغَمَّة والمِكَمَّة: شيءٌ يُوضع على أَنف الحِمار كالكِيس، وكذلك الغِمامةُ والكِمامة. والكِمامُ: ما سُدَّ به. والكِمام، بالكسر، والكِمامة: شيءٌ يُسدُّ به فم البعير والفرس لئلا يَعض. والكَمُّ: قَمْعُ الشيء وستره، ومنه كَممت الشهادة إذا قمَعْتَها وسَترْتَها، والغُمَّة ما غَطَّاك من شيء؛ المعنى بل لو (* قوله «المعنى بل لو إلخ» كذا بالأصل وفيه سقط ظاهر، ولعل الأصل: المعنى بل لو شهدت الناس إذ تكميوا أي غطوا وستروا الأصل تكممت إلخ كما يؤخذ من سابق الكلام). شهدت الأصل تكَمَّمت مثل تَقَمَّيْتُ، الأَصل تقَمَّمْتُ.

قمم (لسان العرب) والقَميم: السويق؛ عن اللحياني؛ وأنشد: تُعَلِّلُ بالنَّبيذةِ حين تُمسي، وبالمَعْوِ المُكَمَّمِ والقَميمِ (* قوله «بالنبيذة» كذا في الأصل والمحكم هنا، والذي في المحكم في كمم وفي معو: بالنهيدة؛ وفسر النهيدة بالزبدة).

وجه (مقاييس اللغة) الواو والجيم والهاء: أصلٌ واحد يدلُّ على مقابلةٍ لشيء. والوجه مستقبِلٌ لكلِّ شيء. يقال وَجْه الرَّجلِ وغيرِه. وأصل جِهَتِهِ وِجْهَته.

1.27

المَرْصُ (القاموس المحيط) المَرْصُ لِلثَّدْيِ ونحوِهِ: الغَمْزُ بالأَصابعِ. والمَرُوصُ، كصَبُورٍ: النَّاقَةُ السَّريعَةُ. ومَرَصَ: سَبَقَ. وتَمَرَّصَ القِشْرُ عن السُّلْتِ: طارَ .

مرص (مقاييس اللغة) الميم والراء والصاد. يقولون: المَرْص مثل المَرْش.

مرش (لسان العرب) المَرْش: شِبْهُ القَرْص من الجِلْد بأَطراف الأَظافير. ويقال: قد أَلطف مَرْشاً وخَرْشاً، والخَرْش أَشدُّه. وامترَشْتُ الشيء إذا اختَلسته. ابن الأَعرابي: الأَمرَشُ الرجلُ الكثيرُ الشرِّ؛ يقال: مَرَشه إذا آذاه.

مرس (لسان العرب) والمَرْسُ: الشيءُ يُمْرَسُ في الماء حتى يتَمَيَّثَ فيه.

مرث (مقاييس اللغة) الميم والراء والثاء كلمةٌ ليست بأصل، بل هي من الإبدال. ومَرَثَ الدواءَ يَمْرُثه مثل مَرَسه يمرُسُه.

مرض (الصِّحَاح في اللغة) المَرَضُ: السَقَمُ. وقد مَرِضَ فلان وأَمْرَضَهُ الله. قال يعقوب: يقال: أَمْرَضَ الرجلُ، إذا وقع في ماله العاهَةُ.

المَرَضُ (القاموس المحيط) المَرَضُ: إظلامُ الطَّبيعةِ، واضْطِرابُها بعدَ صفائِهَا واعْتِدالِها، مَرِضَ، كفَرِحَ، مَرَضاً ومَرْضاً، فهو مَرِضٌ ومَريضٌ ومارِضٌ ج: مِراضٌ ومَرْضَى ومَراضَى، أو المَرْضُ، بالفتح: للقَلْبِ خاصَّةً، وبالتحريكِ أو كلاهُما: الشكُّ، والنِّفاقُ، والفُتورُ، والظُّلْمةُ، والنُّقْصانُ. وتَمَرَّضَ: ضَعُفَ في أمرِه.

مرض (مقاييس اللغة) الميم* والراء والضاد أصلٌ صحيح يدلُّ على ما يخرج به الإنسان عن حدّ الصِّحَة في أيّ شيءٍ كان. منه العِلّة. والنِّفاق مرضٌ في قوله تعالى: في قُلوبِهِمْ مَرَضٌ [البقرة 10] وقال: فَيَطْمَعَ الذي في قَلْبِهِ مَرَضٌ [الأحزاب 32]، قالوا: أراد القَهْر.

مرض (لسان العرب) والمَرَضُ السُّقْمُ نَقيضُ الصِّحَّة. ومَرِضَ فلان مَرَضاً ومَرْضاً، فهو مارِضٌ ومَرِضٌ ومَريض، والأُنثى مَريضةٌ؛ ابن الأَعرابي: أَصل المَرَض النُّقْصانُ، وهو بَدَنٌ مريض ناقِصُ القوّة. ويقال: أتيت فلاناً فأَمرَضْته أي وجدته مريضاً. وليلة مريضةٌ إذا تَغَيَّمَت السماء فلا يكون فيها ضَوء؛ قال أبو حَيَّة: وليْلة مَرِضَتْ من كلّ ناحيةٍ، فلا يُضِيءُ لها نَجْمٌ ولا قَمَرُ ورأْيٌ مَريضٌ: فيه انحراف عن الصواب، وفسر ثعلب بيت أبي حبة فقال: وليلة مَرِضَتْ أظلمت ونقصَ نورها. وليلةٌ مريضةٌ: مُظلِمة لا تُرى فيها كواكِبُها؛ وروي عن ابن الأَعرابي أيضاً قال: المرَضُ إظْلامُ الطبيعةِ واضْطِرابُها بعد صَفائها واعْتدالها، قال: والمرَضُ الظُّلْمةُ.

عبش (لسان العرب) ابن الأَعرابي: العَبْش الصَّلاحُ في كل شيء.

صلح (لسان العرب) الصَّلاح: ضدّ الفساد؛ ورجل صالح في نفسه من قوم صُلَحاء ومُصْلِح في أَعماله وأُموره. وأَصْلَح الشيءَ بعد فساده: أَقامه.

أبش (لسان العرب) الأَبْشُ: الجمْع. وقد أبشه وأَبَش لأهله يَأْبِشُ أَبْشاً: كَسَب. ورجل أَبّاش: مكتسِب.

أبش (مقاييس اللغة) الهمزة والباء والشين ليس بأصل، لأنَ الهمزة فيه مبدلة من هاء. قال ابن دريد: أبَشْتُ الشيء وهَبَشْتُه إذا جمعته .

هبش (الصِّحَاح في اللغة) الهَبْشُ: الجمعُ والكسبُ. يقال: هو يَهْبِشُ لعياله، ويَتَهَبَّشُ فهو هَبَّاشٌ.

عفش (لسان العرب) عَفَشَه يَعْفِشُه عَفْشاً: جمعه.

عفس (مقاييس اللغة) العين والفاء والسين أصل صحيح يدلُّ على ممارسَة ومعالجة. يقولون: هو يعافس الشَيء، إذا عالَجَه.

عفس (لسان العرب) العَفْس: شِدَّة سَوق الإبل. عَفَس الإبلَ يَعْفِسُها عَفْساً: ساقها سَوْقاً شديداً؛ قال: يَعْفِسُها السَّواق كلَّ مَعْفَسِ والعَفْسُ: أن يردَّ الراعي غنمه يثْنِيها ولا يدعُها تمضي على جهاتها. وعَفَسَه عن حاجته أي ردَّه. والعَفْسُ الامتهانُ للشيءِ.

والعَفْسُ الضَّباطة في الصِّراع. والعَفْس الدَّوْس. والمُعافَسَة: المُداعبة والمُمارَسَة؛ يقال: فلان يُعافِس الأُمور أي يُمارِسُها ويُعالجها. والعِفاس: العِلاج. والمُعافَسة: المُعَالجَة. وتَعافسَ القومُ: اعتلجوا في صراع ونحوه. وانعفس في الماء: انغمَسَ. والعَفَّاس: طائر يَنْعَفِس في الماء .

1.28

ألك (لسان العرب) في ترجمة علج: يقال هذا أَلوكُ صِدْقٍ وعَلوك صِدْقٍ وعَلوج صِدْقٍ لما يؤكل، وما تلَوَّكْتُ بأَلوكٍ وما تَعَلَّجْتُ بعَلوج. الليث: الأَلوك الرسالة وهي المَأْلُكة، على مَفْعُلة، سميت أَلوكاً لأَنه يُؤْلَكُ في الفم مشتق من قول العرب: الفرس يَأْلُك اللُّجُم، والمعروف يَلوك أَو يَعْلُك أَي يمضغ. ابن سيده: أَلَكَ الفرسُ اللجام في فيه يَأْلُكه عَلَكه. والأَلوك والمَأْلُكة والمَأْلَكة: الرسالة لأَنها تُؤْلَك في الفم؛ وأَلَكه يأْلِكه أَلْكاً: أَبلغه الأَلوك. والملائكة: جمع مَلأَكة ثم ترك الهمز فقيل مَلَك في الوحدان، وأَصله مَلأَك كما ترى. ويقال: جاء فلان قد استَأْلَكَ مَأْلُكَته أَي حمل رسالته. وأَلَكه يأْلِكه أَلْكاً: أَبلغه الأَلوك. ابن الأَنباري: يقال أَلِكْني إِلى فلان يراد به أَرسلني، وللاثنين أَلِكاني وأَلِكوني وأَلِكيني وأَلِكاني وأَلِكْنَني، والأَصل في أَلِكْني أَلْئِكْني فحولت كسرة الهمزة إلى اللام وأَسقطت الهمزة؛ وأَنشد: أَلِكْني إِليها بخيرِ الرسو ل، أَعْلَمُهُم بنواحي الخَبَرْ قال: ومن بنى على الأَلوك قال: أَصل أَلِكْني أَأْلِكْني فحذفت الهمزة الثانية تخفيفاً؛ وأَنشد: أَلِكْني يا عُيَيْنُ إِليكَ قولا قال أَبو منصور: أَلِكْني أَلِكْ لي، وقال ابن الأَنباري: أَلِكْني إِليه أَي كُنْ رسولي إِليه؛ وقا ل أَبو عبيد في قوله: أَلِكْني يا عُيَيْنُ إِليكَ عني أَي أَبلغ عني الرسالة إِليك، والمَلَكُ مشتق منه، وأَصله مَأْلَك، ثم قلبت الهمزة إِلى موضع اللام فقيل ملأَك، ثم خففت الهمزة بأَن أَلقيت حركتها على الساكن الذي قبلها فقيل مَلَك؛ وقد يستعمل متمماً والحذف أَكثر: فلسْتَ لإِنسيٍّ،

لأك (لسان العرب) المَلأَكُ والمَلأَكَةُ: الرسالة. واسْتَلأَكَ له: ذهب برسالته، عن أَبي علي.

ملك (مقاييس اللغة) الميم واللام والكاف أصلٌ صحيح يدلُّ على قوّةٍ في الشيء وصحة. يقال: أملَكَ عجينَه: قَوّى عَجنَه وشَدَّه. وملَكتُ الشَّيءَ: قَوَيتُه.
ملك (الصّحاح في اللغة) ومِلاكُ الأمرِ ومَلاكُهُ: ما يقوم به. ويقال القلب مِلاكُ الجسد. وما تمالَكَ أن قال ذلك، أي ما تماسك. ويقال أيضاً: الماءُ مَلَكُ أمرٍ، أي يقوم به الأمر.
ملك (لسان العرب) الليث: المَلِكُ هو الله، تعالى ونقدّس، مَلِكُ المُلوك له المُلْكُ وهو مالك يوم الدين وهو مَلِيكُ الخلق أي ربهم ومالكهم. والمُلْكُ معروف وهو يذكر ويؤنث كالسُّلْطان؛ ومُلْكُ الله تعالى ومَلَكُوته: سلطانه وعظمته. والمَلْكُ والمَلِكُ والمَلِيكُ والمالِكُ: ذو المُلْك. وما له مَلْكٌ ومِلْكٌ ومُلْكٌ ومُلُكٌ أي شيء يملكه؛ ومِلاكُ الأمر ومَلاكُه: قِوامُه الذي يُمْلَكُ به وصَلاحُه. وفي التهذيب: ومِلاكُ الأمر الذي يُعْتَمَدُ عليه، ومَلاكُ الأمر ومِلاكُه ما يقوم به. والمَلْكُ: ما ملكت اليد من مال وخَوَل. والمَلَكة مَلْكُكَ، والمَمْلَكة: سلطانُ المَلِك في رعيته.. وتمالَكَ عن الشيء: مَلَكَ نَفْسَه. وفي الحديث: امْلِكْ عليك لسانَك أي لا تُجْرِه إلا بما يكون لك لا عليك. وليس له مِلاكٌ أي لا يَتمالك. وما تَمالَك أن قال ذلك أي ما تماسَكَ ولا يَتماسَك. وما تمالَكَ فلان أن وقع في كذا إذا لم يستطع أن يحبس نفسه؛ قال الشاعر: فلا تَمْلِكُ عن أَرضٍ لها عَمَدُوا ويقال: نفسي لا تُمالِكُني لأن أفعلَ كذا أي لا تُطاوعني. وفلان ما له مَلاكٌ، بالفتح، أي تَماسُكٌ. وفي حديث آدم: فلما رآه أَجْوَفَ عَرَفَ أنه خَلق لا يَتمالَك أي لا يَتماسَك. وإذا وصف الإنسان بالخفة والطَّيْش قيل: إنه لا يَتمالَكُ. ومِلاكُ الأمر ومَلاكُه: قِوامُه الذي يُمْلَكُ به وصَلاحُه. وما تَمالكَ فلان أن وقع في كذا إذا لم يستطع أن يحبس نفسه؛ ومَلْكُ ا لطريق ومَمْلَكَتُه: مُعْظَمه ووسطه؛

جمل (مقاييس اللغة) الجيم والميم واللام أصلان: أحدهما تجمُّع وعِظَم الخَلْق، والآخر حُسْنٌ. فالأوّل قولك أجْمَلْتُ الشَّيءَ، وهذه جُمْلة الشَّيء. وأجمَلْتُه حصَّلته .
جمل (الصّحاح في اللغة) وأَجْمَلْتُ الصنيعة عند فلان، وأَجْمَلَ في صنيعه.
الجَمَلُ (القاموس المحيط) وأجملَ الصَّنيعَةَ: حَسَّنَهَا وكَثَّرها.
جمل (لسان العرب) الجَمَل: الذَّكَر من الإِبل. والتَّجَمُّل تكَلُّف الجَمِيل. والمُجاملة: المُعاملة بالجَمِيل، الفراء: المُجَامِل الذي يقدر على جوابك فيتركه إبقاءً على مَوَدَّتك. والمُجَامِل: الذي لا يقدر على جوابك فيتركه ويَحْقد عليك إلى وقت مَا؛ وأَجْمَلْت الصَّنِيعة عند فلان وأَجْمَل في صنيعه وأَجْمَل في طلب الشيء: اتَّأَد واعتدل فلم يُفرط؛ قال: الرِّزق مقسوم فأَجْمِلْ في الطَّلَب وقد أجْمَلت في الطلب. وجَمَّلْت الشيءَ تجميلاً وجَمَّرْته تجميراً إذا أطلت حبسه. والجُمْلة جماعة الشيء. وأَجْمَل الشيءَ: جَمَعه عن تفرقة؛ وأَجْمَل له الحساب كذلك. والجُمْلة جماعة كل شيء بكماله من الحساب وغيره. يقال: أَجْمَلت له الحساب والكلام؛

gamālu

šu ĝar [CARRY OUT] wr. šu ĝar; šu ĝa2-ĝa2 "to carry out (a task)" Akk. gamālu

طابَ (القاموس المحيط) طابَ يَطِيبُ طاباً وطِيباً وطِيبَةً وتَطْياباً: لَذَّ وزَكَا، و~ الأرضُ: أَكْلأَتْ. والطَّابُ: الطَّيِّبُ، وطابه وأطابه: طَيَّبَه.
واسْتَطابَ: اسْتَنْجى. وطِيبَتُها: أَصفاها. وأَطابَ: تَكَلَّم بكَلامٍ طَيِّبٍ. وطِبْتُ به نَفْساً: طابَتْ به نَفْسي. وطايَبَه: مازَحَه.
طيب (لسان العرب) والطَّابُ الطَّيِّبُ والطِّيبُ أيضاً، يُقالان جميعاً. وأَطابَ الشيءَ وطَيَّبَه واسْتَطابه: وجَدَه طَيِّباً. والطَّيِّبُ من كل شيءٍ: أَفْضَلُه. والطَّيِّباتُ من الكلام: أَفضَلُه وأَحسنُه. وطِيبَةُ الكَلإِ: أَخْصَبُه.

1.29

رب (مقاييس اللغة) الراء والباء يدلُّ على أُصول. فالأول إصلاح الشيءِ والقيامُ عليه. فالرَّبُّ: المالكُ، والخالقُ، والصَّاحب.والرَّبُّ: المُصْلح للشَّيء. يقال رَبَّ فلانٌ ضيعته، إذا قام على إصلاحها. وربَبْتُ الصَّبيَّ أَرُبُّه، وربَّبْته أُرَبِّبُه.
ربا (الصّحاح في اللغة) رَبا الشيءُ يَربو رَبْواً، أي زاد. والرابِيَةُ: الرَبْوُ، وهو ما ارتفعَ من الأرض. ورَبَوْتُ الرابِيَةَ: علوتها. وكذلك الرُبْوَةُ بالضم. وفيها أربع لغات: رُبْوَةٌ ورَبْوَةٌ ورِبْوَةٌ ورَباوَةٌ. والرَبْوُ: النفَسُ العالي.
رَبَا (القاموس المحيط) رَبَا رُبُوًّا، كعُلُوٍّ، ورِباءً: زادَ، ونَما، وارتَبَيْتُه، و~ الرابِيَةَ: عَلاها، ورَبَيْتُ رَباءً ورُبِيًّا: نَشَأْتُ. ورَبَّيْتُه تَرْبِيَةً: غَذَوْتُه، كتَرَبَّيْتُه.
ربى/أ (مقاييس اللغة) الراء والباء والحرف المعتل وكذلك المهموز منه يدلُّ على أصلٍ واحد، وهو الزِّيادة والنَّماء والعُلُوّ. والأُرْبِيَّة من هذا الباب، يقال هو في أُرْبِيَّة قومِه، إذا كان في عالي نسبه من أهل بيته. والرَّبْوُ: الجماعة.

1.30

أسس (الصّحاح في اللغة) وأَسَّ الشاةَ يَؤُسُّها أَسّاً، أي زجرها وقال لها: إسْ إسْ.
زجر (لسان العرب) من زَجَرَ الإِبلَ يَزْجُرُها إذا حَثَّها وحَمَلها على السُّرْعَةِ، والمحفوظ رَاجِزٌ، وسنذكره في موضعه؛ ومنه الحديث: فسمع وراءه زَجْراً؛ أي صِياحاً على الإبل وحَثّاً .
أسس (العباب الزاخر) وأَسَّه يَؤُسَّهُ أَساً -أيضاً-: أي أَزَّهُ

أزز (لسان العرب) والأَزَّةُ: الصوتُ. والأَزِيزُ: النَّشِيشُ. والأَزِيزُ: صوت غليان القدر. وأَزَّهُ: حَثَّه.
أسس (لسان العرب) الأُسُّ والأَسَس والأَساس: كل مُبْتَدإِ شيءٍ. وإِسْ إِسْ: من زجر الشاة، أَسَّها يَؤُسُّها أَسّاً، وقال بعضهم: نَسّاً. وأَزَّ الشيءَ يَؤُزُّه إِذا ضم بعضه إِلى بعض.
نسس (العباب الزاخر) النَّسُّ: السَّوْقُ، يقال: نَسَسْتَ النَاقة أنُسُّها نَسّاً: أي زَجَرتُها، ومنه: المِنَسَّة للعَصا.
النَّسُّ (القاموس المحيط) النَّسُّ: السَّوْقُ، والزَّجْرُ،
نسس (لسان العرب) النَّسُّ: المَضاءُ في كل شيء، وخص بعضهم به السرعة في الوِرْدِ؛ والنَّسُّ: السوق الرقيق. وقال شمر: نَسْنَس ونَسَّ مثل نَشَّ ونَشْنَشَ، وذلك إِذا ساق وطرد، وحديث عمر: كان يَنُسُّ الناس بعد العشاء بالدِّرَّة ويقول: انصرفوا إِلى بيوتكم؛
السُّوسُ (القاموس المحيط) وسُسْتُ الرَّعِيَّةَ سِياسَةً: أمَرْتُها ونَهَيْتُها.
سوس (الصِّحَاح في اللغة) سُسْتُ الرعيَّة سِياسَةً. وسُوِّسَ الرجلُ أمورَ الناس، على ما لم يسم فاعله، إذا مُلِّكَ أمرهم. وفلان مجرَّبٌ قد ساسَ وسِيسَ عليه، أي أَمَرَ وأُمِّرَ عليه.
سوس (لسان العرب) والسَّوْسُ: الرِّيَاسَةُ، يقال ساسوهم سَوْساً، وإِذا رَأَّسُوه قيل: سَوَّسُوه وأَساسوه. وسَاس الأَمر سِياسةً: قام به، ورجل ساسٌ من قوم ساسة وسُوَّاس؛

شكل (الصِّحَاح في اللغة) والمُشاكَلَةُ: الموافَقةُ. والتَشاكُلُ مثله .
الشَّكْلُ (القاموس المحيط) الشَّكْلُ: الشَّبَهُ، والمِثْلُ، ويُكْسَرُ، وما يُوافِقُكَ ويَصْلُحُ لكَ، تقولُ: هذا من هَوايَ ومن شَكْلِي،
شكل (لسان العرب) الشَّكْلُ، بالفتح: الشِّبْه والمِثْل، والجمع أَشكالٌ وشُكُول؛ والشِّكْل، بالكسر: الدَّلُّ، وبالفتح: المِثْل والمَذْهب. والمُشاكِلُ من الأُمور: ما وافق فاعِلَه ونظيره. وشاكِلَة الشيء: جانبُه؛
صقل (لسان العرب) والصُّقْلة والصُّقْل الخاصِرَة، والصُّقْلان القُرْبانِ من الدَّابة وغيرها، وفي التهذيب: من كلِّ دابَّة؛
سقل (لسان العرب) السُّقْل: لغة في الصُّقْل، وهي الخاصِرة.
خصر (لسان العرب) والخاصِرةُ: الشَّاكِلَةُ. وخاصَرَ الرجلُ صاحبه إِذا أَخذ بيده في المشي. والمُخاصَرَةُ: أَخْذُ الرجل بيد الرجل؛ وتَخاصَرَ القومُ: أَخذ بعضهم بيد بعض. وخرج القوم متخاصرين إِذا كان بعضهم آخذاً بيد بعض.

موم (لسان العرب) وقد مَوَّمَها: عَمِلَها.

1.31

كبت (لسان العرب) وفي التنزيل العزيز: كُبِتُوا كما كُبِتَ الذين من قبلهم؛ وفيه: أَو يَكْبِتَهُمْ فيَنْقَلِبُوا خائبين؛ قال أَبو إِسحق: معنى كُبِتُوا أُذِلُّوا وأُخِذُوا بالعذاب بأَن غُلِبُوا، كما نزل بمن كان قبلهم ممن حادَّ اللهَ؛ وقال الفراء: كُبِتُوا أي غِيظُوا وأُحْزِنُوا يوم الخَنْدَق، كما كُبِتَ من قاتَل الأَنبياء قبلهم؛ قال الأَزهري: وقال من احْتَجَّ للفراء: أَصلُ الكَبْتِ الكَبْدُ، فقلبت الدال تاء، أُخذ من الكبِد، وهو مَعْدِنُ الغَيْظ والأَحْقادِ، فكأَن الغَيْظ، لما بَلَغ بهم مَبْلَغه، أَصابَ أَكبادَهم فأَحْرَقها، ولهذا قيل للأَعداء: هم سُودُ الأَكْباد.
وفي الحديث: أَنه رأَى كَلحةَ حَزِيناً مَكْبُوتاً أَي شديدَ الحُزْن؛ قيل: الأَصل فيه مَكْبُودٌ، بالدال، أَي أَصاب الحُزْنُ كَبِدَه، فقلب الدال تاء. الجوهري: الكَبْتُ الصَّرْفُ والإِذْلال، يقال: كَبَتَ اللهُ العَدُوَّ أَي صَرَفه وأَذَلَّه، وكَبَته: أَي صَرَعَه لوجهه.
كبد (لسان العرب) وكَبِدُ كلِّ شيء: وَسَطُه ومعظمه. وكَبِدُ السماءِ: وسطُها الذي تقوم فيه الشمس عند الزوال، فيقال عند انحطاطها: زالت ومالت. الليث: كَبِدُ السماءِ ما استقبلك من وسَطها. وكَبَّدَ النجمُ السماءَ أَي توسَّطها.

1.32

ePSD: arkatu
eĝir [BACK] wr. eĝir; eĝir5(LUM); egir4; eĝir6(MURGU2) "back, rear; after; estate, inheritence" Akk. arkatu
ePSD: şēru
eden [BACK] wr. eden "back, upper side" Akk. şēru

يا (لسان العرب) حَرْفُ نِداء، وهي عامِلَةٌ في الاسم الصَّحيح وإِن كانت حرفاً، والقولُ في ذلك أَنَّ لِيا في قيامِها مَقامَ الفعل خاصةً ليست للحروف، وذلك أَنَّ الحروفَ قد تَنُوبُ عن الأَفعال. وذلك أَنَّ يا نفسَها هي العامِلُ الواقِعُ على زيد، وحالُها في ذلك حال أَدْعُو وأُنادي. ويا نفسُها في المعنى كأَدْعُو. قال الجوهري: وأَما قوله تعالى أَلا يا اسْجدُوا، بالتخفيف، فالمَعْنى يا هَؤُلاء اسْجُدوا، فحُذِفَ المُنادى اكْتِفاء بحَرف النِّداء كما حُذِفَ حَرْفُ النِّداء اكْتِفاء بالمُنادى في قوله تعالى: يُوسُفُ أَعْرِضْ عَن هَذا؛ إِذْ كان المُراد معْلوماً؛ وقال بعضهم: إِنَّ يا في هذا المَوْضِع إِنما هو للتَّنْبِيه كأَنه قال: أَلا اسْجُدُوا، فلما أَدْخل عليه يا التَّنْبيه سَقَطَتِ الأَلِفُ التي في اسْجُدوا لأَنها أَلفُ وَصْلٍ، وذَهَبَت الأَلف التي في يا لاجْتماع الساكِنَيْن لأَنها والسين ساكنتان؛

ظهر (لسان العرب) الظَّهر من كل شيء: خِلافُ البَطْن. وأَظْهَرَ بحاجته واظَّهَرَ: جعلها وراء ظَهْره، أَصله اظْتَهر. أَبو عبيدة: جعلت حاجته بظَهْرٍ أَي يظَهْري خَلْفِي؛ والظَّهْرُ طريق البَرّ. ابن سيده: وطريقُ الظَّهْره طريق البَرّ، وذلك حين يكون فيه مَسْلَك في البر ومسلك في البحر. والظَّهْرُ من الأَرض: ما غلظ وارتفع، والبطن ما لان منها وسَهُلَ ورَقَّ واطْمأَنَّ.

ضهر (لسان العرب) والضَّاهِرُ أَيضاً: الوادي .

1.33

قدم (الصِّحاح في اللغة) وقَيْدومُ الجبل: أنفٌ يَتَقَدَّمُ منه وقَيْدومُ كلِّ شيء: مُقَدَّمُهُ وصدره. والمُقَدَّمُ نقيض المؤخَّر. يقال: ضرب مُقَدَّمَ وجهه. وقُدَّامُ: نقيض وراء، وهما يؤنَّثان ويصغَّران بالهاء: قُدَيْدِمَةٌ وقُدَيْديمَةٌ أيضاً، وهما شاذان، لأنَّ الهاء لا تلحق الرباعيَّ في التصغير.

وثب (الصِّحاح في اللغة) وثب وثباً ووثوباً ووَثَباناً: طَفَرَ. وثَبَ في لغة حِمْيَرَ: اقْعُدْ .

الوَثْبُ (القاموس المحيط) الوثْبُ: الطَّفْرُ، وثَبَ يَثِبُ وثْباً ووثَباناً ووُثُوباً ووثاباً ووثِيباً، والقُعودُ بلُغةِ حِمْيَرَ. ووثَّبَه توْثيباً: أقْعَدَه على وِسادَةٍ.

سكب (لسان العرب) السَّكْبُ: صَبُّ الماء. سَكَبَ الماءَ والدَّمْعَ ونحوَهما يَسْكُبُه سَكْباً وتَسْكاباً، فسَكَبَ وانْسَكَبَ: صَبَّه فانْصَبَّ. وأَسْكُبَّة الباب: أَسْكُفَّته. وقال اللحياني: السَّكْبُ والأُسْكوبُ الهَطَلانُ الدَّائم. وماءٌ أُسْكوبٌ أَي جارٍ؛

سقب (لسان العرب) والسَّقَبُ: القُرْبُ. وقد سَقِبَتِ الدَّارُ، بالكسر، سُقُوباً أَي قَرُبَتْ، وأَسْقَبَتْ؛ وأَسْقَبْتُها أَنا: قَرَّبتها. السَّقَبُ، بالسين والصاد، في الأَصل: القُرْب. يقال: سَقِبَتِ الدارُ وأَسْقَبَتْ إِذا قَرُبَتْ.

صقب (مقاييس اللغة) الصاد والقاف والباء لا يكاد يكون أصلاً؛ لأنَّ الصَّاد يكون مرَّةً فيه السين، والبابان متداخلان، مرَّةً يقال بالسين ومرَّةً بالصاد، إلاَّ أنَّه يدلُّ على القرب ومع الامتداد مع الدِّقَّة.فأمَّا القُرب فالصَّقب. والرَّجُلان يتصاقبان في المحلَّة، إذا تقاربا.وأما الآخر فالصَّقْب: العمودُ يُعمَد به البيت، وجمعه صقوب. قال ذو الرُّمَّة:وأما قولهم: صقبت الشيء، إذا ضَربته فلا يكون إلاَّ على شيءٍ مُصْمَتٍيابس. فممكنٌ أن يكونَ من الإبدال، كأنه من صَقعته، فيكون الباء بدلاً من العين .

أسس (لسان العرب) الأُسُّ والأَسَس والأَساس: كل مُبْتَدإِ شيءٍ. والأُسُّ والأَساس: أَصل البناء، والأَسَسُ مقصور منه، وجمع الأُسِّ إِساس مثل عُسٍّ وعِساس، وجمع الأَساس أُسس مثل قَذال وقُذُل، وجمع الأَسَس آساس مثل سببٍ وأَسباب .

1.35

الفاهُ (القاموس المحيط) الفاهُ والفُوهُ، بالضم، والفِيهُ، بالكسر، والفُوهَةُ والفَمُ: سواءٌ. وفاهَ به: نَطَقَ،

فوه (لسان العرب) الليث: الفُوهُ أَصلُ بناء تأْسيس الفم. قال أَبو منصور: ومما يَدُلُّك على أَن الأَصل في فم وفُو وفا وفي هاءٌ حُذِفت من آخرها قولُهم للرجل الكثيرِ الأَكلِ فَيِّهٌ، وامرأَة فَيِّهةٌ. وفاهَ بالكلام يَفُوهُ: نَطَقَ ولَفَظ به؛

1.36

العَلُّ (القاموس المحيط) والعَليلَةُ: المرأةُ المُطَيَّبَةُ طيباً بعدَ طِيبٍ.

علل (لسان العرب) والعَلِيلة: المرأَة المُطَيَّبة طِيباً بعد طِيب؛ وتَعَلَّلَتِ المرأَةُ من نفاسها وتَعالَّتْ: خَرَجَتْ منه وطَهُرت وحَلَّ وَطْؤُها.

موأ (لسان العرب) ماءَ السِّنَّوْرُ يَمُوءُ مَوْءاً (قوله «يموء موءاً» الذي في المحكم والتكملة مواء أي بزنة غراب وهو القياس في الأصوات.) كمَأَى. قال اللحياني: ماءَتِ الهِرَّةُ تَمُوءُ مثل ماعَتْ تَمُوعُ، وهو الضُّغاء، إِذا صاحت.

وقال: هِرَّةٌ مَؤُوءٌ، على مَعُوعٍ، وصَوتُها المُواءُ، على فُعال. أَبو عمرو: أَمْوَأَ السِّنَّوْرُ إِذا صاحَ.

1.38

مسي (مقاييس اللغة) الميم والسين والحرف المعتلّ كلمتانِ متباينتان جداً.الأولى زمانٌ من الأزمنة، وهو خلاف الإصباح. يقال أصبَحْنا وأمسَيْنا، وأتانا لمُسْيِ خامسةٍ ومِسْيِ خامسة. والمَساء: خِلاف الصَّباح.

عرا (لسان العرب) والعُرَواء: ما بينَ اصْفِرارِ الشَّمْسِ إِلى اللَّيْلِ إِذا اشْتَدَّ البَرْدُ وهاجَتْ رِيحٌ بارِدةٌ. ومن كلامِهم: أَهْلَكَ فقَدْ أَعْرَيْتَ أَي غابت الشمس وبَرَدَتْ .

الفُسْحَةُ (القاموس المحيط) الفُسْحَةُ، بالضم: السَّعَةُ. وفَسُحَ المكانُ، ككَرُمَ، وأفْسَحَ وتَفَسَّحَ وانْفَسَحَ، فهو فَسيحٌ وفُساحٌ وفُسُحٌ وفُسْحُمٌ.

وفَسَحَ له، كمَنَعَ: وسَّعَ، كتَفَسَّحَ. ورَجُلٌ فُسُحٌ وفُسْحُمٌ: واسِعُ الصَّدْرِ .

فسح (لسان العرب) الفُساحةُ: السَّعةُ الواسعةُ (* قوله «الفساحة السعة الواسعة» كذا بالأصل ولعله الفساحة الساحة الواسعة.) في الأَرض. والفُسْحةُ السَّعةُ؛ فَسُحَ المكانُ فَساحةً وتَفسَّحَ وانْفَسَحَ، وهو فَسِيحٌ وفُسُحٌ. وفي التنزيل: إِذا قيل لكم تَفَسَّحُوا في المجالس فافْسَحُوا يَفْسَحِ اللهُ

لكم؛ قال الفراء: قرأها الناس تَفَسَّحُوا، بغير ألف، وقرأها الحسن تفاسَحُوا، بألف؛ قال: وتَفاسَحُوا وتَفَسَّحُوا متقاربٌ في المعنى مثل تَعَهَّدْتُه وتَعاهَدْتُه، وصَعَّرْتُ وصاعَرْتُ.

ظلل (لسان العرب) ظَلَّ نهارَه يفعل كذا وكذا يَظَلُّ ظَلاًّ وظُلولاً وظَلِلْتُ أنا وظَلْتُ وظِلْتُ، لا يقال ذلك إلاَّ في النهار لكنه قد سمع في بعض الشعر ظَلَّ لَيْلَه، وظَلِلت أَعْمَلُ كذا، بالكسر، ظُلُولاً إذا عَمِلته بالنهار دون الليل؛ وقوله تعالى: يَتَفَيَّأُ ظِلاله عن اليمين؛ قال أبو الهيثم: الظِّلُّ كلُّ ما لم تَطْلُع عليه الشمسُ فهو ظِلٌّ، قال: والفَيْءُ لا يُدْعى فَيْئاً إلا بعد الزوال إذا فاءت الشمسُ أي رَجَعَتْ إلى الجانب الغَرْبِيِّ، فما فاءت منه الشمسُ وبَقِيَ ظِلاًّ فهو فَيْء، والفَيْءُ شرقيٌّ والظِّلُّ غَرْبيٌّ، وإنما يُدعى الظِّلُّ ظِلاًّ من أَوَّلِ النهار إلى الزوال، ثم يُدْعى فَيْئاً بعد الزوال إلى الليل؛ وظِلُّ الليل: جُنْحُه، وقيل: هو الليل نفسه، ويزعم المنجِّمون أن الليل ظِلٌّ وإنما اسْوَدَّ جداً لأنه ظِلُّ كُرَة الأرض، وبقَدْر ما زاد بَدَنُها في العِظَم ازداد سواد ظِلِّها. واسْتَظَلَّ بالظِّلِّ: مال إليه وقعَد فيه. وكلُّ شيء أَظَلَّك فهو ظُلَّة. وأَظَلَّني الشيءُ: غَشِيَني، والاسم منه الظِّلُّ؛ كلُّ ما أَطْبَقَ عليك فهو ظُلَّة، وكذلك كل ما أَظَلَّك. والإِظْلالُ: الدُّنُوُّ؛ وأَظَلَّك الشيء: دنا منك حتى أَلقى عليك ظِلَّه من قربه. ويقال: اسْتَظَلَّت العينُ إذا غارت؛ ويقال: ظِلٌّ وظِلالٌ وظُلَّة وظُلَل مثل قُلَّة وقُلَل. والظُّلَّة، بالضم: كهيئة الصُّفَّة، وقرئ: في ظُلَلٍ على الأَرائك مُتَّكئون، وفي التنزيل العزيز: فأَخَذَهُم عذابُ يَوم الظُّلَّة؛ والجمع ظُلَلٌ وظِلال. وأَظَلَّك فلان: دنا منك كأَنه أَلقى عليك ظِلَّه، ثم قيل أَظَلَّك أَمرٌ. ويقال للدم الذي في الجوف مُسْتَظِلٌّ أَيضاً؛ ومنه قوله: مِنْ عَلَقِ الجَوْفِ الذي كان اسْتَظَلّ ويقال: اسْتَظَلَّت العينُ إذا غارت؛

غور (لسان العرب) غَوْرُ كلِّ شيء: قَعْرُه. والتَّغْوير: القَيْلُولة. يقال: غَوِّروا أي انزلوا للقائلة. والغائرة: نصف النهار. والغائرة: القائلة. وغَوَّر القوم تَغْويراً: دخلوا في القائلة. وقالوا: وغَوَّروا نزلوا في القائلة؛ وفي حديث السائب: لما ورد على عمر، رضي الله عنه، بِفَتْحِ نَهاوَنْد قال: وَيْحك ما وراءك؟ فوالله ما بتُّ هذه الليلة إلا تَغْويراً؛ يريد النومة القليلة التي تكون عند القائلة. يقال: غَوَّر القوم إذا قالوا، ومن رواه تَغْريراً جعله من الغِرار، وهو النوم القليل.

(القاموس المحيط) وغِشايَةٌ: غِطاءٌ.

غرر (الصِّحاح في اللغة) والغِرارُ بالكسر: النوم القليل.

غرر (لسان العرب) ويقال: لَبِث اليومَ غِرارَ شهر أَي مِثالَ شهر أَي طُول شهر، والغِرارُ: النوم القليل، وقيل: هوالقليل من النوم وغيره.

غشا (لسان العرب) الغِشاءُ: الغِطاءُ. غَشَّيْت الشيءَ تَغْشِية إذا غَطَّيْته. غُشِي.

غطط (لسان العرب) وغَطِيطُ النائم والمَخْنوقِ: نَخِيرُه. وغَطْغَطَ عليه النومُ: غلب.

غطا (الصِّحاح في اللغة) الغِطاءُ: ما تَغَطَّيت به. وغَطَّيتُ الشيء تَغْطِيَةً. وغَطَّيْتُهُ أيضاً أَغْطي غَطْياً. وغَطا الليل يَغْطو ويَغْطي، أي أظلم.

غطي (لسان العرب) وغَطَى الشيءَ يَغْطِيه غَطْياً وغَطَّى عليه وأَغْطاه وغَطَّاه: سَتَره وعَلاه؛ وقالوا: اللهمَّ أَغْطِ على قَلْبه أَي غَشِّ قَلْبَه. وفعَل به ما غَطاه أَي ما ساءَه. والغِطاءُ: ما تَغَطَّى به أو غُطِّي به غيره.

غطو (مقاييس اللغة) الغين والطاء والحرف المعتل يدلُّ على الغِشاء والسَّتر. يقال: غَطَيت الشَّيءَ وغَطَّيْته. والغِطاء ما تَغَطَّى به. وغَطا اللَّيلُ يَغْطُو، إذا غَشَّى بظلامه .

ضلل (لسان العرب) يقال: أَضْلَلت الشيءَ إذا غَيَّبْته. تقول للشيء الزائل عن موضعه: قد أَضْلَلته، وللشيء الثابت في موضعه إلا أَنك لم تَهْتَدِ إليه: ضَلَلْته؛ يقال: ضَلَّ الشيءُ إذا ضاع، وضَلَّ عن الطريق إذا جار. وضَلَّ الشيءُ: خَفِيَ وغاب. ويقال: ضَلَّني فلانٌ فلم أَقْدِر عليه أَي ذَهَب عَني؛ والضَّلال: النِّسيان. والضَّلَّة: الغَيْبُوبةُ في خير أَو شرّ. وقال مُرَّة: هو تِبْعُ ضِلَّة أَي داهيةٌ لا خير فيه، وقيل: تِبْعُ صِلَّةٍ، بالصاد. وضَلاضِلُ الماء: بقاياه، والصادُ لغةٌ، واحدتها ضُلْضُلَةٌ وصُلْصُلة.

1.39

حلق (لسان العرب) وحلَق الحوضُ: ذهب ماؤُه؛ والحَلْقُ حَلْقُ الشعر. والحَلْقُ مصدر قولك حلق رأْسه. وحَلَقوا رؤُوسهم: شدِّد للكثرة. وحلق الشيءَ يَحْلِقُه حَلْقاً: قشَره.

سبح (لسان العرب) السَّبْحُ والسِّباحة: العَوْمُ. قال ابنُ الفَرَج: سمعت أَبا الجَهْم الجَعْفَرِيَّ يقول: سَبَحْتُ في الأَرض وسَبَخْتُ فيها إذا تباعدت فيها؛ وقيل في قوله تعالى: إن لك في النهار سَبْحاً طويلاً أَي فراغاً للنوم، وقد يكون السَّبْحُ بالليل. والسَّبْحُ أَيضاً: النوم نفسه. والسَّبْحُ أَيضاً: السكون. والسَّبْحُ التقلُّبُ والانتشار في الأَرض والتَّصَرُّفُ في المعاش، فكأَنه ضِدٌّ.

سَبَّهُ (القاموس المحيط) سَبَّهُ: قَطَعَه، وتَسَبْسَبَ الماءُ: جَرى، وسالَ. وسَبْسَبَهُ: أسالَهُ. وسَبْسَبَ بَوْلَه: أرسَلَهُ.

سبه (لسان العرب) السَّبَهُ: ذهاب العقل من الهَرَم.

سفح (مقاييس اللغة) السين والفاء والحاء أصلٌ واحدٌ يدلُّ على إراقة شيء. يقال سفح الدَّم، إذا صبّه. وسفح الدم: هَراقه.

سفح (الصَّحاح في اللغة) سَفْحُ الجبل: أسفله حيثُ يَسْفَح فيه الماءُ، وهو مُضْطَجَعُهُ. وسَفَحْتُ الماءَ: هَرَقْتُه. وسَفَحْتُ دَمَه: سفكته.

سفه (مقاييس اللغة) السين والفاء والهاء أصلٌ واحدٌ، يدلُّ على خفّة وسخافة.

سفه (الصِّحاح في اللغة) السَفَهُ: ضدُّ الحلم، وأصله الخِفَّةُ والحركةُ.

السَّفَهُ (القاموس المحيط) السَّفَهُ، مُحرَّكَةً، وكسَحابٍ وسَحابةٍ: خِفَّةُ الحِلْمِ، أو نَقيضُهُ، أو الجَهْلُ. وسَفِهَ نَفْسَهُ ورأيَهُ، مُثَلَّثَةً: حَمَلَهُ على السَّفَهِ، أو نَسَبَهُ إليه، أو أهْلَكَهُ،

سفه (لسان العرب) السَّفَهُ والسَّفاهُ والسَّفاهة: خِفَّةُ الحِلْم، وقيل: نقيض الحِلم، وأَصله الخفة والحركة، وقيل: الجهل وهو قريب بعضه من بعض. ويجوز على هذا القول سَفِهْتُ زيداً بمعنى سَفَّهْتُ زيداً؛ وقال أَبو عبيدة: معنى سَفِهَ نفسَه أَهلك نفسَه وأَوْبَقَها، وهذا غير خارج من مذهب يونس وأَهل التأْويل؛ وقال الزجاج: القول الجيد عندي في هذا أَن سَفِهَ في موضع جَهِلَ، والمعنى، والله أَعلم، إلا مَنْ جَهِل نَفْسَه أَي لم يُفَكِّرْ في نفسه فوضع سَفِهَ في موضع جَهِلَ، وعُدِّيَ كما عُدِّيَ. ويقال: سَفِهَ فلانٌ رأْيه إذا جهله وكان رأْيه مضطرباً لا استقامة له. والسَّفِيه: الجاهل. وسَفَّه الجهلُ حِلْمَه: أَطاشه وأَخَفَّه؛ وسَفِهْتُ نصيبي: نَسِيتُه؛ عن ثعلب، وتَسَفَّهْتُ فلاناً عن ماله إذا خدعته عنه. وتَسَفَّهْتُ عليه إذا أَسمعته.

1.40

القُلُّ (القاموس المحيط) القُلُّ، بالضم، والقِلَّةُ، بالكسر: ضِدُّ الكَثْرَةِ (والكُثْرِ) قَلَّ يَقِلُّ، فهو قليلٌ.

قهل (لسان العرب) القَهَل: كالقَرَهِ في قَشف الإنسان وقَذَر جلدِه. ورجل مُتَقَهِّل: لا يتعهَّد جسده بالماء والنظافة. ورجل مُتَقَهِّل إذا كان رَثَّ الهيئة متقشِّفاً. وانْقَهَلَ سقط وضعُف؛

قهل (الصّحاح في اللغة) قال الكسائي: التَقَهُّلُ: رَثاثَةُ الهيئة. ورجلٌ مُتَقَهِّلٌ: يابسُ الجِلْدِ سَيِّء الحال، مثل المُتَقَحِّل.

قحل (لسان العرب) وسِقاءٌ قاحِل وشيخ قاحِل وشيخ قَحْل، بالسكون، وقد قَحَل، بالفتح، يَقْحَل قُحُولاً، فهو قاحِل؛ وقد قَحِل يَقْحَل قَحَلاً إذا التزق جلده بعظمه من الهزال والبِلَى، وأَقْحَلْته أَنا؛

قلو (مقاييس اللغة) والمُنْكمش مُقْلَوْلٍ، وفي الحديث: "لو رأيتَ ابنَ عُمَرَ لرأيته مُقلولياً"، أي متجافِياً عن الأرض، كأنّه يريد كَثْرَةَ الصَّلاة. والقِلَى تجافٍ عن الشّيء وذَهابٌ عنه.

سكن (مقاييس اللغة) السين والكاف والنون أصلٌ واحد مطّرِد، يدلُّ على خلاف الاضطراب والحركة. يقال سَكَن الشّيءُ يسكُن سكوناً فهو ساكن.والسَّكْن الأهل الذين يسكُنون الدّار.

سكن (الصّحاح في اللغة) سَكَنَ الشيء سُكوناً: استقرَّ وثبت.

سكن (لسان العرب) وسَكَنَ الرجل: سكت، وقيل: سَكَن في معنى سكت، وسَكَنتِ الريح وسَكَن المطر وسَكَن الغضب.

1.41

سمع (الصّحاح في اللغة) السَمْعُ: سَمْعُ الإنسان، يكون واحداً وجمعاً كقوله تعالى: "ختم الله على قلوبهم وعلى سَمْعِهِمْ" لأنَّه في الأصل مصدرُ قولك: سَمِعْتُ الشيء سَمْعاً وسَماعاً.

السَّمْعُ (القاموس المحيط) السَّمْعُ: حِسُّ الأُذُنِ، والأُذُنُ، وما وَقَرَ فيها من شيءٍ تَسْمَعُه، والذِّكْرُ المَسْموعُ، ويكسرُ، كالسَّماعِ، ويكونُ للواحِدِ والجَمْعِ.

أني (مقاييس اللغة) الهمزة والنون وما بعدهما من المعتل، له أصول أربعة: البُطء وما أشبهه مِن الحِلم وغيره، وساعةٌ من الزمان، وإدراك الشّيء، وظَرف من الظروف.وأمَّا إدراك الشيء*فالإنى، تقول: انتظرنا إِنَى اللَّحم، إي إدراكَه.

وتقول: ما أَنَى لك ولم يأْنِ لك، أي لم يَحِنْ. قال الله تعالى: أَلَمْ يَأْنِ لِلَّذِينَ آمَنُوا [الحديد 16] أي لم يَحِنْ. وآنَ يَئِينُ. واستأنيت الطعامَ، أي انتظرتُ إدراكَه. وَحَمِيمٍ آنٍ [الرحمن 44] قد انتهى حَرُّه. والفعل أَنَى الماءُ المسخَّنُ يأْنِي. و آنيَةٌ" قال عبّاس:

عَلانيَةً والخيلُ يَغْشَى مُتُونها حَمِيمٌ وآنٍ من دَم الجوف ناقِعُ. قال ابنُ الأعرابيِّ: يقال آن يَئِين أيناً وأَنَى لك يأْنِي أَنْياً، أي حان. ويقال: أتَيْتُ فلانا آينَةً بعد آينَةٍ، أي أحياناً بعد أحيان، ويقال تارةً بعد تارة.

أني (لسان العرب) أَنى الشيءُ يأْني أَنْياً وإِنَىً وأَنَىً (* قوله «وأنى» هذه الثالثة بالفتح والقصر في الأصل، والذي في القاموس ضبطه بالمد واعترضه شارحه وصوب القصر)، وهو أَنِيٌّ. وإِنَى الشيء: بلوغُه وإِدراكه. وقد أَنى الشيءُ يأْني إِنىً، وقد آنَ أَوانُك وأَيْنُك وإِينُكَ. ويقال من الأَين: آنَ يَئِين أَيْناً. وآنَيْت وأَنَّيت بمعنى واحد، وفي حديث غزوة حنين: اختاروا إِحدى الطائفتين إِمّا المال وإِمّا السبي وقد كنت اسْتَأْنَيْتُ بكم أَي انتظرت وتربَّصت؛ يقال: آنَيْت وأَنَيْت وتأَنَّيْت واسْتَأْنَيْتُ. الليث: يقال اسْتَأْنَيتُ بفلان أي لم أُعْجِله.

1.42

أزز (لسان العرب) أَزَّت القِدْرُ تَؤُزُّ وتئِزُّ أَزّاً وأَزِيزاً وأَزازاً وائْتَزَّتِ ائْتِزازاً إِذا اشتدَّ غليانها، وقيل: هو غليان ليس بالشديد. وقوله: المسجد يأْزِزُ أَي مُنْغصٌّ بالناس. ويقال: البيت منهم بأَزَزٍ إِذا لم يكن فيه مُتَّسَعٌ، ولا يشتق منه فعل؛ يقال: أَتيت الوالي والمجلسُ أَزَزٌ أَي كثير الزحام ليس فيه متسع، والناس أَزَزٌ إِذا انضم بعضهم إِلى بعض. والأَزَزُ الضِّيق. والأَزُّ: التَّهْييجُ والإِغراء. وأَزَّهُ يَؤُزُّهُ أَزّاً: أَغراه وهيجه. وأَزَّهُ: حَثَّه. وآزاني هو: ضَمَّنِي؛ وأَزَّه أَزّاً وأَزيزاً مثل هَزَّه. وأَزَّ الشيءَ يَؤُزُّه إِذا ضم بعضه إِلى بعض. وأَززْتُ القِدْرَ آؤُزُها أَزّاً إِذا جمعت تحتها الحطب حتى تلتهب النار؛

أزا (لسان العرب) الأَزْوُ: الضِّيِّق؛ عن كراع. وأَزَيْتُ إِليه أَزْياً وأُزِيّاً: انضممت. وأَزى الظِّلُّ أُزِيّاً: قَلَص وتَقَبَّض ودنا بعضه إِلى بعض، فهو آزٍ؛ وأَزى له أَزْياً: أَتاه لِيَخْتِلَه. الليث: أَزَيْتُ لفلان آزي له أَزْياً إِذا أَتيته من وجه مأْمنه لتَخْتِله. ويقال: هو بإِزاء فلان أَي بحذائه ممدوادن. وقد آزَيْتُه إِذا حاذَيْتَه، ولا تقل وازَيْته. وقعدَ إِزاءه أَي قُبالته. وآزاه: قابَلَه.

عز (مقاييس اللغة) العين والزاء أصلٌ صحيح واحد، يدلُّ على شدّةٍ وقوّة وما ضاهاهما، من غلبةٍ وَقهر. واعتزَّ بي وتعزّز. قال: ويقال عَزّه على أمرٍ يَعزُّه، إذا غلبَه على أمره. وفي المثل:"مَن عَزَ بَزَ"، أي من غلب سَلَب. والمُعازّة: المغالَبة. تقول: عازّني فلان عزازاً ومُعَازّة فعزَزْتُه: أي غالَبَني فغلبتُه. قال الخليل: تقول: أعززْتُ بما أصاب فلاناً، أي عظم عليّ واشتدّ. ويقال استعَزَّ عليه الشيطانُ، أي غَلَبَ عليه وعلى عقْله. واستعزَّ عليه الأمر، إذا لجَّ فيه. قال الخليل: العَزَازَة: أرضٌ صلبة ليست بذاتِ حجارة، لا يعلوها الماء.

عَزَ (القاموس المحيط) و~ الشيءُ: قَلَّ، فلا يَكادُ يُوجَدُ، فهو عَزيزٌ. و~ عليَّ أن تَفعَلَ كذا: حَقَّ، واشتَدَّ، يَعِزُّ، كيَقِلُّ، ويَمَلُّ. وعَزِزْتُ عليه أعِزُّ: كَرُمْتُ. وأعْزِزْتُ بما أصابَكَ، بالضم، أي: عَظُمَ عَلَيَّ.

عزز (لسان العرب) والعِزُّ: خلاف الذُّلّ. وفي الحديث: قال لعائشة: هل تدْرين لِمَ كان قومُك رفعوا باب الكعبة؟ قالت: لا، قال: تَعَزُّزاً أن لا يدخلها إلا من أرادوا أي تكبُّراً وتشدُّداً على الناس. والعِزُّ في الأصل: القوة والشدة والغلبة. والعِزُّ والعِزّة: الرفعة والامتناع، والعِزّة لله؛ وفي حديث عليّ، رضي الله عنه، لما رأى طَلْحَةَ قتيلاً قال: أعزِزْ عليّ أبا محمد أن أراك مُجدّلاً تحت نجوم السماء؛ يقال: عَزَّ عليّ يعِزُّ أن أراك بحال سيئة أي يشتدّ ويشق عليّ. وقال ثعلب: في الكلام الفصيح: إذا عَزَّ أخوكَ فهُنْ، والعرب تقوله، وهو مَثَلٌ معناه إذا تَعَظَّم أخوكَ شامخاً عليك فالتَزِمْ له الهوانَ. قال الأزهري: المعنى إذا غلبك وقهرك ولم تقاومْه فتواضع له، فإنَّ اضطرابَكَ عليه يزيدك ذُلاً وخبالاً. وعَزّه يَعُزُّه عَزّاً: قهره وغلبه.

حرم (لسان العرب) الحِرمُ، بالكسر، والحَرامُ: نقيض الحلال، وجمعه حُرُمٌ؛ وبالكسر: الرجل المُحرِمُ؛ وحُرمةُ الرجل: حُرَمُهُ وأهله. وحَرَمُ الرجل وحَريمُه: ما يقاتِلُ عنه ويَحْميه، فجمع الحَرَم أحْرامٌ، وجمع الحَريم حُرُمٌ.

خمر (لسان العرب) خامَرَ الشيءَ: قاربه وخالطه؛ والخِمارُ للمرأة، وهو النَّصيفُ، وقيل: الخمار ما تغطي به المرأة رأسها، وجمعه أخْمِرَةٌ وخُمْرٌ وخُمُرٌ. والحَريمُ: الصديق؛ يقال: فلان حَريمٌ صَريح أي صَديق خالص.

1.43

أجج (لسان العرب) الأجيجُ: تَلَهُّبُ النار. ابن سيده: الأجّةُ والأجيجُ صوت النار؛ وأَجَّجَ بينهم شَرّاً: أوقده. وأجّةُ القوم وأجيجُهم: اختلاطُ كلامهم مع حَفيف مشيهم. وقولهم: القومُ في أجّة أي في اختلاط؛

عج (مقاييس اللغة) العين والجيم أصلٌ واحد صحيح يدلُّ على ارتفاع في شيء، من صوتٍ أو غبارٍ وما أشبه ذلك. من ذلك العجُّ: رفْع الصَّوت. يقال: عجَّ القومُ يَعجُّون عَجّاً وعجيجاً وعجُّوا بالدُّعاء، إذا رفعوا أصواتَهم. وعجيج الماء: صوته؛

عجج (لسان العرب) عَجَّ يَعِجُّ ويَعَجُّ عَجّاً وعجيجاً، وضجَّ يَضِجُّ: رفع صوته وصاحَ؛ وعَجّةُ القوم وعَجِيجُهم: صِياحُهم وجلَبتهم؛ وعَجَّ: صاح.

عدس (لسان العرب) العَدْسُ، بسكون الدال: شدة الوطء على الأرض والكَدْح أيضاً. وعَدَس الرجلُ يَعْدِسُ عَدْساً وعَدَساناً وعُدُوساً وعَدَسَ وحَدَسَ يَحْدِسُ: ذهب في الأرض.

حدس (لسان العرب) الأزهري: الحَدْسُ التوهم في معاني الكلام والأمور؛ بلغني عن فلان أمر وأنا أحْدِسُ فيه أي أقول بالظن والتوهم. والحَدْسُ الظنّ والتخمين. يقال: هو يَحْدِسُ، بالكسر، أي يقول شيئاً برأيه. أبو زيد: تَحَدَّسْتُ ع الأخبار تَحَدُّساً وتَنَدَّسْتُ عنها تَنَدُّساً وتَوَجَّسْتُ إذا كنت تُرِيغُ أخبار الناس لتعلمها من حيث لا يعلمون. ويقال: حَدَسْتُ عليه ظني ونَدَسْتُه إذا ظننت الظن ولا تَحقُّه. وحَدَسَ الكلامَ على عواهِنِه: تعَسَّفه ولم يَتوَقَّه.

حدث (لسان العرب) الحديثُ: نقيضُ القديم. والحديثُ: الجديدُ من الأشياء. والحديث: الخبَرُ يأتي على القليل والكثير، والجمع: أحاديثُ، كقطيع وأقاطيعَ، وهو شاذٌ على غير قياس، وقد قالوا في جمعه: حِدْثانٌ وحُدْثانٌ، وهو قليل؛ وقوله تعالى: إن لم يُؤْمنوا بهذا الحديث أسَفاً؛ عنى بالحديث القرآن؛ عن الزجاج. والحديث: ما يُحَدَّثُ به المُحَدِّثُ تحْديثاً؛ وقد حَدَّثه الحديثَ وحَدَّثه به. الجوهري: المُحادثة والتَحادُث والتَحَدُّثُ والتَّحديثُ: معروفات. وقوله تعالى: وأما بنعمة ربك فَحَدِّثْ؛ أي بَلّغْ ما أُرسلتَ به، وحَدِّث بالنبوّة التي آتاك اللهُ، وهي أجلُّ النِّعَم. ورجل حَدِثٌ وحَدُثٌ وحِدْثٌ وحِدِّيثٌ ومُحَدِّثٌ، بمعنى واحد: كثيرُ الحديثِ، حَسَنُ السِّياق له؛ كلُّ هذا على النَّسَب ونحوه. والأحاديثُ، في الفقه وغيره، معروفة. ويقال: صار فلانٌ أُحْدُوثةً أي أكثروا فيه الأحاديث.

وفلانٌ حِدْثُك أي مُحَدِّثُك، والقومُ يتحادثُون ويتَحَدَّثُون، وتركت البلادَ تَحَدَّثُ أي تَسمَعُ فيها دوِيّاً؛

1.44

لأم (مقاييس اللغة) اللام والألف والميم أصلان: أحدهما الاتّفاق والاجتماع، والآخر خُلق رديء. فالأول قولُهم: لأمْتُ الجُرحَ، ولأمت الصَّدْعَ، إذا سَدَدت.

لأم (لسان العرب) اللُّؤْم: ضد العِتْق والكرم. واللئيمُ: الدَّنِيءُ الأصل الشحيحُ النفس، وقد لَؤُم الرجلُ، بالضم، يَلؤُم لُؤْماً، على فُعْلٍ، ومَلأَمةً على مَفْعَلة، ولآمةً على فعالة، فهو لئيمٌ من قوم لئام ولُؤَماءَ، ومَلأمانٌ؛ وقد جاء في الشعر ألائمُ على غير قياس؛ ويقال للرجل إذا سُبَّ: يا لُؤْمانُ ويا ملأمانُ ويا مَلأمُ. وألأمَ أظهرَ خصالَ اللُّؤم. ويقال قد ألأمَ الرجل إلآماً إذا صنع ما يدعوه الناس عليه لئيماً، فهو مُلْئِمٌ. وألأمَ ولَدَ اللِّئامَ؛ والمُلْئِمُ: الذي يأوي اللِّئام. والمُلْئِمُ: الرجل اللَّئيم.

الكَرمُ (القاموس المحيط) والكَريمُ: الصَّفوحُ.

ندي (لسان العرب) النَّدَى: البَلَلُ. والنَّدَى: ما يَسقُط بالليل، والجمع أَنْداءٍ وأَندِيةٌ ، على غير قياس؛ والنَّداءُ والنُّداءُ: الصوت مثل الدُّعاء والرُّغاء ، وقد ناداه ونادى به وناداه مُناداة ونداء أي صاح به.
نَدَأَهُ (القاموس المحيط) و~ اللَّحْمَ: أَلقاهُ في النارِ، أو دَفَنه فيها.
ندأ (لسان العرب) نَدأَ اللحمَ يَنْدَؤُه نَدْءاً: أَلقاهُ في النار، أو دفَنه فيها.
أدا (لسان العرب) ابن السكيت: آدَيْتُ للسَّفَر فأَنا مُؤْدٍ له إذا كنت متهيِّئاً له. ونحن على أَدِيٍّ للصَّلاة أي تَهيُّؤ. وتَآدَيْتُ للأَمر: أَخذت له أَداته.
ابن بُزُرْج: يقال هل تآدَيْتُم لذلك الأَمر أي هل تأَهَّبْتم. ومَنْ يُؤْدِيني على فلان أي من يُعينني عليه؛ وآداني السلطانُ عليه: أَعْداني. واسْتأْدَيْته عليه: اسْتَعْدَيته. وآدَيْته عليه: أَعَنْتُه، كله منه. ويقال: تآدَى القومُ تآدِياً وتَعادَوْا تَعادِياً أي تَتابَعُوا موتاً. وأَدَّى دَيْنَه تَأْدِيَةً أي قَضاه، والاسم الأَداء.
ويقال: أَدَّى فلان ما عليه أَداءً وتَأْدِيةً. وتأَدَّى إليه الخَبرُ أي انْتَهى.
أدي (مقاييس اللغة) الهمزة والدّال والياء أصلٌ واحد، وهو إيصال الشيء إلى الشيء أو وصوله إليه من تلقاء نفسه. قال الخليل: أَدَّى فلان يؤدِّي ما عليه أداءً وتأْدِيَةً.

1.45

مَن (لسان العرب) والاستفهام كثير وهو كقولك: من تَعْني بما تقول؟ والشرط كقوله: من يَعْمَلْ مثقال ذَرَّةٍ خيراً يره، فهذا شرط وهو عام. ومَنْ للجماعة كقوله تعالى: ومَنْ عَمِلَ صالحاً فلأَنفسهم يَمْهدون؛ وكقوله: ومن الشياطين مَنْ يَغُوصون له. الجوهري: مَنْ اسم لمن يصلح أن يخاطَب، وهو مبهم غير متمكن، وهو في اللفظ واحد ويكون في معنى الجماعة؛ وتحكى بها الأعلام والكُنَى والنكرات في لغة أهل الحجاز إذا قال رأيت زيداً قلت مَنْ زيداً، وإذا قال رأيت رجلاً قلت مَنًا لأنه نكرة، وإن قال جاءني رجل قلت مَنُو، وإن قال مررت برجل قلت مَنِي، وإن قال جاءني رجلان قلت مَنانْ، وإن قال مررت برجلين قلت مَنَينْ، بتسكين النون فيهما؛ ومِنْ، بالكسر: حرف خافض لابتداء الغاية في الأماكن، وذلك قولك مِنْ مكان كذا وكذا إلى مكان كذا وكذا.
ما (لسان العرب) يقول: وتجيء ما الاستفهامية مَحذُوفةً إذا ضممت إليها حرفاً جارًا.

1.46

الذَّوْجُ (القاموس المحيط) الذَّوْجُ: الشُّرْبُ،
ذوق (لسان العرب) الذَّوْقُ: مصدر ذاقَ الشيءَ يذُوقه ذَوقاً وذَواقاً ومَذاقاً، فالذَّواق والمَذاق يكونان مصدرين ويكونان طَعْماً، كما تقول ذَواقُه ومذاقُه طيِّب؛

لو (مقاييس اللغة) اللام والواو كلمةٌ أداة، وهي لو، يُتمنَّى بها. وأهل العربية يقولون: لو يدلُّ على امتناع الشيء لامتناع غيره، ووقوعِهِ لوقوع غيرِه. نحو قولهم لو خرج زيد لخرجت.
لو (الصّحاح في اللغة) لَوْ: حرفُ تَمَنٍ، وهو لامتناع الثاني من أجل امتناع الأوَّل، تقول: لَوْ جِئتني لأكرمتك. وهو خلافُ إنْ التي للجزاء، لأنَّها توقع الثانية من أجل وجود الأول.

شدد (لسان العرب) الشِّدَّةُ: الصَّلابةُ، وهي نَقيضُ اللِّين تكون في الجواهر والأَعراض، والجمع شِدَدٌ؛ وقال تعالى: اشْدُدْ به أَزري. ابن الأَعرابي: يقال حَلَبْتَ بالساعِدِ الأَشَدِّ أي استعَنْتَ بمن يقومُ بأمرِك ويُعْنى بحاجتك. وقال أبو عبيد: يقال حَلَبْتُها بالساعِدِ الأَشَدِّ أي حين لم أَقْدِر على الرِّفْقِ أَخَذْتُه بالقُوَّة والشِّدَّة؛ والأَشُدُّ: مَبْلَغ الرجل الحُنْكَة والمَعْرِفَةِ؛ قال: والشِّدَّة القُوَّة والجَلادَة. وشَدَّ النهارُ أي ارتفع. وشَدُّ النهار: ارتفاعُه، وكذلك شَدُّ الضُّحَى. ويقال: لقِيتُه شَدَّ النهار وهو حين يرتفع، وكذلك امتدَّ. وشَدَّه أي أَوثقه، يَشُدُّوه ويَشِدُّه أَيضاً، وهو من النوادر.
سدد (لسان العرب) السَّدُّ: إغلاق الخَلَلِ ورَدْمُ الثَّلْم. سَدَّه يَسُدُّه سَدّاً فانسدّ واستدّ وسدّده: أصلحه وأَوثقه، والاسم السُّدُّ. قال: وأَما السَّداد، بالفتح، فإِنما معناه الإِصابة في المنطق أَن يكون الرجل مُسَدَّداً. ويقال إِنه لذو سَداً في منطقه وتدبيره، وكذلك في الرمي. يقال: سَدَّ السَّهْمُ يَسِدُّ إِذا استقام. وسَدَّدْتُه تسديداً. واسْتَدَّ الشيءُ إِذا استقام؛ والسَّدَد القصْد في القول والوَفْقُ والإِصابة، وقد تَسَدَّد له واسْتَدَّ. والسَّديدُ والسَّداد: الصواب من القول. يقال: إِنه لَيُسِدُّ في القول وهو أَن يُصِيبَ السَّداد يعني القصد.
سَدَّدَهُ (القاموس المحيط) سَدَّدهُ تَسْديداً: قَوَّمَهُ، ووفَّقهُ لِلسَّدادِ، أي: الصَّواب من القَوْلِ والعَمَلِ. وسَدَّ يَسِدُّ: صارَ سَديداً.

1.47

افل (لسان العرب) أَفَلَ أَي غاب. النوادر: أَفِل الرجلُ إِذا نَشِط، فهو أَفِلٌ على فَعِلٍ؛ قال الليث: إِذا استقر اللَّقاح في قرار الرَّحِم قيل قد أَفَلَ، ثم يقال للحامل آفِل.
فلا (لسان العرب) وفليت الشِّعر إِذا تدبرته واستخرجت معانيه وغريبه؛ عن ابن السكيت. وفَلَيْت الأَمر إِذا تأَملت وجوهه ونظرت إِلى عاقبته. وفَلَوْتُ القوم وفَلَيْتهم إِذا تخللتهم. وفلاه في عَقْله فَلْياً: رازه. أَبو زيد: يقال فَلَيْت الرجل في عقله أَفْليه فَلْياً إِذا نظرت ما عَقْلُه.

1.48

مجر (الصّحاح في اللغة) ويقال أيضاً: ما له مَجْرٌ، أي عقلٌ. والمَجَرُ بالتحريك: الاسم.

مجر (لسان العرب) المَجْرُ: ما في بُطون الحوامل من الإبل والغنم؛ والمَجْرُ: أن يُشتَرى ما في بطونها، وقيل: هو أن يشتري البعير بما في بطن الناقة؛ وقد أَمْجَرَ في البيع وماجَرَ مُماجَرَةً ومِجاراً. الجوهري: والمَجْرُ أن يباع الشيء بما في بطن هذه الناقة. وجَيْشٌ مَجْرٌ: كثيرٌ جداً. الأصمعي: المَجْرُ، بالتسكين، الجيش العظيم المجتمع. وما له مَجْرٌ أي ما له عَقْلٌ. والمَجْرُ الرِّبا. والمَجْرُ القِمارُ. والمُحاقَلَةُ والمُزابَنَةُ يقال لهما: مَجْر.

1.50

أنه (الصَحاح في اللغة) الأصمعي: أَنَهَ يأْنَهُ أَنِهاً وأُنوهاً، مثل أَنَخ يأْنِخ، وذلك إذا تزحَرَ من ثِقَلٍ يجده.
وانَحَه (القاموس المحيط) وانَحَه مُوانَحَةً: وافقَه.
أنَحَ (القاموس المحيط) أنَحَ يأْنِحُ أنْحاً وأَنيحاً وأُنوحاً: زَحَرَ من ثِقَلٍ يَجِدُهُ من مَرَضٍ أو بُهْرٍ، وهو آنِحٌ، ج: أُنَّحٌ، كرُكَّعٍ.
أنح (لسان العرب) أنَح يأْنِحُ أَنْحاً وأَنيحاً وأُنوحاً: وهومثل الزَفِيرِ يكون من الغم والغضب والبِطْنةِ والغَيْرَة، وهو أَنوحٌ؛ قال رؤبة: كزُّ المُحَيَّا أُنَّحٌ إِرْزَبُّ وقال آخر: أَراكَ قَصيراً ثائرَ الشَّعْرِ أَنَّحاً، بعيداً عن الخيراتِ والخُلُقِ الجَزْلِ التهذيب في ترجمة أزح: الأَزُوحُ من الرجال الذي يستأخر عن المكارم، والأَنُوحُ مثله؛
نيح (لسان العرب) ناحَ الغُصْنُ نَيْحاً ونَيَحاناً: مال.
نحا (لسان العرب) وإِبل نَحِيٌّ: مُتَنَحِّيةٌ؛ عن ابن الأَعرابي؛ وأَنشد : ظَلَّ وظَلَّتْ عُصَباً نَحِيَّا، مثل النَّحِيّ اسْتَبرَزَ النَّجِيَّا والنَّحِي من السِّهام: العريضُ النَّصْل الذي إذا أَردت أَن تَرمِي به اضْطَجَعْته حتى تُرْسله.
نوخ (لسان العرب) أَنَخْتُ البعيرَ فاستناخ ونوَّخته فتنوَّخ وأَناخ الإِبلَ: أَبركها فبركت، واستناخت: بركت. والفحلُ يَتَنَوَّخُ الناقة إذا أَراد ضِرابها.
واستناخ الفحل الناقة وتنوَّخها: أَبركها ثم ضربها .

1.51

هدأ (العباب الزاخر) هَدَأَ هَدْءَاً وهُدُوْءَاً: سَكَنَ. ويُقال: نَظَرْتُ إلى هَدئه وهَدْيه -بالهمز وتركه-: أي سِيرته. وأَتَيْته بعد هَدْءٍ من اللَّيل وهَدْءَةٍ وهديءٍ -على فعيلٍ- -ومَهْدَأٍ-على مَفْعَلٍ-: إذا جئتَ بعد نَوْمَةٍ، وكذلك أتانا هُدُوْءً. يُقال: تَرَكْتُ فلاناً على مُهَيْدِئَته: أي على حاله التي كان عليها، تَصغير المَهْدَأة.
هدأ (لسان العرب) ومَرَرْتُ برجل هَدْئِك من رجل، عن الزجاجي، والمعروف هَدِّكَ من رجل.
حدأ (العباب الزاخر) أبو زيد: حَدِئْتُ بالمكان حَدءً -بالتحريك-: إذا لَزِقْتَ به. قال: وحَدِئْتُ إليه: أي لَجأْتُ إليه. قال: وحَدِئْتُ عليه وإليه: إذا حَدِبْتَ عليه ونَصَرْته ومَنَعْته من الظُّلم. أبو عُبَيْد: حَدَأْتُ الشيء حَدْءاً: صرفْته. والتركيب يدلُّ على طائر أو مشبَهٍ به، ومما شَذَّ عن هذا التركيب: حَدِئَ به: أي لَزِقَ به.
حدا (لسان العرب) وحَدَا الشيءَ يَحْدُوه حَدْواً واحْتَداه: تبعه؛ وروى الأَصمعي قال: يقال لَكَ هُدَيَّا هذا وحُدَيّا هذا وشَرْواه وشَكْله كلُّه واحد.
والحِدَوُ هو الحِدَأُ، جمع حِدَأَةٍ وهي الطائر المعروف، فلما سكن الهمز للوقف صارت أَلفاً فقلبها واواً؛
حدا (مقاييس اللغة) الحاء والدال والحرف المعتل أصلٌ واحد، وهو السَّوق. يقال حَدَا بإبله: زَجَر بها وغَنَّى لها.
حدا (الصَحاح في اللغة) الحَدْوُ: سَوْقُ الإل والغناء لها.

المَرْوُ (القاموس المحيط) المَرْوُ: حجارةٌ بيضٌ بَرَّاقَةٌ تُورِي النارَ،
مرا (لسان العرب) المَرْوُ: حجارة بيضٌ بَرَّاقة تكون فيها النار وتُقْدَح منها النار؛ والمارِيُّ: ولد البقرة الأَبيضُ الأَمْلَس. والمُمْرِيةُ من البقر: التي لها ولد مارِيٌّ أي بَرّاقٌ. والمارِيَةُ: البراقة اللَّون.
مور (لسان العرب) وامرأَةٌ مارِيَةٌ: بيضاء بَرَّاقَةٌ كأَنَّ اليَدَ تَمُورُ عليها أي تذهَبُ وتَجِيءُ،
معر (مقاييس اللغة) [و] مَعِرَ الظُّفُر: نصل وتمعَّر لونُه عند غَضَبِه، وذلك أن يتطايَرَ الدَّمُ عنه وتعلوه صُفرة. قال الخليل: وهو أمعَر الشَّعر، وبه مُعْرَةٌ، وهو لونٌ يَضرِب إلى الحُمرة والصُّفرة، وهو أقبَحُ الألوان.
معر (لسان العرب) وغضِبَ فلان فتمَعَّرَ لونُه ووجهُه: تغير وعَلَتْهُ صُفْرَةٌ. وفي الحديث: فتمَعَّرَ وجهُه أي تغير، وأَصله قِلةُ النَضارة وعدمُ إِشْراقِ اللون، من قولهم: مكان أَمْعَرُ وهو الجَدْبُ الذي لا خِصْبَ فيه. ومَعَّرَ وجهَه: غَيَّرَه.

فني (لسان العرب) والفِناء: سَعةٌ أَمامَ الدار. وفي الحديث: رجل من أَفناء الناس أي لم يُعلم ممن هو، الواحد فِنْوٌ، وقيل: هو من الفِناء وهو المُتَّسعُ أَمام الدار، ويجمع الفِناء على أَفْنية.

1.52

كبت (لسان العرب) وفي الحديث: أَنه رأَى كلحةَ حَزيناً مَكْبُوتاً أَي شديدَ الحُزْن؛ قيل: الأَصل فيه مَكْبُودٌ، بالدال، أَي أَصابَ الحُزْنُ كَبِدَه، فقلب الدال تاء. قال الأَزهري: وقال من احْتَجَّ للفراء: أَصلُ الكَبْتِ الكَبْدُ، فقلبت الدال تاء، أُخذ من الكَبِدِ، وهو مَعْدِنُ الغَيْظِ والأَحْقاد،
كبد (مقاييس اللغة) الكاف والباء والدال أصلٌ صحيح يدلُّ على شِدّة في شيء وقُوَّة. من ذلك الكَبَد، وهي المشقّة. يقال: لقِيَ فلانٌ من هذا الأمر كَبَداً، أي مشَقَّة. قال تعالى: لَقَدْ خَلَقْنَا الإنسانَ في كَبَد [البلد 4]. وكابدتُ الأمر: قاسيتُه في مشقَّة.
ومن الباب الكَبِد، وهي معروفة، سمِّيت كَبِداً لتكبُّدها.

الكَبْدُ (القاموس المحيط) وكابَدَهُ مُكابَدَةً وكِباداً: قاساهُ، والاسمُ: الكابِدُ.
كبد (لسان العرب) والكَبِدُ مَعْدِنُ العداوة. والكَبَدُ الشدَّة والمشقَّة. قال أبو منصور: ومكابَدَةُ الأمر معاناة مشقته. وكابَدْت الأمر إذا قاسيت شدته. ويقال: تَكَبَّدْتُ الأَمرَ قصدته؛ وكابَدَ الأَمرَ مُكابَدَة وكِباداً: قاساه، والاسم الكابِدُ كالكاهِلِ والغارِب؛ وكَبِدُ كلِّ شيء: وسَطُه ومعظمه. وكَبَد كل شيء: عِظَمُ وسَطِه وغِلَظُه؛ كَبِدَ كَبَداً، وهو أَكْبَدُ.
الكَبِدُ (القاموس المحيط) والكِبْدُ، كَكَتِفٍ: الجَوْفُ بِكَمالِه، ووسَطُ الشيءِ، ومُعْظَمُهُ،
كبت (أساس البلاغة) كبت الله عدوك: كبّه وأهلكه، وتوقل: لازال خصمك مبكوتًا، وعدوك مكبوتًا. ومن المجاز: فلان يكبت غيظه في جوفه: لا يخرجه. وتقول: من كبت غيظه في جوفه، كبت الله عدوه من خوفه .
كبت (المحيط في اللغة) ورَجل كابِتٌ ومَكْبُوْتٌ ومُكْتَبِتٌ: أي مُمْتَلِىءٌ غَمًّا، وقد كَبَتَه. وهو كابِتٌ ما في نَفْسه: إذا لم يُبْدِهِ لأحَدٍ. والمَكْبُوْتُ: الغَيْظُ نَفْسُه .
كفَتَهُ (القاموس المحيط) كفَتَهُ يَكْفِتُهُ: صَرَفَهُ عن وجْهِهِ فانْكَفَتَ، و~ الشيءَ إليه: ضَمَّهُ، وقَبَضَهُ، كَكَفَّتَهُ، والكِفاتُ، بالكسر: المَوْضِعُ يُكْفَتُ فيه الشيءُ، أي: يُضَمُّ ويُجْمَعُ.
كفت (الصَّحاح في اللغة) كفتُّ الشيء أَكْفِتُهُ كَفْتاً، إذا ضممته إلى نفسك.

دما (الصَّحاح في اللغة) الدَمُ أصله دَمَوٌ بالتحريك، وإنما قالوا دَمِيَ يَدْمى لحال الكسرة التي قبل الياء، كما قالوا رَضِيَ يَرْضى وهو من الرضوان
دمي (لسان العرب) الدَّمُ من الأَخْلاطِ: معروف. الدُّمْية: الصورة المصورة لأَنها يُتَنَوَّقُ في صَنْعتِها ويبالَغُ في تَحْسِينها. وخُذْ ما دَمَّى لك أي ظَهر لك. ودَمَّى له في كذا وكذا إذا قَرَّب؛

1.53

عدر (لسان العرب) والعُدْرةُ الجُرْأَة والإِقدام. والعَدَرُ القَيْلَةُ الكَبيرةُ؛ قال الأَزهري: أَراد بالقيلة الأَدَر، وكأَن الهمزة قلبت عيناً فقيل: عَدِرَ عَدَراً: والأَصل أَدِرَ أَدَراً .
الدَّرُّ (القاموس المحيط) و~ البَيْتِ: قُبالَتُهُ، و~ الشيءَ: حركهُ،
الدارُ (القاموس المحيط) وأَدَرْتُ: اسْتَدَرْتُ.
درر (لسان العرب) ودَرَرُ الطريق: قصده ومتنه، ويقال: هو على دَرَرِ الطريق أَي على مَدْرَجَتِه، وفي الصحاح: أَي على قصده. ويقال: دارِي بِدَرَر دارِك أَي بحذائها. إِذا تقابلتا، ويقال: هما على دَرَرٍ واحد، بالفتح، أَي على قصد واحد. ودَرَرُ الريح: مَهَبُّها؛ وهو دَرَرُك أَي حِذاؤك وقُبالَتُك.
ويقال: دَرَرَك أَي قُبالَتَك؛
دري (مقاييس اللغة) الدال والراء والحرف المعتلّ والمهموز. أمّا الذي ليس بمهموز فأصلان: أحدهما قَصْد الشيء واعتمادُهُ طَلَباً، والآخر حِدَّةٌ تكون في الشَّيء. ودَرَأَ فلانٌ، إذا طَلَع مفاجأةً، وهو من الباب، كأنَّه اندرأَ بنفسه، أي اندفع.
درأ (العباب الزاخر) ودَرَأَ علينا فلان يَدْرَأُ دُرُوءً: أي طلع مفاجأة، وانْدَرَأَ: أي اطلع مفاجأة.
دَرَأَهُ (القاموس المحيط) و~ الرَّجُلُ: طَرَأَ، وخَرَجَ فُجاءَةً،
دور (لسان العرب) دَارَ الشيءُ يَدُورُ دَوْراً ودَوَرَاناً ودُؤُوراً واسْتَدَارَ وأَدَرْتُه أَنا ودَوَّرْتُه وأَدَاره غيره ودَوَّرَ به ودُرْتُ به وأَدَرْتُ اسْتَدَرْتُ، ودَاوَرَهُ مُدَاوَرَةً ودِوَاراً: دَارَ معه؛ والدَّائرة والدَّارَةُ، كلاهما: ما أَحاط بالشيء.
عطر (لسان العرب) أَبو عمرو: تَعَطَّرت المرأَةُ وتأَطَّرت إِذا أَقامت في بيت أَبَوَيْها ولم تزوج.
أطر (لسان العرب) الأَطْرُ: عَطْفُ الشيءِ تَقْبِضُ على أَحَدِ طَرَفَيْهِ فَتُعَوِّجُه؛ قال أَبو عمرو وغيره: قوله تأْطِرُوه على الحق يقول تَعْطِفُوه عليه؛ قال ابن الأَثير: من غريب ما يحكى في هذا الحديث عن نفطويه أَنه قال: بالظاء المعجمة من باب ظأَر، ومنه الظِّئْرُ وهي المرضعة، وجَعَلَ الكلمة مقلوبةً فقدّم الهمزة على الظاء وكل شيء عطفته على شيء، فقد أَطَرْته تأْطِرهُ أَطْراً؛ وتَأَطَّرَ الرُّمحُ: تَثَنَّى؛ ومنه في صفة آدم، عليه السلام: أَنه كان طُوالاً فَأَطَرَ اللَّهُ منه أَي ثَنَاه وقَصَّره ونَقَصَ من طُوله. يقال: أَطَرْتُ الشيء فانْأَطَرَ وتَأَطَّرَ أَي انْثَنَى. وكلُّ ما أَحاط بشيء، فَهُوَ لهُ أُطْرَةٌ وإِطارٌ. وإِطارُ الحافر: ما أَحاط بالأَشْعَرِ، وكلُّ شيء أَحاط بشيء، فهو إِطارٌ له؛ وقال الأَصمعي: إِن بينهم لأَوَاصِرَ رَحِمٍ وأَواطِرَ رَحِمٍ وعَواطِفَ رَحِمٍ بمعنى واحد؛ الواحدة آصِرةٌ وآطِرَةٌ.

قصد (مقاييس اللغة) القاف والصاد والدال أصولٌ ثلاثة، يدلُّ أحدها على إتيانِ شيءٍ وأَمِّه، والآخر على اكتنازٍ في الشيء. والأصل الثالث: الناقة القَصيد: المكتنِزة الممتلئة لحماً.
كَسَدَ (القاموس المحيط) والكَسْدُ: القَسْطُ.
القِسْطُ (القاموس المحيط) ورُكْبَةٌ قَسْطاءُ: يَبِسَتْ، وغَلُظَتْ حتى لا تَكادُ تَنْقبِضُ من يُبْسِها
قسد (لسان العرب) القِسْوَدُّ: الغليظُ الرقبةِ القويُّ؛ وأَنشد: ضَخْمُ الذِّفارى قاسِياً قِسْوَدّا .

1.54

ركب (لسان العرب) وكلُّ ذي أربعٍ، رُكْبَتاه في يَدَيْهِ، وعُرْقُوباهُ في رِجْلَيه، والعُرْقُوبُ: مَوْصِلُ الوظِيفِ. وقيل: الرُّكْبةُ مَرْفِقُ الذّراعِ من كلّ شيءٍ. وحكى اللحياني: بعيرٌ مُسْتَوْقِحُ الرُّكَبِ؛ كأنه جعل كُلَّ جُزْءٍ منها رُكْبةً ثم جَمَع على هذا، والجمعُ في القِلَّة: رُكْباتٌ، ورُكَبات، ورُكُباتٌ، والكثير رُكَبٌ، وكذلك جَمْعُ كلّ ما كان على فُعْلَةٍ، إلا في بناتِ الياءِ فإنهم لا يُحَرِّكونَ مَوْضِعَ العينِ منه بالضم، وكذلك في المُضاعَفة.

برك (مقاييس اللغة) الباء والراء والكاف أصلٌ واحدٌ، وهو ثَباتُ الشيءِ، ثم يتفرع فروعاً يقاربُ بعضُها بعضاً. والبِرْكَة: ما وَلِيَ الأرضَ من جِلد البَطْن وما يليه من الصَّدر، مِنْ كلّ دابة. واشتقاقُه من مَبرَكِ الإبل، وهو الموضع الذي تَبرُكُ فيه، والجمع مبارك. قال يعقوب: البِرْكَة من الفَرَس حيثُ انتصبَتْ فَهْدَتَاه من أسفل، إلى العِرْقين اللذين دون العَضُدين إلى غُضُون الذّراعين من باطن.قال أبو حاتم: البَرْك بفتح الباء: الصدر، فإذا أدخلت الهاء كسرت الباء. قال بعضُهم: البَرْكُ القَصُّ. قال الأصمعيّ: كان أهلُ الكوفة يسمُّون زياداً أشعر بَرْكاً. قال يعقوب: يقول العرب: "هذا أمْرٌ لا يَبْرُك عليه إبلي" أي لا أقرَبُه ولا أقْبَله.

برك (لسان العرب) البَرَكة: النَّماء والزيادة. وبَرَكَ ألقى بَرْكَهُ بالأرض وهو صدره، وبَرَكَتِ الإبل تَبْرُكُ بُروكاً وبَرَّكَتْ: قال الراعي: وإن بَرَكَتْ منها عجاساءُ جِلَّةٌ، بمَحْ◌نيَةٍ، أجلَى العِفاسَ وبَرْوَعا وأبرَكَها هو، وكذلك النعامة إذا جَثَمَتْ على صدرها. والبَرْك والبِرْكَةُ: الصدر، وقيل: هو ما ولي الأرض من جلد صدر البعير إذا بَرَك، وقيل: البَرْك للإنسان والبِرْكة لِما سوى ذلك، وقيل: البَرْك الواحد، والبِركة الجمع، ونظيره حَلْي وحِلْية، وقيل: البَرْكُ باطن الصدر والبِركة ظاهره؛ والبِرْكة من الفرس الصدر؛ قال الأعشى: مُسْتَقْدِم البِرْكة عَبْل الشَّوَى، كَفْتٌ إذا عَضَّ بفأسِ اللّجام الجوهري: البَرْكُ الصدر، فإذا أدخلت عليه الهاء كسرت وقلت بِرْكة؛ قال الجعدي: في مِرْفَقَيْهِ تَقارُبٌ، ولهُ بِرْكَةُ زَوْرٍ كجبأة الخَزَمِ وقال يعقوب: البَرْكُ وسط الصدر؛ قال ابن الزِّبَعْرى: حين حَكَّتْ بقُباءٍ بَرْكَها، واسْتَحَرَّ القتل في عَبْدِ الأَشَلّ وشاهد البِركة قول أبي دواد: جُرْشُعاً أعْظَمُه جَفْرَتُه، نائِئُ البِرْكةِ في غيرِ بَدَدْ وقولهم: ما أحسن بِرْكَة هذه الناقة وهو اسم للبُروك، مثل الرِّكْبة والجِلْسة. وابْتَرك الرجل أي ألقى بِرْكه. وابْتَرَكْتُه إذا صرعته وجعلته تحت بَرْكك.

برخ (مقاييس اللغة) الباء والراء والخاء أصل واحدٌ، إن كانَ عربياً فهو النَّماء والزيادة، ويقال إنها من البَرَكة وهي لغة نَبطيّة .

البَرْخُ (القاموس المحيط) البَرْخُ: النَّماءُ، والزِّيادَةُ، والرَّخيصُ، من الأَسْعارِ، والقَهْرُ، ودَقُّ العُنُقِ والظَّهرِ، وضَرْبٌ يَقْطَعُ بعضَ اللَّحمِ بالسَّيفِ. والبَريخُ: المَكْسورُ الظَّهْرِ. والتَّبْريخُ: الخُضوعُ .

وَسَقهُ (القاموس المحيط) واتَّسَقَ: انْتَظَمَ.

نسق (لسان العرب) النَّسَقُ من كل شيء: ما كان على طريقة نِظامٍ واحد، عامٌّ في الأشياء، وقد نَسقْتُه تَنْسيقاً؛ ويقال: رأيت نَسَقاً من الرجال والمتاع أي بعضُها إلى جنب بعض؛ قال الشاعر: مُسْتَوْسِقات عَصَباً ونَسَقا والنَّسْق، بالتسكين: مصدر نَسَقْتُ الكلام إذا عطفت بعضه على بعض؛ ويقال: نَسَقْتُ بين الشيئين وناسَقْتُ.

عشق (مقاييس اللغة) العين والشين والقاف أصلٌ صحيح يدلُّ على تجاوُزِ حدِّ المحبّة .

عسق (مقاييس اللغة) العين والسين والقاف أُصيلٌ صحيح يدلُّ على لُصوق الشيء بالشيء.

عسق (لسان العرب) عَسِقَ به يَعْسَقُ عَسَقاً: لزق به ولزمه وأُولِعَ به، وكذلك تَعَسَّق؛

عسك (لسان العرب) عَسِكَ به عَسَكاً، فهو عَسِكٌ: لَصِق به ولَزِمَه، وكذلك سَدِكَ، وزعم يعقوب أن كاف عَسِك بدل من قاف عَسِق.

قبل (الصّحاح في اللغة) قبلُ: نقيض بعدُ. وقولهم إذنْ أقْبِلَ قُبْلَكَ، أي أقْصِد قصدَكَ وأتوجّه نحوك. والقُبْلَةُ من التَقْبيلِ معروفةٌ.

1.55

فهر (لسان العرب) وأفْهَر إذا اجتمع لحمه زِيماً زِيماً وتكَتّل فكان مُعَجَّراً، وهو أقبح السمن. والفَهْرُ أن ينكح الرجل المرأة ثم يتحوّل عنها قبل الفراغ إلى غيرها فيُنْزِل، وقد نهي عن ذلك. وفي الحديث: أنه نهى عن الفَهْرِ، وكذلك الفَهَر، مثل نَهْرٍ ونَهَر، بالسكون والتحريك؛ يقال: أفْهَرَ يُفْهِرُ إفْهاراً. ابن الأعرابي: أفْهَر الرجلُ إذا خلا مع جاريته لقضاء حاجته ومعه في البيت أخرى من جواريه، فأكْسَلَ عن هذه أي أَوْلَجَ ولم يُنْزِل، فقام من هذه إلى أخرى فأنزل معها، وقد نهي عنه في الخبر. قال: وأفْهَر الرجل إذا كان مع جاريته والأُخرى تسمع حِسَّه، وقد نهي عنه. وفُهْرُ اليهود، بالضم: موضعُ مِدْراسِهم الذي يجتمعون إليه في عيدهم يصلون فيه، وقيل: هو يوم يأْكلون فيه ويشربون؛ قال أبو عبيد: وهي كلمة نَبَطِيَّة أصلها بُهْر أعجمي، عرّب بالفاء فقيل فُهْر، وقيل: هي عبرانية عرّبت أيضاً، والنصارى يقولون فُخْر. قال ابن دريد: لا أَحسب الفُهْر عربيّاً صحيحاً.

1.57

طلل (لسان العرب) والإطْلال الإشْرافُ على الشيء. ويقال: رأيت نساءً يَتطالَلْنَ من السُّطوح أي يَتشَوَّفْنَ. وتَطالَلْت: تطاوَلْت فنظَرْت. أبو العَمَيْثَل: تطالَلْت للشيء وتطاوَلْت بمعنى واحد، وتطالَّ أي مدّ عُنُقه ينظر إلى الشيء يَبْعُد عنه؛ أبو عمرو: التَّطالُّ الاطّلاع من فَوْق السكان أو من السّتْر. وأَطَلَّ عليه أي أَشْرَف؛ وتطاوَلَ على الشيء واسْتَطَلّ: أَشْرَف؛

ضل (مقاييس اللغة) الضاد واللام أصلٌ صحيحٌ يدلُّ على معنًى واحد، وهو ضَياع الشيء وذهابُهُ في غيرِ حقِّه.

ضلل (لسان العرب) الضَّلالُ والضَّلالةُ: ضدُّ الهُدَى والرَّشاد، ضَلَلْتَ تَضِلُّ هذه اللغة الفصيحة، وضَلِلْتَ تَضَلُّ ضَلالاً وضَلالةً؛ يقال: أَضْلَلْت الشيءَ إذا غَيَّبْتَه. ويقال: ضَلَّ ضَلاله، كما يقال جُنَّ جُنونُه؛ وذَهَب ضِلَّةً أي لم يُدْرَ أين ذَهَب.

الضَّلالُ (القاموس المحيط) والضُّلَّةُ، بالضم: الحِذْقُ بالدَّلالَةِ، وبالفتح: الحَيْرَةُ، والغَيْبَةُ لخَيْرٍ أوشَرٍّ.

دل (مقاييس اللغة) الدال واللام أصلان: أحدهما إبانة الشيء بأمارةٍ تتعلمها، والآخر اضطرابٌ في الشيء.فالأوّل قولهم: دلَلْتُ فلاناً على الطريق.
والدليل: الأمارة في الشيء. وهو بيّن الدَّلالة والدِّلالة.والأصل الآخر قولهم: تَدَلْدَل الشَّيءُ، إذا اضطرَب.
دأل (مقاييس اللغة) الدال والهمزة واللام يدل على خِفّة ونَشْطةٍ. فالدَّألان: المشْيُ بنشاط. يقال منه دَألْتُ أدْأل. والدَّأْل الخَتْل.
دأل (لسان العرب) الدَّأْلُ: الخَتْل، وقد دَألَ يَدْأَلُ دألاً ودَألاناً. أبو زيد في الهمز: دأَلْت للشَّيءِ أَدْأل دأْلاً ودَألاناً، وهي مِشْيَة شبيهة بالخَتْل ومَشْي
المُثقَل، وذكر الأصمعي في صفة مشي الخيل: الدَّألان مشي يقارب فيه الخطو ويبغي فيه كأنه مُثقل من حمل. يقال: الذئب يَدْأل للغزال ليأْكله،
يقول يَخْتِله. وقد دَألْتُ له ودَألْته وقد تكون في سرعة المشي. ابن الأَعرابي: الدَّألانُ عَدْوٌ مُقارِب. ووقع القومُ في دُؤْلول أي في اختلاط من أَمرهم.
دعل (لسان العرب) ابن الأعرابي: الدَّعَل المُخاتَلة بالعين، وهو يُداعله أي يُخاتله.
عدل (مقاييس اللغة) العين والدال واللام أصلان صحيحان، لكنَّهما متقابلان كالمتضادَّين: أحدُهما يدلُّ على استواء، والآخر يدلُّ على اعوجاج.
العَدْلُ (القاموس المحيط) وانْعَدَلَ عنه وعادَلَ: اعْوَجَّ. وهو يُعادِلُ هذا الأمرَ: إذا ارْتَبَكَ فيه، ولم يُمْضِه. و~ فلاناً بفلانٍ: سَوَّى بينهما.
عدل (لسان العرب) ويُعَادِلُ يقول: يُعادِل بين الأَمرين أَيَّهما يَرْكَب. تُميّته: تُذَلّله المَشورات وقولُ الناس أين تَذْهَب. والمُعادَلَةُ: الشَّكُّ في أَمرين،
يقال: أَنا في عِدالٍ من هذا الأَمر أَي في شكٍّ منه: أَأَمضي عليه أَم أَتركه.

ePSD: edēlu
ur [SHUT] wr. ur3 "to shut; protection" Akk. edēlu; kidinnu

1.58

ضَبَطَهُ (القاموس المحيط) ضَبَطَهُ ضَبْطاً وضَباطةً: حَفِظَهُ بالحَزْمِ. ورجُلٌ وجملٌ ضابِطٌ وضَبَنْطَى، كحَبَنْطَى: قويٌّ شديدٌ. وأضْبَطُ: يَعْمَلُ بيدَيْهِ
جميعاً وهي ضبطاء. وتَضَبَّطَهُ: أخَذَهُ على حَبْسٍ وقَهْرٍ،
ضبط (مقاييس اللغة) الضاد والباء والطاء أصلٌ صحيحٌ. ضَبَطَ الشَّيء ضَبْطاً.
ضبط (لسان العرب) الضَّبْطُ: لزوم الشيء وحَبْسُه، ضَبَطَ عليه وضَبَطَه يَضْبُط (* قوله «يضبط» شكل في الأصل في غير موضع بضم الباء،
وهو مقتضى اطلاق المجد وضبط هامش نسخة من النهاية يوثق بها، لكن الذي في المصباح والمختار أنه من باب ضرب.) ضَبْطاً وضَباطةً،
وقال الليث: الضَّبْطُ لزومُ شيء لا يفارقه في كل شيء، وضَبْطُ الشيء حِفْظُه بالحزم، والرجل ضابِطٌ أَي حازِمٌ.

1.59

سطر (لسان العرب) قال أَبو سعيد الضرير: سمعت أَعرابيّاً فصيحاً يقول: أَسْطَرَ فلانٌ اسمي أَي تجاوز السَّطْرَ الذي فيه اسمي، فإذا كتبه قيل:
سَطَرَهُ. وقال ابن بُزُرج: يقولون للرجل إذا أخطأَ فكَنَوْا عن خَطَئِهِ: أَسْطَرَ فلانٌ اليومَ، وهو الإِسْطارُ بمعنى الإِخْطاءِ. قال الأَزهري: هو ما حكاه
الضرير عن الأَعرابي أَسْطَرَ اسمي أَي جاوز السَّطْرَ الذي هو فيه.

الإِتْبُ (القاموس المحيط) الإِتْبُ، بالكسر، والتَّأَتُّبُ: الاسْتِعْدادُ، والتَّصَلُّبُ، وأنْ تَجْعَلَ حِمالَ القَوْسِ في صَدْرِكَ، وتُخْرِجَ مَنْكِبَيْكَ منها. ورجُلٌ
مُؤَتَّبُ الظُّفُرِ، كمُعَظَّمٍ: مُعْوَجُّهُ .
أتب (مقاييس اللغة) الهمزة والتاء والباء أصلٌ واحد، وهو شيءٌ يشتمل به الإبط، قميصٌ غير مَخِيط الجانبين. قال النُّميريّ: المِئْتَبُ المِشْمَل
وقد تأتَّبه إذا ألقاه تحت إبطه ثم اشتمل. ورجل مُؤَتَّب الظهر، ويقال مُؤْتَبٌ، أي أجنَؤُهُ.
أتب (لسان العرب) والمِئْتَبُ: المِشْمَلُ .

لعو (مقاييس اللغة) اللام والعين والحرف المعتلّ كلماتٌ غير راجعةٍ إلى قياسٍ واحد. وقد كتبت الكلبة اللَعوة: الحريصة. والرجُل اللَعْو: السيِّئُ
الخُلُق. واللُّعْوة السَّواد حولَ حَلَمةَ الثَّدي. ويقولون: تَلَعَّى العَسَل: تعَقَّد. ويقولون للعاثر: لعاً لَكَ، دعاء أن ينتعش .
اللَعْوُ (القاموس المحيط) اللَعْوُ: السَّيِّئُ الخُلُقِ، والفَسْلُ، والشَّرِهُ الحريصُ، كاللَّعا، وهي: بهاءٍ ج: لِعاءٌ. واللَّعْوَةُ: السَّوادُ حَوْلَ حَلَمَةِ الثَّدْيِ، ويُضَمُّ،
والكَلْبَةُ، كاللَّعاةِ. وذُو لَعْوَةَ: قَيْلٌ، ورجلٌ آخَرُ. واللاَّعِي: الذي يُفْزِعُه أدْنَى شيءٍ. وتَلَعَّى العَسَلُ: تَعَقَّدَ،
و~ اللُّعاعَ: خَرَجَ يأخُذُهُ.
تلو (مقاييس اللغة) التاء واللام والواو أصلٌ واحد، وهو الاتّباع. يقال: تَلَوْتُه إذا تَبِعْتَه.
تلا (لسان العرب) تَلَوْتُه أَتلُوه وتَلَوْتُ عنه تُلُوّاً، كلاهما: خَذَلته وتركته. وتَلا عَنِّي يَتْلُو تُلُوّاً إذا تركك وتخلَّف عنك، وكذلك خَذَل يَخْذُل خُذُولاً.
وتَلَوْته تُلُوّاً: تبعته. يقال: ما زلت أَتلُوه حتى أَتْلَيْته أَي تقَدَّمْته وصار خلفي. وأَتْلَيْته أَي سبقته. وتَتَلَّى إذا جَمَع مالاً كثيراً. وتَلَوْت القرآن تِلاوةً:
قرأْته، وعم به بعضهم كل كلام؛ وفلان يَتْلو فلاناً أَي يحكيه ويَتْبَع فعله. وهو يُتْلي بَقِيّة حاجته أَي يَقْتَضِيها ويَتَعهَّدها. أَتْلَيْتُه ذمّة أَي أَعطيته
إياها. والتَّلاءُ: الحَوالة. وقد أَتْلَيْت فلاناً على فلان أَي أَحَلْته عليه؛ وأَتْلَيْته أَي أَحلته من الحوالة .
تلع (لسان العرب) تلعَ النهارُ يَتْلَعُ تَلْعاً وتُلوعاً وأَتْلَع: ارْتَفَعَ. وتَلَعَتِ الضُّحَى تُلوعاً وأَتْلَعت: انْبَسَطت. وتَلَعُ الضُّحى: وقتُ تُلوعِها؛ عن ابن
الأَعرابي؛ وأَنشد: أَأَنْ غَرَّدَتْ في بَطنِ وادٍ حَمامةٌ بَكَيْتَ، ولم يَعْذِرْكَ بالجَهْلِ عاذِرُ تعالَيْن في عُبْرِيّه، تَلَعَ الضُّحَى، على فَنَنٍ، قد نَعَّمَتْه السَّرائر وتَلَع
الظَّبْيُ والثَّوْرُ من كِناسه: أَخرج رأْسه وسَمَا بِجِيدِه. وأَتْلَع رأْسَه: أَطْلَعه فنظر؛ وأَتْلَع رأْسَه: أَطْلَعه فنظر؛ قال ذو الرُّمة: كما أَتْلَعَتْ، من تَحْتِ أَرْطَى
صَرِيمةٍ إلى نَبْأَةِ الصوْتِ، الظِّباءُ الكَوانِسُ وتَلَع الرجلُ رأْسَه: أَخرجه من شيء كان فيه، وهو شِبْه طَلَع إلا أَن طلع أَعمّ. قال الأَزهري: في كلام
العرب: أَتْلَع رأْسَه إذا أَطلَع وتَلَع الرأْسُ نفْسُه، وأَنشد بيت ذي الرمة.

طلع (لسان العرب) وطلَع عليهم: أتاهم. وطلَع عليهم: غاب، وهو من الأضداد. وطَلعةُ الرجل: شخْصُه وما طلَع منه. وكلُّ بادٍ من عُلْوٍ طالِعٌ. وفي الحديث: هذا بُسْرٌ قد طَلعَ اليَمَن أي قَصَدها من نجْد. وأطلَع رأسه إذا أشرف على شيء، وكذلك اطّلعَ وأطْلعَ غيرَه واطّلعَه، والاسم الطّلاعُ. واطّلَعْتُ على باطِنِ أمره، وهو افتعَلْتُ، وأطْلَعه على الأمر: أعْلمَه به، والاسم الطّلْعُ. وفي حديث ابن ذي يزن: قال لعبد المطلب: أطْلَعْتُك طِلْعَه أي أعْلَمْتُكه؛ الطِّلع، بالكسر: اسم من اطّلعَ على الشيء إذا عَلِمَه. وطَلعَ على الأمر يَطْلَعُ طُلوعاً واطّلعَ عليهم اطّلاعاً واطّلَعه وتَطَلَّعَه: عَلِمه، وطالَعه إياه فنظر ما عنده؛ يقال: طَلَعْتُ عليهم واطّلَعْتُ وأطْلَعْتُ بمعنًى واحد.واسْتَطْلعَ رأيَه: نظر ما هو. وطالَعْتُ الشيء أي اطّلَعْتُ عليه، وطالَعه بكُتُبه، وتَطَلَّعْتُ إلى وُرودِ كتابِك. والطّلعةُ الرؤيةُ. وطَلَعْتُ عن صاحبي طُلوعاً إذا أدبَرْتَ عنه. وطَلَعْتُ عن صاحبي إذا أقْبلْتَ عليه؛ قال الأزهري: هذا كلام العرب. وقال أبو زيد في باب الأضداد: طَلَعْتُ على القوم أطْلَع طُلوعاً إذا غِبْتَ عنهم حتى لا يَرَوْك، وطلعت عليهم إذا أقبلت عليهم حتى يروك. قال ابن السكيت: طلعت على القوم إذا غبت عنهم صحيح، جعل على فيه بمعنى عن، كما قال الله عز وجل: ويل لمطففين الذين إذا اكتالوا على الناس؛ والطَّلِيعةُ: القوم يُبعثون لمُطالَعةِ خبرِ العدوّ، والواحد والجمع فيه سواء. وامرأة طُلَعةٌ: تكثر التَّطلُّعَ. ويقال امرأة طُلَعةٌ قُبَعةٌ، تَطْلَعُ تنظر ساعة ثم تَخْتَبِئُ. وقول الزِّبْرِقانِ بن بَدْرٍ: إن أبْغَضَ كنائِنِي إليَّ الطُّلَعةُ الخُبَأةُ أي التي تَطْلُعُ كثيراً ثم تَخْتَبِئُ. ونفس طُلَعةٌ: شَهِيّةٌ مُتطلِّعةٌ، على المثل، وكذلك الجمع؛ وتَطلَّعَ الرجلَ: غَلَبَه وأدْرَكَه؛ ويقال: أين مُطّلَعُ هذا الأمر أي مأتاه، وهو موضع الاطّلاع من إشْرافٍ إلى انْحدار. وقول الله عز وجل: نارُ اللهِ المُوقَدةُ التي تَطّلع على الأفْئِدةِ؛ قال الفراءُ: يَبْلُغُ ألَمُها الأفئدة، قال: والاطّلاعُ والبُلوغُ قد يكونان بمعنى واحد، والعرب تقول: متى طَلَعْتَ أرضنا أي متى بَلَغْتَ أرضنا، وقوله تَطّلع على الأفئدة، تُوفي عليها فَتُحرِقُها من اطّلعت إذا أشْرفت؛ قال الأزهري: وقول الفراء أحب إليّ، قال: وإليه ذهب الزجاج. ويقال: عافى اللهُ رجلاً لم يَتَطَلَّعْ في فِيكَ أي لم يتعقَّب كلامك. أبو عمرو: من أسماء الحية الطِّلْعُ والطِّلُّ. وأطْلَعْتُ إليه مَعْروفاً: مثل أزْلَلْتُ. ويقال: أطْلَعَني فلان وأرْهَقَني وأذْلَقَني وأقْحَمَني أي أعْجَلَني.

1.60

سبق (لسان العرب) السَّبْق: القُدْمةُ في الجَرْي وفي كل شيء؛ تقول: له في كل أمر سُبْقةٌ وسابقةٌ وسَبْقٌ، والجمع الأسْباق والسَّوابقُ. والسَّبْقُ مصدر سَبَق. وقد سَبَقَه يَسْبُقُه ويَسْبِقُه سَبْقاً: تقدَّمه. والسَّبَق، بالتحريك: الخَطَرُ الذي يوضع بين أهل السِّباق، وفي التهذيب: الذي يوضع في النِّضال والرِّهان في الخيل، فمن سبَق أخذه، والجمع أسباق. واسْتَبَقَ القومُ وتَسابقوا: تَخاطَرُوا. وأسْبَقَ القومُ إلى الأمر وتسابقوا: بادروا.

1.61

البُضْمُ (القاموس المحيط) البُضْمُ، بالضم: النَّفْسُ، والسُّنْبُلَةُ حين تَخْرُجُ من الحَبَةِ فَتَعْظُمُ. وبضمَ الزَرْعُ: غَلُظ حَبُّهُ، و~ الحَبُّ: اشتَدَّ قليلا .
بذم (الصِّحاح في اللغة) ثوبٌ ذو بُذْمٍ، أي كثير الغَزْلِ. ورجلٌ ذو بُذْمٍ، أي سمين،
البُذْمُ (القاموس المحيط) البُذْمُ، بالضمِّ: الرأيُ، والحزْمُ، والنَّفَسُ، والكثافةُ، والجَلَدُ، واحتِمالُكَ لِمَا حُمِّلْتَ.
بي (لسان العرب) حَيّاكَ اللهُ وبَيّاكَ، قيل: حَيّاكَ مَلّكَكَ، وقيل: أبقاكَ، ويقال: اعتمدك بالمُلك، وقيل: أصْلحك، وقيل: قَرّبَكَ؛ الأخيرة حكاها الأصمعي عن الأحمر. ويقال: بَيّنْتُ الشيء وبَيّيْتُه إذا أوضحته. والتَّبِيُّ التبيين من قرب.
بيض (لسان العرب) وبَيْضَةُ كل شيء حَوْزَتُه. ويقال: بَيَّضْتُ الإناءَ إذا فرَّغْتُه، وبَيَّضْتُه إذا ملأْتُه، وهو من الأضداد.
بثث (لسان العرب) بَثَّ الشيءَ والخبرَ يَبُثُّه ويَبِثُّه بَثّاً، وأبَثَّه، بمعنًى، فانْبَثَّ: فرّقه فتفرَّقَ، ونشره؛ والبَثُّ: الحالُ والحُزْنُ، يقال: أبْثَثْتُك أي أظْهَرْتُ لك بَثِّي. وأبَثَّه الحديثَ: أطْلَعه عليه؛
كان (القاموس المحيط) كانَ يَكِينُ: خضَعَ. وأكانَهُ اللهُ إكانَةً: خَضَعَهُ، وأدخَلَ عليه الذُّلَّ. واكْتانَ: حَزِنَ وهو يُسِرُّهُ.
كين (لسان العرب) واسْتكان الرجلُ: خَضَعَ وذَلَّ، جعله أبو علي استفعل من هذا الباب، وغيره يجعله افتعل من المَسْكنة، ولكل من ذلك تعليل مذكور في بابه. وباتَ فلانٌ بكِينةِ سَوْءٍ، بالكسر، أي بحالة سَوْء. أبو سعيد: يقال أكانَه اللهُ يُكِينُه إكانةً أي أخضعه حتى اسْتكان وأدخل عليه من الذل ما أكانَه؛ وأنشد: لعَمْرُك ما يَشْفي جِراحُ تَكِينُه، ولكِنْ شِفائي أن تئيم حَلائِلُهْ قال الأزهري: وفي التنزيل العزيز: فما اسْتَكانوا لربهم؛ من هذا، أي ما خضعُوا لربهم.
وكن (لسان العرب) وتَوَكَّنَ أي تَمكَّن. والواكِنُ الجالس؛
كنن (لسان العرب) الكِنُّ والكِنّةُ والكِنانُ: وِقاء كل شيء وسِتْرُه. وفي التنزيل العزيز: أو أكْنَنْتُم في أنفسكم؛ أي أخفَيْتم. واسْتَكَنَّ الشيءُ: استَتَرَ؛ وأكْنَنْتُه في نفسي: أسْرَرْتُه. وقال أبو زيد: كَنَنْتُه وأكْنَنْتُه بمعنى في الكِنِّ وفي النَّفس جميعاً، تقول: كَنَنْتُ العلم وأكْنَنْتُه، فهو مَكْنونٌ ومُكَنٌّ.
وصر (مقاييس اللغة) الواو والصاد والراء: كلمةٌ واحدة. قال الخليل: الوَصِيرة: الصَكُ. ويقال الوِصْر: السِّجِلُّ يكتُبه الملك لِمَنْ يُقْطِعُه.
صور (الصِّحاح في اللغة) ومنه قوله تعالى: "يومَ يُنْفَخُ في الصور".قال الكلبيّ: لا أدري ما الصورُ. ويقال: هو جمع صورة، أي يَنْفخُ في صُوَرِ الموتى الأرواحَ. وصارهُ يَصورُهُ، ويَصيرُهُ، أي أماله. وقرئَ قوله تعالى: "فَصُرْهُنَّ إليك" بضم الصاد وكسرها. قال الأخفش: يعني وَجِّهْهُنَّ. يقال: صُرْ إليَّ وصُرْ وجهك إليَّ، أي أقْبِلْ عليَّ.
صور (مقاييس اللغة) الصاد والواو والراء كلماتٌ كثيرةٌ متباينة الأصول. وليس هذا الباب بباب قياسٍ ولا اشتقاق. وقد مضى فيما كتبناه مثله.ومما ينقاس منه قولهم صورَ يَصْوَر، إذا مال. وصُرت الشَيءَ أصُورُهُ، وأصَرْتُه، إذا أملته إليك. ويجيء قياسُه تَصَوَّرَ، لِما ضُرِب، كأنّه مال وسَقَط. فهذا هو المنقاس، وسوى ذلك فكلُّ كلمةٍ منفردةٌ بنفسها. من ذلك الصُّورة صُورة كلِّ مخلوق، والجمع صُوَر، وهي هيئةُ خِلْقته. واللهُ تعالى البارئ المُصَوِّر.

1.62

نكل (مقاييس اللغة) النون والكاف واللام أصلٌ صحيح يدلُّ على مَنع وامتناع، وإليه يرجع فروعه. ونَكَل عنه نُكولاً يَنكِل. وأصل ذلك النِّكْل: القَيْد، وجمعه أنكال، لأنَّه يَنْكُل: أي يَمنَع. والنِّكْل حديدة اللِّجام. وهو ناكلٌ عن الأمور: ضعيفٌ عنها.

نكَلَ (القاموس المحيط) نَكَلَ عنه، كضَرَبَ ونَصَرَ وعَلِمَ نُكولاً: نَكَصَ وجَبُنَ. ونكّل به تنكيلاً: صَنَعَ به صَنيعاً يُحَذِّرُ غيرَه. أو نكله: نَحّاهُ عَمّا قَبْلَهُ،

نكل (لسان العرب) نَكَلَ عنه يَنْكِل (* قوله «نكل عنه ينكل إلخ» عبارة القاموس: نكل عنه كضرب ونصر وعلم نكولاً: نكص وجبن) ويَنْكُل نُكولاً ونَكِلَ: نَكَصَ. يقال: نكل عن العدوّ وعن اليمين يَنْكُل، بالضم، أي جَبُنَ، ونَكَّله عن الشيء: صرفه عنه.

ويقال: نكل الرجل عن الأمر يَنْكُل نُكولاً إذا جَبُنَ عنه، ولغة أخرى نَكِل، بالكسر، يَنْكَل، والأُولى أجود. وفي الحديث: إن الله يحب النَّكَل على النَّكَل، بالتحريك، قيل له: وما النَّكَل على النَّكَل؟ قال: الرجل القويُّ المجرَّب المبدئ المعيدُ أي الذي أبداً في غَزْوِه وأعاد على مثله من الخيل، وفي الصحاح: النَّكَل على النَّكَل يعني الرجل القويَّ المجرَّب على الفرس القوي المجرَّب؛ وأنشد ابن بري للراجز: ضَرْباً بكفَّيْ نَكَلٍ لم يُنْكَل قال ابن الأثير: النَّكَل، بالتحريك، من التَّنْكيل وهو المنع والتنحية عما يريد؛ ومنه النُّكول في اليمين وهو الامتناع منها وترك الإقدام عليها؛ ومنه الحديث: مُضَرُ صَخْرة اللهِ التي لا تُنكل أي لا تُدْفَع عمَّا سُلِّطت عليه لثبوتها في الأرض. يقال: أنكَلْت الرجل عن حاجته إذا دفَعْته عنها؛ ومنه حديث ماعِز: لأَنْكُلَنَّه عنهنَّ أي لأمنَعنَّه.

نقل (مقاييس اللغة) النون والقاف واللام: أصلٌ صحيح يدلُّ على تحويل شيءٍ من مكانٍ إلى مكان، ثم يفرَّع ذلك. يقال: نقلْتُه أنقُله نَقْلاً.

نَقَلَهُ (القاموس المحيط) نَقَلَهُ: حَوَّلَهُ فانْتَقَل. والمُناقَلَةُ في المَنْطِقِ: أن تُحَدِّثَهُ ويُحَدِّثَكَ.

نقل (لسان العرب) والنَّقَلُ سرعة نَقْل القوائم. وفرس مِنْقَل أي ذو نَقَل وذو نِقال. وفرس مِنْقَل ونَقَّال ومُناقِل: سريع نَقْل القوائم، وإنه لذو نَقِيل. والتَّنْقِيل: مثل النَّقَل؛ قال كعب: لهنَّ، من بعدُ، إرْقالٌ وتَنْقِيلٌ والنَّقِيلُ: ضرب من السير وهو المُداومة عليه.

ويقال: انتقَل سار سيراً سريعاً؛ قال الراجز: لو طَلَبونا وجَدُونا نَنْتَقِلْ، مثلَ انْتِقال نفَرٍ على إبِلْ وقد ناقَلَ مُناقلةً ونِقالاً، وقيل: النِّقالُ الرَّدَيان وهو بين العدْو والخَبَب. والفرس يُناقِل في جَرْيه إذا اتَّقى في عَدْوه الحجارة. ومُناقلةُ الفرس: أن يضع يدَه ورجله على غير حجر لحسْن نَقْله في الحجارة؛ والنَّقَلُ مراجعة الكلام في صَخَب؛ قال لبيد: ولقد يعلَم صحْبي كلهم، بعَدانِ السَّيفِ، صَبْري ونَقَلْ أبو عبيد: النَّقَل المُناقَلة في المنطِق. وناقَلْت فلاناً الحديثَ إذا حدَّثته وحدَّثك. ورجل نَقِلٌ: حاضر المنطق والجواب، وأنشد للبيد هذا البيت أيضاً: صَبْري ونَقَل. وقد ناقَله. وتَناقل القومُ الكلامَ بينهم: تنازَعوه؛ فأما ما أنشده ابن الأعرابي من قول الشاعر: كانت إذا غَضِبتْ عليَّ تطلَّمتْ، وإذا طَلَبْتُ كلامَها لم تَنقُل (* قوله «تطلمت» هكذا في الأصل والمحكم بالطاء المهملة). قال ابن سيده: فقد يكون من النَّقَل الذي هو حضور المنطق والجواب، قال: غير أنَّا لم نسمع نَقِل الرجل إذا جاوَب، وإنما نَقِلٌ عندنا على النسب لا على الفعل، إلاَّ أن نجهل ما علم غيرُنا فقد يجوز أن تكون العرب قالت ذلك إلاَّ أنه لم يبلغنا نحن، قال: وقد يكون تَنْقُل تَنْفعِل من القَوْل كقولك لم تَنْقد من الانقياد، غير أنَّا لم نسمعهم قالوا انْقالَ الرجلُ على شكْل انْقادَ، قال: وعسى أن يكون ذلك مَقُولاً أيضاً إلاَّ أنه لم يصل إلينا، قال: والأسبق إليَّ أنه من النَّقَل الذي هو الجواب لأن ابن الأعرابي لمَا فسره قال: معناه لم تُجاوِبني. والنَّقَل المُجادلة.

وتر (لسان العرب) الوِترُ والوَتْرُ: الفَرْدُ أو ما لم يَتشفَّعْ من العَدَدِ. وأَوْتَرَهُ أي أَفَذَّهُ. والتَّواتُرُ التتابُعُ،

فذذ (لسان العرب) الفَذّ: الفَرد، والجمع أفذاذ وفُذوذ. والفذُّ: الواحد، وقد فذ الرجل عن أصحابه إذا شذَّ عنهم وبقي فرداً.

وتر (الصِّحاح في اللغة) والمواتَرةُ المتابعةُ. ولا تكون المُواتَرةُ بين الأشياء إلا إذا وقعت بينهما فترةٌ، وإلاّ فهي مُداركةٌ ومواصلةٌ. وكذلك واتَرْتُ الكتب فتواترَتْ، أي جاءت بعضها في إثر بعض وِتراً وِتراً، من غير أن تنقطع. وتَترى أصلها وَترى من الوِتْر، وهو الفرد. قال الله تعالى: "ثمّ أرسلْنا رُسُلَنا تَتْرى"، أي واحداً بعد واحد.

أتر (لسان العرب) الأُتْرُور: لغة في التُّؤْرُور مقلوب عنه .

تأر (لسان العرب) أتأر إليه النَّظَر: أحَدَّه. عن ابن الأعرابي قال: تأرةٌ، مهموز، فلما كثر استعمالهم لها تركوا همزها؛ قال الأزهري: قال غيره وجمعها تئَر، مهموزة؛ ومنه يقال: أتأرْتُ إليه النظر أي أدمته تارة بعد تارة .

تر (مقاييس اللغة) وأمّا التَّراتِرُ فالأمورُ العِظام، وليست [أصلاً]؛ لأنَ الرّاء مبدلةٌ من لام.

ترر (لسان العرب) وفي حديث ابن زِمْل: رَبْعَةٌ من الرجال تارٌّ؛ التارُّ: الممتلئ البدن، وتَرَّ الرجلُ يَتِرُّ ويَتَرُّ تَرّاً وترارة وتُروراً: امتلأ جسمه وتروّى عظمه؛ والتَّراتِرُ الشدائد والأمور العظام.

سطر (لسان العرب) وقال ابن بُزُرج: يقولون للرجل إذا أخطأ فكَنَوْا عن خَطَئِه: أَسْطَرَ فلانٌ اليومَ، وهو الإسْطار بمعنى الإخْطاء. قال الأزهري: هو ما حكاه الضرير عن الأعرابي أَسْطَرَ اسمي أي جاوز السَّطْرَ الذي هو فيه. والأساطِيرُ: الأباطِيل. والمُسَيْطِرُ والمُصَيْطِرُ: المُسَلَّطُ على الشيء لِيُشرف عليه ويَتَعَهَّدَ أحواله ويكتبَ عَمَلَهُ، وأصله من السَّطر لأن الكتاب مُسَطَّرٌ، والذي يفعله مُسَطِّرٌ ومُسَيْطِرٌ. يقال: سَيْطَرْتَ علينا. وفي القرآن: لست عليهم بِمُسَيطِر؛ أي مُسَلَّطٍ. يقال: سَيْطَر يُسَيطِر وتَسَيطر يتَسَيْطَر، فهو مُسَيْطِرٌ ومتَسَيْطِرٌ، وقد تقلب السين صاداً لأجل الطاء، وقال الفراء في قوله تعالى: أم عندهم خزائن ربك أم هم المُسَيطِرُونَ؛ قال: المصيطرون كتابتها بالصاد وقراءتها بالسين، وقال الزجاج: المسيطرون الأرباب المسلطون. يقال: قد تسيطر علينا وتصيطر، بالسين والصاد، والأصل السين، وكل سين بعدها طاء يجوز أن تقلب صاداً.

يقال: سطر وصطر وسطا عليه وصطا. والسَّطْرُ العَتُودُ من المَعَز، وفي التهذيب: من الغنم، والصاد لغة. والمُسَيْطِرُ: الرقيب الحفيظ، وقيل: المتسلط، وبه فسر قوله عز وجل: لستَ عليهم بمسيطر، وقد سَيْطَرَ علينا وسَوْطَرَ.

تعا (لسان العرب) انفرد الأزهري بهذه الترجمة، وقال ابن الأعرابي: يقال تَعَا إذا عَدَا وتَعا إذا قَذَف. قال: والتَّعَى في الحفظ الحَسَن. وقال في الترجمة أيضاً: والتَّاعِي اللِّبأُ المسترخي، والتَّاعِي القاذف

تعع (لسان العرب) التَّعُّ: الاسترخاء. تَعَّ تعًا وأَتَعَّ: قاء كثَعَّ؛ ووقع القومُ في تَعاتعَ إذا وقعوا في أراجيفَ وتَخليط. وتَعتعةُ الدابة: ارتطامها في الرمل والخَبار والوَحل من ذلك. وقد تَعتَعَ البعيرُ وغيره إذا ساخَ في الخَبار أي في وُعوثةِ الرِّمال؛ قال الشاعر: يُتَعْتِعُ في الخَبارِ إذا علاه، ويَعثُر في الطَّريقِ المُستَقيمِ.

علو (مقاييس اللغة) *العين واللام والحرف المعتل ياءً كان أو واواً أو ألفاً، أصلٌ واحد يدلُّ على السموّ والارتفاع، لا يشذُّ عنه شيء. ومن ذلك العَلاء والعُلُوّ. وأمّا العُلُوّ فالعظمة والتجبُّر. والعالي: الشَّديد. قال الخليل: المَعْلاة: كَسْبُ الشَّرَف، والجمع المعالي. وفلانٌ من عِلْية النّاس أي من أهل الشَّرف. قال: ويقال للمرأة إذا طَهُرت من نِفاسها: قد تعلّت، وهي تتعلَّى.

1.63

مني (لسان العرب) المنى، بالياء: القدر؛ قال الشاعر: دَرَيْتُ ولا أَدْري مَنى الحَدَثانِ مَناهُ اللهُ يَمْنِيه: قَدَّره. والمنى والمَنيَّةُ: الموت لأنه قُدِّر علينا. وقد مَنى اللهُ له الموت يَمْني، ومُنِي له أي قُدِّر؛ وقال الشَّرقي بن القطامي: المَنايا الأَحداث، والحِمامُ الأَجَلُ، والحَتْفُ القَدَرُ، والمَنونُ الزَّمانُ؛ وامْتَنَيْت الشيء: اخْتَلَقْته. ومُنِيتُ بكذا وكذا: ابْتُلِيت به. ومَناه اللهُ بحُبها يَمنِيه ويَمْنُوه أي ابْتلاه بحُبِّها مَنْياً ومَنْواً. وداري بمَنى داره أي بحذائها؛ والمَنى: القَصْدُ؛ وتَمَنَّى الشيءَ: أراده، ومَنَّاه إياه وبه، وهي المُنيةُ والمُنْيةُ والأُمْنيَّةُ. وتَمَنَّى الكتابَ: قرأه وكتبه. وفي حديث الحسن: ليس الإيمانُ بالتَّحَلِّي ولا بالتَّمنِّي ولكن ما وَقَر في القلب وصَدَّقَته الأَعمال أي ليس هو بالقول الذي تُظْهره بلسانك فقط، ولكن يجب أن تَتْبَعه معرفةُ القلب، وقيل: هو من التَّمَنِّي القراءة والتِّلاوة. يقال: تَمنَّى إذا قرأَ. والتَّمنِّي: الكَذِب. وفلان يَتَمَنَّى الأَحاديث أي يَفْتَعِلها، وهو مقلوب من المَيْن، وهو الكذب. وتَمَنَّى الحَديثَ: اخترعه. ويقول الرجل: والله ما تَمَنَّيْت هذا الكلام ولا اخْتَلَقْته. ويقال: لأُمْنِيَنَّك مناوَتَك أي لأَجْزِيَنَّك جزاءك. ومانَيْته مُماناة: كافأْته، غير مهموز. ومانَيْتُك: كافأْتك؛ وأَنشد ابن بري لسَبْرة بن عمرو: نُماني بها أَكْفاءَنا ونُهينها، ونَشْرَبُ في أَثْمانها ونُقامِرُ وقال آخر: أُماني به الأَكْفاءَ في كلِّ مَوْطِنٍ، وأَقْضِي فُروضَ الصَّالحينَ وأَقْتَري ومانَيْته: لَزِمْته. ومانَيْته: انْتَظَرْته وطاوَلْته. والمُماناةُ: المُطاولة. والمُماناةُ: الانْتِظار؛ والمَنا: الكَيْلُ أَو المِيزانُ الذي يُوزَنُ به.

1.64

رحا (لسان العرب) والرَّحَى: معروفة التي يُطْحَنُ بها، والجمع أَرْحٍ وأَرْحاءٌ ورُحِيٌّ ورِحِيٌّ وأَرْحِيَةٌ؛ ورَحَيْتُ الرَّحَى: عَمِلْتُها وأَدَرْتُها. الجوهري: رَحَوْتُ الرَّحا ورَحَيْتُها إذا أَدَرْتَها. إليها لم تكن سبعين سنة ولا كان الدينُ فيها قائماً، ويروى: تزول رَحى الإسلام عِوَض تَدُورُ أي تَزُول عن ثُبُوتها واستقرارها. وترحَّتِ الحَيَّةُ (* قوله «وترحت الحية إلخ» هذه عبارة التهذيب بزيادة قوله ولهذا إلخ من المحكم. وعبارة المحكم: ورحت الحية استدارت كالرحى ولهذا قيل لها إحدى بنات طبق، قال رؤبة إلخ وعليه ينطبق الشاهد). استدارت وتَلَوَّت فهي مُتَرَحِّيَةٌ؛ ورَحى الحَرْب: حَوْمَتُها؛ رها (لسان العرب) رَها الشيءُ رَهْواً: سَكن. وعَيْشٌ راهٍ: خَصِيبٌ ساكنٌ رافِهٌ. وخِمْسٌ راهٍ إذا كان سهلاً. وكلُّ ساكنٍ لا يتحَرَّكُ راهٍ ورَهْوٌ. رخا (لسان العرب) قال ابن سيده: الرَّخْوُ والرِّخْوُ والرُّخْوُ الهَشُّ من كلِّ شيءٍ؛ وأَرْخَيْتُ الشيءَ وغيرَه إذا أَرْسَلْته. والتَّراخي: التَّقاعُدُ عن الشيء. وراخت المرأةُ: حان وِلادُها. وتَراخى عني: تَقاعَس. وراخاه: باعَدَه. وتراخى عن حاجته: فَتَرَ. وتراخى السماء: أَبطأَ المَطَرُ. وتراخى فلان عني أي أَبطأَ عَنِّي، وغيره يقول: تراخى بعُدَ عَنِّي.

1.66

دلف (مقاييس اللغة) الدال واللام والفاء أصلٌ واحد يدلُّ على تقدُّم في رفق فالدَّليف: المشيُ الرُّوَيد. يقال دَلَف دَليفاً؛ وهو فَوقَ الدَّبيب.

دَلَف (القاموس المحيط) دلَفَ الشَّيْخُ يَدْلِفُ دَلْفاً، ويُحَرَّكُ، ودَليفاً ودَلَفاناً، مُحرَّكةً: مَشَى مَشْيَ المُقَيَّدِ، وفوقَ الدَّبيبِ، والمُنْدَلِفُ والمُتَدَلِّفُ: الأَسَدُ الماشي على هِينَتِه. وتدَلَّفَ إليه: تَمَشَّى ودنا.

دلف (لسان العرب) الدَّلِيفُ: المَشْيُ الرُّوَيْدُ. دَلَفَ يَدْلِفُ دَلْفاً ودَلَفاناً ودَلِيفاً ودُلوفاً إذا مشى وقارَب الخَطْو، وقال الأَصمعي: دَلَف الشيخُ فحَصَّص، وقيل: الدَّلِيفُ فوق الدَّبيب كما تَدْلِفُ الكتيبةُ نحو الكتيبة في الحَرْب، وهو الرُّوَيْدُ؛ قال طرفة: لا كبيرٌ دالفٌ من هَرَمٍ أَرْهَبُ الناسَ ولا أَكْبُو لِضُرّ ويقال: هو يَدْلِفُ ويَدْلِتُ دَلِيفاً ودَلِيتاً إذا قارَبَ خَطْوَه مُتقدِّماً، وقد أَدْلَفه الكِبَرُ؛ والدَّالِفُ مثل الدَّالح: وهو الذي يمشي بالحِمْل الثقيل ويُقارِبُ الخَطْو مثل (* قوله «ويقارب الخطو مثل» كذا بالأصل. وعبارة الصحاح: ويقارب الخطو، والجمع دلف مثل إلخ.) وعُقابٌ دَلُوفٌ: سريعة؛ عن ابن الأعرابي؛ وأَنشد: إذا السُّقاةُ اضْطَجَعُوا للأَذْقانْ، عَقَّتْ كما عَقَّتْ دَلُوفُ العِقْبانْ عَقَّتْ: حامتْ، وقيل: ارْتَفعت كارتفاع العُقاب.

كور (لسان العرب) الكُورُ، بالضم: الرحل، وقيل: الرحل بأَداته، والجمع أَكوار وأَكْوُرٌ؛ وتَكْوِيرُ الليل والنهار: أَن يُلْحَق أَحدُهما بالآخر، وقيل: تَكْوِيرُ الليل والنهار تَغْشِيَةُ كل واحد منهما صاحبه، وقيل: إِدخال كل واحد منهما في صاحبه، والمعاني متقاربة؛ وفي الصحاح: وتَكْوِيرُ الليل على النهار تَغْشيته إِياه، ويقال زيادته في هذا من ذلك. وفي التنزيل العزيز: يُكَوِّرُ الليلَ على النهار ويُكَوِّرُ النهارَ على الليل؛ أَي يُدْخِلُ هذا على هذا، وأَصله من تَكْوِيرِ العمامة، وهو لفها وجمعها. وكَوَّر المتاعَ: أَلقى بعضه على بعض. الجوهري: الكارَةُ ما يُحمل على الظهر من الثِّياب، وتَكْوِيرُ المتاع: جمعُه وشدّه. وضربه فكَوَّره أَي صرعه، وكذلك طعنه فكَوَّره أَي أَلقاه مجتمعاً؛ ويقال: كُرْتُ العمامةَ على رأْسي أَكُورُها وكَوَّرْتُها أُكَوِّرُها إِذا لففتها؛ وقال الأَخفش: تُلَفُّ فتُمْحَى؛ وقال أَبو عبيدة: كُوِّرَتْ مثل تكوير العمامة تُلَفُّ فتُمْحَى، وقال قتادة: كُوِّرَتْ ذهب ضوءُها، وهو قول الفراء،

وقال عكرمة: نُزِعَ ضوءُها، وقال مجاهد: كُوِّرَتْ دُهْوِرَتْ، وقال الرَّبيعُ بن خَيثَم: كُوِّرَتْ رُمِيَ بها، ويقال: دَهْوَرْتُ الحائطَ إذا طرحته حتى يَسْقُطَ، وحكى الجوهري عن ابن عباس: كُوِّرَتْ غُوِّرَتْ،

قور (لسان العرب) والاقْوِرارُ تَشَنُّجُ الجلد وانحناءُ الصلب هُزالاً وكِبَراً. واقْوَرَّ الجلدُ اقوراراً: تَشَنَّجَ؛ كما قال رُؤْبةُ بن العَجَّاج: وانْعاجَ عُودي كالشَّظِيفِ الأَخْشَنِ، بعد اقْوِرارِ الجِلْدِ والتَّشَنُّنِ يقال: عُجْتُه فانعاجَ أي عطفته فانعطف. والشظيف من الشجر: الذي لم يَجِدْ رِيَّه فصَلُبَ وفيه نُدُوَّةٌ. واقْوَرَّتِ الأرضُ اقْوِراراً إذا ذهب نباتها. وجاءت الإبل مُقْوَرَّةً أي شاسِفَةً؛ وأنشد: ثم قفَلْنَ قَفَلاً مُقْوَرّا قَفَلْنَ أي ضَمَرْنَ ويَبِسْنَ؛ قال أبو وَجْزَة يصف ناقة قد ضَمُرَتْ: كأنما اقْوَرَّ في أَنْساعِها لَهَقٌ مُرَمَّعٌ، بسوادِ الليل، مَكْحُولُ والمُقْوَرُّ أيضاً من الخيل: الضامر؛ وناقة مُقْوَرَّةٌ وقد اقْوَرَّ جلدُها وانحنَت وهُزِلَتْ. وفي حديث الصدقة: ولا مُقْوَرَّةُ الأَلْياطِ؛ الاقْوِرارُ: الاسترخاء في الجُلود، والأَلْياطُ: جمعُ لِيطٍ، وهو قشر العُود، شبهه بالجلد لالتزاقه باللحم؛ أراد غير مسترخية الجلود لهُزالها. وفي حديث أبي سعيد: كجلد البعير المُقْوَرّ. واقْتَرْتُ حديثَ القوم إذا بَحَثْتُ عنه. وتَقَوَّرَ الليلُ إذا تَهَوَّرَ؛ قال ذو الرمة: حتى تَرَى أَعْجازَه تَقَوَّرُ أي تَذْهَبُ وتُدْبِرُ. وانقارتِ الرَّكِيَّةُ انْقِياراً إذا تَهَدَّمت؛ قال الأزهري: وهو مأخوذ من قولك قُرْتُه فانْقارَ؛ قال الهُذَلي:جادَ وعَقَّتْ مُزْنَهُ الريحُ ، وانْقارَ به العَرْضُ ولم يَشْمَلِ أراد: كأَنَّ عَرْضَ السحاب انْقارَ أي وقعت منه قطعة لكثرة انصباب الماء، وأَصله من قُرْتُ عَيْنَه إذا قلعتها. والقَوَرُ العَوَرُ، وقد قُرْتُ فلاناً فقأت عينه، وتَقَوَّرَتِ الحيةُ إذا تَثَنَّتْ؛

1.67

فطر (مقاييس اللغة) الفاء والطاء والراء أصلٌ صحيحٌ يدلُّ على فَتْحِ شيء وإبرازِه.

فطر (لسان العرب) فَطَرَ الشيءَ يَفْطُرُه فَطْراً فانْفَطَر وفطَّرَه: شقه.

بطر (لسان العرب) وبَطَرَ الشيءَ يَبْطُرُه ويَبْطِرُه بَطْراً، فهو مبطور وبطير: شقه. والبَطْرُ الشَّقُّ؛

ركس (لسان العرب) الرِّكْسُ: الجماعة من الناس، وقيل: الكثير من الناس، والرِّكْسُ شبيه بالرَّجِيع. يقال: رَكَسْتُ الشيء وأَرْكَسْتُه إذا رَدَدْتَه ورَجَعْتَه، وفي رواية: إنه رَكِيس، فعيل بمعنى مفعول؛ ومنه الحديث: اللهم أَرْكِسْهما في الفتنة رَكْساً؛ والرَّكْسُ: قلبُ الشيء على رأسه أو ردُّ أَوله على آخره؛ رَكَسَه يَرْكُسُه رَكْساً، فهو مَرْكوس ورَكِيسٌ، وأَرْكَسَه فارْتَكَس فيهما. والرِّكْسُ، بالكسر: الجِسْرُ؛

ركس (العباب الزاخر) الرَّكْسُ: رَدُّ الشيءِ مقلوباً. وقال الليث: الرَّكْس: قَلْبُ الشيءِ على رأسِهِ ورَدُّ أوَّلِه على آخِرِه. والرِّكْس -بالكسر-: الرِّجْس.

أَجَأ (العباب الزاخر) ابن الأعرابي: أَجَأَ: فَرَّ.

عقا (لسان العرب) العَقْوةُ والعَقَاةُ: الساحة وما حوْلَ الدار والمَحَلَّة، وجمعُهما عِقاءٌ. والعِقْيانُ: ذهبٌ ينبتُ نَباتاً وليس مما يُستَذاب ويُحصَّلُ من الحجارة، وقيل: هو الذَّهبُ الخالصُ. وفي حديث عليّ: لو أراد الله أن يَفْتَحَ عليهم مَعادن العِقْيان؛ قيل: هو الذَّهبَ الخالصُ، وقيل: هو ما يَنبُتُ منه نَباتاً، والألف والنون زائدتان.

عج (مقاييس اللغة) العين والجيم أصلٌ واحد صحيح يدلُّ على ارتفاعٍ في شيء، من صوتٍ أو غبارٍ وما أشبه ذلك.

شحط (العباب الزاخر) ويقال لأثرِ سحج يصيبُ جنْباً أو فخذاً أو نحو ذلك: أصابتهُ شحطةَ. وقال غيره: شحَطتُ البعيرَ في السوم حتى بلغْتُ به أقص نهاهُ في الثمنِ؛ أشحطاً، ومنه حديثُ ربيعة أنهُ قال في الرَّجلِ يعتقُ الشقصَ من العبدِ: إنه يكون على المعتقِ قيمةُ أنصباءِ شركائهُ يشحطُ الثمنُ ثم يعتقُ كله يريدُ: يبلغُ بقيمةِ العبدَ أقصَ الغايةِ. وقيل: معنىَ: "يشحطُ" يجمعُ، من شَحَطتُ الإناءَ وشمطته: إذا ملأته، عن الفراء. وقال ابن الأعرابيّ: شحطتهُ العقربُ: أي لدَغتهُ. وشحطَ الطائرُ: أي سقسقَ. والمشحط -بالكسر-: عودٌ يوضعُ عند القضيبِ من قُضبانِ الكرمِ يقيهِ من الأرض، عن الليثِ وقال الطائفيّ: الشحطُ: عودٌ يرفع به الحبلة حتىَ تستقلّ إلى العريشِ: وقال أبو الخطاب: شحطتها: أي وضعتُ إلى جنْبها خشبةَ حتىَ ترتفعَ إليها. وقال الليثُ: الشحطَ: الاضطرابُ في الدمِ. وقال غيرهُ: يقال جاءَ فلان سابقاً قد شحطَ الخيلَ: أي فاتها. ويقال: شَحَطتْ نبو هاشمِ العربَ: أي فأتوهم فضلاً وسبقوهم.

شحط (لسان العرب) الشَّحْطُ والشَّحَطُ: البُعْدُ، والتشحُّطُ الاضْطرابُ في الدَّم. ابن سيده: الشحْطُ الاضطراب في الدم. وتشَحَّطَ الولد في السَّلى: اضْطرب فيه؛ قال النابغة: ويَقْذِفْنَ بالأَوْلادِ في كلّ مَنْزِلٍ، تَشَحَّطُ، في أَسْلائها، كالوَصائلِ الوصائلُ: البُرودُ الحُمْر. وشَحَطَه يَشْحطُه شَحْطاً وسَحَطَه: ذبحه، قال ابن سيده: والسين أَعْلى.

سَحَطَه (القاموس المحيط) والمَسْحوطُ من الشَّرابِ كُلِّه: المَمْزوجُ. وانْسَحَطَ من يده: انْمَلَصَ فَسَقَطَ، و~ عن النخلةِ وغيرِها: تَدَلَّى عنها حتى يَنْزِلَ، لا يُمْسِكُها بيده .

سحط (لسان العرب) السَّحْطُ مثل الذَّعْطِ: وهو الذبْحُ. سَحَطَ الرجلَ يَسْحَطُه سَحْطاً وشَحَطَه إذا ذبحه. وقال ابن دريد: أَكل طعاماً فسحَطَه أي أَشْرَقَه؛ قال ابن مقبل يصف بقرة: كاد اللُّعاعُ من الحَوْذانِ يَسْحَطُها، ورِجْرِجٌ بَيْنَ لَحْيَيْها خَناطِيلُ وقال يعقوب: يَسْحَطُها هنا يذْبَحُها، والرِّجْرِجُ: اللُّعابُ يَتَرَجْرَجُ. وسحَط شرابَه سَحْطاً: قتله بالماء أَي أَكثر عليه. وانْسحَطَ الشيء من يدي: امَّلَسَ فسقط، يمانية. ابن بري: قال أَبو عمرو: المَسْحُوطُ اللبن يُصبّ (* قوله «اللبن يصب» كذا بالأصل وشرح القاموس ولم يزيدا على ذلك شيئاً.)؛ وأَنشد لابن حبيب الشيباني: متى يأْته ضَيفٌ فليس بذائقٍ لَماجاً، سوى المَسْحُوطِ واللَّبَنِ الإِدْلِ.

1.68

حدق (مقاييس اللغة) الحاء والدال والقاف أصلٌ واحدٌ، [وهو الشيء] يحيط بشيء.

علم (مقاييس اللغة) العين واللام والميم أصلٌ صحيح واحد، يدلُّ على أثرٍ بالشيء يتميَّزُ به عن غيره.من ذلك العَلامة، وهي معروفة. ومن الباب العالَمون، وذلك أنَ كلَّ جنسٍ من الخَلق فهو في نفسه مَعْلَم وعَلَم. وقال قوم: العالم سمّي لاجتماعه. قال الله تعالى: وَالْحَمْدُ لِلَّهِ رَبِّ الْعَالَمِينَ [الأنعام 45، الصافات 182]، قالوا: الخلائق أجمعون. وقال في العالَم: * فخِنْدِفٌ هامةُ هذا العالَمِ *والذي قاله القائلُ في أنّ في ذلك ما يدلّ على الجمع والاجتماع فليس ببعيد، وذلك أنّهم يسمون العَيْلم، فيقال إنّه البحر، ويقال إنّه البئر الكثيرةُ الماء .

علم (لسان العرب) من صفات الله عز وجل العَلِيم والعالِمُ والعَلاَّمُ؛ قال الشاعر: ولَئِنْ السُّبُوبَ خِمَرَةَ قُرَشِيَّةً دُبَيْرِيَّةً، يَعْلَمْنَ في لَوْثِها عَلما وقَدَحُ مُعْلَمٌ: فيه عَلامةٌ؛ ومنه قول عنترة: رَكَدَ الهَواجِرُ بالمَشُوفِ المُعْلَمِ والعَلامةُ: السِّمَةُ، والجمع عَلامٌ، وهو من الجمع الذي لا يفارق واحده إلاَّ بإلقاء الهاء؛

لمم (لسان العرب) اللَّمُّ: الجمع الكثير الشديد. ورجُل مِلَمٌّ: يَلُمُّ القوم أي يجمعهم. وتقول: هو الذي يَلُمّ أهل بيته وعشيرته ويجمعهم؛ قال رؤبة: فابْسُط علينا كَنَفَيْ مِلَمَ أي مُجمِّع لِشَمْلِنا أي يَلُمُّ أَمرَنا. ورجل مِلَمٌ معَمٌّ إذا كان يُصْلِح أُمور الناس ويَعُمّ الناس بمعروفه. والمُلِمَّة النازلة الشديدة من شدائد الدهر ونوازل الدنيا؛ وأما قول عقيل بن أبي طالب: أَعِيذُه من حادثات اللَّمَّهْ فيقال: هو الدهر. ويقال: الشدة، ووافَق الرجزَ من غير قصد؛ وبعده: ومن مُرِيدٍ هَمَّه وغَمَّهْ وأنشد الفراء: علَّ صُروفَ الدَّهْرِ أو دُولاتِها تُدِيلنا اللَّمَّة من لَمّاتِها، فتَسْتَريحَ النَّفسُ من زَفْراتِها قال ابن بري وحكي أن قوماً من العرب يخفضون بلعل، وأنشد: لعلَّ أَبي المِغْوارِ منكَ قريبُ وجَمَلٌ مَلْمومٌ ومُلَمْلَم: مجتمع، وكذلك الرجل، ورجل مُلَمْلَم: وهو المجموع بعضه إلى بعض.

وحجَر مُلَمْلم: مُدَمْلَكٌ صُلْب مستدير، وقد لَمْلمه إذا أَداره. وكتيبة مَلْمومة ومُلَمْلَمة: مجتمعة، وحجر مَلْموم وطين مَلْموم؛ وقدح مَلْموم: مستدير؛ عن أَبي حنيفة. وجَيْش لَمْلَمٌ: كثير مجتمع، وحَيٌّ لَمْلَمٌ كذلك، قال ابن أحمر: منْ دُونِهم، إن جِئْتَهم سَمَراً، حَيٌّ حلالٌ لَمْلَمٌ عَسكر وكتيبة مُلَمْلَمة ومَلْمومة أيضاً أي مجتمعة مضموم بعضها إلى بعض. وصخرة مَلْمومة ومُلَمْلمة أي مستديرة صلبة. واللِّمَّة: شعر الرأس، بالكسر، إذا كان فوق الوَفْرة، وفي الصحاح؛ يُجاوز شحمة الأُذن، فإذا بلغت المنكبين فهي جُمَّة. ولِمَّةُ الوتد: ما تشَعَّثَ منه؛

لم (مقاييس اللغة) اللام والميم أصله صحيحٌ يدلُّ على اجتماعٍ ومقاربَة ومُضامَّة. يقال: لَمَمْتُ شَعَثَه، إذا ضممت ما كان من حالِه متشعِّثاً منتشِراً. والمُلِمَّة النَّازلة من نَوازل الدُّنيا. فأمَّا العين اللاَّمَّة، فيقال: الأصل مُلِمَّة، لمَا قُرِنت بالسّامّة قيل لامَّة، وهي التي تُصيب بالسُّوء.

1.69

قمع (لسان العرب) القَمْعُ: مصدر قَمَعَ الرجل يَقْمَعُه قَمْعاً وأَقْمَعه فانْقَمَعَ قَهَره وذَلّله فذَلَّ. أَقْمَعَ الرجلَ، بالأَلف، إذا طَلَعَ عليه فرَدَّه؛ وقَمَعه: قَهره.

قما (مقاييس اللغة) القاف والميم والحرف المعتلُّ كلمةٌ تدلُّ على حقارة وذُلّ. يقال: هو قَمِيٌّ بيّن القماءة، أي الحقارة. وأقْمَيْته أنا: أذللته. وإذا هُمِز كان له معنىً آخر، وذلك قولهم: تقمَّأت الشَّيء، إذا طلبته، تَقَمُّؤاً.

كمأ (لسان العرب) وقَدْ أَكْمأَتْهُ السِّنُّ أي شَيَّخَته، عن ابن الأَعرابي. وعنه أيضاً: تَلَمَّعَتْ عليه الأَرضُ وتودَّأَت عليه الأَرض وتكَمَّأَت عليه إذا غَيَّبَتْه وذهَبَتْ به.

كمي (لسان العرب) كَمى الشيءَ وتَكَمّاه: سَتَرَه؛ وقد تأَوَّل بعضهم قوله: بَلْ لو شَهِدْتَ الناسَ إذْ تُكُمُّوا إنه من تكَمَّيت الشيء. وكَمَى الشهادة يَكْمِيها كَمْياً وأَكْماها: كَتَمها وقَمَعَها؛ وانْكَمى أي اسْتَخْفى. وتكَمَّتْهم الفِتَنُ إذا غَشِيَتْهم. والكَمُوُّ الستر (* قوله« والكمو الستر » هذه عبارة النهاية ومقتضاها أن يقال كما يكمو.)

نحر (لسان العرب) والنَّحْرُ في اللَّبَّة: مثلُ الذبح في الحلق. ويقال: انْتَحر الرجلُ اي نَحر نفسه. وفي المثل: سُرِقَ السارقُ فانْتَحَر.

هر (لسان العرب) وأَنْهَرَ الطَّعْنَةَ: وسَّعها؛ قال قيس بن الخطيم يصف طعنة: مَلَكْتُ بها كَفِّي فأَنْهَرْتُ فَتْقَها، يرى قائمٌ من دونها ما وراءَها ملكت أي شددت وقوّيت. ويقال: طعنه طعنة أَنهر فَتْقَها أي وسَّعه؛ وأَنشد أَبو عبيد قول أَبي ذؤيب. وأَنْهَرْتُ الدمَ أي أَسلته. وفي الحديث: أَنْهِرُوا الدمَ بما شئتم إلا الظُّفُرَ والسِّنَّ. وفي حديث آخر: ما أَنْهَرَ الدمَ فكُلْ؛ وأَنْهرَ دَمَه أي أَسال دمه. ويقال: أَنْهَرَ بطنُه إذا جاء بطنه مثلَ مجيء النَّهَرِ. وقال أَبو الجَرَاحِ: أَنْهَر بطنُه واسْتَطْلَقَتْ عُقَدُه. ويقال: أَنْهَرْتُ دَمَه وأَمَرْتُ دَمَه وهَرَقْتُ دَمَه.

1.70

سأر (لسان العرب) السُّؤْرُ بقيّة الشيء، وجمعه أَسآر، وسُؤْرُ الفأْرة وغيرها؛ وقوله أَنشده يعقوب في المقلوب: إنَّا لَنَضْرِبُ جَعْفَراً بِسُيوفِنا، ضَرْبَ الغَريبةِ تَرْكَبُ الآسارا أَراد الأَسآر فقلب، ونظيره الآبار والآرام في جمع بئْر ورئْم. وَأَسْأَر منه شيئاً: أَبْقى.

سور (لسان العرب) سَوْرَةُ الخمرِ وغيرها وسُوَارُها: حِدَّتُها؛ وسارَ الرجلُ يَسُورُ سَوْراً ارتفع؛ وأَنشد ثعلب: تَسُورُ بَيْنَ السَّرْجِ والحِزام، سَوْرَ السَّلُوقيِّ إلى الأَحْذام وقد جلس على المِسْوَرَة. قال أَبو العباس: إنما سميت المِسْوَرَةُ مِسْوَرَةً لعلوها وارتفاعها، من قول العرب سار إذا ارتفع؛ وأَنشد: سُرْتُ إليه في أَعالي السُّورِ أَراد: ارتفعت إليه. وفي الحديث: لا يَضُرُّ المرأَة أَن لا تَنْقُض شعرها إذا أَصاب الماء سُورَ رأْسها؛ أَي أَعلاه. وكلُّ مرتفع: سُورٌ. وفي رواية: سُورَة الرأْس، ومنه سُورُ المدينة؛

أسر (لسان العرب) الأُسْرَةُ: الدِّرْعُ الحصينة؛ وتقول: اسْتَأْسِرْ أَي كن أَسيراً لي. والأَسيرُ: الأَخِيذُ، وأَصله من ذلك. وكلُّ محبوس في قِدٍّ أَو سِجْنٍ: أَسِيرٌ. والأَسْرُ القوة والحبس؛

فرق (مقاييس اللغة) الفاء والراء والقاف أُصَيلٌ صحيحٌ يدلُّ على تمييزٍ وتزييلٍ بين شيئين. من ذلك الفَرْق: فرق الشعر. يقال: فرقْتُه فَرقاً. والفِرق الفِلْق من الشَّيء إذا انفلَق. والفارق من الناس: الذي يَفرِق بين الأمور، يَفْصِلُها. وفَرَقُ الصُّبحِ وفَلَقُه واحد.

فرقَ (القاموس المحيط) فَرقَ بينهما فَرقاً وفُرقاناً بالضم: فَصلَ. و{فيها يُفرَقُ كلُّ أمرٍ حكيم}، أي: يُقضى. {وقُرآناً فرَقْناهُ}: فَصَّلْناهُ وأحْكَمْناهُ. {وإذ فرَقْنا بكمُ البَحرَ}: فَلَقْناهُ. وفرَقَ: مَلَكهُ، والفِلقُ من الشيءِ: المُنفَلِقُ، والجَبَلُ، والهَضْبَةُ، والمَوْجَةُ. وكفرِحَ: دَخلَ فيها وغاصَ، وشَرِبَ بالفَرَقِ. وكَنَصَرَ ذَرَقَ. وأفْرَقه: أذْرَقه.

فرق (لسان العرب) وفارَقَ الشيءَ مُفارقةً وفِراقاً: بايَنَهُ، والاسم الفُرقة. وتَفارق القومُ: فارَقَ بعضهم بعضاً. وفارقَ فلان امرأته مُفارقةً وفِراقاً: بايَنها. والفَرْقُ الفصل بين الشيئين. وقوله تعالى: وقرآناً فَرقْناه، أي فصلناه وأحكمناه، مَنْ خففَ قال بَيّناه من فرَق يَفرُق، ومن شدَّد قال أنزلناه مُفرّقاً في أيامٍ. وفرَقَ له عن الشيء: بيَّنه له؛ عن ابن جني. وكل ما فُرِقَ به بين الحق والباطل، فهو فُرقان، ولهذا قال الله تعالى: ولقد آتينا موسى وهرون الفرقان. والفُرقان الحُجَّة. والفَرَقُ، بالتحريك: الخوف. وفَرِقَ منه، بالكسر، فَرَقاً: جزع؛ وفي حديث أبي بكر: أباللهِ تُفَرِّقُني؟ أي تخوّفني. وحكى اللحياني: فَرَقْتُ الصبيَ إذا رُعْته وأفزعته؛

فرك (مقاييس اللغة) الفاء والراء والكاف أصلٌ يدلُّ على استرخاءٍ في الشيء وتفتيلٍ له. وأمّا قوله: فاركتُ صاحبي، مثل تاركته، فهذا من باب الإبدال .

ترك (لسان العرب) التَّرْكُ: وَدْعُك الشيء، تركه يَترُكه تَركاً واتّركه. وترَكْتُ الشيءَ تَرْكاً: خليته. ولا بارك الله فيه ولا تارَكَ ولا دارَكَ: كل ذلك إتباع، وقال ابن الأعرابي: تارَكَ أبقى. والتَّرْكُ الجعل في بعض اللغات، يقال: تركْتُ الحبل شديداً أي جعلته شديداً، قال: ولا يعجبني.

1.72

صرر (لسان العرب) والصَّرَّة العَطْفة. والصِّرار الخيط الذي تُشَدُّ به التَّوادِي على أطراف الناقة وتُذَيّرَ الأَطباءُ بالبَعَر الرَّطب لئلاّ يُؤثِّرَ الصِّرارُ فيها. الجوهري: وصَررْتُ الناقة شددت عليها الصِّرار، وهو خيط يُشدُّ فوق الخِلْف لئلاّ يرضعَها ولدها.

وفي الحديث: لا يَحِلُّ لرجل يُؤمن بالله واليوم الآخر أن يَحُلَّ صِرارَ ناقةٍ بغير إذْنِ صاحبها فإنه خاتَمُ أَهْلِها. قال ابن الأثير: من عادة العرب أن تَصُرَّ ضُروعَ الحَلُوبات إذا أرسلوها إلى المَرْعَى سارحَة، ويسمُّون ذلك الرِّباطَ صِراراً، فإذا راحَتْ عَشِياً حُلَّت تلك الأَصِرَّة وحُلِبَتْ، فهي مَصْرُورة ومُصَرَّرة؛ ومنه حديث مالك بن نُوَيْرَة حين جَمَعَ بَنُو يَرْبُوع صَدَقاتهم ليُوَجِّهوا بها إلى أبي بكر، رضي الله عنه، فمنعَهم من ذلك وقال: وقُلْتُ: خُذُوها هذه صَدَقاتكمْ مُصَرَّرَة أخلافها لم تُحَرَّد سأجْعَلُ نفسي دُونَ ما تَحْذَرُونه، وأرْهَنُكُم يَوْماً بما قُلْتُهُ يَدِي قال: وعلى هذا المعنى تأَوَّلوا قولَ الشافعي فيما ذهب إليه من أمرِ المُصَرَّاة. وصَرَّ الناقة يَصُرُّها صَرّاً وصَرَّ بها: شدَّ ضَرعَها. والصِّرارُ ما يُشدُّ به، والجمع أَصِرَّة؛ وصَررْت الصُّرَّة: شددتها. وفي الحديث: أنه قال لجبريل، عليه السلام: تأْتِيني وأنت صارٌّ بين عَيْنَيْك؛ أي مُقبِّض جامعٌ بينهما كما يفعل الحَزين. وأَصل الصَّرّ: الجمع والشدُّ. وفي حديث عمران بن حصين: تَكاد تَنْصَرُّ من المِلْء، كأنه من صَرَرْته إذا شَدَدْته؛ وصَرَّرَتِ الناقةُ: تقدَّمتْ؛ عن أبي ليلى؛

طمح (لسان العرب) وطَمَحَ ببصره يَطْمَحُ طَمْحاً: شَخَصَ، وقيل: رمى به إلى الشيء. وطَمَّحَ ببوله وبالشيء: رمى به في الهواء؛ الأزهري: إذا رميت بشيء في الهواء قلت طَمَّحْتُ به تَطْميحاً. وطَمَح به: ذَهَب به؛ وطَمَح أي أبْعَدَ في الطلب. وطَمَحاتُ الدهر: شدائده؛

تمه (مقاييس اللغة) التاء والميم والهاء كلمةٌ واحدةٌ تدلّ على تغيّر الشَّيء. يقال تَمِه الطَّعامُ إذا فسَدَ.

كلل (لسان العرب) الكَلُّ: اسم يجمع الأجزاء. وكَلَّ يَكِلُّ كَلاًّ وكَلالاً وكَلالةً؛ الأَخيرة عن اللحياني: أَعْيا. وكَلَلْت من المشي أكِلُّ كَلالاً وكَلالة أي أعْيَيْت، وكذلك البعيرِ إذا أعيا. وأكَلَّ الرجلُ بعيره أي أعياه. وأكَلَّ الرجلُ أيضاً أي كَلَّ بعيرُه. ابن سيده: أكَلَّه السيرُ وأكَلَّ القومُ كَلَّت إبلُهم. وكَلَّ الرجل إذا تعب. وكَلَّ إذا توكَّل؛ وكَلَّلَ الرجلُ: ذهب وترك أهلَه وعياله بمضْيَعَةٍ. وكَلَّل عن الأمر: أحْجَم. والمُكَلِّل الجادُّ، يقال: حَمَل وكَلَّل أي مضى قُدُماً ولم يَخِم؛ وأنشد الأصمعي: حَسَمَ عِرْقَ الداءِ عنه فقضَبْ، تَكْلِيلَةَ اللَّيْثِ إذا الليثُ وَثَبْ قال: وقد يكون كَلَّل بمعنى جَبُن، يقال: حمل فما كَلَّل أي فما كَذَب وما جبُن كأنه من الأضداد؛ قال: والمُكَلِّل الذي يحمِل فلا يرجع حتى يقع بقِرنه، والمُهَلِّل يحمل على قِرنه ثم يُحجِم فيرجع؛ وقال النابغة الجعدي: بَكَرَتْ تلوم، وأَمْسِ ما كَلَّلتها، ولقد ضَلَلْت بذاك أيَّ ضَلال ما: صِلة، كَلَّلتها: أدْعَصْتها. يقال: كَلَّ فلان فلاناً أي لم يُطِعه. وتكَلَّله الشيءُ: أحاط به. واكْتَلَّ الغمامُ بالبرق أي لمع. وانكَلَّ السحاب عن البرق واكْتَلَّ: تبسم؛

الكَلُّ (القاموس المحيط) و~ فُلاناً: ألْبَسهُ الإِكْليلَ.

كل (مقاييس اللغة) الكاف واللام أصولٌ ثلاثةٌ صِحاح. فالأول يدلُّ على خلاف الحدَة، والثاني يدلُّ على إطافة شيء بشيء، والثالث عضوٌ من الأعضاء. وكَلَّ فلانٌ مثل نَكل، وقال قومٌ: كَلَّ: حَمَلَ؛ وهذا خلاف الأوّل، ولعله أنْ يكون من المتضادّات.

نكل (مقاييس اللغة) النون والكاف واللام أصلٌ صحيح يدلُّ على مَنعٍ وامتناع، وإليه يرجع فروعه. ونَكَل عنه نُكولاً يَنكل. وأصل ذلك النِّكْل: القَيْد، وجمعه أنكال، لأنَه يَنكل: أي يَمنَع. والنِّكل حديدة اللِّجام.

وكل (لسان العرب) ووَكَل إليه الأمرَ: سلَّمه. ووكيلُ الرجل: الذي يَقوم بأمره، سمِّي وَكيلاً لأن مُوَكِّله قد وَكَل إليه القيام بأمره فهو مَوْكولٌ إليه الأمرُ.

أكل (الصِّحاح في اللغة) وآكَلْتُك فلاناً، إذا أمكنته منه.

1.73

أصد (مقاييس اللغة) الهمزة والصاد والدال، شيء يشتمل على الشيء. يقولون للحظيرة أصيدةٌ، سمّيت بذلك لاشتمالها على ما فيها .

صادَه (القاموس المحيط) صادَه يَصيدُه ويَصادُه: اصْطادَه، وخَرَجَ يَتَصَيَّدُ. وأصادَه: آذاهُ، وداواهُ من الصَّيَدِ، ضِدٌّ. والأَصْيَدُ: المَلِكُ، ورافِعُ رأسِه كِبْراً، والأَسَدُ، كالمُصْطادِ والصَّادِ.

صيد (لسان العرب) صاد الصَّيْدَ يَصِيدُه ويَصادُه صَيْداً إذا أخذه وتَصَيَّده واصطاده وصاده إياه.

صيد (الصَحّاح في اللغة) صادَهُ يَصيدُهُ ويَصادُهُ صَيْداً، أي اصطاده والصَيْدُ أيضاً: المَصيدُ. والصَيَدُن بالتحريك: مصدر الأَصْيدِ، وهو الذي يرفع رأسه كِبْراً.
سأد (الصَحّاح في اللغة) وسَأَدَهُ سَأْداً وسَأَداً: خَنَقَهُ.
سأد (لسان العرب) وقيل: الإِسْآد أن تسير الإِبل بالليل مع النهار؛ وقول ساعدة بن جؤية الهذلي يصف سحاباً: سادٍ تَجَرَّمَ في البَضِيعِ ثمانياً، يَلْوي بعَيْقاتِ البحارِ ويَجْنُبُ قيل: هو من الإِسْآد الذي هو سير الليل كله؛ قال ابن سيده: وهذا لا يجوز إِلا أَن يكون على قلب موضع العين إِلى موضع اللام كأَنه سائد أَي ذو إِسآد، كما قالوا تامر ولابن أَي ذو تمر وذو لبن، ثم قلب فقال سادئ فبالغ، ثم أَبدل الهمزة إِبدالاً صحيحاً فقال سادي، ثم أَعل كما أَعل قاض ورام؛ قال: وإِنما قلنا في سادٍ هنا إِنه على النسب لا على الفعل لأَنَّا لا نعرف سأد البتة، وإِنما المعروف أَسأد، وقيل: ساد هنا مهمل فإِذا كان ذلك فليس بمقلوب عن شيء، وهو مذكور في موضعه. قال: وقد جاء الساءد [السائد؟؟] إِلاَّ أَني لم أَر فعلاً؛ قال الشماخ: حَرْفٌ صَمُوتُ السُّرَى، إِلاَّ تَلَفُّتَها بالليل في سأْدِ منها وإِطْراق وأَسْأَد السَّيْرَ: أَدأَبه؛ أَنشد اللحياني: لم تلْقَ خَيْلٌ قبلها ما قد لقت من غبِّ هاجرة وسير مُسْأَد أَراد: لقِيتْ وهي لغة طيِّء. الجوهري: الإِسْآد الإِغْذاذُ في السير وأَكثر ما يستعمل ذلك في سير الليل؛
أسد (لسان العرب) الأَسَد: من السباع معروف، والجمع آساد وآسُد، مثل أَجبال وأَجبل، وأُسُود وأُسُد، مقصور مثل، وأُسْدٌ مخفف، وأُسْدانٌ، والأُنثى أَسَدة، وأَسَدٌ آسد على المبالغة، كما قالوا عَرادٌ عَرِدٌ؛ عن ابن الأَعرابي. وآسَدَ السيرَ كأَسْأَدَهُ؛ عن ابن جني؛ قال ابن سيده: وعسى أَن يكون مقلوباً عن أَسأَد. ويقال للوسادة: الإِسادة كما قالوا للوشاح إِشاح. واستأْسد النبت: طال وعظم، وقيل: هو أَن ينتهي في الطول ويبلغ غايته، وقيل: هو إِذا بلغ والتف وقوي؛
وسد (لسان العرب) وأَوْسَدَ في السير: أَغذَّ. وأَوْسَدَ الكلبَ: أَغْراه بالصَّيْدِ مثل آسَدَه .

1.74

رنن (الصَحّاح في اللغة) الرَنَّةُ: الصوت. يقال: رَنَّتِ المرأة تَرِنُّ رَنيناً، وأَرَنَّتْ أيضاً: صاحت.
رن (مقاييس اللغة) الراء والنون أصلٌ واحدٌ يدلُّ على صوتٍ. فالإرنان: الصوت والرَّنّة والرَّنين: صَيحةُ ذِي الحُزْن. ويقال أرنَّت القوسُ عند إنباض الرّامي عنها. قال:أي أنْبَضَ. والمِرْنانُ: القوس؛ لأنَّ لها رنيناً.
رنن (لسان العرب) الرَّنَّةُ: الصَّيْحَةُ الحَزِينةُ. يقال: ذو رَنَّةٍ. والرَّنينُ: الصياح عند البكاء. ابن سيده: الرَّنَّةُ والرَّنينُ والإِرْنانُ الصيحة الشديدة والصوت الحزين عند الغناء أَو البكاء. رَنَّت تَرِنُّ رنيناً ورَنَّنَتْ تَرْنيناً وتَرْنية وأَرَنَّتْ: صاحت. وفي كلام أَبي زُبَيدٍ الطائي: شجْراؤه مُغِنَّة، وأَطياره مُرِنَّة؛ قال الشاعر: عَمْداً فعلْتُ ذاكَ، بَيْدَ أَني أَخافُ إِن هَلَكْتُ لم تُرِنِّي وقيل: الرَّنِينُ الصوت الشَّجِيُّ. والإِرْنانُ الشديد. ابن الأَعرابي: الرَّنَّة صوت في فَرَحٍ أَو حُزْنٍ، وجمعها رَنّات، قال: والإِرنان صوتُ الشَّهيق مع البكاء. والرَّنَنُ: شيء يصيح في الماء أَيام الصيف؛ وقال: ولم يَصْدَحْ له الرَّنَنُ والرَّنَنُ: الماء القليل، والرَّنَبُ: الماء الكثير. والرَّنَّاءُ: الطَّرَبُ على بَدَلِ التضعيف، رواه ثعلب بالتشديد، وأَبو عبيد بالتخفيف، وهو أَقيس لقولهم رَنَوْتُ أَي طَرِبْتُ ومددت صوتي، ومن قال رَنَوْتُ فالرَّنَّاءُ عنده معتل. ويوم أَرونانٌ: شديد في كل شيء، أَفْوعالٌ من الرَّنين فيما ذهب إِليه ابن الأَعرابي، وهو عند سيبويه أَفْعلانٌ من قولك: كشف الله عنك رُونَةَ هذا الأَمر أَي غُمَّته وشدَته، وهو مذكور في موضعه. أَبو عمرو: الرُّنَّى شهر جمادى (* قوله «الرنى شهر جمادى» الذي في القاموس: ورنى، بلا لام، شهر جمادى). أَبو عمرو: الرُّنَّى شهر جُمادى (* قوله «الرنى شهر جمادى» الذي في القاموس: ورنى، بلا لام، شهر جمادى). وجمعها رُنَنٌ. قال أَبو عمر الزاهد: يقال لجمادى الآخرة رُنَّى، ويقال رُنَةٌ، بالتخفيف؛ وأَنه قال: يا آلَ زَيْدٍ، احْذَرُوا هذي السَّنَهْ من رُنَةٍ حتى تُوافِيها رُنَهْ قال: وأَنكر رُبَّى، بالباء، وقال: هو تصحيف إِنما الرُّبَّى الشاة النُّفَساء؛ وقال قُطْرُبٌ وابن الأَنباري وأَبو الطيب عبد الواحد وأَبو القاسم الزجاجي: هو بالباء لا غير؛ قال أَبو القسم الزجاجي: لأَن فيه يعلم ما نُتِجَتْ حُرُوبُهم إِذا ما انجلت عنه، مأْخوذ من الشاة الرُّبَّى؛ وأَنشد أَبو الطيب: أَتَيْتُك في الحَنِينِ فقلت: رُبَّى وماذا بين رُبَّى والحَنِينِ؟ والحَنينُ: اسم لجمادى الأُولى.
أرن (مقاييس اللغة) الهمزة والراء والنون أصلان، أحدهما النَّشاط. والآخر مأوىً يأوي إليه وحشيٌّ أو غيره. فأما الأول فقال الخليل: الأَرَنُ النَّشاط، أرِنَ يأْرَنُ أرَناً. والرَّنَاءُ: الطَّرَبُ على بَدَلِ التضعيف، رواه ثعلب بالتشديد، وأبو عبيد بالتخفيف، وهو أقيس لقولهم رَنَوْتُ أَي طَرِبْتُ ومددت صوتي، ومن قال رَنَوْتُ فالرَّنَاءُ عنده معتل.
أرن (لسان العرب) الأَرَنُ: النشاطُ، أَرِنَ يأْرَنُ أَرَناً وإِراناً وأَريناً؛ قال الزمخشري: كلُّ مَن علاكَ وغَلَبكَ فقد رانَ بك.

زأز (لسان العرب) تَزَأْزَ منه: هابه وتصاغر له وزَأْزَأَه الخوف. وتَزَأْزَأَ منه: اختبأَ. الليث: تَزَأْزَأَ عني فلان إِذا هابك وفرقك، وتَزَأْزَأَتِ المرأَةُ إِذا اختبأَت؛ قال جرير: تَدْنُو فتُبْدِي جمالاً زانه خَفَرٌ، إِذا تَزَأْزَأَتِ السُّودُ العَناكِيبُ أَبو زيد: تَزَأْزَأْتُ من الرجل تَزَأْزُؤاً شديداً إِذا تصاغرت له وفرقت منه. وزَأْزَأَ عدا. وزَأْزَأَ الظَّلِيم: مشى مسرعاً ورفع قُطْرَيْه.
زأز (الصَحّاح في اللغة) الزَأْزاء بالمدّ: ما غلظ من الأرض. والزئزاءَةُ أخصُّ منه وهي الأكمة.
فرق (مقاييس اللغة) الفاء والراء والقاف أُصَيلٌ صحيحٌ يدلُّ على تمييزٍ وتزييلٍ بين شيئين. من ذلك الفَرْق: فرق الشعر. يقال: فَرَقْته فَرْقاً. والفارق من الناس: الذي يَفرق بين الأمور، يَفصِلُها. وفَرْقُ الصُّبح وفَلَقُه واحد.
فرق (لسان العرب) والفِرْقُ القِسْم، والجمع أَفراق. والفُرْقُ الفصل بين الشيئين. والفُرْقان النصر. وأَفْرَقَتِ الناقة: أَخرجت ولدها فكأَنها فارَقَتْه. والفَرَقُ، بالتحريك: الخوف. وفَرِقَ منه، بالكسر، فَرَقاً: جَزِع؛ والفِرق الفِلْق من الشَّيء إِذا انفلَق، ورجل فَرِقٌ وفَرُق وفَرُوق وفَرُوقَةٌ وفَرُّوق وفَرُّوقَةٌ وفاروق وفارُوقَةٌ: فَزِعٌ شديد الفَرَق؛

فلق (مقاييس اللغة) الفاء واللام والقاف أصلٌ صحيحٌ يدلُّ على فُرجةٍ وبَيْنُونةٍ في الشيء، وعلى تعظيمِ شيء. من ذلك: فَلَقْتُ الشَّيءَ أَفْلِقُه فَلْقاً. والفَلَق الصُّبح؛ لأنَّ الظَّلام يَنْفلِقُ عنه. والفَلَق مطمئنٌّ من الأرض كأنَّه انفلَق، وجمعه فِلْقانٌ. والفلق الخَلق كله، كأنَّه شيءٌ فُلِق عنه شيء حَتَّى أبرزَ وأظْهِر.

فَلَقَهُ (القاموس المحيط) فَلَقَهُ يَفْلِقُه: شَقَّهُ، كفَلَّقَهُ فانْفَلَقَ وتَفَلَّقَ. وأفْلَقَ الشاعرُ: أَتَى بالعَجيبِ، كافْتَلَقَ.

زوي (لسان العرب) وزَوْزَيْته وزَوْزَيْت به إذا طَرَدْته. الليث: الزَّوْزاةُ شِبْهُ الطَّرْدِ والشَّلِّ، تقول: زَوْزى به. أبو عبيد: الزَّوْزاةُ مصدرُ قولك زَوْزى الرجلُ يُزَوْزِي زَوْزاةً، وهو أن ينصِب ظَهْره ويُسْرع ويُقاربَ الخَطْوَ؛

عزز (الصِّحاح في اللغة) وعَزَّهُ أيضاً يَعُزُّهُ عَزًّا: غلبه. وفي المثل: مَنْ عَزَّ بَزَّ، أي من غلب سلب. والاسم العِزَّةُ، وهي القوة والغلبة. والعَزَّةُ بالفتح: بِنْتُ الظَبية. وعَزَّهُ في الخطاب وعازَّهُ، أي غالَبه.

عَزَّ (القاموس المحيط) وتَعَزَّزَ لَحْمُه: اشْتَدَّ، وصَلُبَ. ويقولون: تُحِبُّني، فيقولُ: لَعَزَّ ما، أي: لَشَدَّ ما.

عز (مقاييس اللغة) العين والزاء أصلٌ صحيح واحد، يدلُّ على شدَّةٍ وقوَّةٍ وما ضاهاهما، من غلبةٍ وَقهر.

عزز (لسان العرب) والعِزُّ: خلاف الذُّلّ. والعِزُّ في الأَصل: القوة والشدة والغلبة. والعِزُّ والعِزَّة: الرفعة والامتناع، والعِزَّة لله؛ وفي حديث عمر، رضي الله عنه: اخْشَوْشِنوا وتَمَعْزَزُوا أَي تشدَّدوا في الدين وتصلَّبوا، من العِزِّ القوَّة والشدة، والميم زائدة، كتَمَسْكَن من السكون، وقيل: هو من المَعَز وهو الشدة، وسيجيءُ في موضعه. وعَزَزْتُ القومَ وأَعْزَزْتُهم وعَزَّزْتُهم: قَوَّيْتُهم وشَدَّدْتُهم. والعَزَزُ والعَزازُ: المكان الصُّلْب السريع السيل. واسْتَعَزَّ الرَّمْلُ: تماسَكَ فلم يَنْهَلْ.

أزز (الصِّحاح في اللغة) وائْتَزَّتِ القِدْرُ ائْتِزازاً، إذا اشتدَّ غليَانُها.

جرأ (لسان العرب) وفي الحديث: وقومُه جُرَآءُ عليه، بوزن عُلماء، جمع جَرِيءٍ: أَي مُتَسَلِّطين غيرَ هائِبين له.

1.75

كمي (مقاييس اللغة) الكاف والميم والحرف المعتلُّ يدلُّ على خفاءِ شيء. ولذلك سُمِّي الشُّجاعُ الكَمِيَّ. قالوا: هو الذي يتكمَّى في سِلاحِه، أي يتغطَّى به.

كمي (لسان العرب) كَمى الشيءَ وتَكَمَّاه: سَتَرَه؛ وتَكَمَّى: تَغَطَّى. وتَكَمَّى في سِلاحه: تَغَطَّى به.

كَمَى (القاموس المحيط) كَمَى شَهادَتَه، كرَمَى: كتَمَها، وتَكَمَّى: تَعَهَّدَ، وسَتَرَ.

قمم (لسان العرب) ويقال: أَلْقِ قُمامة بيتك على الطريق أَي كُناسة بيتك. وتَقَمَّمَ أَي تتبع القُمامَ في الكُناسات. قال ابن بري: والقُمَّةُ، بالضم، المَزْبَلة؛ والقِمَّةُ: أَعلى الرأْسِ وأَعلى كلِّ شيء. وقِمَّةُ النخلة: رأْسها. وتَقَمَّمها ارتقى فيها حتى يبلغ رأْسَها. وقِمَّةُ كل شيء: أَعلاه ووسطه.

كمم (لسان العرب) كُمُّ كل نَوْر: وعاؤُه، والجمع أَكْمام وأَكاميم، وهو الكِمام، وجمعه أَكِمَّةٌ. والكِمَّةُ: كلُّ ظَرْف غطيْت به شيئاً وأَلبسته إياه فصار له كالغِلاف، ومن ذلك أَكمام الزرع غُلُفها التي يَخرج منها. وكَمّ الفَصِيل (* قوله «وكم الفصيل» كذا بالصاد في الأصل، وفي بيت ابن مقبل الآتي والذي في الصحاح والقاموس: بالسين، وبها في المحكم أيضاً في بيت طفيل الآتي وياقوت في بيت ابن مقبل: كالفسيل المكمم) إذا أُشْفِقَ عليه فسُتِر حتى يَقْوَى؛ قال العجاج: بَل لو شَهِدْتَ الناسَ إذْ تُكُمُّوا بِغُمَّةٍ، لو لم تُفَرَّجْ غُمُّوا وتُكُمُّوا أَي أُغْمِيَ عليهم وغُطُّوا. والكِمَّةُ: القُلْفة. والكُمَّة: القَلَنسوة، وفي الصحاح: الكمة القلنسوة المدوَّرة لأنها تغطي الرأس. والكَمُّ: قَمْعُ الشيء وستره، ومنه كَممت الشهادة إذا قمعْتها وستَرتها، والغُمَّة ما غَطَّاك من شيء؛

1.76

عشر (لسان العرب) والعُشْرُ والعَشِيرُ: جزء من عَشَرة، يطَّرِد هذان البناءان في جميع الكسور، والجمع أَعْشارٌ وعُشُورٌ، وهو المِعْشار؛ وفي التنزيل: وما بَلَغوا مِعْشارَ ما آتيْناهم؛ أَي ما بلغ مُشْرِكُو أَهل مكة مِعْشارَ ما أُوتِيَ مَن قَبْلَهم من القُدْرةِ والقُوَّة. والعَشِيرُ: الجزءُ من أَجْزاء العَشرة، وجمع العَشِيرِ أَعْشِراء مثل نَصِيب وأَنْصِباء، ولا يقولون هذا في شيء سوى العُشْر. والعُشَارة: القطعةُ من كل شيء، قوم عُشارة وعُشَارات؛

1.77

ePSD: gipāru

<u>ĝipar</u> <u>[CLOISTER]</u> wr. ĝi$_6$-par$_4$; ĝi$_6$-par$_3$; ^{ĝeš}gipar$_x$(KISAL); ĝipar$_x$(KISAL) "cloister" Akk. gipāru

جبر (لسان العرب) الْجِيمُ وَالْبَاءُ وَالرَّاءُ أَصْلٌ وَاحِدٌ، وَهُوَ جِنْسٌ مِنَ الْعَظَمَةِ وَالْعُلُوِّ وَالِاسْتِقَامَةِ. فَالْجَبَّارُ: الَّذِي طَالَ وَفَاتَ الْيَدَ، يُقَالُ فَرَسٌ جَبَّارٌ، وَنخلَةٌ جَبَّارَةٌ. وَيُقَالُ لِلْخَشَبِ الَّذِي يُضَمُّ بِهِ الْعَظْمُ الْكَسِيرُ جِبَارَةٌ، وَالْجَمْعُ جَبَائِرُ. وَشُبِّهَ السِّوَارُ فَقِيلَ لَهُ جِبَارَةٌ. وَالْمَعْدِنُ جُبَارٌ، قَوْمٌ يَحْفِرُونَهُ بِكِرَاءٍ فَيَنْهَارُ عَلَيْهِمْ، فَذَلِكَ جُبَارٌ، لِأَنَّهُمْ يَعْمَلُونَ بِكِرَاءٍ. وَيُقَالُ أَجْبَرْتُ فُلَانًا عَلَى الْأَمْرِ، وَلَا يَكُونُ ذَلِكَ إِلَّا بِالْقَهْرِ وَجِنْسٍ مِنَ التَّعَظُّمِ عَلَيْهِ.

شارَ (القاموس المحيط) و~ إليه: أوْمَأَ، كأشارَ، ويكونُ بالكفِّ والعَيْنِ والحاجِبِ .

شور (لسان العرب) والمُشِيرَةُ: هي الإِصْبَع التي يقال لها السَّبَّابة، وهو منه. ويقال للسَّبَّابَتين: المُشِيرَتان. وأَشار الرجل يُشِيرُ إِشارةً إِذا أَوْمأَ بيديه. ويقال: شَوَّرْت إِليه بيَدِي وأَشرت إِليه أَي لَوَّحْت إِليه وأَلَحْتُ أَيضاً. وأَشارَ إِليه باليَدِ: أَوْمأَ، وأَشارَ عليه بالرَّأْي. ويقال للمكان الذي تُشَوَّرُ فيه الدوابّ وتعرض: المِشْوار.

رشد (مقاييس اللغة) الراء والشين والدال أصلٌ واحدٌ يدلُّ على استقامةِ الطريق. فالمَراشِد: مقاصد الطُّرُق.

رصد (الصَحَاح في اللغة) والمِرْصادُ: الطريق.
رصد (مقاييس اللغة) الراء والصاد والدال أصلٌ واحد، وهو التهيُّؤ لِرِقْبةِ شيءٍ على مَسْلكِه، ثم يُحمَل عليه ما يشاكله. يقال أرصدتُ له كذا، أي هيأْتُه* له، كأنك جعلتَه على مَرصَده.
رصد (لسان العرب) وأَرْصَدْت له شيئاً أُرْصِدُه: أَعددت له.

1.78

قين (مقاييس اللغة) القاف والياء والنون أصلٌ صحيح يدلُّ على إصلاحٍ وتزيين .
قين (لسان العرب) وقانَنِي اللّهُ على الشيء يَقِينُني: خلَقَني.
الكَوْنُ (القاموس المحيط) الكَوْنُ: الحَدَثُ، كالكَيْنونَةِ. والكائنَةُ: الحادِثَةُ. وكَوَّنَهُ: أحْدَثَهُ، و~ الله الأشياء: أوْجَدها.
كون (لسان العرب) الكَوْنُ: الحَدَثُ، وقد كان كَوْناً وكَيْنُونة؛ وكَوَّنَه فتكَوَّن: أَحدَثَه فحدث.
ضمك (لسان العرب) اضْمَأَكَّتِ الأَرضُ اضمِئْكاكاً: كاضْبأَكَّتْ إِذا خرج نبتها. والمُضْمَئِكُّ: الزرع الأَخضر كالمُضْبَئِكِّ، عن كراع. أَبو زيد: اضمأَكَّ النبت إِذا رَوِيَ واخْضَرَّ. واضْمأَكَّ السحاب: لم يُشكَّ في مطره؛ هذه عن أَبي حنيفة.
دأم (مقاييس اللغة) وقال: والبحر نفسُه الدَأْماء. وتداءمَت السَماءُ: توالت أمطارُها .
دَعَمَهُ (القاموس المحيط) دعَمَهُ، كمنعهُ: مالَ فأقامَهُ، وادَّعَمَ، كافْتَعَلَ: اتَّكأَ عليها. و~ المَرْأةَ: جامَعَها، أو طَعَنَ فيها، أو أوْلَجَهُ أجْمَعَ .
دعم (لسان العرب) ابن شميل دَعَمَ الرجلُ المرأَة بأَيره يَدْعَمُها ودَحَمَها، والدَّعْمُ والدَّحْمُ: الطعن وإِيلاجُهُ أَجمعَ، ويُسَمَّى السيدُ الدِّعامَةَ.
دأم (لسان العرب) ودأَمْتُ الحائط أَي رفعته مثل دعَمْتُهُ.

ePSD: DAM
dam [SPOUSE] wr. dam "spouse" Akk. aššatu; mutu

4.135

أنح (لسان العرب) وقال آخر: أَراكَ قَصِيراً ثائِرَ الشَّعْرِ أَنَّحاً، بعيداً عن الخيراتِ والخُلُقِ الجَزْلِ التهذيب في ترجمة أزح: الأَزْوَحُ من الرجال الذي يستأْخر عن المكارم، والأَنُوحُ مثله؛
أنه (لسان العرب) الأَنِيهُ: مثل الزَّفِيرِ، والآنهُ كالآنح. وأَنَهَ يَأْنِهُ أَنْهاً وأُنُوهاً: مثل أَنَحَ يَأْنِحُ إذا تَزَحَّرَ من ثِقَلٍ يَجِدُه، والجمع أُنَّهٌ مثل أُنَّحٍ؛
نخخ (لسان العرب) ابن الأَعرابي: نَخْنَخَ إِذا سار سيراً شديداً.
نحا (لسان العرب) والنَّحْوُ: القَصْدُ والطَّرِيقُ، يكون ظرفاً ويكون اسماً، نَحاه يَنْحُوه ويَنْحاه نَحْواً وانْتَحاه، ونَحْوُ العربيةِ منه، إِنما هو انْتِحاء سَمْتِ كلام العرب في تَصَرُّفه من إِعراب وغيره كالتثنية والجمع والتحقير والتكبير والإِضافة والنسب وغير ذلك، ليَلْحَق مَن ليس من أَهل اللغة العربية بأَهلها في الفصاحة فيَنطِق بها وإِن لم يكن منهم، أَو إِن شَذَّ بعضهم عنها رُدَّ به إِليها، وهو في الأَصل مصدر شائع أَي نَحَوْتُ نَحْواً كقولك قَصَدْت قَصْداً، ثم خُصَّ به انْتِحاء هذا القَبِيلِ من العلم، كما أَن الفِقْه في الأَصل مصدر فَقِهْت الشيء أَي عَرَفْته، ثم خُصَّ به علم الشريعة من التحليل والتحريم، وكما أَن بيت الله عز وجل خُصَّ به الكعبة، وإِن كانت البيوت كلها لله عز وجل؛ ونَحى الشيءَ يَنْحاه نَحْياً ونَحّاه فتَنَحَّى: أَزاله.
التهذيب: يقال نَحَّيْت فلاناً فتَنَحَّى، وفي لغة: نَحَيْتُه وأَنا أَنْحاه نَحْياً بمعناه؛ وأَنشد: أَلا أَيُّهذا الباخِعُ الوَجْدُ نفسَه لِشيءٍ نَحَتْهُ، عن يَدَيْه، المَقادِرُ أَي باعَدَتْه. ونَحَّيْته عن موضعه تَنْحِيةً فتنَحَّى، وقال الجعدي: أَمَرَّ ونُحِّيَ عن زَوْرِه، كتَنْحِيةِ القَتَبِ المُجْلَبِ ويقال: فلان نَحِيَّةُ القَوارِعِ إِذا كانت الشَّدائد تَنْتَحِيه؛ وأَنشد: نَحِيَّةُ أَحْزانٍ جَرَتْ مِنْ جُفُونِه نُضاضةُ دَمْعٍ، مِثْلُ ما دَمَعَ الوَشْلُ ويقال: استخذَ فلانٌ فلاناً أُنْحِيَّةً أَي انْتَحى عليه حتى أَهلك ما له أَو ضَرَّه أَو جَعل به شَرّاً؛

برو/ي (مقاييس اللغة) الباء والراء والحرف المعتلّ بعدهما وهو الواو والياء أصلان: أحدهما تسويةُ الشَيء نحتاً، والثاني التعرُّض والمحاكاة. والأصل الآخَر المحاكاة في الصَنيع والتعرُّض. قال الخليل: تقول: بارَيْتُ فلاناً أي حاكيتهُ. والمباراة أن يباري الرَجلُ آخَر فيصنع كما يصنَعُ. ومنه قولهم: فلانٌ يُباري جيرانَه، ويُباري الرِيحَ، أي يُعطي ما هبّتِ الرِيح، وقال الراجز: أي يعارضها. قال الأصمعي: يقال انْبَرى له وبَرى له أي تَعَرَّضَ، وقال: وقال ذو الرمّة: قال ابن السكيت: تبرَّيتُ مَعروفَ فلانٍ وتَبَرَّيْتُ لمعروفه، أي تعرَّضْتُ.

سلم (الصَحَاح في اللغة) والسَلَمُ أيضاً: شجرٌ من العِضاهِ، الواحدة سَلَمَةٌ. والسَلِمَةُ أيضاً: واحدةُ السِلامِ، وهي الحجارة.

4.136

عضو (مقاييس اللغة) العين والضاد والحرف المعتل أصلٌ واحدٌ يدلُّ على تجزئةِ الشَيء. من ذلك العِضو والعُضْو. والتَعضية أن يُعَضِّيَ الذَبيحة أعضاء. والعِضَةُ: القِطعة من الشيء، تقول: عَضَيْتُ الشيء أي وزَّعته. قال رؤبة:أي بالمفرَق. قال الخليل: وقوله تعالى: الَّذِينَ جَعَلُوا القُرْآنَ عِضِينَ [الحجر 91]، أي عِضَةً عِضَة، ففرَقوه، آمنوا ببعضه وكفَروا ببعضه.

عضا (لسان العرب) العُضْوُ والعِضْوُ: الواحدُ من أعضاءِ الشاةِ وغيرِها، وقيل: هو كلُّ عَظْمٍ وافِرٍ بلَحمه، وجمعُهما أعضاءٌ. وعَضَّى الذَّبيحة: قَطَعها أعْضاءً. وعَضَّيْتُ الشاةَ والجَزُورِ تَعْضِيةً إذا جعلْتها أعضاءً وقسَمْتَها. وفي حديث جابر في وقت صلاة العصر: ما لو أَنَّ رجُلاً نَحَرَ جَزُوراً وعَضَّاها قبل غُروب الشمسِ أي قَطَّعَها وفَصَّلَ أعضاءَها. وعَضَّى الشيءَ: وزَّعه وفرَّقه؛ قال: وليس دينُ اللهِ بالمُعَضَّى ابن الأعرابي: وعَضا مالاً يَعْضُوه إذا فَرَّقه وفي الحديث: لا تَعْضِيةَ في مِيراثٍ إلاَّ فيما حَمَلَ القَسْمَ؛ معناه أن يموتَ المَيّت ويَدَعَ شيئاً إن قُسِمَ بينَ وَرَثَته كان في ذلك ضَرَرٌ على بعضهم أو على جميعهم، يقول فلا يُقسَم. وعَضَّيت الشيءَ تَعْضِيةً إذا فَرَّقْته. والتَّعْضِيةُ: التَّفْرِيقُ، وهو مأْخُوذٌ من الأَعْضاءِ.

كبب (لسان العرب) والكُبَّةُ: الإِبلُ العظيمة. وكبَّ إذا ثَقُلَ. وأَلْقَى عليه كُبَّتَه أي ثِقْلَه.

4.137

AALD: hepû (hebû, hapû, habû): يحطم، يدمر، يقطع، يسحق، يشطر الى شطرين

حفف (لسان العرب) وحَفَّ رأْسَه وشاربه يَحُفُّ حَفّاً أي أَحْفاه. قال ابن سيده: وحَفَّ اللِّحية يَحُفُّها حَفّاً: أخذ منها، وحَفَّه يَحُفُّه حَفّاً: قَشَره، والمرأَة تَحُفُّ وَجْهها حَفّاً وحِفافاً: تزيل عنه الشعر بالمُوسَى وتَقْشِرُهُ، مشتق من ذلك. والحِفافان: ناحيتا الرأْس والإِناء وغيرهما، وقيل: هما جانباه، والجمع أَحِفَّةٌ. وحِفافا الجبلِ: جانباه. وحفافا كل شيء: جانباه؛

حفي (مقاييس اللغة) ويقال احتفأته، إذا اقتلعته .

حفا (لسان العرب) وحَفا شاربَه حَفْواً وأَحْفاه: بالَغ في أَخْذه وأَلْزَق حَزَّه. واحْتَفَى البَقْلَ: اقْتَلعه من وجه الأَرض. وكلُّ شيء اسْتُؤْصِل فقد احْتُفِيَ، ومنه إحْفاءُ الشَّعَر. قال: واحْتَفَى البقْلَ إذا أَخَذَه من وجه الأَرض بأَطراف أَصابعه من قصره وقلته؛ ال: ومن قال تَحْتَفِئُوا بالهمز من الحَفَإِ البَرْدِيّ فهو باطل لأَن البَرْدِيَّ ليس من البقل، والبُقول ما نبت من العُشْب على وجه الأَرض مما لا عِرْق له، قال: ولا بَرْدِيَّ في بلاد العرب، ويروى: ما لم تَجْتَفِئُوا، بالجيم، قال: والاجْتِفاء أَيضاً بالجيم باطل في هذا الحديث لأَن الاجْتِفاء كَبُّكَ الآنِيَةَ إذا جَفَأْتَها، ويروى: ما لم تَحْتَفُّوا، بتشديد الفاء، من احْتَفَفْتُ الشيءَ إذا أَخذتَه كله كما تَحُفُّ المرأَة وجهها من الشعر، ويروى بالخاء المعجمة، وقال خالد ابن كلثوم: احْتَفَى القومُ المَرْعَى إذا رَعَوْهُ فلم يتركوا منه شيئاً؛

النُّونُ (القاموس المحيط) النُّونُ: من حُرُوفِ الزِّيادةِ، ولو قيلَ: نُنْ في الشِّعْرِ، جازَ، والدَّواةُ، والحُوتُ. وذُو النُّونِ: لَقَبُ يُونُسَ عليه الصلاةُ والسلامُ، واسمُ سَيْفِ لَهُمْ، لكونِهِ على مِثالِ سَمَكَةٍ. والنُّونَةُ: الكَلِمَةُ من الصَّوابِ، والسَّمَكَةُ، والنُّقْرَةُ في ذَقَنِ الصَّبِيِّ الصَّغيرِ.

أشش (لسان العرب) وأَشَّ القومُ يَؤُشُّون أَشّاً: قام بعضهم إلى بعض وتحرّكوا؛ قال ابن دريد: وأَحسبهم قالوا أَشَّ على غَنَمه يَؤُشُّ أَشّاً مثل هَشَّ هَشّاً، قال: ولا أَقف على حقيقته. ابن الأَعرابي: الأَشُّ الخبز اليابس الهَشّ؛ وأَنشد شمر: رُبَّ فَتاةٍ من بَني العِنازِ، حَيَّاكةٍ ذاتِ هَنٍ كِنازِ ذي عَضَدَيْن مُكْلَئِزٍّ نازي، تأَشُّ لِلقُبْلةِ والمَحازِ شمر عن بعض الكلابيين: أَشَّت الشَّحْمة ونشَّت، قال: أَشَّت إذا أَخذَت تحَلَّب، ونشَّت إذا قطَرت .

حشش (لسان العرب) الحَشِيشُ: يابسُ الكلإِ، وحَشَّت اليدُ وأَحَشَّت وهي مُحِش: يَبِسَت، وأَكثر ذلك في الشَّلَل. وفي الحديث: أَن رجُلاً أَراد الخروج إلى تبوك فقالت له أُمُّه أَو امرأَته: كيف بالوَدِيّ؟ فقال: الغَزْوُ أَنمى لِلوَدِيَ، فما ماتَتْ منه وَدِيَّةٌ ولا حَشَّت أَي يَبِسَت. قال أَبو عبيد: حَشَّ ولدُها في بطنها أَي يَبِس. وحَشَّ النارَ يَحُشُّها حَشّاً: جمع إليها ما تفرق من الحطب، وقيل: أَوقدها، وقال الأَزهري: حَشَشْتُ النار بالحطب، فزاد بالحطب؛ قال الشاعر:تاللهِ لولا أَنْ تَحُشَّ الطُّبَّخُ بِيَ الجَحِيمَ، حينَ لا مُسْتَصْرَخُ يعني بالطُّبَّخِ الملائكة الموكَّلين بالعذاب. وحَشَّ الحرب يَحُشُّها حَشّاً كذلك على المَثَل إذا أَسعرها وهيجها تشبيهاً بإِسْعار النار؛ وحَشْحَشَتْه النَّارُ: أَحرَقَتْه.

4.138

ظلل (لسان العرب) ظَلَّ نهارَه يفعل كذا وكذا يَظَلُّ ظَلاًّ وظُلولاً وظَلِلْتُ أَنا وظَلْتُ وظِلْتُ، لا يقال ذلك إلاَّ في النهار لكنه قد سمع في بعض الشعر ظَلَّ لَيلَه، وظَلِلْت أَعْمَلُ كذا، بالكسر، ظُلولاً إذا عَمِلته بالنهار دون الليل؛ وقوله تعالى: يَتَفَيَّأُ ظِلالُه عن اليمين؛ قال أَبو الهيثم: الظِّلُّ كُلُّ ما لم تَطْلُع عليه الشمسُ فهو ظِلٌّ، قال: والفَيْءُ لا يُدْعى فَيْئاً إلا بعد الزوال إذا فاءت الشمسُ أَي رَجَعَتْ إلى الجانب الغَرْبِيِّ، فما فاءت منه الشمسُ وبَقِيَ ظِلاًّ فهو فَيْء، والفَيْءُ شرقيٌّ والظِّلُّ غَرْبِيٌّ، وإِنما يُدْعى الظِّلُّ ظِلاًّ من أَوَّل النهار إلى الزوال، ثم يُدْعى فيئاً بعد الزوال إلى الليل؛ وظِلُّ الليل: جُنْحُه، وقيل: هو الليل نفسه، ويزعم المنجِّمون أَن الليل ظِلٌّ وإِنما اسْوَدَّ جداً لأَنه ظِلُّ كُرَة الأَرض، وبِقَدْر ما زاد بَدَنُها في العِظَم ازداد سواد ظِلِّها. واسْتَظَلَّ بالظِّلِّ: مال إليه وقعَد فيه. وكُلُّ شيء أَظَلَّك فهو ظُلَّة. وأَظَلَّني الشيءُ: غَشِيَني، والاسم منه الظِّلُّ؛ كُلُّ ما أَطْبَق عليك فهو ظُلَّة، وكذلك كل ما أَظَلَّك. والإِظلالُ: الدُّنُوُّ؛ وأَظَلَّك الشيءُ: دَنا منك حتى أَلقى عليك ظِلَّه من قربه. ويقال: اسْتَظَلَّت العينُ إذا غارت؛ ويقال: ظِلٌّ وظِلالٌ وظُلَّة وظُلَل مثل قُلَّة وقُلَل. والظُّلَّة، بالضم: كهيئة الصُّفَّة، وقرئ: في ظُلَلٍ على الأَرائك مُتَّكئون، وفي التنزيل العزيز: فأَخذَهُم عذابُ يَوْمِ الظُّلَّة؛ والجمع ظُلَلٌ وظِلال. وأَظَلَّك فلان: دَنا منك كأَنه أَلقى عليك ظِلَّه، ثم قيل أَظَلَّك أَمرٌ. ويقال للدم الذي في الجوف مُسْتَظِلٌّ أَيضاً؛ ومنه قوله: مِنْ عَلَقِ الجَوْفِ الذي كان اسْتَظَلَّ ويقال: اسْتَظَلَّت العينُ إذا غارت؛

4.139

شدد (الصَّحاح في اللغة) وشَدَّ النهار، أي ارتفع .

شدد (لسان العرب) الشِّدَّةُ: الصَّلابةُ، وهي نَقيضُ اللِّينِ تكون في الجواهر والأَعراض، والجمع شِدَدٌ؛ وشَدَّ النهارُ أي ارتفع. وشَدُّ النهار: ارتفاعُه، وكذلك شَدُّ الضُّحَى. يقال: جئتك شَدَّ النهار وفي شَدِّ النهار، وشَدَّ الضُّحَى وفي شَدِّ الضحى. ويقال: لقيتُه شَدَّ النهار وهو حين يرتفع، وكذلك امتدَّ. وفي حديث عِتْبانَ بن مالك: فَغَدا عليَّ رسول الله، صلى الله عليه وسلم، بعْدَما اشْتَدَّ النهارُ أي علا وارتفعت شمسه؛

فرك (لسان العرب) الفَرْكُ: دَلْكُ الشيء حتى ينقلع قِشْرُه عن لبِّه كالجَوْز، فَرَكه يَفْرُكه فَرْكاً فانْفرَك. والفرِكُ المُتفرِّك قشره .

AALD: maşşaru (s.) (maşşuru) (See naşāru) الحارس، المراقب
ePSD: naşāru
ennuĝ ak [GUARD] wr. en-nu-uĝ3 ak "to guard, to watch" Akk. naşāru

مصر (مقاييس اللغة) المِصْر، وهو الحدّ؛
مَصَرَ (القاموس المحيط) واشترى الدار بِمُصُورِها: بحُدُودِها.
مصر (لسان العرب) والمِصْرُ الحاجزُ والحدُّ بين الشيئين؛ قال أُمية يذكر حِكْمة الخالق تبارك وتعالى: وجَعَلَ الشمسَ مِصْراً لا خَفاءَ به، بين النهارِ وبين الليل قد فَصَلا قال ابن بري: البيت لعدي بن زيد العبادي وهذا البيت أورده الجوهري: وجاعل الشمس مصراً، والذي في شعره وجعل الشمس كما أوردناه عن ابن سيده وغيره؛ وقبله: والأرضَ سَوَّى بِساطاً ثم قَدَّرَها، تحتَ السماءِ، سَواءً مثل ما ثَقُلا قال: ومعنى ثَقُلَ تَرَفَّعَ أي جعل الشمس حَدّاً وعلامةً بين الليل والنهار؛ قال ابن سيده: وقيل هو الحدُّ بين الأَرضين، والجمع مُصُور. والمِصْرُ الحدّ في كل شيء، وقيل: المصر الحَدُّ في الأرض خاصة. والمِصْران الكوفةُ والبصْرةُ؛ قال ابن الأَعرابي: قيل لهما المصران لأَن عمر، رضي الله عنه، قال: لا تجعلوا البحر فيما بيني وبينكم، مَصِّروها أي صيروها مِصْراً بين البحر وبيني أي حدّاً. وقال الليث: المِصْر في كلام العرب كل كُورة تقام فيها الحُدود ويقسم فيها الفيءُ والصدَقاتُ من غير مؤامرة للخليفة.

4.140

صيص (لسان العرب) ابن الأَعرابي: أَصاصَت النَّخلة إِصاصةً وصَيَّصَت تَصْيِيصاً إِذا صارت شِيصاً، قال: وهذا من الصِّيصِ لا من الصِّيصَاء، يقال: من الصِّيصَاء صأْصأَت صِيصاءً. والصِّيصُ والصِّيصاءُ: لُغَةٌ في الشِّيص والشِّيصاء.
الصِّيصُ (القاموس المحيط) الصِّيصُ، بالكسر: الشِّيصُ،
شيص (لسان العرب) ويقال: أَشاصَ به إِذا رفعَ أَمرَه إِلى السلطان؛
شصا (الصّحاح في اللغة) شصا بصرُه يشصو شُصُوّاً: شخَصَ. وأشصاه صاحبه: رفعه. وفي المثل: إذا ارْجَحَنَّ شاصِياً فارفعْ يداً، أي إذا سقط ورفع رجليه فاكْفُفْ عنه. وشصا السحاب، أي ارتفع في الهواء.

مَرَّ (القاموس المحيط) و~ الماءَ: جَعَلَهُ يَمُرُّ على وجْهِ الأرض.
مار (لسان العرب) المِئرَةُ، بالهمزة: الذَّحْلُ والعَداوةُ، وجمعها مِئَرٌ. ومَأَر السِّقاءَ مَأْراً: وَسَّعه .

5.53

صدغ (لسان العرب) الصُّدْغُ: ما انحدر من الرأْس إِلى مَرْكَبِ اللَّحيين، وقيل: هو ما بين العين والأُذن، وقيل: الصدغان ما بين لِحاظَي العينين إِلى أَصل الأُذن؛

سجد (مقاييس اللغة) السين والجيم والدال أصلٌ واحدٌ مطرد يدلُّ على تطامُن وذلّ. يقال سجد، إذا تطامَن. وكلُّ ما ذلّ فقد سجد. قال أبو عمرو: أسْجَدَ الرَّجُل، إذا طأطأ رأسَهُ وانحنى.
سجد (الصّحاح في اللغة) سَجَدَ: خضع. ومنه سُجودُ الصلاة، وهو وضع الجَبْهة على الأرض .

كور (مقاييس اللغة) الكاف والواو والراء أصلٌ صحيحٌ يدلّ على دَوْرٍ وتجمُّع. من ذلك الكَوْر: الدَّور. يقال كار يَكُورُ، إذا دار.
الكُورُ (القاموس المحيط) والكُورَةُ، بالضم: المدينةُ، والصُّقْعُ.
كور (لسان العرب) ويقال: كُرْتُ العمامةَ على رأْسي أَكُورُها وكَوَّرْتُها أُكَوِّرُها إِذا لففتها؛ وقال الأَخفش: تُلَفُّ فَتُمْحَى؛ وقال أَبو عبيدة: كُوِّرَتْ مثل تَكْوِير العمامة تُلَفُّ فَتُمْحَى، وقال قتادة: كُوِّرَتْ ذهب ضوءُها، وهو قول الفراء، وقال عكرمة: نُزِعَ ضوءُها، وقال مجاهد: كُوِّرَتْ دُهْوِرَتْ، وقال الرَّبيعُ بن خَيْثَم: كُوِّرَتْ رُمِيَ بها، ويقال: دَهْوَرْتُ الحائط إِذا طرحته حتى يَسْقُطَ، وحكى الجوهري عن ابن عباس: كُوِّرَتْ غُوِّرَتْ، وفي الحديث: يُجاءُ بالشمس والقمر ثَوْرَيْنِ يُكَوَّرانِ في النار يوم القيامة أَي يُلَفَّانِ ويُجْمَعانِ ويُلْقَيانِ فيها، والرواية ثورين، بالثاء، كأَنهما يُمْسَخانِ؛ قال ابن الأَثير:

وقد روي بالنون، وهو تصحيف. الجوهري: الكُورَةُ المدينة والصُّقْعُ، والجمع كُوَرٌ. ابن سيده: والكُورَةُ من البلاد المِخْلافُ، وهي القرية من قُرَى اليمن؛ قال ابن دريد: لا أَحْسبه عربيّاً. وكُرْت الأَرض كَوْراً: حفرتُها.
صقع (مقاييس اللغة) والصَّوقعة: العِمامة؛ لأنَّها تُغشِّي الرأس.وما بقي من الباب فهو من الإبدال؛ لأنَّ الصُّقْع النَّاحية. والأصل، فيما ذكر الخليل، السِّين كأنه في الأصل سقع. ويكون من هذا الباب قولهم: ما أدري أين صقع، أي ذهب، والمعنى إلى أيِّ صقْعٍ ذهبَ.
صقع (لسان العرب) والصُّقْعُ ناحيةُ الأَرضِ والبيت.
قور (لسان العرب) والقارَةُ: الجُبَيْلُ الصغير، وقال اللحياني: هو الجُبَيْلُ الصغير المُنْقَطع عن الجبال. والقارَةُ: الصخرة السوداء، وقيل: هي الصخرة العظيمة، وهي أصغر من الجبل، وقيل: هي الجبيل الصغير الأَسود المنفردُ شِبْهُ الأَكَمَة .

سفك (مقاييس اللغة) السين والفاء والكاف كلمة واحدة. يقال سَفَكَ دمَه يسفِكه سفْكاً ، إذا أساله، وكذلك الدَّمع .
سبك (مقاييس اللغة) السين والباء والكاف أُصَيلٌ يدل على التناهي في إمهاء الشيء. من ذلك: سَبَكْتُ الفضة وغيرَها أَسْبِكُها سَبْكاً.
سفق (لسان العرب) السَّفْق: لغة في الصَّفْق. وفي حديث أَبي هريرة: كان يَشْغَلُهم السَّفْقُ بالأَسْواق، يروى بالسين والصاد، يريد صَفْقَ الأَكُفّ عند البيع والشراء، والسينُ والصادُ يتعاقبان مع القاف والخاء، إلا أن بعض الكلمات يكثر في الصاد وبعضها يكثر في السين، وهكذا يُرْوَى حديث البَيْعة: أَعْطاه صَفْقَة يمينِه، بالسين والصاد، وخصَّ اليَمينَ لأنَّ البَيْعَ والبَيْعةَ يقع بها.

5.54

نقب (مقاييس اللغة) النون والقاف والباء أصلٌ صحيح يدلُّ على فَتح في شيء. ونقَب الحائطَ ينقُبه نَقْباً. والبَيطار ينقُبُ سُرّةَ الدَّابّة ليخرج منها ماء.

فتح (الصّحاح في اللغة) والفَتْحُ الماء يجري من عينٍ أو غيرها. وتقول: افْتَحْ بيننا، أي احكم. والفُتاحة بالضم: الحُكْم.
فتَحَ (القاموس المحيط) فتَحَ، كمَنَعَ: ضِدُّ أغْلَقَ، كفَتَّحَ وافْتَتَحَ. والفَتْحُ: الماءُ الجاري،
فتي (مقاييس اللغة) الفاء والتاء والحرف المعتل أصلان: أحدهما يدلُّ على طَراوة وجِدّة، والآخرة على تبيين حكم.
فتا (لسان العرب) ويقال: أَفْتَيْت فلاناً رؤيا رآها إذا عبرتها له، وأَفْتَيته في مسألته إذا أَجبته عنها. وفي الحديث: أَن قوماً تَفاتَوا إليه؛ معناه تحاكموا إليه وارتفعوا إليه في الفُتْيا. يقال: أَفْتاه في المسأَلة يُفْتِيه إذا أَجابه، والاسم الفَتْوى؛
فتت (لسان العرب) فَتَّ الشيءَ يَفُتُّه فَتّاً، وفَتَّتَه: دَقَّه. وقيل: فَتَّه كَسَره؛ وقيل: كسره بأَصابعه.
الفَتُّ (القاموس المحيط) الفَتُّ: الدَّقُّ والكسرُ بالأصابعِ، والشَّقُّ في الصَّخْرَةِ.

سبي (لسان العرب) وجَاءَ السيلُ بِعُودٍ سَبِيٍّ إذا احْتَمَلَه من بلد إلى بلد، وقيل: جاء به من مكانٍ غريب فكأَنه غَرِيب؛ وقال الأَصمعي والأَحمر: السابِياءُ هو الماءُ الذي يَخْرُج على رأْسِ الولَدِ إذا وُلِد، والإسْبَة (* قوله «والاسبة إلخ» هكذا في الأصل.) الطَّرِيقَةُ من الدَّم. والأَسابِيُّ: الطُّرق من الدَّم. وأَسَابِيُّ الدماء: طَرائِقُها؛ وقال الليث: إذا كثر نَسلُ الغَنَم سُمِّيَت السابِياءَ فيقعُ اسمُ السابياءِ على المال الكثير والعدد الكثير؛ والإسْباءَة أَيضاً: خيطٌ من الشَّعر مُمْتدٌّ. وأَسابِيُّ الطريق: شَوْكه. وسَبَى الماءَ: حَفَر حتى أَدركه؛ قال رؤبة: حتى اسْتفاضَ الماءُ يَسْبِيه السابْ .
الإسْبُ (القاموس المحيط) الإسْبُ، بالكسر: شَعرُ الرَّكَبِ أو الفَرْجِ أو الاسْتِ. وكَبْشٌ مُؤَسَّبٌ، كمُعَظَّمٍ: كثيرُ الصُّوفِ. وآسَبَتِ الأرضُ: أعْشَبَتْ .

صأب (لسان العرب) صَئِبَ من الشَّراب صأْباً: رَوِيَ وامتلأَ، وأَكثر من شرب الماء.
صوب (لسان العرب) الصَّوْبُ: نُزولُ المَطَر. صَابَ المَطَرُ صَوْباً، وانْصابَ: كلاهما انْصَبَّ. وصاب الغيثُ بمكان كذا وكذا، وصابَتِ السَّماءُ الأَرضَ: جادَتْها. وصابَ الماءَ وصَوَّبه: صبَّه وأَراقَه؛

5.55

فرت (لسان العرب) الفُراتُ: أَشَدُّ الماء عُذوبةً. وفي التنزيل العزيز: هذا عَذْبٌ فُراتٌ، وهذا مِلْحٌ أُجاجٌ. وقد فَرُتَ الماءُ يَفْرُتُ فُروتةً إذا عَذُبَ، فهو فُراتٌ. والفُراتانِ: الفُراتُ ودُجَيْلٌ؛ والفُراتُ: اسم نهر الكوفة، معروف.

يا (لسان العرب) حَرْفُ نِداء، وهي عامِلةٌ في الاسم الصَّحِيح وإن كانت حرفاً، والقولُ في ذلك أَنَّ لِيا في قيامِها مَقامَ الفعل خاصةً ليست للحروف، وذلك أَنَّ الحروفَ قد تَنُوبُ عن الأَفعال. وذلك أَنَّ يا نفسَها هي العامِلُ الواقعُ على زيد، وحالُها في ذلك حال أَدْعُو وأُنادي. ويا نفسُها في المعنى كأَدْعُو. قال الجوهري: وأَما قوله تعالى أَلا يا اسْجدُوا، بالتخفيف، فالمَعْنى يا هَؤُلاءِ اسْجُدوا، فحُذِفَ المُنادى اكْتِفاء بحَرف النَّداء كما حُذِفَ حَرْفُ النَّداء اكْتِفاء بالمُنادى في قوله تعالى: يُوسُفُ أَعْرِضْ عَن هَذا؛ إذْ كانَ المُراد مَعْلوماً؛ وقال بعضهم: إنَّ يا في هذا المَوْضِع إنما هو للتَّنْبيه كأَنه قال: أَلا اسْجُدُوا، فلما أُدْخل عليه يا التَّنْبيه سَقَطتِ الأَلفُ التي في اسْجُدوا لأَنها أَلفُ وَصْلٍ، وذَهَبَت الأَلفُ التي في يا لاجْتماع الساكنين لأَنها والسين ساكنتان؛

دجل (لسان العرب) ودَجَل الشيءَ غَطّاه. ودِجْلة اسم نهر، من ذلك لأنها غَطَّت الأرض بمائها حين فاضت، وحكى اللحياني في دِجلة دَجْلة، بالفتح؛ غيره: دِجْلة اسمٌ معرفة لنهر العراق، وفي الصحاح: دِجْلة نهر بغداد، قال ثعلب: تقول عبرت دِجْلة، بغير ألف ولام. ودُجَيل: نهر صغير متشعب من دِجْلة.

5.56

نخر (مقاييس اللغة) النون والخاء والراء أصلٌ صحيح يدلُّ على صوتٍ من الأصوات ثم يفرَع منه. النخير: صوتٌ يخرج من المَنْخِرين، وسمّي المَنخران من جهة النَّخير الخارج منهما. وفُرّع منه فقيل لخَرقَي الأنف النُّخرتان. والنَّخُور الناقة لا تدُرّ حتّى تُدخِل الإصبع في مَنْخِرها. ويقولون النُّخْرة: الأنف نفسُه.

فيح (لسان العرب) فاحَ الحرُّ يفيحُ فَيْحاً: سَطَعَ وهاجَ. وشَجَّةٌ تَفيحُ بالدم: تَقْذِفُ. وفاحت الشَّجَّةُ، فهي تَفيحُ فَيْحاً: نَفَحَتْ بالدم أيضاً؛ وفي حديث أبي بكر: مُلكاً عَضُوضاً ودماً مُفاحاً أي سائلاً؛ مُلكٌ عَضُوضٌ يَنال الرعيَّة منه ظُلمٌ وعَسْفٌ كأَنهم يُعَضُّون عَضّاً.
وأَفَحْتُ الدم: أَسَلْته. والفَيْحُ والفَيَحُ: السَّعَةُ والانتشار.
فحا (لسان العرب) الفحا والفِحا، مقصور: أَبْزارُ القِدْر، بكسر الفاء وفتحها، والفتح أكثر، وفي المحكم: البزر، قال: وخص بعضهم به اليابس منه، وجمعه أفحاء. وعرَفت ذلك في فَحْوى كلامِه وفحْوائه وفَحْوائه وفُحَوائِه أي مِعراضِه ومَذْهَبِه، وكأنه من فَحَيت القِدْر إذا أَلْقَيْتَ الأبزار، والباب كله بفتح أوله مثل الحَشا الطَّرَفِ من الأَطْراف، والغفا والرَّحى والوغَى والشَّوَى .
فحا (الصّحّاح في اللغة) والفَحا مقصورٌ: أَبزارُ القِدر، بكسر الفاء والفتح أكثر، والجمع أفْحاءٌ. يقال: فَحِّ قِدرَكَ تَفْحِيَةً .

عق (مقاييس اللغة) العين والقاف أصل واحد يدلُّ [على الشَّقّ]، وإليه يرجع فروع الباب بلطف نظر. قال الخليل: أصل العقّ الشقّ.
عقق (لسان العرب) عَقَّه يَعُقُّه عَقّاً، فهو مَعْقوقٌ وعَقِيقٌ: شقَّه. والعَقّ: حفر في الأرض مستطيل سمي بالمصدر. والعَقَّةُ: حفرة عميقة في الأرض، وجمعها عَقّات. وانْعقَّ الوادي: عَمُقَ. ويقال: عَقَّت الريحُ المُزْنَ تَعُقُّه عَقاً إذا استدَرَّته كأنها تشقه شقّاً؛ قال الهذلي يصف غيثاً: حارَ وعَقَّتْ مُزْنَهُ الريحُ، وانْقارَ به العَرْضُ، ولم يُشمَلِ حارَ: تحيَّر وتردد واستَدَرّته ريح الجَنوب ولم تهب به الشَّمال فتقَشْعَه، وانْقار به العَرْضُ أي كأن عرضَ السحاب انْقار بِهِ أي وقعت منه قطعة وأصله من قُرتُ جَيْبَ القميص فانْقار، وقُرْتُ عينه إذا قلعتها. وسحبة مَعْقُوقة إذا عُقَّت فانعَقَّت أي تبَعَّجت بالماء. وسحابة عَقّاقة إذا دفعت ماءها وقد عَقَّت؛ قال عبدُ بني الحَسْحاس يصف غيثاً: فمرَّ على الأنهاء فانْثَجَّ مُزْنُه، فَعَقّ طويلاً يَسْكُبُ الماءَ ساجِيَا واعْتَقَّت السحابة بمعنى؛ قال أبو وَجْزة: واعْتَقَّ مُنْبَعِجٌ بالوَبْل مَبْقُور ويقال للمُعْتذر إذا أفرط في اعتذاره: قد اعْتَقَّ اعْتِقاقاً. ويقال: سحابة عَقّاقة منشقة بالماء. وعَقَّ البرقُ وانْعَقَّ: انشق.
بعج (مقاييس اللغة) الباء والعين والجيم أصل واحدٌ، وهو الشَّقّ والفَتْح.
طعج (لسان العرب) طَعَجَها يَطْعَجُها طَعْجاً: نَكَحَها.

ePSD: TAG
guruš [CUT] wr. guruš3; guruš4 "to cut, fell, trim, peel off; a cutting; stubble" Akk. kismu; nakāsu; šarāmu
[i.e.: In Iraqi accent, even today, this verb/root means: to dent; therefor TAG means the dent or cut]

عزب (مقاييس اللغة) العين والزاء والباء أصلٌ صحيحٌ يدلُّ على تباعدٍ وتنحٍّ. يقال: عَزَب يعزُبُ عُزُوباً. والعَزَب الذي لا أهلَ له. وقد عَزَب يَعْزُبُ عُزُوبةً. وقالوا: والمِعزابةُ: الذي طالت عُزْبته حتى ما له في الأهل من حاجة. يقال: عَزَب حِلمُ فلانٍ، أي ذهب، وأَعْزَبَ اللهُ حِلمَه، أي أذهَبَه. قال الأعشى: والعازب من الكلأ: البَعيد المَطْلَب. قال أبو النجم: وكلُّ شيءٍ يفوتُك لا تَقْدِر عليه فقد عَزَب عنك.
عزب (الصّحّاح في اللغة) وعَزِبت الأرض، إذا لم يكن بها أحدٌ، مخصبةً كانت أو مجدبة .
عزب (لسان العرب) وعَزَبَ يَعْزُبُ، فهو عازِبٌ: أَبْعَدَ.

5.57

صري (لسان العرب) وقال ابن بزرج: صَرِتِ الناقةُ تَصْرِي من الصَّرِيِ، وهو جمع اللبن في الضَّرْع: وصَرَّيْت الشاة تَصْرِيةً إذا لم تَحْلُبْها أياماً حتى يجتمعَ اللَّبَنُ في ضَرعِها، والشاةُ مُصَرَّاة. قال ابن بري: ويقال ناقةٌ صَرْياءُ وصَرِيَةٌ؛ والصَّرَى: اللبن الذي قد بَقِيَ فتغيَّر طَعْمهُ، وقيل: هو بقيَّةُ اللبَنِ، وقد صَرِيَ صَرىً، فهو صَرٍ، كالماء. وصرِيَتِ الناقةُ صَرىً وأَصْرَتْ: تَحفَّل لبنُها في ضَرعها؛ وأنشد: مَنْ للجَعافِرِ يا قَوْمِي، فقد صَرِيَتْ، وقد يُساقُ لذاتِ الصَّرْيةِ الحَلَبُ الليث: صَرِيَ اللبَنُ يَصْرى في الضَّرع إذا لم يُحْلَبْ ففسَدَ طَعْمُهُ، وهو لبَنٌ صَرىً. وفي حديث أبي موسى: أَنَّ رجلاً اسْتَفْتاه فقال: امرأَتي صَرِيَ لبنُها في ثَدْيِها فدَعَتْ جارِيةً لها فمَصَّته، فقال: حَرُمَت عليك، أي اجْتمَعَ في ثدْيها حتى فَسَدَ طَعْمُه، وتَحْريمُها على رأْيِ من يَرى أَنَّ إرْضاعَ الكبيرِ يُحَرِّم.
صر (مقاييس اللغة) والأصل في هذا الصِّرار، وهي أماكنُ مرتفعةٌ لا يكادُ الماء يعلوها.

سدد (لسان العرب) والسُّدُّ والسَّدُّ: الجبل، وقيل: ما قابلك فسَدَّ ما وراءَه فهو سَدٌّ وسُدٌّ.

بحر (الصَحاح في اللغة) البَحْرُ: خلاف البرّ. يقال: سمّي بحراً لعُمقه واتساعه. والبَحْرَةُ البلدةُ. يقال: هذه بَحْرَتُنا، أي بلدتنا وأرضنا.

5.58

نبع (مقاييس اللغة) النون والباء والعين كلمتان: إحداهما نُبوع الماء، والموضع الذي يَنْبَع منه يَنْبُوع. والنَّوابع من البعير: المواضع التي يَسيل منها عرقُه. ومنابع الماء: مَخارِجُه من الأرض .

نبع (لسان العرب) نَبَعَ الماءُ ونبَعَ ونَبُعَ؛ عن اللحياني، يَنْبعُ وينْبَعُ ويَنْبُعُ؛ الأَخيرة عن اللحياني، نَبْعاً ونُبُوعاً: تفَجَّر، وقيل: خرج من العين، ولذلك سميت العين يَنْبُوعاً؛ واليَنْبُوعُ: الجَدْوَلُ الكثير الماء، وكذلك العين؛ ومنه قوله تعالى: حتى تَفْجُرَ لنا من الأَرض يَنْبوعاً، والجمع اليَنابيعُ؛ والنَّبَّاعةُ: الاسْتُ، يقال: كَذَبَتْ نَبّاعَتُك إذا رَدَمَ، ويقال بالغين المعجمة أيضاً .

سته (لسان العرب) السَّتَهُ والسَّتَهُ والاسْتُ: معروفة، وهو من المحذوف المُجْتَلَبَة له ألفُ الوصل، وقد يستعار ذلك للدهر؛ الجوهري: والاسْتُ العَجُزُ، وقد يُرادُ بها حَلْقة الدبر، وأصله سَتَهٌ على فَعَلٍ، بالتحريك، يدل على ذلك أن جمعه أَسْتاه مثل جَمَلٍ وأجمال، ولا يجوز أن يكون مثل جِزْعٍ وقُفْلٍ اللذين يجمعان أيضاً على أفعال، لأنك إذا رَدَدْتَ الهاء التي هي لام الفعل وحذفت العين قلت سَهٌ، بالفتح؛ ويقال للرجل الذي يُسْتَذَلُّ: أنت الاسْتُ السُّفْلى وأنت السَهُ السُّفْلى. ويقال لأَرذالِ الناس: هؤلاء الأَسْتاه، ولأَفاضلهم: هؤلاء الأَعْيانُ والوُجوهُ؛

فلذ (مقاييس اللغة) الفاء واللام والذال أُصَيلٌ يدلُّ على قَطْعِ شيءٍ من شيء .

فلذ (الصَحاح في اللغة) والفِلْذَةُ القطعةُ من الكبدِ والحمِ والمالِ وغيرِها، والجمع فِلَذٌ. يقال: فَلَذْتُ له من مالي، أي قطعت له منه. وافْتَلَذْتُهُ المالَ، أي أخذتُ من ماله فِلْذَةً.

فلذ (لسان العرب) فلذ له من المال يَفْلِذُ فَلْذاً: أَعطاه منه دَفْعَةً، وقيل: قطع له منه، وقيل: هو العطاء بلا تأْخير ولا عِدَةٍ، وقيل: هو أَن يكثر له من العطاء. وافْتَلَذْتُ له قطعة من المال افتلاذاً إِذا اقتطعته. وافتلذته المالَ أَي أَخذت من ماله فِلْذَةً؛ والفِلْذَةُ من اللحم: ما قطع طولاً. ويقال: فَلَّذْتُ اللحم تفليذاً إِذا قطعته. التهذيب: والفُولاذُ من الحديد معروف، وهو مُصاصُ الحديد المنقى من خَبَثِه.

فلس (مقاييس اللغة) ويقولون: أَفْلَسَ الرَجل، قالوا: معناه صار ذا فُلوسٍ بعد أن كان ذا دراهم.

ePSD: palāšu; šapālu

burud [PERFORATE] wr. burudx(U) "breach, hole; depression, low-lying area, depth; to perforate; (to be) deep"

Akk. palāšu; šapālu; pilšu; šupālu; šuplu

بلم (مقاييس اللغة) الباء واللام والميم أصلان: أحدهما ورمٌ أو ما يشبهه، والثاني نَبتٌ.فالأول بَلَمٌ، وهو داءٌ يأخُذ الناقةَ في حَلْقة رَحِمِها. يقال أَبلَمتِ الناقةُ إذا أخَذَها ذلك. الفرّاء: أَبلَمَتْ وبَلِمَتْ إذا ورِمَ حَياؤُها.

البَلَمُ (القاموس المحيط) وبَلِمَت الناقة وأبلَمَتْ: اشْتَهتِ الفَحلَ. والبَلَمَةُ، محرَكَةً: الضَبَعَةُ، أو وَرَمُ الحَياءِ من شدَّةِ الضَّبَعَةِ، كالبَلَمِ، ووَرَمُ الشَّفَةِ والأَبلَمُ: الغليظُ الشَّفتينِ، وبَقْلَةٌ لها قُرونٌ كالباقِلَّى، وخُوصُ المُقْلِ، ويُثَلَّثُ أوّله، كالإِبْلَمَةِ، مُثَلَّثَةَ الهَمْزَةِ واللامِ،
والمالُ بيننا شِقَّ الأَبْلَمَةِ، أي: نِصْفَيْنِ .

كفف (الصَحاح في اللغة) الكَفُّ: واحدة الأَكُفِّ. وكُفَّةُ القميص: ما استدار حولَ الذيل. وكَفَّةُ اللِثة، وهي ما انحدر منها. قال: ويقال أيضاً: كِفَّةُ الميزان بالفتح، والجمع كِفَفٌ. والكِفَفُ في الوشم: داراتٌ تكون فيه. وكِفافُ الشيء: حتارُهُ. وكان الأصمعي يقول: كلُّ ما استطال فهو كُفَّةٌ بالضم، نحو كُفَّة الثوب وهي حاشيته، وكُفَّةُ الرملِ وجمعه كِفافٌ. وكلُّ ما استدار فهو كِفَّةٌ بالكسر، نحو كِفَّةِ الميزان، وكِفَّةِ الصائد وهي حِبالته.

كبب (لسان العرب) كَبَّ الشيءَ يَكُبُّه، وكَبْكَبَه: قَلَبه. وأَكَبَّ الرَجلُ يُكِبُّ إكْباباً إذا ما نَكَسَ. وكَبْكَبَ الشيءَ: قَلَبَ بعضَه على بعض.

قبب (لسان العرب) والقَبُّ: ما بَين الوَرِكَين. وقَبُّ الدُّبُرِ: مَفْرَجُ ما بين الأَلْيَتَيْنِ. والقِبُّ، بالكسر: العَظم النَاتِئ من الظهر بين الأَلْيَتَيْنِ؛ يقال: أَلزِقْ قِبَّكَ بالأَرض. وفي نسخة من التهذيب، بخط الأَزهري: قَبَّكَ، بفتح القاف. والقَبُّ: ضَرْبٌ من اللُّجُم، أَصْعَبُها وأَعظمها. والأَقَبُّ: الضامر، وجمعه قُبٌّ؛ وفي الحديث: خَيرُ الناسِ القُبِّيُّون. والقَبْقابُ: النعل المتخذة من خَشَب، بلغة أهل اليمن. والقَبْقابُ: الفرج. يُقال: بَلَّ البَوْلُ مَجامِعَ قَبْقابه.

5.59

عجر (مقاييس اللغة) العين والجيم والراء أصلٌ واحد صحيح يدلُّ على تعقد في الشيء ونُتوّ مع التواء. والعُجْرة: كلُّ عقدةٍ في خشبةٍ أو غيرها من نحو عروق البدَن، والجمع عُجَر. ومن الباب الاعتجار، وهو لفُّ العِمامة على الرأس من غير إدارةٍ تحت الحنك. وإنما سمّيَ اعتجاراً لما فيه من لَيّ ونُتوّ.

عجر (الصَحاح في اللغة) وتَعَجَّر بطنه، أي تَعَكَّن. والمِعْجَرُ ما تشدُّهُ المرأة على رأسها. يقال: اعْتَجَرَتِ المرأة. والاعْتِجار أيضاً: لفُّ العمامة على الرأس. وعَجَرَ الفرسُ، أي مدَّ ذنبَه نحو عَجُزِه في العَدْو.

عجر (لسان العرب) وعَجَرَ الفرسُ يَعْجِرُ إذا مدَّ ذنبه نحو عَجُزه في العَدْوِ؛ وقال أبو زيد: وهَبَّتْ مَطاياهُم، فَمِنْ بَيْنَ عاتِب، ومِنْ بَيْنِ مُودٍ بالبَسِيطَةِ يَعْجِرُ أي هالك قد مدَّ ذنبه. وعَجَر الفرسُ يَعْجِرُ عَجْراً وعَجَراناً وعاجَر إذا مَرَّ مَرّاً سريعاً من خوف ونحوه. والعَجْرُ لَيُّك عنق الرَجل.

وفي نوادر الأعراب: عَجَر عنقه إلى كذا وكذا يَعْجِره إذا على وجه فأراد أن يرجع عنه إلى شيء خلفه، وهو منهيّ عنه، أو أمرته بالشيء فعَجَر عنقه ولم يرد أن يذهب إليه لأمرك. وعَجَر عنقه يَعْجِرها عَجْرا: ثناها.

زب (مقاييس اللغة) الزاء والباء أصلان: أحدهما يدل على وُفُور في شَعَر، ثم يحمل عليه. فالزَّبَب: طُول الشَّعْر، وكثرتُه.
زبب (الصّحاح في اللغة) الزُّبّ: الذكَر. والزُّبُّ: اللحية بلغة اليمن. والزَّبَبُ طول الشعَر وكثرتُه.
زبب (لسان العرب) الزَّبَبُ: مصدر الأزَبّ، وهو كثْرة شَعَر الذِّراعَيْن والحاجِبين والعينين، والجمعُ الزُّبُّ. والزَّبَبُ طولُ الشعَرِ وكثرته؛ والزَّبَّاءُ: الاست لشعرها.
زنب (لسان العرب) زُنابةُ العَقْرب وزُناباها: كلتاهما إبْرتُها التي تَلْدَغ بها.
ذبب (لسان العرب) الذَّبُّ: الدَّفْعُ والمَنْعُ. والذَّبْذَبُ: اللِّسانُ، وقيلَ الذَّكَر. والتَّذَبْذُبُ: التَّحرُّكُ. والذَّبْذَبةُ: نَوْسُ الشيءِ المُعَلَّق في الهواءِ. وتذَبْذَب الشيءُ: ناسَ واضْطَرب ، وذَبْذَبَه هو؛
ذنب (لسان العرب) والذَّنَبُ معروف، والجمع أَذْنابٌ.

درم (القاموس المحيط) دَرِمَ الساقُ، كفرِح: اسْتَوى، و~ الكَعْبُ أو العَظْمُ: واراهُ اللَّحْمُ حتى لم يَبِنْ له حَجْمٌ، والأَدْرَمُ: المُسْتوِي، وع. ودَرَّمَ أظفارَهُ تَدْريماً: سَوَّاها بعدَ القصّ. ودِرْعٌ دَرِمَةٌ، كفرِحَةٍ ومُعَظَّمةٍ: مَلْساءُ، أو لَيِّنَةٌ. والأَدْرَمُ: الذي لا أسْنانَ له.
درم (لسان العرب) الليث: الدَّرَمُ استواء الكعب وعَظْم الحاجب ونحوه إذا لم يَنْتبِرْ فهو أَدْرَمُ، والفعل دَرِمَ يَدْرَمُ فهو دَرِمٌ. ومكان أَدْرَمُ: مستوٍ، وكعب أَدْرَمُ؛
الدَّرْمَكُ (القاموس المحيط) الدَّرْمَكُ، كجَعْفَرٍ: دَقيقُ الحُوَّارَى، والتُّرابُ الناعِمُ .

5.60

سيف (مقاييس اللغة) السين والياء والفاء أصلٌ يدلُّ على امتدادٍ في شيء وطول. من ذلك السَّيف، سمِّيَ بذلك لامتداده .
وظف (لسان العرب) والوَظِيفُ لكل ذي أربع: ما فوق الرُّسْغ إلى مَفْصِل الساق. ووَظِيفا يدي الفرس: ما تحت رُكْبَتَيْه إلى جنبيه، ووظيفا رجليه: ما بين كعبيه إلى جنبيه. وقال ابن الأعرابي: الوظِيفُ من رُسْغَي البعير إلى ركبتيه في يديه، وأما في رجليه فمن رُسغيه إلى عُرقوبيه، والجمع من كل ذلك أَوْظِفة ووُظف.

5.61

خل (مقاييس اللغة) فأمَا الفُرجة فالخَلل بين الشَيئين.
الخَلُّ (القاموس المحيط) والخَلَلُ: مُنْفرَجُ ما بين الشَّيْئَيْنِ،
خلل (لسان العرب) والخَلل الفُرْجة بين الشيئين. والخلَة: الثُّقْبة الصغيرة، وقيل: هي الثُّقْبة ما كانت؛
حل (مقاييس اللغة) الحاء واللام له فروع كثيرة ومسائل، وأصلها كلُّها عندي فتح الشيء، لا يشذُّ عنه شيء.

رتا (لسان العرب) رَتَا الشيءَ يَرْتُوه رَتْواً: شدّه وأَرخاه، ضِدٌّ. وروي عن النبي، صلى الله عليه وسلم، أنه قال في الحَساءِ: إنَّه يَرْتُو فُؤادَ الحَزِين ويَسْرو عن فؤادِ السَّقِيم؛ قال الأَصمعي: يَرْتُو فُؤادَ الحَزِين يَشُدُّه ويُقَوِّيه؛ وقال لبيد في الشَّدِّ يصف دِرعاً: فَخْمَةٌ دفراء تُرْتَى بالعُرى قُرْدُمانِيّاً وتَرْكاً كالبَصَلْ يعني الدُّروعَ أَنه ليس لها عُرىً في أَوساطها، فيُضَمّ ذَيلها إلى تلك العُرى وتُشَدُّ إلى فوقُ لتنشمِر عن لابسها، فذلك الشَدُّ هو الرَّتْوُ. ابن الأَعرابي: الرَّتْوُ يكون شدّاً ويكون إرخاءً؛ وأَنشد للحرث يذكر جَبَلاً وارتفاعه: مُكْفَهِراً على الحَوادِثِ لا يَرْ تُوهُ لِلدَّهْرِ مُؤْيِدٌ صَمَّاءُ أَي لا تُرْخِيه ولا تُدْهِيه داهِيةٌ ولا تُغَيّرُه. وقال أَبو عبيد: معناه لا تَرْتُوهُ لا تَرْمِيه، وأَصل الرَّتْوِ الخَطْوُ، أَراد أَنَّ الداهية لا تَخَطّاه ولا تَرْمِيه فتُغَيِّره عن حاله ولكنه باقٍ على الدهر. وفي الحديث: إنَّ الخَزِيرَة تَرْتُو فُؤادَ المَرِيضِ أَي تَشُدُّه وتُقَوِّيه. ورَتَوْته ضَمَمْته. ورَتَى في ذَرْعِه: كَفُتَّ في عَضُده. والرَّتْوة الدَّرَجة والمَنْزلة عندَ السُّلْطان. والرَّتْيَة والرَّتْوة: الخَطْوة، وقال ابن سيده في موضع آخر: قال اللحياني ولَسْت منها على ثقة. وقد رَتَوْت أَرْتُو رَتْواً إذا خطَوْت. وروي عن معاذ أَنه قال: تَتَقدَّم العلماءُ يومَ القيامة بِرَتْوَة؛ قال أَبو عبيد: الرَّتْوة الخَطْوة ههنا أَي بخَطْوة، ويقال بدَرَجة. وقال ابن الأَثير: أَي برَمْيَة سَهْم، وقيل: بميل، وقيل: مدى البَصر. وفي حديث أَبي جهل: فَيَغيب في الأَرض ثم يَبْدو رَتْوَة. وفي حديث فاطمة، رضي الله عنها: أَنها أَقبلت إلى النبي، صلى الله عليه وسلم ، فقال لها ادْني يا فاطمة، فدَنَتْ رَتْوة، ثم قال ادْني يا فاطمة، فدَنَتْ رَتْوة؛ الرَّتْوة ههنا: الخَطْوة، وقيل: الرَّتْوة البَسْطة، والرَّتْوةُ نحوٌ منْ ميل، والرَّتْوة الدَّعْوة، والرَّتْوة الزيادة في الشرف وغيره، والرَّتْوة العُقْدة الشَّدِيدة، والرَّتْوة العُقْدة المسترخية، قال: ورتا برأسه يَرْتو رَتْواً ورُتُوّاً أَوْمأَ، وقيل: هو مِثْل الإيماء، وقيل: هو أَن يقول نعم وتعال بالإيماء. ورتا بالدَّلْو يَرْتُو رَتْواً: مَدَّ بها مدّاً رَفِيقاً. ورَتَوْت رمَيْت. والرَّتْوة رَمية بسَهْم. والرَّتْوة نحوٌ من مِيل، وقيل: مَدُّ البَصر والرَّتْوة: سُوَيْعة. والرَّتْوة شَرَفٌ من الأَرض نحو الرَّبْوة.
رَتاهُ (القاموس المحيط) رَتاهُ: شَدَّه، وأرْخاهُ، ضِدٌّ، و~ القلبَ: قَوّاهُ، و~ الدَّلْوَ: جَذَبَها رَفيقاً، و~ برأْسِه رَتْواً ورُتُوّاً: أشار، وضم، وخَطا.

5.62

ظلل (لسان العرب) كلُّ ما أَطْبَقَ عليك فهو ظُلّة، وكذلك كل ما أَظلَّك.
الكَتَنُ (القاموس المحيط) والمُكْتَتِنُ: ضِدُّ المُطْمَئِنِّ، وبزنته. وأكْتَنَ: ألْصَق.

كتن (لسان العرب) لكَتَنُ: الدَّرَنُ والوَسَخُ وأثر الدُّخان في البيت. وكَتِنَ الوَسَخُ على الشيء كَتناً: لَصِقَ به. والكَتَنُ لَطْخُ الدخان بالحائط أي أنها لَزُوق بمن يَمَسُّها أو أنها دَنِسةُ العِرْضِ. الليث: الكَتَنُ لَطْخ الدخانِ بالبيت والسَّوادِ بالشَّفَة ونحوه. يقال للدابة إذا أكلت الدَّرِين: قد كَتِنَتْ جَحافِلُها أي اسودَت؛

كتل (لسان العرب) ويقال: كَتِنَتْ جَحافِل الخيل من العُشب وكَتِلَت، بالنون واللام، إذا لزِجَتْ. وكَتِل الشيء، فهو كَتِل: تلزَّق وتلزَّج؛ قال: وفي مراغٍ جلدُها منه كَتِلْ قال: وقد تكون لام كَتِل بدلاً من نون كَتِنَ، وهما بمعنى واحد.

كدن (لسان العرب) والكَوْدانة: الناقة الغليظة الشديدة؛ قال ابن الرقاع: حَمَلَتْهُ بازِلٌ كَوْدانةٌ في مِلاطٍ ووعاءٍ كالجراب وكَدِنَتْ شَفَتُه كَدَناً، فهي كَدِنةٌ: اسْودَّت من شيءٍ أكله، لغة في كَتِنَتْ، والتاء أعلى. ابن السكيت: كَدِنَتْ مشافر الإبل وكَتِنَتْ إذا رَعتِ العشبَ فاسْوَدَّت مشافرُها من مائه وغلُظت. ويقال: أدْرِكوا كَدَنَ مائكم أي كَدَرَه. قال أبو منصور: الكَدَنُ والكَدَرُ والكَدَلُ واحد.

6.1

Ancient Mesopotamian Gods and Goddesses (http://oracc.museum.upenn.edu/amgg/listofdeities/marduk/): "The etymology of Marduk's name is controversial. It is difficult to determine whether the logographic writing of his name dAMAR.UD, Sumerian for "calf of the sun/sun-god," is in any way significant or not. The suggestion to translate this spelling as "calf of the storm" should probably be rejected as there is no evidence for Marduk originally having been a storm god nor is there evidence for his association with the storm god Iškur/Adad."

"In gratitude the other gods then bestow 50 names upon Marduk and select him to be their head. The number 50 is significant, because it was previously associated with the god Enlil, the former head of the pantheon, who was now replaced by Marduk. This replacement of Enlil is already foreshadowed in the prologue to the famous Code of Hammurabi, a collection of "laws," issued by Hammurabi (r. 1792-1750 BCE), the most famous king of the first dynasty of Babylon. In the prologue, Hammurabi mentions that the gods Anu and Enlil determined for Marduk to receive the "Enlil-ship" (stewardship)

of all the people, and with this elevated him into the highest echelons of the Mesopotamian pantheon."

"The interpretation of líl as 'wind' is apparently a secondary development of the first millennium BCE, which has led to an interpretation of Enlil's name as 'Lord Wind' or 'Lord Air'."

Written Forms Logographic spellings: AMAR.UD/UTU, dAMAR.UD/UTU, dAMAR.UD/UTU.KAM, dAMAR.UD/UTU.KÁM, dDUMU.Ú.TUK, dŠÀ.ZU, dMES, dTUŠ.A(?), dŠÚ, dKU, dEN

Syllabic spellings

ma-ru-tu-uk, dma-ru-tu-uk-ku, ma-ru-tu-UD, dmar-duk

ePSD: AMAR

amar [YOUNG] wr. amar "calf; young, youngster, chick; son, descendant" Akk. būru; māru

ePSD: UD

ud [STORM] wr. ud "storm; storm demon" Akk. ūmu

ud [SUN] wr. ud "day; heat; a fever; summer; sun" Akk. immu; ummedu; umšu; šamšu; ūmu

ردك (لسان العرب) قال الأزهري: ومَرْوَدك إن جعلت الميم أصلية فهو فَعْوَلَل، وإن كانت الميم غير أصلية فإني لا أعرف له في كلام العرب نظيراً، قال: وقد جاء مَرْدَك في الأسماء وما أراه عربياً صحيحاً.

أمر (الصَّحاح في اللغة) والإمَّرُ أيضاً: الصغيرُ من وَلَدِ الضأن؛ والأنثى إمَّرَةٌ. يقال: ما له إمَّرٌ ولا إمَّرَةٌ، أي شيءٌ.

أمر (لسان العرب) وأمِرَ الشيءُ أمَراً وأمَرةً، فهو أمِرٌ: كَثُرَ وتَمَّ؛ قال: أمُّ عِيالٍ ضَنؤُها غيرُ أمِرْ والاسم: الإمْرُ. والأمَرَةُ الزيادة والنماءُ والبركة. أمِرَ المالُ إذا كَثُرَ. والإمَّرُ الصغيرُ من الحُمْلان أوْلادِ الضأنِ، والأُنثى إمَّرَةٌ، وقيل: هما الصغيران من أولادِ المعز. والإمَّرُ الخروف. والإمَّرَةُ الرِّخْلُ، والخروف ذكر، والرِّخْلُ أُنثى.

دوك (مقاييس اللغة) الدال والواو والكاف أصلٌ واحد يدلُّ على ضَغْطٍ وتزاحُم. فيقولون: دُكْتُ الشيءَ دَوْكاً.

دوك (لسان العرب) وداكَ الطِّيبَ والشيءَ يَدُوكه دوكاً ومَداكاً أي سحقه. الدَّوْكُ: دق الشيء وسحقه وطحنه كما يَدُوك البعيرُ الشيء بكَلْكَلِه. وفي حديث خيبر: أن النبي، صلى الله عليه وسلم، قال: لأُعطينَّ الراية غداً رجلاً يفتح الله على يديه، فبات الناس يَدُوكون تلك الليلة فيمن يدفعها إليه؛ قوله يَدُوكون أي يخوضون ويموجون ويختلفون فيه. والدَّوْك الإختلاط. وباتوا يَدوكون دَوْكاً إذا باتوا في اختلاط ودَوران.

دك (مقاييس اللغة) الدال والكاف أصلان: أحدهما يدلُّ على تطامُن وانسطاحٍ. والأصل الآخر يقرب من باب الإبدال، فكأنَّ الكاف فيه قائمةٌ مَقام القاف. يقال دكَكْت الشيء، مثل دقَقته، وكذلك دكّكته.

الدَّكُّ (القاموس المحيط) الدَّكُّ: الدَّقُّ والهَدْمُ، ودكَّكَهُ: خَلَطَهُ.

داقَ (القاموس المحيط) دَاقَ دَوْقاً ودَواقةً ودُؤوقاً ودُؤوقةً، بضمهما: حَمُقَ، فهو دائِقٌ، والدَّوْقةُ والدَّوْقانِيَّةُ: الفَسادُ، والحُمْقُ. وأداقوا به: أحاطوا.

دوق (الصّحاح في اللغة) الدوقُ بالضم: الموقُ والحُمْق. يقال: أحمقُ مائقٌ دائقٌ. وقد داقَ يَدوقُ دَوْقاً ودُؤوقاً ودَواقَةً .

دوق (لسان العرب) الدُّوقُ، بالضم: المُوقُ والحُمْقُ. والدَّائقُ: الهالِك حُمْقاً. يقال: هو أَحْمقُ مائقٌ دائقٌ؛ وقد ماقَ وداقَ يَمُوقُ ويَدُوقُ مَواقةً ودواقةً ودَوْقاً ومُؤوقاً ودُؤوقاً. ورجل مُدَوَّق: مُحَمَّق. أبو سعيد: داقَ الرَّجلُ في فعله وداكَ يَدُوقُ ويَدُوك إذا حَمُق.

مأق (لسان العرب) المَأْقةُ: الحِقْد. الأَصمعي: امتَأَق غضبهُ امتِئاقاً إذا اشتدَ. وقال غيره: المَأْقةُ الأَنَفةُ وشدة الغضب والحميَّة.

دوغ (لسان العرب) وقال أَبو سعيد: في فلان دوغة ودَوْكة أي حُمْقٌ.

دوخ (لسان العرب) داخ يَدُوخ دَوْخاً: ذَلَّ وخضَع. ودَوَّخ الرجلُ والبعيرَ: ذَلَّله، يائية وواوية. وأَدَخْتُه أنا فداخ. ودَوَّخَ المكانَ: جالَ فيه. ودَوَّخ الوجعُ رأسَه: أداره.

توك (لسان العرب) أحمق تائِكٌ: شديد الحمق، ولا فعل له؛ قال ابن سيده: لذلك لم أخص به الواو دون الياء ولا الياء دون الواو.

تكك (لسان العرب) وتَكَّ الإِنسان إذا حَمُق.

حمق (لسان العرب) الحُمْقُ: ضِدّ العَقْل. والمُحْمِقاتُ من الليالي: التي يَطلعُ القمر فيها ليلة كلَّه فيكون في السماء ومن دونه سَحاب، فترى ضَوءاً ولا ترى قمراً،فتظنُّ أنك قد أَصبحت وعليك ليل، مشتق من الحُمْق. وفي المثل: غَرَّني غُرُورَ المُحْمِقات. ويقال سِرْنا في ليال مُحمِقات إذا استتر القمر فيها بغيم أَبيض فيسير الراكب ويظن أنه قد أَصبح حتى يَملَّ، قال: ومنه أُخذ اسم الأَحْمق لأنه يغُرك في أول مجلسه بتَعاقُله، فإذا انتهى إلى آخر كلامه تبيّن حمقه فقد غرك بأول كلامه.

عود (لسان العرب) وكل من أتاك مرة بعد أخرى، فهو عائد، وأما قول أبي النجم: حتى إذا الليلُ تَجلَّى أَصْحَمُه، وانْجابَ عن وجْهِ أَغَرَّ أَدْهَمُه، وتَبِعَ الأَحْمَرَ عَوْدٌ يَرْجُمُه فإنه أراد بالأحمر الصبح، وأراد بالعود الشمس. قال الأزهري: قال بعضهم: العَوْد تثنية الأمر عَوْداً بعد بَدْءٍ. يقال: بَدأَ ثم عاد، والعَوْدَةُ عَوْدَةٌ مرة واحدةٌ.

أود (لسان العرب) والتأَوّد التثنِي.

أبَى (لسان العرب) ويقال: أَبَيَ فلان إذا أَطلَّ عليه العدوُّ. وقد أُتيتَ يا فلان إذا أُنذِر عدواً أَسرف عليه.

عدو (مقاييس اللغة) العين والدال والحرف المعتل أصلٌ واحدٌ صحيحٌ يرجع إليه الفروعُ كلُّها، وهو يدلُّ على تجاوُزٍ في الشيء وتقدُّمٍ لما ينبغي أن يقتصر عليه.

عتا (لسان العرب) عَتَا يَعْتُو عُتُوّاً وعِتِيّاً: اسْتَكْبَرَ وجاوزَ الحَدَّ.

عتك (مقاييس اللغة) العين والتاء والكاف أصلٌ صحيح يدلُّ على قريبٍ من الذي قبله، وليس ببعيدٍ أن يكونَ من باب الإبدال، وهو من الإقدام والقَدَم. قال الخليلُ وغيره: عَتك فلانٌ [بفلان]، إذا أَقْدَمَ عليه ضَرباً لا يَنهنهُه شيء. قال الأصمعيّ: هو أن يَحمِلَ عليه حملةَ أَخْذٍ وبَطْش. قال الخليل: عَتَكَ الرَّجُل يَعْتِك عَتْكاً وعُتُوكاً، إذا ذَهَب في الأرض.

عدك (مقاييس اللغة) العين والدال والكاف ليس بشيء، إلا كلمةٌ من هَنَواتِ ابن دُرَيد، قال: العَدْك: ضَرب الصُّوف بالمِطْرَقة .

6.2

شأي (لسان العرب) الشَّأْوُ: الطَّلَقُ والشَّوْطُ. والشَّأْوُ: الغايةُ والأَمدُ، وفي الحديث: فَطَلَبْته أَرْفَعُ فرَسي شَأْواً وأَسِيرُ شَأْواً؛ الشَّأْوُ: الشَّوْطُ والمدَى؛ وقوله: وما شأْوَنكَ نَقْرَةً أي لم يُحرِّكْنَ مِن قَلْبِكَ أَدْنى شيء. وشُؤْتُ بالرَّجُلِ شَوْءاً: سُرِرْتُ. وشاءاهُ على فاعَله أي سابقه. وشاءَه: مثل شآهُ على القلب أي سَبقه. ورجلٌ شَيْئانٌ بوزن شَيْعان: بعيدُ النظر، ويُنْعَتُ به الفرس، وهو يحتمل أن يكون مقلوباً من شأى الذي هوسبق لأن نظره يَسْبِقُ نظر غيره، واشْتأَى: اسْتَمَع. أبو عبيد: اشْتأْيتُ اسْتمَعْت؛ وقد أَشِئْتُ إلى فلانٍ وأَجِئْتُ إليه أي أُلجِئْتُ إليه. والشَّأْوُ: ما أُخْرِجَ من تُراب البِئْرِ بمِثل المِشآة. وشَأَوْتُ البِئرَ شأْواً: نَقَّيْتها وأَخرَجْت تُرابها، واسمُ ذلك التّراب الشَّأْوُ أَيضاً.

سأي (لسان العرب) والسَّأْوُ: الوَطن؛ قال ذو الرمة: كأَنَّني من هَوَى خَرْقاءَ مُطَّرِفٌ دامِي الأَظَلِّ، بعيد السَّأْوِ مَهْيُوم والسَّأْوُ: الهِمَّة. يقال: فلان بَعيد السَّأْوِ أي بَعيدُ الهِمَّة، وأنشد أيضاً بيت ذي الرمة. قال: وفسره فقال يَعني هَمَّه الذي تُنازِعُه نفسُه إليه، ويروى هذا البيت بالشين المعجمة من الشَّأْوِ، وهو الغاية؛ والسَّأْوُ بُعْدُ الهَمِّ والنِّزاع، يقال: إنك لذُو سَأْوٍ بعيد أي لَبَعيد الهَمّ. والسَّأْوُ: النِّيَّة والطِّيَّة

6.4

تمم (لسان العرب) تَمَ الشي يَتِمُ تَماً وتُماً وتمامةً وتماماً وتِمامةً وتُماماً وتِماماً وتُمَّةً وأَتمَّه غيره وتَمَّمه واسْتَتمَّه بمعنىً، وتَمَّمه الله تَتْميماً وتَتِمَّةً، وتَمامُ الشيءِ وتِمامتُه وتَتِمَّته: ما تَمَّ به.

مَدَنَ (القاموس المحيط) ومَدَّنَ المَدائنَ تَمْديناً: مَصَّرَها.

مدن (الصّحاح في اللغة) وفلان مَدَّنَ المَدائنَ، كما يقال: مَصَّرَ الأَمْصار.

مدن (لسان العرب) مَدَنَ بالمكان: أَقام به، فِعْلٌ مُمات، ومنه المَدِينة، وهي فَعِيلة، وتجمع على مَدائن، بالهمز، ومُدْنٍ ومُدُن بالتخفيف والتثقيل؛ وفيه قول آخر: أَنه مَفْعِلة من دِنْتُ أَي مُلِكْتُ؛ قال ابن بري: لو كانت الميم في مدينة زائدة لم يجز جمعها على مُدْنٍ. وفلان مَدَّنَ المَدائن: كما يقال مَصَّرَ الأَمصار.

مصر (مقاييس اللغة) ومصَّرت عليه الشَّيء: أعطيتُه إيّاه قليلاً قليلاً.

ندا (الصّحاح في اللغة) والنّدى: الجود. ورجلٌ نَدٍ، أي جواد. وفلان أَندى من فلان، إذا كان أكثر خيراً منه. وفلان يَتَندَّى على أصحابه، أي يتسخَّى. ولا تقل يُندِّي على أصحابه.
ندي (لسان العرب) وما نَدِيَني منه شيء أي نالني ، وما نَديت منه شيئاً أي ما أَصبْت ولا علمت ، وقيل: ما أَتَيْت ولا قارَبْت. ولا يَنداك مني شيء تكرهه أي ما يَصِيبك ؛ عن ابن كيسان. والنَّدى: السَّخاء والكرم. وتندَّى عليهم ونَدِيَ : تَسخَّى ، وأَندى نَدًى كثيراً كذلك. وأَنْدَى عليه: أَفضل. وأَنْدَى الرَّجلُ: كثُر نداه أي عَطاؤه، وأَندى إذا تَسخَّى، وأَندَى الرجلُ إذا كثُر نداه على إخوانه، وكذلك انْتدى وتَندَّى. وفلان يَتَندَّى على أَصحابه: كما تقول هو يَتسخَّى على أَصحابه، ولا تقل يُندِّي على أَصحابِه. وفلان نَدِي الكَفِّ إذا كان سَخِيًا. ونَدَوتُ من الجُود.

6.5

عظم (لسان العرب) وفي التنزيل: فَخَلَقْنا المُضْغةَ عِظاماً فكَسَونا العِظامَ لحماً؛ وعَظْمُ الفَدّانِ: لَوْحُه العَريضُ الذي في رأسِه الحديدةُ التي تُشَقُّ بها الأرضُ، والضاد لغة. والعَظْم خَشَبُ الرَّحْلِ بلا أَنْساعٍ ولا أَداةٍ، وهو عَظْمُ الرَّحْلِ.
عظم (مقاييس اللغة) العين والظاء والميم أصلٌ واحد صَحيح يدلُّ على كِبَرٍ وقوّة. ومن الباب العَظْم، معروف، وهو سمّي بذلك لقوّته وشدّته .
عضم (لسان العرب) العَضْمُ في القَوْسِ: المَعْجِس، وهو مَقبِضُ القَوْسِ، والعَضْمُ والعَجْسُ والمَقْبِضُ كله بمعنًى واحدٍ، والجمع عِضامٌ؛ وعَضْمُ الفدّانِ: لَوْحُه العريضُ الذي في رأْسِه الحديدةُ التي تَشُقُّ الأرض، والجمعُ أَعْضِمةٌ وعُضُمٌ، كلاهما نادرٌ، وعندي أَنهم كَسَّرُوا العَضْمَ الذي هو الخشبةُ وعَضْمَ الفَدّانِ على عِضامٍ، كما كَسَّرُوا عليه عَضْمَ القَوْسِ، ثم كَسَّرُوا عِضاماً على أَعْضِمة وعُضُمٍ كما كَسَّروا مِثالاً على أَمْثِلةٍ ومُثُلٍ، والظاءُ في كل ذلك لغةٌ؛ حكاه أَبو حنيفة بعد أَن قَدَّمَ الضَّاد. والعَضُومُ: الناقةُ الصُّلْبةُ في بدنها القَوِيَّةُ على السَّفَر. والعَصُومُ، بالصاد المُهْمَلَة: الكثيرةُ الأَكْلِ. وامرأَةٌ عَيْضُومٌ: كثيرةُ الأَكلِ؛ عن كراع؛ قال: أَرْجِدَ رأْسُ شَيْخةٍ عَيْضُوم والصاد أَعلى؛ قال أَبو منصور: هذا تصحيف قبيح، والصوابُ العَيْصُومُ، بالصاد؛ كذلك رواه أَبو العباس أَحمد بن يحيى عن ابن الأَعرابي، وقال في موضع آخر: هي العَصُومُ للمرأَة إذا كثُر أَكلها، وإِنما عَصُومٌ وعَيْصُومٌ لأَن كثرة أَكلِها تَعْصِمها من الهُزالِ وتُقَوِّيها، والله أَعلم .
عَصَمَ (القاموس المحيط) والعَصومُ: الأَكولُ، كالعَيْصُوم .
عصم (مقاييس اللغة) العين والصاد والميم أصلٌ واحدٌ صحيحٌ يدلُّ على إمساكٍ ومنْعٍ وملازمة. وأثر الخِضاب عَصيم، والمُعصَم: الجِلد لم يَنْحَ وبرُه عنه، بل أُلزِم شعرَه لأنه لا يُنْتَفع به.
عصم (لسان العرب) والعَيْصومُ: الكثيرُ الأَكْلِ، الذَّكرُ والأُنثى فيه سواء؛ قال: أَرْجِدَ رأْسُ شَيْخةٍ عَيْصُوم ويروى عَيْضُوم، بالضاد المعجمة. قال الأَزهريّ: العَيْصوم من النّساء الكثيرةُ الأكْلِ الطَّويلةُ النَّوْم المُدَمْدِمةُ إذا انْتَبهتْ. ورجلٌ عَيْصُومٌ وعَيْصامٌ إذا كان أَكولاً. والعَصُومُ، بالصادِ: الناقةُ الكثيرةُ الأَكْلِ.
عصن (لسان العرب) أَعْصَنَ الرجلُ إذا شَدَّدَ على غريمه وتمكَّكَه، وقيل: أَعْصَنَ الأَمرُ إذا اعْوَجَّ وعَسُر .
عظن (لسان العرب) ابن الأَعرابي: أَعْظَنَ الرجلُ إذا غَلُظ جسمه .
عضنك (لسان العرب) العَضَنَّكُ: المرأَةُ العَجْزاء اللَّفَّاءُ الكثيرة اللحم المُضْطَرِبة، وقيل: هي العظيمة الرَّكَب، وقال ابن الأَعرابي: هي العَضَنَّكة، وقال الليث: العَضَنَّكُ المرأَة التي ضاق مُلْتَقى فخذيها مع ترارتها وذلك لكثرة اللحم .

6.6

لألأ (العباب الزاخر) وقال الفَرّاءُ: سَمِعتُ العَرَبَ تقول لصاحب اللُؤلُؤ: لأّل -مثالُ لَعّالٍ-، والقياس: لأّءٌ مثالُ لَعّاع.
وني (لسان العرب) وقال أَبو العباس: الوَنى واحدته ونيَةٌ وهي اللُّؤْلؤة؛ قال أَبو منصور: واحدة الوَنى وناةٌ لا وَنيةٌ، والوَنْيةُ الدُّرَّة؛ أَبو عمرو: هي الوَنيةُ والوَناة للدرَّة؛ قال ابن الأَعرابي: سميت وَنيَةً لثقبها .
لعل (الصّحاح في اللغة) لعَلَّ كلمةُ شكٍّ، وأَصلها عَلَّ، واللام في أوّلها زائدة.
لَعَلَّ (القاموس المحيط) لَعَلَّ ولَعَلَ: كَلِمَةُ طَمَعٍ وإشْفاقٍ،كعَلَّ وعَنَّ وغَنَّ وأنَّ ولأَنَّ ولَونَّ ورَعَلَّ ولَعَنَّ ولَغَنَّ ورَغَنَّ. ويقالُ: عَلِّي أَفْعَلُ وعَلَّني ولَعَلِّي ولَعَلِّني ولَعَنِّي ولَعَنِّني ولَغَنِّي ولَغَنَّني ولَوَنِّي ولَوَنَّني ولأَنِّي ولأَنَّني وأَنِّي وأَنَّني ورَغَنِّي ورَغَنَّني .
عل (مقاييس اللغة) واسم اللَّبن العُلالة. ومما شذَّ عن هذه الأصول إن صحَّ قولُها إنّ العُلْعُل: الذّكر من القنابر. والعُلْعُل رأس الرَّهابة مما يلي الخاصرة. والعُلْعُل عُضو الرَّجُل. ويقولون: علّ في معنى لعلّ.
علل (لسان العرب) والعَلُّ الذي يزور النساء. والعَلُّ التَّيْس الضَّخم العظيم؛ والعُلْعُل والعَلْعَل؛ الفتح عن كراع: اسمُ الذَّكر جميعاً. الفراء: العرب تقول للعاثر لَعاً لكَ وتقول: عَلَّ ولَعَلَّ وعَلَّكَ ولَعَلَّكَ بمعنىً واحد؛ قال الكسائي: العرب تُصَيِّرُ لَعَلَّ مكان لَعاً وتجعل لَعاً مكان لَعَلَّ.
أمل (لسان العرب) ابن الأَعرابي: الأَمَلة أَعوان الرجل، واحدهم آمل.
عمل (مقاييس اللغة) العين والميم واللام أصلٌ واحدٌ صحيح، وهو عامٌ في كلّ فِعلٍ يُفعَل. قال الخليل: عَمِل يَعمَل عَمَلاً، فهو عامل؛
عمل (لسان العرب) والعَوامِلُ: الأَرجل؛ قال الأَزهري: عَوامِلُ الدابة قوائمه، واحدتها عامِلة.
رجل (مقاييس اللغة) الراء والجيم واللام مُعظم بابه يدلُّ على العُضو الذي هو رِجْلُ كلِّ ذي رِجْل. ويكون بعد ذاك كلماتٌ تشذُّ عنه. فمعظم الباب الرِّجل: رِجْلُ الإنسانِ وغيره. والرَّجْل: الرَّجّالة. وإنما سُمُّوا رَجْلاً لأنهم يمشون على أرجُلِهم، والرُّجّال والرُّجالَى: الرَّجال. والرَّجْلانُ: الراجل، والجماعة رَجْلى.
اللَّغْوُ (القاموس المحيط) اللَّغْو: السَّيِّئُ الخُلُقِ، والفَسْلُ، والشَّرِهُ الحريصُ. وذُو لَغْوَة: قَيْلٌ، ورجلٌ آخرُ.

لعا (الصّحاح في اللغة) ويقال: ما بها لاعي قَرْوٍ، أي ما بها مَن يلحس عُسًا، معناه ما بها أحدٌ. ويقال: خرجنا نَتَلعَّى، أي نأخذ اللعاعَ، وهو أول النبت.

لعا (لسان العرب) واللَعو السيء الخُلق، واللَعْوُ الفسْلُ، واللَّعْوُ واللَّعا الشَّرِه الحَريص، رجل لَعْوٌ ولَعاً، منقوص، وهو الشَره الحريص، والأُنثى بالهاء وكذلك هما من الكلاب والذئاب؛

6.8

الدَّوْلةُ (القاموس المحيط) وأدالَنا اللهُ تعالى من عَدُوِّنا: من الدَّوْلةِ. والإِدالةُ: الغَلَبةُ. ودالتِ الأيّامُ: دارتْ، واللهُ تعالى يُداولها بينَ الناس. والدَّوْلُ لُغةٌ في الدَّلْوِ، وانقِلابُ الدَّهْرِ من حالٍ إلى حالٍ، وبالتحريكِ: النَّبَلُ المتداوَلُ.

دألَ (القاموس المحيط) دألَ، كمنَع، دَألاً، ويُحرَكُ، وكجمَزى: وهو مِشيةٌ فيها ضَعفٌ، أو عَدْوٌ مُتقارِبٌ، أو مَشْيٌ نَشيطٌ، و~ له دألاً ودألاناً، محرَكتينِ: خَتَلَه.

دول (مقاييس اللغة) الدال والواو واللام أصلان: أحدُهما يدلُّ على تحوُّل شيءٍ من مكان إلى مكان، والآخر يدلُّ على ضَعْفٍ واسترخاء. قال أبو زيد: دال الثَّوبُ يَدول، إذا بَلِيَ. وقد جعل [وُدُّه] يَدُول، أي يبلى. ومن هذا الباب انْدالَ بَطنُه، أي استرخَى .

دول (لسان العرب) الدَّولةُ والدُّولةُ: العُقْبةُ في المال والحَرْب سَواء، وقيل: الدُّولةُ، بالضم، في المال، والدَّولةُ، بالفتح، في الحرب، وقيل: هما سواء فيهما، يضمان ويفتحان، وقيل: بالضم في الآخرة، وبالفتح في الدنيا، وقيل: هما لغتان فيهما، والجمع دُوَلٌ ودِوَلٌ وتداولته الأيدي: أخذته هذه مرَّة وهذه مرَّة. ودالَ الثوبُ يَدُول أي بَلِيَ. وقد جَعَل وِدُّه يَدُول أي يَبْلى. الليث: الدَّوْلة والدُّولة لغتان، ومنه الإدالةُ الغَلَبة. وأَدالَنا الله من عدوِّنا: من الدَّوْلة؛ يقال: اللهم أَدِلْني على فلان وانصرني عليه. وفي حديث وفد ثقيف: نُدالُ عليهم ويُدالون علينا؛ الإدالةُ: الغَلَبة، يقال: أُدِيل لنا على أعدائنا أي نُصِرنا عليهم، وكانت الدَّوْلة لنا، والدَّوْلة: الانتقال من حال الشدَّة إلى الرَّخاء؛ ومنه حديث أَبي سُفْيان وهِرَقْل: نُدالُ عليه ويُدالُ علينا أي نَغْلِبه مرة ويَغلبنا أخرى. الليث: الدَّوْلة والدُّولة لغتان، ومنه الإدالةُ الغَلَبة. وتَداوَلْنا الأَمرَ: أَخذناه بالدُّوَل. وقالوا دَوالَيْك أَي مُداولة على الأَمر؛ قال سيبويه: وإِن شئت حملته على أَنه وقع في هذه الحال. ودالَت الأَيامُ أَي دارت، والله يُداولها بين الناس. وتَداولته الأَيدي: أَخذته هذه مرَّة وهذه مرَّة.

ودالَ الثوبُ يَدُول أَي بَلِي.

عند (لسان العرب) وعَقَبةٌ عَنُودٌ: صَعْبَةُ المُرْتقى. وما لي عنه عُنْدَدٌ وعُنْدُدٌ أَي بُدٌّ؛ أَبو زيد: يقال إِنَّ تحتَ طريقتك لَعِنْدَأْوَةً، والطريقةُ: اللينُ والسكونُ، والعِنْدَأْوَةُ: الجَفْوَةُ والمَكْرُ؛ قال الأَصمعي: معناه إِن تحت سكونك لَنَزْوَةً وطِماحاً؛ وقال غيره: العِنْدَأْوَةُ الالتواء والعَسَرُ، وقال: هو من العَداء، وهمزه بعضهم فجعل النون والهمزة زائدتين (* قوله «النون والهمزة زائدتين» كذا بالأصل وفيه يكون بناء عندأوة فنعالة لا فنعلوة) على بناء فِنْعَلْوة، وقال غيره: عِنْداوةٌ فِعْلَلْوة. وطَعْنٌ عَنِدٌ، بالكسر، إِذا كان يَمْنَةً ويَسْرَةً. قال أَبو عمرو: أَخَفُّ الطَّعْن الوَلْقُ، والعانِدُ مثله.

بدد (لسان العرب) والبَدُّ والبِدُّ والبِدَّة، بالكسر، والبُدَّة، بالضم، والبَداد: النصيب من كل شيء؛

عدد (لسان العرب) العَدُّ: إِحصاءُ الشيء، عدَّه يعُدُّه عدّاً وتَعْداداً وعَدَّةً وعَدَّده. والعِدادُ والبِدادُ: المناهَدَة. يقال: فلانٌ عِدُّ فلان وبِدُّه أَي قِرْنُه، والجمع أَعْدادٌ وأَبْدادٌ. ويقال: فلان إِنما يأْتي أَهلَه العِدَّةَ وهي من العِداد أَي يأْتي أَهله في الشهر والشهرين. ويقال: به مرضٌ عِدادٌ وهو أَن يَدَعه زماناً ثم يعاوده، وقد عادَه مُعادَةً وعِداداً، وكذلك السليم والمجنون كأَنّ اشتقاقه من الحساب من قِبَل عدد الشهور والأَيام أَي أَن الوجع كأَنه يَعُدُّ ما يمضي من السنة فإِذا تمت عاود الملدوغ. ومعنى قول النبي، صلى الله عليه وسلم: تَعادُّني تُؤْذِيني وتراجعني في أَوقاتٍ معلومة ويعاودني أَلمُ سمها؛ كما قال النابغة في حية لدغت رجلاً: تُطَلِّقُهُ حِيناً وحِيناً تُراجِعُ ويقال: به عِدادٌ من أَلمٍ أَي يعاوده في أَوقات معلومة. والعُدَّةُ ما أُعِدَّ لأَمر يحدث مثل الأُهْبةِ. يقال: أَعْدَدْتُ للأَمر عُدَّته. وأَعَدَّه لأَمر كذا: هيَّأَه له. والاستعداد للأَمر: التَّهَيُّؤُ له.

6.12

طيم (لسان العرب) طامَهُ الله على الخيرِ يَطِيمُه طَيماً: جَبَله. وطانَه يَطِينُه أَي جَبَله، ومنه الطِّيماءُ، وهي الجِبلَّة، والطِّيماءُ الطبيعةُ.

طعم (لسان العرب) ورجل ذو طَعْمٍ أَي ذو عَقلٍ وحَزْمٍ؛ وأَنشد: فلا تأْمُري، يا أُمَّ أَسماءَ، بالتي تُجِرُّ الفتى ذا الطَّعْمِ أَن يتكلما أَي تُخرِسُ، وأَصله من الإِجْرارِ، وهو أَن يُجْعَلَ في فَمِ الفَصيل خشَبةٌ تمنعه من الرَّضاع. ويقال: ما بفلان طَعْمٌ ولا نَوِيصٌ أَي ليس له عَقْل ولا به حَراكٌ. قال أَبو بكر: قولُهم ليس لما يَفْعلُ فلانٌ طَعْمٌ، معناه ليس له لَذَّة ولا مَنْزِلَةٌ من القلب، وقال في قوله للمُزَلَّجِ ذا طَعْم في بيت أَبي خِراش: معناه ذا منزلة من القلب، والمُزَلَّجُ البخيلُ، وقال ابن بَرِّي: المُزَلَّجُ من الرجال الدونُ الذي ليس بكامل؛ وأَنشد: أَلا ما لِنفسٍ لا تموتُ فيَنْقضِي شَقاها، ولا تَحْيا حَياةً لها طَعْمُ معناه لها حلاوةٌ ومنزلة من القلب. وليس بذي طَعْمٍ أَي ليس له عقْلٌ ولا نفْسٌ.

6.14

بتت (لسان العرب) البَتُّ: القَطْعُ المُسْتأْصِل. يقال: بَتَتُّ الحبلَ فانْبَتَّ. ابن سيده: بَتَّ الشيءَ يَبُتُّه، ويَبِتُّه بَتّاً، وأَبَتَّه: قطعه قَطْعاً مُسْتأْصِلاً؛ وبَتَّ عليه القضاءَ بَتّاً، وأَبَتَّه: قطعه. وأَبَتَّ يَمينَه: أَمْضاها.

عبط (مقاييس اللغة) العين والباء والطاء أصلٌ صحيح يدلُّ على شِدَّةٍ تُصيبُ من غير استحقاق. وهذه عبارةٌ ذكرها الخليل، وهي صحيحةٌ منقاسة. فالعَبْط: أن تُعبَط النّاقةُ صحيحةً من غير داءٍ ولا كَسْر. قالوا: والعَبيط: الطريُّ من كلِّ شيء. وهذا الذي ذكروهُ في الطريِّ توسُّعٌ منهم،

وإنّما الأصل ما ذكر. يقال من الأوّل: عُبِطت النّاقةُ واعتُبِطت اعتباطاً، إذا نُحِرت سمينةً فتيّةً من غير داء. قالوا: والرّجُل يَعبِط بنفسه في الحرب عَبْطاً، إذا ألقاها فيها غيرَ مُكرَه.

عَبَطَ (القاموس المحيط) عَبَطَ الذبيحةَ يَعْبِطُها: نَحَرَها من غيرِ عِلَّةٍ، وهي سَمينةٌ فَتِيَّةٌ، فهو عَبيطٌ .

عبط (الصّحاح في اللغة) عَبَطَ الثوبَ يَعْبِطُه، أي شقَّه، فهو مَعبوطٌ وعَبيطٌ؛ وعَبَطْتُ الناقة واعْتَبَطْتُها، إذا ذبحتها وليس بها علة فهي عَبيطَةٌ، ولحمها عَبيطٌ.

عبط (لسان العرب) عَبَطَ الذَّبيحةَ يَعْبِطُها عَبْطاً واعْتَبَطَها اعْتِباطاً: نَحَرَها من غير داء ولا كسر وهي سَمينة فَتِيَّةٌ، وهو العَبْطُ، وناقة عَبِيطةٌ ومُعْتَبَطةٌ ولحمها عَبِيط، وكذلك الشاة والبقرة، وعمّ الأَزهريّ فقال: يقال للدابة عَبِيطةٌ ومُعْتَبَطةٌ، والجمع عُبُطٌ وعِباطٌ؛ قال: ومن رواها العُبُط أَراد بها جمعَ عَبِيطٍ، وهو الذي يُنْحَرُ لغير علة، فإِذا كان كذلك كان خُروجُ الدم أَشدّ. والعَوْبَطُ: لُجَّةُ البحر، مقلوب عن العَوْطَبِ. ويقال عَبَطَ الحمارُ التُّرابَ بحَوافِره إِذا أَثاره، والتّرابُ عَبيطٌ. وعَبَطَتِ الرِّيحُ وجهَ الأَرض إِذا قَشَرَتْه. وعَبَطْنا عَرَقَ الفرسِ أَي أَجْرَيْناه حتى عرِقَ؛ قال الجَعْديّ: وقد عَبَطَ الماءَ الحَمِيمَ فأَسْهَلا.

عوج (لسان العرب) العَوَجُ: الانعطاف فيما كان قائماً فمالَ كالرُّمْحِ والحائط؛ والرُّمْح وكلُّ ما كان قائماً يقال فيه العَوَجُ، بالفتح، ويقال: شجرتك فيها عَوَجٌ شديد. ورجل أَعْوَجُ بَيِّنُ العَوَجِ أَي سَيِءُ الخُلُق.

الأَوْجُ (القاموس المحيط) الأَوْجُ: ضِدُّ الهُبوطِ .

عج (مقاييس اللغة) العين والجيم أصلٌ واحد صحيح يدلُّ على ارتفاعٍ في شيء، من صوتٍ أو غبارٍ وما أشبه ذلك.

عنّ (لسان العرب) عَنَّ الشيءُ يَعِنُّ ويَعُنُّ عَنَناً وعُنُوناً: ظَهَرَ أَمامك؛ وفي حديث قَيْلَة: تَحْسَبُ عَنِّي نائمة أَي تحسب أَني نائمة؛ ومنه حديث حُصَين بن مُشَمِّت: أَخبرنا فلان عَنَّ فلاناً حَدَّثه أَي أَن فلاناً؛ قال ابن الأَثير: كأَنهم يفعلون لبَحَحٍ في أَصواتهم، والعرب تقول: لأَنَّكَ ولعَنَّك، تقول ذاك بمعنى لعَلَّك. ابن الأَعرابي: لعَنَّكَ لبني تميم، وبنو تَيْم الله بن ثعْلبة يقولون: رَعَنَّك، يريدون لعلك. ومن العرب من يقول: رَعَنَّكَ ولَغَنَّك، بالغين المعجمة، بمعنى لعَلَّكَ، والعرب تقول: كنا في عُنَّةٍ من الكلأ وفُنَّةٍ وثُنَّةٍ وعانكَةٍ من الكلأ واحدٌ أَي كنا في كَلاءٍ كثيرٍ وخِصْبٍ. وعَنّي: بمعنى عَلِّي أَي لَعَلِّي؛

عَلْوُ (القاموس المحيط) و~ الكِتابَ: عَنْوَنَهُ، كعَلْوَنَهُ عَلْوَنَةً وعُلْواناً. وعالَوْا نَعِيَّهُ: أظْهَرُوهُ. والعِلْيانُ، بالكسر: الضَّخْمُ، والطَّويلُ، والمَتاعُ، والناقةُ المُشْرِفَةُ، و~ من الأَصْواتِ: الجَهيرُ،

فتق (مقاييس اللغة) الفاء والتاء والقاف أصلٌ صحيح يدلُّ على فتحٍ في شيء. من ذلك: فتقت الشّيء فَتْقاً. والفَتْق شقُّ عصا الجماعة. والفَتْق الصُّبح. وأعوام الفَتَق: أعوام الخِصْب. قال:ويقال: أَفتَقَ القمر، إذا صادَفَ فتقاً من سَحابٍ وطَلَع منه.

فتق (لسان العرب) الفَتْق: خلاف الرَّتْق. فَتَقَهُ يَفْتُقُه ويَفْتِقه فَتْقاً: شقه؛ والفَتَقُ الخصب، سمّي بذلك لانشقاق الأرض بالنبات؛

6.16

أرن (لسان العرب) والأَرُون: السَّمُّ، وقيل: هو دماغُ الفيل وهو سمٌّ؛

عرن (لسان العرب) ورجل عِرْنةٌ: شديد لا يطاق، وقيل: هو الصِّرِّيحُ. الفراء: إذا كان الرجل صِرّيعاً خبيثاً قيل: هو عِرْنةٌ لا يُطاق؛

عنّ (لسان العرب) والعِنَّةُ والعُنَّةُ: الاعتراض بالفُضول. ورجل مِعَنٌّ: يعْرِض في شيء ويدخل فيما لا يعنيه، والأُنثى بالهاء.

الكَنّ (القاموس المحيط) والمُكْتَنُّ: ضِدُّ المُطْمَئِنّ، وبزِنَته. وأكْتَنَ: ألْصَقَ.

6.18

تر (مقاييس اللغة) التاء والراء قريبٌ من الذي قبلَه. وفيه من اللغة الأصلية كلمةٌ واحدة، وهو قولهم بَدَنٌ ذو تَرارة، إذا كانَ ذا سِمَنٍ وبَضاضة. وأمّا التَّراتِرُ فالأمورُ العِظام، وليست [أصلاً]؛ لأنّ الرّاء مبدلةٌ من لام.

التَّرتَةُ (القاموس المحيط) التُّرتَةُ، بالضم: رَدَّةٌ قَبيحةٌ في اللّسانِ من العَيْبِ .

ترر (لسان العرب) وتَرَّ بِسَلْحه يَتِرُّ: قذف به. وتَرَّ النَّعامُ: أَلقى ما في بطنه. وتَرْتَرَ: تكلم فأَكثر؛ قال: قُلْتُ لِزَيْدٍ: لا تُتَرْتِرْ، فإِنَّهُمْ يَرَوْنَ المنايا دونَ قَتْلِكَ أَوْ قَتْلي ويروى: تُثَرْثِرْ وتُبَرْبِرْ. والتَّراتِرُ: الشدائد والأُمور العظام.

تلل (لسان العرب) والتَّلْتَلة: التحريك والإِقْلاق. التهذيب في ترجمة ترر: التَّرْتَرة أَن تُحرّك وتُزَعْزِع، قال: وهي التَّرْتَرة والتَّلْتَلة والمَزْمَزة؛ قال ذو الرمة يصف جملاً: بَعِيدُ مَسافِ الخَطْوِ عَوْجٌ شَمَرْدَلٌ، يُقَطِّعُ أَنفاسَ المَهاري تلاتِله وتَلْتَله أَي زَعْزَعه وأَقْلَقه وزَلْزله. وفي حديث ابن مسعود: أُتِيَ بشارب فقال تَلْتِلوه؛ هو أَن يُحرَّك ويُسْتَنْكه ليُعلَم أَشرب أَم لا، وهو في الأَصل السَّوْق بعُنْف. وتَلْتَل الرجلَ: عَنُف بسَوْقه. والتَّلْتَل: الشِّدَّة؛

تير (لسان العرب) وفَعلَ ذلك تارَةً بعد تارة أَي مرة بعد مرة، والجمع تاراتٌ وتِيَرٌ. قال الراجز: بالوَيْلِ تاراً والثُّبُورِ تارا وأَتاره: أَعاده مرة بعد مرة .

تأر (لسان العرب) ابن الأَعرابي: التَّائِرُ المداوم على العمل بعد فتور. الأَزهري في التَّأْرَة: الحين. عن ابن الأَعرابي قال: تأْرَةٌ، مهموز، فلما كثر استعمالهم لها تركوا همزها؛ قال الأَزهري: قال غيره وجمعها تِئَرٌ، مهموزة؛ ومنه يقال: أَتْأَرْتُ إِليه النظر أَي أَدمته تارةً بعد تارة.

6.19

البوقُ (القاموس المحيط) وباقَ بك: طَلَعَ عليك من غَيْبَةٍ، و~ به: حاقَ،

حاقَ (القاموس المحيط) حاقَ به يَحيقُ حَيْقاً وحُيوقاً وحَيَقاناً: أحاطَ به،

6.21

كانَ (القاموس المحيط) كانَ يَكينُ: خَضَعَ. واكْتانَ: حَزِنَ. والكَيْنَةُ: النَّبقَةُ، والكَفالَةُ، والمُكْتانُ: الكَفيلُ.
كين (لسان العرب) ثعلب عن ابن الأعرابي: الكَيْنةُ النَّبقةُ، والكَيْنة الكفالة، والمُكْتانُ الكَفِيلُ.
نوف (لسان العرب) نافَ الشيءُ نَوْفاً: ارتفع وأَشرف. وحكى الأَصمعي: ضع النيف في موضعه أَي الفضْل؛ وقد نيّف العددُ على ما تقول. قال: والنَّيفُ والنَّيِّفُ، كميْت وميِّت، الزيادة. ونيّف العَدَد على ما تقول: زاد، وأَورد الجوهري النيف الزيادة، والنِّياف في ترجمة نيف، قال: وأَصله الواو؛
النَّوْفُ (القاموس المحيط) والنَّيِّفُ: الفضْلُ، والإِحسانُ، ومن واحدةٍ إلى ثلاثٍ. ونافَ وأنافَ على الشيءِ: أشْرَفَ.
نعف (مقاييس اللغة) النون والعين والفاء كلمةٌ تدلُّ على ارتفاعٍ في شيءٍ. منه النَّعَف: مكانٌ مرتفع في اعتراض. وانتَعَفَ الرَّجُل الشيءَ، إذا تركَهُ إلى غيره، كأنَّه سَمَا بنفسه عنه. ومن الكلمة الأولى ناعفْتُ الرَّجُلَ: عارضتُه.
نعب (مقاييس اللغة) النون والعين والباء: أصلانِ صحيحان: أحدُهما يدلُّ على صوتٍ، والآخرُ على حركةٍ من الحركات.

6.22

نأم (لسان العرب) النَّأْمةُ، بالتسكين: الصوتُ. نأَم الرجلُ يَنْئِمُ ويَنْأَمُ نَئِيماً، وهو كالأَنِينِ، وقيل: هو كالزَّحِيرِ، وقيل: هو الصوت الضعيف الخفيّ أَيّاً كان. ويقال: أَسْكتَ اللهُ نَأْمَته، مهموزة مخففة الميم، وهو من النَّئِيم الصوت الضعيف أَي نَغْمَته وصوته. والنَّأْمةُ والنَّئِيمُ: صَوتُ القوس؛ والنَّأْمةُ الحركة .
نمم (لسان العرب) والنَّمِيمة: الهَمس والحركة. وأَسكت الله نامّته أَي جَرْسَه، وما يَنِمُّ عليه من حَرَكته؛ قال: وقد يهمز فيجعل من النَّئِيم. وسَمِعْتُ نامَّته ونَمَّته أَي حِسَّه، والأَعرفُ في ذلك نأْمته.
نوم (لسان العرب) النَّوْم: معروف. ابن سيده: النَّوْمُ النُّعاسُ. نامَ يَنامُ نَوْماً ونِياماً؛ عن سيبويه، والاسمُ النِّيمةُ، وهو نائمٌ إذا رَقَدَ.
النِّيمُ (القاموس المحيط) النِّيمُ، بالكسر: النِّعْمَةُ التامَّةُ، ومن يُسْتَنامُ إليه ويُؤْنَسُ به،

6.23

تقن (مقاييس اللغة) التاء والقاف والنون أصلان: أحدهما إحكام الشيء، والثاني الطين والحَمأة.فالقول الأوّل أتقَنْت الشيء أحكمتُه. ورجل تقِن: حاذقٌ. وابن تِقن: رجلٌ كان جيِّد الرَّمي يُضرَبُ به المثل.
تقن (لسان العرب) وتِقْنٌ اسم رجل كان جيِّد الرَّمي، يُضرَب به المثل، ولم يكن يَسْقُط له سَهْم؛

6.24

بلك (لسان العرب) ابن الأَعرابي: البُلْك أَصوات الأَشداق إذا حركتها الأَصابع من الوَلَع، وقد بَلَكَ الشيءَ: كلَبَكَهُ، وسنذكره .
بَلَكَهُ (القاموس المحيط) بَلَكَهُ: لَبَكَهُ.
لبك (مقاييس اللغة) اللام والباء والكاف أصلٌ صحيح يدلُّ على خَلْط شيء بشيء. يقال لبكتُ على فلانٍ الأمرَ ألبكه، إذا خلَطْتَه عليه. وسأل رجلٌ الحسن عن شيء فلم يبيّنْ فقال: "لَبَكت عليَّ ."
لبك (لسان العرب) اللَّبْكُ: الخَلْط، لَبكْتُ الأَمرَ أَلْبُكه لَبْكاً. اللَّبَكُ واللَّبَكةُ: الشيء المخلوط. لَبَكه يَلْبُكه لَبْكاً: خلطه، ولَبكَ الأَمْرَ لَبْكاً. وسأَل الحسنَ رجلٌ عن مسأَلة ثم أَعاد عليه فغيَّر مسأَلته فقال له الحسن: لَبَكْتَ عليَّ أَي خلطت عليّ، ويروى: بَكَلْتَ، والتَبَكَ الأَمْرُ: اختلط والتبس. وأَمر مُلْتَبِكٌ: ملتبس، على النسب؛

كسر (مقاييس اللغة) الكاف والسين والراء أصلٌ صحيح يدلُّ على هَشْم الشيء وهَضْمه. من ذلك قولُك كَسَرْت الشيءَ أكسِره كَسْراً.
قسر (مقاييس اللغة) القاف والسين والراء يدلُّ على قهرٍ وغلَبَة بشدة. من ذلك القَسْر: الغَلَبة والقَهْر.
كصر (لسان العرب) أَبو زيد: الكَصِيرُ لغة في القَصِير لبعض العرب .
قصر (مقاييس اللغة) القاف والصاد والراء أصلانِ صحيحان، أحدهما يدلُّ على ألا يبلُغَ الشَّيءُ مداه ونهايته، والآخر على الحَبْس. والأصلان متقاربان. فالأوّل القِصَر: خلافُ الطُّول. يقول: هو قصيرٌ بيّن القِصَر.

الحَوْزُ (القاموس المحيط) الحَوْزُ: الجمعُ، وضمُّ الشيء، كالحِيازَةِ والاحتِيازِ، والسَّوْقُ اللَّيِّنُ، والشديدُ، ضِدٌّ، والسيرُ اللَّيِّنُ، والمَوْضِعُ تُتَّخَذُ حَوالَيْهِ مُسَنَّاةٌ، والمِلْكُ، والنِّكاحُ، والإِغْراقُ في نَزْعِ القَوْسِ، ومَحَلَّةٌ بأَعْلى بَعْقُوبا، منها عبدُ الحَقِّ بنُ محمود الفَرَّاشُ الزاهِدُ، و~ القَوْمُ: تَرَكوا مَرْكَزَهم إلى آخَرَ. وتَحاوَزَ الفَرِيقانِ: انْحازَ كلُّ واحدٍ عن الآخَرِ. و"حَوَّازُ القُلوبِ" في حديثِ ابنِ مسعود: ما يَحُوزُها ويَغْلِبُها، حتى تَرْكَبَ ما لا يُحَبُّ. ويُرْوَى: حَوازُّ: جمعُ حازَّةٍ، وهي الأُمورُ التي تَحُزُّ في القُلوبِ، وتَحُكُّ، وتُؤَثِّرُ، ويَتَخالَجُ فيها أن تكونَ مَعاصِيَ، لِفَقْدِ الطُّمَأْنِينَةِ إليها. والحَوْزاءُ: الحَرْبُ التي تَحُوزُ القَومَ.

6.31

مخر (مقاييس اللغة) الميم والخاء والراء أصلٌ يدل على شَقٍّ وفَتْح. يقال مَخَرت السَفينةُ الماءَ مخراً: شَقَّته. قال الراجز في نساءٍ يختصمن ويستعنَّ بأيديهنَّ، كما يفعل السَّابح: ويقال: مَخَرْتُ الأرضَ، إذا أرسلْتَ فيها الماء. ويقال استمخَرْتُ الرِّيحَ، إذا استقبلتَها بأنفِك. وقياسُه صحيح، كأنَّك تشقُّ الرِّيح بأنفك. وقولهم: امتخَرْتُ القومَ، إذا انتقيْتَ خِيارَهم، كأنَّه شقَّ النَّاس إليه حتَّى انتخَبَه .

6.32

أمد (مقاييس اللغة) الهمزة والميم والدال، الأمد: الغاية. كلمةٌ واحدة لا يقاس عليها .

عمد (لسان العرب) العَمْدُ: ضدّ الخطإِ في القتل وسائر الجنايات. وقد تعَمَّده وتعمد له وعَمَده يعْمِده عَمْداً وعَمَدَ إليه وله يَعْمَّد عمداً وتعمَّده واعتَمَده: قصده، والعمد المصدر منه. وعَمَد الشيءَ يَعْمِدُه عمداً: أَقامه. والعِمادُ: ما أُقِيم به. وعمود الأمر: قِوامُه الذي لا يستقيم لا به.

عمد (مقاييس اللغة) العين والميم والدال أصلٌ كبير، فروعه كثيرة ترجع إلى معنىً، وهو الاستقامة في الشيء، منتصباً أو ممتدّاً، وكذلك في الرَّأي وإرادة الشيء.

فتَر (لسان العرب) الفَتْرَةُ: الانكسار والضعف. وقال الأصمعي: فَتَّر مَطر وفرغ ماؤُه وكَفَّ وتحيّر. والفَتَر الضعف. وفتَرَ الماءُ: سكن حرّه.

فتَرَ (القاموس المحيط) فَتَرَ يَفْتُرُ ويَفْتِرُ فُتوراً وفُتاراً: سَكَن بعدَ حِدَّةٍ، ولانَ بعدَ شِدَّةٍ. وفَتَّرَهُ تَفْتِيراً. وفتَرَ الماءُ: سَكَنَ حَرُّهُ فهو فاتِرٌ وفاتورٌ،

6.34

مسر (لسان العرب) مَسَرَ الشيءَ يَمْسُرُه مَسْراً: استخرجه من ضيق، والمَسْرُ فعل الماسِرِ. ومَسَرْتُ به ومَحَلْتُ به أي سَعَيْتُ به. والماسِرُ: الساعِي .

6.35

عرس (لسان العرب) العَرَسُ، بالتحريك: الدَّهَشُ. وعَرِسَ الرجل وعَرِشَ، بالكسر والسين والشين، عَرَساً، فهو عَرِسٌ: بطِرَ، وقيل: أَعْيَا ودَهِشَ؛

2

Part 1-2 References

1.3

صير (مقاييس اللغة) الصاد والياء والراء أصلٌ صحيح، وهو المآلُ والمرجِع. من ذلك صار يصير صَيْراً وصَيرورة. ويقال أنا على صِيرِ أمرٍ، أي إشرافٍ من قضائه، وذلك هو الذي يُصار إليه.

صير (لسان العرب) ورجل صَيِّرٌ شَيِّرٌ أي حسن الصُّورَة والشَّارَة؛ عن الفراء. وتَصَيَّر فلانٌ أباه: نزع إليه في الشَّبَه. وصارَ وجهَه يَصِيره: أقبل به. وفي قراءة عبدالله بن مسعود وأبي جعفر المدني: فصِرهن إليك، بالكسر، أي قطّعهن وشققهن، وقيل: وجِّهْهن. الفراء: ضمَّت العامة الصاد وكان أصحاب عبدالله يكسرونها، وهما لغتان، فأما الضم فكثير، وأما الكسر ففي هذيل وسليم؛ قال وأنشد الكسائي: وفَرْعٍ يَصِير الجِيدَ وحْفٍ كأنّه، على اللِّيت، قِنْوانُ الكُرُومِ الدَّوالِحُ يَصِير: يميل، ويروى: يَزِينُ الجيد، وكلهم فسروا فصُرْهن أَمِلْهن، وأما فصِرْهن، بالكسر، فإنه فسر بمعنى قَطّعهن؛ قال: ولم نجد قطّعهن معروفة؛ قال الأزهري: وأراها إن كانت كذلك من صَريتُ أَصْري أي قطعت فقدمت ياؤها.

صور (الصّحاح في اللغة) وصارهُ يصورُهُ، ويَصيرُهُ، أي أماله: وقرئ قوله تعالى: "فَص◌ُرْهُنَّ إليك" بضم الصاد وكسرها. قال الأخفش: يعني وَجِّهْهُنَّ. يقال: صُرْ إليَّ وصُرْ وجهك إليَّ، أي أَقْبِلْ عليَّ. وصُرتُ الشيءَ أيضاً: قَطَّعْتُهُ وفصَّلته.

الصُّورَةُ (القاموس المحيط) الصُّورَةُ، بالضم: الشَّكْلُ. والصَّيِّرُ، كالكَيِّسِ: الحَسَنُها، وقد صَوَّره فتَصَوَّر، وصارَ وجْهَهُ يَصُورُهُ ويَصيرُهُ: أقْبَلَ به، و~ الشيءَ: قَطَعَه وفَصَّلَه.

وصر (لسان العرب) الوِصْرُ: السِّجِلُّ؛ وجمعه أَوْصارٌ. والوَصِيرَةُ: الصَّكُّ، كلتاهما فارسية معرَبة. الليث: الوَصَرَّةُ معربة وهي الصك وهو الأَوْصَرُ؛ الجوهري: الوِصْرُ لغة في الإِصْر، وهو العهد، كما قالوا إرث ووِرْثٌ وإسادَةٌ ووِسادَةٌ، والوِصْرُ: الصَّكُّ وكتاب العهد، والله أعلم.

أصر (مقاييس اللغة) الهمزة والصاد والراء، أصلٌ واحدٌ يتفرع منه أشياء متقاربة. فالأصر الحبسُ والعَطف وما في معناهما. وتفسيرُ ذلك أنَّ العهد يقال له إصْرٌ، والقرابة تسمى آصِرَةٌ، وكل عقدٍ وقرابةٍ وَعهدٍ إصرٌ. والبابُ كلُّه واحد.

أصر (لسان العرب)

أَصَرَ الشيءَ يَأْصِرُه أَصْراً: كسره وعَطَفه. والأَصْرُ والإِصْرُ: ما عَطَفك على شيء. والإِصْرُ العَهْد الثقيل. الفرَاء: الإِصْرُ العهد؛ وأَصل الإِصْر: الثِّقْل والشَّدُّ لأَنها أَثْقَل الأَيمان وأَضْيَقُها مَخْرَجاً؛ يعني أَنه يجب الوفاء بها ولا يُتَعَوَّضُ عنها بالكفارة. والعَهْدُ يقال له: إِصْر.

1.4

نمق (مقاييس اللغة) النون والميم والقاف أُصَيلٌ يدلُّ على تحسينِ شيء وتجويده. ونَمَقْتُ الكتاب ونَمَّقْتُه: نقشتُه وصَوَّرْتُه.

نمق (لسان العرب) نَمَق الكتاب يَنْمُقُه، بالضم، نَمْقاً: كتبه، ونَمَّقه: حسّنه وجوَّده. ونَمّق الجلد ونَبّقه: نقشه وزينه بالكتابة، ونَبّقه ونَمّقه واحد؛ قال النابغة الذبياني: كأَنَّ مَجَرَّ الرامِساتِ ذُيُولَها عليه قَضيمٌ نَمَّقَتْهُ الصوانع ويروى حصير نمّقته. أبو زيد: نَمَقْتُه أَنْمُقُه نَمْقاً ولَمَقْتُه أَلْمُقُه لَمْقاً.

نبق (مقاييس اللغة) النون والباء والقاف كلمةٌ تدلُّ على تسويةٍ وتهذيب. والنخل إذا كان غِراسُه على استواءٍ منبَّق. وقد نَبَّقه صاحبُه. وكذلك كلُّ شيءٍ مستوٍ مهذَّب.

بنق (لسان العرب) بَنَّقَ الكِتابَ: لغة في نَبَّقه. وبَنَّق كلامَه: جمعَه وسوّاه، ومنه بَنائقُ القَميصِ أي جمع شيء. (* كذا بالأصل). وقد بَنَّق كتابه إذا جوَّده وجمعَه.

دين (مقاييس اللغة) وأدَنْتُ أقْرَضْت وأعطيت دَيْناً.

دور (مقاييس اللغة) الدال والواو والراء أصلٌ واحد يدلُّ على إحداق الشيء بالشيء من حواليه. يقال دارَ يدُور دَوَراناً. والدار أصلها الواو.

دور (الصّحاح في اللغة) الدارُ مؤنَّثةٌ. والدائرة: واحدةُ الدوائر. والدَّوَّاريُّ: الدَهْرُ يدور بالإنسان أحْوالاً.

دامَ (القاموس المحيط) دامَ يَدُومُ ويَدامُ دَوْماً ودَواماً ودَيْمومَةً، ودِمْتَ، بالكسرِ، تَدُومُ نادِرَةٌ. وأدامَه واسْتَدامه وداوَمَهُ: تأنَّى فيه، أو طَلَبَ دَوامَهُ. والدَّيُّومُ والدَّوْمُ: الدائمُ.
دوم (لسان العرب) دامَ الشيءُ يَدُومُ ويَدامُ؛

1.5

بقل (لسان العرب) بَقَلَ الشيءُ: ظهَر.
بكل (لسان العرب) البَكْل: الدَّقِيق بالرُّبِّ؛ قال: ليس بغشٍّ هَمُّه فيما أَكل، وأَزْمةٌ وَزْمتُه من البَكل (* قوله «ليس بغش» الغش كما في اللسان والقاموس عظيم السرَّة، قال شارحه والصواب: عظيم الشره، بالشين محركة). أراد البَكْل فحرَّك للضرورة. والمُتبكِّل المخلِّط في كلامه. وتَبكَّلوا عليه: عَلَوْه بالشَّتْم والضرب والقَهْر. وتَبكَّل في مِشْيَتِه. اختالَ. والإنسان يَتَبكَّل أي يَخْتال. ورجل جَميل بَكيل: مُتَنَوِّق في لِبْسَته ومَشْيه. والبَكِيلة: الهيئة والزِّيُّ. والبِكْلة الخُلُق. والبِكْلة الحَالُ والخِلْقة؛ حكاه ثعلب؛ وأَنشد: لَسْتُ إذاً لِزَعْبَلَه، إنْ لم أُغَيِّرْ بِكْلَتِي، إن لم أُسَاوِ بالطُّولْ قال ابن بري: وهذا البيت من مُسَدَّس الرَّجَز جاء على التمام. والبَكْل الغَنِيمة وهو التَّبكُّل، اسم لا مصدر، ونظيره التَّنَوُّط؛ قال أوسبن حَجَر: عَلى خَيْرِ ما أَبْصَرْتها من بِضَاعة، لِمُلْتَمِسٍ بَيْعاً لها أو تَبكُّلا أي تَغَنُّماً. وبَكَّله إذا نَحَّاه قبله كائناً ما كان.
فكل (لسان العرب) الأَفْكَلُ، على أَفْعَل: الرِّعْدة، ولا يبنى منه فِعْل. التهذيب عن الليث وغيره: الأَفْكَل رِعْدة تعلو الإنسان ولا فعل له؛ وأَنشد ابن بري: بعَيْشِكِ هاتِي فغَنِّي لنا، فإِن نَداماكِ لم يَنْهَلُوا فباتَتْ تُغَنِّي بغِرْبالها غِناءً رُوَيداً، له أَفْكَلُ وقال الأَخطل: لَها بعد إِسْآدٍ مِراحٌ وأَفْكَل ابن الأَعرابي: افْتَكل فلان في فِعْله افْتِكالاً واحْتَفَل احْتِفالاً بمعنى واحد.
حفل (لسان العرب) الحَفْل: اجتماع الماء في مَحْفِله، تقول: حَفَل الماءُ يَحْفِل حَفْلاً وحُفُولاً وحَفِيلاً، وحَفَل الوادي بالسَّيْل واحْتَفَل: جاء بِملْءِ جَنْبَيْه؛ وقول صخر الغَيّ: أنا المثلَّم أَقْصِرْ قبل فاقِرَة، إذا تُصِيبُ سَواءَ الأَنف تَحْتَفِل معناه تأْخذ مُعْظَمه. وروي عن ابن الأَعرابي قال: الحُفَال الجَمْع العظيم. ومَحْفِل الماء: مُجْتَمَعُه. ورجل ذو حَفْل وحَفْلة: مُبالغ فيما أَخذ فيه من الأُمور. وكانَ حَفِيلَةً ما أَعطى دِرْهَماً أَي مَبْلَغُ ما أَعطى. الأَزهري: ومُحْتَفَل الأَمر مُعْظَمُه. ويقال للمرأَة: تَحَفَّلي لزوجك أَي تَزَيَّني لتَحْظَيْ عنده. وحَفَلْت الشيءَ أَي جَلوته فتَحَفَّل واحْتَفَل. وطريق مُحْتَفِل أَي ظاهر مُسْتَبِين، وقد احْتَفَل أَي استبان، واحتفل الطريقُ: وَضَح؛ وما حَفَله وما حَفَل به يَحْفِل حَفْلاً وما احْتَفَل به أَي ما بالى. والحَفْل: المُبَالاة. يقال: ما أَحْفِل بفلان أَي ما أُبالي به؛
بجل (لسان العرب) التَّبجيل: التعظيم. بَجَّل الرجلَ: عَظَّمَه. ورجل بَجَال وبَجِيل: يُبَجِّله الناسُ، وقيل: هو الشيخ الكبير العظيم السيد مع جَمال ونُبْل، وقد بَجُلَ بَجَالة وبُجُولاً، ولا توصف بذلك المرأَة. شمر: البَجَال من الرجال الذي يُبَجِّله أَصحابه ويسوِّدونه.
والبَجِيل: الأَمر العظيم. ورجل بَجَال: حَسَن الوجه. وشيخ بَجَال وبَجِيل أَي جَسِيم؛ ورجل باجِل وقد بَجَل يَبْجُل بُجولاً: وهو الحسَن الجَسِيمُ الخَصِيب في جِسْمه؛ وأَنشد: وأَنت بالبابِ سَمِينٌ باجِل وبَجِلَ الرجلُ بَجَلاً: حسنت حاله، وقيل: فَرِحَ. والبَجَلُ العَجَب. يقال: ذو بَجْلة وذو بَجَالة، وهو الرُّوَاءُ والحُسْن والحَسَب والنُّبْل، وبه سمي الرجل بَجَالة. إِنه لذو بَجْلة أَي شارة حَسَنة، وقيل: كانت هذه أَلْقاباً لهم، وقيل: البَجَال الذي يُبَجِّله الناس أَي يعظمونه .

1.6

رأد (لسان العرب) غُصن رَؤُودٌ: وهو أَرطب ما يكون وأَرخصه، وقد رَؤُدَ وتَرَأَّدَ وقيل: تَرَؤُّده تَفَيُّؤه وتذبُّله وتراؤده، كقولك تَواعُدَه: تميُّله وتميُّحه يميناً وشمالاً. الجوهري: الرَّأْد والرُّؤْدُ من النساء الشابة الحسنة؛ قال أَبو زيد: هما مهموزان، ويقال أَيضاً: رَأْدة ورُؤْدةٌ. وتَرَأَّدَ الشيءُ: التوى فذهب وجاءَ، وقد تَرَأَّد إِذا تفيأَ وتثنى، وتَرَأَّد وتَمايَحَ إِذا تميَّل يميناً وشمالاً، والرِّئْدُ: التِّرب، وربما لم يهمز وسنذكره في ريد.
رود (مقاييس اللغة) الراء والواو والدال معظمُ بابِه [يدلُّ] على مجيءٍ وذَهابٍ من انطلاقٍ في جهة واحدة. تقول: راودْتُه على أن يَفعل كذا، إذا أردتَه على فعله. والرَّوْد: فِعلُ الرَّائد.
رود (لسان العرب) الرَّوْدُ: مصدر فعل الرائد، والرائد: الذي يُرْسَل في التماس النُّجْعَة وطلب الكلإِ، والجمع رُوَّاد مثل زائر وزُوَّار. وأَصل الرائد الذي يتقدم القوم يُبْصِر لهم الكلأَ ومساقط الغيث؛ ورجل رادٌ: بمعنى رائد، وهو فَعَل، بالتحريك، بمعنى فاعل كالفَرَط بمعنى الفارط. ويقال: بعثنا رائداً يرود لنا الكلأَ والمنزل ويرتاد والمعنى واحد أَي ينظر ويطلب ويختار أَفضله. التهذيب: والرِّيدة اسم يوضع موضع الارتياد والإِرادة، وأَراد الشيءَ: أَحبه وعُنِيَ به، والاسم الرِّيدُ.
ريد (لسان العرب) التهذيب: والرِّيدة اسم يوضع موضع الارتياد والإرادة .

مسك (مقاييس اللغة) الميم والسين والكاف أصلٌ واحد صحيح يدلُّ على حَبْس الشيء أو تحبُّسه.
مسك (الصّحاح في اللغة) أَمْسَكْتُ الشيء، وتَمَسَّكْتُ به، واسْتَمْسَكْتُ به، وامْتَسَكْتُ به، كلّه بمعنى اعتصمت به.

1.7

أبّ (مقاييس اللغة) اعلم أن للهمزة والباء في المضاعف أصلين: أحدهما المرعَى، والآخر القَصْدَ والتهيُّؤ.
أبب (لسان العرب) الأَبُّ: الكَلأُ، وعَبَّر بعضهم (قوله بعضهم: هو ابن دريد كما في المحكم.) عنه بأَنه المَرْعَى. وقال عطاء: كلُّ شيءٍ يَنْبُتُ على وَجْهِ الأَرضِ فهو الأَبُّ. وفي حديث أَنس: أَنَّ عُمَر بن الخَطاب، رضي الله عنهما، قرأَ قوله، عز وجل، وفاكِهَةً وأَبّاً، وقال: فما الأَبُّ، ثم قال: ما كُلِّفْنا وما أُمِرْنا بهذا. والأَبُّ: المَرْعَى المُتَهَيِّئُ للرَّعْيِ والقَطْعِ. ومنه حديث قُسّ بن ساعدة: فَجعل يَرْتَعُ أَبّاً وأَصِيدُ ضَبّاً. وأَبَّ للسير يَئِبُّ ويَؤُبُّ أَبّاً

وأبيباً وأبابة: تَهَيَّأَ للذَّهابِ وتجَهَّز. قال الأعشى: صَرمْتُ، ولم أصْرِمْكُم، وكصارِمٍ؛ * أخٌ قد طَوى كَشحاً، وأبَّ لِيَذْهَبا أي صَرمْتُكم في تَهَيُّئي لمُفارَقتِكم، ومن تَهَيَّأَ للمُفارقةِ، فهو كمن صَرَمَ. وكذلك ائتَبَّ. قال أبو عبيد: أَبَبْتُ أَؤُبُّ أَبّاً إذا عَزَمْتَ على المَسيرِ وتَهَيَّأْتَ. وهو في أَبابِه وإبابَتِه وأَبابَتِه أي في جَهازِه. التهذيب: والوَبُّ: التَّهَيُّؤُ للحَمْلةِ في الحَرْبِ، يقال: هَبَّ ووَبَّ إذا تَهَيَّأَ للحَمْلة. قال أبو منصور: والأَصل فيه أَبَّ فقُلبت الهمزة واواً. ابن الأعرابي: أَبَّ إذا حَرَّك، وأَبَّ إذا هَزَم بحَمْلةٍ لا مَكْذُوبة فيها. والأَبُّ: النِّزاعُ إلى الوَطَنِ.وأَبَّتْ أَبابةُ الشيءِ وإبابَتُه: اسْتَقامت طَريقَتُه. وقالوا للظِّباءِ: إن أَصابَتِ الماءَ، فلا عَباب، وإنْ لم تُصِبِ الماءَ، فلا أَباب. أي لم تَأْتَبَّ له ولا تَتَهَيَّأْ لطلَبه، وهو مذكور في موضعه.

علل (لسان العرب) وتَعَلَّلَتِ المرأَةُ من نفاسها وتَعالَّتْ: خَرَجَتْ منه وطَهُرت وحَلَّ وَطْؤُها.
العَلُّ (القاموس المحيط) والعَليلَةُ: المرأةُ المُطَيَّبَةُ طيباً بعدَ طِيبٍ.
علا (لسان العرب) وتَعَلَّتِ المرأَةُ: طهرت من نفاسِها. وفي حديث سُبَيْعة: أَنها لما تَعَلَّتْ من نِفاسها أَي خرجت من نفاسها وسَلِمَت، وقيل: تَشَوَّفَتْ لخُطَّابها، ويروى: تعالت أَي ارْتَفَعت وظهرت، قال: ويجوز أَن يكون من قولهم تَعَلَّى الرجلُ من عِلَّته إذا برأَ؛ ومنه قول الشاعر: ولا ذات بَعْلٍ من نفاس تَعَلَّتِ وتَعَلَّى المريضُ من عِلَّتِه: أَفاق منها.

قتو (مقاييس اللغة) القاف والتاء والواو. يقولون: القَتْو: حُسْنُ الخدمة.
القَتْوُ (القاموس المحيط) القَتْوُ والقَتا، مثلثةً: حُسْنُ خِدْمةِ المُلوكِ، كالمَقْى، وبهاءٍ: النَّميمةُ. والمَقْتَوُونَ والمَقاتِوَةُ والمَقاتِيَةُ: الخُدَّامُ، الواحدُ: مَقْتَوِيٌّ ومَقْتًى أو مَقْتَوِينٌ، وتُفْتَحُ الواوُ غيرَ مَصْروفَيْنِ، وهي للواحِدِ والجمعِ والمُؤَنَّثِ سواءٌ، أو الميمُ فيه أصْلِيَّةٌ، من مَقَتَ: خَدَمَ.
قتا (لسان العرب) القَتْوُ: الخِدْمة. وقد قَتَوْتُ أَقْتُو قَتْواً ومَقْتًى أَي خَدَمْت مثل غَزَوْت أَغْزُو غَزْواً ومَغْزًى، وقيل: القَتْو حُسْنُ خِدمة الملوك، وقد قتاهم. الليث: تقول هو يَقْتُو الملوك أَي يَخْدُمهم؛ وقال شمر: المَقْتَوُون الخُدَّام، واحدهم مَقْتَوِيٌّ؛ اقتوته أَي استخدَمْته.

فسس (لسان العرب) والفِسْفِسُ: البيت المُصوَّر بالفُسَيْفِساء؛ قال: كصَوْتِ اليَراعَة في الفِسْفِس يعني بيتاً مُصوَّراً بالفُسَيْفِساء. قال أَبو منصور: ليس الفُسَيْفِساس عربيَّة. والفِسْفِسة: لغة في الفِصْفِصة، وهي الرَّطْبَة، والصاد أَعرب، وهما معربان والأَصل فيهما إِسْبَسْت .
بسس (لسان العرب) بَسَّ السَّويقَ والدقيقَ وغيرهما يَبُسُّه بَسّاً: خلطه بسمن أَو زيت، وهي البَسِيسَةُ. قال اللحياني: هي التي تُلَتُّ بسمن أَو زيت ولا تُبلُّ. والبَسُّ: اتخاذ البَسِيسة، وهو أَن يلتَّ السَّويقُ أَو الدقيق أَو الأَقِطُ المطحون بالسمن أَو بالزيت ثم يؤكل ولا يطبخ. وقال يعقوب: هو أَشد من اللَّتِّ بللاً؛

فرص (لسان العرب) الفُرْصةُ: النُّهْزةُ والنَّوبةُ، والسين لغة، وقد فَرَصَها فَرْصاً وافْتَرَصَها وتفَرَّصها: أَصابها، وقد افْتَرَصْتُ وانتهزْتُ. وأَفْرَصَتْكَ الفُرصةُ: أَمْكَنَتْكَ. وأَفْرَصَتْني الفُرْصةُ أَي أَمكنَتْني، وافْتَرَصْتُها: اغتَنَمْتُها. ابن الأَعرابي: الفَرْصاءُ من النُّوق التي تقوم ناحيةً فإِذا خلا الحوضُ جاءت فشربت؛ قال الأَزهري: أُخِذَت من الفُرْصة وهي النُّهْزَة. يقال: وجد فلان فُرْصة أَي نهزة. وجاءت فُرْصَتُكَ من البئر أَي نَوْبَتُك. وانتهَزَ فلانٌ الفُرْصة أَي اغْتنَمها وفاز بها. والفُرْصةُ والفِرْصةُ والفَرِيصةُ؛ الأَخيرة عن يعقوب: النوبة تكون بين القوم يتناوبُونها على الماء. والفَرْسُ، بالسين: الكسرُ. والفَرْصُ الشَّقُّ. والفَرْصُ القطعُ. وفَرَصَ الجِلْدَ فَرْصاً: قطَعه.
فرس (العباب الزاخر) وقال ابن الأعرابي: الفُرْسَة: الفُرْصَة.
فرض (لسان العرب) فرَضْت الشيءَ أَفْرِضه فَرْضاً وفَرَّضْتُه للتكثير: أَوْجَبْتُه. وفَرائضُ الله: حُدودُه التي أَمرَ بها ونهى عنها، وكذلك الفَرائضُ بالمِيراثِ. والفارِضُ والفَرَضِيُّ: الذي يَعْرِف الفرائضَ ويسمى العِلْمُ بقسْمةِ المَوارِيث فَرائضَ. وكلُّ واجبٍ مؤقَّتٍ، فهو مَفْرُوضٌ. وأَصلُ الفرض القَطْعُ.

1.10

نحت (لسان العرب) النَّحْتُ: النَّشْرُ والقَشْر. والنَّحْتُ: نَحْتُ النَّجَّارِ الخَشَبَ. نَحَت الخشبةَ ونحوَها يَنْحِتُها ويَنْحَتُها نَحْتاً، فانْتَحَتَتْ. والنُّحاتة ما نُحِتَ من الخَشَب. ونَحَتَ الجبلَ يَنْحِتُه: قَطَعَه، وهو من ذلك. وفي التنزيل العزيز: وتَنْحِتُون من الجبال بيوتاً آمنين.
والنَّحائتُ: آبار معروفة، صفة غالبة لأَنها نُحِتَتْ أَي قُطِعَتْ؛ والنَّحِيتة: الطبيعة التي نُحِتَ عليها الإِنسانُ أَي قُطِعَ، وقال اللحياني: هي الطبيعة والأَصل.

1.13

ركز (مقاييس اللغة) الراء والكاف والزاء أصلان: أحدهما إثبات شيءٍ في شيء يذهب سُفْلاً، والآخر صَوت.
ركس (مقاييس اللغة) الراء والكاف والسين أصلٌ واحد، وهو قلبُ الشَّيء على رأسه وردُّ أوّله على آخره.

فسر (لسان العرب) الفَسْرُ: البيان. فَسَر الشيءَ يفسِرُه، بالكسر، وتَفْسُرُه، بالضم، فَسْراً وفَسَّرَهُ: أَبانه، والتَّفْسيرُ مثله.
الفَسْرُ (القاموس المحيط) الفَسْرُ: الإِبانَةُ، وكَشْفُ المُغَطَّى،
بذر (مقاييس اللغة) الباء والذال والراء أصلٌ واحد، وهو نَثْرُ الشيءِ وتفريقُه.

بذر (لسان العرب) وبَذَرَ الله الخلق بَذْراً: بَثَّهُمْ وفرّقهم. وفي حديث فاطمة عند وفاة النبي، صلى الله عليه وسلم، قالت لعائشة: إني إذاً لَبَذِرَةٌ؛ البَذِرُ: الذي يفشي السر ويظهر ما يسمعه، وقد بَذُرَ بَذارَةً.

ePSD: pašāru
bur [SPREAD] wr. bur2; bur Akk. pašāru; šuparruru

1.14

با (لسان العرب) الباء حرف هجاء من حروف المعجم، وأكثر ما تَرِد بمعنى الإلصاق لما ذُكِر قَبْلها من اسم أو فعل بما انضمت إليه، وقد تَرِدُ بمعنى المُلابسة والمُخالطة، وبمعنى من أجل ، وبمعنى في ومن وعن ومع، وبمعنى الحال والعوض، وزائدة، وكلّ هذه الأقسام قد جاءت في الحديث، وتعرف بسياق اللفظ الواردة فيه، والباء التي تأتي للإلصاق كقولك: أمسَكْت بزيد، وتكون للاستعانة كقولك: ضَرَبْتُ بالسيف، وتكون للإضافة كقولك: مررت بزيد. قال ابن جني: أما ما يحكيه أصحاب الشافعي من أن الباءَ للتبعيض فشيء لا يعرفه أصحابنا ولا ورد به بيت، وتكون للقسم كقولك: بالله لأفْعَلَنَّ. وقوله تعالى: أولم يَرَوا أن الله الذي خَلَقَ السمواتِ والأرضَ ولم يَعْيَ بخلقهن بقادر؛ إنما جاءَت الباء في حَيّز لم لأنها في معنى ما وليس، ودخلت الباءُ في قوله: وأَشْرَكوا بالله، لأن معنى أَشرَكَ بالله قَرَنَ بالله عز وجل غيره، وفيه إضمار. والباء للإلصاق والقِرانِ، ومعنى قولهم: وَكَّلت بفلان، معناه قَرَنْتُ به وَكيلاً.
لا (القاموس المحيط) لا: تكونُ نافِيَةً، وهي على خَمْسَةِ أوْجُهٍ :

البَتْرُ (القاموس المحيط) البَتْرُ: القَطْعُ، أو مُسْتأْصِلاً. وسيفٌ باتِرٌ: قاطِعٌ، وبَتّارٌ وبُتارٌ، كغُرابٍ.
بتر (لسان العرب) والبَتْرُ القطعُ.
بطر (مقاييس اللغة) الباء والطاء والراء أصلٌ واحد وهو الشَّقُّ. وسُمّي البيطار لذلك. ويقال له أيضاً المُبَيْطِر.
بطر (لسان العرب) وبَطَرَ الشيءَ يَبْطُره ويَبْطِره بَطْراً، فهو مبطور وبطير: شقه. والبَطْرُ الشَّقُّ؛ وبه سمي البَيْطارُ بَيْطاراً والبَطِيرُ والبَيْطَرُ والبَيْطارُ والبيَطْرُ، مثل هِزَبْرٍ، والمُبَيْطِرُ، مُعالجُ الدوابّ: من ذلك؛
الفَطْرُ (القاموس المحيط) الفَطْرُ: الشَّقُّ.
فطر (مقاييس اللغة) الفاء والطاء والراء أصلٌ صحيحٌ يدلُّ على فَتْح شيء وإبرازه.

1.15

علب (لسان العرب) والعُلْبةُ قَدَحٌ ضخم من جلود الإبل. وقيل: العُلْبة من خشب، كالقَدَحِ الضَخْمِ يُحْلَبُ فيها. وقيل: إنها كهيئة القَصْعَةِ من جلد، ولها طَوْق من خشب. وقيل: مِحْلَبٌ من جلد. وفي حديث وفاة النبي، صلى الله عليه وسلم: وبين يديه رَكْوَة أو عُلْبةٌ فيها ماءٌ؛ العُلْبة: قدحٌ من خشب؛ وقيل: من جلدٍ وخشبٍ يُحْلَبُ فيه. ومنه حديث خالد: أعطاهم عُلْبَةَ الحالبِ أي القَدَحَ الذي يُحْلَبُ فيه؛ والجمعُ: عُلَبٌ وعِلابٌ.

مخر (لسان العرب) مَخَرَتِ السفينةُ تَمْخَرُ وتَمْخُر مَخْراً ومُخُوراً: جرت تَشُقُّ الماءَ مع صوت، وقيل: استقبلتِ الريح في جريتها، فهي ماخِرَةٌ. ومَخَرَتِ السفينةُ مَخْراً إذا استقبلت بها الريح. وفي التنزيل: وترى الفُلْكَ فيه مَواخِرَ؛
بحر (لسان العرب) البَحْرُ: الماءُ الكثيرُ، مِلْحاً كان أو عَذْباً، وهو خلاف البَرِّ، سمي بذلك لعُمقِهِ واتساعه، قد غلب على المِلْح حتى قَلَّ في العَذْبِ، وجمعه أَبْحُرٌ وبُحُورٌ وبِحارٌ. وسمي البَحْرُ بَحْراً لاسْتبحاره، وهو انبساطه وسعته. ويقال: إنما سمي البَحر بَحْراً لأنه شَقَّ في الأَرض شقّاً وجعل ذلك الشق لمائه قراراً. والبَحْرُ في كلام العرب: الشَّقُّ .

بأر (لسان العرب) أبو زيد: بَأَرْتُ أَبْأَرُ بَأْراً حفرتُ بُؤْرَةً يطبخ فيها، وهي الإرَةُ. وبَأَرَ الشيءَ يَبْأَرُه بَأْراً وابتَأَره، كلاهما: خَبَأَه وادَّخَرَه؛ ومنه قيل للحُفرَة: البُؤْرَةُ. والبُؤْرَةُ والبِئْرَةُ والبَئِيرَةُ، على فَعِيلَةٍ: ما خُبِئَ وادُّخِرَ. وفي الحديث: أن رجلاً آتاه الله مالاً فلم يَبْتَئِرْ خيراً: أي لم يُقَدِّمْ لنفسه خَبِيئَةَ خَيْرٍ ولم يَدَّخِرْ. وابْتَأَر الخيرَ وبَأَرَهُ: قَدَّمَهُ، وقيل: عمله مستوراً. وقال الأمويُّ في معنى الحديث: هو من الشيء يُخْبَأُ كأنه لم يُقدِّمْ لنفسه خيراً خَبَأَهُ لها. ويقال للذَّخيرة يدخرها الإنسان: بَئِيرَةٌ. قال أبو عبيد: في الابْتِئار لغتان: يقال ابْتَأَرْتُ وائْتَبَرْتُ ابْتِئاراً وائتباراً؛
أبر (مقاييس اللغة) الهمزة والباء والراء يدلُّ بناؤها على نخس الشيء بشيءٍ محدَّد. قال الخليل: الإبرة معروفة، وبائعها أبّار.
أبر (الصِّحاح في اللغة) الإبْرَةُ: واحدة الإبَر. وإبْرَةُ الذراع: مُسْتَدَقُّها .
أبر (لسان العرب) والإِبْرة مِسَلَّة الحديد، والجمع إِبَرٌ وإِبارٌ، قال القطامي: وقَوْلُ المرء يَنْفُذُ بعد حين أَماكِنَ، لا تُجاوِزُها الإِبارُ وصانعها أَبّار. والإِبْرة واحدة الإِبَر. التهذيب: ويقال للمِخْيط إِبرة، وجمعها إِبَر، والذي يُسوّي الإِبر يقال له الأَبّار. ويقال للسان: مِئْبر ومِذْرَبٌ ومِفْصَل ومِقْول. وإِبرة العقرب: التي تلدَغُ بها، وفي المحكم: طرف ذنبها. وأَبَرَتْه تَأْبُرُه وتأْبِرُه أَبْراً: لسعته أي ضربته بإِبرتها.
AALD: bâ'iru (s.) صياد بالشبك (سمّاك)، صياد، صنف من الجنود See: ŠU.HA

شاة (القاموس المحيط) وتَشَوَّهَ شاةً: اصْطادَها،
شوه (مقاييس اللغة) ويقولون: لا تَشَوَّهْ عَلَيَّ، إذا قال ما أحسَنَك، أي لا تُصِبْني بعينك. ومما شذ عن الباب: الشّاة. قالوا: أصل بنائها من هذا، يقال تشوَّهْت شاةً، أي أخذتها .

شوه (الصّحاح في اللغة) ويقال رجلٌ أَشْوَهُ بيّن الشَوه، إذا كان سريعَ الإصابة بالعين. ابن السكيت: يقال لا تَشْوَهْ عليَ، أي لا تقل ما أحْسَنَكَ فتصيبني بالعين. ويقال أيضاً: تشوَّهَ له، أي تنكر له وتغوَّل. ورجلٌ شائِهُ البصر، أي حديد البصر. والشاةُ من الغنم تذكَّر وتؤنث. وفلان كثير الشاة والبعير، وهو في معنى الجمع، لأنَّ الألف واللام للجنس. وأصل الشاة شاهةٌ، لأنَّ تصغيرها شُوَيْهَةٌ، والجمع شِياهٌ بالهاء في أدنى العدد. تقول ثلاث شِياهٍ إلى العَشر، فإذا جاوزتَ فبالتاء، فإذا كثرت قيل: هذه شاءٌ كثيرةٌ. وجمع الشاءِ شَوِيٌّ. والشاةُ أيضاً: الثور الوحشيّ. وتَشَوَّهْتُ شاةً، إذا اصدته.

داكَهُ (القاموس المحيط) داكَهُ دَوْكاً ومَداكاً: سَحَقَهُ،
دوك (لسان العرب) الدَوْكُ: دق الشيء وسحقه وطحنه كما يَدُوك البعيرُ الشيء بكَلْكَلِه .
والدَكّ: الدقّ، وقد دَكَكْتُ الشيء أَدُكُّه دكّاً إذا ضربته وكسرته حتى سوّيته بالأرض؛ ومنه قوله عز وجل: فَدُكَّتا دَكَّةً واحدة.

1.16

أدف (العباب الزاخر) ابن الأعرابي: الداف -بالضم-: الذَّكَر،
أدف (لسان العرب) الأُدافُ: الذَّكَرُ؛ قال الراجز: أَوْلَجَ في كَعْثَبِها الأُدافا، مِثْلَ للذِّراع يَمْتَطِي النِّطافا وفي حديث الدِّيات: في الأُدافِ الدِّيةُ، يعني الذكر إذا قُطِعَ، وهمزته بدل من الواو من ودَفَ الإِناءُ إذا قَطَر. ودَفَتِ الشَّحْمَةُ إذ قَطَرَتْ دُهْناً، ويروى بالذال المعجمة .
ودف (لسان العرب) وَدَفَ الإِناءُ: قطَر. والوَدَفةُ الشحمة. ودَفَ الشحمُ ونحوه يَدِفُ: سالَ وقطَر. واسْتَوْدَفْت الشحمة أي اسْتَقْطَرتها فوَدفت. واسْتَوْدَفَتِ المرأَةُ ماء الرجل إذا اجتمعت تحته وتقبّضت لئلاَّ يفرق الماء فلا تحمل؛ عن ثعلب. والأُدافُ: الذكر لقَطَرانه، الهمزة فيه بدل من الواو، وهو مما لزم فيه البدل إذ لم نسمعهم قالوا وُداف. وفي الحديث: في الأُداف الدية، يعني الذكر. قال ابن الأَثير: سماه بما يَقْطُر منه مجازاً وقلب الواو همزة. التهذيب: والأُدافُ والأُذافُ، بالدال والذال، فرج الرجل؛ قال الشاعر: أَوْلَجَ في كعثَبِها الأُدافا قال أَبو منصور: قيل له أُداف لما يَدِفُ منه أَي يقطُر من المني والمَذْي والبول، وكان في الأَصل وُدافاً، قلبت الواو همزة لانضمامها كما قال تعالى: وإِذا الرسل أُقّتت، وهو في الأَصل وُقّتت. ابن الأَعرابي: يقال لبُظارة المرأَة الوَدَفةُ والوَذَفةُ والوَذَرة. قال ابن بري: حكى أَبو الطيب اللغوي أَن المني يسمى الوَدْف والوُداف، بضم الواو. وفي الحديث: في الوداف الغسل؛ الوُداف الذي يقطر من الذكر فوق المذي .
الذَّكَرُ (القاموس المحيط) والذَّكَرُ: خلافُ الأُنثى

أدب (الصّحاح في اللغة) الأدَبُ: أدَبُ النَفْس والدَرْس، تقول منه: أدُبَ الرجلُ بالضم فهو أديبٌ، وأدَّبْتُهُ فتأدَّبَ. والأدْبُ أيضاً: مَصدرُ أدَبَ القَوْمَ يَأْدِبُهُمْ إذا دَعاهُمْ إلى طعامه. والآدِبُ الداعي. ويقال أيضاً: آدَبَ القَوْمَ إلى طعامِهِ يُؤْدِبُهُمْ إيداباً.
أدب (لسان العرب) الأَدَبُ: الذي يَتَأَدَّبُ به الأَديبُ من الناس؛ سُمِّيَ أَدَباً لأَنه يَأْدِبُ الناسَ إِلى المَحامِد، ويَنْهاهم عن المقَابِح. وأَصل الأَدْب الدُّعاءُ، ومنه قيل للصَّنِيع يُدْعَى إِليه الناسُ: مَدْعاةٌ ومَأْدُبَةٌ. ابن بُزُرْج: لقد أَدُبْتُ آدُبُ أَدَباً حسناً، وأَنت أَديبٌ. وقال أَبو زيد: أَدُبَ الرَّجلُ يَأْدُبُ أَدَباً، فهو أَديبٌ، وأَرُبَ يَأْرُبُ أَرابةً وأَرَباً، في العَقْلِ، فهو أَريبٌ. غيره: الأَدَبُ: أَدَبُ النَّفْسِ والدَّرْسِ. والأَدَبُ الظَّرْفُ وحُسْنُ التَّناوُلِ. وأَدُبَ، بالضم، فهو أَديبٌ، من قوم أُدَباءَ. وأَدَّبه فتَأَدَّبَ: عَلَّمه، واستعمله الزجاج في الله، عز وجل، فقال: وهذا ما أَدَّبَ اللهُ تعالى به نَبيَّه، صلى الله عليه وسلم. وفلان قد اسْتَأْدَبَ: بمعنى تَأَدَّبَ.
دبب (لسان العرب) وأَدَبَّ البلادَ: مَلأَها عَدْلاً، فدَبَّ أَهلُها، لِمَا لَبِسُوه من أَمْنِه، واسْتَشْعَرُوه من بَرَكته ويُمْنِه؛

أدم (لسان العرب) الأُدْمةُ: القَرابةُ والوسيلةُ إِلى الشيء. يقال: فلان أُدْمَتي إِليك أَي وَسِيلَتي. ويقال: بينهما أُدْمةٌ ومَلْحة أَي خُلْطةٌ، وقيل: الأُدْمة الخُلْطة، وقيل: المُوافقةُ. والأَدْمُ الأُلْفةُ والاتِّفاق؛ وأَدَمَ الله بينهم يَأْدِمُ أَدْماً. قال أَبو عبيد: لا أَرى الأَصل فيه إِلا من أَدْمِ الطعام لأَن صَلاحَه وطِيبَه إِنما يكون بالإِدام، ولذلك يقال طعام مَأْدُومٌ. والإِدامُ: معروف ما يُؤْتَدَمُ به مع الخبز. وفي الحديث: نِعْمَ الإِدام الخلُّ؛ الإِدام، بالكسر، والأُدْمُ، بالضم: ما يؤكل بالخبز أَيَّ شيء كان. وفي الحديث: سَيِّدُ إِدامِ أَهْلِ الدُّنيا والآخرة اللحمُ؛ جعل اللحم أُدْماً وبعض الفقهاء لا يجعله أُدْماً ويقول: لو حَلَفَ أَن لا يأْتَدِمَ ثم أَكل لَحْماً لم يحنَثْ، والجمع آدِمةٌ وجمع الأُدْمِ آدامٌ، وقد ائتدَمَ به. وأَدَمَ الخبز يأْدِمُه، بالكسر، أَدْماً: خلطه بالأُدْم، وقال غيره: أَدَمَ الخبزَ باللحم؛ وأَنشد ابن بري: إِذا ما الخُبْزُ تَأْدِمه بلحمٍ، فذاكَ أَمانةَ اللهِ الثَّرِيدُ وقال آخر: تَطْبُخه ضُروعُها وتَأْدِمُهْ قال: وشاهد الإِدام قولُ الشاعر: الأَبْيَضانِ أَبْرَدا عِظامِي: الماءُ والفَثُّ بلا إِدامِ وفي حديث أُمِّ مَعْبَد: أَنا رأَيت الشاةَ وإِنها لَتَأْدُمُها وتَأْدُم صِرْمَتها (* قوله «وانها لتأدمها وتأدم صرمتها» ضبط في الأصل والنهاية بضم الدال). وفي حديث أَنس: وعَصَرَتْ عليه أُمُّ سُلَيم عُكَّةً لها فأَدَمَتْه أَي خَلَطته وجعلت فيه إِداماً يؤكل، يقال فيه بالمَدِّ والقَصْرِ، وروي بتشديد الدال على التكثير. وأَدَمَ القومَ: أَدَمَ لهم خُبْزَهم؛ أَنشد يعقوب في صفة كلاب الصيد: فهي تُباري كلَّ سارٍ سَوْهَقِ، وتُؤْدِمُ القوم إِذا لم تُغْبَقِ (* قوله «فهي تباري إلخ» هكذا في الأصل هنا، وتقدم في مادة سهق عل غير هذا الوجه وأتى بمشطورين بين هذين المشطورين). وقولهم: سَمْنُهم في أَديمهم، يعني طَعامَهم المأْدُوم أَي خَيْرُهم راجع فيهم. التهذيب: من أَمثالهم: سَمْنُكم هُرِيقَ في أَدِيمِكم أَي في مَأْدُومكم، ويقال: في سِقائكم. واختلف في اشتقاق اسم آدم فقال بعضهم: سُمِّي آدم لأَنه خُلِق من أُدْمةِ الأَرض، وقال بعضهم: لأُدْمةٍ جعلها الله تعالى فيه، وقال الجوهري: آدَمُ أَصله بهمزتين لأَنه أَفْعَل، إِلا أَنهم لَيَّنُوا الثانية، فإِذا احتجْت إِلى تحريكها جعلتها واواً وقلت أَوادِم في الجمع، لأَنه ليس لها أَصل في الياء معروف، فَجُعِلَ الغالبُ عليها الواوَ؛ عن الأَخفش؛ قال ابن بري: كل أَلِفٍ مجهولة لا يُعْرف عَمَّاذا انْقِلابها، وكانت عن همزة بعد همزة يدعو أَمْرٌ إِلى تحريكها، فإِنها تبدل واواً حملاً على ضَوارِب وضُوَيْرِب، فهذا حكمُها في كلام العرب إِلا أَن تكون طَرفاً رابعةً فحينئذ تبدل ياء؛ وقال الزجاج (*قوله «وقال الزجاج إلخ» كذا في الأصل، وعبارة التهذيب: وقال الزجاج يقول أهل اللغة

في آدم إن اشتقاقه من أديم الأرض لأنه خلق من تراب): يقول أهلُ اللغة إنَّ اشْتِقاق آدم لأنه خُلِق من تُراب، وكذلك الأُدْمةُ إنّما هي مُشَبَّهة بلَوْن التّراب؛ وقوله: سادُوا الملُوكَ فأصْبَحوا في آدَمٍ، بَلَغُوا بها غُرَّ الوُجوه فُحُولا جعل آدمَ اسْماً للقبيلة لأنه قال بَلَغوا بها، فأنَّث وجمَع وصرف آدم ضرورة؛ وقوله: الناسُ أَخْيافٌ وشَتَّى في الشِّيَمْ، وكلُّهم يَجْمَعُهم بيتُ الأَدَمْ قيل: أراد آدَم، وقيل: أراد الأرض؛ قال الأَخفش: لو جعلت في الشعر آدَم مع هاشم لجَاز؛ قال ابن جني: وهذا هو الوجه القويّ لأنه لا يحقِّق أحدٌ همزةَ آدَم، ولو كان تحقيقُها حَسَناً لكان التحقيقُ حَقيقاً بأَن يُسْمَع فيها، وإذا كان بَدلاً البتّة وجَب أن يُجْرى على ما أَجْرَتْه عليه العرب من مُراعاة لفظِه وتنزيل هذه الهمزة الأَخيرة منزلة الألفِ الزائدة التي لا حظّ فيها للهمزة نحو عالم وصابر، أَلا تَرهم لما كَسَروا قالوا آدم وأَوادِم كسالِم وسَوالِم؟ والأَدْمانُ في النَّخْل: كالدَّمانِ وهو العَفَن، وسيأْتي ذكره؛ وقيل: الأَدْمانُ عَفَن وسَوادٌ في قلب النَّخْلة وهو وَدِيُّه؛ عن كُراع، ولم يقل أَحد في القَلْب إنه الوَدِيُّ إلاَّ هو. وأَدام: بلد؛

1.17

وَأَلَ (القاموس المحيط) وَأَلَ إليه يَئِلُ وَأْلاً ووُؤُولاً ووَئِيلاً وواءَلَ مُواءَلَةً ووَآلاً: لَجأَ وخَلَص.

وأل (لسان العرب) وَأَلَ إليه وَأْلاً ووُؤُولاً وَوَئِيلاً وواءَلَ مُواءَلَةً ووِئالاً: لجأَ. وقال أبو الهيثم: يقال وَأَلَ يَئِلُ وأْلاً وَوَأْلَةً وواءَل يُوائِل مُواءَلةً ووِئالاً؛ قال ذو الرمة: حتى إذا لم يَجِدْ وَأْلاً ونَجْنَجَها، مَخافة الرَّمْي حتى كلُّها هِيمُ يروى: وَغْلاً؛ ويروى: وَغْلاً، فالوَأْل المَوْئِل، والوَغْل المَلْجَأُ يَغِل فيه أَي يدخل فيه. يقال: وغل يَغِل فهو واغِل، وكل ملجاءٍ يُلجأُ إليه وَغْل ومَوْغِل، ومَن رواه وَغْلاً فهو مثل الوَأْل سواءً، قُلبت الهمزة عيناً؛ ونَجْنَجَها أَي حَرَّكها وردَّدها مخافة صائد أَن يرميها. الليث: الوَأْلُ والوَعْل الملجأ. وقالوا: رَدَدْته إلى إيلته أَي إلى أَصله؛ وأَنشد:ولم يكن في إلَيَ غوالي يريد أَهلَ بيته وهذا من نوادره. قال أبو منصور: أَمّا إِلَةُ الرجل فهم أَهلُ بيته الذين يَئِلُ إليهم أَي يَلجأُ إليهم، من وَأَل يئل.

أول (لسان العرب) الأَوْلُ: الرجوع. آل الشيءُ يَؤُول أَولاً ومآلاً: رَجَع.

آل (تهذيب اللغة) آل: ثعلب، عن ابن الأعرابي: الأَوْلُ الرُّجوع. وقد آل يَؤُول أَوْلاً. والإيَال، مصدر: آل يَؤُول أَوْلا وإيَالاً.

آلَ (القاموس المحيط) آلَ إليه أَوْلاً ومآلاً: رَجَعَ،

سد (مقاييس اللغة) السين والدال أصل واحد، وهو يدلُّ على ردم شيء ومُلاءَمته من ذلك سَدَدت الثُّلمة سدّاً. وكلُّ حاجزٍ بين الشيئين سَدٌّ.

سدد (لسان العرب) السَّدُّ: إغلاق الخَلَلِ ورَدْمُ الثَّلَم. سَدَّه يَسُدُّه سَدّاً فانسدَّ واستدَّ وسدَّده: أَصلحه وأَوثقه، والاسم السُّدُّ. وحكى الزجاج: ما كان مسدوداً خلقه، فهو سُدٌّ، وما كان من عمل الناس، فهو سَدٌّ، وعلى ذلك وُجِّهت قراءة من قرأَ بين السُّدَّيْن والسَّدَّيْن. التهذيب: السَّدُّ مصدر قولك سَدَدْتُ الشيءَ سَدّاً. والسَّدُّ والسُّدّ: الجبل والحاجز. وقرئ قوله تعالى: حتى إذا بلغ بين السَّدَّين، بالفتح والضم. والسَّد، بالفتح والضم: الردم والجبل؛ ومنه سدّ الرَّوْحاء وسد الصهباء وهما موضعان بين مكة والمدينة.

وقوله عز وجل: وجعلنا من بين أيديهم سدّاً ومن خلفهم سدّاً؛ والسَّدّ: الرَّدْمُ لأَنه يُسدُّ به، والسُّدُّ والسَّدُّ: كل بناء سُدَّ به موضع. وسُدَّة المسجد الأَعظم: ما حوله من الرِّواق، وسمي إسمعيل السُّدِّيُّ بذلك لأَنه كان تاجراً يبيع الخُمُر والمقانع على باب مسجد الكوفه، وفي الصحاح: في سُدَّة مسجد الكوفة. قال أَبو عبيد: وبعضهم يجعل السُّدَّة الباب نفسه.

1.18

سجر (لسان العرب) سَجَرَه يَسْجُرُه سَجْراً وسُجوراً وسَجَّرَه: ملأَه. وسَجَرْتُ النهَرَ: ملأْتُه. وقوله تعالى: وإذا البِحارُ سُجِّرت؛ فسره ثعلب فقال: مُلِئَتْ، قال ابن سيده: ولا وجه له إلا أَن تكون مُلِئَت ناراً. وقوله تعالى: والبحرِ المَسْجُور؛ جاء في التفسير: أَن البحر يُسْجَر فيكون نارَ جهنم.

وسَجَرَ يَسْجُر وانْسَجَرَ: امتلأَ. وكان علي بن أَبي طالب، عليه السلام، يقول: المسجورُ بالنار أَي مملوء. قال: والمسجور في كلام العرب المملوء.

وقد سَكَرْتُ الإناء وسَجَرْته إذا ملأْته؛ وسَجَرْت الماء في حلقه: صببته؛ قال مزاحم: كما سَجَرَتْ ذا المَهْدِ أُمٌّ حَفِيَّةٌ، بِيُمْنَى يَدَيْها، مِنْ قَدِيٍّ مُعَسَّلِ القَدِيُّ: الطَّيِّبُ الطَّعْمِ من الشراب والطعام. وسَجَرَ التَّنُّورَ يَسْجُرُه سَجْراً: أَوقده وأَحماه، وقيل: أَشبع وَقُودَه. والسَّجُورُ: ما أُوقِدَ به. والساجِرُ والمَسْجُورُ: الساكن. أبو عبيد: المَسْجُورُ الساكن والمُمْتَلِئُ معاً.والساجُورُ: القِلادةُ أَو الخشبة التي توضع في عنق الكلب. وسَجَرَ الكلبَ والرجلَ يَسْجُرُه سَجْراً: وضع الساجُورَ في عنقه؛ وحكى ابن جني: كلبٌ مُسَوْجَرٌ، فإِن صح ذلك فشاذٌّ نادر. أَبو زيد: كَتب الحجاج إلى عامل له أَنِ ابْعَثْ إليَّ فلاناً مُسَمَّعاً مُسَوْجَراً أَي مُقَيَّداً مغلولاً. وكلب مَسْجُورٌ: في عنقه ساجورٌ.

išaru

ĝeš [PENIS] wr. ĝeš3; mu "penis; male" Akk. išaru; zikaru

سرر (لسان العرب) والسريرةُ: عمل السر من خير أَو شر. والسرُّ: الذَّكرُ؛ وإِنه لَسُرْسُورُ مالٍ أَي حافظ له. أَبو عمرو: فلان سُرْسُورُ مالٍ وسُوبانُ مالٍ إذا كان حسن القيام عليه عالماً بمصلحته. أَبو حاتم: يقال فلان سُرْسُوري وسُرْسُورَتِي أَي حبيبي وخاصَّتِي. ويقال: فلان سُرْسُورُ هذا الأَمر إذا كان قائماً به. ويقال للرجل سُرْسُرْ (* قوله: «سرسر» هكذا في الأَصل بضم السينين). إذا أَمرته بمعالي الأُمور .

2.11

سَأَته (القاموس المحيط) سَأَتَه، كمَنَعَهُ: خَنَقَهُ. والسَّأْتانِ، مُحَرَّكَةً: جانِبا الحُلْقُوم، الواحِدُ: سَأَت؟؟ .

سأت (لسان العرب) سَأَتَه يَسْأَتُه سأْتاً: خَنَقه بشدَّة، وقيل: إذا خَنَقه حتى يقتله. الفراء: السَّأْتانِ جانبا الحُلقوم، حيث يقع فيهما اصبعا الخانق، والواحد سأْتٌ، بالفتح والهمز .

ذأت (لسان العرب) ذأته يذأته ذأتاً: خنقه، مثل دغته دغتاً. وقال أبو زيد: ذأته إذا خنقه أشدَّ الخنق حتى أدلع لسانه .

جنب (لسان العرب) الجَنْبُ والجَنَبةُ والجانِبُ: شِقُّ الإِنْسانِ وغيرِه. تقول: قعدْتُ إِلى جَنْب فلان وإِلى جانِبِه، بمعنى، والجمع جُنُوبٌ وجَوانِبُ وجَنائِبُ، الأَخيرة نادرة. والجَنُوبُ ريح تُخالِفُ الشَّمالَ تأْتي عن يمين القِبْلة. وقال ثعلب: الجَنُوبُ مِن الرِّياحِ: ما اسْتَقْبَلَكَ عن شِمالك إِذا وقَفْتَ في القِبْلة. والجَنُوبُ ريح تُخالِفُ الشَّمالَ تأْتي عن يمين القِبْلة. وقال ثعلب: الجَنُوبُ مِن الرِّياحِ: ما اسْتَقْبَلَكَ عن شِمالك إِذا وقَفْتَ في القِبْلةِ.

وقال الأَصمعي: إِذا جاءَت الجَنُوبُ جاءَ معها خَيْرٌ وتَلْقِيح، وإِذا جاءَت الشَّمالُ نَشَّفَتْ.

وتقول العرب للاثنين، إِذا كانا مُتصافِيَيْن: رِيحُهما جَنُوبٌ، وإِذا تفرَّقا قيل: شَمْلَتْ رِيحُهما، ولذلك قال الشاعر: لَعَمْري، لَئِنْ رِيحُ المَوَدَّةِ أَصْبَحَتْ * شَمالاً، لقد بُدِّلْتُ، وهي جَنُوبُ وقول أَبي وجزة: مَجْنُوبةُ الأُنْسِ، مَشْمُولٌ مَواعِدُها، * مِن الهِجانِ، ذواتِ الشَّطْبِ والقَصَبِ يعني: أَن أُنْسَها على مَحَبَّته، فإِن التَمَس منها إِنجازَ مَوْعِدٍ لم يَجِدْ شيئاً. وقال ابن الأَعرابي: يريد أَنها تَذْهَب مَواعِدُها مع الجَنُوب ويَذْهَبُ أُنْسُها مع الشَّمال. وتقول: جَنَبَت الرِّيحُ إِذا تَحوَّلَتْ جَنُوباً. وسَحابةٌ مَجْنُوبةٌ إِذا هَبَّتْ بها الجَنُوب. التهذيب: والجَنُوبُ من الرياح حارَّةٌ، وهي تَهُبُّ في كلِّ وَقْتٍ، ومَهَبُّها ما بين مَهَبَّي الصَّبا والدَّبُور مِمَّا يَلي مَطْلَعَ سُهَيْلٍ. وجَمْعُ الجَنُوبِ: أَجْنُبٌ. وفي الصحاح: الجَنُوبُ الريحُ التي تُقابِلُ الشَّمالَ. وحُكي عن ابن الأَعرابي أَيضاً أَنه قال: الجَنُوب في كل موضع حارَّة إِلاَّ بنجْدٍ فإِنها باردة، وبيتُ كثير عَزَّةَ حُجَّة له: جَنُوبٌ، تُسامِي أَوْجُهَ القَوْمِ، مَسُّها * لَذِيذٌ، ومَسْراها، من الأَرضِ، طَيِّبُ وهي تكون اسماً وصفة عند سيبويه، وأَنشد: رَيحُ الجَنُوبِ مع الشَّمالِ، وتارةً * رِهَمُ الرَّبيعِ، وصائبُ التَّهْتانِ وهَبَّتْ جَنُوباً: دليل على الصفة عند أَبي عثمان. قال الفارسي: ليس بدليل، أَلا ترى إِلى قول سيبويه: إِنه قد يكون حالاً ما لا يكون صفة كالقَفِيزِ والدِّرْهم. والجمع: جَنائِبُ. وقد جَنَبَتِ الرِّيحُ تَجْنُبُ جُنُوباً، وأَجْنَبَتْ أَيضاً، وجُنِبَ القومُ: أَصابَتْهم الجَنُوبُ أَي أَصابَتْهم في أَمْوالِهِم. قال ساعدة بن جُؤَيَّة: سادٍ، تَجَرَّمَ في البَضِيعِ ثمانياً، * يُلْوَى بعَيْقاتِ البِحارِ، ويُجْنَبُ أَي أَصابَتْه الجَنُوبُ. وأَجْنَبُوا دَخَلُوا في الجَنُوبِ. وجُنِبُوا أَصابَهُم الجَنُوبُ، فهم مَجْنُوبُونَ، وكذلك القول في الصَّبا والدَّبُورِ والشَّمالِ.

كفف (لسان العرب) كفَّ الشيءَ يَكُفُّه كَفّاً: جمعه. وفي حديث الحسن: أَنَّ رجلاً كانت به جراحة فسأَله: كيف يتوضأُ؟ فقال: كُفَّه بخِرْقة أَي اجمَعها حوله. والكفُّ: اليد، أُنثى. وكِفافُ الشيءِ: حِتارُه. ابن سيده: والكِفة، بالكسر، كل شيء مستدير كدارة الوشم وعُود الدُّفِّ وحِبالة الصيْد، والجمع كِفَفٌ وكِفافٌ. قال: وكفة الميزان الكسر فيها أَشهر، وقد حكي فيها الفتح وأَباها بعضهم. وكُفَّة كل شيء، بالضم: حاشيته وطرَّته. وفي حديث عليّ، كرَّم الله وجهه، يصف السحاب: والتمع بَرْقُه في كُفَفِه أَي في حواشيه؛ وفي حديثه الآخر: إِذا غَشِيكم الليلُ فاجعلوا الرِّماح كُفَّةً أَي في حواشي العسكر وأَطرافه. وكُفَفُ السحاب وكِفافُه: نواحيه. وكُفَّة السحاب: ناحيته.

قفف (لسان العرب) القُفَّة: الزَّبيل، والقُفَّة: قرعة يابسة، وفي المحكم: كهيئة القَرْعة تُتَّخذ من خوص ونحوه تجعل فيها المرأَةُ قُطنها؛ وأَنشد ابن بري شاهداً على قول الجوهري القُفَّة القرعة اليابسة للراجز: رُبَّ عَجُوزٍ رأْسُها كالقُفَّهْ تَمْشي بخُفٍّ، معها هِرْشَفَّهْ ويروى كالكُفَّه.

عبر (مقاييس اللغة) العين والباء والراء أصلٌ صحيح واحدٌ يدلُّ على النفوذ والمضيِّ في الشيء. يقال: عَبرت النَّهر عُبوراً.

عبر (الصِّحاح في اللغة) وعَبَرْتُ النهر وغيره أَعْبُرُهُ عَبْراً، وعُبوراً. وعَبَرْتُ الرؤيا أَعْبُرُها عِبارةً: فَسَّرتها، وعَبَّرْتُ الرؤيا تَعْبيراً: فَسَّرتها. وعَبَّرت عن فلانٍ أيضاً، إذا تكلمت عنه. واللسان يُعَبِّرُ عما في الضمير. وتَعْبيرُ الدراهم: وزنُها جملة بعد التفاريق. واسْتَعْبَرْتُ فلاناً لرؤياي، أي قصصتُها عليه ليَعْبُرَها.

عَبَرَ (القاموس المحيط) عَبَرَ الرُّؤيا عَبْراً وعِبارةً. وعَبَّرَها: فَسَّرَها، وأخْبَرَ بآخِرِ ما يؤُولُ إليه أمْرُها. واسْتَعْبَرَه إيَّاها: سَأَلَهُ عَبْرَها. وعَبَّرَ عما في نفسه: أعْرَبَ، وعَبَّرَ عنه غيرُه فأعْرَبَ عنه، والاسم: العَبْرَةُ والعِبارَةُ. وعِبْرُ الوادِي، ويفتحُ: شاطِئُه، وناحِيَتُه. وعَبَرَه عَبْراً وعُبوراً: قَطَعَه من عِبْرِه إلى عِبْرِه.

سبر (لسان العرب) السَّبْرُ: التَّجْرِبَةُ. وسَبَرَ الشيءَ سَبْراً: حَزَرَه وخَبَرَه. واسْبُرْ لي ما عنده أي اعْلَمْه. والسَّبْر اسْتِخْراجُ كُنْهِ الأمر.

2.57

مَن (لسان العرب) والاستفهام كثير وهو كقولك: من تَعْني بما تقول؟

البَنْيُ (القاموس المحيط) البَنْيُ: نَقِيضُ الهَدْمِ، بَناهُ يَبْنِيهِ بَنْياً وبِناءً وبُنْياناً وبِنْيَةً وبِنايَةً، وابْتَنَاهُ وبَنَّاهُ. وتكونُ البِنايةُ في الشَّرَفِ.

بني (لسان العرب) بَنَا في الشرف يَبْنُو؛ وعلى هذا تُؤُوِّلَ قول الحطيئة: أُولئك قومٌ إِنْ بَنَوا أَحْسنُوا البُنا قال ابن سيده: قالوا إِنه جمعُ بُنْوَة أَو بِنْوَة؛ قال الأَصمعي: أَنشدت أَعرابياً هذا البيت أَحسنوا البِنا، فقال: أَي بُنا أَحسنوا البِنَاء، أَراد بالأَول أَي بَنَى .

2.58

وكل (لسان العرب) ووَكَلَ إِليه الأَمرَ: سلَّمه. ووكيلُ الرجل: الذي يَقوم بأَمره، سمِّي وَكيلاً لأَن مُوَكِّله قد وَكَلَ إِليه القيامَ بأَمره فهو مَوْكولٌ إِليه الأَمرُ.

أكل (الصِّحاح في اللغة) وآكَلْتُكَ فلاناً، إذا أمكنته منه .

2.59

كفر (مقاييس اللغة) الكاف والفاء والراء أصلٌ صحيحٌ يدلُّ على معنىً واحد، وهو السَّتْر والتَّغْطية. يقال لمن غطَّى درعَه بثوب: قد كَفَر درعَه. والمُكَفِّر الرَّجل المتغطِّي بسلاحه. فيقال: إنَّ الكافر: مَغِيب الشَّمس. ويقال: بل الكافر: البحر. والنهر العظيم كافر، تشبيهٌ بالبحر. قال:والكَفْر:

ضِدّ الإيمان، سمّي لأنّه تَغْطِيَةُ الحق. وكذلك كُفران النّعمة: جُحودها وسَتْرها. والكافور: كِمّ العِنَب قبل أن يُنوّر. وسمّي كافوراً لأنّه كفر الوَليع، أي غطّاه.

كفر (لسان العرب) والكَفْرُ، بالفتح: التغطية. وكَفَرْتُ الشيء أَكْفِرُه، بالكسر، أي سترته. والكافِر: الليل، وفي الصحاح: الليل المظلم لأنه يستر بظلمته كل شيء. وكَفَرَ الليلُ الشيءَ وكَفَرَ عليه: غَطّاه. وكَفَرَ الليلُ على أثر صاحبي: غَطّاه بسواده وظلمته.

وكَفَرَ الجهلُ على علم فلان: غَطّاه. والكافر: البحر لسَتْرِه ما فيه، ويُجْمَعُ الكافِرُ كِفاراً؛ والكافِرُ من الأرضين: ما بعد واتسع.

القَفْرُ (القاموس المحيط) القَفْرُ والقَفْرَةُ: الخَلاءُ من الأرضِ،

قفر (الصّحاح في اللغة) القَفْرُ: مفازةٌ لا ماء فيها ولا نبات، والجمع قِفارٌ. يقال: أرضٌ قَفْرٌ، وقَفْرَةٌ أيضاً، ومِقْفارٌ. والقَفُّورُ: كافور النخل.

قفر (لسان العرب) القَفْرُ والقَفْرة: الخلاءُ من الأرض، وجمعه قِفارٌ وقُفُورٌ؛ وأَقْفَر الرجلُ: أكل طعامَه بلا أُدْم. وأكل خُبزَه قفاراً: بغير أُدْم. وأَقْفَر الرجلُ إذا لم يبق عنده أُدْمٌ. وفي الحديث: ما أَقْفَر بيتٌ فيه خَلّ أي ما خلا من الأُدام ولا عَدِمَ أهلُه الأُدْمَ؛ قال أبو عبيد: قال أبو زيد وغيره: هو مأخوذ من القَفار، وهو كل طعام يؤكل بلا أدم. والقَفار، بالفتح: الخبز بلا أُدم. والقَفار: الطعام بلا أدم. يقال: أكلت اليوم طعاماً قَفَاراً إذا أكله غير مأدوم؛ قال: ولا أرى أصله إلا مأخوذاً من القَفْر من البلد الذي لا شيء به. والقفار والقَفِير: الطعام إذا كان غير مأدوم.

قبر (مقاييس اللغة) القاف والباء والراء أصلٌ صحيحٌ يدلُّ على غموضٍ في شيء وتطامُن. من ذلك القَبْر: قَبْر الميّت .

قبر (لسان العرب) وقَبَره يَقْبِره ويَقْبُره: دفنه.

كبر (مقاييس اللغة) الكاف والباء والراء أصلٌ صحيح يدلُّ على خِلاف الصِّغَر. يقال: هو كَبيرٌ، وكُبار، وكُبّار. ويقال أكبَرْتُ الشَّيءَ: استعظمتُه .

2.60

بلط (لسان العرب) البَلاطُ: الأرضُ، وقيل: الأرض المُسْتَوِيةُ المَلْساء، ومنه يقال بالَطْناهم أي نازَلْناهم بالأرض؛ والبَلاطُ: المسْتوي

البَلاطُ (القاموس المحيط) البَلاطُ، كسحابٍ: الأرضُ المُسْتَوِيةُ المَلْساءُ، والبُلْطةُ، بالضم، في قولِ امرئِ القيس: نَزَلْتُ على عَمْرِو بن دَرْماءَ بُلْطَةً. البُرْهَةُ، أو الدَّهْرُ، أو المُفْلِسُ، أو الفَجْأةُ، أو هَضْبَةٌ بعَيْنِها، أو أرادَ دارَهُ، وأنها مُبَلَّطَةٌ. وانْبَلَطَ: بَعُدَ.

2.61

ليق (لسان العرب) ولاقَ الشيءُ بقلبي لَيْقاً ولَياقاً ولَيقاناً والْتاق، كلاهما: لَزِق. وما لاقَ ذلك بصَفَري أي لم يوافقني. وفلان ما يَليقُ ببلد أي ما يمتسك، وما يُليقُه بلد أي ما يمسكه. والالْتِياقُ: لزوم الشيء الشيءَ. وقد الْتاق فلانٌ بفلان إذا صافاهُ كأنه لَزِقَ به.

لاقَ (القاموس المحيط) ولا يَليقُ بكَ: لا يَعْلَقُ. وما يَليقُ دِرْهَماً من جُودِه: ما يُمْسِكُهُ. و~ له: لَزِمَهُ،

لقا (لسان العرب) ولَقِيَ فلان فلاناً لِقاء ولقاءةً، بالمدّ، ولُقِيّاً ولِقِيّاً، بالتشديد، ولُقْياناً ولِقْياناً ولِقْيانة واحدة ولُقْية واحدة ولُقًى، بالضم والقصر، ولَقاةً؛ الأخيرة عن ابن جني، واستضعفها ودَفَعها يعقوب فقال: هي مولّدة ليست من كلام العرب؛ قال ابن بري: المصادر في ذلك ثلاثة عشر مصدراً، تقول لقِيته لِقاءً ولقاءةً وتلقاءً ولُقِيّاً ولِقِيّاً ولُقْياناً ولِقْياناً ولِقْيانَةً ولُقْيةً ولُقْياً ولُقًى ولِقًى، فيما حكاه ابن الأعرابي، ولَقاةً؛ وجلس تِلْقاءه أي حِذاءه؛ وتقول: لاقيتُ بين فلان وفلان. ولاقيْتُ بين طَرَفي قضيب أي حَنَيْته حتى تلاقيا والتَقيا. وكلُّ شيءٍ استقبل شيئاً أو صادفه فقد لقِيَه من الأشياء كلها. واللِّقْيان: كل شيئين يَلْقَى أحدهما صاحبه فهما لِقْيَان. فسر الزجاج قوله تعالى: وإنَّك لَتُلَقَّى القرآن؛ أي يُلْقَى إليك وحياً من عند الله. واللَّقَى: كل شيء مطروح متروك كاللُّقَطة.

والأُلْقِيَّةُ: ما أُلقِيَ. وقد تَلاقَوْا بها: كتَحاجَوْا؛ وتَلَقّاه أي استقبله. وفلان يَتَلَقَّى فلاناً أي يَسْتَقْبِله. والرجل يُلَقَّى الكلام أي يُلَقَّنه. وقوله تعالى: إذ تَلَقَّوْنَه بألسنتكم؛ أي يأخذ بعض عن بعض. وأما قوله تعالى: فتلقَّى آدمُ من ربه كلماتٍ؛ فمعناه أنه أخذها عنه، ومثله لقِنها وتلَقَّنها ، وقيل: فتلقَّى آدمُ من ربه كلماتٍ، أي تعلّمها ودعا بها. قال: قال ابن أحمر في اللقى أيضاً: تَروي لَقًى أُلْقِيَ في صَفْصَفٍ، تَصْهَرُه الشمس فما يَنْصَهِر وأَلْقَيْتُه أي طَرَحته . تقول: أَلْقِه مِن يدِك وأَلْقِ به من يدك، وأَلْقَيْتُ إليه المودّةَ وبالمودّةِ.

2.63

اللِّبْنُ (القاموس المحيط) ولِبْنُ القَميصِ، كَكَتِفٍ، ولِبْنَتُهُ ولِبْنَتُهُ، بالكسر: بَنيقَتُه.

لبن (الصّحاح في اللغة) ولِبنةُ القَميصِ: جُرُبّانُهُ.

بنق (لسان العرب) بَنَّقَ الكِتابَ: لغة في نَبَّقه. وبَنَّق كلامَه: جمعه وسوّاه، ومنه بَنائقُ القَميص أي جمع شيء. (* كذا بالأصل). وقد بَنَّق كتابه إذا جوّده وجمعه. والبنَقة والبَنِيقةُ: رُقْعة تكون في الثوب كاللِّبنِة ونحوها، مشتق من ذلك، وقيل: البَنيقة لَبِنة القميص، والجمع بَنائقُ وبَنِيقٌ؛

بنق (مقاييس اللغة) الباء والنون والقاف كلمةٌ واحدة، وأراها من الحواشي غير واسطة. وهي البَنيقة، وهو جُ◌رُ◌بان القَميص. ويقال: البَنيقة كلُّ رُقعةٍ في الثوب كاللِّبنةِ ونحوها.

ستي (لسان العرب) سَدى الثَّوْبَ يَسْديه وسَتاه يَسْتيه؛ وقال ابن سيده: السَّتى والأُسْتِيُّ خلاف لُحمةِ الثوب كالسَّدى والأُسْدِيّ. أبو عبيدة: اسْتاتَتِ الناقةُ اسْتِياتاءً إذا اسْتَرْخت من الضَّبعة؛ قال ابن بري: وليس هذا من هذا الفصل، وحقُّه أن يُذْكر في فصل أتى لأن وزنه اسْتَفْعَلت، والأصل فيه الهمز فترك الهمز، ويقوّي أنه من أتى رواية من روى الهمز فيها فقال اسْتأْتت اسْتِئْتاءً، قال: ولو كان افتعلت من السَّتى لقال في فعلها اسْتَتَت الناقةُ وفي مصدرها اسْتِتاءً.

سدو (مقاييس اللغة) ومن الباب: أَسْدَى النَخلُ، إذا استرخت ثفاريقُه، وذلك يكون كالشَيء المخلّى من اليدِ، والواحدة من ذلك السَّدِية.
والسَّدَى: النَّدَى؛ يقال سَدِيَتْ ليلتُنا، إذا كثُر نَداها.
سدا (الصَّحَاح في اللغة) والسَدا: نَدى الليل، وهو حياة الزرع. قال الكميتُ، وسَدِيَتِ الأرضُ، إذا كثُر نداها، من السماء كان أو من الأرض، فهي سَدِيَةٌ .
سدا (لسان العرب) السَّدْوُ: مَدُّ اليَد نحوَ الشيء كما تَسْدُو الإبلُ في سيرها بأيديها وكما يَسدو الصِّبيانُ إذا لعِبُوا بالجَوْز فرمَوْا به في الحَفيرة، والزَّدْوُ لغة كما قالوا للأَسْدِ أَزْدٌ، وللسَّرَادِ زَرَادٌ. وسَدا يديه سَدْواً واسْتَدَى: مَدَ بهما؛ وكلُّ رطبٍ ندٍ فهو سَدٍ؛

2.64

سمن (لسان العرب) السِّمنُ: نقيض الهُزال. والسَّمْنُ سِلاءُ اللَّبن. والسَّمْنُ سِلاءُ الزُّبْد، والسَّمْنُ للبقر، وقد يكون للمِعْزى؛
سمن (الصَّحَاح في اللغة) وسَمَنْتُ لهم الطعام أسمُنُهُ سَمْناً، إذا لَتَتُّهُ بالسمن.

2.65

بسس (لسان العرب) بَسَّ السَّويقَ والدقيقَ وغيرهما يَبُسُّه بَساً: خلطه بسمن أو زيت، وهي البسيسَةُ. قال اللحياني: هي التي تُلَتُّ بسمن أو زيت ولا تُبلُّ. والبَسُّ: اتخاذ البَسيسَة، وهو أن يُلتَّ السَّويقُ أو الدقيق أو الأَقِطُ المطحون بالسمن أو بالزيت ثم يؤكل ولا يطبخ. وقال يعقوب: هو أشد من اللَّتِّ بللاً؛

2.66

دجل (لسان العرب) ورُفْقة دَجَّالة: عظيمة تُغطِّي الأرض بكثرة أهلها، وقيل: هي الرُّفْقة تحمل المتاع للتجارة؛ وأنشد: دَجَّالة من أعظم الرِّفاق وكلُّ شيء مَوَّهته بماء ذهب وغيره فقد دَجَّلته. والدَّجَّال الذهب، وقيل: ماء الذهب؛ حكاه كراع وأنشد: ووَقْع صفائح مَخْشوبةٍ عليها يد الدهر دَجَّالها وهو اسم كالقَذَّاف والجَبَّان؛ وقال النابغة الجعدي: ثم نَزَلْنا وكَسَّرنا الرِّماحَ، وجرَ رَّدْنا صَفيحاً كَسْته الرُّومُ دَجّالا ودَجَّل الشيءَ بالذَّهَب.
التهذيب: يقال لماء الذهب دَجّال وبه شُبِّه الدَّجّال لأنه يُظْهِر خلاف ما يُضْمِر؛ قال أبو العباس: سمي الدَّجّال دَجّالاً لضربه في الأرض وقطعه أكثر نواحيها، ويقال: قد دَجَل الرجلُ إذا فعل ذلك. قال: وقال مرة أخرى سُمِّي دَجّالاً لتمويهه على الناس وتلبيسه وتزيينه الباطل، يقال: قد دَجَل إذا مَوَّه ولَبَّس، وفي الحديث: أن أبا بكر، رضي الله عنه، خَطَب فاطمة، رضي الله عنها، إلى سيدنا رسول الله، صلى الله عليه وسلم، فقال: إني وَعَدْتها لِعَليٍّ ولستُ بدَجّال، أي بخدّاع، ولا مُلَبِّس عليك أمرك.
دغل (مقاييس اللغة) الدال والغين واللام أصلٌ يدلُّ على التباسٍ والتواءٍ من شيئين يتداخلان. من ذلك الدَّغلُ، وهو الشَّجَر الملتفّ. ومنه الدَّغل في الشَّيء، وهو الفساد. ويقولون أدْغَلَ في الأمر، إذا أدْخَلَ فيه ما يخالفُه .
دغل (لسان العرب) ودَغَل في الشيء: دَخَل فيه دُخول المُريب كما يدخل الصائد في القُتْرة ونحوها ليخْتِل الصَّيد؛ يقال ذلك للرجل إذا دَخَل مَدْخَل مُريب. أبو عمرو: الدَّغل ما استرت به؛ قال الكميت: لا عَيْنُ نارك عن سارٍ مُغَمَّضَةٌ، ولا مَحَلَّتُك الطَّأْطاء والدَّغل ومكان داغِلٌ ودَغِلٌ ومُدْغِلٌ: خَفِيٌّ؛

صخخ (لسان العرب) وتقول: صخَّ الصوتُ الأُذُنَ يَصُخُّها صخّاً. وفي نسخة من التهذيب أَصخ إصخاخاً، ولا ذكر له في الثلاثي. وفي حديث ابن الزبير وبناء الكعبة: فخاف الناس أن يصيبهم صاخة من السماء؛ هي الصيحة التي تَصُخُّ الأَسماع أي تقرعها وتصمها.
صيخ (لسان العرب) أصاخ لهُ يصيخُ إصاخةً: استمع وأنصت لصوت؛ قال أبو دواد: ويصيخ أحياناً، كما اسـتمع المضلّ لصوت ناشد وفي حديث ساعة الجمعة: ما من دابة إلا وهي مُصيخة أي مستمعة منصتة، ويروى بالسين وقد تقدم.
صيح (لسان العرب) الصِّياحُ: الصوتُ؛ وفي التهذيب: صوتُ كل شيء إذا اشتدَ. صاحَ يَصيحُ صَيْحة وصِياحاً وصُياحاً، بالضم، وصَيْحاً وصَيَحاناً، بالتحريك، وصَيَّح: صَوَّت بأقصى طاقته، يكون ذلك في الناس وغيرهم؛ والصائِحَةُ: صَيْحَةُ المَناحة؛

ePSD: ṣīhu
isiš [SORROW] wr. i-si-iš; isiš3 "to laugh; laughter; wailing, lamentation, sorrow; to whisper" Akk. dimmatu; nissatu; ratāmu; tassistu; ṣiāhu; ṣīhu

محح (لسان العرب) ومُحُّ كل شيءٍ: خالصه. والمُحُّ والمُحَّةُ: صُفْرة البيض، قال ابن سيده: وإنما يريدون فصَّ البيضة لأن المُحَّ جوهر والصفرة عرض، ولا يعبر بالعرض عن الجوهر، اللهم إلا أن تكون العرب قد سمت مُحَّ البيضة صُفْرَةً، قال: وهذا ما لا أعرفه وإن كانت العامّة قد أُولِعَتْ بذلك؛ وأنشد الأزهري لعبد الله بن الزِّبَعْرى: كانت قُرَيْشٌ بَيْضَةً فتفَلَّقتْ، فالمُحُّ خالِصُها لعبد مَنافِ قال ابن بري: من روى خالصة، بالتاء، فهو في الأصل مصدر كالعافية؛ ومنه قوله تعالى: إنا أخلصناهم بخالصة ذِكْرى الدار، فذكرى فاعلة بخالصة، تقديره بأن خلصت لهم ذكرى الدار، وقد قرئَ بالإضافة، وهي في القِراءتين مصدر؛ ومن روى خالصه بالهاء فلا إشكال فيه. وقال ابن شُمَيل: مُحُّ البيض ما في جوفه من أصفر وأبيض، كلُه مُحٌّ، قال: ومنهم من قال: المُحَّةُ الصفراء، والغِرْقِئُ البياضُ الذي يؤكل. أبو عمرو: يقال لبياض البيض الذي يؤكل الآحُ، ولصفرتها الماحُ.
محت (لسان العرب) عَرَبِيٌّ مَحْتٌ بَحْتٌ أي خالص.
محط (لسان العرب) ويقال: مَحَطْتُ الوتر، وهو أن تُمِرّ عليه الأصابع لتُصْلِحه، وكذلك تَمْحِيطُ العَقَب تخليصه.

المَيْحُ (القاموس المحيط) والماحَةُ: السَّاحَةُ. والماحُ: صُفْرَةُ البَيْضِ، أو بَياضُهُ.
بوح (لسان العرب) والباحَةُ: باحةُ الدار، وهي ساحتها. والباحة: عَرْصة الدار، والجمع بُوحٌ، وبُحْبُوحة الدار، منها؛ ويقال: نحن في باحَة الدار، وهي أوسطها،
موخ (لسان العرب) الليث: ماخَ يَميخ مَيْخاً وتميَّخَ تميُّخاً، وهو التبختر في الأمر؛
ميح (لسان العرب) ماحَ في مِشْيته يَميحُ مَيْحاً ومَيْحُوحة: تَبَخْتر،
مخخ (الصّحَاح في اللغة) وخالصُ كلِّ شيءٍ مُخُّهُ.
مخ (مقاييس اللغة) الميم والخاء كلمةٌ تدلُّ على خالصِ كلِّ شيء.

2.68

أنس (لسان العرب) الإنسان: معروف؛ وقوله: أَقَلْ بَنو الإنسانِ، حين عَمَدْتُمُ إلى من يُثير الجنَّ، وهي هُجُودُ يعني بالإنسان آدم، على نبينا وعليه الصلاة والسلام. النَّاسُ هھنا أهل مكة الأُناسُ لغة في الناس، قال سيبويه: والأصل في الناس الأُناسُ مخففاً فجعلوا الألف واللام عوضاً عن الهمزة وقد قالوا الأُناس؛ قال الشاعر: إنَّ المَنايا يَطَّلِعْـ نَ على الأُناس الآمِنينا وحكى سيبويه: الناسُ الناسُ أي الناسُ بكل مكان وعلى كل حال كما نعرف؛ والنَّاتُ: لغة في الناس على البدل الشاذ؛

دأل (مقاييس اللغة) الدال والهمزة واللام يدل على خِفَّة ونَشْطَة. فالدَّأَلانُ: المشْيُ بنَشاط. يقال منه دَأَلْتُ أَدْأَل.
دأل (لسان العرب) الدَّأْلُ: الختْل، وقد دَأَلَ يَدْأَلُ دأْلاً ودأَلاناً. والدُّؤْلول الداهية، والجمع الدَّآلِيل. ووقع القومُ في دُؤْلول أي في اختلاط من أمرهم. أبو زيد: وقعوا من أمرهم في دُولول أي في شِدَّة وأَمر عظيم، قال الأزهري: جاء به غير مهموز. وفي حديث خزيمة: إن الجَنَّة محظور عليها بالدَّآلِيل أي بالدواهي والشدائد، وهذا كقوله: حُفَّتْ بالمَكاره .
الدَّوْلَةُ (القاموس المحيط) الدَّوْلَةُ: انْقِلابُ الزمانِ، و~ الشيءُ: ناسَ وتَعَلَّقَ. وأدالَنا اللهُ تعالى من عَدُوِّنا: من الدَّوْلَةِ. والإدالَةُ: الغَلَبَةُ. ودالَتِ الأَيَّامُ: دارَتْ، واللهُ تعالى يُداولها بينَ الناس. والدَّوَلُ: لُغَةٌ في الدَّلْوِ، وانْقِلابُ الدَّهْرِ من حالٍ إلى حالٍ، وبالتحريكِ: النَّبْلُ المُتَداوَلُ .
دول (لسان العرب) الدَّوْلةُ والدُّولةُ: العُقْبة في المال والحَرْب سَواء، والدَّوْلة: الانتقال من حال الشدَّة إلى الرَّخاء؛ وقالوا: دَواليْك أي مُداوَلةً على الأَمر؛ قال سيبويه: وإن شئت حملته على أنه وقع في هذه الحال. ودالَت الأَيامُ أي دارت، والله يُداوِلها بين الناس. وتَداولته الأَيدي: أَخذته هذه مرَّة وهذه مرَّة. ودالَ الثوبُ يَدُول أي بَلِي. وقد جَعَل وُدُّه يَدُول أي يَبْلى.

2.70

القَرُّ (القاموس المحيط) و~ بالمكانِ يَقِرُّ، بالكسر والفتح، قَراراً وقُروراً وقَرَاً وتَقِرَّةً: ثَبتَ، وسَكَن، كاسْتَقَرَّ وتَقارَّ. وأقَرَّهُ في مكانِهِ، فاسْتَقَرَّ،
قر (مقاييس اللغة) ويوم القَرِّ: يومَ يستقرُّ الناسُ بمِنىً، وذلك غداةَ يومِ النَّحر.
قرا (لسان العرب) القَرْو: من الأَرض الذي لا يكاد يَقْطعه شيء، والجمع قُرُوٌّ. وقال بعضهم: ما زلت أَسْتَقْري هذه الأَرض قَرْيَةً قَرْيَة. الأَصمعي: قَرَوْتُ الأَرضَ إذا تَتَبَّعت ناساً بعد ناس فأَنا أَقْرُوها قَرْواً. والقَرِيّ: مجرى الماء إلى الرياض، وجمعه قُرْيانٌ وأَقْراء؛ وأَنشد: كأَنَّ قُرْيانَها الرِّجال وتقول: تَقَرَّيْتُ المياه أي تتبعتها. واسْتَقْرَيْت فلاناً: سأَلته أن يَقْرِيَني.

3

Part 1-4 References

A.11

كحح (لسان العرب) الكُحّ: الخالص من كل شيء كالقُحّ، والأُنثى كُحّة كقُحّة. وعبد كُحٌّ: خالصُ العُبودةِ. وعربيٌّ كُحٌّ وأعراب أَكْحاحٌ إِذا كانوا خُلَصاءَ؛ وزعم يعقوب أَنَّ الكاف في كل ذلك بدل من القاف. والأَكَحُّ: الذي لا سِنَّ له. وأُمُّ كُحَّةَ: امرأة نزلت في شأْنها الفرائض .

A.12

مَنَّ (القاموس المحيط) مَنَّ عليه مَنًّا ومِنِّيَى، كخِلِّيفَى: أَنْعَمَ، واصْطَنَعَ عندَهُ صَنِيعَةً ومِنَّةً، امْتَنَّ، والمَنَّانُ: من أَسْماءِ الله تعالى، أي: المُعْطِي ابْتِداءً،
مون (لسان العرب) مانَهُ يَمُونه مَوْناً إِذا احتمل مؤونته وقام بكفايته، فهو رجل مَمُونٌ؛ عن ابن السكيت. ومانَ الرجلُ أَهله يَمُونُهُمْ مَوْناً ومَؤُونةً: كفاهم وأَنفق عليهم وعالهم. ومِنَ فلانٌ يُمانُ، فهو مَمُونٌ، والاسم المائِنةُ والمَوُونة بغير همز على الأَصل، ومن قال مَؤُونٌ قال مَؤُونةٌ.
مأن (لسان العرب) وجاءه أَمرٌ ما مأَنَ له أَي لم يشعر به. وما مأَنَ مأْنه؛ عن ابن الأَعرابي، أَي ما شعرَ به. وأَتاني أَمرٌ ما مأَنْتُ مأْنه وما مأَلْتُ مأْله ولا شأَنْتُ شأْنه أَي ما تهيَّأْتُ له؛ قال اللحياني: أَتاني ذلك وما مأَنْتُ مأْنه أَي ما علِمْتُ عِلْمَه، وقال بعضهم: ما انتبهت له ولا شعرْتُ به ولا تهيَّأْتُ له ولا أَخذْتُ أُهْبته ولا احتَفلْتُ به؛ ويقال: هو يَمْأَنُه أَي يَعْلمه. ومأَنْتُ القومَ أَمأَنُهم مأْناً إِذا احتملت مَؤُونتهم، ومن ترك الهمز قال مُنْتُهم أَمُونهم.
مني (لسان العرب) ومَنَيْت الرجل مَنْياً ومَنَوْتُه مَنْواً أَي اختبرته، ومُنِيتُ به مَنْياً بُليت، ومُنِيتُ به مَنْواً بُلِيت، ومانَيْته جازَيْته. ويقال: لأَمْنِيَنَّك مِناوَتَك أَي لأَجْزِيَنَّك جزاءك. ومانَيْته مُماناة: كافأْته، غير مهموز. ومانَيْتُك: كافأْتك؛
منا (الصّحاح في اللغة) ويقال: مُنِيَ له، أي قُدِّر. وقال: حتَّى تُلاقِيَ ما يَمْني لك الماني أي يقدِّر لك القادر.

ePSD: dim2
dim [CREATE] wr. dim2 "to create, make, manufacture; to replace?; to bring forth?" Akk. banû
طيم (لسان العرب) طامَهُ الله على الخَير يَطِيمُه طَيْماً: جَبَله. يقال: ما أَحْسَنَ ما طامَه اللهُ. وطانَه يَطِينُه أي جَبَله، ومنه الطِّيماءُ، وهي الجِبِلَّة، والطِّيماءُ الطبيعةُ. يقال: الشِّعْر مِنْ طِيمائِه أي من سُوسِه؛ حكاها الفارسي عن أَبي زيد، قال: ولا أَقول إنها بدلٌ من نون طانَ لأَنهم لم يقولوا طِيناء .
طيم (الصّحاح في اللغة) ابن السكيت: طامَهُ الله على الخير يَطيمُهُ، أي جَبَلَهُ، مثله طانَهَ .
طين (لسان العرب) وطِينةُ الرجل: خِلْقَتُه وأَصله، وطَيْناً مصدر من طانَ، ويروى طِيمَ عليه، بالميم، وهو بمعناه. ويقال لقد طانَنِي اللهُ على غير طِينَتِك. ابن الأَعرابي: طانَ فلانٌ وطامَ إذا حَسُنَ عَمَلُه .

ePSD: dim2-ma
dimma [THOUGHT] wr. dim2-ma; dimma "thought, planning; instruction" Akk. ţēmu
طعم (لسان العرب) ورجل ذو طَعْمٍ أَي ذو عَقْلٍ وحَزْمٍ؛ وليس بذي طَعْم أَي ليس له عقْلٌ ولا نفْسٌ. ومنه حديثُ ميراثِ الجَدّ: إن السدسَ الآخَرَ طُعْمةٌ له أَي أَنه زيادة على حقّه. والطُّعْمة والطِّعْمة، بالضم والكسر: وَجْهُ المَكْسَبِ. ويقال فلانٌ تُجْبَى له الطُّعَمُ أَي الخَراجُ والإتاواتُ؛ ورجل مُطْعَمٌ، بضم الميم: مرزوق. والطعام: اسم لما يؤْكل، والشراب: اسم لما يُشْرَبُ؛ ويقال: إنه لمُتَطاعِمُ الخَلْقِ أَي مُتَتابِعُ الخَلْق. ويقال: هذا رجل لا يَطَّعِمُ، بتثقيل الطاء، أَي لا يَتأَدَّبُ ولا يَنْجَعُ فيه ما يُصْلِحه ولا يَعْقِلُ.

A.13

ePSD: nig2

niĝ [THING] wr. niĝ2; aĝ2 "thing, possesion; something" Akk. bušu; mimma
عج (مقاييس اللغة) العين والجيم أصلٌ واحد صحيح يدلُّ على ارتفاعٍ في شيء، من صوتٍ أو غبارٍ وما أشبه ذلك. ومن الباب: فرس عجعاج، أي عدّاء. قال: وإنّما سمّي بذلك لأنه يثير العَجاج. والعَجاجة: الكثيرة من الغنم والإبل.
نأج (الصّحاح في اللغة) نأجَ في الأرض يَنأجُ نُؤوجاً: ذَهَبَ. ونأجتِ الريحُ تَنأجُ نَئيجاً: تحركت، فهي نَؤوجٌ.
نأجَ (القاموس المحيط) نأجَ في الأرض، كمَنَعَ، نُؤوجاً: ذَهَبَ. و~ الرّيحُ نَئيجاً: تَحرَّكَتْ، فهي نَؤوجٌ، ولِلرّيحِ نَئيجٌ، أي: مَرٌّ سَريعٌ بصوتٍ.
وجج (لسان العرب) ابن الأعرابي: الوَجُّ السُّرعة. والوُجُجُ النعام السريعة العَدْوِ؛
نعج (الصّحاح في اللغة) والناعِجَةُ البيضاء من النوق، ويقال هي التي يُصادُ عليها نِعاج الوحش. والناعِجَةُ من الأرض: السهلة. والنَواعِجُ من الإبل: السِراع. وقد نَعَجَت الناقةُ في سيرها، بالفتح: أسرعتْ؛ لغة في مَعَجَتْ.
نعج (لسان العرب) النَّعْجَة: الأُنثى من الضأْن والظِّباء والبقرِ الوَحْشيّ والشَّاءِ الجَبَلِيّ، والجمع نِعاجٌ ونَعَجات، والعربُ تَكْني بالنعجة والشاة عن المرأَة، ويسمون الثَّوْرَ الوحْشِيَّ شاةً؛ قال الجوهري: نَعَجَ يَنْعُجُ نَعجاً مثل طَلَبَ يَطْلُبُ طَلَباً.
معج (مقاييس اللغة) الميم والعين والجيم أصلٌ صحيح يدلُّ على تقلُّبٍ وسُرعة في شيء. ومعج الحمارُ مَعْجاً: تقلَّب في جريه .
مَعَجَ (القاموس المحيط) مَعَجَ، كمَنَعَ: أسْرَعَ،
معج (الصّحاح في اللغة) المَعْجُ: سُرعة السير. يقال: مَعَجَ الحمار والريحُ. وفرس مَعوج على فَعولٍ. وقد مَرَّ يَمْعَجُ، أي يَمُرُّ مَرًا سَهلاً.
معج (لسان العرب) المَعْجُ: سُرعةُ المَرِّ. وريح مَعُوجٌ: سريعةُ المَرِّ؛ ومَعَجَ في سيره إذا سارَ في كل وجه،

ePSD: gilim
gilim [BARRIER] wr. ĝešgilim "barrier, bolt" Akk. napraku
gilim [CLASP] wr. gigilim "type of clasp" Akk. hannāqu
gilim [CROSS] wr. gilim; gilibx(|GI%GI|)ib; gi16-il; gil-gilil "to lie across; to be entwined; to entwine, twist; to block; (to be) difficult to understand" Akk. egēru; parāku
gilim [FOLIAGE] wr. gigilim; ĝešgilim "foliage; forest" Akk. gūru; halbu
gilim [RODENT] wr. gilim2; gir12 "(wild) animals, moving things" Akk. nammaštû
gilim [ROPE] wr. gilim; kilib "rope of twined reeds" Akk. kilimbu
niĝgilim
ePSD: niĝgilim [RODENT] wr. niĝ2-gilim; niĝ2-gilim2 "vermin; a rodent" Akk. iškarissu
جَلَمَهُ (القاموس المحيط) جَلَمَهُ يَجْلِمُه: قَطَعهُ، و~ الجَزُورَ: أخَذَ ما على عِظامها من اللَّحم، كاجْتَلَمَه، و~ الصُّوفَ: جَزَّهُ. وكثُمامةٍ: ما جُزَّ منه. والجِلْمُ، بالكسر: شَحْمُ ثَرْبِ الشاةِ. وهو مَجْلومٌ: مَحْلوقٌ. والجَلَمةُ، محرَكةً: الشاةُ المسلوخَةُ إذا ذَهَبَتْ أكارعُها وفُضولُها، وجميعُ الشيءِ، كالجَلْمةِ، ويضم. وكزُنَّارٍ: التُّيوسُ المَحْلوقةُ. والجَلَمُ، محرَكَةً: غَنَمٌ طِوالُ الأَرْجُلِ لا شَعَرَ على قوائمِها، تكونُ بالطائِفِ، وتَيسُ الظِّباءِ والغَنَمِ.
جلم (لسان العرب) جَلَمَ الشيءَ يَجْلِمُه جَلْماً: قطعه. والجَلَمانِ المِقْراضانِ، واحدهما جَلَمٌ للذي يُجَزُّ به؛ قال سالم بن وابِصَة: داوَيْتُ صَدْراً طويلاً غِمْرُه حَقِداً منه، وقَلَّمْتُ أظفاراً بلا جَلَمِ والجَلَمُ: اسم يقع على الجَلَمَيْنِ كما يقال المِقْراضُ والمِقْراضان والقَلَمُ والقَلَمانِ؛ وقيل: الجِلامُ غنم من غنم الطائف صغار؛ قال: قُدْنا إلى هَمْدانَ، من أرضِنا، شُعْثَ النَّواصي شُزَّباً كالجِلام أبو عبيد: الجِلامُ شاءُ أهل مكة، واحدتها جَلَمَةٌ؛ وأنشد: شَواسِفٌ مثلُ الجِلام قُبّ. والجَلَمُ من سِماتِ الإبل (* قوله «والجلم من سمات الإبل إلخ» كذا في المحكم أيضاً، والذي في التكملة: والجلم أي محرَكاً سمة لبني فزارة في الفخذ.) شبيه بالجَلَم في الخَدّ؛ عن ابن حبيب من تذكرة أبي علي؛ وأنشد: هو الفَزارِيُّ الذي فيه عَسَمْ، في يده نَعْلٌ وأُخْرى بالقَدَمْ يَسُوقُ أشْباهاً عَلَيهِنَّ الجَلَمْ والجَلَمُ: الهلالُ ليلة يُهَلُّ (* قوله «ليلة يهل» زاد في التكملة: الجيلم كصقيل القمر ليلة البدر)؛ شُبِّه بالجَلَم. التهذيب: والجَلَمُ القمر.
قلم (مقاييس اللغة) القاف واللام والميم أصلٌ صحيح يدلُّ على تسويةِ شيء عند بَرْيه وإصلاحه. من ذلك: قَلَمْتُ الظُّفْر وقلَّمته.
قلم (الصّحاح في اللغة) والقَلَمُ الجَلَمُ.
قلم (لسان العرب) وكلُّ ما قطعت منه شيئاً بعد شيء فقد قلَّمته؛

ePSD: mu-lu
lu [PERSON] wr. lu2; mu-lu; mu-lu2; lu10; lu6 "who(m), which; man; (s)he who, that which; of; ruler; person" Akk. amēlu; ša
مأل (لسان العرب) رجل مَأْلٌ ومَئِلٌ: ضخم كثير اللحم تارٌ، والأُنثى مَأْلةٌ ومَئِلةٌ، وقد مَأَلَ يَمْأَلُ: تَمَلأَ وضخم؛ التهذيب: وقد مَئِلتْ تمأل ومُؤِلت تَمْؤُل. وجاءه أَمرٌ ما مَأَلَ له مَأْلاً وما مَأَلَ مَأْلَهُ؛ الأَخيرة عن ابن الأَعرابي، أَي لم يستعدّ له ولم يشعُر به؛ وقال يعقوب: ما تَهيَّأَ له .
ملأ (لسان العرب)والمُلأَة، بالضم مثال المُتْعةِ، مَلأَ الشيءَ يَمْلَؤُه مَلأً، فهو مَمْلوءٌ، ومَلأَه فامْتَلأَ، وتَمَلأَ، وإِنه لحَسَنُ المِلأَةِ أَي المَلْءِ، لا التَّمَلُّؤ. وتَمَلَّى إِخوانَه: مُتِّعَ بهم. يقال: مَلاَّكَ الله حَبِيبَكَ أَي مَتَّعَك به وأَعاشَك معه طويلاً؛ والإِمْلاءُ والإِمْلالُ على الكاتب واحد. وأَمْلَيْتُ الكتاب أُمْلي وأَمْلَلْتُه أُمِلُّه لغتان جَيِّدتان جاءَ بهما القرآن.
ملل (الصّحاح في اللغة) مَلِلْتُ الشيءَ بالكسر، ومَلِلْتُ منه أيضاً مَلَلاً ومَلَّةً ومَلالَةً، إذا سئمته.

ملا (الصَحاح في اللغة) يقال: ملاَّكَ الله حبيبَك، أي متَّعكَ به وأعاشك معه طويلاً .

A.14

ePSD: maš2-anše
mašanše [ANIMALS] wr. maš2-anše; maš-anše "animals, livestock" Akk. būlu
maš2
maš [GOAT] wr. maš2; maš "goat; extispicy; sacrificial animal for omens" Akk. bīru; urīşu
maš [INTEREST] wr. maš; maš2 "interest (on a loan); an irrigation tax" Akk. şibtu
anše
ePSD: anše [EQUID] wr. anše "donkey; equid" Akk. imēru

المَيْسُ (القاموس المحيط) المَيْسُ والمَيَسانُ والتَّمَيُّسُ: التَبَخْتُرُ، ماسَ يَميسُ، فهو مائِسٌ ومَيُوسٌ ومَيَّاسٌ. و~ اللهُ المَرَضَ فيه: كَثَّرَهُ.
ميس (لسان العرب) المَيْس: التَبَخْتُر، ماسَ يَميسُ ميساً ومَيَساناً: تَبَخْتَر واختالَ. وغصن مَيَّاسٌ: مائِلٌ. والمَيْس شجر تُعمل منه الرحال؛
المَيْشُ (القاموس المحيط) وماشُوا الأرضَ مَيْشَةً: مَرُّوا بها.
عنس (مقاييس اللغة) العين والنون والسين أصلٌ صحيح واحدٌ يدلُّ على شدّةٍ في شيء وقوّة. قال الخليل: العَنْس: اسمٌ من أسماء الناقة، يقال إنما سميت عنساً إذا تمَت سنُّها، واشتدَّت قوَّتُها ووفرت عظامُها وأعضاؤها؛
العَنْسُ (القاموس المحيط) العَنْسُ: الناقةُ الصُلْبَةُ، والعُقابُ، وعَطْفُ العُودِ، وقَلْبُهُ .
عنش (لسان العرب) عَنَشَ العُودَ والقضيبَ والشيءَ يَعْنِشُه عَنْشاً: عطَفه. والعَنْشَنْشُ الطويلُ، وقيل: السريعُ في شَبابه. وفرسٌ عَنْشَنَشَةٌ: سريعة؛

ePSD: ur
ur [BASE] wr. ur2; ĝešur2 "base, legs of a table"
ur [ROOT] wr. ur2; ur5 "root, base; limbs; loin, lap" Akk. išdu; mešrêtu; sūnu; utlu
ur [ROAM] wr. ur4; ur-ru-ur "to roam around" Akk. parāru
ur [KEEL?] wr. ur2 "keel?"

عرو/ي (مقاييس اللغة) العين والراء والحرف المعتل أصلان صحيحان متباينان يدلُّ أحدُهما على ثباتٍ ومُلازمةٍ وغِشيان، والآخر يدلُّ على خلوٍّ ومفارقة ويقال للفرس الطَّويل القوائم عُريان، وهو من الباب، يراد أنَّ قوائمه متجرِّدة طويلة .
عرر (لسان العرب) وعُرّا الوادي: شاطِئاه. وكلُّ شيءٍ باءَ بشيءٍ، فهو له عَرَار؛ وأنشدَ للأعشى: فقد كان لهم عَرار وقيل: العَرارُ القَوَدُ. والعَرارةُ الشدةُ؛ وعُرْعُرةُ كل شيء، بالضم: رأسُه وأعلاه. والعراعِرُ: أطراف الأَسْنِمة في قول الكميت: سَلَفي نِ○زار، إِذْ تحوَّلت المناسمُ كالعَراعِرْ وعَرْعَرَ عينَه: فقأها، وقيل: اقتلعها؛ عن اللحياني.
العَرْيُ (القاموس المحيط) واعْرَوْرَى: سارَ في الأرضِ وحدَهُ، والعَراءُ: الفضاءُ لا يُستَتَرُ فيه بشيءٍ ج: أعراءٌ، وأعْرَى: سارَ فيه، وأقامَ،
العَرُّ (القاموس المحيط) وعارَرْتُ: تَمَكَّثْتُ.

ePSD: edin
eden [PLAIN] wr. eden "plain, steppe, open country" Akk. edinu

عدن (مقاييس اللغة) العين والدال والنون أصلٌ صحيح يدلُّ على الإقامة.
عدن (الصَحاح في اللغة) عَدَنْتُ البلد: توطنته. وعَدَنت الإبل بمكانٍ كذا: لزمته فلم تبرح.
عَدَنَ (القاموس المحيط) عَدَنَ بالبَلَدِ يَعْدِنُ ويَعْدُنُ عَدْناً وعُدوناً: أقامَ، ومنه: {جَنَّاتُ عَدْنٍ}،
عدن (لسان العرب) عَدَنَ فلان بالمكان يَعْدِنُ ويَعْدُنُ عَدْناً وعُدُوناً: أَقام. وعَدَنْتُ البلدَ: تَوَطَّنْتُه. ومركَزُ كل شيء مَعْدِنُه، وجنَاتُ عَدْنٍ منه أي جنات إقامة لمكان الخُلْد، وجناتُ عَدْنٍ بُطْنانُها، وبُطْنانها وسَطُها. وبُطْنانُ الأَودية: المواضعُ التي يَستَرِيضُ فيها ماءُ السيل فيَكْرُمُ نباتُها، واحدها بَطْنٌ. واسم عَدْنان مشتق من العَدْنِ، وهو أَن تلزَمَ الإِبلُ المكانَ فتأْلفه ولا تبرَحه. تقول: تركْتُ إبل بني فلان عَوادِنَ بمكان كذا وكذا؛ قال: ومنه المَعْدِن، بكسر الدال، وهو المكان الذي يَثْبُتُ فيه الناس لأَن أَهله يقيمون فيه ولا يتحوّلون عنه شتاء ولا صيفاً، ومَعْدِنُ كل شيء من ذلك، ومعْدِنُ الذهب والفضة سمي مَعْدِناً لإِنْبات الله فيه جوهرهما وإِثباته إِياه في الأَرض حتى عَدَنَ أَي ثبت فيها. وعَدَنَتِ الإِبل بمكان كذا تَعْدِنُ وتَعْدُنُ عَدْناً وعُدُوناً: أَقامت في المَرْعَى، وخص بعضهم به الإِقامةَ في الحَمْض، وقيل: صَلَحَتْ واستَمرأَت المكانَ ونَمتْ عليه؛ قال أَبو زيد: ولا تَعْدِنُ إِلا في الحَمْض، وقيل: يكون في كل شيء، وهي ناقة عادِنٌ، بغير هاء. والعَدَنُ موضع باليمن، ويقال له أَيضاً عَدَنُ أَبْيَنَ، نُسب إِلى أَبْيَنَ رجلٍ من حِمْير لأَنه عَدَنَ به أَي أَقام؛

ePSD: me-te
mete [APPROPRIATE THING] wr. me-te; te "appropriate thing, ornament" Akk. simtu

mete [IMAGE] wr. me-te "image" Akk. simtu
mete [ONE'S OWN] wr. me-te; ni2-te "one's own" Akk. ramānu

ميت (لسان العرب) داري بِميتاءِ داره أي بِحذائها. ويقال: لم أدْرِ ما مِيداءُ الطريقِ ومِيتاؤه؛ أي لم أدْرِ ما قَدْرُ جانبيه وبُعْدِه؛ وأنشد: إذا اضْطَمَّ مِيتاءُ الطريقِ عليهما، مَضَتْ قُدُماً مَوْجُ الجبالِ زَهُوقُ ويروى مِيداءُ الطريق. والزَّهُوقُ: المُتقدِّمَةُ من النُّوقِ. وفي حديث أبي ثَعلبة الخُشَنيِّ: أنه اسْتَفْتَى رسولَ الله، صلى الله عليه وسلم، في اللُّقَطة، قال: ما وَجَدْتَ في طَريقٍ مِيتاءٍ فَعَرِّفْه سَنَةً. قال شمر: مِيتاءُ الطريق ومِيداؤه ومَحَجَّته واحدٌ، وهو ظاهره المسلوكُ. وقال النبي، صلى الله عليه وسلم، لابنه إبراهيم وهو يَجود بنَفْسه: لولا أنه طَريقٌ مِيتاءٌ لَحَزِنَّا عليك أكثر مما حَزِنَّا؛ أراد أنه طريق مسلوك، وهو مِفْعال من الإتْيان، فإن قلتَ طريقٌ مَأْتِيٌّ، فهو مفعول من أَتَيْتُه .

متع (مقاييس اللغة) الميم والتاء والعين أصلٌ صحيح يدلُّ على منفعة وامتداد مُدَّةٍ في خيرٍ. منه استمتعت بالشَّيء. والمُتْعة والمَتَاع: المنفعة في قوله تعالى: بُيُوتاً غَيْرَ مَسْكُونَةٍ فيها مَتاعٌ لَكُمْ [النور 29].

متع (لسان العرب) ومَتَعَ الرجلُ ومَتُعَ: جادَ وظَرُفَ، وقيل: كا ما جادَ فقد مَتُعَ، وهو ماتِعٌ. والماتِعُ من كل شيء: البالغُ في الجَوْدةِ الغاية في بابه؛ والمُتْعةُ والمِتْعةُ والمَتْعةُ أيضاً: البُلْغةُ؛ ويقول الرجل لصاحبه: ابْغِني مُتْعةً أَعِيشُ بها أي ابْغِ لي شيئاً آكُله أو زاداً أتزَوَّدُه أو قوتاً أَقتاته؛ والمَتاعُ أيضاً: المنفعة وما تَمَتَّعْتَ به. وفي حديث ابن الأَكْوَع: قالوا يا رسول الله لولا مَتَّعْتنا به أي تركتنا ننتفع به.

ePSD: ĝal2
ĝal [BE] wr. ĝal2; ma-al; ga2gal2 "to be (there, at hand, available); to exist; to put, place, lay down; to have" Akk. bašû; šakānu
ĝal [CVNE] wr. ĝal2 "(compound verb nominal element)"
ĝal [GUARD] wr. ĝal2 "to guard, protect" Akk. naṣāru
ĝal [OPEN] wr. ĝal2 "to open" Akk. petû

بجل (الصَحاح في اللغة) وأَبْجَلَهُ الشيء، أي كَفاهُ.

بَجَّلَهُ (القاموس المحيط) بَجَّلَهُ تَبْجيلاً: عَظَّمَهُ، أو قال له: بَجَلْ، كنَعَمْ، أي حَسْبُكَ حيثُ انْتَهَيْتَ. وبَجَلْكَ وبَجَلْنِي، ساكِنَتَي اللامِ، أي يَكْفيكَ ويَكْفيني، اسمُ فِعْلٍ. وبَجَلْ: كنَعَمْ زِنَةً ومعنًى. وأَبْجَلَهُ الشيءُ: كفاهُ .

بجل (لسان العرب) التَّبجيل: التعظيم. بَجَّل الرجلَ: عَظَّمه.

جل (مقاييس اللغة) الجيم واللام أصولٌ ثلاثة: جَلَّ الشَيءُ: عَظُمَ، وجُلُّ الشيء مُعْظَمُه. وجلال الله: عَظَمته. والجُلالة: النَاقة العظيمة. والجَليلة: خلافُ الدَّقيقة. ويقال ما له دقيقة ولا جليلة، أي لا ناقةَ ولا شاة.

C.7

ePSD: kug
kug [METAL] wr. kug "metal, silver; (to be) bright, shiny"
kug [PURE] wr. kug "(to be) pure" Akk. ellu
ku3
kug [METAL] wr. kug "metal, silver; (to be) bright, shiny"
kug [PURE] wr. kug "(to be) pure" Akk. ellu

خوق (لسان العرب) الخَوْقُ: الحَلْقة من الذهب والفِضة، وقيل هي حَلْقة القُرط والشَّنْف خاصَّة؛ والخَوْقاء من النساء: الواسعة، وقيل: هي التي لا حجاب بين فرجها ودُبرها، وقيل: هي المُفْضاة. والخَوْقاء: الحَمْقاء من النساء. والخَوْقاء من النساء: الطويلة الدقيقةُ، ونساء خُوقٌ. وخاقُ المفازة: طولها، وخَوَقُّها: سَعَتُها، ويقال: خَوَقها طولها وعَرْض انبساطها وسَعة في جَوْفها، وخَرْقٌ أَخْوقٌ؛ قال: تخَوَّق تباعَدَ عنه؛ وخاقَ الرجلُ المرأَة إذا فَعل بها. وخاقَ الشيءَ: اسْتأْصَله وذَهَب به؛

كأج (لسان العرب) التهذيب: أَهمله الليث، وروى أَبو العباس عن ابن الأَعرابي، قال: كأَجَ الرجلُ إذا زاد حُمْقُه. والكِئاجُ: الفَدامةُ والحَماقةُ .

كيج (لسان العرب) الكِياجُ: الفَدامةُ والحَماقةُ .

قهو (مقاييس اللغة) القاف والهاء والحرف المعتلّ أصلٌ يدلُّ على خِصْب وكَثْرة. يقال للرَّجُل المُخصِب الرَحْلِ: قاهٍ.

قها (لسان العرب) القَهْو والقَهْوة: خَصِيبٌ، وهذه يائية وواوية. الجوهري القاهِي الحَديدُ الفؤاد المُستطارُ؛

ePSD: ug3
uĝ [PEOPLE] wr. uĝ3 "people" Akk. nišu

ePSD: BI

bad [OPEN] wr. bad; ba; be2 "(to be) remote; to open, undo; to thresh grain with a threshing sledge" Akk. be'ēšû; nesû; petû
biz [TRICKLE] wr. bi-iz; biz "to trickle, drip" Akk. baṣāṣu
dug [POT] wr. dug; dugx(BI) "(clay) pot; a unit of liquid capacity" Akk. karpatu
e [SPEAK] wr. e; na-be2-a; be2; ne; da-me; na-be2; e7 "perfect plural and imperfect stem of dug[to speak]" Akk. atwû; dabābu; qabû
ešemen [ROPE] wr. ešemen; ešemen2; e-šen; ešemen3; ešemen5 "game, play; skipping rope" Akk. keppû; mēlultu
kaš [BEER] wr. kaš; kaš2 "beer; alcoholic drink" Akk. šikaru

ePSD: be2
bad [OPEN] wr. bad; ba; be2 "(to be) remote; to open, undo; to thresh grain with a threshing sledge" Akk. be'ēšû; nesû; petû
e [SPEAK] wr. e; na-be2-a; be2; ne; da-me; na-be2; e7 "perfect plural and imperfect stem of dug[to speak]" Akk. atwû; dabābu; qabû

بحح (لسان العرب) البُحَّة والبَحَحُ والبَحاحُ والبُحُوحةُ والبَحاحةُ: كلُّه غِلَظٌ في الصوت وخُشُونة، وربماكان خِلْقَةً. بَحَّ يَبَحُّ (* قوله «بح يبح إلخ» بابه فرح ومنع كما في القاموس. ويقال: ما زِلْتُ أَصِيحُ حتى أَبَحَّنِي ذلك. قال الأَزهري: بِحِحْتُ أَبَحُّ هي اللغة العالية، قال: وبَحَحْتُ، بالفتح، أَبَحُّ، لغة؛ وقول الجعْدي يصف الدينار: وأَبَحَّ جُنْدِيٍّ، وثاقِبةٍ سُبِكَتْ، كثاقِبةٍ من الجَمْرِ أَراد بالأَبَحِّ: ديناراً أَبَحَّ في صوته. جُنْدِيّ: ضُرِبَ بأَجْنادِ الشام. والثاقبة: سَبِيكَة من ذهب تَثْقُبُ أَي تتقد. والبَحَحُ في الإِبل: خُشُونة وحَشْرَجةٌ في الصدر. بعير أَبَحُّ وعيودٌ أَبَحُّ: غليظ الصوت. والبَمُّ يُدْعى الأَبَحَّ لغلظ صوته. وتَبَحْبَحَ في المجدِ أَي أَنه في مَجْدٍ واسع. وجعل الفراء التَّبَحْبُحَ مِن الباحة، ولم يجعله من المضاعف. ويقال: القوم في ابْتِحاح أَي في سَعَةٍ وخِصْب. وبُحْبُوحة كل شيء وسطه وخياره. ويقال: قد تَبَحْبَحْتُ في الدار إِذا تَوَسَّطْتَها وتمكنت منها. والتَّبَحْبُح: التمكن في الحلول والمُقامِ. وقد بَحْبَحَ وتَبَحْبَحَ إِذا تمكن وتوسط المنزل والمقام؛

ePSD: še
še [BARLEY] wr. še "barley; grain; a unit of length; a unit of area; a unit of volume; a unit of weight" Akk. uṭṭatu; û; uṭṭatu
še [CALL] wr. še21 "to call by name" Akk. nabû
še [CONE] wr. ĝešše "(conifer) cone"
še [CVNE] wr. še "(compound verb nominal element)"
še [HOOK?] wr. še "hook?"
še [PLANT] wr. šesar "a plant"
še [SHAPE] wr. še "a geometric shape"
še [TEAR] wr. šex(|IGI@g|) "tear"
še [THAT] wr. še "that"
še [UNMNG] wr. še3 "?" Akk. ?

ePSD: anir
anir [GRASS] wr. u2a-nir "a grass"
anir [LAMENT] wr. a-nir; a-še-er "lament" Akk. tanēhu
anir [PROFESSION] wr. a-nir "a profession"

نعر (مقاييس اللغة) النون والعين والراء: أصلانِ مُتقارِبان: أحدهما صوتٌ من الأصوات، والآخر حركةٌ من الحركات. فالأوّل نَعَرَ الرّجُل، وهو صَوتٌ من الخيشوم. وجُرْحٌ نَعّارٌ ونَعور، إذا صَوَّتَ دمُه عِند خُروجِه منه. والنّاعور: ضَربٌ من الدِّلاء يُستقَى به، سمِّي لصوته. والثاني نَعَرَ في الفِتنة: سعَى وجاءَ وذهبَ. وهو نَعّارٌ في الفِتَن: سَعّاء. ونَعَرَ في البِلاد: ذهب. وهو نَعِير الهَمّ: بَعيدُه. وإنَّ في رأسه نُعَرَةً، أي نَخوةً وتكبُّراً، ورُكوبَ رأسٍ، يمضي به على جَهله.
النُّعَرَةُ (القاموس المحيط) والنَّعيرُ: الصُّراخُ، والصِّياحُ في حَرْبٍ أو شَرٍّ. وامرأةٌ نَعّارَةٌ، كشَدّادٍ: صَخّابَةٌ فاحِشَةٌ. والنَّعْرَةُ: صَوتٌ في الخَيْشومِ. والنَّعُورُ من الرِّياحِ: ما فاجَأَكَ بِبَرْدٍ، وأنتَ في حَرٍّ، أو عَكْسُهُ. ونَعَرَ، كمَنَعَ: خالَفَ، وأبَى، و~ القومُ: هاجُوا، اجْتَمَعُوا، و~ إليه: أتاه، و~ في الأَمْرِ: نَهَضَ، وسَعَى.

نعر (لسان العرب) النُّعْرَةُ والنُّعَرَةُ: الخَيْشُوم، ومنها يَنْعِرُ النَّاعِرُ. والنَّعِيرُ: الصِّياحُ. والنَّعِيرُ: الصُّراخُ في حَرْب أو شَرّ. وفي رأسه نُعَرَةٌ ونَعَرَةٌ أي أَمْرٌ يَهُمُّ به. ونِيَّةٌ نَعُورٌ: بعيدة؛ قال: ومنتُ إذا لم يَصِرْني الهَوَى ولا حُبُّها، كان هَمِّي نَعُورَا وفلان نَعِيرُ الهَمّ أي بَعِيدُه. وهِمَّةٌ نَعُورٌ: بعيدةٌ. والنَّعُورُ من الحاجات: البعيدة. ويقال: سَفَرٌ نَعُورٌ إذا كان بعيداً؛ ومنه قول طرفة: ومِثْلِي، فاعْلَمِي يا أُمَّ عَمرٍو، إذا ما اعْتادَهُ سَفَرٌ نَعُورُ ورجل نَعَّارٌ في الفتن: خَرَّاجٌ فيها سَعَّاءٌ، لا يراد به الصوتُ وإنما تُعْنَى به الحركةُ.

والنَّعَّارُ أيضاً: العاصي؛ عن ابن الأعرابي. ونَعَرَ القومُ: هاجوا واجتمعوا في الحرب. وقال الأصمعي في حديث ذكره: ما كانت فتنةٌ إلاَّ نَعَرَ فيها فلانٌ أي نَهَضَ فيها. وفي حديث الحَسَنِ: كلما نَعَرَ بهم ناعِرٌ اتَّبَعُوه أي ناهِضٌ يدعوهم إلى الفتنة ويصيح بهم إليها. ونَعَر الرجل: خالف وأَبى؛

ePSD: ga2

ĝa [HOUSE] wr. ĝa2; ma "house" Akk. bītu

ĝar [PLACE] wr. ĝar; ĝa2; ĝa2-ar; ĝa2ĝar; ĝarar; mar; ĝa2ĝarar "to put, place, lay down; to give in place of something, replace; to posit (math.)" Akk. šakānu

جاءَ (القاموس المحيط) جاءَ يَجِيءُ جَيئاً جَيْئَةً وَمَجِيْئاً: أتَى، والاسم كالجيعَةِ. وإنَّه لَجِيَّاءٌ وجَئَّاءٌ وجَائِيٌّ. وأجَأْتُه: جِئْتُ به، و إليه: ألْجَأْتُه. وجاءَأَنِي، وهِمَ فيه الجوْهَرِيُّ، وصَوَابُهُ: جَايأَنِي، لأنَّهُ مُعْتَلُّ العَيْنِ مَهْمُوزُ اللاَّمِ، لا عكسُهُ، فَجِئْتُه أجِيئُهُ: غَالبَنِي بكَثْرَةِ المجيءِ، فغَلَبْتُه. والجَيْئَةُ والجايئَةُ: القَيْحُ والدَّمُ. والجَيْءُ والجِيءُ: الدُّعَاءُ إلى الطَّعامِ والشَّرابِ. وجَأْجَأَ بالإِبِلِ: دَعاهَا للشُّرْبِ. وجَيَّأَ القِرْبَةَ: خاطَهَا. والمُجَيَّأُ، كمُعَظَّمٍ: العِذْيَوْطُ، وبهاءٍ: المُفْضَاةُ تُحْدِثُ إذا جُومِعَتْ. والمُجَايَأَةُ: المُقابَلَةُ والمُوافَقَةُ كالجِيَاءِ. والجَيْئَةُ: المَوْضِعُ يَجْتَمِعُ فيه الماءُ، كالجِئَةِ، كَجِعَةٍ وجِيعَةٍ، والأعْرَفُ الجِيَّةُ، مُشَدَّدَةً، و : قِطْعَةٌ تُرْقَعُ بها النَّعلُ، أو سَيْرٌ يُخاطُ به، وقد أجاءَها. وما جَاءَتْ حاجَتُك: ما صَارَتْ.

C.8

ePSD: šag4

šag [HEART] wr. šag4; ša; ša3-ab "inner body; heart; in, inside" Akk. libbu

سوق (لسان العرب) وساقَ بنفسه سياقاً: نَزَع بها عند الموت. تقول: رأيت فلاناً يَسُوق سُوُقاً أي يَنْزِع نَزْعاً عند الموت، يعني الموت؛ الكسائي: تقول هو يَسُوق نفْسَه ويَفِيظ نفسَه وقد فاظت نفسُه وأفاظَه الله نفسَه. ويقال: فلان في السِّياق أي في النَّزْع. ابن شميل: رأيت فلاناً بالسَّوْق أي بالموت يُساق سوقاً، وإنه نَفْسه لتُساق. والسِّياق: نزع الروح. وفي الحديث: دخل سعيد على عثمان وهو في السَّوْق أي النزع كأَنّ روحه تُساق لتخرج من بدَنه، ويقال له السِّياق أيضاً، وأصله سِواق، فقلبت الواو ياء لكسرة السين، وهما مصدران من ساقَ يَسُوق. وفي الحديث: حَضَرْنا عمرو بن العاصِ وهو في سِياق الموت .

شوق (لسان العرب) الشَّوْقُ والاشْتياقُ: نِزاعُ النفس إلى الشيء، والجمع أَشْواقٌ، شاقَ إليه شَوْقاً وتَشَوَّق واشتاقَ اشْتياقاً. والشَّوْقُ: حركة الهوى. والشُّوق: العُشّاق. ويقال: شاقَنِي الشيءُ يَشُوقُني، فهو شائِقٌ وأنا مَشوقٌ؛

ePSD: ni2

ni [BIRD] wr. ni2mušen "a bird"

ni [FEAR] wr. ni2; e; ne4 "fear, aura" Akk. puluhtu

ni [SELF] wr. ni2 "self" Akk. ramānu

nidib [BIRD] wr. ni2mušen "a bird"

نأي (لسان العرب) النَّأْيُ: البُعدُ. نَأَى يَنْأَى: بَعُدَ، بوزن نَعى يَنْعَى. ونَأَوْتُ: بَعُدْت، لغة في نأَيْتُ. والنَّأْيِ المُفارقة؛ قال المنذري: أَنشدني المبرد: أَعاذِلَ، إنْ يُصْبحْ صَدايَ بقَفْرةٍ بَعِيداً، نآني زائِرِي وقَرِيبي قال المبرد: قوله نآني فيه وجهان: أَحدهما أَنه بمعنى أَبعدني كقولك زِدْته فزاد ونقصته فنقص، والوجه الآخر في نآني أَنه بمعنى نَأَى عني،قال أَبو منصور: وهذا القول هو المعروف الصحيح. والنُّؤْي والنِّئْي والنَّأْيُ والنُّؤَى، بفتح الهمزة على مثال النُّقَى؛

نعا (لسان العرب) والنُّعاء: صوت السِّنَّوْر؛ قال ابن سيده: وإِنما قضينا على همزتها أَنها بدل من واو لأَنهم يقولون في معناه المُعاء، وقد مَعا يَمْعُو، قال: وأَظنُّ نون النُّعاء بدلاً من ميم المعاء. واسْتَنْعى القومُ: تفَرَّقوا نافرين. والاسْتِنْعاء: شبه النِّفار. يقال: اسْتَنْعى الإِبلُ والقوم إِذا تفرَّقوا من شيء وانتشروا .

نَوَى (القاموس المحيط) نَوَى الشيءَ يَنْوِيه نِيَّةً، ويُخَفَّفُ: قَصَدَه، كانْتَواهُ وتَنَوَّاهُ، و~ اللهُ فُلاناً: حَفِظَهُ. والنِيَّةُ: الوجهُ الذي يُذْهَبُ○ فيه، والبُعْدُ،

نوي (لسان العرب) نَوى الشيءَ نِيَّةً ونِيَةً، بالتخفيف؛ عن اللحياني وحده، وهو نادر، إِلاَّ أَن يكون على الحذف، وانْتَواه كلاهما: قصده واعتقده. ونَوى المنزلَ وانْتَواه كذلك. والنِّيَّةُ: الوجه يُذْهَب فيه؛ والنِّيَّة والنَّوى جميعاً: البُعْد؛ والنَّوى: النِّيَّة وهي النِّيَة، مخففة، ومعناها القصد لبلد غير البلد الذي أَنت فيه مقيم. وفلان يَنْوي وجه كذا أَي يقصده من سفر أَو عمل. والنَّوى: الوجهُ الذي تقصده. التهذيب: وقال أَعرابي من بني سُليم لابن له سماه إِبراهيم ناوَيْتُ به إِبراهيمَ أَي قصدت قَصْدَه فتبرَّكت باسمه.

وقوله في حديث ابن مسعود: ومَنْ يَنْو الدنيا تُعْجِزْه أي من يَسْعَ لها يَخِبْ، يقال: نَوَيْتُ الشيءَ إذا جَدَدْتَ في طلبه. وأنوى إذا تباعد. ونَواهُ اللهُ: حفظه؛ الجوهري: وناواه أي عاداه، وأصله الهمز لأنه من النَّوْء وهو النُّهوض. والنَّواةُ في الأصل: عَجَمةُ التمرة.

نحا (لسان العرب) الأزهري: ثبت عن أهل يُونانَ، فيما يَذْكُر المُتَرْجِمُون العارِفُون بلسانهم ولغتهم، أنهم يسمون عِلْمَ الألفاظ والعِناية بالبحث عنه نَحْواً، ويقولون كان فلان من النَّحْوِيينَ، ولذلك سُمي يُوحنَّا الإسكَنْدَرانيُّ يَحْيَى النَّحْويَّ للذي كان حصل له من المعرفة بلغة اليُونانِيِّين.

والنَّحْوُ: إعراب الكلام العربي. والنَّحْوُ: القَصدُ والطَّرِيقُ، يكون ظرفاً ويكون اسماً، نَحاه يَنْحُوه ويَنْحاه نَحْواً وانْتَحاه، ونَحْوُ العربية منه، الليث: النَّحْوُ القَصْدُ نَحْوَ الشيء. وأَنْحَىْ عليه وانْتَحَى عليه إذا اعتمد عليه. ابن الأَعرابي: أَنْحَى ونَحَى وانْتَحى أي اعْتَمَدَ على الشيء. وانتَحَى له وتَنَحَّى له: اعتمد .

ePSD: te-na

ten [COOL] wr. te-na; te-en "to be cool, become cool"

طعن (لسان العرب) وفي حديث علي، كرم الله وجهه: والله لوَدَّ معاويةُ أنه ما بقي من بني هاشم نافِخُ ضَرمةٍ إلا طَعَنَ في نَيْطِه؛ يقال: طَعَنَ في نَيْطِه أي في جنازته. ومن ابتدأ بشيء أو دخله فقد طَعَنَ فيه، ويروى طُعِنَ، على ما لم يسم فاعله؛ والنَّيْطُ: نِياطُ القَلْبِ وهو عِلاقَتُه. وطَعَن الليلَ: سار فيه، كله في المثل. والفرس يَطْعُنُ في العِنانِ إذا مَدَّه وتَبَسَّط في السير؛ قال لبيد: تَرْقى وتَطْعُنُ في العِنانِ وتَنْتَحي وِرْدَ الحَمامةِ، إذْ أَجَدَّ حَمامُها أي كوِرْدِ الحَمامة، والفراء يجيز الفتح في جميع ذلك

تعا (لسان العرب) انفرد الأزهري بهذه الترجمة، وقال ابن الأَعرابي: يقال تَعا إذا عَدَا وثَعا إذا قَذَف. قال: والتَّعَى في الحفظ الحَسَن. وقال في الترجمة أَيضاً: والتَّاعِي اللِّبأ المسترخي، والثَّاعِي القاذف. وحكي عن ا لفراء: الأَتْعاءُ ساعات الليل، والثُّعَى القَذْف.

تعع (لسان العرب) التَّعُّ: الاسْتِرْخاء. تَعَّ تَعّا وأَتَعَّ: قاء كثَعَّ؛ ووقع القومُ في تعاتِعَ إذا وقعوا في أراجِيفَ وتَخْلِيط.

طعع (لسان العرب) والطَّعْطَعُ من الأرض: المطمئن .

طعا (لسان العرب) حكى الأزهري عن ابن الأعرابي: طَعا إذا تباعَد. غيره: طَعا إذا ذَلَّ. أبو عمرو: الطاعِي بمعنى الطائِع إذا ذَلَّ. قال ابن الأَعرابي: الإِطْعاءُ: الطَّاعَةُ.

ePSD: ad

ad [BEAD] wr. ad "bead"

ad [LOG] wr. ad; ĝešad "log; plank; raft"

ad [VOICE] wr. ad "voice; cry; noise" Akk. rigmu

adda [FATHER] wr. ad-da; ad "father" Akk. abu

أدد (لسان العرب) الإِدُّ والإِدَّةُ: العَجبُ والأَمر الفظيع العظيم والداهية، وكذلك الآدّ مثل الفاعل، وجمعُ الإِدَّة إِدَدٌ؛ وأَمر إِدٌّ وصف به؛ هذه عن اللحياني. والأَدُّ: الغلبةُ والقوّةُ؛ قال: نَضَوْنَ عنّي شدّةً وأَدّا، من بعدِ ما كنتُ صُمُلاً نَهدا وأَدّت الناقة: والإِبل تؤدّ أَدّاً: رجّعت الحنين في أَجوافها. وأَدُّ الناقة: حنينها ومدّها لصوتها؛ عن كراع. وأَدّ البعيرُ يؤدّ أَدّاً: هَدَر. وأَدّ الشيءَ والحبل يؤدّه أَدّاً: مدّه. وأَدّ في الأَرض يؤدّ أَدّاً: ذهب. وأَددُ الطريق: دَررُه. والأَدُّ: صوتَ الوطء؛ قال الشاعر:يَتْبَعُ أَرضاً جِنُّها يُهوّلُ، أَدٌّ وسَجْعٌ ونَهيمٌ هَتْمَلُ والأَديد: الجبلة.

أدد (الصّحاح في اللغة) أَدَّتِ الناقة تَؤُدُّ أَدّاً، إذا رَجَعَتْ الحنينَ في جوفها. والأَديدُ: الجلبةُ. والأَدُّ أيضاً: القوة.

ePSD: gi4

gi [KILL] wr. gi4 "kill" Akk. dâku

gi [TURN] wr. gi4; gi "to turn, return; to go around; to change status; to return (with claims in a legal case); to go back (on an agreement)" Akk. lamû; târu

قيأ (لسان العرب) وتَقَيَّأَتِ المرأَةُ: تَعرَّضَتْ لبَعْلِها وأَلْقَتْ نَفْسَها عليه. الليث: تَقَيَّأَتِ المَرأَةُ لزوجها، وتَقَيُّؤُها: تَكسُّرها له وإِلقاؤُها نفسَها عليه وتَعرُّضُها له. قال الشاعر: تَقَيَّأَتْ ذاتُ الدَّلالِ والخَفَرْ * لِعابسٍ، جافِي الدَّلالِ، مُقْشَعِرّ قال الأزهري: تقَيَّأَت، بالقاف، بهذا المعنى عندي: تصحيف، والصواب تفَيَّأَتْ،بالفاءِ، وتفَيُّؤُها: تثنّيها وتكسُّرها عليه، من الفَيْءِ، وهو الرُّجوع .

جيأ (لسان العرب) المَجِيء: الإِتيان. جاء جَيْئاً ومَجِيئاً. وأَجاءَه إِلى الشيء: جاءَ به وأَلجأَه واضطرَّه اليه؛ وأَجأْتُه أي جِئتُ به. وجايأَني، على فاعَلني، وجاءاني فَجئْتُه أَجيئه أي غالبَني بكثرة المَجيء فغلَبْتُه. وجايا: لغة في جاءا، وهو من البَدليّ. ابن الأَعرابي: جايأَني الرجل من قُرْب أي قابلَني ومَرَّ بي، مُجايأَة أي مقابلة؛ قال الأَزهري: هو من جِئْتُه مَجيئاً ومَجيئةً: فأَنا جاءٍ. أَبو زيد: جايأْتُ فلاناً: إذا وافَقْت مَجيئَه. ويقال: لو قد جاوَزْتَ هذا المكان لجايأْتَ الغَيْث مُجايأَةً وجِياءً أي وافقته. وأَجاءَه إِلى الشيء: جاءَ به وأَلجأَه واضطرَّه اليه؛

ePSD: ad gi4

ad gi [ADVISE] wr. ad gi4 "to advise, give advice" Akk. malāku

القُوقُ (القاموس المحيط) والقاقُ: الأَحْمَقُ الطائِشُ. وقاقَتِ الدَّجاجَةُ: صوَّتَتْ، كَقَوْقَأَتْ .

قوق (لسان العرب) وقَاقَ النعامُ: صَوَّت؛ والقَيْقُ والقَقْوُ والقَوْقُ: صوت الغِرْغِرَة إذا أرادت السِّفاد وهي الدجاجة السندية
قيق (لسان العرب) ابن الأَعرابي: القَيْقُ صوت الدجاجة إذا دعت الديك للسِّفاد، وقال أيضاً: القِيقُ الجبل المحيط بالدنيا .
القَيْقُ (القاموس المحيط) القَيْقُ: صَوْتُ الدَّجاجَةِ إذا دَعَتِ الديكَ للسِّفادِ، وبالكسر: الأَحْمَقُ الطائِشُ، والجَبَلُ المُحيطُ بالدُّنيا.

C.9

ePSD: AN
an [SKY] wr. an "sky, heaven; upper; crown (of a tree)" Akk. šamû
an [SPADIX] wr. a2-an; an "date spadix" Akk. sissinnu
diĝir [DEITY] wr. diĝir; dim3-me-er; dim3-me8-er; dim3-mi-ir; di-me2-er "deity, god, goddess" Akk. iltu; ilu
ilu [GOD] wr. ilu "god" Akk. ilu

عن (مقاييس اللغة) العين والنون أصلان، أحدهما يدلُّ على ظهورِ الشيء وإعراضه، والآخر يدلُّ على الحَبْس. قال طُفيل: ويقال إنّ الجبلَ الذاهبَ في السّماء يقال [له] عان، وجمعها عَوَانٍ.
عَنَّ (القاموس المحيط) عَنَّ الشيءُ يَعِنُّ ويَعُنُّ عَنَاً وعَنَناً وعُنوناً: إذا ظَهَرَ أمامَكَ، واعْتَرَضَ، و"عَنْ"، مُخَفَّفَة على ثَلاثَةِ أوْجُهٍ: تكونُ حَرْفاً جارًا، ولها عشرةُ مَعانٍ: المُجَاوَزَةُ: سافَرَ عن البَلَدِ، البَدَلُ: {لا تَجْزي نَفْسٌ ع نَفْسٍ شيئاً}، الاسْتِعْلاءُ: {فإنّما يَبْخَلُ عن نَفْسِه}، التَّعْليلُ: {وما كان اسْتِغْفارُ إبراهيمَ لأبيهِ إلاَّ عن مَوْعِدَةٍ}، مُرادَفَةُ بَعْدَ: {عَمّا قَليلٍ لَيُصْبِحُنَّ نادمينَ}، الظَّرْفِيَّةُ: ولا تَكُ عن حَمْلِ الرِّباعَةِ وانِيا بدَليل: {ولا تَنِيا في ذِكْري}، مُرادَفَة مِنْ: {وهو الذي يَقْبَلُ التَّوْبَةَ عن عبادِهِ}، مرادفة الباءِ: {وما يَنْطِقُ عن الهَوى}، الاسْتِعانَةُ: رَمَيْتُ عن القَوْسِ، أي: به. قاله ابنُ مالِكٍ، الزائِدَةُ للتَّعويضِ عن أُخْرَى مَحْذوفَةٍ: أتَجْزَعُ إن نَفْسٌ أتاها حِمامُها **** فَهَلاَّ التي عن بَيْنَ جَنْبَيْك تَدْفَعُ فَحُذِفَتْ "عن" من أوّلِ المَوْصولِ، وزِيدَتْ بَعْدَهُ. وتكونُ مَصْدَرِيَّةً، وذلك في عَنْعَنَةِ تَميمٍ: أعْجَبَنِي عن تَفْعَلَ. وتكونُ اسْماً بمَعْنَى جانِبٍ: مِنْ عَنْ يَميني مَرَّةً وأمامِي وكقَوْله: على عن يَميني مَرَّتِ الطَّيْرُ سُنَّحا .
عنن (لسان العرب) عَنَّ الشيءُ يَعِنُّ ويَعُنُّ عَنَناً وعُنُوناً: ظَهَرَ أَمامك؛ وامرأَة مِعَنَّة: تَعْتَنُّ وتَعْتَرِض في كل شيء؛ وفي حديث طهفة: بَرِئنا إليك من الوَثَن والعَنَن؛ الوَثَنُ: الصنم، والعَنَن: الاعتراض، من عَنَّ الشيء أي اعترض كأَنه قال: برئنا إليك من الشرك والظلم، وقيل: أراد به الخلافَ والباطل؛ ومنه حديث سطيح: أَم فازَ فازْلَمَّ به شَأْوُ العَنَنْ. يريد اعتراض الموت وسَبْقَه. والمُعانَّة: المعارضة. وفي الحديث: لو بَلَغَتْ خَطيئَتُه عَنانَ السماء؛ العَنَان، بالفتح: السحاب، ورواه بعضهم أَعْنان، بالأَلف، فإِن كان المحفوظ أَعْنان فهي النواحي؛ قاله أَبو عبيد؛ قال يونس بن حبيب: أَعْنانُ كل شيء نواحيه، فأَما الذي نحكيه نحن فأَعْناءُ السماء نواحيها؛ قاله أَبو عمرو وغيره. وفي الحديث: مَرَّتْ به سحابةٌ فقال: هل تدرون ما اسم هذه؟ قالوا: هذه السحابُ، قال: والمُزْنُ، قالوا: والمزن، قال: والعَنان، قالوا: والعَنانُ؛ وقيل: العَنان التي تُمسِكُ الماءَ، وأَعْنانُ السماء نواحيها، واحدها عَنَنٌ وعَنٌّ. وأَعْنان السماء: صَفائحُها وما اعترَضَ من أَقطارها كأَنه جمع عَنَن. قال يونس: ليس لمَنْقوصِ البيان بَهاءٌ ولو حَكَّ بيافُوخِه أَعْنان السماء، والعامة تقول: عَنان السماء، وقيل: عَنانُ السماء ما عَنَّ لك منها إِذا نظرت إِليها أَي ما بدا لك منها. وعَنِّ: بمعنى عَلِّي أَي لَعَلِّي؛ قال القُلاخُ: يا صاحِبَيَّ، عَرِّجا قَليلا، عَنَّا نُحَيّي الطَّلَلَ المُحِيلا. وأَعْنانُ الشجر: أَطرافُه ونواحيه . وعَنانُ الدار: جانبها الذي يَعُنُّ لك أَي يَعْرِضُ.

C.10

ePSD: pad
pad [BREAK] wr. pad "to break (into bits)" Akk. kasāpu
pad [FIND] wr. pad3 "to find, discover; to name, nominate" Akk. atû; nabû

فود (لسان العرب) واستفاده: اقْتَناه. وأَفَدْتُه أَنا: أَعطيْتُه إِياه وسيأْتي بعض ذلك في ترجمة فيد لأَن الكلمة يائية وواوية.
الفَوْدُ (القاموس المحيط) وأفادَهُ واسْتَفادَهُ وتَفَيَّدَهُ: اقْتَناهُ. وأفَدْتُهُ أنا: أعْطَيْتُهُ إيّاهُ، ورجلٌ مِتْلافٌ مِفْوادٌ ومِفْيادٌ، أي: مُتْلِفٌ مُفيدٌ، ويقالُ: هُما يَتَفاوَدانِ العِلْمَ، والصَّوابُ: يتفايَدانِ، أي: يُفيدُ كُلٌّ صاحِبَهُ .
فيد (لسان العرب) الفائدةُ: ما أَفادَ اللهُ تعالى العبدَ من خيرٍ يَسْتَفيدُه ويَسْتَحْدِثُه، وجمعها الفَوائِدُ. ابن شميل: يقال إِنهما لَيَتَفايَدانِ بالمال بينهما أَي يُفِيدُ كل واحد منهما صاحبه.
فادَ (القاموس المحيط) و~ الفائدَةُ: حَصَلَتْ. والفائدةُ: ما اسْتَفَدْتَ من عِلْمٍ أو مالٍ، ج: فَوائِدُ. وفَيَّدَ تَفْييداً: تَطَيَّرَ من صَوْتِ الفَيَّادِ. وأفَدْتُ المالَ: اسْتَفَدْتُهُ، وأعْطَيْتُه، ضِدٌّ. وهُما يَتَفايَدانِ بالمالِ: يُفيدُ كُلٌّ صاحبَه، ولا تَقُل: يَتفاوَدانِ.

ePSD: mu
mu [CRUSH] wr. mu11; ma5; mu7 "to crush, mangle" Akk. hašû
mu [FISH] wr. mu11(|KAxSAR|)ku6 "a fish"
mu [GOOD] wr. mu5 "good, beautiful" Akk. banû
mu [GROW] wr. mu2; mu2-mu2 "to grow"
mu [INCANTATION] wr. mu7 "incantation, spell" Akk. šiptu

mu [MANLY] wr. mu6 "manly; young man" Akk. eṭlu
mu [NAME] wr. mu "name; line of text; son" Akk. šumu
mu [SOUND] wr. mu7 "to make a sound"
mu [YEAR] wr. mu "year" Akk. šattu

مع (الصّحاح في اللغة) مَعَ: كلمةٌ تدلُّ على المصاحبة. قال محمد بن السَريّ: الذي يدلُّ على أنَّ مَعَ اسمٌ حركةُ آخرِه مع تحرُّك ما قبله، وقد يسكَّن وينوَّن تقول: جاءوا معاً .

معع (لسان العرب) ومَعَ، بتحريك العين: كلمة تضم الشيء إلى الشيء وهي اسم معناه الصحبة وأَصلها مَعاً، وذكرها الأَزهري في المعتلّ؛ قال محمد بن السريّ: الذي يدل على أن مَعَ اسمٌ حركة آخره مع تحرك ما قبله، وقد يسَكن وينَوّنُ، تقول: جاؤوا مَعاً. الأَزهري في ترجمة معاً: وقال الليث كنا معاً معناه كنا جميعاً.

E.1

ePSD: zi
zi [CHIRP] wr. zi "to chirp (birds)" Akk. ṣabāru ša iṣṣuri
zi [CUT] wr. zi2; zi; zix(|IGI@g|) "to cut, remove; to erase" Akk. baqāmu; barāšu; naṭāpu; nasāhu
zi [LIFE] wr. zi; ši; ši-i "life" Akk. napištu

ذا (لسان العرب) قال أَبو العباس أَحمد بن يحيى ومحمد بن زيد: ذا يكون بمعنى هذا، وم نه قول الله عز وجل: مَنْ ذا الذي يَشْفع عِنده إلا بإذنه؛وقد استُعْمِلت ذا مكان الذي كقوله تعالى: ويَسأَلونك ماذا يُنْفِقُون قل العَفْوُ؛ أَي ما الذي ينفقون فيمن رفع الجواب فَرَفْعُ العَفْوِ يدلّ على أَن ما مرفوعة بالابتداء وذا خبرها ويُنْفِقُون صِلةُ ذا، وأَنه ليس ما وذا جميعاً كالشيء الواحد، هذا هو الوجه عند سيبويه، وإِن كان قد أَجاز الوجهَ الآخر مع الرفع. وذي، بكسر الذال، للمؤنث وفيه لُغاتٌ: ذِي وذِهْ، الهاء بدل من الياء،

نفس (لسان العرب) النَّفْس: الرُّوحُ، قال ابن سيده: وبينهما فرق ليس من غرض هذا الكتاب، قال أَبو إِسحق: النَّفْس في كلام العرب يجري على ضربين: أَحدهما قولك خَرَجَتْ نَفْس فلان أَي رُوحُه، وفي نفس فلان أَن يفعل كذا وكذا أَي في رُوعِه، والضَّرْب الآخر معْنى النَّفْس فيه معْنى جُمْلَةِ الشيء وحقيقته. ويقال: ما رأَيت ثَمَّ نفساً أَي ما رأَيت أَحداً. ابن الأَعرابي: النَّفْس العَظَمَةُ والكِبر والنَّفْس العِزَّة والنَّفْس الهِمَّة والنَّفْس عين الشيء وكُنْهه وجَوْهَره، والنَّفْس الأَنَفة والنَّفْس العين التي تصيب المَعِين.

زَدَى (القاموس المحيط) والزَّدْوُ: مَدُّ اليَدِ نحوَ الشيء. وأزْدَى: صَنَعَ معروفاً. وأحمدُ بنُ محمدِ بن مُزْدَى: مُحَدِّثُ الحَرَمِ، ويقالُ: مُسْدَى.

زدا (لسان العرب) الزَّدْوُ: كالسَّدْوِ؛ وفي التهذيب: لغة في السَّدْوِ، وهو من لعب الصبيان بالجوز. قال ابن بري: قال يعقوب الزَّدَى الزيادة من قولك أَزْدَى على كذا أَي زادَ عليه؛ قال كثير: له عَهْدُ وُدٍّ لَمْ يُكَدَّرْ، يَزِينُه زَدَى قَوْلِ مَعْروفٍ حديثٍ ومُزْمِنِ أَبو عبيد: الزَّدْو لغة في السَّدْو، وهو مَدُّ اليَدِ نحوَ الشيء كما تَسْدُو الإِبلُ في سَيْرِها بأَيْدِيها .

سدو (مقاييس اللغة) قال الخليل: زَدْوُ الصِّبيان بالجوز إنّما هو السَّدو .

سدا (لسان العرب) السَّدْوُ: مَدُّ اليَدِ نحوَ الشيء كما تَسْدُو الإِبلُ في سيرها بأَيديها وكما يَسدو الصِّبيانُ إِذا لعِبُوا بالجَوْز فرَمَوْا به في الحَفِيرة، والزَّدْوُ لغة كما قالوا للأَسْدِ أَزْدٌ، وللسَّرَادِ زَرَادٌ. وسَدا يديه سَدْواً واسْتَدَى: مَدّ بهما؛ والسَّدَى: المعروفُ، وقد أَسْدى إِليه سَدىً وسَدّاه عليه. أَبو عمرو: أَزْدى إِذا اصْطَنع معروفاً، وأَسدى إِذا أَصْلح بين اثنين، وأَصدى إِذا مات، وأَصْدى إِناءَه إِذا مَلأَه (* قوله «واصدى اناءه إذا ملأه» هكذا في الأَصل). وفي الحديث: من أَسْدى إِليكم معروفاً فكافِئُوه، أَسْدى وأَوْلى وأَعْطَى بمعنًى.

زأد (مقاييس اللغة) الزاء والهمزة والدال كلمة واحدة، تدلُّ على الفزع. يقال زُئِد الرّجُل، إذا فزِع، زُؤْداً.

ePSD: he
he [BE] wr. he2; he2-a "be it, be he"

ePSD: dalla
dalla [BRIGHT] wr. dalla "(to be) bright; (to be) impetuous, fierce" Akk. ellu
dalla [RING] wr. dalla "ring; crown" Akk. kamkammatu

دول (لسان العرب) الليث: الدَّوْلة والدُّولة لغتان، ومنه الإدالةُ الغَلَبة. وأَدالَنا الله من عدوِّنا: من الدَّوْلة؛ يقال: اللهم أَدِلْني على فلان وانصرني عليه. وفي حديث وفد ثقيف: نُدالُ عليهم ويُدالون علينا؛ الإِدالةُ: الغَلَبة، يقال: أُدِيل لنا على أَعدائنا أَي نُصِرْنا عليهم، وكانت الدَّوْلة لنا، والدَّوْلة: الانتقال من حال الشدَّة إِلى الرَّخاء؛ ومنه حديث أَبي سُفْيان وهِرَقْل: نُدالُ عليه ويُدالُ علينا أَي نَغْلِبه مرة ويَغلبنا أُخرى. ودالَت الأَيامُ أَي دارت، والله يُداوِلها بين الناس. وتداولته الأَيدي: أَخذته هذه مرَّة وهذه مرَّة.

E.3

ePSD: ed

ed [ASCEND] wr. ed3; |UD×U+U+U.DU| "to go up or down; to demolish; to scratch; to rage, be rabid" Akk. arādu; elû; naqāru; šegû
ed [PIERCE] wr. e11 "pierce"
ed [STRENGTHEN] wr. e11 "strengthen"
عدا (لسان العرب) وأَعْدَيْتُ فرسي: اسْتَحضَرته. وأَعْدَيْت في مَنْطِقِكَ أَي جُرت. ويقال للخَيْل المُغِيرة: عادِيَة؛ والعَدَوانُ والعَدَّاء، كلاهما: الشَّديدُ العَدْوِ؛ وتعادَى القومُ على نصرهم أَي تَوالَوْا وتَتابَعوا.

مَارَ (القاموس المحيط) مَارَ يَمُورُ مَوْراً: تَرَدَّدَ في عَرْضٍ، وأَتَى نَجداً، و~ الدَّمُ: جَرَى. وأَمَارَهُ: أسالَهُ. والمَوْرُ: المَوْجُ، والاضْطِرابُ، والجَرَيانُ على وَجْهِ الأرضِ، والتَّحرُّكُ، والطريقِ المَوْطوءُ المُسْتَوِي، والشيءُ اللَّيِّنُ، ونَتْفُ الصُّوفِ، وساحِلٌ لِقُرى اليَمَنِ شِمالِيَّ زَبِيدَ، وبالضم: الغُبارُ المُتَرَدِّدُ، والتُّرابُ تُثيرُهُ الريحُ. وناقةٌ مَوَّارَةٌ: سَهْلَةُ السَّيْرِ، سَرِيعَةٌ.
مور (لسان العرب) والمَوْرُ: السرعة؛ وأَنشد: ومَشْيُهُنَّ بالحَبِيبِ مَوْر ومارَتِ الناقةُ في سيرها مَوْراً: ماجَتْ وتَرَدّدتْ؛ وناقة مَوّارَةُ اليد، وفي المحكم: مَوّارَةٌ سَهْلَةُ السيْرِ سَرِيعة؛

E.5

ePSD: še
še [BARLEY] wr. še "barley; grain; a unit of length; a unit of area; a unit of volume; a unit of weight" Akk. uţţatu; û; uţţatu
še [CALL] wr. še21 "to call by name" Akk. nabû
še [CONE] wr. ĝešše "(conifer) cone"
še [CVNE] wr. še "(compound verb nominal element)"
še [HOOK?] wr. še "hook?"
še [PLANT] wr. šesar "a plant"
še [SHAPE] wr. še "a geometric shape"
še [TEAR] wr. šex(|IGI@g|) "tear"
še [THAT] wr. še "that"
še [UNMNG] wr. še3 "?" Akk. ?

ePSD: la
la [STRETCH] wr. la2 "to stretch out; to be in order" Akk. tarāşu

لعا (لسان العرب) واللاعي: الذي يُفزعه أَدنى شيء؛ واللاعي: الخاشِي؛ وقال ابن الأَعرابي في قول الشاعر: داوِيَة شَتَّتْ على اللاعي السَّلِعْ، وإنما النَّوْمُ بها مِثْلُ الرَّضع قال الأَصمعي: اللاعي من اللَّوْعةِ. قال الأَزهري: كأَنه أَراد اللاَّئع فقلب، وهو ذو اللَّوعة، والرَّضع: مصة بعد مصة. أَبو سعيد: يقال هو يَلْعى به ويَلْغى به أَي يتولع به. ابن الأَعرابي: الأَلْعاء السُّلامَياتُ. قال الأَزهري في هذه الترجمة: وأَعْلاء الناسِ الطِّوال من الناس. ولَعاً كلمة يُدعَى بها للعاثر معناها الارتفاع؛

ePSD: giri
giri [CRY] wr. giri16 "a cry"
giri [SEAT] wr. girix(|GIŠ.LU2|); girix(|GIŠ.ŠU.LU2|) "a seat" Akk. nēmedu
giri [UNMNG] wr. girix(LU2) ""
جعر (لسان العرب) الجِعَارُ: حبل يَشُدُّ به المُسْتَقِي وَسَطَهُ إذا نزل في البئر لئلا يقع فيها، وطرفه في يد رجل فإن سقط مَدَّه به؛
جأر (لسان العرب) جَأَرَ يَجْأَرُ جَأْ◌راً وجُؤَاراً: رفع صوته مع تضرع واستغاثة. وفي التنزيل: إذا هُمْ يَجْأَرُون؛ وقال ثعلب: هو رفع الصوت إليه بالدعاء. وجَأَر الرجلُ إلى الله عز وجل إذا تضرّع بالدعاءِ. وجَأَرَ النبتُ: طال وارتفع، وجَأَرت الأَرض بالنبات كذلك؛

ePSD: sub
sub [COAT] wr. sub6 "to complete, perfect; to coat" Akk. šuklulu
sub [GO] wr. sub2 "imperfect plural stem of ĝen[to go]" Akk. alāku
sub [RUB] wr. su-ub; sub; sub6 "to suck; to rub" Akk. naşābu

sub [SEDGE] wr. sub5 "rush, sedge" Akk. šuppatu
sub [UNMNG] wr. subx(KAL) "?" Akk. ?

نصب (لسان العرب) النَّصَبُ: الإِعْياءُ من العَناءِ. والفعلُ نَصِبَ الرجلُ، بالكسر،نَصَباً: أَعيا وتَعِبَ؛ وأَنْصَبه هو، وأَنْصَبَنِي هذا الأَمْرُ. وهَمٌّ ناصِبٌ مُنْصِبٌ: ذو نَصَبٍ، مثل تامِرٍ ولابِنٍ، وهو فاعلٌ بمعنى مفعول، لأَنه يُنْصَبُ فيه ويُتْعَبُ. وفي الحديث: فاطمةُ بَضْعةٌ مِنِّي، يُنْصِبُنِي ما أَنْصَبَها أَي يُتْعِبُني ما أَتْعَبَها. والنَّصَبُ التَّعَبُ؛ قال النابغة: كِلِيني لِهَمٍّ، يا أُمَيْمَةَ، ناصِبِ قال: ناصِب، بمعنى مَنْصُوب؛ وقال الأَصمعي: ناصِب ذي نَصَبٍ، مثلُ لَيْلٌ نائمٌ ذو نوم يُنامُ فيه، ورجل دارِعٌ ذو دِرْعٍ؛ ويقال: نَصَبٌ ناصِبٌ، مثل مَوْتٌ مائِت، وشِعْرٌ شاعر؛ وقال سيبويه: هَمٌّ ناصِبٌ، هو على النَّسَب. وحكى أَبو عليٍّ في التَّذْكرة: نَصَبه الهَمُّ؛ فناصِبٌ إِذاً على الفِعْل. قال الجوهري: ناصِبٌ فاعل بمعنى مفعول فيه، لأَنه يُنْصَبُ فيه ويُتْعَبُ، كقولهم: لَيْلٌ نائمٌ أَي يُنامُ فيه، ويوم عاصِفٌ أَي تَعْصِفُ فيه الريح. قال ابن بري: وقد قيل غير هذا القول، وهو الصحيح، وهو أَن يكون ناصِبٌ بمعنى مُنْصِبٍ، مثل مكان باقلٌ بمعنى مُبْقِل، وعليه قول النابغة؛ وقال أَبو طالب: أَلا مَنْ لِهَمٍّ، آخِرَ اللَّيْلِ، مُنْصِبِ قال: فناصِبٌ، على هذا، ومُنْصِب بمعنًى. قال: وأَما قوله ناصِبٌ بمعنى مَنْصوب أَي مفعول فيه، فليس بشيء. وفي التنزيل العزيز: فإِذا فَرَغْتَ فانْصَبْ؛ قال قتادة: فإِذا فرغتَ من صَلاتِكَ، فانْصَبْ في الدُّعاءِ؛ قال الأَزهري: هو من نَصِبَ يَنْصَبُ نَصَباً إِذا تَعِبَ؛ وقيل: إِذا فرغت من الفريضة، فانْصَبْ في النافلة.

صب (مقاييس اللغة) الصاد والباء أصلٌ واحدٌ، وهو إراقة الشيء، وإليه ترجع فروعُ الباب كلّه.من ذلك صَبَبت الماءَ أصبُّه صَبّاً. ويُحمَل على ذلك فيقال لِما انحدرَ من الأرض صَبَبٌ، وجمعه أصباب، كأنَّه شيءٌ منصبٌّ في انحداره. وفي الحديث: "أنَّه كان صلى الله عليه وآله وسلم إذا مشى فكأنّما يمشي في صَبَب. الراجز:والصُّبَّة: القِطعةُ من الخيل، كأنَّها تنصبُّ في الإغارة انصباباً، والقِطعةُ من الغَنَم أيضاً صُبَّة، لذلك المعنى. ويقال للحيّات الأساود: الصُّبُّ، وذلك أنها إذا أرادت النكزَ انصبَّتْ على الملدوغ انصباباً .

صبب (لسان العرب) صبَّ الماءَ ونحوه يَصُبُّه صبّاً فَصُبَّ وانْصَبَّ وتَصَبَّبَ: أَراقه، وصَبَبْتُ الماءَ: سَكَبْتُه. ويقال: صَبَبْتُ لفلان ماءً في القَدَحِ ليشربه، واصْطَبَبْتُ لنفسي ماءً من القِربة لأَشربه، واصْطَبَبْتُ لنفسي قدحاً. وفي الحديث: فقام إِلى شَجْبٍ فاصْطَبَّ منه الماءَ؛ هو افتعل من الصَّبِّ أَي أَخذه لنفسه. والماءُ يَنْصَبُّ من الجبل، ويَتَصَبَّبُ من الجبل أَي يَتَحَدَّر. والصُّبَّة: السُّفرة لأَن الطعام يُصَبُّ فيها؛ وقيل: هي شبه السُّفْرة. وفي صفة النبي، صلى الله عليه وسلم، أَنه كان إِذا مشى كأَنه يَنْحَطُّ في صَبَبٍ أَي في موضع مُنْحدر؛ وقال ابن عباس: أَراد به أَنه قويّ البدن، فإِذا مشى فكأَنه يمشي على صَدْر قدميه من القوة؛ وحديث الصلاة: لم يَصُبَّ رأْسَه أَي يُمَيِّله إِلى أَسفل. ومنه حديث أُسامة: فجعل يَرْفَعُ يده إِلى السماءِ ثم يَصُبُّها عليَّ، أَعرف أَنه يدعو لي.

سبب (لسان العرب) والسَّبَّةُ: الاسْتُ. والسَّبَبُ كلُّ شيءٍ يُتَوَصَّلُ به إِلى غيره؛ وفي نُسْخةٍ: كلُّ شيءٍ يُتَوَسَّلُ به إِلى شيءٍ غيرِه، وقد تَسَبَّبَ إِليه، والجمعُ أَسْبابٌ؛ وكلُّ شيءٍ يُتَوصَّلُ به إِلى الشيءِ، فهو سَبَبٌ. وقال أَبو عبيدة: السَّبَبُ كلُّ حَبْلٍ حَدَرْتَه من فوق.

سيب (لسان العرب) والسِّيبُ: مَجْرى الماءِ، وجَمْعُه سُيُوبٌ. وسابَ يَسِيبُ: مشى مُسْرِعاً. وسابَتِ الحَيَّةُ تَسِيبُ إِذا مَضَتْ مُسْرِعةً؛ سابَ الماءُ وانْساب إِذا جرى .

الصَّوْبُ (القاموس المحيط) الصَّوْبُ: الانْصِبابُ، كالانْصِيابِ، والصَّيِّبُ، كالصَّيُّوبِ، وضِدُّ الخَطأَ،

ePSD: ba
ba [ALLOT] wr. ba "to divide into shares, share, halve; to allot" Akk. qiāšu; zâzu
ba [ANIMAL] wr. ba "a marine creature?"
ba [GARMENT] wr. tug2ba13 "a garment" Akk. nalbašu
ba [HALF] wr. ba3; ba7 "half; thirty" Akk. bāmtu; mišlu; šalāšā
ba [TOOL] wr. ĝešba "a cutting tool" Akk. suppīnu
ba [VESSEL] wr. dugba "type of vessel"

با (لسان العرب) الباء حرف هجاء من حروف المعجم، وأكثر ما ترد بمعنى الإلصاق لما ذُكر قبلها من اسم أو فعل بما انضمت إليه، وقد ترِدُ بمعنى المُلابسة والمُخالَطة، وبمعنى من أجل ، وبمعنى في ومن وعن ومع، وبمعنى الحال والعوض، وزائدة، وكلُّ هذه الأقسام قد جاءت في الحديث، وتعرف بسياق اللفظ الواردة فيه، والباء التي تأتي للإلصاق كقولك: أمسكت بزيد، وتكون للاستعانة كقولك: ضربتُ بالسيف، وتكون للإضافة كقولك: مررت بزيد. قال ابن جني: أما ما يحكيه أصحاب الشافعي من أن الباءَ للتبعيض فشيء لا يعرفه أصحابنا ولا ورد به بيت، وتكون للقسم كقولك: بالله لأَفْعَلَنَّ.

ePSD: gub
gub [BATHE] wr. gub2 "to bathe, wash oneself; (to be) pure" Akk. ramāku
gub [STAND] wr. gub "to stand; (to be) assigned (to a task)" Akk. izuzzu
gub [~SHEEP] wr. gub "a designation of sheep or goats"

جبب (لسان العرب) الجَبُّ: القَطْعُ. جَبَّه يَجُبُّه جَبّاً وجِباباً واجْتَبَّه وجَبَّ خُصاه جَبّاً: اسْتأْصَله. وخَصِيٌّ مَجْبُوبٌ بَيِّنُ الجِبابِ. والمَجْبُوبُ: الخَصِيُّ الذي قد اسْتُؤْصِلَ ذكره وخُصْياه. وقد جُبَّ جَبّاً. وفي حديث مَأْبُورٍ الخَصِيِّ الذي أَمر النبيُّ، صلى الله عليه وسلم، بقَتْله لَمَّا اتُّهِمَ بالزنا: فإِذا هو مَجْبُوبٌ. أَي مقطوع الذكر. وفي حديث زِنْباعٍ: أَنه جَبَّ غُلاماً له.

الجَبَبُ (القاموس المحيط) والجَبْجَبُ: المُسْتَوِي من الأرضِ. وجَبْجَبَ: ساخَ في الأرضِ.

جوب (لسان العرب) والجَوْبةُ فَضاءٌ أَملَسُ سَهْلٌ بَيْنَ أَرْضَيْنِ. وقال أَبو حنيفة: الجَوْبةُ من الأَرضِ: الدارةُ، وهي المكانُ المُنْجابُ الوطِيءُ من الأَرض، القليلُ الشجرِ مِثْلُ الغائط المُسْتَدير، ولا يكون في رَمْلٍ ولا جَبَلٍ، إِنما يكون في أَجلاد الأَرض ورحابِها، سمي جَوْبةً لانْجِيابِ الشجر عنها، والجمع جَوْباتٌ، وجُوَبٌ، نادر. وقال غيره: الأَصل جاب يجوب مثل طاع يَطُوعُ. قال: والأَصل الإِصابةُ مِن صاب يَصُوبُ إِذا قَصَدَ، وانجابَتِ الناقةُ: مَدَّت عُنُقَها للحَلَبِ، قال: وأُراه مِن هذا كأَنَّها أَجابَتْ حالِبَها، على أَنـا لم نَجِدِ انْفَعَل مِنْ أَجابَ. قال أَبو سعيد قال لي أَبو عَمْرو بن العلاءِ: اكْتُبْ لي الهمز، فكتبته له فقال لي: سَلْ عن انْجابَتِ الناقةُ أَمَهْموز أَمْ لا؟ فسأَلت، فلم أَجده مهموزاً.
وجب (لسان العرب) وَجَبَ الشيءُ يَجِبُ وُجوباً أَي لزمَ. وأَوجَبهُ هو، وأَوجَبَه الله، واسْتَوْجَبَه أَي اسْتَحَقَّه.

E.6

ePSD: mi
mi [CVNE] wr. mi2 "(compound verb nominal element)"
mi [PRAISE] wr. mi2 "praise"

معس (العباب الزاخر) المَعْسُ والمَعْكُ: الدَّلْكُ، يقال: مَعَسْتُ المَنِيئَةَ في الدِّباغ: إذا دَلَكْتَها دَلْكاً شَدِيداً.
محس (لسان العرب) ابن الأَعرابي: الأَمْحَسُ الدَّبّاغُ الحاذِقُ. قال الأَزهري: المَحْسُ والمَعْسُ دَلْك الجِلْدِ ودِباغُه، أَبْدِلَت العينُ حاء .
معش (لسان العرب) ابن الأَعرابي: المَعْشُ، بالشين المعجمة، الدَّلْكُ الرفيق، قال الأَزهري: وهو المَعْسُ، بالسين المهملة أَيضاً. يقال: مَعَشَ إِهابَه مَعْشاً، وكأَن المَعْش أَهْونُ من المَعْس .
معت (لسان العرب) مَعَتَ الأَدِيمَ يَمْعَتُه مَعْتاً: دَلَكه، وهو نحوٌ من الدَّلْكِ .

ePSD: dug
dug [BIRD] wr. dug3mušen; dumušen "a bird"
dug [GOOD] wr. dug3; ze2-eb; du-uq "(to be) good; (to be) sweet; goodness, good (thing)" Akk. ţābu
dug [POT] wr. dug; dugx(BI) "(clay) pot; a unit of liquid capacity" Akk. karpatu
dug [SPEAK] wr. dug4 "to speak, talk, say; to order; to do, perform; to negotiate" Akk. atwû; dabābu; epēšu; qabû

ضجج (لسان العرب) ضَجَّ يَضِجُّ ضَجّاً وضَجيجاً وضَجَاجاً وضُجاجاً، الأَخيرة عن اللحياني: صاح، والاسم الضَّجَّة.

E.7

ePSD: til
til [COMPLETE] wr. til; til3 "(to be) complete(d); (to be) old, long-lasting; to end" Akk. gamāru; labāru; qatû
til [LIVE] wr. til3 "to live; to sit (down); to dwell" Akk. ašābu; balāţu
til [POLE] wr. til "a pole, part of a wooden object"

طالَ (القاموس المحيط) طالَ طُولاً، بالضم: امْتَدَّ، والطِّيلَةُ، بالكسر: العُمُرُ.
طول (لسان العرب) وأَطَلْتُ الشيءَ وأَطْوَلْت على النقصان والتمام بمعنى. وأَطال الله طِيلَتَه أَي عُمْره. وطالَ طِوَلُك وطِيَلُك أَي عُمْرك، ويقال غَيْبتك؛

ePSD: gin
gin [ESTABLISH] wr. gin6; gi-na; gi-in; ge-en; gin "(to be) permanent; to confirm, establish (in legal contexts), verify; (to be) true; a quality designation; medium quality" Akk. kânu; kīnu
gin [GRASS] wr. gin4; u2|ZI&ZI|; u2|A.ZI&ZI|; u2|ZI&ZI.A|; u2|ZI&ZI.EŠ2.ŠE| "a grass" Akk. kuštu

جعن (لسان العرب) جَعْوَنةُ: من أَسماء العرب. ورجل جَعْوَنة إِذا كان قصيراً سميناً. وقال ابن دريد: الجَعْنُ فعل مُمات، وهو التقبض، قال: ومنه اشتقاق جَعْوَنة، وقد وجدت حاشية قال أَبو جعفر النحاس في كتاب الاشتقاق له: جَعْونةُ اسم رجل مشتق من الجَعْن، وهو وَجَعُ الجسد وتكسُّره، قال: ويجوز أَن يكون مشتقاً من الجَعْو، وهو جمع الشيء، وتكون النون زائدة .
جَحِنَ (القاموس المحيط) جَحِنَ الصَّبِيُّ، كفرِحَ، فهو جَحِنٌ: ساء غِذاؤُهُ، وأَجْحَنَهُ غيرُه. وجَحْوَانُ: اسمٌ. والجَحِنُ، ككتِفٍ: البَطِيءُ الشَّبابِ، والنَّباتُ الضعيفُ الصغيرُ،
جحن (لسان العرب) والجَحِن البَطِيءُ الشباب؛ وكلُّ نبت ضعف فهو جَحِنٌ. والمُجْحَن، بضم الميم، من النبات: القصيرُ القليل الماء.

ePSD: šum
šum [FISH] wr. šumku6 "a fish"

šum [GARLIC] wr. šum2; šum2sar "garlic; onion" Akk. šūmū
šum [GIVE] wr. šum2; ze2-eĝ3 "to give" Akk. nadānu
šum [SLAUGHTER] wr. šum "to slaughter" Akk. ţabāhu

E.8

ePSD: dari
dari [ETERNAL] wr. da-ri2; da-ri; du-ri "(to be)eternal" Akk. dārû
dari [SUPPORT] wr. da-ri "to support"
دور (لسان العرب) دَارَ الشيءُ يَدُورُ دَوْراً ودَوَرَاناً ودُؤُوراً واسْتَدَارَ وأَدَرْتُه أنا ودَوَّرْتُه وأَدَارَه غيره ودَوَّرَ به ودُرْتُ به وأَدَرْت اسْتَدَرْتُ، ودَاوَرَهُ مُدَاوَرَةً ودِوَاراً: دَارَ معه؛ والدهر دَوَّارٌ بالإِنسان ودَوَّارِيٌّ أَي دائر به على إِضافة الشيء إِلى نفسه؛

E.9

ePSD: udbita
udbita [FORMER] wr. ud-bi-ta "former (lit. from those days)"
عود (مقاييس اللغة) العين والواو والدال أصلان صحيحان، يدلُّ أحدهما على تثنيةٍ في الأمر، والآخر جنسٌ من الخشب.فالأوّل: العَوْد، قال الخليل: هو تثنية الأمر عوداً بعد بَدْء. تقول: بدأ ثُمَّ عاد.
با (لسان العرب) الباء حرف هجاء من حروف المعجم، وأَكثر ما تَرِد بمعنى الإِلْصاق لما ذُكِر قَبْلها من اسم أَو فعل بما انضمت إليه، وقد تَرِدُ بمعنى المُلابسة والمُخالَطة، وبمعنى من أَجل ، وبمعنى في ومن وعن ومع، وبمعنى الحال والعوض، وزائدةً، وكلُّ هذه الأَقسامِ قد جاءت في الحديث، وتعرف بسياق اللفظ الواردة فيه، والباء التي تأْتي للإِلصاق كقولك: أَمْسَكْت بزيد، وتكون للاستعانة كقولك: ضَرَبْتُ بالسَّيْف، وتكون للإِضافة كقولك: مررت بزيد. قال ابن جني: أَما ما يحكيه أَصحاب الشافعي من أَن الباءَ للتبعيض فشيء لا يعرفه أَصحابنا ولا ورد به بيت، وتكون للقسم كقولك: بالله لأَفْعَلَنَّ.

E.10

ePSD: numun
numun [GRASS] wr. u2numun2; u2|ZI&ZI|; šu-mu; u2|A.ZI&ZI|; u2|ZI&ZI.A|; u2|ZI&ZI.EŠ2.ŠE|; šu-mu-un "alfalfa grass" Akk. elpetu
numun [INSECT] wr. numun3 "insect(s), bug(s); caterpillar" Akk. kalmatu; nāpû
numun [SEED] wr. numun "seed" Akk. zēru

ePSD: nam
nam [FATE] wr. nam; na-aĝ2 "determined order; will, testament; fate, destiny" Akk. šīmtu
nam [LORD] wr. nam2 "lord"
nam [THOUGHT] wr. nam2 "(fore)thought, plan(ning); understanding; instruction" Akk. ţēmu
النَّمّ (القاموس المحيط) والنامَّةُ: الحِسُّ، والحركَةُ، وحياةُ النَّفْسِ. وأسْكَتَ الله تعالى نامَّتَه: أماته. ونَمَّ المِسْكُ: سَطَعَ.
نأم (لسان العرب) والنامَّةُ: الحِسُّ، والحركَةُ، وحياةُ النَّفْسِ. وأسْكَتَ الله تعالى نامَّتَه: أماته. ونَمَّ المِسْكُ: سَطَعَ. وما بها نُمِّيٌّ أي ما بها أَحدٌ.
والنُّمِّيَّةُ: الطبيعة؛ قال الطرماح: بلا خَدَبٍ ولا خَوَرٍ، إذا ما بَدَتْ نُمِّيَّةُ الخُدْبِ النُّفاةِ ونُمِّيُّ الرجلِ: نُحاسُه وطَبْعُه؛ قال أَبو وجزة: ولولا غيرُهُ لكشَفْتُ عنه، وعن نُمِّيَّةِ الطَّبْعِ اللَّعِينِ
نعم (مقاييس اللغة) النون والعين والميم فروعُه كثيرة، وعندنا أنَّها على كثرتها راجعةٌ إلى أصلٍ واحدٍ يدلُّ على ترفُّهٍ وطِيب عيش وصلاح. منه النِّعمة: ما يُنعِم الله تعالى على عبدِه به من مالٍ وعيش. يقال: للهِ تعالى عليه نِعمة. والنِّعمة المِنَّة، وكذا النَّعْماء .
نعم (لسان العرب) والنَّعامة: الطريق. وشالَتْ نَعامَتُهم: تفرقت كلِمَتُهم وذهب عزُّهم ودَرَسَتْ طريقتُهم وولَّوْا، وقيل: تَحَوَّلوا عن دارهم، وقيل: قَلَّ خَيْرُهم وولَّتْ أُمورُهم؛ والنَّعامة: الجهل، يقال: سكَنَتْ نَعامتُه؛ والنعامة: الرجْل. والنعامة: الساق. والنَّعامة: الفَيْجُ المستعجِل. والنَّعامة: الفَرَح. والنَّعامة: الإكرام. والنَّعامة: المحَجَّة الواضحة. والنَّعَم واحد الأَنْعام وهي المال الراعية؛ قال ابن سيده: النَّعَم الإبل والشاء، يذكر ويؤنث، والنَّعْم لغة فيه؛ عن ثعلب؛ وأَنشد: وأَشْطانُ النَّعامِ مُرَكَّزاتٌ، وحَوْمُ النَّعْمِ والحَلَقُ الحُلول والجمع أَنعامٌ، وأَناعيمُ جمع الجمع؛ قال ذو الرمة: دانى له القيدُ في دَيْمومةٍ قُذُفٍ قَيْنَيْهِ، وانْحَسَرَتْ عنه الأَناعِيمُ وقال ابن الأَعرابي: النعم الإبل خاصة، والأَنعام الإبل والبقر والغنم.
ePSD: lu2-ulu3
lulu [MAN] wr. lu2-lu7; lu2-lu7lu "man; humanity" Akk. amēlu; lullû

ePSD: ak
ak [DO] wr. ak; a "to do; to make; to act, perform; to proceed, proceeding (math.)" Akk. epēšu
عكك (لسان العرب) وعَكَّ الرجلَ يَعُكّه عَكّاً: حَدثه بحديث فاستعاده مرتين أو ثلاثاً، وكذلك عَكَّكْته الحديث: وفي حواشي بعض التهذيب الموثوق بها عن ابن الأَعرابي: أنه سئل عن شيء فقال: سوف أَعُكُّه لك:؛ يريد أُفسّره. وعَكّه يَعُكّه عَكّاً: حبسه. وإِبل مَعْكُوكة أَي محبوسة. وعَكّه عن حاجته يَعُكُّه عَكّاً: عَقله وصَرفه مثل عَجَسَه، وكذلك إِذا مَطَله بحق؛ وقال ابن الأَعرابي في قول رؤبة:ماذا ترى رَأْيَ أَخ قد عَكّا (* قوله «ماذا ترى إلخ» صدره كما في شرح القاموس: يا ابن الرفيع حسباً وبنكا). قال: عَكَّ الرجلُ إِذا أَقام واحْتَبس، وعَكّه بالحجة يَعُكّه عَكّاً: قهره. وعَكّني بالأَمر عَكّاً إِذا ردّده عليك حتى يُتْعِبَك، وكذلك عَكّه بالقول عَكّاً إِذا ردّه عليه متعنتاً. وعَكَّ عليه: عَطَف كَعاكَ .
عكا (لسان العرب) وعَكاهُ عَكْواً: شدَّه. وعكا بالمكان: أَقامَ.
عكو (مقاييس اللغة) العينَ والكاف والحرف المعتلّ أصلٌ صحيحٌ يدلُّ على تجمُّع وغِلَظٍ أيضاً. وهذا صحيح لأنَّه إذا عَقَد ثوبَه فقد عكاه وجمّعه.
ePSD: uru
uru [FISH] wr. uru6ku6; uru7ku6 "a fish" Akk. āru
uru [FLOOD] wr. uru2; uru18; uru5 "flood, deluge" Akk. abūbu
uru [LITTER] wr. uru12 "bedding place; litter; lair, dwelling; dung" Akk. mūšabu; rubşu
uru [SEAT] wr. uru5 "seat, dwelling" Akk. šubtu
uru [SOW] wr. uru4; uru11ru; i-ru "to sow; to cultivate" Akk. erēšu
uru [SUBSCRIPT] wr. uruuru16; u18-ru "a literary subscript"
uru [SUPPORT] wr. uru9 "support; imposition; repair" Akk. imdu; takšīru
uru [VICINITY] wr. uru9 "immediate vicinity, adjacent (place)" Akk. ţēhu
uru [UNMNG] wr. uru10 ""

أور (مقاييس اللغة) والأُوَار: المكانُ.
الأُوَارُ (القاموس المحيط) الأُوَارُ، كغُرابٍ: حَرُّ النارِ والشَّمْسِ، والعَطَشُ، والدُّخانُ، واللَّهَبُ، والجَنوبُ، ج: أُورٌ. والأَوْرُ: الشَّمالُ،
عرا (لسان العرب) وأَعْرَى القومُ صاحِبَهُم: تركوه في مكانه وذَهَبُوا عنه. والعِرْو الناحيةُ، والجمع أَعْراءٌ. والعَرى والعَراةُ: الجنابُ والناحِية والفِناء والساحة. ونزَل في عَراه أَي في ناحِيَتِه؛
العَوَرُ (القاموس المحيط) وعارَهُ يَعُورُهُ ويَعيرُهُ: أخَذَهُ، وذهبَ به، أو أتْلَفَهُ.
عور (لسان العرب) وعارَه يَعُوره أَي أَخذه وذهب به. وحكى اللحياني: أَراك عُرْته وعِرْته أَي ذهبت به.

E.11

ePSD: kur
kur [BURN] wr. kur "to burn, light up" Akk. napāhu
kur [DIFFERENT] wr. kur2; gur "(to be) different; (to be) strange; (to be)estranged; (to be) hostile; to change; to become strange; to alternate (math.)" Akk. nakāru; šanû
kur [ENTER] wr. kur9; kurx(DU); kurx(LIL) "to enter" Akk. erēbu
kur [MOUNTAIN] wr. kur; kir5 "underworld; land, country; mountain(s); east; easterner; east wind" Akk. erşetu; mātu; šadû; šadû
kur [UNIT] wr. kur2; gur2 "unit of capacity based on a vessel size"

ePSD: bal
bal [DIG] wr. ba-al; bal; bal3; bal4; pe-el "to dig, excavate; to unload (a boat)" Akk. herû
bal [RECOVER] wr. ba-al "to recover (goods, property)"
bal [STONE] wr. na4bal "type of stone
ePSD: kurbal
kurbal [COUNTRY] wr. kur-bal "overseas country"
بل (مقاييس اللغة) الباء واللام في المضاعف له أصولٌ خمسة هي معظم الباب. والأصل الثالث: أخذ الشّيءِ والذّهابُ به. يقال بَلَّ فلانٌ بكذا، إذا وَقَعَ في يده. قال ذو الرّمّة:ويقولون: "لئن بَلَّ به لَيَبَلَّنَّ بما يودّه. ومنه قوله: إنّ عليكِ فاعلمنَّ سائقا بَلا بأعْجازِ المَطِيِّ لاحقا، أي ملازماً لأعجازها. ويقال : إنّه لَبَلٌّ بالقرينة. وأنشد وإنّي لَبَلٌّ بالقَرينَةِ ما ارعَوَتْ وإنّي إذا صارَمْتُها لَصَرُومُ، وقال آخر: بَلّتْ عُرَيْنَةُ في اللّقاء بفارسٍ لا طائشٍ رَعِشٍ ولا وَقّافِ، ويقولون: إنّه ليَبَلُّ بهِ الخَيْرُ، أي يوافِقُه.
بلل (شمس العلوم) وبَلِلْتُ بالشيء بَلالَةً: أي ظفرت، يقال: لئن بلَت يدي بك لا تفارقني: أي ظفرت،

بلل (لسان العرب) وبَلِلْتُ بِهِ بَلَلًا: ظَفِرْتُ بِهِ. وَقِيل: بَلِلْتُ أَبَلُّ ظَفِرت بِهِ؛ حَكَاهَا الأَزهري عَن الأَصمعي وَحْدَهُ. وبَلِلت بِهِ بَلَلًا وبَلَالة وبُلُولًا وبَلَلْت: مُنِيت بِهِ وعَلِقْته. وبَلِلْته: لَزِمْته؛ الْجَوْهَرِيُّ: بَلِلْت بِهِ، بِالْكَسْرِ، إِذا ظَفِرت بِهِ وَصَارَ فِي يَدِكَ؛

ePSD: dilmun
dilmun [IMPORTANT] wr. dilmun "(to be) made manifest; (to be) heavy; (to be) important; ritually unclean, impure person; instruction" Akk. kabtu; musukku; têrtu; šûpû
دلم (مقاييس اللغة) الدال واللام أصلٌ يدلُّ على طولٍ وتهدُّل في سواد. فالأدلم من الرِّجال: الطويل الأسود؛ وكذلك هو من الجِمال والجِبال. وزعم ناسٌ أن الدَّيلم: سوادُ اللَّيل وظُلْمته .
دَلِمَ (القاموس المحيط) والأَدْلَمُ: الآدَمُ، والشديدُ السَّوادِ مِنَّا ومن الجبالِ، والأَسَدُ. وكسَحابٍ: السَّوادُ، والأَسْوَدُ. وجبلُ ديلَميٌّ: مُطِلٌّ على المَرْوَةِ. وأبو دُلامَةَ، كثُمامةٍ: رَجُلٌ، وجَبَلٌ مُطِلٌّ على الحَجونِ.
دلم (لسان العرب) الأَدلَم: الشديد السواد من الرجال والأُسْد والحمير والجبال والصَّخرِ في ملوسة، وقيل: هو الآدَمُ، وقد دلِمَ دلَماً. التهذيب: الأَدْلَمُ من الرجال الطويلُ الأَسْودُ، ومن الجبل كذلك في مَلُوسَةِ الصَّخْر غير جدّ شديد السواد؛ قال رؤبة يصف فيلاً: كان دَمْخاً ذا الهِضابِ الأَدْلَما وقال ابن الأَعرابي: الأَدْلَمُ من الأَلوان الأَدْغَمُ. وقال شمر: رجل أَدْلَمُ وجبل أَدْلَمُ، وقد دلِمَ دلَماً، وقد ادلامَّ الرجلُ والحمار ادْليماماً؛ وقول عنترة: ولقد هَمَمْتُ بِغارةٍ في ليلةٍ سَوْداءَ حالِكَةٍ، كلَوْنِ الأَدْلَمِ قالوا: الأَدْلَمُ هَهنا الأَرَنْدَجُ.

ePSD: na
na [CVNE] wr. na "(compound verb nominal element)"
na [MAN] wr. na "man" Akk. amēlu
na [PESTLE] wr. na4na "pestle; a stone" Akk. na'u
na [STONE] wr. na4; na; na4na "stone; stone weight" Akk. abnu
نَاءَ (القاموس المحيط) ناءَ نَوْءاً وتَنْوَاءً: نَهَضَ بِجَهْدٍ ومَشَقَّةٍ، و~ بالحِمْلِ: نَهَضَ مُثْقَلاً، و~ به الحِمْلُ: أَثْقَلَهُ، وأَمالَهُ، كأَناءَهُ،

ePSD: e
e [BARLEY?] wr. e "barley?"
e [CHAFF] wr. e3 "chaff" Akk. hāmū
e [HOUSE] wr. e2; ĝa2; e4 "house; temple; (temple) household; station (of the moon)?; room; house-lot; estate" Akk. bītu
e [INTERJECTION] wr. e "a vocative interjection"
e [LEATHER] wr. e; e6 "strip or piece of leather; leather bearing" Akk. ya'u
e [LEAVE] wr. e3; i; e "to leave, to go out; to thread, hang on a string; to remove, take away; to bring out; to enter; to bring in; to raise, rear (a child); to sow; to rave; to winnow; to measure (grain) roughly (with a stick); to rent" Akk. aṣû; erēbu; mahû; rubbû; zarû; šakāku
e [PRINCELY?] wr. e; e5 "princely?"
e [SPEAK] wr. e; na-be2-a; be2; ne; da-me; na-be2; e7 "perfect plural and imperfect stem of dug[to speak]" Akk. atwû; dabābu; qabû
e [TRUST] wr. e7 "trust" Akk. tukultu
e [TUBE] wr. ĝeše11 "tube, socket" Akk. uppu
e [WATCH] wr. e3 "watch"
عيا (لسان العرب) الأزهري: قال الليث العِيُّ تأْسيسٌ أَصله من عين وياءَيْن وهو مصدر العَيِّ، قال: وفيه لغتان رجل عَيِيٌّ، بوزن فعيل؛ وقال العجاج: لا طائِشٌ قاقٌ ولا عَيِيٌّ ورجل عَيٌّ: بوزن فَعْلٍ، وهو أَكثر من عَيِيٍّ، قال: ويقال عَيِيَ يَعْيا عن حُجَّته عَيًّا، وعَيَّ يَعْيَا، وكلُّ ذلك يقال مثل حَيِيَ يَحْيَا وحَيَّ؛ قال الله عز وجل: ويَحْيا مَنْ حَيَّ عن بَيِّنَةٍ ، قال: والرَّجلُ يَتَكلَّف عملاً فيَعْيا به وعنه إذا لم يَهْتَدِ لوجه عَمَله. وحكي عن الفراء قال: يقال في فِعْلِ الجميع من عَيِيَ عَيُوا؛ وتَعَيَّا بالأَمر: كتَعَيَّى ؛ عن ابن الأَعرابي؛ ويقال أَيضاً: عَيَّ بأَمرِه وعَيِيَ إذا لم يَهْتَدِ لوجهه، وحكى الأَزهري عن الأَصمعي: عَيِيَ فلان، بياءَين، بالأَمر إذا عَجَز عنه، ولا يقال أَعْيا به. قال: ومن العرب من يقول عَيَّ به، فيُدْغِمُ. وأَعْيا الماشي: كَلَّ.
الحَيُّ (القاموس المحيط) وحايَيْتُ النارَ بالنَّفْخِ: أحْيَيْتُها. وحَيَّ على الصلاةِ، بفتح الياءِ، أي: هَلُمَّ وأقْبِلْ. وحَيَّ هلاً، وحَيَّ هَلاً على كذا، و~ إلى كذا، وحَيَّ هَلْ، كخمسة عَشَرَ، وحَيَّ هَلْ، كصَهْ ومَهْ، وحَيَّهَلَ، بسكون الهاءِ: حَيَ، أي: اعْجَلْ، وهَلاً، أي: صِلْهُ، أو حَيَّ، أي: هَلُمَّ، وهَلاً، أي: حَثِيثاً، أو أسْرِعْ، أو هَلاً، أي: اسْكُنْ، ومعناهُ: أسْرِعْ عند ذِكْرِه، واسْكُنْ حتى تَنْقَضِيَ. وحَيَّ هَلاً بفُلانٍ، أي: عليكَ به، وادْعُهُ. وإذا قلتَ حَيَّ هَلاً مُنَوَّنَةً، فكأنَّكَ قلتَ: حَثًّا. وإذا لم تُنَوِّنْ، فكأنَكَ: قلتَ: الحَثَّ، جعلوا التنوينَ عَلَماً على النَّكِرَةِ، وتَرْكَهُ عَلَماً لِلمَعْرِفَةِ، وكذا في جميعِ ما هذا حالُهُ من المَبْنِيَّاتِ. ولا حَيَّ عنه: لا مَنْعَ.

حيا (لسان العرب) الحَياةُ: نقيض الموت، كُتِبَتْ في المصحف بالواو ليعلم أن الواو بعد الياء في حَدّ الجمع، وقيل: على تفخيم الألف، وحكى ابن جني عن قُطْرُب: أن أَهل اليمن يقولون الحَيَوْةُ، بواو قبلها فتحة، فهذه الواو بدل من أَلف حياةٍ وليست بلام الفعل من حَيِوْتُ، أَلا ترى أَن لام الفعل ياء؟ وكذلك يفعل أَهل اليمن بكل أَلف منقلبة عن واو كالصلوة والزكوة. حَيِيَ حَياةً (* قوله «حيي حياة إلى قوله خفيفة» هكذا في الأصل والتهذيب). وحَيَّ يَحْيَا ويَحَيُّ فهو حَيٌّ، وللجميع حَيُّوا، بالتشديد، قال: ولغة أُخرى حَيَ وللجميع حَيُوا، خفيفة. وربما أَظهرت العرب الإدغام في الجمع إرادةَ تأْليفِ الأَفعال وأَن تكون كلها مشددة، فقالوا في حَيِيتُ حَيُوا، وفي عَيِيتُ عَيُوا؛ قال: وأَنشدني بعضهم: يَحِدْنَ بنا عن كلّ حَيٍّ، كأَننا أَخاريسُ عَيُّوا بالسَّلام وبالكتب (* قوله «وبالكتب» كذا بالأصل، والذي في التهذيب: وبالنسب). قال: وأَجمعت العرب على إدغام التَّحِيَّة لحركة الياء الأَخيرة، كما استحبوا إدغام حَيَّ وعَيَّ للحركة اللازمة فيها، فأَما إذا سكنت الياء الأَخيرة فلا يجوز الإدغام مثل يُحْيِي ويُعْيِي، وقد جاء في الشعر الإدغام وليس بالوجه، وأَنكر البصريون الإدغام في مثل هذا الموضع، ولم يَعْبإِ الزجاج بالبيت الذي احتج به الفراء، وهو قوله: وكأَنها، بينَ النساء، سَبِيكةٌ تَمْشِي بسُدَّةِ بَيْتِها فتُعِيِّي وأَحْياه اللهُ فَحَيِيَ وحَيَّ أَيضاً، والإدغام أَكثر لأَن الحركة لازمة، وإذا لم تكن الحركة لازمة لم تدغم كقوله: أَليس ذلك بقادر على أَن يُحْيِيَ المَوْتَى. والمَحْيا مَفْعَلٌ من الحَياة. وقال أَبو حنيفة: أَحْيَيْت الأَرض إذا اسْتُخْرِجَت. وفي الحديث: أَنه كان يصلي العصر والشمس حَيَّة أَي صافية اللون لم يدخلها التغيير بدُنُوِّ المَغِيب، كأَنه جعل مَغِيبَها لها مَوْتاً وأَراد تقديم وقتها. والحِيُّ، بكسر الحاء: جمعُ الحَياة. وقال ابن سيده: الحِيُّ الحَياةُ زَعَمُوا؛ قال العجاج: كأَنَّها إذِ الحَياةُ حِيُّ، وإذْ زَمانُ النَّاسِ دَغْفَلِيُّ وكذلك الحيوان. وفي التنزيل: وإن الدارَ الآخرةَ لَهِيَ الحَيَوانُ؛ والحيوانُ: اسم يقع على كل شيء حيٍّ، وسمى الله عز وجل الآخرة حَيَواناً فقال: وإنَّ الدارَ الآخرةَ لَهِيَ الحَيَوان؛ قال قتادة: هي الحياة. الأَزهري: المعنى أَن من صار إلى الآخرة لم يمت ودام حيّاً فيها لا يموت، فمن أُدخل الجنة حَيِيَ فيها حياة طيبة، ومن دخل النار فإنه لا يموت فيها ولا يَحْيا، كما قال تعالى. والحَيُّ: الواحد من أَحْياءِ العَرب. وأَحْيا اللهُ الأَرْضَ: أَخرج فيها النبات، وقيل: إنما أَحْياها من الحَياة كأَنها كانت ميتة بالمَحْل فأَحْياها بالغيث. والتَّحِيَّة: السلام، وقد حَيَّاهُ تَحِيَّةً، وحكى اللحياني: حَيَّاكَ اللهُ تَحِيَّةَ المؤمن. والتَّحِيَّة: البقاءُ. حَيَّاك اللهُ أَي أَبقاك اللهُ، صحيحٌ، من الحياة، وهو البقاء. وحَيَا الخَمْسين: دنا منها؛ عن ابن الأَعرابي. الأَزهري: والحَيُّ فرج المرأَة. والحَيَّةُ: الحَنَشُ المعروف، اشتقاقه من الحَياة في قول بعضهم؛ الجوهري: وقولهم حَيَّ على الصلاة معناه هَلُمَّ وأَقْبِلْ. وهَلا: حَثٌّ واستعجال؛ وقال ابن بري: صَوْتان زُكْبا، ومعنى حَيَّ أَعْجِلْ؛

أَيي (مقاييس اللغة) ويقال: ليست هذه بدار تَئِيَّة، أي مُقام. وأصلٌ آخر، وهو التعمُّد، يقال تآيَيْتُ، على تفاعلت، وأصله تعمَّدت آيَتَه وشخصَه. قال: وقالوا: الآيَة العلامة، وهذه آيةٌ مَأْيَاةٌ، كقولك علامَة مَعْلَمَة. الهمزة والياء والياء أصلٌ واحد، وهو النَّظَر. يقال تأَيَّا يتأيّا تأيِّياً، أي تمكّث. قالوا: وأصل آية أَأْيَة بوزن أَعْيَة، مهموز همزتين، فخفِّفت الأخيرة فامتدّت. قال سيبويه: موضع العين من الآية واو؛ لأنَ ما كان* موضع العين [منه] واواً، واللام ياءً، أكثرُ ممَّا موضع العينِ واللامِ منه ياءان، مثل شوَيتُ، هو أكثر في الكلام حَيِيتُ. قال الأصمعيّ: آيةُ الرَّجُل شخْصُه. قال الخليل: خَرَجَ القوم بآيتهم أي بجماعتهم.

أيا (لسان العرب)
إيّا من علامات المضمر، تقول: إيّاك وإيّاهُ وإيّاكَ أنْ تَفْعَل ذلك وهِيّاكَ، الهاء على البدل مثل أراق وهَراق؛ وأنشد الأخفش:فهِيّاكَ والأَمْرَ الذي إنْ تَوسَّعَتْ مَوارِدُه، ضاقَتْ عَلَيكَ مَصادِرُهْ وفي المُحكم: ضاقَتْ عليكَ المَصادِرُ؛ وقال آخر: يا خال، هَلاَّ قُلْتَ، إذْ أَعْطَيْتَني، هِيّاكَ هِيّاكَ وحَنْواءَ العُنُقْ وتقول: إيّاكَ وأنْ تَفْعَلَ كذا، ولا تقل إيّاكَ أنْ تَفْعَل بلا واو؛ قال ابن بري: الممتنع عند النحويين إيّاكَ الأَسَدَ، ولا بُدّ فيه من الواو ، فأَمَّا إيّاكَ أنْ تَفْعَل فجائز على أن تجعله مفعولاً من أجله أي مَخافةَ أنْ تَفْعَل. الجوهري: إيّا اسم مبهم ويَتَّصِلُ به جميع المضمرات المتصلة التي للنصب، تقول إيّاكَ وإيّايَ وإيّاه وإيّانا، وجعلت الكاف والهاء والياء والنون بياناً عن المقصود ليُعْلَم المخاطَب من الغائب، ولا موضع لها من الإعراب، فهي كالكاف في ذلك وأرَأَيْتَكَ، وكالألف والنون التي في أنت فتكون إيّا الاسم وما بعدها للخطاب، وقد صار كالشيء الواحد لأن الأسماء المبهمة وسائر المَكْنِيّات لا تُضافُ لأنها مَعارِفُ؛ وقال بعض النحويين: إنّ إيّا مُضاف إلى ما بعده، واستدل على ذلك بقولهم إذا بَلَغَ الرجل السِّتِّينَ فإيّاهُ وإيّا الشَّوابِّ، فأَضافوها إلى الشَّوابِّ وخَفَضُوها؛ وقال ابن كيسان: الكاف والهاء والياء والنون هي الأسماء ، وإيّا عِمادٌ لها، لأنها لا تَقُومُ بأَنْفُسها كالكاف والهاء والياء في التأخير في يَضْرِبُكَ ويَضْرِبُه ويَضْرِبُني، فلما قُدِّمت الكاف والهاء والياء عُمِدَتْ بإيّا، فصار كله كالشيء الواحد، ولك أن تقول ضَرَبْتُ إيّايَ لأنه يصح أن تقول ضَرَبْتُني، ولا يجوز أن تقول ضَرَبْتُ إيّاك، لأنك إنما تحتاجُ إلى إيّاكَ إذا لم يُمكِنْكَ اللفظ بالكاف، فإذا وصَلْتَ إلى الكاف تَركْتَها ؛ قال ابن بري عند قول الجوهري ولك أن تقول ضَرَبْتُ إيايَ لأنه يصح أن تقول ضَرَبْتَني ولا يجوز أن تقول ضَرَبْتُ إيّاكَ، قال: صوابه أن يقول ضَرَبْتُ إيّايَ، لأنه لا يجوز أن تقول ضَرَبْتُني، ويجوز أن تقول ضَرَبْتُكَ إيّاكَ لأن الكاف اعْتُمِدَ بها على الفِعل، فإذا أَعَدْتَها احتَجْتَ إلى إيّا؛ وأما قولُ ذي الإصْبَعِ العَدْوانيّ: كأنّا يومَ قُرَّى إنْـ نَما نَقْتُلُ إيّانا قَتَلْنا منهُم كلَّ فَتًى أَبْيَضَ حُسّانا فإنه إنما فصلَها من الفعل لأن العرب لا تُوقع فِعْلَ الفاعل على نفسه بإيصال الكناية، لا تقول قَتَلْتُني، إنما تقول قَتَلْتُ نفسي، كما تقول ظَلَمْتُ نَفْسِي فاغفر لي، ولم تقل ظَلَمْتُني ، فأَجْرَى إيّانا مُجْرَى أَنْفُسَنا، وقد تكون للتحذير، تقول: إيّاكَ والأَسَدَ، وهو بدل من فعل كأَنك قُلْتَ باعِدْ، قال ابن حَرّى: وروينا عن قطرب أَن بعضهم يقول أَيّاك ، بفتح الهمزة، ثم يبدل الهاء منها مفتوحة أَيضاً، فيقول هَيّاكَ، واختلف النحويون في إيّاكَ، فذهب الخليل إلى أَنّ إيّا اسم مضمر مضاف إلى الكاف، وحكي عن المازني مثل قول الخليل؛ قال أبو عليّ: وحكى أبو بكر عن أبي العباس عن أبي الحسن الأَخفش وأَبو إسحق عن أبي العباس عن منسوب إلى الأَخفش أَنه اسم مفرد مُضمر، يتغير آخره كما يتغير آخر المُضمَرات لاختلاف أَعداد المُضْمَرِينَ، وأَنَّ الكاف في إيّاكَ كالتي في ذلِكَ في أنه دلالة على الخطاب فقط مَجَرَّدَةٌ من كَوْنها عَلامة الضمير، ولا يُجيزُ الأَخفش فيما حكي عنه إيّاكَ وإيّا زَيْدٍ وإيّايَ وإيّا الباطِلِ، قال سيبويه: حدّثني من لا أَتَّهِمُ عن الخليل أَنه سمع أَعرابيّاً يقول إذا بلَغ الرجل السِّتِّينَ فإيّاه وإيّا الشَّوابِّ، وحكى سيبويه أَيضاً عن الخليل أَنه قال: لو أَن قائلاً قال إيّاكَ نَفْسِكَ لم أُعنفه لأَن هذه الكلمة مجرورة، وحكى ابن كيسان قال : قال بعض النحويين إيّاكَ بكمالها اسم،

قال: وقال بعضهم الياء والكاف والهاء هي أسماء وإيّا عِمادٌ لها لأنها لا تَقُوم بأنفسها، قال: وقال بعضهم إِيّا ايم مُبْهَم يُكْنَى به عن المنصوب ، وجُعِلَت الكاف والهاء والياء بياناً عن المقصود لِيُعْلَم المُخاطَبُ من الغائب، ولا موضع لها من الإِعراب كالكاف في ذلك وأَرَأَيْتَك، وهذا هو مذهب أَبي الحسن الأَخفش ؛ قال أَبو منصور: قوله اسم مُبهم يُكْنَى به عن المنصوب يدل على أَنه لا اشتاق له؛ وقال أَبو إِسحق الزَّجاجُ: الكافُ في إِيَّاكَ في موضع جرّ بإضافة إِيّا إليها، إلا أَنه ظاهر يُضاف إِلى سائر المُضْمَرات، ولو قلت إِيّا زَيدٍ حدَّثت لكان قبيحاً لأَنه خُصَّ بالمُضْمَر، وحكى ما رواه الخليل من إِيّاهُ وإِيّا الشَّوابِّ؛ قال ابن جني: وتأَملنا هذه الأَقوال على اختلافها والاعْتِلالَ لكل قول منها فلم نجد فيها ما يصح مع الفحص والتنقير غيرَ قَوْلِ أَبي الحسن الأَخفش، أَما قول الخليل إِنَّ إِيّا اسم مضمر مضاف فظاهر الفساد، وذلك أَنه إِذا ثبت أَنه مضمر لم تجز إِضافته على وجه من الوجوه، لأَن الغَرَض في الإِضافة إِنما هو التعريف والتخصيص والمضمر على نهاية الاختصاص فلا حاجة به إِلى الإِضافة ، وأَمّا قول من قال إِنَّ إِيّاك بكمالها اسم فليس بقويّ، وذلك أَنَّ إِيّاك في أَن فتحة الكاف تفيد الخطاب المذكر، وكسرة الكاف تفيد الخطاب المؤنث، بمنزلة أَنت في أَنَّ الاسم هو الهمزة، والنون والتاء المفتوحة تفيد الخطاب المذكر، والتاء المكسورة تفيد الخطاب المؤنث، فكما أَن ما قبل التاء في أَنت هو الاسم والتاء هو الخطاب فكذا إِيّا اسم والكاف بعدها حرف خطاب، وأَمّا مَن قال إِن الكاف والهاء والياء في إِيّاكَ وإِيّاه وإِيّايَ هي الأَسماء، وإِنَّ إِيّا إِنما عُمِدَت بها هذه الأَسماء لقلتها، فغير مَرْضِيّ أَيضاً، وذلك أَنَّ إِيّا في أَنها ضمير منفصل بمنزلة أَنا وأَنت ونحن وهو وهي في أَن هذه مضمرات منفصلة ، فكما أَنَّ أَنا وأَنت ونحوهما تخالف لفظ المرفوع المتصل نحو التاء في قمت والنون والأَلف في قمنا والأَلف في قاما والواو في قامُوا، بل هي أَلفاظ أُخر غير أَلفاظ الضمير المتصل، وليس شيء منها معموداً له غَيْرُه، وكما أَنَّ التاء في أَنتَ، وإِن كانت بلفظ التاء في قمتَ، وليست اسماً مثلها بل الاسم قبلها هو أَن والتاء بعده للمخاطب وليست أَنْ عِماداً للتاء، فكذلك إِيّا هي الاسم وما بعدها يفيد الخطاب تارة والغيبة تارة أُخرى والتكلم أُخرى، وهو حرف خطاب كما أَن التاء في أَنت حرف غير معمود بالهمزة والنون من قبلها، بل ما قبلها هو الاسم وهي حرف خطاب، فكذلك ما قبل الكاف في إِيّاكَ اسم والكاف حرف خطاب ، فهذا هو محض القياس، وأَما قول أَبي إِسحق: إِنَّ إِيّا اسم مظهر خص بالإِضافة إِلى المضمر، ففاسد أَيضاً، وليس إِيّا بمظهر، كما زعم والدليل على أَنَّ إِيّا ليس باسم مظهر اقتصارهم به على ضَرْبٍ واحد من الإِعراب وهو النصب؛ قال ابن سيده: ولم نعلم اسماً مُظْهَراً اقْتُصِرَ به على النَّصب البتة إِلاَّ ما اقْتُصِرَ به من الأَسماء على الظَّرْفيَّة، وذلك نحو ذاتَ مَرَّة وبُعَيْداتِ بَيْنٍ وذا صَباحٍ وما جرى مَجْراهُنَّ، وشيئاً من المصادر نحو سُبْحانَ اللهِ ومَعاذَ اللهِ ولَبَّيْكَ، وليس إِيّا ظرفاً ولا مصدراً فيُلحق بهذه الأَسماء، فقد صح إِذاً بهذا الإِيراد سُقُوطُ هذه الأَقوالِ، ولم يَبْقَ هنا قول يجب اعتقاده ويلزم الدخول تحته إِلا قول أَبي الحسن من أَنَّ إِيّا اسم مضمر، وأَن الكاف بعده ليست باسم، وإِنما هي للخطاب بمنزلة كاف ذلك وأَرَأَيْتك وأَبْصِرْكَ زيداً ولَيْسَكَ عَمْراً والنَّجاكَ. قال ابن جني:وسئل أَبو إِسحق عن معنى قوله عز وجل: إِيّاكَ نَعْبُد، ما تأْويله؟ فقال: تأْويله حَقيقَتَكَ نَعْبُد، قال: واشتقاقه من الآيةِ التي هي العَلامةُ؛ قال ابن جني: وهذا القول من أَبي إِسحق غير مَرْضِيّ، وذلك أَنَّ جميع الأَسماء المضمرة مبني غير مشتق نحو أَنا وهِيَ وهُوَ، وقد قامت الدلالة على كونه اسماً مضمراً فيجب أَن لا يكون مشتقّاً. وتكون أَيٌّ جزاء، وتكون بمعنى الذي، والأُنثى من كل ذلك أَيّة، وربما قيل أَيُّهن منطلقةٌ، يريد أَيّتهن؛ وتأَيّا الشيءَ: تَعَمَّد آيَتَهُ أَي شَخْصَه. وآية الرجل: شَخْصُه. ابن السكيت وغيره: يقال تآيَيْتُه، على تَفاعَلْتُه، وتَأَيَّيْتُه إِذا تعمدت آيته أَي شخصه وقصدته؛ وأَيّا آيةً: وضع علامة. وخرج القوم بآيَتهم أَي بجماعتهم لم يَدعوا وراءهم شيئاً؛

4

Part 1-5 References

1.26

عسس (العباب الزاخر) واعْتَسَ -أيضاً-: أي اكْتَسَبَ.
عسا (لسان العرب) وعَسَتْ يَدُه تَعْسُو عُسُوّاً: غَلُظَتْ من عَمَلٍ؛ قال ابن سيده: وهذا هو الصواب في مصدرِ عَسا.
عَسَى (القاموس المحيط) وإنَّهُ لَمَعْساةٌ بِكذا، أيْ: مَخْلَقَةٌ. وأعْسِ به: أخْلِقْ. وهو عَسِيٌّ بِهِ، وعَسٍ: خَليقٌ.

ادم (لسان العرب) ورجل مُؤْدَمٌ مُبْشَرٌ: حاذقٌ مُجَرَّب قد جمع لِيناً وشدَّةً مع المعرفة بالأُمور، وأَصلُه من أَدَمَةِ الجلد وبَشَرته، فالبَشَرةُ ظاهِرةُ، وهو مَنْبتُ الشعَر. والآدَمُ من الناس: الأَسْمَرُ. ابن سيده: الأُدْمَةُ في الإبل لَوْنٌ مُشْرَب سَواداً أو بياضاً، وقيل: هو البياضُ الواضِحُ، وقيل: في الظِّباء لَوْنٌ مُشْرَبٌ بياضاً وفي الإنسان السُّمرة. قال أبو حنيفة: الأُدْمَةُ البياضُ، وقد أَدِمَ وأَدُمَ، فهو آدمُ، والجمع أُدْمٌ، كسَّروه على فُعْل كما كسَّروا فَعُولاً على فُعُل، نحو صَبور وصُبُر، لأَن أَفْعَل من الثلاثة (* قوله «لأن أفعل من الثلاثة إلخ» هكذا في الأصل، ولعله لان أفعل من ذي الثلاثة وفيه زيادة كما أن فعولا إلخ). واختُلف في اشتقاق اسم آدَم فقال بعضهم: سُمِّيَ آدَم لأَنه خُلِق من أُدْمةِ الأَرض، وقال بعضهم: لأُدْمةٍ جعلَها الله تعالى فيه، وقال الجوهري: آدَمُ أَصله بهمزتين لأَنه أَفْعَل، إلا أَنهم لَيَّنُوا الثانية، فإذا احتَجْت إلى تحريكها جعلتها واواً وقلت أَوادِم في الجمع، لأَنه ليس لها أَصل في الياء معروف، فَجُعِلَ الغالبُ عليها الواو؛ عن الأَخفش؛ قال ابن بري: كل أَلِفٍ مجهولة لا يُعْرَف عَمَّاذا انْقِلابُها، وكانت عن همزة بعد همزة يدعو أَمْرٌ إلى تحريكها، فإنها تبدَل واواً حملاً على ضَوارب وضُوَيْرب، فهذا حكمُها في كلام العرب إلا أَن تكون طَرفاً رابعةً فحينئذ تبدل ياءً؛ وقال الزجاج (*قوله «وقال الزجاج إلخ» كذا في الأصل، وعبارة التهذيب: وقال الزجاج يقول أهل اللغة في آدم إن اشتقاقه من أديم الأرض لأنه خلق من تراب): يقول أَهلُ اللغة إنَّ اشْتِقاق آدم لأَنه خُلِق من تُراب، وكذلك الأُدْمَةُ إنَّما هي مُشَبَّهة بلَوْن التُّراب؛ وقوله: سادُوا الملُوكَ فأَصْبَحوا في آدَمٍ، بَلَغُوا بها غُرَّ الوُجوه فُحُولا جعل آدَمَ اسماً للقَبيلة لأَنه قال بَلَغوا بها، فأَنَّث وجمَع وصرف آدم ضرورة؛ وقوله: الناسُ أَخْيافٌ وشَتَّى في الشِّيَمْ، وكلُّهم يَجْمَعُهم بيتُ الأَدَمْ قيل: أَراد آدَم، وقيل: أَراد الأَرضَ؛ قال الأَخفش: لو جعلت في الشعر آدَم مع هاشم لجاز؛ قال ابن جني: وهذا هو الوجه القويُّ لأَنه لا يحقِّق أَحدٌ همزةَ آدَم، ولو كان تحقيقُها حَسَناً لكان التحقيقُ حَقيقاً بأَن يُسْمَع فيها، وإذا كان بَدلاً البتَّة وجَب أَن يُجْرى على ما أَجْرَتْه عليه العرب من مُراعاة لفظِه وتنزيل هذه الهمزةِ الأَخيرة منزلةَ الأَلفِ الزائدة التي لا حظ فيها للهمزة نحو عالم وصابر، أَلا ترَهم لما كسَّروا قالوا آدَم وأَوادِم كسالِم وسَوالِم؟ والأَدَمانُ في النَّخْل: كالدَّمانِ وهو العفَن، وسيأْتي ذكره؛
أدم (مقاييس اللغة) والأَدَمَةُ الوسيلة إلى الشيء، وذلك أنَّ المخالِف لا يُتوسَّل به. فإن قال قائلٌ: فعلى أيِّ شيء تحمل الأدمة وهي باطن الجلد؟ قيل له: الأدمة أحسن ملاءمة للَّحم من البشرة، ولذلك سُمّي آدم عليه* السلام؛ لأنَّه أخذ من أدمة الأرض. ويقال هي الطبقة الرابعة. والعرب تقول مُؤْدَمٌ مُبْشَرٌ، أي قد جمع لِينَ الأدَمة وخشونة البشَرة. فأما اللَّون الآدَم فلأنّه الأغلبُ على بني آدم. وناس تقول: أديم الأرض وأدَمَتُها وجهها.
الأُدْمَةُ (القاموس المحيط) وككتابٍ: كلُّ مُوافِقٍ، وامرأةٌ، وبئرٌ على مَرْحلةٍ من مَكَّةَ، وما يُؤْتَدَمُ به ج: آدِمَةٌ وآدامٌ. والأَدِيمُ: الطَّعامُ المأْدومُ، وع ببلادِ هُذَيْلٍ، وفَرَسُ الأَبْرَشِ الكَلْبِيِّ، أو الجِلْدُ، أو أحْمَرُهُ، أو مَدْبوغُهُ ج: آدِمَةٌ وأُدُمٌ وآدامٌ. والأَدَمُ: اسمٌ للجَمْعِ. والأُدْمَةُ، بالضم، في الإِبلِ: لَوْنٌ مُشْرَبٌ سَواداً أو بياضاً، أو هو البياضُ الواضِحُ، أو في الظِّباءِ: لَوْنٌ مُشْرَبٌ بياضاً، وفينا السُّمْرَةُ، أدُ◌مَ كعَلِمَ وكَرُمَ فهو آدمُ ج: أُدْمٌ وأُدْمانٌ، بضمِّهما، وهي: أدْماءُ، وشذَّ أدْمانَةٌ ج: أُدْمٌ، بالضم. وآدَمُ: أبو البَشَرِ، صلواتُ الله عليه وسلامُهُ. وشذَّ أَدَمٌ، محرَّكةً، ج: أوادِمُ .
أدم (الصّحاح في اللغة) الأَدَمُ: جمع الأديمِ، وقد يجمع على آدِمَةٍ وربما سُمِّيَ وجهُ الأرض أديماً. والآدَمُ من الناس: الأسمر، والجمع أُدْمانٌ. وآدَمُ عليه السلام: أبو البشر.

البَشَرُ (القاموس المحيط) البَشَرُ، محرَّكَةً: الإِنْسانُ ذَكَراً أو أُنْثَى، واحداً أو جَمْعاً، وقد يُثَنَّى، ويُجْمَعُ أبْشاراً،

دمي (لسان العرب) وقال أَبو إسحق: أَصله دَمَيٌ، قال: ودليل ذلك قوله دَمِيَتْ يَدُه؛ وكلُّ شيءٍ في لوْ◌نِهِ سَوادٌ وحُمْرة فهو مُدَمَّىً. وكل أَحْمَرَ شديد الحمرة فهو مُدَمَّىً. ويقال: كُمَيْتٌ مُدَمَّىً؛ والمُدَمَّى من الأَلْوانِ: ما كان فيه سوادٌ. ومنه الحديث: لا والدِّماءِ أَي دماءِ الذَّبائحِ، ويُرْوى: لا والدُّمى،

جمع دُمْيَةٍ وهي الصورة ويريد بها الأَصْنام. والدُّمْيَةُ الصَّنَم، وقيل: الصورة المُنَقَّشة العاجُ ونحوه، وقال كُراع: هي الصورة فعَمَّ بها. ويقال للمرأ◌ة: الدُّمْيَة، يكنى عن المرأة بها، عربية، وجمع الدُّمْيةِ دُمىً؛ وفي صفته، صلى الله عليه وسلم: كأَن عُنُقَه عُنُقُ دُمْيةٍ؛ الدُّمْية: الصورة المصورة لأَنها يُتَنَوَّقُ في صَنْعتِها وي◌ُبالَغُ في تَحْسِينِها. وخُذْ ما دَمَّى لك أَي ظَهَرَ لك. ودَمَّى له في كذا وكذا إذا قَرَّب.
دما (الصّحَاح في اللغة) الدَمُ أصله دَمَوٌ بالتحريك، وإنما قالوا دَمِيَ يَدْمى لحال الكسرة التي قبل الياء، كما قالوا رَضِيَ يَرْضى وهو من الرضوان. والدَمَةُ أخصُ من الدَمِ. والدُمْيَةُ: الصنمُ، والجمع الدُمى، وهي الصورة من العاج ونحوه.
الدَمُ (القاموس المحيط) الدَّمُ: م، أَصْلُه دَمَيٌ، تَثْنِيَتُه دَمانِ ودَمَيانِ. ج: دِماءٌ ودُمِيٌّ، وقِطْعَتُه: دَمَةٌ، أَو هي لغةٌ في الدَّمِ، وقد دَمِيَ، كرَضِيَ، دَمًى، وأَدْمَيْتُه ودَمَّيْتُه. والدُّمْيَةُ، بالضم: الصُّورةُ المُنَقَّشَةُ من الرُّخامِ، أو عامٌّ، والصَّنَمُ. ج: دُمًى.

ردد (الصّحَاح في اللغة) وهذا الأمرُ أَرَدُّ عليه، أي أَنْفَعُ له. وهذا أمرٌ لا رادَّةَ له: أي لا فائدة له ولا رُجوع.

دجا (الصّحَاح في اللغة) والدُجى: جمع دُجْيَةٍ بالضم، وهي قُترة الصائد، والظُلمة أيضاً.

هيم (لسان العرب) هامَت الناقةُ تَهِيم: ذهَبَت على وجهها لرَعْيٍ كهَمَتْ، وقيل: هو مقلوب عنه. وقلبٌ مُسْتهامٌ أَي هائمٌ.

عوف (العباب الزاخر) وقال شمر: عافَتِ الطير تَعُوْفُ عَوْفاً: إذا استدرت على شيء.
العَوْفُ (القاموس المحيط) العَوْفُ: الحالُ، والشأنُ، والذَّكَرُ، والضَّيْفُ، والجَدُّ، والحَظُّ، وطائرٌ، والديكُ، وصَنَمٌ، وجَبَلٌ، والأَسَدُ، لأنه يَتعَوَّفُ بالليلِ، والذئبُ، وحُسْنُ الرِّعْيَةِ، والكادُّ على عِيالِهِ، ونباتٌ طَيِّبُ الرائحةِ، وبه سَمَوْا.

رمس (لسان العرب) ابن شُمَيْل: الرَّوامِسُ الطير الذي يطير بالليل، قال: وكل دابة تخرج بالليل، فهي رَامِسٌ تَرْمُس: تَدْفِنُ الآثار كما يُرْمَسُ الميت، قال؛ وأَصلُ الرَّمْسِ: الستر والتغطية. ويقال لما يُحْثَى من التراب على القبر: رَمْسٌ.

1.27

ها (لسان العرب) الهاء: بفخامة الأَلف: تنبيهٌ، وبإِمالة الأَلف حرفُ هِجاء. الجوهري: الهاء حرف من حروف المُعْجَمِ، وهي من حُروف الزِّيادات، قال: وها حرفُ تنبيه. قال الأَزهري: وأَما هذا إِذا كان تنبيهاً فإِن أَبا الهيثم قال: ها تَنْبيهٌ تَفْتَتِحُ العرب بها الكلام بلا معنى سوى الافتتاح، تقولُ: هذا أَخوك، ها إِنَّ ذا أَخُوكَ؛ الكسائي: يقال في الاستفهام إِذا كان بهمزتين أَو بهمزة مطولة بجعل الهمزة الأُولى هاء، فيقال هأَلرجُل فَعلَ ذلك، يُريدون آلرجل فَعل ذلك، وهأَنت فعلت ذلك، وكذلك الذَّكَرَيْنِ هالذَّكَرَيْنِ، فإِن كانت للاستفهام بهمزة مقصورة واحدة فإِن أَهل اللغة لا يجعلون الهمزة هاء مثل قوله: أَتَخَذْتُم، أَصْطفى، أَفْتَرى، لا يقولون هاتَّخَذْتم، ثم قال: ولو قِيلت لكانتْ. وطيِّءٌ تقول: هَزَيْدٌ فعل ذلك، يُريدون أَزيدٌ فَعلَ ذلك. ويقال: أَيا فلانُ وهَيا فلانُ؛ وأَما قول شَبيب بن البَرْصاء: نُفَلِّقُ، ها مَنْ لم تَنَلْه رِماحُنا، بأَسْيافِنا هامَ المُلوكِ القَماقِمِ فإِنَّ أَبا سعيد قال: في هذا تقديم معناه التأَخر إِنما هو نُفَلِّقُ بأَسيافنا هامَ المُلوك القَماقِمِ، ثم قال: ها مَنْ لم تَنَلْه رِماحُنا، فها تَنْبيه.
ها (لسان العرب) وقال الكسائي: بعضهم يُلقِي الواور من هُو إِذا كان قبلها أَلف ساكنة فيقول حتَّاهُ فعل ذلك وإِنَّماهُ فعل ذلك؛ وقال الكسائي: لم أَسمعهم يلقون الواو والياء عند غير الأَلف، وتَثْنِيَتُه هما وجمعُه هُمُو، فأَما قوله هُم فمحذوفة من هُمُو كما أَن مُذْ محذوفة من مُنْذُ، فأَما قولُك رأَيتُهو فإِنَّ الاسام إِنما هو الهاء وجيء بالواو لبيان الحركة، وكذلك لَهُو مالٌ إِنما الاسم منها الهاء والواو لما قدَّمنا، ودَلِيلُ ذلك أَنَّك إِذا وقفت حذفت الواو فقلت رأَيته والمالُ لَهْ، ومنهم من يحذفها في الوصل مع الحركة التي على الهاء ويسكن الهاء؛

علم (مقاييس اللغة) العين واللام والميم أصلٌ صحيح واحد، يدلُّ على أثَرٍ بالشيء يتميَّزُ به عن غيره. من ذلك العَلامة، وهي معروفة. يقال: عَلَّمت على الشيء علامة. والعِلْم نقيض الجهل، وقياسه قياس العَلَم والعلامة، والدَّليل على أنَّهما من قياسٍ واحد قراءة بعض القُرّاء : وَإِنَّهُ لَعَلَمٌ لِلسَّاعَةِ [الزخرف 61]، قالوا: يراد به نُزول عيسى عليه السلام، وإنّ بذلك يُعلَمُ قُرب الساعة. وتعلّمت الشَّيء، إذا أخذت علمَه. والعرب تقول: تعلَّمْ أنّه كان كذا، بمعنى اعلَمْ. والباب كلُّه قياس واحد. ومن الباب العالَمُون، وذلك أنّ كلَّ جنسٍ من الخَلْق فهو في نفسه مَعْلَم وعَلَم.
علم (لسان العرب) والعَلامةُ: السِّمَةُ، والجمع عَلامٌ، وهو من الجمع الذي لا يفارق واحده إِلاَّ بإِلقاء الهاء؛ قال عامر بن الطفيل: عَرَفْت بِجَوِّ عارِمَةَ المُقاما بِسَلْمَى، أَو عَرَفْت بها عَلاما والمَعْلَمُ مكانُها. وقوله تعالى: وله الجَوارِ المُنْشآتُ في البحر كالأَعلام؛ قالوا: الأَعْلامُ الجِبال. والعَلَمُ العَلامةُ. والعالَمُ الخَلْق كلُّه، وقيل: هو ما احتواه بطنُ الفَلك؛ والعَلَمُ الجبل الطويل. وقال اللحياني: العَلَمُ الجبل فلم يَخُصَّ الطويلَ؛ والعَيْلَم: البحر.

ذكر (صحاح اللغة) الذَكَرُ: خلاف الأُنْثى.
ذكر (لسان العرب) وقَوْلٌ ذَكَرٌ: صُلْبٌ مَتِينٌ.

نَقَبَ (مقاييس اللغة) النُّونُ وَالْقَافُ وَالْبَاءُ أَصْلٌ صَحِيحٌ يَدُلُّ عَلَى فَتْحٍ فِي شَيْءٍ.

برأ (لسان العرب) وَفِي التنزيلِ العزيز: الْبارئُ الْمُصَوِّرُ. وقالَ تعالى: فَتُوبُوا إِلى بارِئِكُمْ. قالَ ابنُ سِيدَة: برأَ اللهُ الخَلْقَ يَبْرَؤُهم بَرءاً وبُرُوءاً: خَلَقَهُم، يكونُ ذلكَ فِي الجَواهِرِ والأَعْراضِ. وَفِي التنزيل: {مَا أَصابَ مِنْ مُصِيبَةٍ فِي الأَرْضِ وَلا فِي أَنْفُسِكُمْ إِلَّا فِي كِتابٍ مِنْ قَبْلِ أَنْ نَبْرَأَها} وَفِي التَّهْذِيبِ: والبَرِيَّةُ أَيضًا: الخَلْق، بِلَا هَمْزٍ. قالَ الفَرَّاءُ: هِيَ مِنْ بَرَأَ اللهُ الخَلْقَ أَي خَلَقَهُم.

وا (لسان العرب) ومنها واو العطف والفرقُ بينها وبين الفاء في المعطوف أَو الواو يُعْطَفُ بها جملة على جملةٍ ،لا تدلُّ على الترتيب في تَقْديم المُقَدَّم ذِكْرُه على المؤخَّر ذكره، وأَما الفراء فإِنه يُوصَلُ بها ما بَعْدَها بالذي قبلها والمُقَدَّمُ هو الأَوَّل، وقال الفراء: إِذا قلت زُرْتُ عبدَ اللهِ وزيداً فأَيَّهما شئت كان هو المبتدأَ بالزيارة، وإِن قلت زُرْتُ عبدَ الله فزَيْداً كان الأَولُ هو الأَولَ والآخِرُ هو الآخر؛

2.7

صير (لسان العرب) صارَ الأَمرُ إِلى كذا يَصِيرُ صَيْراً ومَصِيراً وصَيْرُورةً وصَيَّرَه إِليه وأَصاره، والصَّيْرُورةُ مصدر صار يَصِيرُ. وصَيَّرته أَنا كذا أَي جعلته. وصِرْتُ الشيءَ: قطعته.

صرر (لسان العرب) وأَصل الصَّرِّ: الجمع والشدُّ.

هوأ (لسان العرب) هاءَ بِنَفْسِه إِلى المَعالي يَهُوءُ هَوْءاً: رَفَعَها وسَما بها إِلى المَعالي.

عفر (لسان العرب) العَفْرُ والعَفَرُ: ظاهر التراب، والجمع أَعفارٌ. وعَفَرَه في التُّراب يَعْفِره عَفْراً وعَفَّره تَعْفِيراً فانْعَفَر وتَعَفَّرَ: مَرَّغه فيه أَو دَسَّه. والعَفَر التراب؛

فحح (لسان العرب) وفَحَّ الرجل في نومه يَفُحُّ فَحِيحاً وفَحْفَحَ: نَفَخَ؛ قال ابن دريد: هو على التشبيه بفَحِيح الأَفْعى.

هيه (لسان العرب) هِيهِ وهِيهَ، بالكسر والفتح: (* قوله «بالكسر والفتح» أي كسر الهاء الثانية وفتحها، فأما الهاء الأولى فمكسورة فقط كما ضبط كذلك في التكملة والمحكم). في موضع إِيهِ وإِيهَ. وفي حديث أُميَّةَ وأَبي سفيان قال: يا صَخْرُ هِيهِ، فقلت: هِيهاً؛ هِيه: بمعنى إِيهِ فأَبدل من الهمزة هاء، وإِيهِ اسم سمي به الفعل، ومعناه الأَمر، تقول للرجل إِيهِ، بغير تنوين، إِذا استزدته من الحديث المعهود بينكما، فإِن نوَّنْتَ استزدتَهُ من حديثٍ مَّا غير معهود، لأَن التنوين للتنكير، فإِذا سَكَّنْتَهُ وكففته قلت إِيهاً، بالنصب، فالمعنى أَن أُميَّةَ قال له: زِدْني من حديثك، فقال له أَبو سفيان: كُفَّ عن ذلك. ابن سيده: إِيهِ كلمة استزادة لكلام، وهاهْ كلمة وعيدٍ، وهي أَيضاً حكايةُ الضحك والنَّوْح. وهَيْهاتَ وهَيْهاتِ: كلمة معناها البُعْدُ، وقيل: هَيْهاتَ كلمة تبعيد؛

أيه (لسان العرب) إِيهِ: كلمةُ اسْتزادة واسْتِنْطاقٍ، وهي مبنية على الكسر، وقد تُنَوَّنُ. تقول للرجل إِذا اسْتَزَدته من حديث أَو عمل: إِيهِ، بكسر الهاء. وفي الحديث: أَنه أَنشد شعر أُمية بن أَبي الصَّلْتِ فقال عند كل بيت إِيهِ؛ قال ابن السكيت: فإِن وصلت نوّنت فقلت إِيهٍ حَدِّثْنا، وإِذا قلت إِيهاً بالنصب فإِنما تأْمره بالسكوت، قال الليث: هِيهِ وهِيهَ، بالكسر والفتح، في موضع إِيهِ وإِيهَ. ابن سيده: وإِيه كلمة زجر بمعنى حَسْبُكَ، وتنوَّن فيقال إِيهاً. وقال ثعلب: إِيهٍ حَدِّثْ؛ وأَنشد لذي الرمة: وَقَفْنا فقلنا: إِيهِ عن أُمِّ سالمٍ وما بالُ تَكْليم الديارِ البَلاقِعِ؟ أَراد حَدِّثْنا عن أُم سالم، فترك التنوين في الوصل واكتفى بالوقف؛ قال الأَصمعي: أَخطأَ ذو الرمة إِنما كلام العرب إِيهٍ، وقال يعقوب: أَراد إِيهٍ فأَجراه في الوصل مُجْراه في الوقف، وذو الرمة أَراد التنوين، وإِنما تركه للضرورة؛ قال ابن سيده: والصحيح أَن هذه الأَصوات إِذا عنيت بها المعرفة لم تنوَّن، وإِذا عنيت بها النكرة نونت، وإِنما استزاد ذو الرمة هذا الطَّلل حديثاً معروفاً، وقال بعض النحويين: إِذا نونت فقلت إِيهٍ فكأَنك قلت استزادة، كأَنك قلت هاتِ حديثاً مَا، لأَن التنوين تنكير، وإِذا قلت إِيه فلم تنوّن فكأَنك قلت الاستزادة، فصار التنوين علم التنكير وتركه علم التعريف؛ واستعار الحَذْلَمِيُّ هذا للإِبل فقال: حتى إِذا قالتْ له إِيهٍ إِيهْ وإِن لم يكن لها نطق كأَنَّ لها صوتاً ينحو هذا النحو. قال ابن بري: قال أَبو بكر السراج في كتابه الأُصول في باب ضرورة الشاعر حين أَنشد هذا البيت: فقلنا إِيهِ عن أُم سالم، قال: وهذا لا يعرف إِلا منوَّناً في شيء من اللغات، يريد أَنه لا يكون موصولاً إِلا منوَناً، أَبو زيد: تقول في الأَمر إِيهِ افْعَلْ، وفي النهي: إِيهاً عَنّي الآنَ وإِيهاً كُفَّ. وفي حديث أُصَيْل الخُزاعِيّ حين قدمَ عليه المدينة فقال له: كيف تركتَ مكة؟ فقال: تركتها وقد أَحْجَنَ ثُمامها وأَعْذَقَ إِذْخِرُها وأَمْشَرَ سَلَمُها، فقال: إِيهاً أُصَيْلُ دَعِ القُلوبَ تَقِرُّ أَي كُفَّ واسكت. الأَزهري: لم يُنَوِّنْ ذو الرُّمَّةِ في قوله إِيهِ عَنْ أُمِّ سالم، قال: لم ينوِّن وقد وصَل لأَنه نوى الوقف، قال: فإِذا أَسْكَتَّهُ وكَفَفْتَهُ قلتَ إِيهاً عَنَّا، فإِذا أَغْرَيْتَهُ بالشيء قلت وَيْهاً يا فلانُ، فإِذا تعجبت من طيب شيء قلتَ واهاً ما أَطْيبه وحكي أَيضاً عن الليث: إِيهِ وإِيهٍ في الاستزادة والاستنطاق وإِيهِ وإِيهاً في الزَّجْر، كقولك إِيهِ حَسْبُكَ وإِيهاً حَسْبُكَ؛ قال ابن الأَثير: وقد ترد المنصوبة بمعنى التصديق والرضا بالشيء. ومنه حديث ابن الزبير لما قيل له يا ابْنَ ذاتِ النِّطاقَيْنِ فقال: إِيهاً والإِلهِ أَي صدَّقْتُ ورضيتُ بذلك، ويروى: إِيهٍ، بالكسر، أَي زدني من هذه المَنْقَبة، وحكى اللحياني عن الكسائي: إِيهِ وهِيهِ، على البَدَلِ، أَي حَدِّثْنا، الجوهري: إِذا أَسكته وكَفَفْتَهُ قلت إِيهاً عَنّا؛

2.21

فل (مقاييس اللغة) الْفَاءُ وَاللَّامُ أَصْلٌ صَحِيحٌ يَدُلُّ عَلَى انْكِسَارٍ وَانْثِلَامٍ.

ردم (لسان العرب) والرَّدْمُ: ما يَسْقُطُ من الجِدارِ المُتَهَدِّمِ، نَقَلَه ابنُ سِيْدَه. ورَدَمَ الشَّيءُ يَرْدِمُ رَدْمًا: سَالَ، وهذه عن كُراع.

أسن (لسن العرب) وأَسِنَ الرجلُ أَسَنًا، فَهُوَ أَسِنٌ، وأَسِنَ يأْسَنُ ووَسِنَ: غُشِيَ عَلَيْهِ مِنْ خُبْثِ رِيحِ الْبِئْرِ. وأَسِنَ لَا غَيْرُ: استدارَ رأْسُه مِنْ رِيحٍ تُصيبه. أبو زَيْد: ركِيَّة مُوسِنةٌ يَوْسَنُ فِيهَا الإِنسانُ وَسَنًا، وَهُوَ غَشْيٌ يأْخذه، وَبَعْضُهُمْ يَهْمِزُ فَيَقُولُ أَسِن. الجَوْهَرِيُّ :أَسِنَ الرجلُ إِذَا دَخَلَ الْبِئْرَ أَصابته رِيحٌ مُنْتِنة مِنْ رِيحِ الْبِئْرِ أو غَيْرِ ذَلِكَ فغُشِيَ عَلَيْهِ أو دَارَ رأْسه، وأَنشد بَيْتَ زُهَيْرٍ أَيضًا.

قح (معجم العين) والقُحُّ الجافي من الناس والأشياء، يقالُ للبَطِّيخة التي لم تَنْضَج: إنّها لقُحٌّ. والفعلُ: قَحَّ يقُحُّ قُحوحةً، يحكي سعال الشَّرِقِ الأَبَحّ. والقُحُّ: الشَّيخُ الفاني. والقُحّ: الخالصُ من كُلّ شَيْءٍ.
قحا (لسان العرب) وفِي النوادر: اقْتَحَيْتُ المالَ وقَحَوْتُه واجْتَفَفْته وازْدَفَفْتُه أَي أَخذته.

سجر (لسان العرب) سَجَره يَسْجُره سَجْرًا وسُجورًا وسَجَّره: ملأَه. وسَجَرْتُ النهرَ: ملأْتُه. وَقَوْلُهُ تعالى: {وَإِذَا الْبِحارُ سُجِّرَتْ}؛ فَسَرَهُ ثَعْلَبٌ فَقَالَ: مُلِئَتْ، قالَ ابْنُ سِيدَهْ: وَلَا وَجْهَ لَهُ إِلا أَن تكُونَ مُلِئَت نَارًا. قَالَ: وَالْمَسْجُورُ فِي كَلَامِ الْعَرَبِ الْمَمْلُوءُ.

بسر (مقاييس اللغة) الباء والسين والراء أصلان: أحدُهما الطَّراءة وأن يكون الشَّيءُ قَبل إناه.

تحت (لسان العرب) تَحْتَ: إِحْدى الجهاتِ السِّتِّ المُحيطة بالجِرْم، تَكُونُ مَرَّةً ظَرْفًا، ومرَّة اسْمًا، وَتُبْنى فِي حَالِ الاسْمِيَّةِ عَلى الضَّمِّ، فَيُقَالُ: مِنْ تَحْتُ.

2.22

لقح (لسان العرب) وأَنشد: يَشْهدُ مِنهَا مَلْقَحًا ومَنْتَحا وقالَ فِي قَوْلِ أَبي النَّجْمِ: وَقَدْ أَجَنَّتْ عَلَقًا مَلْقُوحَا، يَعْنِي لَقِحَتْه مِنَ الفَحل أَي أَخذته.

باء (تهذيب اللغة) وقال الفَرَاء فِي قول الله تعالى: {وَالَّذِينَ آمَنُوا وَعَمِلُوا الصَّالِحَاتِ لَنُبَوِّئَنَّهُمْ مِنَ الْجَنَّةِ غُرَفًا} [العنكبوت: 58]. يُقال: بَوَّأته منزِلًا، وأثْويته منزِلًا، سواء، معناهما: أنزلته. وقال الأخفش: أبأت بالمكان: أَقَمت به. وبَوَّأك بَيْتًا: اتَّخذت لك بَيْتًا. وفي حديث النبيِّ صلى الله عليه وسلم: "من استطاع منكم الباءة فَلْيَتَزَوَّج، ومَن لم يَستطع فعليه بالصَّوم فإنه له وجاء" .أراد ب «الباءة»: النِّكاح والتَّزويج. ويُقال: في أرض فلان فلاةٌ تُبِيء في فلاة، أي: تذهب. وبَوَّأته منزلًا، أي: جعلته: ذا منْزِل.
بوأ (مختار الصحاح) (تَبَوَّأَ) مَنْزِلًا نَزَلَهُ وَ(بَوَّأَ) لَهُ مَنْزِلًا وَ(بَوَّأَهُ) مُنْزِلًا هَيَّأَهُ وَمَكَّنَ لَهُ فِيهِ.

أنس (لسان العرب) الإِنسان: معروف؛ وقوله: أَقَلْ بَنو الإِنسانِ، حين عَمَدْتُمْ إِلى من يُثير الجِنَّ، وهي هُجُودُ يعني بالإِنسان آدم، على نبينا وعليه الصلاة والسلام.
إنس (العباب الزاخر) الإنْسُ: البَشَرُ، الواحِدُ: إنْسي وأنَسِيٌّ. والجمع: أناسِيُّ، قال الله تعالى: (وأَنَاسِيَّ كَثِيرا)، وقرأ الكسائي ويحيى بن الحارث: "وأناسي" بتخفيف الياء، أسقطا الياء التي تكون فيما بين عين الفعل ولامه، مثل قراقير وقراقِر. ويبيِّن جواز أناسِي -بالتخفيف- قولهم: أناسِيَةٌ كثيرة. وقال أبو زيد: إنسيٌّ وإنْسٌ -مثال جِنِّيٍّ وجِنٍّ- وإنْسٌ وآناسٌ -مثال إجْلٍ وآجالٍ- قال: وإنْسانٌ وأناسِيَةٌ؛ كصيارِفةٍ وصياقِلةٍ. وقال الفرّاء: واحِدُ الأناسِيّ إنْسِيٌّ، وإن شئت جعلته إنساناً ثم جمعته أناسِيَّ، فتكون الياء عوضاً من النون. ويقال للمرأة: إنْسانٌ -أيضاً-، ولا يقال إنسانة، والعامة تقولها،
أيسَ (القاموس المحيط) والإِيسانُ: الإِنسانُ
أنس (الصِّحَاح في اللغة) الإنْسُ: البَشَر، الواحد إنْسِيٌّ وأَنَسِيٌّ أيضاً بالتحريك، والجمع أناسِيٌّ.
الإِنْسُ (القاموس المحيط) الإِنْسُ: البَشَرُ، كالإِنْسَانِ، الواحد إِنْسِيٌّ وأَنَسِيٌّ.
إِنْسَانٌ (شمس العلوم) الكلمة: إِنْسَانٌ. الجذر: ءنس. الوزن: فِعْلَان. [إِنْسَانٌ]: هو الإِنسان. وهو بمعنى النَّاس في قوله تعالى: {إِنَ الْإِنْسانَ لَفِي خُسْرٍ} لأن الإِنسان بمعنى الجنس. وسمِّي إِنسانًا لظهوره، من آنستَ الشيءَ: إِذا أبصرتُه، وجمعه أَناسِيُّ، وأصله أَناسِينُ، مثل سِرْحان وسَرَاحِين، فأبدل من النون ياء، هذا أحد قولي الفراء.

2.23

فعم (لسان العرب) فعم: الفَعْمُ والأَفْعَم: الممتلئ، وقِيل: الْفَائِضُ امتِلَاءً. وساعدٌ فَعْمٌ، فَعُمَ يَفْعُمُ فَعامة وفُعومة فَهُوَ فَعْم: مُمْتَلِئٌ. ووَجْه فَعْم وَجَارِيَةٌ فَعْمة، وافْعَوْعَمَ،

2.24

عزب (مقاييس اللغة) الْعَيْنُ وَالزَّاءُ وَالْبَاءُ أَصْلٌ صَحِيحٌ يَدُلُّ عَلَى تَبَاعُدٍ وَتَنَحٍّ.

2.25

عرو (المحيط في اللغة) وهو عِرْوٌ منه: أي خِلْوٌ.
عرو (معجم العين) والعَراءُ: كلّ شيءٍ أعْرَيْتَهُ من سُتْرته، تقول: استُرْهُ من العَراء،

كشش (لسان العرب) كشَّت الأفعى تَكِشّ كشًا وكشيشًا: وَهُوَ صَوْتُ جِلْدِهَا إذا حكَّت بعضها ببَعْض، وَقِيلَ: الكشيشُ للأُنثى مِنَ الأساود، وَقِيلَ: الكَشِيشُ للأفعى، وَقِيلَ: الكَشِيشُ صوتٌ تُخْرِجُهُ الأفعى مِنْ فِيهَا؛ عَنْ كُرَاع، وَقِيلَ: كَشِيشُ الأَفْعى صوتُها منْ جلْدها لا من فمها فإن ذلك فَحيحُها، وَقَدْ كَشَّت تَكِش، وكشْكَشَت مِثْلُه. أَبو نَصْر: سَمِعْتُ فَحِيحَ الأَفْعَى وَهُوَ صَوْتُها مِنْ فَمِها، وسَمِعْتُ كَشِيشَها وفَشِيشَها وَهُوَ صَوْتُ جِلْدِهَا. وكَشَّ الضبُّ والوَرَلُ والضِفدعُ يَكِشُّ كَشِيشًا: صوَت. وكَشَّت البقرة: صاحَتْ. والكَشْكَشَةُ: كالكَشيش.

3.21

كتن (تاج العروس) والكِتْنَةُ، بالكسْر: شَجرةٌ طَيِّبَةُ الرِّيح. والكَتَنُ، محرَكَةً: لُغَةٌ في الكتّان؛
كتن (مقاييس اللغة) الْكَافُ وَالتَّاءُ وَالنُّونُ أَصْلٌ يَدُلُّ عَلَى لَطْخٍ وَدَرَنٍ. يُقَالُ الْكَتَنُ: لَطْخُ الدُّخَانِ الْبَيْتَ. وَكَتِنَ السِّقَاءُ، إِذَا لَصِقَ بِهِ اللَّبَنُ مِنْ خَارِجٍ فَغَلُظَ. وَالْكَتَّانُ مَعْرُوفٌ، وَزَعَمُوا أَنَّ نُونَهُ أَصْلِيَّةٌ. وَسَمَّاهُ الْأَعْشَى الْكَتَنَ. قَالَ ابْنُ دُرَيْدٍ: هُوَ عَرَبِيٌّ مَعْرُوفٌ، وَإِنَّمَا سُمِّيَ بِذَلِكَ لِأَنَّهُ يُلْقَى بَعْضُهُ عَلَى بَعْضٍ حَتَّى يَكْتَنَ.

عور (لسان العرب) قَالَ شِمْرٌ: عَوَّرت عُيونَ المِيَاهِ إذا دَفَنْتها وسدَدْتها، وعَوَّرت الرَّكِيَّة إذا كبَسْتها بالتُّراب حَتَّى تَنْسَدَّ عُيُونُها. وَفَلَاةٌ عَوْرَاءُ: لَا مَاءَ بِهَا. والعَوارُ والعُوار، بفَتْحِ العَيْنِ وَضَمِّهَا: خَرْقٌ أَو شَقٌّ فِي الثَّوْبِ، وَقِيلَ: هُوَ عَيْبٌ فِيهِ فَلَمْ يُعيَّنْ ذَلِكَ؛
عرر (لسان العرب) وعَرْعَرَةُ الإِنسان: جلدةُ رأْسه.

3.22

رعع (لسان العرب) ورعاعُ النَّاسِ: سُقاطهم وسَفِلَتُهم.

عتا (لسان العرب) وعَتَّى: بِمَعْنَى حتَّى، هُذَلِيَّةٌ وثَقَفِيَّة، "وقرأَ بعْضُهم: عَتَّى حِينٍ"؛ أي حَتَّى حينٍ.
عت (مقاييس اللغة) وَعَتَتُّ عَلَى فُلَانٍ قَوْلَهُ، إِذَا رَدَدْتَ عَلَيْهِ الْقَوْلَ مَرَّةً بَعْدَ مَرَّةٍ.

جما (تهذيب اللغة) جما: سَلَمة، عن الفرَاء: جُماءُ كلّ شيءٍ حَزْرُه ومقدارُه، ممدود. ابن السِّكيت: تَجمَّى القومُ، إذا اجتمع بعضهم إلى بعض، وقد تجمَّوا عليه. وقال ابن بُزرج: جَماءُ كلّ شيء اجتماعُه وحركته. أبو بكر: يقال جَماءُ الترس وجُماؤه وهو اجتماعه ونتوّه، قال: وجُماء الشيء قدره.
أبو بكر: يقال جَماءُ الترس وجُماؤه وهو اجتماعه ونتوّه، قال: وجُماء الشيء قدره.
عصص (لسان العرب) عصص: العَصُّ: هُوَ الأَصلُ الكَرِيمُ وَكَذَلِكَ الأُصُّ. وعَصَّ يَعَصُّ عَصًّا وعَصَصًا: صَلُبَ واشْتَدّ.
عصا (لسان العرب) وَفِي الْحَدِيثِ: « أَنه حَرَّمَ شَجَرَ الْمَدِينَةِ إِلَّا عَصَا حَدِيدَةٍ» أَي عَصَا تَصْلُحُ أَن تَكُونَ نِصابًا لِآلَةٍ مِنَ الْحَدِيدِ. واعْتَصى الشجرةَ: قَطَعَ مِنْهَا عَصًا؛

5.1

سفر (مقاييس اللغة) والسَّفر: الكتابة. والسفرة الكتبة، وسُمي بذلك لأنَّ الكتابة تُسفِرُ عما يُحتاج إليه من الشيء المكتوب.

6.1

حل (مقاييس اللغة) الحاء واللام له فروع كثيرة ومسائلُ، وأصلها كلُّها عندي فتح الشيء، لا يشذُّ عنه شيء.
حلل (لسان العرب) والحِلَّة: مُجْتَمَع القوم؛ هذه عن اللحياني. ورَوْضة مِحْلال إذا أكثر الناسُ الحُلول بها.

ربب (الصّحاح في اللغة) وفلان مَرَبٌّ بالفتح، أي مَجمعٌ يَرُبُّ الناسَ أي يجمعهم. ومكانٌ مَرَبٌّ، أي مَجْمَعٌ
ربب (لسان العرب) الرَّبُّ: هو اللهُ عزَّ وجل، هو رَبُّ كلِّ شيءٍ أي مالكه، وله الرُّبوبيَّة على جميع الخَلْق، لا شريك له، وهو رَبُّ الأَرْباب، ومالِكُ المُلوكِ والأَمْلاكِ. والسَّحابُ يَرُبُّ المَطر أي يَجْمَعُه ويُنَمِّيه. وقيل: المَرْبابُ من الأَرضِين التي كَثُر نبتُها ونأْمَتُها، وكلُّ ذلك مِنَ الجَمْع. والمَرَبُّ: المَحَلُّ، ومكانُ الإِقامةِ والاجتماعِ. والتَّرَبُّبُ الاجْتماعُ. ومَكانٌ مَرَبٌّ، بالفتح: مَجْمَعٌ يَجْمَعُ الناسَ؛.

6.2

بحر (لسان العرب) وأَبحَرَ إذا صادف إِنسانًا على غير اعتمادٍ وقَصدٍ لرؤيته، وهو من قولهم: لقيته صَحْرَةَ بَحْرَةَ أي بارزًا ليس بينك وبينه شيء.
وتبحَّر الخبرَ: تَطَلَّبه.

6.3

دون (لسان العرب) التهذيب: ويقال هذا دون ذلك في التقريب والتحقير، فالتحقير منه مرفوع، والتقريب منصوب لأنه صفة. ويقال: دُونَك زيدٌ في المنزلة والقرب والبُعْد؛
دون (مقاييس اللغة) الدال والواو والنون أصل* واحد يدلُّ على المداناةِ والمقاربة. يقال هذا دُونَ ذاك، أي هو أقربُ منه. وإذا أردْتَ تحقيره قلتَ دُوَيْنَ.

الشُّجُمُ (القاموس المحيط) الشُّجُمُ، بضَمَّتَيْن: الطِّوالُ الخَبَثاءُ الدَّواهي، وبالتَّحريكِ: الهَلاكُ.

6.14

تبت (لسان العرب) هذه ترجمة لم يترجم عليها أحدٌ من مُصَنِّفي الأُصول، وذكره ابن الأَثير لمراعاته ترتيبه، في كتابه، وترجمنا نحن عليها لأن الشيخ أبا محمد بن بري، رحمه الله، قال في ترجمة توب، راداً على الجوهري لمَا ذكر تابوت في أثنائها، قال: إن الجوهري أساء تصريفه حتى ردّه إلى تابوت، قال: وكان الصواب أن يذكره في فصل تبت، لأن تاءه أصلية، ووزنه فاعول، كما ذكرناه هناك في توب؛ وذكره ابن سيده أيضاً في ترجمة تبه، وقال: التابُوه لغة في التَّابُوتِ، أنصارية؛ وقد ذكرناه نحن أيضاً في ترجمة تبه، ولم أرَ في ترجمة تبت شيئاً في الأُصول، وذكرتها أنا هنا مراعاة لقول الشيخ أبي محمد بن بري: كان الصواب أن يذكر في ترجمة تبت؛ ولما ذكره ابن الأَثير، قال في حديث دعاء قيام الليل: اللهم اجْعَل في قَلْبِي نوراً، وذكر سبعاً في التَّابُوتِ. التَّابُوتُ: الأَضْلاعُ وما تَحْوِيه كالقَلْب والكبِد وغيرهما، تشبيهاً بالصُّنْدُوق الذي يُحْرزُ فيه المَتاع أي أنه مكتوب موضوع في الصُّنْدُوقِ .
تُبَتُ (القاموس المحيط) والتَّبُوتُ: التَّابوتُ.
تبه (لسان العرب) ا لتابُوه: لغة في التابوت، أنصاريّة. قال ابن جني: وقد قرئ بها، قال: وأراهم غَلطوا بالتاء الأَصلية فإنه سُمِعَ بعضُهم يقول قَعَدْنا على الفُراه، يريدون على الفرات.
تابَ (القاموس المحيط) والتَّابوتُ: أصلهُ تَأْبُوَةٌ، كتَرْقُوةٍ، سُكِّنَتِ الواوُ فانْقَلَبَتْ هاءُ التَّأْنيثِ تاءً، ولُغَةُ الأَنْصار: التَّابُوهُ بالهاءِ.

عصو/ي (مقاييس اللغة) العين والصاد والحرف المعتل أصلان صحيحان، إلاّ أنّهما متباينان يدلُّ أحدهما على التجمُّع، ويدلُّ الآخر على الفُرْقة.فالأوّل العصا، سمّيت بذلك لاشتمالِ يد مُمْسِكِها عليها، ثم قيس ذلك فقيل للجماعة عَصاً.
عصا (لسان العرب) العَصا: العُودُ، أُنْثَى .

جفر (لسان العرب) والجُفْرَةُ جَوْفُ الصدر، وقيل: ما يجمع البطن والجنبين، وقيل: هو مُنحَنَى الضلوع، وكذلك هو من الفرس وغيره، وقيل: جُفْرةُ الفرس وسَطُه، والجمع جُفَرٌ وجِفَارٌ. والجُفَرَاء والجُفَرَاةُ: الكافور من النخل؛ حكاهما أبو حنيفة.
كفر (لسان العرب) والكَفَرُ والكُفُرَّى والكِفِرَّى والكَفَرَّى: وعاء طلع النخل، وهو أيضاً الكافورُ، ويقال له الكُفَرَّى والجُفَرَّى.
غفر (لسان العرب) والمَغافرُ والمَغافِيرُ: صمغ شبيه بالناطِفِ ينضحه العُرْفط فيوضع في ثوب ثم يُنْضح بالماء فيُشْرب، واحدها مِغْفَر ومَغْفَر ومُغْفُر ومُغْفور ومِغْفار ومِغْفِير. والمَغْفوراء: الأَرضُ ذات المَغافِير؛ وحكى أبو حنيفة ذلك في الرباعي؛ وأَغْفَر العُرْفُط والرِّمْثُ: ظهر فيهما ذلك، وأخرج مَغافِيرَه وخرج الناس يَتَغَفَّرُون ويَتَمَغْفَرُون أي يجتنُون المَغافِيرَ من شجره؛ ومن قال مُغْفور قال: خرجنا نتَمَغْفَر؛ ومن قال مُغْفُر قال: خرجنا نتَغَفَّر، وقد يكون المُغْفورُ أيضاً العُشَر والسَّلَم والثُّمام والطلح وغير ذلك. التهذيب: يقال لصمغ الرِّمْث والعرفط مَغافِير ومَغاثِيرُ، الواحد مُغْثور ومُغْفور ومُغْفُر ومِغْثَر، بكسر الميم. روي عن عائشة، رضي الله عنها، أن النبي، صلى الله عليه وسلم، شَرِبَ عند حَفْصة عسلاً فتواصَيْنا أن نقول له: أَكَلْتَ مَغافِيرَ، وفي رواية: فقالت له سَوْدة أَكلتَ مَغافِيرَ؛ ويقال له أَيضاً مَغاثِير، بالثاء المثلثة، وله ريح كريهة منكرة؛ أَرادت صَمْغَ العرفط. والمَغافِير: صمغٌ يسيل من شجر العرفط غير أَن رائحته ليست بطيبة. قال الليث: المِغْفارُ ذَوْبَةٌ تخرج من العرفط حلوة تُنْضح بالماء فتشرب. قال: وصَمْغُ الإِجَّاصة مِغْفارٌ. أَبو عمرو: المَغافيرُ الصمغ يكون في الرمث وهو حلو يؤكَل، واحدُها مُغْفور، وقد أَغْفَر الرِّمْثُ. وقال ابن شميل: الرمث من بين الحمض له مَغافِيرُ، والمَغافيرُ: شيء يسيل من طرف عِيدانها مثل الدِّبْس في لونه، تراه حُلواً يأْكله الإِنسان حتى يَكْدَن عليه شِدْقاه، وهو يُكْلِع شَفته وفمه مثل الدِّبْق والرُّبّ يعلق به، وإِنما يُغْفِر الرمثُ في الصفريَّة إِذا أَوْرَسَ؛ يقال: ما أَحسن مَغافِيرَ هذا الرمث. وقال بعضهم: كلُّ الحمض يُورِس عند البرد وهو بروحه وارباده يخرج (* قوله «بروحه وارباده يخرج» إلخ هكذا في الأصل) . مغافيره تجدُ ريحَه من بعيد. ومَثَلُ العربِ: هذا الجَنى لا أَن يُكَدَّ المُغْفُر؛ يقال ذلك للرجل يصيب الخير الكثير، والمُغْفُرُ هو العود من شجر الصمغ يمسح به ما ابيضّ فيتخذ منه شيء طيب؛

قنا (مقاييس اللغة) القاف والنون والحرف المعتلُّ أصلان يدلُّ أحدهُما على ملازمة ومُخالَطة، والآخرَ على ارتفاعٍ في شيء. والقِنْو: العِذْقُ بما عليه، لأنّه ملازمٌ لشجرته.ومن الباب المَقْنَاة من الظِّلّ فيمَنْ لا يَهمِزُها، وهو مكانٌ لا تُصيبه الشّمس. وإنّما سمّي بذلك لأنَّ الظلّ مُلازِمُه لا يكادُ يُفارِقُه. ويقول أهلُ العلم بالقُرآن: إنّ كهفَ أصحابِ الكهف في مَقْناةٍ من جبل.
قنا (لسان العرب) وأَغناه الله وأَقْناه أي أَعطاه ما يَسكُن إِليه. والقِنا، مقصور: مِثْل القِنْو. قال ابن سيده: القِنْوُ والقِنا الكِباسةُ، والقَنا، بالفتح: لغة فيه؛ والقُنْوُ: الكِباسة، وهي القِنا أَيضاً، مقصور، ومن قال قِنْوٌ فإِنه يقول للاثنين قِنْوانِ، بالكسر، والجمع قُنْوانٌ، بالضم، ومثله صِنْوٌ وصِنْوانٌ. وشجرة قَنْواء: طويلة. وقُنِيَتِ الجارية تُقْنَى قِنْيةً، على ما لم يُسمَّ فاعله، إِذا مُنعَتْ من اللَّعب مع الصبيان وسُتِرَت في البيت؛

كفر (لسان العرب) وأصل الكفر تغطية الشيء تغطية تستهلكه. وكل من ستر شيئاً، فقد كفره وكَفَّره. والكافر الزرَّاعُ لستره البذر بالتراب. والكُفَّار: الزُّرَّاعُ. وتقول العرب للزَّرَّاع: كافر لأنه يَكْفُر البَذْر المَبْذورَ بتراب الأرض المُثارة إذا أمَرّ عليها مالقَهُ؛ وقال الليث: يقال إنما سمي الكافر كافراً لأن الكفر غطى قلبه كله؛ والكُفْر القِيرُ الذي تُطلى به السُّفُنُ لسواده وتغطيته؛ عن كراع. ابن شميل: القِيرُ ثلاثة أَضْرُب: الكُفْرُ والزِّفْتُ والقِيرُ، فالكُفْرُ تُطلى به السُّفُنُ، والزفت يُجْعَل في الزقاق، والقِيرُ يذاب ثم يطلى به السفن.

بيت (لسان العرب) وأتاهم الأمر بَياتاً أي أتاهم في جوف الليل.

حوط (لسان العرب) حاطه يَحُوطُه حَوْطاً وحِيطةً وحِياطةً: حَفِظه وتعهَّده؛ وقول الهذلي: وأَحْفَظُ مَنْصِبي وأَحُوطُ عِرْضِي، وبعضُ القوم ليس بذِي حِياطِ أراد حِياطة، وحذف الهاء كقول الله تعالى: وإِقام الصلاة، يريد الإقامة، وكذلك حَوْطه؛ قال ساعدة ابن جُؤيَّة: عليَّ وكانُوا أهلَ عِزٍّ مُقدَّمٍ ومَجْدٍ، إذا ما حُوِّطَ المَجْدُ نائل (* قوله «حوط المجد» وقوله «ويروى حوص» كذا في الأصل مضبوطاً.) ويروى: حُوِّصَ، وهو مذكور في موضعه.

6.15

زها (لسان العرب) وزُهاءُ الشيء وزِهاؤُه: قَدْرُه، يقال: هُمْ زُهاءُ مائةٍ وزِهاءُ مائةٍ أي قدرها. وهُم قومٌ ذَوُو زُهاءٍ أي ذَوُو عَدَدٍ كثير؛ وأنشد: تَقَلَّدَتْ إبْريقاً، وعلَّقَتْ جَعْبَةً لتُهْلِكَ حَيّاً ذَا زُهاءٍ وجَامِلِ الإبريق: السيف، ويقال قوس فيها تلاميع. وزُهاءُ الشيء: شخصُه. وزَهَوْت فلاناً بكذا أزْهاهُ أي حَزَرْته. وكم زُهاؤُهم أي قدرُهم وحزرُهم؛ وأنشد للعجاج؛ كأنما زُهاؤُهم لمن جَهَرْ وقولُهم: زُهاءُ مائة أي قدر مائة. وفي حديث: قيل له كم كانوا؟ قال: زُهاءَ ثلثمائة أي قدر ثلثمائة، من زَهَوْت القومَ إذا حَزَرْتَهم.

أرك (لسان العرب) وأرَكَ الرجل بالمكان يأرُكُ ويأرِكُ أُرُوكاً وأرِكَ أرَكاً، كلاهما: أقام به.
طول (لسان العرب) يقال: طَوِّلْ لفرسك يا فلان أي أرْخِ له حَبْلَه في مَرْعاه. الجوهري: طَوَّلْ فرسك أي أَرْخِ طَوِيلَتَه في المَرْعى؛

أمت (لسان العرب) أمَتَ الشيءَ يأمِتُه أمْتاً، وأمَّتَه: قَدَّرَهُ وحَزَرَه. ويُقال: كم أَمْتُ ما بَيْنَكَ وبين الكُوفة؟ أي قَدْرُ. وأمتُّ القوم آمِتُهم أمْتاً إذا حَزَرْتَهم. وأمَتُّ الماءَ أمْتاً إذا قَدَّرْتَ ما بينك وبينه؛

رحب (لسان العرب) الرُّحْبُ، بالضم: السَّعةُ. رَحُبَ الشيءُ رُحْباً ورَحابةً، فهو رَحْبٌ ورَحِيبٌ ورُحابٌ، وأرْحَبَ: اتَّسَع. وأرْحَبْتُ الشيءَ: وسَّعْتُه.

قوم (مقاييس اللغة) القاف والواو* والميم أصلانِ صحيحان، يدلُّ أحدهما على جماعةِ ناس، وربّما استعير في غيرهم. والآخر على انتصابٍ أو عَزْم.

6.16

صهر (لسان العرب) والصَّهْرُ الحارُّ؛ حكاه كراع، وأنشد: إذ لا تزالُ لكُمْ مُغَرْغِرة تَغْلي، وأَعْلى لوْنِها صَهْرُ فعلى هذا يقال: شيء صَهْرٌ حارٌّ.
والصَّاهُورُ: غِلافُ القمر، أعجمي معرب.
الصِّهْرُ (القاموس المحيط) واصْهارَّ: تلألأ ظَهْرُهُ من حَرِّ الشمس.

خلل (الصِّحَاح في اللغة) وتَخَلَّلَ الشيء، أي نفذ. وتَخَلَّلَ المطر، إذا خصَّ ولم يكن عاماً. وتَخَلَّلْتُ القومَ، إذا دخلت بين خَلَلِهِمْ وخِلالِهِمْ.

صدد (لسان العرب) وصُدَّا الجبل: ناحيتاه في مَشْعَبِه. والصُّدَّان: ناحيتا الشِّعْب أو الجبل أو الوادي، الواحد صُدٌّ، وهما الصَّدَفان أيضاً؛ وقال حميد: تَقَلْقَلَ قِدْحٌ، بين صُدَّين، أَشْخَصَتْ له كفُّ رامٍ وجْهَةً لا يُريدُها قال: ويقال للجبل صُدٌّ وسُدٌّ. قال أبو عمرو: يقال لكل جبل صُدٌّ وصَدٌّ وسَدٌّ وسُدٌّ. قال أبو عمرو: الصُّدَّان الجبلان، وأنشد بيت ليلى الأخيلية. وقال: الصُّدَيُّ شِعْبٌ صغير يَسيل فيه الماء، والصَّدُّ الجانب.

8.4

نحا (لسان العرب) وفي حديث الخضر. عليه السلام: وتَنَحَّى له أي اعْتَمد خَرْقَ السَّفينة. وفي حديث عائشة، رضي الله عنها: فلم أَنْشَبْ حتى أَنْحَيْتُ عليها. وفي حديث الحسن: قد تنحَّى في بُرْنُسِه وقامَ الليلَ في حِنْدِسِه أي تعَمَّدَ العِبادة وتوجَّه لها وصار في ناحيتها وتَجَنَّب الناس وصار في ناحية منهم . وتَنَحَّى وانْتَحى: اعْتَمَدَ. يقال: انْتَحَى له بسهم ونحا عليه بشَفْرته، ونحا له بسهم. ونحا الرَّجل وانْتَحَى: مالَ على أحد شِقَّيْه أو انْحَنَى في قَوْسِه. وأنْحَى في سَيره أي اعْتَمَد على الجانب الأيسر. قال الأصمعي: الانتحاء في السير الاعْتماد على الجانب الأيسر، ثم صار الاعتماد في كل وجه؛

حدث (لسان العرب) الحَدِيثُ: نقيضُ القديم. وأخذَ الأمر بحِدْثانه وحَداثته أي بأوّله وابتدائه. والحديثُ: الجديدُ من الأشياء.

هرر (لسان العرب) وقولهم في المثل: ما يعرف هِرّاً من برٍّ؛ قيل: معناه ما يعرف من يَهُرُّه أي يكرهه ممن يَبَرُّه وهو أحسن ما قيل فيه. وقال الفَزاريُّ: البِرُّ اللُّطف، والهِرُّ العُقُوق، وهو من الهَرير؛ ابن الأعرابي: البِرُّ الإكرام والهِرُّ الخُصُومةُ، وقيل: الهِرُّ ههنَا السِّنَّوْرُ والبِرُّ الفأر. والسُّنَّارُ والسِّنَّوْرُ: الهِرُّ، مشتق منه، وجمعه السَّنَانِيرُ. والسنانير: رؤساء كل قبيلة، الواحد سِنَّوْرٌ. والسِّنَّوْرُ السَّيِّدُ.

Wikipedia: Ararat (sometimes Ararad) is the Greek version of the Hebrew spelling (אֲרָרָט; RRṬ) of the name Urartu, a kingdom that existed in the Armenian Highlands in the 9th–6th centuries BC.
In the Assyrian annals the term Uruatri (Urartu) as a name for this league was superseded during a considerable period of years by the term "land of Nairi".

Wikipedia: Nairi (Armenian: Նայիրի in TAO or Նաիրի in RAO) was the Assyrian name (KUR.KUR Na-i-ri, also Na-'i-ru) for a confederation of tribes in the Armenian Highlands, roughly corresponding to the modern Van and Hakkâri provinces of modern Turkey. The word is also used to describe the Armenian tribes who lived there. Nairi has sometimes been equated with Nihriya, known from Mesopotamian, Hittite, and Urartian sources.

رَاط (القاموس المحيط) والرُّوطُ، بالضم: النَّهْرُ، مُعَرَّبُ رُود.
أرط (العباب الزاخر) وأرَاطَةُ: ماء لبني عملية شَرقي سميراء.
رطط (العباب الزاخر) ابن دريدٍ: ذكرَ عن أبي مالك أنه قال: اللرطراطُ: الماءُ الذي أسْأرتهُ الإبل في الحياض نحوُ الرجرَج؛
جوف (لسان العرب) ومنه قوله: الجَوْفُ خيرٌ لكَ من أغْواطِ، ومنْ ألاءاتٍ ومنْ أراطِ (* قوله «أراط» في معجم ياقوت: أراط، بالضم، من مياه بني نمير، ثم قال: وأراط باليمامة. وفي اللسان في مادة أرط: فأما قوله الجوف إلخ فقد يجوز أن يكون أراط جمع أرطاة وهو الوجه وقد يكون جمع أرطى ا هـ. وفيه أيضاً ان الغوط والغائط المتسع من الأرض مع طمأنينة وجمعه اغواط ا هـ. وألاءات بوزن علامات وفعالات كما في المعجم وغيره موضع.)

10.5

أبي (مقاييس اللغة) الهمزة والياء والياء أصلٌ واحد، وهو النَظَر. قال: وقالوا: الآية العلامة، وهذه آيةٌ مأياةٌ، كقولك علامة مَعْلَمَة.

أيا (لسان العرب) وآية الرجل: شَخْصُه. ابن السكيت وغيره: يقال تآيَيْتُه، على تفاعَلْتُه، وتأَيَّيْتُه إذا تعمدت آيته أي شخصه وقصدته؛ وأيَا آيةً: وضع علامة. وقال الجوهري: قال سيبويه موضع العين من الاية واو لأن ما كان مَوْضَعَ العين منه واوٌ واللام ياء أكثر مما موضع العين واللام منه ياءان، مثل شَوَيْتُ أكثر من حَيِيت، قال: وتكون النسبة إليه أوويٌّ؛ قال الفراء: هي من الفعل فاعلة، وإنما ذهبت منه اللام، ولو جاءت تامة لجاءت آيِيَة، ولكنها خُففت، وجمع الآية آيٌ وآياتٌ؛ وأنشد أبو زيد: لم يبق هذا الدهر من آيايه قال ابن بري: لم يذكر سيبويه أن عين آية واو كما ذكر الجوهري، وإنما قال أصلها أيَّة، فأبدلت الياء الساكنة ألفا؛ وحكي عن الخليل أن وزنها فَعْلة، وأجاز في النسب إلى آية آيِيٌّ وآئِيٌّ وآوِيٌّ، قال: فأما أوويٌّ فلم يقله أحد علمته غير الجوهري.
أيا (لسان العرب) إيَّا من علامات المضمر، تقول: إيّاكَ وإيّاهُ وإيّاكَ أنْ تَفْعَل ذلك وهيّاكَ، الهاء على البدل مثل أراقَ وهَراقَ؛ الجوهري: إيَّا اسم مبهم ويَتَّصِلُ به جميع المضمرات المتصلة التي للنصب، تقول إيّاكَ وإيّايَ وإيّاه وإيّانا، وجعلت الكاف والهاء والياء والنون بيانا عن المقصود ليُعْلَم المخاطب من الغائب، ولا موضع لها من الإعراب، فهي كالكاف في ذلك وأرأَيْتَكَ، وكالألف والنون التي في أنت فتكون إيّا الاسم وما بعدها للخطاب، وقد صار كالشيء الواحد لأن الأسماء المبهمة وسائر المَكْنِيّات لا تُضافُ لأنها معارفُ؛
أيا (القاموس المحيط) أيَا: حَرْفٌ لِنداءِ البَعيدِ لا القَريبِ، ووَهِمَ الجوهريُّ، وتُبْدَلُ هَمْزَتُه هاءً. وايَّا، بالكسر والفتح: اسْمٌ مُبْهَمٌ تَتَّصِلُ به جَميعُ المُضْمَراتِ المُتَّصِلَةِ التي للنَّصْبِ: إيَّاكَ وإيّاهُ وإيّايَ، وتُبْدَلُ هَمْزَتُه هاءً، وتارةً واواً، تقولُ ويَّاكَ. الخَليلُ: إيّا: اسمٌ مُضْمَرٌ مُضافٌ إلى الكافِ.

Wikipedia: The word goy means "nation" in Biblical Hebrew. In the Torah, goy and its variants appear over 550 times in reference to Israelites and to gentile nations. The first recorded usage of goyim occurs in Genesis 10:5 and applies innocuously to non-Israelite nations. The first mention of goy in relation to the Israelites comes in Genesis 12:2, when God promises Abraham that his descendants will form a goy gadol ("great nation"). In Exodus 19:6, the Israelites are referred to as a goy kadosh, a "holy nation".[11] While the books of the Hebrew Bible often use goy to describe the Israelites, the later Jewish writings tend to apply the term to other nations.[citation needed]

Some Bible translations leave the word Goyim untranslated and treat it as the proper name of a country in Genesis 14:1, where it states that the "King of Goyim" was Tidal. Bible commentaries suggest that the term may refer to Gutium. In all other cases in the Bible, goyim is the plural of goy and means "nations".[1]
One of the more poetic descriptions of the chosen people in the Hebrew Bible, and popular among Jewish scholarship, as the highest description of themselves: when God proclaims in the holy writ, goy ehad b'aretz, or "a unique nation upon the earth!" (2 Samuel 7:23 and 1 Chronicles 17:21).
Because of the idolatry and immoralities of the surrounding nations, the biblical writings show a passionate intolerance of these nations. Thus the seven goyim, i.e., nations (Deuteronomy 7:1, 12:2), were to be treated with but little mercy; and, more especially, marriages with them were not to be tolerated (Deut. 7:3; comp. Exodus 34:16).

جوي (مقاييس اللغة) الجيم والواو والياء أصلٌ يدلُّ على كراهة الشيء. يقال اجتوَيْت البلاد، إذا كرِهتَها وإنْ كنت في نَعْمةٍ، وجَويتُ. فأمّا الجِوَاءُ فهي الأرض الواسعة، وهي شاذّةٌ عن الأصل الذي ذكرناه.
الجَوَى (القاموس المحيط) الجَوَى: هَوًى باطنٌ، والحُزْنُ، والماءُ المُنْتِنُ، والحُرْقةُ، وشِدَّةُ الوَجْدِ، والسُّلُّ، وتَطاوُلُ المَرَضِ، وداءٌ في الصَّدْرِ.
جَوِيَ جَوًى، فهو جَوٍ وجَوًى، وصْفٌ بالمَصْدَرِ. وجَوِيَهُ، كرَضِيَهُ، واجْتَواهُ: كرِهَهُ. وأرضٌ جَوِيَةٌ وجَوِيَّةٌ: غيرُ مُوافِقةٍ، وجَوِيَتْ نفسهُ منه، و~ عنه.
جوا (الصّحاح في اللغة) ويقال أيضاً: جَوِيَتْ نفسي، إذا لم يوافِقْك البلد. واجْتَوَيْتُ البلد، إذا كرهتَ المُقام به وإن كنت في نعمة.
جوا (لسان العرب) وجَوِيَ الشيءَ جَوىً واجْتواه: كرهه؛ قال: فقدْ جعَلَتْ أكبادُنا تَجْتَويكُم، كما تَجْتَوي سُوقُ العِضاهِ الكَرازِما وجَوِيَ الأرضَ جَوىً واجْتواها: لم توافقه. وأرض جَوِيَةٌ وجَوِيَّةٌ غير موافقة. وتقول: جَوِيَتْ نفسي إذا لم يُوافِقْك البلدُ. واجْتَوَيْتُ البلدَ إذا كرهتَ المُقامَ فيه وإن كنت في نعمة. وفي حديث العُرَنِيِّينَ: فاجْتَوَوُا المدينةَ أي أصابهم الجَوَى، وهو المرض وداءُ الجَوْف إذا تَطاوَلَ، وذلك إذا لم يوافقهم هواؤُها واسْتَوْخَمُوها. واجْتَوَيْتُ البلدَ إذا كرهتَ المُقام فيه وإن كنت في نِعْمة. وفي الحديث: أن وفْد عُرَيْنَة قدموا المدينة فاجْتَوَوْها. أبو زيد: اجْتَوَيْتُ البلادَ إذا كرهتها وإن كانت موافقة لك في بدنك؛ وقال في نوادره: الاجْتِواءُ النِّزاعُ إلى الوطن وكراهةُ المكان الذي أنت فيه وإن كنت في نِعْمة، قال: وإن لم تكن نازِعاً إلى وطنك فإنك مُجْتَوٍ أيضاً.

سفح (لسان العرب) والتَّسافُحُ والسِّفاحُ والمُسافحة: الزنا والفجور؛ وفي التنزيل: مُحْصِنينَ غيرَ مُسافِحين؛ وأَصل ذلك من الصبّ، تقول: سافَحْته مُسافَحة وسِفاحاً، وهو أَن تقيم امرأَةٌ مع رجل على فجور من غير تزويج صحيح؛ ويقال لابن البَغِيّ: ابنُ المُسافِحةِ؛ وفي الحديث: أَوّله سِفاحٌ وآخِره نِكاح، وهي المرأَة تُسافِحُ رجلاً مدة، فيكون بينهما اجتماع على فجور ثم يتزوّجها بعد ذلك، وكره بعض الصحابة ذلك، وأَجازه أَكثرهم. والمُسافِحة: الفاجرة؛ وقال تعالى: مُحْصَناتٍ غيرَ مُسافِحات؛ وقال أَبو إِسحق: المُسافِحة التي لا تمتنع عن الزنا؛ قال: وسمي الزنا سِفاحاً لأَنه كان عن غير عقد، كأَنه بمنزلة الماء المَسْفوح الذي لا يحبسه شيء؛ وقال غيره: سمي الزنا سفاحاً لأَنه ليس ثَمّ حرمة نكاح ولا عقد تزويج. وكل واحد منهما سَفَحَ مَنِيّته أَي دفقها بلا حرمة أَباحت دَفْقَها؛ ويقال: هو مأْخوذ من سَفَحْت الماء أَي صببته؛ وكان أَهل الجاهلية إِذا خطب الرجل المرأَة، قال: أَنكحيني، فإِذا أَراد الزنا، قال: سافحيني.
سفح (مقاييس اللغة) والسِّفاح: صبُّ الماء بلا عَقد نكاح، فهو كالشيء يُسفَح ضَياعاً. وأمّا سَفْح الجبل فهو من باب الإبدال، والأصل فيه صَفح، وقد ذُكر في بابه.
شعب (لسان العرب) قال الشيخ ابن بري: الصحيح في هذا ما رَتَّبه الزُّبَيرُ ابنُ بكَّار: وهو الشَّعْبُ، ثم القبيلةُ، ثم العِمارةُ، ثم البطنُ، ثم الفَخِذُ، ثم الفصيلةُ؛ قال أَبو أُسامة: هذه الطَّبَقات على ترتيب خَلْق الإِنسانِ، فالشَّعبُ أَعظمُها، مُشْتَقٌّ من شَعْبِ الرَّأْسِ، ثم القبيلةُ من قبيلةِ الرأْس لاجْتماعِها، ثم العِمارةُ وهي الصَّدرُ، ثم البَطنُ، ثم الفَخِذُ، ثم الفصيلة، وهي الساقُ.
الصَّفْحُ (القاموس المحيط) والصَّفائِحُ: قَبائِلُ الرَّأْسِ،

10.32

بقر (الصّحاح في اللغة) وبَقَرْتُ الشيءَ بَقْراً: فَتَحْتَهُ ووسَّعْته. ومنه قولهم: ابْقَرها عن جَنينها، أي شُقَّ بطنها عن ولدها. والتَبَقُّرُ التَوَسُّعُ في العِلم والمال.
بقر (لسان العرب) وأَصل البقر: الشق والفتح والتوسعة. بَقَرْتُ الشيءَ بَقْراً: فتحته ووسعته. وتَبَقَّر فيها وتَبَيْقَر: توسع. وبَيْقَرَ الرجلُ: هاجر من أَرض إِلى أَرض. وبَيْقَرَ: خرج إِلى حيث لا يَدْري. وبَيْقَر الدار إِذا نزلها واتخذها منزلاً.

بلل (لسان العرب) والبِلال: الماءُ. والبُلالة: البَلَل.

12.2

جَدَلَهُ (القاموس المحيط) جَدَلَهُ يَجْدُلُهُ ويَجْدِلُهُ: أحْكم فتْلَهُ. ورجُلٌ مَجدولٌ: لَطيفُ القَصَبِ، مُحْكَمُ الفَتْلِ، وساعِدٌ أجْدَلُ. وساقٌ مَجْدولَةٌ وجَدْلاءُ: حَسَنَةُ الطَّيِّ، و~ من الدُّروعِ: المُحْكَمَةُ، وجَدَلَ جُدولاً، فهو جَدِلٌ، كَكَتِفٍ وعَدْلٍ: صَلُبَ .

جدل (مقاييس اللغة) الجيم والدال واللام أصلٌ واحدٌ، وهو من باب استحكام الشيء في استرسالٍ يكون فيه، وامتدادِ الخصومة ومراجعةِ الكلام.
جدل (لسان العرب) الجَدْل: شِدَّة الفَتْل. وجَدَلْتُ الحَبْلَ أَجْدِلُه جَدْلاً إِذا شددت فَتْله وفتَلْتَه فَتْلاً مُحْكماً؛ ومنه قيل لزمام الناقة الجَدِيل. ابن سيده: جدل الشيءَ يَجْدُله ويَجْدِله جَدْلاً أَحكم فَتْله؛ ومنه جارية مَجْدُولة الخَلْق حَسَنة الجَدْل. ورجل مَجْدول، وفي التهذيب: مَجْدول الخَلْق لَطيف القَصَب مُحْكَم الفَتْل. والمجدول: القَضِيف لا من هُزَال. وغلام جادل: مُشْتَدّ. والجَدَالة: الأَرض لشِدَّتها، وقيل: هي أَرض ذات رمل دقيق؛ وقد جُدِلَت الدروعُ جُدْلاً إِذا أُحكمت.

17.2

أتي (لسان العرب) الإِتْيان: المَجيء. أَتَيْته أَتْياً وأُتِيّاً وإِتِيّاً وإِتْياناً وإِتْيانةً ومَأْتاةً: جِئْته؛ وأَتَى للماء: وَجَّه له مَجْرًى. وفي التنزيل العزيز: أَينما تكونوا يأْتِ بكم الله جميعاً؛ قال أَبو إِسحق: معناه يُرْجِعُكم إِلى نَفْسه، وأَتَى الأَمرَ من مأْتاه ومَأْتاتِه أَي من جهته ووَجْهه الذي يُؤْتَى منه، كما تقول: ما أَحسَنَ مَعْناةَ هذا الكلام، تُريد معناه؛ قال الراجز: وحاجةٍ كنتُ على صُماتِها أَتَيْتُها وحْدِيَ من مَأْتاتِها وآتَى إِليه الشيءَ: ساقَه. والأَتِيُّ النهر يَسوقه الرجل إِلى أَرْضه، وقيل: هو المَفْتَح، وكلُّ مَسيل سَهَّلته لماءٍ أَتِيٌّ، وهو الأَتِيُّ؛ حكاه سيبويه، وقيل: الأَتِيُّ جمعٌ. وأَتَّى لأَرْضِه أَتِيّاً: ساقَه؛ ويقال: أَتِّ لهذا الماء فتَهَيِّئَ له طريقه. وسَيْل أَتِيٌّ وأَتاوِيٌّ: لا يُدْرى من أَين أَتَى؛ ورُوِي أَن النبي، صلى الله عليه وسلم، سأَل عاصم بن عَدِيَ الأَنصاري عن ثابت بن الدحْداح وتُوُفِّيَ، فقال: هل تعلمون له نَسَباً فيكم؟ فقال: لا، إِنما هو أَتِيٌّ فينا، قال: فقَضَى رسول الله، صلى الله عليه وسلم، بميراثه لابن أُخته؛ قال الأَصمعي: إِنما هو أَتِيٌّ فينا؛ الأَتِيُّ الرجل يكون في القوم ليس منهم، ولهذا قيل للسيل الذي يأْتي من بلد قد مُطر فيه إِلى بلد لم يُمطر فيه أَتِيٌّ. ويقال أَتَّيْت للسيل فأَنا أُؤَتِّيه إِذا سهَّلْت سبيله من موضع إِلى موضع ليخرُج إِليه، وأَصل هذا من الغُرْبة، أَي هو غَريبٌ؛ يقال: رجل أَتِيٌّ وأَتاوِيٌّ أَي غريبٌ. يقال: جاءنا أَتاوِيٌّ إِذا كان غريباً في غير بلاده. وآتاه الشيءَ أَي أَعطاه إِيَّاه. وفي التنزيل العزيز: وأُوتِيَتْ من كلّ شيء؛ أَراد وأُوتِيَتْ من كل شيء شيئاً، قال: وليس قولُ مَنْ قال إِنَّ معناه أُوتِيَتْ كل شيء يَحْسُن، لأَن بلْقِيس لم تُؤْتَ كل شيء، أَلا ترى إِلى قول سليمان، عليه السلام: ارْجِعْ إِليهم فلنأْتِيَنَّهم بجنود لا قِبَل لهم بها؟ فلو كانت بلْقِيسُ أُوتِيَتْ كلَّ شيء لأُوتِيَتْ جنوداً تُقاتلُ بها جنود سليمان، عليه السلام، أَو الإِسلام لأَنها إِنما أَسلمت بعد ذلك مع سليمان، عليه السلام. وآتاه: جازاه. ورجل مِيتاءٌ: مُجازٍ مِعْطاء. وتأَتَّى له الشيءُ: تَهَيَّأَ.

البِرُّ (القاموس المحيط) البِرُّ: الصِّلَةُ، والجَنَّةُ، والخَيْرُ، والاتِّساعُ في الإِحْسانِ، والحَجُّ، ويقالُ: بَرَّ حَجُّكَ، وبُرَّ، بفتح الباءِ وضمِّها، فهو مَبْرُورٌ، و~: الصِّدْقُ، والطَّاعَةُ، كالتَّبَرُّرِ، واسْمُه: بَرَّةُ مَعْرِفَةٌ، وضِدُّ العُقوقِ، كالمَبَرَّةِ، بَرِرْتُهُ أَبَرُّهُ، كَعَلِمْتُهُ وضَرَبْتُهُ. وأَبَرَّ: رَكِبَ البَرَّ، وكَثُرَ وَلَدُهُ، و~ القَوْمُ: كَثُرُوا .

أرب (لسان العرب) الإِرْبَةُ والإِرْبُ: الحاجةُ. وقد أَرِبَ الرجلُ، إِذا احتاج إِلى الشيءِ وطَلَبَه، يَأْرَبُ أَرَباً. والتَّأْرِيبُ: تَمامُ النَّصِيب. وروى المغيرة بن عبدالله عن أَبيه: أَنه أَتَى النبيَّ، صلى الله عليه سلم، بِمِنًى، فَدنا منه ،فنُحِّيَ، فقال النبي ، صلى الله عليه وسلم: دَعُوه فأَرِبٌ مَا لَهُ. قال: فَدَنَوْتُ. ومعناه: فحاجَةٌ ما لَه، فدَعُوه يَسْأَلُ. قال أَبو منصور: وما صلة. قال: ويجوز أَن يكون أَراد فَأَرِبٌ منالآراب جاءَ به، فدَعُوه. وأَرَّبَ العُضْوَ: قَطَّعه مُوَفَّراً. يقال: أَعْطاه عُضْواً مُؤَرَّباً أَي تاماً لم يُكَسَّر. وتأْرِيبُ الشيءِ: تَوْفيرُه، وقيل: كلُّ ما وُفِرَ فقد أُرِّبَ، وكلُّ مُوفَرٍ مُؤَرَّبٌ.
أرب (مقاييس اللغة) الهمزة والراء والباء لها أربعةُ أصولٍ إليها ترجِع الفروع: وهي الحاجة، والعقل، والنَّصيب، والعَقْد. وأما النَّصيب فهو والعُضْو من بابٍ واحد، لأنهما جزء الشَّيء. قال الكُمَيت: ولانْتَشَلَتْ عُضْوين منها يُحابِرٌ وكانَ لعبْدِ القَيْسِ عُضْوٌ مُؤَرَّبُ. أي صار لهم نصيبٌ وافر.

مأد (لسان العرب) المَأْدُ من النبات: اللَّيِّنُ الناعم. قال الأَصمعي: قيل لبعض العرب: أَصِبْ لنا موضعاً، فقال رائدُهم: وجدت مكاناً ثَأْداً مَأْداً. ومَأْد الشباب: نَعْمَتُه. ومَأَدَ العُودُ يَمْأَدُ مَأْداً إِذا امتلأَ من الريِّ في أَول ما يجري الماء في العود فلا يزال مائداً ما كان رطباً. والمَأْدُ من النبات: ما قد ارتوى؛ يقال: نبات مَأْدٌ. وقد مَأَدَ يَمْأَدُ، فهو مَأْدٌ. وأَمْأَده الريّ والربيع ونحوه وذلك إِذا جرى فيه الماء أَيام الربيع. ويقال للجارية التارَّة: إِنها لمأْدةُ الشباب وهي يَمؤُود ويمؤُودة. ويقال للغصن إِذا كان ناعماً يهتز: هو يَمْأَدُ مَأْداً حسناً. ومأَد النباتُ والشجر يمأَدُ مأْداً: اهتزَّ وترَوَّى وجرى فيه الماء، وقيل: تنعم ولان؛ وقد أَمْأَده الرِّيّ. وغصن مَأْدٌ ويَمؤُود أَي ناعم، وكذلك الرجل والأُنثى مأْدة ويَمْؤُودة شابة ناعمة، وقيل: المأْد الناعم من كل شيء؛ وامتأَد فلان خيراً أَي كسبه.

17.3

برهم (لسان العرب) وإبراهيم اسم أعجمي وفيه لغات: إبْراهامُ وإبْراهَم وإبْراهِم، بحذف الياء؛ وقال عبد المطلب: عُذْتُ بما عاذَ به إبْراهِمُ مُسْتَقْبِلَ القِبلَة، وهْو قائمُ، إِني لك اللهمَّ عانٍ راغِمُ وتصغيرُ إبراهيم أُبَيْرِهٌ، وذلك لأَن الأَلف من الأَصل لأَن بعدها أَربعة أَحرف أُصول، والهمزة لا تُلحق بَبنات الأَربعة زائدة في أَوّلها، وذلك يُوجِب حَذْفَ آخره كما يُحذف من سَفَرْجَل فيقال سُفَيْرِج، وكذلك القولُ في إسمعيل وإسرافيل، وهذا قولُ المبرّد، وبعضُهم يتوهّم أَن الهمزة زائدة إِذا كان الاسم أَعجميّاً فلا يُعْلَم اشتِقاقُه، فيصغّره على بُرَيْهِيمٍ وسُمَيْعِيلٍ وسُرَيْفِيلٍ، وهذا قول سيبويه وهو حسن، والأَوّل قِياسٌ، ومنهم مَن يقول بُرَيْهٌ بطَرْح الهمزة والميم.
أبَرَ (القاموس المحيط) أبَرَ النَّخْلَ والزَّرْعَ، يأْبُرُهُ ويأْبِرُهُ، أبْراً وإباراً وإبارةً: أصْلَحَهُ، كأَبَّرَه. وأبِرَ، كفرِحَ: صَلَحَ.

دبر (لسان العرب) ودَبَّر الحديثَ عنه: رواه. ويقال: دَبَرْتُ الحديث عن فلان حَدَّثْتُ به عنه بعد موته، وهو يَدْبُرُ حديث فلان أَي يرويه. ودَبَرْتُ الحديث أَي حدّثت به عن غيري. قال شمر: دبَرْتُ الحديث ليس بمعروف؛ قال الأَزهري: وقد جاء في الحديث: أَمَا سَمِعْتَهُ من معاذ يُدَبِّرُه عن رسول الله، صلى الله عليه وسلم؟ أَي يحدث به عنه؛ وقال: إِنما هو يُذَبِّرُه، بالذال المعجمة والباء، أَي يُتْقِنُه؛ وقال الزجاج: الذَّبْر القراءةُ، وأَما

أَبو عبيد فإِن أَصحابه رووا عنه يُدَبِّره كما ترى، وروى الأَزهري بسنده إِلى سَلاَّم بن مِسْكِين قال: سمعت قتادة يحدّث عن فلان، يرويه عن أَبي الدرداء، يُدَبِّره عن رسول الله، صلى الله عليه وسلم، قال: ما شَرَقَتْ شمسٌ قَطُّ إِلا بجَنْبَيْها ملكان يُنادِيانِ أَنهما يُسْمِعانِ الخلائقَ غيرَ الثَّقَلَيْن الجن والإِنس، أَلا هَلُمُّوا إِلى ربكم فإِنَّ ما قَلَّ وكَفَى خيرٌ مما كَثُرَ وأَلْهَى، اللهم عَجِّلْ لِمُنْفِقٍ خَلَفاً وعَجِّلْ لِمُمْسِكٍ تَلَفاً. ابن سيده: ودَبَرَ الكتابَ يَدْبُرُه دَبْراً كتبه؛ عن كراع، قال: والمعروف ذَبَره ولم يقل دَبَره إِلا هو.
دبر (مقاييس اللغة) ودَبَرْتُ الحديثَ عن فُلانٍ، إذا حدَّثْتَ به عنه، وهو من الباب؛ لأنَّ الآخِر المحدِّثَ يَدْبُر الأوَّلَ يجيءُ خَلْفَه.

17.5

أبي (لسان العرب) والأَبُ: أَصله أَبَوٌ، بالتحريك، لأَن جمعه آباءٌ مثل قَفاً وأَقفاء، ورَحىً وأَرْحاء، فالذاهب منه واوٌ لأَنك تقول في التثنية أَبَوانِ، وبعض العرب يقول أَبانِ على النَّقْص، وفي الإِضافة أَبَيْك، وإِذا جمعت بالواو والنون قلت أَبُون، وكذلك أَخُونَ وحَمُون وهَنُونَ؛ ابن سيده: الأَبُ الوالد، والجمع أَبُونَ وآباءٌ وأُبُوٌّ وأُبُوَّةٌ؛ عن اللحياني؛

مون (لسان العرب) قال ابن الأَعرابي: التَّمَوُّنُ كثرة النفقة على العيال، والتَّوَمُّنُ كثرة الأَولاد.

17.6

فرت (لسان العرب) الفُراتُ: أَشَدُّ الماء عُذوبةً.

صوي (مقاييس اللغة) الصاد والواو والياء أصلٌ صحيحٌ يدلُّ على شدَّةٍ وصَلابة ويُبْس. عن ابن دريد: "صَوَى الشَّيء، إذا يَبِس، فهو صاوٍ. ويقال صويَ يَصوَى". والصَّوَّانُ: حجارةٌ فيها صلابة. وربَّما استُعِير من هذا وحُمِلَ عليه فقيل صَوَّيْت لإِبلي فَحْلاً، إذا اخترته لها. ولا يكون الاختيار وحدَه تصويةً، لكن يُصنَع لذلك حتَّى يقوى ويصلُب.

17.8

حوز (مقاييس اللغة) الحاء والواو والزاء أصلٌ واحد، وهو الجمع والتجمّع، يقال لكلِّ مَجْمَعٍ وناحيةٍ حَوْزٌ وحَوْزَة. وكلُّ مَن ضمَّ شيئاً إلى نفسه فقد حازَهُ حَوْزاً.
حوز (لسان العرب) وقال الليث: يقال ما لك تَتَحَوَّز إِذا لم يستقر على الأَرض، والاسم منه التَّحَوُّز. وحُزت الأَرض إِذا أَعلَمتها وأَحييت حدودها. والحَوز الملْك. وكل ناحية على حِدَةٍ حَيِّز، بتشديد الياء، وأَصله من الواو. والحَيْز: تخفيف الحَيِّز مثل هَيْن وهَيِّن ولَيْن ولَيِّن، والجمع أَحْيازٌ نادر. فأَما على القياس فَحَيائِز، بالهمز، في قول سيبويه، وحَياوِزُ، بالواو، في قول أَبي الحسن. قال الأَزهري: وكان القياس أَن يكون أَحْواز بمنزلة الميت والأَموات ولكنهم فرقوا بينهما كراهة الالتباس. وفي الحديث: فحَمَى حَوْزَةَ الإِسلام أَي حدوده ونواحيه. وفلان مانع لحَوْزَته أَي لما في حَيِّزه. والحَوْزة، فَعْلَةٌ، منه سميت بها الناحية .

References, Nicknames, and Meanings for Idim and Enlil

^{d}Ea *(also* ^{d}IDIM, ^{d}Niššiku, ^{d}Nudimmud, ^{d}Enki, ^{d}EN.KI-GA-KAM, ^{d}gašam); Adam

Ancient Mesopotamian Gods and Goddesses:
Enki is spelled in Sumerian as ^{d}en-ki or ^{d}am-an-ki. In Akkadian, Ea's name is commonly spelled ^{d}E2.A but it is unclear to which language this name belonged originally. In literary texts, Enki/Ea was sometimes known by the alternative names Nudimmud or Niššiku, the latter originally being a Semitic epithet TT (nas(s)iku "prince") that was then reinterpreted as a pseudo-logogram TT ^{d}nin-ši-kù. He had a number of epithets TT, including 'stag of the abzu' and 'little Enlil'.

Written forms:
^{d}é-a; ^{d}EN.KI; EN.KI-GA.KAM2; ^{d}40; ^{d}60; ^{d}IDIM, ^{d}nu-dím-mud, ^{d}nin-ši-kù

Normalized forms:
Enki, Enkig, Nudimmud, Niššiku, Ea

Wikipedia:
Enki is a god in Sumerian mythology, later known as Ea in Akkadian and Babylonian mythology. He was the deity of crafts (gašam); mischief; water, seawater, lakewater (a, aba, ab), intelligence (gestú, literally "ear") and creation (Nudimmud: nu, likeness, dim mud, make beer). In Sumerian E-A means "the house of water". Enki (Ea) (Samael) (NUDIMMUD) of the Immortals (Lord of the Earth and Waters).

^{d}é-a

From Arabic references:
é-a = ẖaya = of rain and land fertility
é-a = haya = of creation

حَيا = المطرُ والخِصْبُ
هيا = الخلق

حيا (لسان العرب) أحْيا القومُ، أي صاروا في الحَيا، وهو الخِصْبُ. وقد أتيت الأرض فأحْيَيْتُها، أي وجدتها خِصبةً.
هيا (لسان العرب) هَيُّ بن بَيّ، وهَيَّانُ بن بَيَانَ: لا يُعرف هو ولا يُعرف أبوه. يقال: ما أدري أيُّ هَيِّ بن بَيٍّ هو، معناه أي أيُّ الخَلْقِ هو.

Therefore:
é-a = god of rain and land fertility; god of creation

dIDIM

From Arabic references:
Adam (v.): to make water flow; to water
Adīm (adj.) one who makes water flow; flat land; top soil

أدَمَ، أدِمَ، أدُمَ، فهو آدِم، آدَمْ (فَعَلَ، فَعِلَ، فَعُلَ فهو فاعِلْ، فاعَلْ)
أأْدَمَ، أيْدمَ، أوْدمَ، فهو أيْدِيم (آدِم)، أوْدُوم (آدَمْ) (فَعْلَلَ، فَيْعلَ، فَوْعلَ فهو فَيْعِيلْ (فاعِلْ)، فَوْعُولْ (فاعَلْ))

أدم (لسان العرب) الأُدْمةُ: القَرابةُ والوَسيلةُ إلى الشيء. يقال: فلان أُدْمَتي إليك أي وَسيلَتي. ويقال: بينهما أُدْمةٌ ومُلْحة أي خُلْطةٌ، وقيل: الأُدْمة الخُلْطة، وقيل: المُوافَقةُ. والأُدْمُ الأُلْفَةُ والاتِّفاق؛ وأَدَمَ الله بينهم يَأْدِمُ أَدْماً. قال أبو عبيد: لا أرى الأَصل فيه إلا من أدْمِ الطعام لأَن صَلاحَه وطِيبَه إنما يكون بالإِدامِ، ولذلك يقال طعام مَأْدُومٌ. والإِدامُ: معروف ما يُؤْتَدَمُ به مع الخبز. وفي الحديث: نِعْمَ الإِدام الخَلُّ؛ الإِدام، بالكسر، والأُدْمُ، بالضم: ما يؤكل بالخبز أَيَّ شيء كان. وفي الحديث: سَيِّدُ إدامِ أَهْل الدُّنيا والآخرة اللحمُ؛ جعل اللحم أُدْماً وبعض الفقهاء لا يجعله أُدْماً ويقول: لو حَلَفَ أَن لا يَأْتَدِمَ ثم أَكل لَحْماً لم يحنَث، والجمع آدِمةٌ وجمع الأُدْمِ آدامٌ، وقد ائتَدَمَ به. وأَدَمَ الخبز يَأْدِمُه، بالكسر، أَدْماً: خلطه بالأُدْم، وقال غيره: أَدَمَ الخبزَ باللحم؛ وأنشد ابن بري: إذا ما الخُبْزُ تَأْدِمُه بلَحْمٍ، فذاك أَمانَةَ الله الثَّرِيدُ وقال آخر: تَطْبُخه ضُروعُها وتَأْدِمُهْ قال: وشاهد الإِدامِ قولُ الشاعر: الأَبْيَضانِ أَبْرَدا عِظامِي: الماءُ والفَثُّ بلا إدامِ وفي حديث أُمّ مَعْبَد: أنا رأَيت الشاةَ وإنها لَتَأْدُمُها وتَأْدُم صِرْمَتَها (* قوله «وانها لتأدمها وتأدم صرمتها» ضبط في الأصل والنهاية بضم الدال). وفي حديث أنس: وعَصَرَتْ عليه أُمُّ سُلَيْم عُكَّةً لها فأَدَمَتْه أي خَلَطته وجعلت فيه إداماً يؤْكل، يقال فيه بالمَدّ والقَصْر، وروي بتشديد الدال على التكثير. وأَدَمَ القومَ: أَدَمَ لهم خُبْزَهم؛ وقولهم: سَمْنُهم في أَديمهم، يعني طَعامَهم المَأْدُوم أَي خُبزهم راجع فيهم. التهذيب: من أَمثالهم: سَمْنُكم هُريقَ في أَديمِكم أَي في مَأْدُومِكم، ويقال: في سِقائكم. وأَدَمَةُ الأَرض: وجهُها؛ قال الجوهري: وربما سمي وجهُ الأَرض أَديماً؛ وأَدَمَةُ الأَرض: باطِنُها، وأَدِيمُها، وَجْهُها، وأَدِيمُ الليل: ظلمته؛ والأُدْمة في الإِبل: البياض مع سواد المُقْلَتَيْن، قال: وهي في الناس السُّمرة الشديدة، وقيل: هو من أُدْمة الأَرض، وهو لوْنُها، قال: وبه سمي آدم أَبو البَشَر، على نبينا وعليه الصلاة والسلام. واختُلف في اشتِقاق اسم آدَم فقال بعضهم: سُمِّيَ آدَم لأَنه خُلِق من أَدَمةِ الأَرض، وقال بعضهم: لأُدْمةٍ جعلَها الله تعالى فيه، الأُدْمَةُ (القاموس المحيط) وائْتَدَمَ العودُ: جَرَى فيه الماءُ. و~ القَوْمَ: أَدَمَ لهم خُبْزَهُم.
بني (لسان العرب) ويقال للسَّقاء: ابنُ الأَدِيم، فإذا كان أَكبر فهو ابن أَدِيمَين وابنُ ثلاثةِ آدِمَةٍ.

Therefore:
IDIM = aydim = ādim = one who makes water flow (waters); one of (who makes) the fertile land
أيْدِيم = آدِم = ساقي الارض = ذا (سيد، أبو) الارض (التراب)

dnin-ši-kù

According to al-Jiburi rules:
ninšikù = niššiku

From Arabic references:
našaka (v.) = to pour water on
nāšiku (adj.) = green, fertile, watered

"نَسَكْتُ الشيء: غسلته بالماء وطهّرته، فهو مَنْسوكٌ. ونَسَكَ الثَّوبَ أو غيرَهُ: غَسَلَهُ بالماءِ فَطَهَّرَهُ. وأرضٌ ناسِكَةٌ: خَضْراءُ حَديثَةُ المَطَرِ."

Therefore:
niššiku = the one who waters the land; the one who makes green and watered (fertile) land

نِسَيك = نِنسِكُ = المُنَسَكُ، المُطهِّر، الغاسلُ، الذي يسقي الماء، الذي يُمطر، الذي يجعل الارض خضراء مُسقاة (خصبة)

ᵈnu-dím-mud

From Arabic references:

nu = for us, our; distant; keeper

dímu = steady quite rain, continuance, survival, land watering (fertility), mud

mud = to keep

dím-mud = survival (existence)

"والمُدام: المَطَرُ الدائمُ. دامَ يَدُومُ ويَدامُ دَوْماً ودَواماً ودَيْمومةً، ودِمْتَ، بالكسر. تَدُومُ نادِرَةٌ. والدَّيُّومُ والدَّوْمُ: الدائمُ. ودامَ: سَكَنَ، ومنه: الماءُ الدائمُ، والدِيمَةُ، بالكسر: مَطَرٌ يدومُ في سُكونٍ بلا رَعْدٍ وبَرْقٍ. وأرض مَدِيمةٌ ومُدَيَّمَةٌ: أصابتها الدِّيَمُ، وأصلها الواو؛"

"ونَوَّيْتُه تَنْوِيةً أي وَكَلْتُه إلى نِيَّتِه. ونَوِيُّك: صاحبُك الذي نيته نيّتك؛ ونَواهُ اللهُ: حفظه؛"

Therefore:
nu-dím-mud = keeper of (our) land fertility; keeper of (our) survival (existence)

نؤديمُدْ = حافظ الخِصْب؛ حافظ الدَيمومة = المُديم = الدَّيُّومُ

ᵈEN.KI

From references Arabic and the Assyriology method:

En = lord

KI = earth

"العَنوة: الطاعة. ويقولون: العاني: العبد."

"والقاعُ والقاعةُ والقِيعُ: أرض واسعةٌ سَهْلة مطمئنة مستوية حُرَّةٌ لا حُزُونةَ فيها ولا ارتفاعَ ولا انْهِباطَ، تَنْفَرِجُ عنها الجبالُ والآكامُ، ولا حَصَى فيها ولا حجارةَ ولا تُنْبِتُ الشجر، وما حوالَيْها أرْفَعُ منها وهو مَصَبُّ المِياه، وقيل: هو مَنْقَعُ الماء في حُرِّ الطين."

Therefore:
EN.KI = lord of the land (earth)

عَن كِع؛ عَن قِع = عَن كِي = سيد الأرض

ᵈEN.KI-GA-KAM

From Arabic references:

GA = watered land

KAM = kham

"الجَعْوُ: الطين. يقال: جَعَّ فلانٌ فلاناً إذا رماه بالجَعْوِ وهو الطين. والجَيْئَةُ -بالفتح أيضاً-: الموضعُ الذي يجتمع فيه الماء، وكذلك الجِئَةُ مثال جِعَةٍ، الجِيَة، بغير همز: الموضع الذي يجتمع فيه الماء كالجِيئَةِ، وقيل: هي الركيَّة المُنْتِنة. وقال ثعلب: الجِيَّة الماءُ المُسْتَنْقِعُ في الموضع."
"الخامَةُ: الرَّطْبة من النَّبات والزَّرْع. أرضٌ خامَةٌ: وخِمَةٌ. والخامةُ الغَضَّةُ الرَّطْبَةُ من النبات."

<u>Therefore:</u>
EN.KI-GA-KAM = lord of the wet (fertile) watered land (earth)

عَن كِع جَأ خَم ؛ عَن قِع جَأ خَم = عَن كِي جَأ خَم = سيد الأرض المسقية الرطبة (الخصبة)

^{d}Enkig

EN.KI-G = EN.KI-GA = lord of the watered land

عَن كِعَج [قِعَج] = سيد الأرض المسقية

^{d}gašam

<u>From Arabic references:</u>
jasama = to cover land with water
jašam = jassam = one who covers land with water

"والجَسِيمُ: ما ارتفع من الأرض وعلاه الماء؛"

<u>Therefore:</u>
gašam = God who covers land with water

<u>Author's Notes:</u> Compare the consistent rational meanings offered by the Arabic references with some of the bizarre meanings provided through the Assyriology method decipherment tools, like "the house of water", “likeness make beer”, “god of crafts”, or "the prince".

^{d}Enlil (*also* ^{d}Ellil, ^{d}Amurri, ^{d}KUR.GAL, ^{d}nun-nam-nir); Hilal; Hurun; Iblīs; Shayṭān

<u>Ancient Mesopotamian Gods and Goddesses:</u>
There has been much debate concerning the writing, etymology, and hence meaning of Enlil's name. These elements are important to discuss because they also relate to an analysis of this deity's functions. The writing and reading of this deity's name is not certain (see below), and even if we do read den-líl, the translation of "líl" is contentious. The Sumerian word "líl", whose Akkadian equivalent is zaqīqu, means "ghost, phantom, haunted" but a translation of Enlil's name as "Lord Ghost" makes little sense in the context of his mythological attestations. The interpretation of líl as "wind" is apparently a secondary development of the first millennium BCE, which has led to an interpretation of Enlil's name as "Lord Wind" or "Lord Air". This interpretation has led some scholars to reconstruct a vertically ordered cosmology that consisted of the gods An (heavens), Enlil (atmosphere), and Enki (earth), but this remains very problematic.

<u>Written forms:</u> ^{d}en-líl, ^{d}50, ^{d}nu-nam-nir
<u>Normalized forms:</u> Enlil, Ellil

<u>Wikipedia:</u>
Enlil (nlin) EN (Lord) + LÍL (Wind), "Lord (of the) Storm" is the God of breath, wind, loft and breadth (height and distance). Sometimes rendered in translations as "Ellil" in later Akkadian. Enlil was one of the supreme deities of the Mesopotamian pantheon. He decreed the fates, his command could not be altered, and he was the god who granted kingship.

^{d}Enlil & ^{d}Ellil

<u>From references of Arabic and the Assyriology method</u>
ePSD: lil
<u>lil</u> [<u>FOOL</u>] wr. lil; $^{lu}{}_{2}$lil$_2$; lil$_3$; lil$_5$; lil$_8$ "fool" Akk. lillu
<u>lil</u> [<u>GHOST</u>] wr. lil$_2$ "wind, breeze; ghost" Akk. zīqīqu
<u>lil</u> [<u>ILL</u>] wr. lil$_2$ "(to be) ill"

ePSD: lillu
lil [FOOL] wr. lil; lu2lil2; lil3; lil5; lil8 "fool" Akk. lillu

ePSD: lilû
lillilgi [DEMON] wr. |LIL2.LIL2|-gi4 "demon" Akk. Lilû

ePSD: zīqīqu
lil [GHOST] wr. lil2 "wind, breeze; ghost" Akk. zīqīqu

ePSD: zīqīqu?
sisig [BREEZE] wr. sig-sig; tumusi-si-ig; si-si-ga; sig3-sig3 "ghost?; storm; breeze, wind" Akk. mehû; zīqīqu?; šāru

هلل (لسان العرب) وكل شيء ارتفع صوتُه فقد استهلَّ. وأَهَلَّ الرجل واستهلَّ إذا رفع صوتَه. والإهْلال: التلبية، وأصل الإهْلال رفعُ الصوتِ. وكل رافِع صوتَه فهو مُهِلّ، وكذلك قوله عز وجل: وما أُهِلَّ لغير الله به؛ وقال أبو الخطاب: كلّ متكلم رافع الصوت أو خافضِه فهو مُهِلّ ومُسْتَهِلّ؛ وتَهَلّل السحابُ بالبَرَق: تلألأ. والهِلالُ: الحيَّة ما كان، وقيل: هو الذكر من الحيات؛ ومنه قول ذي الرمة: إليك ابْتَذَلنا كلَّ وَهْمٍ، كأنه هِلالٌ بدا في رَمْضةٍ يَتقَلّب يعني حيَّة. والهِلال: الحيَّة إذا سُلِخَت؛
ألّ (مقاييس اللغة) والهمزة واللام في المضاعف ثلاثة أصول: اللّمعان في اهتزاز، والصّوت، والسَّبَب يحافَظ عليه. قال الخليل وابن دريد: ألّ* الشيءُ، إذا لمع. قال ابن الأعرابيّ: في جوفه أليلٌ وصليل. وسمعت أليل الماء أي صوته.
ألل (الصّحاح في اللغة) ألّهُ يَؤُلُّهُ ألاًّ: طعنه بالحَرْبة. يقال: ما له ألَّ وغُلَّ. وألّ لونُه يَؤُلُّ ألاًّ: صَفا وَبَرَقَ. وألَّ أيضاً، بمعنى أسرع.
ألل (لسان العرب) الأَلُّ: السرعة، والأَلُّ الإسراع. وألَّ الفرسُ يَئِلُّ ألاًّ: اضطرب. وفرس مِئَلّ أي سريع. وألَّ الشيءُ يَؤُلُّ ويَئِلُّ؛ الأَخيرة عن ابن دريد، ألاًّ: برق. وقد ألَّ يَؤُلُّ ألاًّ: بمعنى أسرع؛ ويقال: ما له ألَّ وغُلَّ؛ قال ابن بري: ألَّ دُفع في قفاه، وغُلَّ أي جُنَّ. والأَلُّ الصّياحُ. والإلُّ الربوبية. والإلُّ الحِقد.
علل (لسان العرب) والعُلْعُول: الشَّرُّ؛ الفراء: إنه لفي عُلْعُولِ شَرٍّ وزُلْزُولِ شَرٍّ أي في قتال واضطراب.
عل (مقاييس اللغة) العين واللام أصول ثلاثة صحيحة: أحدها تكرُّرٌ أو تكرير، والآخر عائق يعوق، والثالث ضَعف في الشَّيء. وقال أبو عمرو: بئرٌ يعاليلُ صار فيها المطرُ والماءُ مرّةً بعد مرة. قال: وهو من العَلَل.
زقا (لسان العرب) والزَّقْيةُ: الصَّيْحةُ.
زقا (الصّحاح في اللغة) الزَقْو والزَقْيُ: مصدرٌ. وقد زَقا الصَدى يَزْقو ويَزْقى زُقاءً، أي صاح. وكلُّ صائحٍ زاقٍ. والزَقْيَةُ: الصيحةُ.

غلل (لسان العرب) والغِلُّ، بالكسر، والغَلِيلُ: الغِشُّ والعَداوة والضِّغْنُ والحقْد والحسد. واغْتَلَّت الثوبَ: لَبِسته تحت الثياب، والغَلْغَلة: سرعة السير، وقد تغَلْغَل.

غلل (الصّحاح في اللغة) والغليلُ الضِغْنُ والحقدُ، مثل الغُلّ.

غل (مقاييس اللغة) والغِلالة: شِعارٌ يُلبَس تحت الثُّوب، الغَلغلة: سُرعة السَّير.

ليل (لسان العرب) اللَّيْلُ: عقيب النهار ومَبْدَؤُه من غروب الشمس. وليلٌ أَلْيَلُ: شديد الظلمة؛ وأَلال القومُ وأَلْيَلوا: دخلوا في الليل.

عشا (لسان العرب) ويقال أَخَذْتُ عَلَيْهِم بالعَشْوة أي بالسَّوادِ من اللَّيل. والعُشوة، بالضم والفتح والكسر: الأَمْرُ المُلْتَبس. وركب فلانٌ العَشْواءَ إذا خَبَطَ أمرَه على غيرِ بَصِيرة. وعَشْوَةُ اللَّيلِ والسَّحَر وعَشواؤه: ظُلْمَتُه.

لبس (لسان العرب) اللُّبْسُ، بالضم: مصدر قولك لَبِسْتُ الثوبَ أَلْبَس، واللَّبْس، بالفتح: مصدر قولك لَبَسْت عليه الأَمر أَلْبِسُ خَلَطْت. واللَّبْسُ واللُّبْسُ: اختلاط الأَمر. لَبَسَ عليه الأَمرَ يَلْبِسُه لَبْساً فالْتَبَسَ إذا خلَطَه عليه حتى لا يعرِف جِهَتَه. وفي المَوْلِدِ والمَبْعَثِ: فجاء المَلَكُ فشقَّ عن قلبه، قال: فَخِفْتُ أن يكون قد الْتُبِسَ بي أي خُولِطْت في عَقْلي، من قولك في رَأْيِه لَبْسٌ أي اختلاطٌ، ويقال للمجنون: مُخالَط. والْتَبَسَ عليه الأَمر أي اختلَطَ واشْتَبه. والمِلْبَسُ الليل بعَيْنه كما تقول إزارٌ ومِئْزَرٌ ولِحافٌ ومِلْحَفٌ؛ واللَّبْسُ اختِلاطُ الظلام. ورجل البِيسٌ: أحمق (قوله «البيس أحمق» كذا في الأصل).

بلس (لسان العرب) وأَبْلَسَ من رحمة الله أي يَئِسَ ونَدِمَ، ومنه سمي إبليس وكان اسمه عزازيلَ. وفي التنزيل العزيز: يومئذ يُبْلِسُ المجرمون. وإبليس، لعنة الله: مشتق منه لأنه أُبْلِسَ من رحمة الله أي أُويِسَ. وقال أبو إسحق: لم يصرف لأنه أعجمي معرفة. والمُبْلِسُ اليائسُ، ولذلك قيل للذي يسكت عند انقطاع حجته ولا يكون عنده جواب: قد أَبْلَسَ؛ وقال العجاج: قال: نَعَمْ أَعْرِفُه، وأَبْلَسا أي لم يُحِرْ إِلَيَّ جواباً. ونحو ذلك قيل في المُبلِس، وقيل: إن إبليس سمي بهذا الاسم لأنه لما أُويِسَ من رحمة الله أَبْلَسَ يأساً. وفي الحديث. فتأَشَّبَ أَصحابُه حوله وأَبْلَسُوا حتى ما أَوضحوا بضاحِكة؛ أَبلسوا أَي سكتوا. والمُبْلِسُ الساكت من الحزن أَو الخوف. والإِبْلاسُ: الحَيْرة؛ ومنه الحديث: أَلم تر الجِنَّ وإِبلاسَها أَي تَحَيُّرها ودَهَشَها. والإِبْلاسُ: الحَيْرة؛ ومنه الحديث: أَلم تر الجِنَّ وإِبلاسَها أَي تَحَيُّرها ودَهَشَها.

جنن (لسان العرب) جَنَّ الشيءَ يَجُنُّه جَنّاً: سَتَره. وجِنُّ الليلِ وجُنونُه وجَنانُه: شِدَّةُ ظُلْمته وادْلِهْمامُه، وقيل: اختلاطُ ظلامِه لأَن ذلك كلَّه ساترٌ؛

جن (مقاييس اللغة) والجِنّة: الجنون؛ وذلك أنّه يغطّي العقل. وجَنَانُ الليل: سوادُه وسَتْره الأشياء. ويقال جُنُون الليل، والمعنى واحد. جَنّة الجنون. فأمّا الحيّة الذي يسمَّى الجانّ فهو تشبيهٌ له بالواحد من الجانّ.

زيق (لسان العرب) وزِيقُ الشيطانِ: لُعابُ الشمس؛ قال أبو منصور: هذا تصحيف والصواب رِيقُ الشمس، بالراء، ومعناه لعاب الشمس،

لعب (لسان العرب) ولُعابُ الشَّمْس: شيء تَراه كأنه يَنْحَدِر من السماء إذا حَمِيَتْ وقامَ قائمُ الظَّهيرة؛ قال جرير: أَنِخْنَ لتَهْجِيرٍ، وقَدْ وَقَدَ الحَصَى،

* وذابَ لُعابُ الشَّمْسِ فَوْقَ الجماجم قال الأَزهري: لُعابُ الشَّمْسِ هو الذي يقال له مُخاطُ الشَّيْطانِ، وهو السَّهام، بفتح السين، ويقال له: ريق الشمس، وهو شِبْهُ الخَيْطِ، تَراه في الهَواءِ إذا اشْتَدَّ الحَرُّ ورَكَدَ الهَواءُ؛ ومَن قال: إن لُعابَ الشَّمْسِ السَّرابُ، فقد أَبطَلَ؛

شطن (لسان العرب) وشَطَنَ عنه: بَعُدَ. وأَشْطَنَه أَبعده. والشيطان: معروف، وكل عاتٍ متمرد من الجن والإنس والدواب شيطان؛ والشيطانُ: حَيَّةٌ له عُرْفٌ. والشاطِنُ: الخبيث.

شطن (مقاييس اللغة) الشين والطاء والنون أصلٌ مطّرد صحيح يدلُّ على البُعد. يقال شَطَنت الدار تَشْطُن شطوناً إذا غَرَبَت. ونوىً شَطونٌ، أي بعيدة.

حرن (الصّحاح في اللغة) فرسٌ حَرونٌ: لا ينقاد، وإذا اشتدَّ به الجريُ وقف. وقد حَرَنَ يَحْرُنُ حُروناً. وحَرُنَ بالضم، أي صار حَروناً. ويقال: حَرَنَ في البيع، إذا لم يزد ولم يُنقِص

<u>Using al-Jibouri's rules:</u>

Elílu >> Enlillu

<u>Therefore:</u>

Elíl = Ellil = Enli [ilīl = illil = inlil] = ilbīs = iblīs = Satan = the fool devil; the creator of the jinn (genies, the ghosts) and crazy ones; the desperate; the creator of storms, turbulences, anxiety, and chaos; the instigator of hate, jealousy, and skepticism

إلِيلْ = إلّيل = إنليل = إلْبِيسْ = إبْلِيسْ = الشيطان الاحمق؛ اليائسْ، مُولد العواصف والاضطرابات والخوف والفوضى؛ مولد الجِنْ والمجانين؛ المحرض على الحقد والغيرة والشك

or:

EN.LIL = Lord (creator) of the Jinn (genies, the ghosts); Lord (creator) of storms, turbulences, anxiety, chaos; Lord (creator) hate, jealousy, and skepticism = Satan

عَنْ ليلْ = سيد (مولد) الجِنْ؛ سيد (مولد) العواصف والفوضى والاضطرابات؛ سيد (مولد) الحِقدْ و الغيرة والشك = إبليس، الشيطان

dnun-nam-nir

From Arabic references, and using al-Jibbouri's rules:
namara = to threaten, to be angry, to bluster

"ونَمَرَ وتَنَمَّرَ: غَضِبَ، وساءَ خُلُقُهُ. وتَنَمَّرَ: تَمَدَّدَ في الصَّوْتِ عندَ الوَعِيدِ، وتَشَبَّهَ بالنَّمِرِ، و~ له: تَنَكَّرَ، وتَغَيَّرَ، وأوعَدَهُ، لأَنَّ النَّمِرَ لا يُلْقَى إلاَّ مُتَنَكِّراً غَضْبانَ، وسَمَّوْا: نِمْرانَ، بالكسر. ونَمِرَ الرجلُ ونَمَّر وتَنَمَّرَ: غَضِبَ"

Therefore:
numma-nir >> nu-nam-nir = the angry one who threatens and blusters = Enlil = Satan

نمَرَ، نمْرَ فهو نُمَيْرَ >> نُنمْنِر = المتوعَدْ، المهدّدْ، الغاضبْ = إنليل = الشيطان

dKUR.GAL

Wikipedia:
Although the word for earth was Ki, Kur came to also mean land, and Sumer itself, was called "Kur-gal" or "Great Land". "Kur-gal" also means "Great Mountain" and is a metonym for both Nippur and Enlil who rules from that city. Ekur, "mountain house" was the temple of Enlil at Nippur. A second, popular meaning of Kur was "underworld", or the world under the earth. Kur was sometimes the home of the dead, it is possible that the flames on escaping gas plumes in parts of the Zagros mountains would have given those mountains a meaning not entirely consistent with the primary meaning of mountains and an abode of a god. The eastern mountains as an abode of the god is popular in Ancient Near Eastern mythology. The underworld Kur is the void space between the primeval sea (Abzu) and the earth (Ma). Kur is almost identical with "Ki-gal", "Great Land" which is the Underworld (thus the ruler of the Underworld is Ereshkigal "Goddess of The Great Land".

From references of Arabic and the Assyriology method, and using al-Jiburi's rules:
KUR = underworld
GAL = great, almighty
KUR.GAL = great of the underworld; great of twisting

كور = قور = قُعر = باطن الارض
جل = عظيم
كُرجَل = عظيم باطن الارض؛ عظيم اللَف والبرم

"والكُرَّجِيُّ: المُخَنَّثُ. وكَرَّجَ وتَكَرَّجَ أي فَسَدَ وعَلاهُ خُضْرَةٌ."
"كور: الكاف والواو والراء أصلٌ صحيحٌ يدلّ على دُوْرٍ وتجمُّع. من ذلك الكَوْر: الدَّور. يقال كار يَكُورُ، إذا دار. وقال النضر: كل دارة من العمامة كَوْرٌ، وكل دَوْرٍ كَوْرٌ. وتَكْوِيرُ العمامة: كَوْرُها. وكارَ العِمامَةَ على الرأس يَكُورُها كَوْراً: لاثَها عليه وأَدارها؛ الجوهري: الكُورَةُ المدينة والصُّقْعُ، والجمع كُوَرٌ. والصَّقْعُ: رَفْعُ الصَّوْتِ؛ وصَقَع في كل النَواحي يَصْقَعُ: ذَهَبَ؛ ابن سيده: والكُورَةُ من البلاد المِخْلافُ، وهي القرية من قُرَى اليمن؛ وقيل: التَّكْوِير الصَّرْع، ضَرَبه أو لم يضرِبْه. والاكتيارُ: صرعُ الشيءِ بعضَه على بعضٍ. واسْتَكارَ: أَسْرَع. وكُور وكُوَيْرٌ والكَوْر: جبال معروفة؛ وكُرت الأَرض كَوْراً: حفرتُها. وقيل: كَرَيْت النهر كَرْياً إذا حفرته. وكَرا الأَرضَ كَرْواً: حفرها وهو من ذوات الواو والياء. وفي حديث فاطمة، رضي الله عنها: أنها خرجت تُعَزِّي قوماً، فلما انصرفت قال لها: لَعَلكِ بَلَغْتِ معهم الكُرَى؟ قالت: معاذَ اللهِ هكذا جاء في رواية بالراء، وهي القُبور جمع كُرْيَةٍ أو كُرْوةٍ،

من كَرَيْتُ الأرض وكَرَوْتُها إذا حفرتها كالحُفرة؛ ومنه الحديث: أن الأنصار سألوا رسول الله، صلى الله عليه وسلم، في نهر يَكْرُونه لهم سَيْحاً أي يَحْفِرُونه ويُخْرِجون طينه."

Therefore:

KUR.GAL = Master of the underworld (the jinn); Master of twisters (storms) = Enlil = Satan

كَرجَلْ = عظيم باطن الارض (الجن)؛ عظيم اللَف والبرم (الاعاصير)

dAmurri

From Arabic references:

‘amr = what rises of voice or wind; mixer

‘amru = name of Satan

zbu ‘amrah = that who brings death and destruction

عمر = كل ما يرتفع من صوت او ريح

العومرة = الاختلاط والجُلبة

عمرو = اسم شيطان

ابو عَمْرة = اذا حل هو بقوم حل بهم البلاء

"عمر: العين والميم والراء أصلان صحيحان، أحدهما يدلُّ على بقاءٍ وامتداد زمان، والآخر على شيءٍ يعلو، من صوتٍ أو غيره. وأيُّ ذلك كان فهو من العلوّ والارتفاع على ما ذكرنا. قال أهلُ اللغة: والعَمَار: كلُّ شيء جعلتَه على رأسك، من عِمامةٍ، أو قَلَنْسُوة أو إكليل أو تاج، أو غير ذلك، كلُّه عَمار. وقال قوم: العَمار يكون من رَيحَان أيضاً. قال ابنُ السِّكِّيت: العَمَار: التَّحيَّة. يقال عمَّرك الله، أي حيّاك. ويجوز أن يكون هذا لرفع الصوت. وممكن أن يكون الحيُّ العظيم يسمى عمارة لما يكون ذلك من جلبة وصياح. والعَوْمَرَةُ: الاختلاط، والجَلَبَةُ، وجَمْعُ الناسِ، وحَبْسُهم في مكانٍ. وعَمْرو: اسْمٌ، جمعه أعْمُرٌ وعُمُورٌ، واسمُ شَيْطانِ الفَرَزْدَق، وعامِرٌ: اسمٌ، وقد يُسَمَّى به الحَيُّ، وعُمَرُ، مَعْدولٌ عنه في حالِ التَّسْميَةِ. وعُمَيْرٌ وعُوَيْمِرٌ وعَمَّارٌ ومَعْمَرٌ وعِمْرانُ وعُمارَةُ ويَعْمَرُ، كيَفْعَلُ: أسْماءٌ. وأبو عَمْرَة: كُنْيَةُ الإفلاسِ والجُوعِ، ورجُلٌ كان إذا حَلَّ بِقومٍ، حَلَّ بِهِم البلاءُ من القَتْلِ والحَرْبِ. وأبو عَمْرة: الإقْلالُ؛ قال: إن أبا عَمْرة شرُّ جار وقال: حلَ أبو عَمْرة وَسْطَ حُجْرَتي وأبو عَمْرة: كنية الجوع."

Therefore:

Ammuri = one who cause rising wind; that who brings death and distruction = Enlil = Satan

عَمْرٌ = جالب الرياح والاصوات العالية، جالب البلاء = ابليس ابو الجن = الشيطان

www.ingramcontent.com/pod-product-compliance
Lightning Source LLC
Chambersburg PA
CBHW081132300726
48982CB00005B/935

* 9 7 8 0 9 8 4 9 8 4 3 9 8 *